'Two of the most delightful characters in the history of fantast : literature' Neil Gaiman

'Mos fantasy writers, if asked, admit that Fritz Leiber is our s tual father, and for the most part we're sweating to keep let alone overtake him' Raymond E. Feist

'Ma prose and urbane wit' Michael Moorcock

'The st literate and important sword and sorcery serie Mike Ashley

'[A] ter of major importance' *The Encyclopedia of Fant*

ALSO BY FRITZ LEIBER

Fantasy Masterworks

THE FIRST BOOK
OF LANKHMAR

FRITZ LEIBER

This edition Copyright © Fritz Leiber 2001

The right of Fritz Leiber to be identified as the author
of this work has been asserted by him in accordance with the Copyright,
Designs and Patents Act 1988.

This edition published in Great Britain in 2001 by
Gollancz
An imprint of the Orion Publishing Group
Orion House, 5 Upper St Martin's Lane,
London WC2H 9EA

10 9 8 7

A CIP catalogue record for this book is available
from the British Library

ISBN 978-1-85798-327-2

Typeset at The Spartan Press Ltd,
Lymington, Hants

Printed in Great Britain by
Clays Ltd, St Ives plc

www.orionbooks.co.uk

CONTENTS

Fritz Leiber (1910–1992) was born in Chicago. Both his parents were Shakespearean actors and his father appeared in a number of films. He majored in psychology and physiology at the University of Chicago and then spent a year at a theological seminary. He joined his father's acting company in 1934 and even had a few roles in films, including a small part in *Camille*, which starred Greta Garbo. In 1936 he married and turned to writing, although his career also included periods as an editor, mainly with *Science Digest*, and as a drama teacher. His long and distinguished writing career covered science fiction and horror as well as his ground-breaking fantasy, and included such acclaimed titles as *The Big Time*, *The Wanderer*, both of which won Hugos, and *Our Lady of Darkness*. In all, Fritz Leiber won six Hugos and four Nebulas, and more than twenty other awards, including the 1975 Grand Master of Fantasy (Gandalf) Award and the 1976 Life Achievement Lovecraft Award. The 1981 Grand Master Nebula Award was presented for his work as a whole.

SWORDS AND
DEVILTRY

CONTENTS

I
INDUCTION

Sundered from us by gulfs of time and stranger dimensions dreams the ancient world of Nehwon with its towers and skulls and jewels, its swords and sorceries. Nehwon's known realms crowd about the Inner Sea: northward the green-forested fierce Land of the Eight Cities, eastward the steppe-dwelling Mingol horsemen and the desert where caravans creep from the rich Eastern Lands and the River Tilth. But southward, linked to the desert only by the Sinking Land and further warded by the Great Dike and the Mountain of Hunger, are the rich grainfields and walled cities of Lankhmar, eldest and chiefest of Nehwon's lands. Dominating the Land of Lankhmar and crouching at the silty mouth of the River Hlal in a secure corner between the grainfields, the Great Salt Marsh, and the Inner Sea is the massive-walled and mazy-alleyed metropolis of Lankhmar, thick with thieves and shaven priests, lean-framed magicians and fat-bellied merchants – Lankhmar the Imperishable, the City of the Black Toga.

In Lankhmar on one murky night, if we can believe the runic books of Sheelba of the Eyeless Face, there met for the first time those two dubious heroes and whimsical scoundrels, Fafhrd and the Gray Mouser. Fafhrd's origins were easy to perceive in his near seven-foot height and limber-looking ranginess, his hammered ornaments and huge longsword: he was clearly a barbarian from the Cold Waste north even of the Eight Cities and the Trollstep Mountains. The Mouser's antecedents were more cryptic and hardly to be deduced from his childlike stature, gray garb, mouse-skin hood shadowing flat swart face, and deceptively dainty rapier; but somewhere about him was the suggestion of cities and the south, the dark streets and also the sun-drenched spaces. As the twain eyed each other challengingly through the murky fog lit indirectly by distant torches, they were already dimly aware that they were two long-sundered, matching fragments of a greater hero and that each had found a comrade who would outlast a thousand quests and a lifetime – or a hundred lifetimes – of adventuring.

No one at that moment could have guessed that the Gray Mouser was once named Mouse, or that Fafhrd had recently been a youth whose voice was by training high-pitched, who wore white furs only, and who still slept in his mother's tent although he was eighteen.

II
THE SNOW WOMEN

At Cold Corner in midwinter, the women of the Snow Clan were waging a cold war against the men. They trudged about like ghosts in their whitest furs almost invisible against the new-fallen snow, always together in female groups, silent or at most hissing like angry shades. They avoided Godshall with its trees for pillars and walls of laced leather and towering pine-needle roof.

They gathered in the big, oval Tent of the Women, which stood guard in front of the smaller home tents, for sessions of chanting and ominous moaning and various silent practises designed to create powerful enchantments that would tether their husbands' ankles to Cold Corner, tie up their loins, and give them sniveling, nose-dripping colds, with the threat of the Great Cough and Winter Fever held in reserve. Any man so unwise as to walk alone by day was apt to be set upon and snowballed and, if caught, thrashed – be he even skald or mighty hunter.

And a snowballing by Snow Clan women was nothing to laugh at. They threw overarm, it is true, but their muscles for that had been greatly strengthened by much splitting of fire-wood, lopping of high branches, and pounding of hides, including the iron-hard one of the snowy behemoth. And they sometimes froze their snowballs.

The sinewy, winter-hardened men took all of this with immense dignity, striding about like kings in their conspicuous black, russet, and rainbow-dyed ceremonial furs, drinking hugely but with discretion, and trading as shrewdly as Ilthmarts their bits of amber and ambergris, their snow-diamonds visible only by night, their glossy animal pelts, and their ice-herbs, in exchange for woven fabrics, hot spices, blued and browned iron, honey, waxen candles, fire-powders that flared with a colored roar, and other products of the civilized south. Nevertheless, they made a point of keeping generally in groups, and there was many a nose a-drip among them.

It was not the trading the women objected to. Their men were good at that and they – the women – were the chief beneficiaries. They greatly preferred it to their husbands' occasional piratings, which took those lusty men far down the eastern coasts of the Outer Sea, out of reach of immediate matriarchal supervision and even, the women sometimes feared, of their potent female magic. Cold Corner was the farthest south ever got by the entire Snow Clan, whose members spent most of their lives on the Cold Waste and among the foothills of the untopped Mountains of the Giants and the even more northerly Bones of the Old Ones, and so this midwinter camp was their one yearly chance to trade peaceably with venturesome Mingols, Sarheenmarts, Lankhmarts, and even an occasional Eastern desert-man, heavily beturbaned, bundled up to the eyes, and elephantinely gloved and booted.

Nor was it the guzzling which the women opposed. Their husbands were great quaffers of mead and ale at all times and even of the native white snow-potato brandy, a headier drink than most of the wines and boozes the traders hopefully dispensed.

No, what the Snow Women hated so venomously and which each year caused them to wage cold war with hardly any material or magical holds barred, was the theatrical show which inevitably came shivering north with the traders, its daring troupers with faces chapped and legs chilblained, but hearts a-beat for soft northern gold and easy if rampageous audiences – a show so blasphemous and obscene that the men pre-empted Godshall for its performance (God being unshockable) and refused to let the women and youths view it; a show whose actors were, according to the women, solely dirty old men and even dirtier scrawny southern girls, as loose in their morals as in the lacing of their skimpy garments, when they went clothed at all. It did not occur to the Snow Women that a scrawny wench, her dirty nakedness all blue goosebumps in the chill of drafty Godshall, would hardly be an object of erotic appeal besides her risking permanent all-over frostbite.

So the Snow Women each midwinter hissed and magicked and sneaked and sniped with their crusty snowballs at huge men retreating with pomp, and frequently caught an old or crippled or foolish, young, drunken husband and beat him soundly.

This outwardly comic combat had sinister undertones. Particularly when working all together, the Snow Women were reputed to wield mighty magics, particularly through the element of cold and its consequences: slipperiness, the sudden freezing of flesh, the gluing of skin to metal, the frangibility of objects, the menacing mass of snow-laden trees and branches, and the vastly greater mass of avalanches. And there was no man wholly unafraid of the hypnotic power in their ice-blue eyes.

Each Snow Woman, usually with the aid of the rest, worked to maintain absolute control of her man, though leaving him seemingly free, and it was whispered that recalcitrant husbands had been injured and even slain, generally by some frigid instrumentality. While at the same time witchy cliques and individual sorceresses played against each other a power game in which the brawniest and boldest of men, even chiefs and priests, were but counters.

During the fortnight of trading and the two days of the Show, hags and great strapping girls guarded the Tent of the Women at all quarters, while from within came strong perfumes, stenches, flashes and intermittent glows by night, clashings and tinklings, cracklings and quenchings, and incantational chantings and whisperings that never quite stopped.

This morning one could imagine that the Snow Women's sorcery was working everywhere, for the weather was windless and overcast, and there were wisps of fog in the moist freezing air, so that crystals of ice were rapidly forming on every bush and branch, every twig and tip of any sort, including the ends of the men's moustaches and the eartips of the tamed lynxes. The crystals were as blue and flashing as the Snow Women's eyes and even mimicked in their forms, to an imaginative mind, the Snow

Women's hooded, tall, and white-robed figures, for many of the crystals grew upright, like diamond flames.

And this morning the Snow Women had caught, or rather got a near certain chance of trapping, an almost unimaginably choice victim. For one of the Show girls, whether by ignorance or foolhardy daring, and perhaps tempted by the relatively mild, gem-begetting air, had strolled on the crusty snow away from the safety of the actors' tents, past Godshall on the precipice side, and from thence between two sky-thrusting copses of snow-laden evergreens, out onto the snow-carpeted natural rock bridge that had been the start of the Old Road south to Gnampf Nar until some five man-lengths of its central section had fallen three score years ago.

A short step from the up-curving, perilous brink she had paused and looked for a long while south through the wisps of mist that, in the distance, grew thin as pluckings of long-haired wool. Below her in the canyon's overhung slot, the snow-capped pines flooring Trollstep Canyon looked tiny as the white tents of an army of Ice Gnomes. Her gaze slowly traced Trollstep Canyon from its far eastern beginnings to where, narrowing, it passed directly beneath her and then, slowly widening, curved south, until the buttress opposite her with its matching, jutting section of the one-time rock bridge, cut off the view south. Then her gaze went back to trace the New Road from where it began its descent beyond the actors' tents and clung to the far wall of the canyon until, after many a switchback and many a swing into great gully and out again – unlike the far swifter, straighter descent of the Old Road – it plunged into the midst of the flooring pines and went with them south.

From her constant yearning look, one might have thought the actress a silly homesick soubrette, already regretting this freezing northern tour and pining for some hot, flea-bitten actors' alley beyond the Land of the Eight Cities and the Inner Sea – except for the quiet confidence of her movements, the proud set of her shoulders, and the perilous spot she had chosen for her peering. For this spot was not only physically dangerous, but also as near the Tent of the Snow Women as it was to Godshall, and in addition the spot was taboo because a chief and his children had plunged to their deaths when the central rock-span had cracked away three score years ago, and because the wooden replacement had fallen under the weight of a brandy-merchant's cart some two score years later. Brandy of the fieriest, a loss fearsome enough to justify the sternest of taboos, including one against ever rebuilding the bridge.

And as if even those tragedies were not sufficient to glut the jealous gods and make taboo absolute, only two years past the most skillful skier the Snow Clan had produced in decades, one Skif, drunk with snow brandy and an icy pride, had sought to jump the gap from the Cold Corner side. Towed to a fast start and thrusting furiously with his sticks, he had taken off like a gliding hawk, yet missed the opposite snowy verge by an arm's length; the prows of his skis had crashed into rock, and he himself smashed in the rocky depths of the canyon.

The bemused actress wore a long coat of auburn fox fur belted with a light, gold-washed brass chain. Icy crystals had formed in her high-piled, fine, dark brown hair.

From the narrowness of her coat, her figure promised to be scrawny or at least thinly muscular enough to satisfy the Snow Women's notion of female players, but she was almost six feet tall – which was not at all as actresses should be and definitely an added affront to the tall Snow Women now approaching her from behind in a silent white rank.

An over-hasty white fur boot sang against the glazed snow.

The actress spun around and without hesitation raced back the way she had come. Her first three steps broke the snowcrust, losing her time, but then she learned the trick of running in a glide, feet grazing the crust.

She hitched her russet coat high. She was wearing black fur boots and bright scarlet stockings.

The Snow Women glided swiftly after her, pitching their hard-packed snowballs.

One struck her hard on the shoulder. She made the mistake of looking back.

By ill chance two snowballs took her in jaw and forehead, just beneath painted lip and on an arched black eyebrow.

She reeled then, turning fully back, and a snowball thrown

almost with the force of a slinger's stone struck her in the midriff, doubling her up and driving the breath from her lungs in an open-mouthed *whoosh*.

She collapsed. The white women rushed forward, blue eyes a-glare.

A big, thinnish, black-moustached man in a drab quilted jacket and a low black turban stopped watching from beside a becrystalled, rough-barked living pillar of Godshall, and ran toward the fallen woman. His footsteps broke the crust, but his strong legs drove him powerfully on.

Then he slowed in amaze as he was passed almost as if he were at a standstill by a tall, white, slender figure glide-running so swiftly that it seemed for a moment it went on skis. Then for another instant, the turbaned man thought it was another Snow Woman, but then he noted that it wore a short fur jerkin rather than a long fur robe – and so was presumably a Snow Man or Snow Youth, though the black-turbaned man had never seen a Snow Clan male dressed in white.

The strange, swift figure glide-ran, with chin tucked down and eyes bent away from the Snow Women, as if fearing to meet their wrathful blue gaze. Then, as he swiftly knelt by the felled actress, long reddish-blond hair spilled from his hood. From that and the figure's slenderness, the black-turbaned man knew an instant of fear that the intercomer was a very tall Snow Girl, eager to strike the first blow at close quarters.

But then he saw a jut of downy male chin in the reddish-blond hair and also a pair of massive silver bracelets of the sort one gained only by pirating. Next the youth picked up the actress and glide-ran away from the Snow Women, who now could see only their victim's scarlet-stockinged legs. A volley of snowballs struck the rescuer's back. He staggered a little, then sped determinedly on, still ducking his head.

The biggest of the Snow Women, one with the bearing of a queen and a haggard face still handsome, though the hair falling to either side of it was white, stopped running and shouted in a deep voice, 'Come back, my son! You hear me, Fafhrd, come back now!'

The youth nodded his ducked head slightly, though he did

not pause in his flight. Without turning his head, he called in a rather high voice, 'I will come back, revered Mor my mother . . . later on.'

The other women took up the cry of 'Come back now!' Some of them added such epithets as 'Dissolute youth!' 'Curse of your good mother Mor!' and 'Chaser after whores!'

Mor silenced them with a curt, sidewise sweep of her hands, palms down. 'We will wait here,' she announced with authority.

The black-turbaned man paused a bit, then strolled after the vanished pair, keeping a wary eye on the Snow Women. They were supposed not to attack traders, but with barbarian females, as with males, one could never tell.

Fafhrd reached the actors' tents, which were pitched in a circle around a trampled stretch of snow at the altar end of Godshall. Farthest from the precipice was the tall, conical tent of the Master of the Show. Midway stretched the common actors' tent, somewhat fish-shaped, one-third for the girls, two-thirds for the men. Nearest Trollstep Canyon was a medium-size, hemi-cylindrical tent supported on half hoops. Across its middle, an evergreen sycamore thrust a great heavy branch balanced by two lesser branches on the opposite side, all spangled with crystals. In this tent's semicircular front was a laced entry-flap, which Fafhrd found difficult to open, since the long form in his arms was still limp.

A swag-bellied little old man came strutting toward him with something of the bounce of youth. This one wore ragged finery touched up with gilt. Even his long gray moustache and goatee glittered with specks of gold above and below his dirty-toothed mouth. His heavily pouched eyes were rheumy and red all around, but dark and darting at center. Above them was a purple turban supporting in turn a gilt crown set with battered gems of rock crystal, poorly aping diamonds.

Behind him came a skinny, one-armed Mingol, a fat Easterner with a vast black beard that stank of burning, and two scrawny girls who, despite their yawning and the heavy blankets huddled around them, looked watchful and evasive as alley cats.

'What's this now?' the leader demanded, his alert eyes taking in every detail of Fafhrd and his burden. 'Vlana slain? Raped and slain, eh? Know, murderous youth, that you'll pay high for your fun. You may not know who I am, but you'll learn. I'll have reparations from your chiefs, I will! Vast reparations! I have influence, I have. You'll lose those pirate's bracelets of yours and that silver chain peeping from under your collar. Your family'll be beggared, and all your relatives, too. As for what *they'll* do to you—'

'You are Essedinex, Master of the Show,' Fafhrd broke in dogmatically, his high tenor voice cutting like a trumpet through the other's hoarse, ranting baritone. 'I am Fafhrd, son of Mor and of Nalgron the Legend-Breaker. Vlana the culture dancer is not raped or dead, but stunned with snowballs. This is her tent. Open it.'

'We'll take care of her, barbarian,' Essedinex asserted, though more quietly, appearing both surprised and somewhat intimidated by the youth's almost pedantic precision as to who was who, and what was what. 'Hand her over. Then depart.'

'I will lay her down,' Fafhrd persisted. 'Open the tent!'

Essedinex shrugged and motioned to the Mingol, who with a sardonic grin used his one hand and elbow to unlace and draw aside the entry-flap. An odor of sandalwood and closetberry came out. Stooping, Fafhrd entered. Midway down the length of the tent he noted a pallet of furs and a low table with a silver mirror propped against some jars and squat bottles. At the far end was a rack of costumes.

Stepping around a brazier from which a thread of pale smoke wreathed, Fafhrd carefully knelt and most gently deposited his burden on the pallet. Next he felt Vlana's pulse at jaw-hinge and wrist, rolled back a dark lid and peered into each eye, delicately explored with his fingertips the sizable bumps that were forming on jaw and forehead. Then he tweaked the lobe of her left ear and, when she did not react, shook his head and, drawing open her russet robe, began to unbutton the red dress under it.

Essedinex, who with the others had been watching the proceedings in a puzzled fashion cried out, 'Well, of all— Cease, lascivious youth!'

'Silence,' Fafhrd commanded and continued unbuttoning.

The two blanketed girls giggled, then clapped hands to mouths, darting amused gazes at Essedinex and the rest.

Drawing aside his long hair from his right ear, Fafhrd laid that side of his face on Vlana's chest between her breasts, small as half pomegranates, their nipples rosy bronze in hue. He maintained a solemn expression. The girls smothered giggles again. Essedinex strangledly cleared his throat, preparing for large speech.

Fafhrd sat up and said, 'Her spirit will shortly return. Her bruises should be dressed with snow-bandages, renewed when they begin to melt. Now I require a cup of your best brandy.'

'My best brandy—!' Essedinex cried outragedly. 'This goes too far. First you must have a help-yourself peep show, then strong drink! Presumptuous youth, depart at once!'

'I am merely seeking—' Fafhrd began in clear and at last slightly dangerous tones.

His patient interrupted the dispute by opening her eyes, shaking her head, wincing, then determinedly sitting up – whereupon she grew pale and her gaze wavered. Fafhrd helped her lie down again and put pillows under her feet. Then he looked at her face. Her eyes were still open and she was looking back at him curiously.

He saw a face small and sunken-cheeked, no longer girlish-young, but with a compact catlike beauty despite its lumps. Her eyes, being large, brown-irised and long-lashed, should have been melting, but were not. There was the look of the loner in them, and purpose, and a thoughtful weighing of what she saw.

She saw a handsome, fair-complexioned youth of about eighteen winters, wide-headed and long-jawed, as if he had not done growing. Fine red-gold hair cascaded down his cheeks. His eyes were green, cryptic, and as staring as a cat's. His lips were wide, but slightly compressed, as if they were a door that locked words in and opened only on the cryptic eyes' command.

One of the girls had poured a half cup of brandy from a bottle on the low table. Fafhrd took it and lifted Vlana's head for her to drink it in sips. The other girl came with powder snow folded in woolen cloths. Kneeling on the far side of the pallet, she bound them against the bruises.

After inquiring Fafhrd's name and confirming that he had

rescued her from the Snow Women, Vlana asked, 'Why do you speak in such a high voice?'

'I study with a singing skald,' he answered. 'They use that voice and are the true skalds, not the roaring ones who use deep tones.'

'What reward do you expect for rescuing me?' she asked boldly.

'None,' Fafhrd replied.

From the two girls came further giggles, quickly cut off at Vlana's glance.

Fafhrd added, 'It was my personal obligation to rescue you, since the leader of the Snow Women was my mother. I must respect my mother's wishes, but I must also prevent her from performing wrong actions.'

'Oh. Why do you act like a priest or healer?' Vlana continued. 'Is that one of your mother's wishes?' She had not bothered to cover her breasts, but Fafhrd was not looking at them now, only at the actress's lips and eyes.

'Healing is part of the singing skald's art,' he answered. 'As for my mother, I do my duty toward her, nor less, nor more.'

'Vlana, it is not politic that you talk thus with this youth,' Essedinex interposed, now in a nervous voice. 'He must—'

'Shut up!' Vlana snapped. Then, back to Fafhrd, 'Why do you wear white?'

'It is proper garb for all Snow Folk. I do not follow the new custom of dark and dyed furs for males. My father always wore white.'

'He is dead?'

'Yes. While climbing a tabooed mountain called White Fang.'

'And your mother wishes you to wear white, as if you were your father returned?'

Fafhrd neither answered nor frowned at that shrewd question. Instead he asked, 'How many languages can you speak – besides this pidgin-Lankhmarese?'

She smiled at last. 'What a question! Why, I speak – though not too well – Mingol, Kvarchish, High and Low Lankhmarese, Quarmallian, Old Ghoulish, Desert-talk, and three Eastern tongues.'

Fafhrd nodded. 'That's good.'

'Forever why?'

'Because it means you are very civilized,' he answered.

'What's so great about that?' she demanded with a sour laugh.

'You should know, you're a culture dancer. In any case, I am interested in civilization.'

'One comes,' Essedinex hissed from the entry. 'Vlana, the youth must—'

'He must not!'

'As it happens, I must indeed leave now,' Fafhrd said, rising. 'Keep up the snow-bandages,' he instructed Vlana. 'Rest until sundown. Then more brandy, with hot soup.'

'Why must you leave?' Vlana demanded, rising on an elbow.

'I made a promise to my mother,' Fafhrd said without looking back.

'Your mother!'

Stooping at the entry, Fafhrd finally did stop to look back. 'I owe my mother many duties,' he said. 'I owe you none, as yet.'

'Vlana, he *must* leave. It's *the* one,' Essedinex stage-whispered hoarsely. Meanwhile he was shoving at Fafhrd, but for all the youth's slenderness, he might as well have been trying to push a tree off of its roots.

'Are you afraid of him who comes?' Vlana was buttoning up her dress now.

Fafhrd looked at her thoughtfully. Then, without replying in any way whatever to her question, he ducked through the entry and stood up, waiting the approach through the persistent mist of a man in whose face anger was gathering.

This man was as tall as Fafhrd, half again as thick and wide, and about twice as old. He was dressed in brown sealskin and amethyst-studded silver except for the two massive gold bracelets on his wrists and the gold chain about his neck, marks of a pirate chief.

Fafhrd felt a touch of fear, not at the approaching man, but at the crystals which were now thicker on the tents than he recalled them being when he had carried Vlana in. The element over which Mor and her sister witches had most power was cold – whether in a man's soup or loins, or in his sword or climbing rope, making them shatter. He often wondered whether it was Mor's magic that had made his own heart so cold. Now the cold would close in on the dancer. He should warn her, except she was civilized and would laugh at him.

The big man came up.

'Honorable Hringorl,' Fafhrd greeted softly.

For reply, the big man aimed a backhanded uppercut at Fafhrd with his near arm.

Fafhrd leaned sharply away, slithering under the blow, and then simply walked off the way he had first come.

Hringorl, breathing heavily, glared after him for a couple of heartbeats, then plunged into the hemicylindrical tent.

Hringorl was certainly the most powerful man in the Snow Clan, Fafhrd reflected, though not one of its chiefs because of his bullying ways and defiances of custom. The Snow Women hated, but found it hard to get a hold of him, since his mother was dead and he had never taken a wife, satisfying himself with concubines he brought back from his piratings.

From wherever he'd been inconspicuously standing, the black-turbaned and black-moustached man came up quietly to Fafhrd. 'That was well done, my friend. And when you brought in the dancer.'

Fafhrd said impassively, 'You are Vellix the Venturer.'

The other nodded. 'Bringing brandy from Klelg Nar to this mart. Will you sample the best with me?'

Fafhrd said, 'I am sorry, but I have an engagement with my mother.'

'Another time then,' Vellix said easily.

'Fafhrd!'

It was Hringorl who called. His voice was no longer angry. Fafhrd turned. The big man stood by the tent, then came striding up when Fafhrd did not move. Meanwhile, Vellix faded back and away in a fashion as easy as his speech.

'I'm sorry, Fafhrd,' Hringorl said gruffly. 'I did not know you had saved the dancer's life. You have done me a great service. Here.' He unclasped from his wrist one of the heavy gold bracelets and held it out.

Fafhrd kept his hands at his sides. 'No service whatever,' he said. 'I was only saving my mother from committing a wrong action.'

'You've sailed under me,' Hringorl suddenly roared, his face reddening though he still grinned somewhat, or tried to. 'So you'll take my gifts as well as my orders.' He caught hold of Fafhrd's hand, pressed the weighty torus into it, closed Fafhrd's lax fingers on it, and stepped back.

Instantly Fafhrd knelt, saying swiftly, 'I am sorry, but I may not take what I have not rightly won. And now I must keep an engagement with my mother.' Then he swiftly rose, turned, and walked away. Behind him, on an unbroken crust of snow, the golden bracelet gleamed.

He heard Hringorl's snarl and choked-back curse, but did not look around to see whether or not Hringorl picked up his spurned gratuity, though he did find it a bit difficult not to weave in his stride or duck his head a trifle, in case Hringorl decided to throw the massive wristlet at his skull.

Shortly he came to the place where his mother was sitting amongst seven Snow Women, making eight in all. They stood up. He stopped a yard short. Ducking his head and looking to the side, he said, 'Here I am, Mor.'

'You took a long while,' she said. 'You took too long.' Six heads around her nodded solemnly. Only Fafhrd noted, in the blurred edge of his vision, that the seventh and slenderest Snow Woman was moving silently backward.

'But here I am,' Fafhrd said.

'You disobeyed my command,' Mor pronounced coldly. Her haggard and once beautiful face would have looked very unhappy, had it not been so proud and masterful.

'But now I am obeying it,' Fafhrd countered. He noted that the seventh Snow Woman was now silently running, her great white cloak a-stream, between the home tents toward the high white forest that was Cold Corner's boundary everywhere that Trollstep Canyon wasn't.

'Very well,' Mor said. 'And now you will obey me by following me to the dream tent for ritual purification.'

'I am not defiled,' Fafhrd announced. 'Moreover, I purify myself after my own fashion, one also agreeable to the gods.'

There were clucks of shocked disapproval from all Mor's coven. Fafhrd had spoken boldly, but his head was still bent, so that he did not see their faces, and their entrapping eyes, but only their long-robed white forms, like a clump of great birches.

Mor said, 'Look me in the eyes.'

Fafhrd said, 'I fulfill all the customary duties of a grown son, from food-winning to sword-guarding. But as far as I can ascertain, looking my mother in the eyes is not one of those duties.'

'Your father always obeyed me,' Mor said ominously.

'Whenever he saw a tall mountain, he climbed her, obeying no one but himself,' Fafhrd contradicted.

'Yes, and died doing so!' Mor cried, her masterfulness controlling grief and anger without hiding them.

Fafhrd said hardly, 'Whence came the great cold that shattered his rope and pick on White Fang?'

Amidst the gasps of her coven, Mor pronounced in her deepest voice, 'A mother's curse, Fafhrd, on your disobedience and evil thinking!'

Fafhrd said with strange eagerness, 'I dutifully accept your curse, Mother.'

Mor said, 'My curse is not on you, but on your evil imaginings.'

'Nevertheless, I will forever treasure it,' Fafhrd cut in. 'And now, obeying myself, I must take leave of you, until the wrath-devil has let you go.'

And with that, head still bent down and away, he walked rapidly toward a point in the forest east of the home tents, but west of the great tongue of forest that stretched south almost to Godshall. The angry hissings of Mor's coven followed him, but his mother did not cry out his name, nor any word at all. Fafhrd would almost rather that she had.

Youth heals swiftly, on the skin-side. By the time Fafhrd plunged into his beloved wood without jarring a single becrystalled twig, his senses were alert, his neck-joint supple, and the outward surface of his inner being as cleared for new experience as the unbroken snow ahead. He took the easiest path, avoiding bediamonded thorn bushes to left and huge pinescreened juttings of pale granite to right.

He saw bird tracks, squirrel tracks, day-old bear tracks; snow birds snapped their black beaks at red snowberries; a furred snow-snake hissed at him, and he would not have been startled by the emergence of a dragon with ice-crusted spines.

So he was in no wise amazed when a great high-branched pine opened its snow-plastered bark and showed him its dryad – a merry, blue-eyed, blonde-haired girl's face, a dryad no more than seventeen years old. In fact, he had been expecting such an apparition ever since he had noted the seventh Snow Woman in flight.

Yet he pretended to be amazed for almost two heartbeats. Then he sprang forward crying, 'Mara, my witch,' and with his two arms separated her white-cloaked self from her camouflaging background, and kept them wrapped around her while they stood like one white column, hood to hood and lips to lips for at least twenty heartbeats of the most thuddingly delightful sort.

Then she found his right hand and drew it into her cloak and, through a placket, under her long coat, and pressed it against her crisply-ringleted lower belly.

'Guess,' she whispered, licking his ear.

'It's part of a girl. I do believe it's a—' he began most gayly, though his thoughts were already plunging wildly in a direly different direction.

'No, idiot, it's something that belongs to you,' the wet whisper coached.

The dire direction became an iced chute leading toward certainty. Nevertheless he said bravely, 'Well, I'd hoped you hadn't been trying out others, though that's your right. I must say I am vastly honored—'

'Silly beast! I meant it's something that belongs to us.'

The dire direction was now a black icy tunnel, becoming a pit. Automatically and with an appropriately great heart-thump, Fafhrd said, 'Not—?'

'Yes! I'm certain, you monster. I've missed twice.'

Better than ever in his life before, Fafhrd's lips performed their office of locking in words. When they opened at last, they and the tongue behind them were utterly under control of the great green eyes. There came forth in a joyous rush: 'O gods! How wonderful! I am a father! How clever of you, Mara!'

'Very clever indeed,' the girl admitted, 'to have fashioned anything so delicate after your rude handling. But now I must pay you off for that ungracious remark about "trying out others".' Hitching up her skirt behind, she guided both his hands under her cloak to a knot of thongs at the base of her spine. (Snow women wore fur hoods, fur boots, a high fur stocking on each leg gartered to a waist thong, and one or more fur coats and cloaks – it was a practical garb, not unlike the men's except for the longer coats.)

As he fingered the knot, from which three thongs led lightly off, Fafhrd said, 'Truly, Mara dearest, I do not favor these chastity girdles. They are not a civilized device. Besides, they must interfere with the circulation of your blood.'

'You and your fad for civilization! I'll love and belabor you out of it. Go on, untie the knot, making sure you and no other tied it.'

Fafhrd complied and had to agree that it was his knot and no other man's. The task took some time and was a delightful one to Mara, judging from her soft squeals and moans, her gentle nips and bites. Fafhrd himself began to get interested. When the task was done, Fafhrd got the reward of all courteous liars: Mara loved him dearly because he had told her all the right lies and she showed it in her beguiling behavior, and his interest in her and his excitement became vast.

After certain handlings and other tokens of affection, they fell to the snow side by side, both mattressed and covered entirely by their white fur cloaks and hoods.

A passerby would have thought that a snow mound had come alive convulsively and was perhaps about to give birth to a snowman, elf, or demon.

After a while the snow-mound grew utterly quiescent and the hypothetical passerby would have had to lean very close to catch the voices coming from inside it.

MARA: Guess what I'm thinking.

FAFHRD: That you're the Queen of Bliss. Aaah!

MARA: Aaaah back at you, and ooooh! And that you're the King of Beasts. No, silly, I'll tell you. I was thinking of how glad I am that you've had your southward adventurings before marriage. I'm sure you've raped or even made indecent love to dozens of southern women, which perhaps accounts for your wrongheadedness about civilization. But I don't mind a bit. I'll love you out of it.

FAFHRD: Mara, you have a brilliant mind, but just the same you greatly exaggerate that one pirate cruise I made under Hringorl, and especially the opportunities it afforded for amorous adventures. In the first place, all the inhabitants, and especially all the young women of any shore town we sacked, ran away to the hills before we'd even landed. And if there were any women raped, I being youngest would have been at the bottom of the list of rapists and so hardly tempted. Truth to tell, the only interesting folk I met on that dreary voyage were two old men held for ransom, from whom I learned a smattering of Quarmallian and High Lankhmarese, and a scrawny youth apprenticed to a hedge-wizard. He was deft with the dagger, that one, and had a legend-breaking mind, like mine and my father's.

MARA: Do not grieve. Life will become more exciting for you after we're married.

FAFHRD: That's where you're wrong, dearest Mara. Hold, let me explain! I know my mother. Once we're married, Mor will expect you to do all the cooking and tent-work. She'll treat you as seven-eighths slave and – perhaps – one-eighth my concubine.

MARA: Ha! You really will have to learn to rule your mother, Fafhrd. Yet do not fret, dearest, even about that. It's clear you know nothing of the weapons a strong and untiring young wife has against an old mother-in-law. I'll put her in her place, even if I have to poison her – oh, not to kill, only to weaken sufficiently. Before three moons have waxed, she'll be trembling at my gaze and you'll feel yourself much more a man. I know that you being an only child and your wild father perishing young, she got an unnatural influence over you, but—

FAFHRD: I feel myself very much the man at this instant, you immoral and poisoning witchlet, you ice-tigress; and I intend to prove it on you without delay. Defend yourself! Ha, would you—!

Once more the snow-mound convulsed, like a giant ice-bear dying of fits. The bear died to a music of sistrums and triangles, as there clashed together and shattered the flashing ice crystals which had grown in unnatural numbers and size on Mara's and Fafhrd's cloaks during their dialogue.

The short day raced toward night, as if even the gods who govern the sun and stars were impatient to see the Show.

Hringorl conferred with his three chief henchmen, Hor, Harrax, and Hrey. There was scowling and nodding, and Fafhrd's name was mentioned.

The youngest husband of the Snow Clan, a vain and thoughtless cockerel, was ambushed and snowballed unconscious by a patrol of young Snow Wives who had seen him in brazen converse with a Mingol stage girl. Thereafter, a sure casualty for the two-day run of the Show, he was tenderly but slowly nursed back toward life by his wife, who had been the most enthusiastic of the snowballers.

Mara, happy as a snow dove, dropped in on this household and helped. But as she watched the husband so helpless and the wife so tender, her smiles and dreamy grace vanished. She grew tense and, for an athletic girl, fidgety. Thrice she opened her lips to speak, then pursed them, and finally left without saying a word.

In the Women's Tent, Mor and her coven put a spell on Fafhrd to bring him home and another to chill his loins, then went on to discuss weightier measures against the whole universe of sons, husbands, and actresses.

The second enchantment had no effect on Fafhrd, probably because he was taking a snow-bath at the time – it being a well-known fact that magic has little effect on those who are already inflicting upon themselves the same results which the spell is trying to cause. After parting with Mara, he had stripped, plunged into a snowbank, then rubbed every surface, crack and cranny of his body with the numbing powdery stuff. Thereafter he used thickly-needled pine branches to dust himself off and beat his blood back into motion. Dressed, he felt the pull of the first enchantment, but opposed it and secretly made his way into the tent of two old Mingol traders, Zax and Effendrit, who had been his father's friends, and he snoozed amidst a pile of pelts until evening. Neither of his mother's spells were able to follow him into what was, by trading custom, a tiny area of Mingol territory though the Mingols' tent did begin to sag with an unnaturally large number of ice crystals, which the Mingol oldsters, wizened and nimble as monkeys, beat off janglingly with poles. The sound penetrated pleasantly into Fafhrd's dream without arousing him, which would have irked his mother had she known – she believed that both pleasure and rest were bad for men. His dream became one of Vlana dancing sinuously in a dress made of a net of fine silver wires from the intersections of which hung myriads of tiny silver bells, a vision which would have irked Mor beyond endurance; fortunate indeed that she was not at that moment using her power of reading minds at a distance.

Vlana herself slumbered while one of the Mingol girls, paid a half smerduk in advance by the injured actress, renewed the snow-bandages as necessary and, when they looked dry, wet Vlana's lips with sweet wine, of which a few drops trickled between. Vlana's mind was a-storm with anticipations and plots, but whenever she waked, she stilled it with an Eastern circle-charm that went something like, 'Creep, sleep; rouse, drowse; browse, soughs; slumber, umber; raw, claw; burnt, earn'd; cumber, number; left, death; cunt, won't; count, fount; mount, down't; leap, deep; creep, sleep,' and so on back around the incestuous loop. She knew that a woman can get wrinkles in her mind as well as her skin. She also knew that only a spinster looks after a spinster. And finally she knew that a trouper, like a soldier, does well to sleep whenever possible.

Vellix the Venturer, idly slipping about, overheard some of Hringorl's plottings, saw Fafhrd enter his tent of retreat, noted that Essedinex was drinking beyond his wont, and eavesdropped for a while on the Master of the Show.

In the girls' third of the actors' fish-shaped tent, Essedinex was arguing with the two Mingol girls, who were twins, and a barely nubile Ilthmarix, about the amount of grease they proposed to smear on their shaven bodies for tonight's perfor-mance.

'By the black bones, you'll beggar me,' he wailingly expostulated. 'And you'll look no more lascivious than lumps of lard.'

'From what I know of Northerners, they like their women well larded, and why not outside as well as in?' the one Mingol girl demanded.

'What's more,' her twin added sharply, 'if you expect us to freeze off our toes and tits, to please an audience of smelly old bearskins, you've got your head on upside-down.'

'Don't worry, Seddy,' the Ilthmarix said, patting his flushed cheek and its sparse white hairs, 'I always give my best performance when I'm all gooey. We'll have them chasing us up the walls, where we'll pop from their grabs like so many slippery melon seeds.'

'Chasing—?' Essedinex gripped the Ilthmarix by her slim shoulder. 'You'll provoke no orgies tonight, do you hear me? Teasing pays. Orgies don't. The point is to—'

'We know just how far to tease, daddy-pooh,' one of the Mingol girls put in.

'We know how to control them,' her sister continued.

'And if we don't, Vlana always does,' the Ilthmarix finished.

As the almost imperceptible shadows lengthened and the mist-wreathed air grew dark, the omnipresent crystals seemed to be growing even a little more swiftly. The palaver at the trading tents, which the thick snowy tongue of the forest shut off from the home tents, grew softer-voiced then ceased. The unending low chant from the Women's Tent became more noticeable and also higher pitched. An evening breeze came from the north making all the crystals tinkle. The chanting grew gruffer and the breeze and the tinkling ceased as if on command. The mist came wreathing back from east and west, and the crystals were growing again. The women's chanting faded to a murmur. All the Cold Corner grew tautly and expectantly silent with the approach of night.

Day ran away over the ice-fanged western horizon as if she were afraid of the dark.

In the narrow space between the actors' tents and Godshall there was movement, a glimmer, a bright spark that sputtered for nine, ten, eleven heartbeats, then a flash, a flaring, and there rose up – slowly at first, then swifter and swifter – a comet with a brushy tail of orange fire that dribbled sparks. High above the pines, almost on the edge of heaven – twenty-one, twenty-two, twenty-three – the comet's tail faded and it burst with a thunderclap into nine white stars.

It was the rocket signaling the first performance of the Show.

Godshall on the inside was a tall crazy longship of chill blackness inadequately lit and warmed by an arc of candles in the prow, which all the rest of the year was an altar, but now a stage. Its masts were eleven vast living pines thrusting up from the ship's bow, stern, and sides. Its sails – in sober fact, its walls – were stitched hides laced tautly to the masts. Instead of sky overhead there were thickly interthrusting pine branches, white with drifting snow, beginning a good five man's-heights above the deck.

The stern and waist of this weird ship, which moved only on the winds of imagination, were crowded with Snow Men in their darkly colorful furs seated on stumps and thick blanket rolls. They were laughing with drink and growling out short talk and jokes at each other, but not very loudly. Religious awe and fear touched them on entering Godshall, or more properly, God's Ship, despite or more likely because of the profane use to which it was being put tonight.

There came a rhythmic drumming, sinister as the padding of a snow leopard and at first so soft that no man might say exactly when it began, except that one moment there was talk and movement in the audience and the next none at all, only so many pairs of hands gripping or lightly resting on knees, and so many pairs of eyes scanning the candlelit stage between two screens painted with black and gray whorls.

The drumming grew louder, quickened, complicated itself into weaving arabesques of tapped sound, and returned to the leopard's padding.

There loped onto the stage, precisely in time with the drum beats, a silver-furred, short-bodied, slender feline with long legs, long ears a-prick, long whiskers, and long, white fangs. It stood about a yard high at the shoulder and rump. The only human feature was a glossy mop of long, straight black hair falling down the back of its neck and thence forward over its right shoulder.

It circled the stage thrice, ducking its head and sniffing as if on a scent and growling deep in its throat.

Then it noticed the audience and with a scream crouched back from them rampant, menacing them with the long, glittering claws which terminated its forelegs.

Two members of the audience were so taken in by the illusion that they had to be restrained by neighbors from pitching a knife or hurling a short-handled axe at what they were certain was a genuine and dangerous beast.

The beast scanned them, writhing its black lips back from its fangs and lesser teeth. As it swiftly swung its muzzle from side to side, inspecting them with its great brown eyes, its short-furred tail lashed back and forth in time.

Then it danced a leopardly dance of life, love, and death, sometimes on hind legs, but mostly on all fours. It scampered and investigated, it menaced and shrank, it attacked and fled, it caterwauled and writhed cat-lasciviously.

Despite the long black hair, it became no easier for the audience to think of it as a human female in a close-fitting suit of fur. For one thing, its forelegs were as long as its hindlegs and appeared to have an extra joint in them.

Something white squawked and came fluttering upward from behind one of the screens. With a swift leap and slash of foreleg, the great silvery cat struck.

Everyone in Godshall heard the scream of the snow pigeon and the crack of its neck.

Holding the dead bird to its fangs, the great cat, standing womanly now, gave the audience a long look, then walked without haste behind the nearest screen. There came from the audience a sigh compounded of loathing and longing, of a wonder as to what would happen next and of a wish to see what was going on now.

Fafhrd, however, did not sigh. For one thing, the slightest movement might have revealed his hiding place. For another, he could clearly see all that was going on behind both whorl-marked screens.

Being barred from the Show by his youth, let alone by Mor's wishes and witcheries, half an hour before showtime he had mounted one of the trunk-pillars of Godshall on the precipice side when no one was looking. The strong lacings of the hide walls made it the easiest of climbs. Then he had cautiously crawled out onto two of several stout pine branches growing inward close together over the hall, being very careful to disturb neither browning needles nor drifted snow, until he had found a good viewing hole, one opening toward the stage, but mostly hidden from the audience. Thereafter, it had been simply a matter of holding still enough so that no betraying needles or snow dropped down. Anyone looking up through the gloom and chancing to see parts of his white garb would take it for snow, he hoped.

Now he watched the two Mingol girls rapidly pull off from Vlana's arms the tight fur sleeves together with the fur-covered, claw-tipped, rigid extra lengths in which they ended and which her hands had been gripping. Next they dragged from Vlana's legs *their* fur coverings, while she sat on a stool and, after drawing her fangs off her teeth, speedily unhooked her leopard mask and shoulder piece.

A moment later she slouched back on stage – a cave woman in a brief sarong of silvery fur and lazily gnawing at the end of a long, thick bone. She mimed a cave woman's day: fire-and-baby-tending, brat-slapping, hide-chewing, and laborious sewing. Things got a bit more exciting with the return of her husband, an unseen presence made visible by her miming.

Her audience followed the story easily, grinning when she demanded what meat her husband had brought, showed dis-satisfaction with his meager kill, and refused him an embrace. They guffawed when she tried to clobber him with her chewing bone and got knocked sprawling in return, her children cow-ering around her.

From that position she scuttled off stage behind the other screen, which hid the actors' doorway (normally the Snow Priest's) and also concealed the one-armed Mingol, whose flickering five fingers did all the drum music on the instrument clutched between his feet. Vlana whipped off the rest of her fur, changed the slant of her eyes and eyebrows by four deft strokes of makeup, seemingly in one movement shouldered into a long gray gown with hood, and was back on stage in the persona of a Mingol woman of the Steppes.

After another brief session of miming, she squatted gracefully down at a low, jar-stocked table stage front, and began carefully to make up her face and do her hair, the audience serving as her mirror. She dropped back hood and gown, revealing the briefer red silk garment her fur one had hidden. It was most fascinating to watch her apply the variously colored salves and powders and glittering dusts to her lips, cheeks, and eyes, and see her comb up her dark hair into a high structure kept in place by long, gem-headed pins.

Just then Fafhrd's composure was tested to the uttermost, when a large handful of snow was clapped to his eyes and held there.

He stayed perfectly still for three heartbeats. Then he captured a rather slender wrist and dragged it down a short distance, meantime gently shaking his head and blinking his eyes.

The trapped wrist twisted free and the clot of snow fell down the neck of the wolfskin coat of Hringorl's man Hor seated immediately below. Hor gave a strange low cry and started to glare upward, but fortunately at that moment Vlana pulled down her red silk sarong and began to anoint her nipples with a coral salve.

Fafhrd looked around and saw Mara grinning fiercely at him from where she lay outstretched on the two branches next to his, her head level with his shoulder.

'If I'd been an ice gnome, you'd be dead!' she hissed at him. 'Or if I'd set my four brothers to trap you, as I should have. Your ears *were* dead, your mind all in your eyes straining toward that skinny harlot. I've heard how you challenged Hringorl for her! And refused his gift of a gold bracelet!'

'I admit, dear, that you slithered up behind me most skillfully and silently,' Fafhrd breathed at her softly, 'while you seem to have eyes and ears for all things that transpire – and some that don't – at Cold Corner. But I must say, Mara—'

'Hah! Now you'll tell me I shouldn't be here, being a woman. Male prerogatives, intersexual sacrilege, and so forth. Well, neither should you be here.'

Fafhrd gravely considered part of that. 'No, I think all the women should be here. What they would learn would be much to their interest and advantage.'

'To caper like a cat in heat? To slouch about like a silly slave? Yes, I saw those acts too – while you were drooling dumb and deaf! You men will laugh at anything, especially when your stupid, gasping, red-faced lust's been aroused by a shameless bitch making a show of her scrawny nakedness!'

Mara's heated hissings were getting dangerously loud and might well have attracted the attention of Hor and others, but once again good fortune intervened, in that there was a ripple of drumming as Vlana streaked off the stage, and then there began a wild, somewhat thin, but galloping music, the one-armed Mingol being joined by the little Ilthmarix playing a nose flute.

'I did not laugh, my dear,' Fafhrd breathed somewhat loftily, 'nor did I drool or flush or speed my breath, as I am sure you noted. No, Mara, my sole purpose in being here is to learn more about civilization.'

She glared at him, grinned, then of a sudden smiled tenderly. 'You know, I honestly think you believe that, you incredible infant,' she breathed back wonderingly. 'Granting that the decadence called civilization could possibly be of interest to anyone, and a capering whore able to carry its message, or rather absence of message.'

'I neither think nor believe, I *know* it,' Fafhrd replied, ignoring Mara's other remarks. 'A whole world calls and have we eyes only for Cold Corner? Watch with me, Mara, and gain wisdom. The actress dances the cultures of all lands and ages. Now she is a woman of the Eight Cities.'

Perhaps Mara was in some small part persuaded. Or perhaps it was that Vlana's new costume covered her thoroughly – sleeved green bodice, full blue skirt, red stockings, and yellow shoes – and that the culture dancer was panting a trifle and showing the cords in her neck from the stamping and whirling dance she was doing. At any rate, the Snow Girl shrugged and smiled indulgently and whispered, 'Well, I must admit it all has a certain disgusting interest.'

'I knew you'd understand, dearest. You have twice the mind of

31

any woman of our tribe, aye, or of any man,' Fafhrd cooed, caressing her tenderly but somewhat absently as he peered at the stage.

In succession, always making lightning costume changes, Vlana became a houri of the Eastern Lands, a custom-hobbled Quarmallian queen, a languorous concubine of the King of Kings, and a haughty Lankhmar lady wearing a black toga. This last was theatrical license; only the men of Lankhmar wear the toga, but the garment was Lankhmar's chiefest symbol across the world of Nehwon.

Meanwhile Mara did her best to share the eccentric whim of her husband-to-be. At first she was genuinely intrigued and made mental notes on details of Vlana's dress styles and tricks of behavior which she might herself adopt to advantage. But then she was gradually overwhelmed by a realization of the older woman's superiority in training, knowledge and experience. Vlana's dancing and miming clearly couldn't be learned except with much coaching and drill. And how, and especially where, could a Snow Girl ever wear such clothes? Feelings of inferiority gave way to jealousy and that to hatred.

Civilization was nasty, Vlana ought to be whipped out of Cold Corner, and Fafhrd needed a woman to run his life and keep his mad imagination in check. Not his mother, of course – that awful and incestuous eater of her own son – but a glamorous and shrewd young wife. Herself.

She began to watch Fafhrd intently. He didn't look like an infatuated male, he looked cold as ice, but he was certainly utterly intent on the scene below. She reminded herself that a few men were adept at hiding their true feelings.

Vlana shed her toga and stood in a wide-meshed tunic of fine silver wires. At each crossing of the wires a tiny silver bell stood out. She shimmied and the bells tinkled, like a tree of tiny birds all chirruping together a hymn to her body. Now her slenderness seemed that of adolescence, while from between the strands of her sleekly cascading hair, her large eyes gleamed with mysterious hints and invitations.

Fafhrd's controlled breathing quickened. So his dream in the Mingols' tent had been true! His attention, which had half been off to the lands and ages Vlana had danced, centered wholly on her and became desire.

This time his composure was put to an even sorer test for, without warning, Mara's hand clutched his crotch.

But he had little time in which to demonstrate his composure. She let go and crying, 'Filthy beast! You are lusting!' struck him in the side, below the ribs.

He tried to catch her wrists, while staying on his branches. She kept trying to hit him. The pine boughs creaked and shed snow and needles.

In landing a clout on Fafhrd's ear, Mara's upper body over-balanced, though her feet kept hooked to branchlets.

Growling, 'God freeze you, you bitch!' Fafhrd gripped his stoutest bough with one hand and lunged down with the other to catch Mara's arm just beneath the shoulder.

Those looking up from below – and by now there were some, despite the strong counter-attraction of the stage – saw two struggling, white-clad torsos and fair-haired heads dipping out of the branchy roof, as if about to descend in swan dives. Then, still struggling, the figures withdrew upward.

An older Snow Man cried out, 'Sacrilege!' A younger, 'Peepers! Let's thrash 'em!' He might have been obeyed, for a quarter of the Snow Men were on their feet by now, if it hadn't been that Essedinex was keeping a close eye on things through a peephole in one of the screens and that he was wise in the ways of handling unruly audiences. He shot a finger at the Mingol behind him, then sharply raised that hand, palm upward.

The music surged. Cymbals clashed. The two Mingol girls and the Ilthmarix bounded on stage stark naked and began to caper around Vlana. The fat Easterner clumped past them and set fire to his great black beard. Blue flames crawled up and flickered before his face and around his ears. He didn't put the fire out – with a wet towel he carried – until Essedinex hoarsely stage-whispered from his peephole, 'That's enough. We've got 'em again.' The length of the black beard had been halved. Actors make great sacrifices, which the yokels and even their co-mates rarely appreciate.

Fafhrd, dropping the last dozen feet, lighted in the high drift outside Godshall at the same instant Mara finished her downward climb. They faced each other calf-deep in crusted snow, across which the rising, slightly gibbous moon threw streaks of white glimmer and made shadow between them.

Fafhrd asked, 'Mara, where did you hear that lie about me challenging Hringorl for the actress?'

'Faithless lecher!' she cried, punched him in the eye, and ran off toward the tent of the women, sobbing and crying, 'I *will* tell my brothers! You'll see!'

Fafhrd jumped up and down, smothering a howl of pain, sprinted after her three steps, stopped, clapped snow to his pain-stabbed eye and, as soon as it was only throbbing, began to think.

He looked around with the other eye, saw no one, made his way to a clump of snow-laden evergreens on the edge of the precipice, concealed himself among them, and continued to think.

His ears told him that the Show was still going at a hot pace inside Godshall. There were laughs and cheers, sometimes drowning the wild drumming and fluting. His eyes – the hit one was working again – told him there was no one near him. They swiveled to the actors' tents at that end of Godshall which lay nearest the new road south, and at the stables beyond them, and at the traders' tents beyond the stables. Then they came back to the nearest tent: Vlana's hemicylindrical one. Crystals clothed it, twinkling in the moonlight, and a giant crystal flatworm seemed to be crawling across its middle just below the evergreen sycamore bough.

He slitheringly walked toward it across the bedia-monded snow crust. The knot joining the lacings of its doorway was hidden in shadow and felt complex and foreign. He went to the back of the tent, loosened two pegs, went on belly through the crack like a snake, found himself amongst the hems of the skirts of Vlana's racked garments, loosely replaced the pegs, stood up, shook himself, took four steps and lay down on the pallet. A little heat radiated from a banked brazier. After a while he reached to the table and poured himself a cup of brandy.

At last he heard voices. They grew louder. As the lacings of the door were being unknotted and loosened, he felt for his knife and also prepared to draw a large fur rug over him.

Saying with laughter but also decision, 'No, no, *no*,' Vlana swiftly stepped in backward over the slack lashings, held the door closed with one hand while she gave the lashings a tightening pull with the other, and glanced over her shoulder.

Her look of stark surprise was gone almost before Fafhrd marked it, to be replaced by a quick welcoming grin that wrinkled her nose comically. She turned away from him, carefully drew the lashings tight, and spent some time tying a knot on the inside. Then she came over and knelt beside him where he lay, her body erect from her knees. There was no grin now as she looked down at him, only a composed, enigmatic thoughtfulness, which he sought to match. She was wearing the hooded robe of her Mingol costume.

'So you changed your mind about a reward,' she said quietly but matter-of-factly. 'How do you know that I too may not have changed mine since?'

Fafhrd shook his head, replying to her first statement. Then, after a pause, he said, 'Nevertheless, I have discovered that I desire you.'

Vlana said, 'I saw you watching the show from . . . from the gallery. You almost stole it, you know – I mean the show. Who was the girl with you? Or was it a youth? I couldn't be quite sure.'

Fafhrd did not answer her inquiries. Instead he said, 'I also wish to ask you questions about your supremely skillful dancing and . . . and acting in loneliness.'

'Miming.' She supplied the word.

'Miming, yes. *And* I want to talk to you about civilization.'

'That's right, this morning you asked me how many languages I knew,' she said, looking straight across him at the wall of the tent. It was clear that she too was a thinker. She took the cup of brandy out of his hand, swallowed half of what was left, and returned it to him.

'Very well,' she said, at last looking down at him, but with unchanged expression. 'I will give you your desire, my dear boy. But now is not the time. First, I must rest and gather strength.

Go away and return when the star Shadah sets. Wake me if I slumber.'

'That's an hour before dawn,' he said, looking up at her. 'It will be a chilly wait for me in the snow.'

'Don't do that,' she said quickly. 'I don't want you three-quarters frozen. Go where it's warm. To stay awake, think of me. Don't drink too much wine. Now go.'

He got up and made to embrace her. She drew back a step, saying, 'Later. Later – everything.' He started toward the door. She shook her head, saying, 'You might be seen. As you came.'

Passing her again, his head brushed something hard. Between the hoops supporting the tent's middle, the supple hide of the tent bulged down, while the hoops themselves were bowed out and somewhat flattened bearing the weight. He cringed down for an instant, ready to grab Vlana and jump any way, then began methodically to punch and sweep at the bulges, always striking outward. There was a crashing and a loud tinkling as the massed crystals, which outside had reminded him of a giant flatworm – must be a giant snow serpent by now! – broke up and showered off.

Meanwhile he said, 'The Snow Women do not love you. Nor is Mor my mother your friend.'

'Do they think to frighten me with ice crystals?' Vlana demanded contemptuously. 'Why, I know of Eastern fire sorceries compared to which their feeble magickings—'

'But you are in *their* territory now, at the mercy of *their* element, which is crueler and subtler than fire,' Fafhrd interposed, brushing away the last of the bulgings, so that the hoops stood up again and the leather stretched almost flat between them. 'Do not underrate their powers.'

'Thank you for saving my tent from being crumbled. But now – and swiftly – go.'

She spoke as if of trivial matters, but her large eyes were thoughtful.

Just before snaking under the back wall, Fafhrd looked over his shoulder. Vlana was gazing at the side wall again, holding the empty cup he had given her, but she caught his movement and, now smiling tenderly, put a kiss on her palm and blew it toward him.

Outside the cold had grown bitter. Nevertheless, Fafhrd went to his clump of evergreens, drew his cloak closely around him, dropped its hood over his forehead, tightened the hood's drawstring, and sat himself facing Vlana's tent.

When the cold began to penetrate his furs, he thought of Vlana.

Suddenly he was crouching and had loosened his knife in its sheath.

A figure was approaching Vlana's tent, keeping to the shadows when it could. It appeared to be clad in black.

Fafhrd silently advanced.

Through the still air came the faint sound of fingernails scratching leather.

There was a flash of dim light as the doorway was opened.

It was bright enough to show the face of Vellix the Venturer. He stepped inside and there was the sound of lacings being drawn tight.

Fafhrd stopped ten paces from the tent and stood there for perhaps two dozen breaths. Then he softly walked past the tent, keeping the same distance.

There was a glow in the doorway of the high, conical tent of Essedinex. From the stables beyond, a horse whickered twice.

Fafhrd crouched and peered through the low, glowing doorway a knife-cast away. He moved from side to side. He saw a table crowded with jugs and cups set against the sloping wall of the tent opposite the doorway.

To one side of the table sat Essedinex. To the other, Hringorl.

On the watch for Hor, Harrax, or Hrey, Fafhrd circled the tent. He approached it where the table and the two men were faintly silhouetted. Drawing aside his hood and hair, he set his ear against the leather.

'Three gold bars – that's my top,' Hringorl was saying surlily. The leather made his voice hollow.

'Five,' Essedinex answered, and there was the *slup* of wine mouthed and swallowed.

'Look here, old man,' Hringorl countered, his voice at its most gruffly menacing, 'I don't need you. I can snatch the girl and pay you nothing.'

'Oh no, that won't do, Master Hringorl.' Essedinex sounded merry. 'For then the Show would never return again to Cold Corner, and how would your tribesmen like that? Nor would there be any more girls brought you by me.'

'What matter?' the other answered carelessly. The words were muffled by a gulp of wine, yet Fafhrd could hear the bluff in them. 'I have my ship. I can cut your throat this instant and snatch the girl tonight.'

'Then do so,' Essedinex said brightly. 'Only give me a moment for one more quaff.'

'Very well, you old miser. Four gold bars.'

'Five.'

Hringorl cursed sulfurously. 'Some night, you ancient pimp, you will provoke me too far. Besides, the girl is old.'

'Aye, in the ways of pleasure. Did I tell you that she once became an acolyte of the Wizards of Azorkah? – so that she might be trained by them to become a concubine of the King of Kings and their spy in the court at Horborixen. Aye, and eluded those dread necromancers most cleverly when she had gained the erotic knowledge she desired.'

Hringorl laughed with a forced lightness. 'Why should I pay even one silver bar for a girl who has been possessed by dozens? Every man's plaything.'

'By hundreds,' Essedinex corrected. 'Skill is gained only by experience, as you know well. And the greater the experience, the greater the skill. Yet this girl is never a plaything. She is the instructress, the revelator; she plays with a man for his pleasure, she can make a man feel king of the universe and perchance – who knows? – even *be* that. What is impossible to a girl who knows the pleasure-ways of the gods themselves – aye, and of the arch-demons? And yet – you won't believe this, but it's true – she remains in her fashion forever virginal. For no man has ever mastered her.'

'That will be seen to!' Hringorl's words were almost a laughing shout. There was the sound of wine gulped. Then his voice dropped. 'Very well, five gold bars it is, you usurer. Delivery after tomorrow night's Show. The gold paid against the girl.'

'Three hours after the Show, when the girl's drugged and all's quiet. No need to rouse the jealousy of your fellow tribesmen so soon.'

'Make it two hours. Agreed? And now let's talk of next year. I'll want a black girl, a full-blooded Kleshite. And no five-gold-bar deal ever again. I'll not want a witchy wonder, only youth and great beauty.'

Essedinex answered, 'Believe me, you won't ever again desire another woman, once you've known and – I wish you luck – mastered Vlana. Oh, of course, I suppose—'

Fafhrd reeled back from the tent a half dozen paces and there planted his feet firm and wide, feeling strangely dizzy, or was it drunk? He had early guessed they were almost certainly talking of Vlana, but hearing her name spoken made a much greater difference than he'd expected.

The two revelations, coming so close, filled him with a mixed feeling he'd never known before: an overmastering rage and also a desire to laugh hugely. He wanted a sword long enough to slash open the sky and tumble the dwellers in paradise from their beds. He wanted to find and fire off all the Show's sky-rockets into the tent of Essedinex. He wanted to topple Godshall with its pines and drag it across all the actors' tents. He wanted—

He turned around and swiftly made for the stable tent. The one groom was snoring on the straw beside an empty jug and near the light sleigh of Essedinex. Fafhrd noted with a fiendish grin that the horse he knew best happened to be one of Hringorl's. He found a horse collar and a long coil of light, strong rope. Then, making reassuring mumbles behind half-closed lips, he led out the chosen horse – a white mare – from the rest. The groom only snored louder.

He again noted the light sleigh. A risk-devil seized him and he unlaced the stiff, pitchy tarpaulin covering the storage space behind the two seats. Beneath it among other things was the Show's supply of rockets. He selected three of the biggest – with their stout ash tails they were long as ski sticks – and then took time to replace the tarpaulin. He still felt the mad desire for destruction, but now it was under a measure of control.

Outside he put the collar on the mare and firmly knotted to it one end of the rope. The other end he fashioned into a roomy noose. Then, coiling the rest of the rope and gripping the rockets under his left elbow, he nimbly mounted the mare and walked it near the tent of Essedinex. The two dim silhouettes still confronted each other across the table.

He whirled the noose above his head and cast. It settled around the apex of the tent with hardly a sound, for he was quick to draw in the slack before it rattled against the tent's wall.

The noose tightened around the top of the tent's central mast. Containing his excitement, he walked the mare towards the forest across the moon-bright snow, paying out the rope. When there were only four coils of it left, he urged the mare into a lope. He crouched over the collar, holding it firm, his heels clamped to the mare's sides. The rope tightened. The mare strained. There was a satisfying, muffled *crack* behind him. He shouted a triumphant laugh. The mare plunged on against the rope's irregular restraint. Looking back, he saw the tent dragging after them. He saw fire and heard yells of surprise and anger. Again he shouted his laughter.

At the edge of the forest he drew his knife and slashed the rope. Vaulting down, he buzzed approvingly in the mare's ear and gave her a slap on the flank that set her cantering toward the stable. He considered firing off the rockets toward the fallen tent, but decided it would be anticlimactic. With them still clamped under his elbow, he walked into the edge of the woods. So hidden, he started home. He walked lightly to minimize footprints, found a branch of fringe pine and dragged it behind him and, when he could, he walked on rock.

His mountainous humor was gone and his rage too, replaced by black depression. He no longer hated Vellix or even Vlana, but civilization seemed a tawdry thing, unworthy of his interest. He was glad he had spilled Hringorl and Essedinex, but they were woodlice. He himself was a lonely ghost, doomed to roam the Cold Waste.

He thought of walking north through the woods until he found a new life or froze, of fetching and strapping on his skis and attempting to leap the tabooed gap that had been the death of Skif, of getting sword and challenging Hringorl's henchmen all at once, and of a hundred other doom-treadings.

The tents of the Snow Clan looked like pale mushrooms in the light of the crazily glaring moon. Some were cones topping a squat cylinder; others, bloated hemispheres, turnip shapes. Like mushrooms, they did not quite touch the ground at the edges. Their floors of packed branches, carpeted with hides and supported by heavier boughs, stood on and overhung chunky posts, so that a tent's heat would not turn the frozen ground below it to a mush.

The huge, silvery trunk of a dead snow oak, ending in what looked like a giant's split fingernails, where an old lightning bolt had shattered it midway up, marked the site of Mor's and Fafhrd's tent – and also of his father's grave, which the tent overlay. Each year it was pitched just so.

There were lights in a few of the tents and in the great Tent of the Women lying beyond in the direction of Godshall, but Fafhrd could see no one abroad. With a dispirited grunt he headed for his home door then, remembering the rockets, he veered toward the dead oak. It was smooth surfaced, the bark long gone. The few remaining branches were likewise bare and broken off short, the lowest of them appearing well out of reach.

A few paces away he paused for another look around. Assured of secrecy, he raced toward the oak and making a vertical leap more like a leopard's than a man's, he caught hold of the lowest branch with his free hand and whipped himself up onto it before his upward impetus was altogether spent.

Standing lightly on the dead branch with a finger touching the trunk, he made a final scan for peepers and late walkers, then with pressure of fingers and tease of fingernails, opened in the seemingly seamless gray wood a doorway tall as himself but scarcely half as wide. Feeling past skis and ski sticks, he found a long thin shape wrapped thrice around with lightly oiled seal-skin. Undoing it, he uncovered a powerful-looking bow and a quiver of long arrows. He added the rockets to it, replaced the wrappings, then shut the queer door of his tree-safe and dropped to the snow below, which he brushed smooth.

Entering his home tent, he felt again like a ghost and made as little noise as one. The odors of home comforted him uncomfortably and against his will; smells of meat, cooking, old smoke, hides, sweat, the chamber pot, Mor's faint, sour-sweet stench. He crossed the springy floor and, fully clad, he stretched himself in his sleeping furs. He felt tired as death. The silence was profound. He couldn't hear Mor's breathing. He thought of his last sight of his father, blue and shut-eyed, his broken limbs straightened, his best sword naked at his side with his slate-colored fingers fitted around the hilt. He thought of Nalgron now in the earth under the tent, worm-gnawed to a skeleton, the sword black rust, the eyes open now – sockets staring upward through solid dirt. He remembered his last sight of his father alive: a tall wolfskin cloak striding away with Mor's warnings and threats spattering against it. Then the skeleton came back into his mind. It was a night for ghosts.

'Fafhrd?' Mor called softly from across the tent.

Fafhrd stiffened and held his breath. When he could no longer, he began to let it out and draw it in, open-mouthed, in noiseless draughts.

'Fafhrd?' The voice was a little louder, though still like a ghost cry. 'I heard you come in. You're not asleep.'

No use keeping silent. 'You haven't slept either, Mother?'

'The old sleep little.'

That wasn't true, he thought. Mor wasn't old, even by the Cold Waste's merciless measure. At the same time, it *was* the truth. Mor was as old as the tribe, the Waste itself, as old as death.

Mor said composedly – Fafhrd knew she had to be lying on her back, staring straight upward – 'I am willing that you should take Mara to wife. Not pleased, but willing. There is need for a strong back here, so long as you daydream, shooting your thoughts like arrows loosed high and at random, and prank about and gad after actresses and such gilded dirt. Besides, you have got Mara with child and her family does not altogether lack status.'

'Mara spoke to you tonight?' Fafhrd asked. He tried to keep his voice dispassionate, but the words came out strangledly.

'As any Snow Girl should. Except she ought to have told me

earlier. And you earlier still. But you have inherited threefold your father's secretiveness along with his urge to neglect his family and indulge himself in useless adventurings. Except that in you the sickness takes a more repulsive form. Cold mountaintops were his mistresses, while you are drawn to civilization, that putrid festering of the hot south, where there is no natural stern cold to punish the foolish and luxurious and to see that the decencies are kept. But you will discover that there is a witchy cold that can follow you anywhere in Nehwon. Ice once went down and covered all the hot lands, in punishment for an earlier cycle of lecherous evil. And wherever ice once went, witchery can send it again. You will come to believe that, and shed your sickness, or else you will learn as your father learned.'

Fafhrd tried to make the accusation of husband-murder that he had hinted at so easily this morning, but the words stuck, not in his throat, but in his very mind, which felt invaded. Mor had long ago made his heart cold. Now, up in his brain, she was creating among his most private thoughts crystals which distorted everything and prevented him from using against her the weapons of duty coldly performed and joined by a cold reason which let him keep his integrity. He felt as if there were closing in on him forever the whole world of cold, in which the rigidity of ice and the rigidity of morals and the rigidity of thought were all one.

As if sensing her victory and permitting herself to joy in it a little, Mor said in the same dead, reflective tones, 'Aye, your father now bitterly regrets Gran Hanack, White Fang, the Ice Queen, and all his other mountain paramours. They cannot help him now. They have forgotten him. He stares up endlessly from lidless sockets at the home he despised and now yearns for, so near, yet so impossibly far. His fingerbones scrabble feebly against the frozen earth, he tries futilely to twist under its weight . . .'

Fafhrd heard a faint scratching, perhaps of icy twigs against tent leather, but his hair rose. Yet he could move no other part of him, he discovered as he tried to lift himself. The blackness all around him was a vast weight. He wondered if Mor had magicked him down under the ground beside his father. Yet it

43

was a greater weight than that of eight feet of frozen earth that pressed on him. It was the weight of the entire Cold Waste and its killingness, of the taboos and contempts and shutmindedness of the Snow Clan, of the pirate greed and loutish lust of Hringorl, of even Mara's merry self-absorption and bright, half-blind mind, and atop them all Mor with ice crystals forming on her fingertips as she wove them in a binding spell.

And then he thought of Vlana.

It may not have been the thought of Vlana that did it. A star may have chanced to crawl across the tent's tiny smoke-hole and shoot its tiny silver arrow into the pupil of one of his eyes. It may have been that his held breath suddenly puffed out and his lungs automatically sucked another breath in, showing him that his muscles *could* move.

At any rate he shot up and dashed for the doorway. He dared not stop for the lashings, because Mor's ice-jagged fingers were clutching at him. Instead he ripped the brittle, old leather with one downward sweep of his clawed right hand and then *leaped* from the door, because Nalgron's skeletal arms were straining toward him from the narrow black space between the frozen ground and the tent's elevated floor.

And then he ran as he had never run before. He ran as if all the ghosts of the Cold Waste were at his heels – and in some fashion they were. He passed the last of the Snow Clan's tents, all dark, and the faintly tinkling Tent of the Women, and sprinted out onto the gentle slope, all silvered by the moon, leading down to the upcurving lip of Trollstep Canyon. He felt the urge to dash off that verge, challenging the air to uphold him and bear him south or else hurl him to instant oblivion – and for a moment there seemed nothing to choose between those two fates.

Then he was running not so much away from the cold and its crippling, supernatural horrors, as toward civilization, which was once again a bright emblem in his brain, an answer to all small-mindedness.

He slowed down a little and some sense came back into his head, so that he peered for living late-walkers as well as for demons and fetches.

He noted Shadah twinkling blue in the western treetops.

He was walking by the time he reached Godshall. He went between it and the canyon's rim, which no longer tugged him.

He noted that Essedinex's tent had been set up again and was once more lit. No new snow worm crawled across Vlana's tent. The snow sycamore bough above it glittered with crystals in the moonlight.

He entered without warning by the back door, silently drawing out the loosened pegs and then thrusting together under the wall and the hems of the racked costumes his head and right fist, the latter gripping his drawn knife.

Vlana lay asleep alone on her back on the pallet, a light red woolen blanket drawn up to her naked armpits. The lamp burned yellow and small, yet brightly enough to show all the interior and no one but her. The unbanked and newly stoked brazier radiated heat.

Fafhrd came all the way in, sheathed his knife, and stood looking down at the actress. Her arms seemed very slender, her hands long-fingered and a shade large. With her big eyes shut, her face seemed rather small at the center of its glory of outspread, dark brown hair. Yet it looked both noble and knowing and its moist, long, generous lips, newly and carefully carmined, roused and tempted him. Her skin had a faint sheen of oil. He could smell its perfume.

For a moment Vlana's supine posture reminded him of both Mor and Nalgron, but this thought was instantly swept away by the brazier's fierce heat, like that of a small wrought-iron sun, by the rich textures and graceful instruments of civilization all around him, and by Vlana's beauty and couth grace, which seemed self-aware even in sleep. She was civilization's sigil.

He moved back toward the rack and began to strip off his clothes and neatly fold and pile them. Vlana did not wake, or at least her eyes did not open.

Getting back under the red blanket again some time later, after crawling out to relieve himself, Fafhrd said, 'Now tell me about civilization and your part in it.'

Vlana drank half of the wine Fafhrd had fetched her on his

way back, then stretched luxuriously, her head resting on her intertwined hands.

'Well, to begin with, I'm not a princess, though I liked being called one,' she said lightly. 'I must inform you that you have not got yourself even a lady, darlingest boy. As for civilization, it stinks.'

'No,' Fafhrd agreed, 'I have got myself the skillfullest and most glamorous actress in all Nehwon. But why has civilization an ill odor for you?'

'I think I must disillusion you still further, beloved,' Vlana said, somewhat absently rubbing her side against his. 'Otherwise you might get silly notions about me and even devise silly plans.'

'If you're talking about pretending to be a whore in order to gain erotic knowledge and other wisdoms—' Fafhrd began.

She glanced at him in considerable surprise and interrupted rather sharply: 'I'm worse than a whore, by some standards. I'm a thief. Yes, Red Ringlets, a cutpurse and filchpocket, a roller of drunks, a burglar and alleybasher. I was born a farm girl, which I suppose makes me lower still to a hunter, who lives by the death of animals and keeps his hands out of the dirt and reaps no harvest except with the sword. When my parents' plot of land was confiscated by the law's trickery to make a tiny corner of one of the new, vast, slave-worked, Lankhmar-owned grain farms, and they in consequence starved to death, I determined to get my own back from the grain merchants. Lankhmar City would feed me, aye, feed me well! – and be paid only with lumps and perhaps a deep scratch or two. So to Lankhmar I went. Falling in there with a clever girl of the same turn of mind and some experience, I did well for two full rounds of moons and a few more. We worked only in black garb, and called ourselves to ourselves the Dark Duo.

'For a cover, we danced, chiefly in the twilight hours, to fill in the time before the big-name entertainers. A little later we began to mime too, taught by one Hinerio, a famous actor fallen by wine on evil days, the darlingest and courtliest old trembler who ever begged for a drink at dawn or contrived to fondle a girl one quarter his age at dusk. And so, as I say, I did quite well . . .until I fell afoul, as my parents had, of the law. No, not the Overlord's courts, dear boy, and his prisons and racks and head-and-hand-chopping blocks, though they are a shame crying to the stars. No, I ran afoul of a law older even than Lankhmar's and a court less merciful. In short, my friend's and my own cover was finally blown by the Thieves' Guild, a most ancient organization with locals in every city of the civilized world with a hidebound law against female membership and with a deep detestation of all freelance pilferers. Back on the farm I had heard of the Guild and hoped in my innocence to become worthy to join it, but soon learned their byword, "Sooner give a cobra a kiss, than a secret to a woman." Incidentally, sweet scholar of civilization's arts, such women as the Guild must use as lures and attention-shifters and such, they hire by the half hour from the Whores' Guild.

'I was lucky. At the moment when I was supposed to be slowly strangling somewhere else, I was stumbling over my friend's body, having looped swiftly home to get a key I'd forgot. I lit a lamp in our close-shuttered abode and saw the long agony in Vilis' face and the red silken cord buried deep in her neck. But what filled me with the hottest rage and coldest hate – besides a second measure of knee-melting fear – was that they had strangled old Hinerio too. Vilis and I were at least competitors and so perhaps fair game by civilization's malodorous standards, but he had never even suspected us of thievery. He had assumed merely that we had other lovers or else – and also – erotic clients.

'So I scuttled out of Lankhmar as swiftly as a spied crab, eyes behind me for pursuit, and in Ilthmar encountered Essedinex's troupe, headed north for the off-season. By good fortune they needed a leading mime and my skill was sufficient to satisfy old Seddy.

'But at the same time, I swore an oath by the morning star to avenge the deaths of Vilis and Hinerio. And some day I shall! With proper plans and help and a new cover. More than one high potentate of the Thieves' Guild will learn how it feels to have his weasand narrowed a fingerclip's breadth at a time, aye, and worse things!

'But this is a hellish topic for a comfy morning, lover, and I raise it only to show you why you must not get deeply involved with a dirty and vicious one such as me.'

Vlana turned her body then so that it leaned against Fafhrd's and she kissed him from the corner of the lip to the lobe of the ear, but when he would have returned these courtesies in full measure and more, she carried away his groping hands and, bracing herself on his arms, thereby confining them, pushed herself up and gazed at him with her enigmatic look, saying, 'Dearest boy, it is the gray of dawn and soon comes the pink and you must leave me at once, or at most after a last engagement. Go home, marry that lovely and nimble tree-girl – I'm sure now it was not a male youth – and live your proper, arrow-straight life far from the stinks and snares of civilization. The Show packs up and leaves early, day after tomorrow, and I have my crooked destiny to tread. When your blood has cooled, you will feel only contempt for me. Nay, deny it not – I know men! Though there is a tiny chance that you, being you, will recall me with a little pleasure. In which case I advise one thing only: never hint of it to your wife!'

Fafhrd matched her enigmatic look and answered, 'Princess, I've been a pirate, which is nothing but a water thief, who often raids folk poor as your parents. Barbarism can match civilization's every stench. Not one move in our frostbit lives but is strictured by a mad god's laws, which we call customs, and by black-handed irrationalities from which there is no escape. My own father was condemned to death by bone-breaking by a court I dare not name. His offense: climbing a mountain. And there are murders and thievings and pimpings and – Oh, there are tales I could tell you if—'

He broke off to lift his hands so that he was holding her half above him, grasping her gently below the armpits, rather than she propped on her arms. 'Let me come south with you, Vlana,' he said eagerly, 'whether as member of your troupe or moving alone – though I *am* a singing skald, I can also sword dance, juggle four whirling daggers, and hit with one at ten paces a mark the size of my thumbnail. And when we get to Lankhmar City, perhaps disguised as two Northerners, for you are tall, I'll be your good right arm of vengeance. I can thieve by land, too, believe me, and stalk a victim through alleys, I should think, as sightlessly and silently as through forests. I can—'

Vlana, supported by his hands, laid a palm across his lips while her other hand wandered idly under the long hair at the back of his neck. 'Darling,' she said, 'I doubt not that you are brave and loyal and skillful for a lad of eighteen. And you make love well enough for a youth – quite well enough to hold your white-furred girl and mayhap a few more wenches, if you choose. But, despite your ferocious words – forgive my frankness – I sense in you honesty, nobility even, a love of fair play, and a hatred of torture. The lieutenant I seek for my revenge must be cruel and treacherous and fell as a serpent, while knowing at least as much as I of the fantastically twisty ways of the great cities and the ancient guilds. And, to be blunt, he must be old as I, which you miss by almost the fingers of two hands. So come kiss me, dear boy, and pleasure me once more and—'

Fafhrd suddenly sat up, and lifted her a little and sat her down, so that she sat sideways on his thighs, he shifting his grasp to her shoulders.

'No,' he said firmly. 'I see nothing to be gained by subjecting you once more to my inexpert caresses. But—'

'I was afraid you would take it that way,' she interrupted unhappily. 'I did not mean—'

'But,' he continued with cool authority, 'I want to ask you one question. Have you already chosen your lieutenant?'

'I will not answer that,' she replied, eyeing him as coolly and confidently.

'Is he—?' he began and then pressed his lips together, catching the name 'Vellix' before it was uttered.

She looked at him with undisguised curiosity as to what his next move would be. 'Very well,' he said at last, dropping his hands from her shoulders and propping himself with them. 'You have tried, I think, to act in what you believe to be my best interests, so I will return like with like. What I have to reveal indites barbarism and civilization equally.' And he told her of Essedinex' and Hringorl's plan for her.

She laughed heartily when he was done, though he fancied she had turned a shade pale.

'I must be slipping,' she commented. 'So that was why my somewhat subtle mimings so easily pleased Seddy's rough and ready tastes, and why there was a place open for me in the troupe, and why he did not insist I whore for him after the Show, as the other girls must.' She looked at Fafhrd sharply. 'Some pranksters overset Seddy's tent this midnight. Was it—?'

He nodded. 'I was in a strange humor, last night, merry yet furious.'

Honest, delighted laughter from her then, followed by another of the sharp looks. 'So you did not go home when I sent you away after the Show?'

'Not until afterward,' he said. 'No, I stayed and watched.'

She looked at him in a tender, mocking, wondering way which asked quite plainly, 'And what did you see?' But this time he found it very easy not to name Vellix.

'So you're a gentleman, too,' she joked. 'But why didn't you tell me about Hringorl's base scheme earlier? Did you think I'd become too frightened to be amorous?'

'A little of that,' he admitted, 'but it was chiefly that I did not decide until this moment to warn you. Truth to tell, I only came back to you tonight because I was frightened by ghosts, though later I found other good reasons. Indeed, just before I came to your tent, fear and loneliness – yes, and a certain jealousy too – had me minded to hurl myself into Trollstep Canyon, or else don skis and attempt the next-to-impossible leap which has teased my courage for years . . .'

She clutched his upper arm, digging in fingers. 'Never do that,' she said very seriously. 'Hold onto life. Think only of yourself. The worst always changes for the better – or oblivion.'

'Yes, so I was thinking when I would have let the air over the canyon decide my destiny. Would it cradle me or dash me down? But selfishness, of which I've a plenty whatever you think – that and a certain leeriness of all miracles – quashed that whim. Also, I was earlier half minded to trample your tent before pulling down the Show Master's. So there *is* some evil in me, you see. Aye, and a shut-mouthed deceitfulness.'

She did not laugh, but studied his face most thoughtfully. Then for a time the enigma-look came back into her eyes. For a moment Fafhrd thought he could peer past it, and he was troubled, for what he thought he glimpsed behind those large, brown-irised pupils was not a sibyl surveying the universe from a mountaintop, but a merchant with scales in which he weighed objects most carefully, at whiles noting down in a little book old debts and new bribes and alternate plans for gain.

But it was only one troubling glimpse, so his heart joyed when Vlana, whom his big hands still held tilted above him, smiled down into his eyes and said, 'I will now answer your question, which I would and could not earlier. For I have only this instant decided that my lieutenant will be . . . *you*. Hug me on it!'

Fafhrd grappled her with eager warmth and a strength that made her squeal, but then just before his body had fired unendurably, she pushed up from him, saying breathlessly, 'Wait, wait! We must first lay our plans.'

'Afterward, my love. Afterward,' he pleaded, straining her down.

'No!' she protested sharply. 'Afterward loses too many battles to Too Late. If you are lieutenant, I am captain and give directions.'

'Harkening in obedience,' he said, giving way. 'Only be swift.'

'We must be well away from Cold Corner before kidnap time,' she said. 'Today I must gather my things together and provide us with sleigh, swift horses, and a store of food. Leave all that to me. You behave today exactly as is your wont, keeping well away from me, in case our enemies set spies on you, as both Seddy and Hringorl are most like to do—'

'Very well, very well,' Fafhrd agreed hurriedly. 'And now, my sweetest—'

'Hush and have patience! To cap your deception, climb into the roof of Godshall well before the Show, just as you did last night. There just might be an attempt to kidnap me during the Show – Hringorl or his men becoming overeager, or Hringorl seeking to cheat Seddy of his gold – and I'll feel safest with you on watch. Then when I exit after wearing the toga and the silver bells, come you down swiftly and meet me at the stable. We'll escape during the break between the first and second halves of the Show, when one way or another all are too intent on what more's coming, to take note of us. You've got that? Stay far away today? Hide in the roof? Join me at the halves break? Very well! And now, darlingest lieutenant, banish all discipline. Forget every atom of respect you owe your captain and—'

But now it was Fafhrd's turn to delay. Vlana's talk had allowed time for his own worries to rouse and he held her away from him although she had knit her hands behind his neck and was straining to draw their two bodies together.

He said, 'I will obey you in every particular. Only one warning more, which it's vital you heed. Think as little as you can today about our plans, even while performing actions vital to them. Keep them hid behind the scenery of your other thoughts. As I shall mine, you may be sure. For Mor my mother is a great reader of minds.'

'Your mother! Truly she has overawed you inordinately, darling, in a fashion which makes me itch to set you wholly free – oh, do not hold me off! Why, you speak of her as if she were the Queen of Witches.'

'And so she is, make no mistake,' Fafhrd assured her dourly. 'She is the great white spider, while the whole Cold Waste, both above and below, is her web, on which we flies must go tippy-toe, o'erstepping sticky stretches. You *will* heed me?'

'Yes, yes, yes! And now—'

He brought her slowly down toward him, as a man might put a wineskin to his mouth, tantalizing himself. Their skins met. Their lips poised.

Fafhrd became aware of a profound silence above, around, below as if the very earth were holding her breath. It frightened him.

They kissed, drinking deeply of each other, and his fear was drowned.

They parted for breath. Fafhrd reached out and pinched the lamp's wick so that the flame fled and the tent was dark except for the cold silver of dawn seeping in by cranny and crack. His fingers stung. He wondered why he'd done it – they'd loved by lamplight before. Again fear came.

He clasped Vlana tightly in the hug that banishes all fears.

And then of a sudden – he could not possibly have told why –

he was rolling over and over with her toward the back of the tent. His hands gripping her shoulders, his legs clamping hers together, he was hurling her sideways over him and then himself over her in swiftest alteration.

There was a *crack* like thunder and the jolt of a giant's fist hammered against the granite-frozen ground behind them, where the middle of the tent became nothing high, while the hoops above them leaned sharply that way, drawing the tent's leather skin after.

They rolled into the racked garments spilling down. There was a second monster *crack* followed by a crashing and a crunching like some super-giant beast snapping up a behemoth and crunching it between its jaws. Earth quivered for a space.

Then all was silent after that great noise and ground-shaking, except for the astonishment and fear buzzing in their ears. They clutched each other like terrified children.

Fafhrd recovered himself first. 'Dress!' he told Vlana and squirmed under the back of the tent and stood up naked in the biting cold under the pinkening sky.

The great bough of the snow sycamore, its crystals dashed off in a vast heap, lay athwart the middle of the tent, pressing it and the pallet beneath into the frozen earth.

The rest of the sycamore, robbed of its great balancing bough, had fallen entire in the opposite direction and lay mounded around with shaken-off crystals. Its black, hairy, broken-off roots were nakedly exposed.

All the crystals shone with a pale flesh-pink from the sun.

Nothing moved anywhere, not even a wisp of breakfast smoke. Sorcery had struck a great hammerstroke and none had noted it except the intended victims.

Fafhrd, beginning to shake, slithered under again. Vlana had obeyed his word and was dressing with an actress's swiftness. Fafhrd hurried into his own garments, piled so providentially at this end of the tent. He wondered if he had been under a god's directions in doing that and in snuffing out the lamp, which else by now would have had the crushed tent flaming.

His clothes felt colder than the icy air, but he knew that would change.

He crawled with Vlana outside once more. As they stood up, he faced her toward the fallen bough with the great crystal heap around it and said, 'Now laugh at the witchy powers of my mother and her coven and all the Snow Women.'

Vlana said doubtfully, 'I see only a bough that was over-weighted with ice.'

Fafhrd said, 'Compare the mass of crystals and snow that was shaken off that bough with those elsewhere. Remember: hide your thoughts!'

Vlana was silent.

A black figure was racing toward them from the traders' tents. It grew in size as it grotesquely bounded.

Vellix the Venturer was gasping as he stamped to a stop and seized Vlana's arms. Controlling his breathing, he said, 'I dreamed a dream of you struck down and pashed. Then a thunderclap waked me.'

Vlana answered, 'You dreamed the beginning of the truth, but in a matter like this, almost is as good as not at all.'

Vellix at last saw Fafhrd. Lines of jealous anger engraved his face and his hand went to the dagger at his belt.

'Hold!' Vlana commanded sharply. 'I had indeed been mashed to a mummy, except that this youth's senses, which ought to have been utterly engrossed in something else, caught the first cues of the bough's fall, and he whipped me out of death's way in the very nick. Fafhrd's his name.'

Vellix changed his hand's movement into part of a low bow, sweeping his other arm out wide.

'I am much indebted to you, young man,' he said warmly and then after a pause, 'for saving the life of a notable *artiste*.'

By now other figures were in view, some hurrying toward them from the nearby actors' tents, others at the doors of the far-off Snow Tribe's tents and not moving at all.

Pressing her cheek to Fafhrd's, as if in formal gratitude, Vlana whispered rapidly, 'Remember my plan for tonight and for all our future rapture. Do not depart a jot from it. Efface yourself.'

Fafhrd managed, 'Beware ice and snow. Act without thought.'

To Vellix, Vlana said more distantly, though with courtesy

and kindness, 'Thank you, sir, for your concern for me, both in your dreams and your wakings.'

From out a fur robe, whose collar topped his ears, Essedinex greeted with gruff humor, 'It's been a hard night on tents.' Vlana shrugged.

The women of the troupe gathered around her with anxious questions and she talked with them privately as they walked to the actors' tent and went in through the girls' door-flap.

Vellix frowned after her and pulled at his black moustache.

The male actors stared and shook their heads at the beating the hemicylindrical tent had taken.

Vellix said to Fafhrd with warm friendliness, 'I offered you brandy before and now I'd guess you need it. Also, since yestermorning I've had a great desire to talk with you.'

'Your pardon, but once I sit I will not be able to stay awake for a word, were they wise as owls', nor for even a brandy swig,' Fafhrd answered politely, hiding a great yawn which was only half feigned. 'But I thank you.'

'It appears I am fated always to ask at the wrong time,' Vellix commented with a shrug. 'Perhaps at noon? Or mid-afternoon?' he added swiftly.

'The latter, if it please you,' Fafhrd replied and rapidly walked off, taking great strides toward the trading tents. Vellix did not seek to keep up with him.

Fafhrd felt more satisfied than he ever had in his life. The thought that tonight he would forever escape this stupid snow world and its man-chaining women almost made him nostalgic about Cold Corner. Thought-guard! he told himself. Feelings of eerie menace or else his hunger for sleep turned his surroundings spectral, like a childhood scene revisited.

He drained a white porcelain tankard of wine given him by his Mingol friends Zax and Effendrit, let them conduct him to a glossy pallet hidden by piles of other furs, and fell at once into a deep sleep.

After eons of absolute, pillowy darkness, lights came softly on. Fafhrd sat beside Nalgron his father at a stout banquet table crowded with all savory foods smoking hot and all fortified wines in jugs of earthenware, stone, silver, crystal and gold.

There were other feasters lining the table, but Fafhrd could make nothing of them except their dark silhouettes and the sleepy sound of their unceasing talk too soft to be understood, like many streams of murmuring water, though with occasional bursts of low laughter, like small waves running up and returning down a gravelly beach. While the dull clash of knife and spoon against plate and each other was like the clank of the pebbles in that surf.

Nalgron was clad and cloaked in ice-bear furs of the whitest with pins and chains and wristlets and rings of purest silver, and there was silver also in his hair, which troubled Fafhrd. In his left hand he held a silver goblet, which at intervals he touched to his lips, but he kept his eating hand under his cloak.

Nalgron was discoursing wisely, tolerantly, almost tenderly of many matters. He directed his gaze here and there around the table, yet spoke so quietly that Fafhrd knew his conversation was directed at his son alone.

Fafhrd also knew he should be listening intently to every word and carefully stowing away each aphorism, for Nalgron was speaking of courage, of honor, of prudence, of thoughtfulness in giving and punctilio in keeping your word, of following your heart, of setting and unswervingly striving toward a high, romantic goal, of self-honesty in all these things but especially in recognizing your aversions and desires, of the need to close your ears to the fears and naggings of women, yet freely forgive them all their jealousies, attempted trammelings, and even extremest wickednesses, since those all sprang from their ungovernable love, for you or another, and of many a different matter most useful to know for a youth on manhood's verge.

But although he knew this much, Fafhrd heard his father only in snatches, for he was so troubled by the gauntness of Nalgron's cheek and by the leanness of the strong fingers lightly holding the silver goblet and by the silver in his hair, and a faint overlay of blue on his ruddy lips, although Nalgron was most sure and even sprightly in every movement, gesture, and word, that he was compelled to be forever searching the steaming platters and bowls around him for especially succulent portions to spoon or fork onto Nalgron's wide, silver plate to tempt his appetite.

Whenever he did this, Nalgron would look toward him with a smile and a courteous nod, and with love in his eyes, and then touch his goblet to his lips and return to his discoursings, but never would he uncover his eating hand.

As the banquet progressed, Nalgron began to speak of matters yet more important, but now Fafhrd heard hardly one of the precious words, so greatly agitated was he by his concern for his father's health. Now the thin skin seemed stretched to bursting on the jutting cheekbone, the bright eyes ever more sunken and dark-ringed, the blue veins more bulgingly a-crawl across the stout tendons of the hand lightly holding the silver goblet – and Fafhrd had begun to suspect that although Nalgron often let the wine touch his lips he drank never a drop.

'Eat, father,' Fafhrd pleaded in a low voice taut with concern. 'At least drink.'

Again the look, the smile, the agreeable nod, the bright eyes warmer still with love, the brief tipping of goblet against unparted lips, the looking away, the tranquil, unattendable discourse resumed.

And now Fafhrd knew fear, for the lights were growing blue and he realized that none of the black, unfeatured fellow-feasters were or had all the while been lifting so much as hand, let alone cup-rim, to mouth, though making an unceasing dull clatter with their cutlery. His concern for his father became an agony and before he rightly knew what he was doing, he had brushed back his father's cloak and gripped his father's right forearm and wrist and so shoved his eating hand toward his high-piled plate.

Then Nalgron was not nodding, but thrusting his head at Fafhrd, and not smiling, but grinning in such fashion as to show all his teeth of old ivory hue, whilst his eyes were cold, cold, cold.

The hand and arm that Fafhrd gripped felt like, looked like, *were* bare brown bone.

Of a sudden shaking violently in all his parts, but chiefly in his arms, Fafhrd recoiled swift as a serpent down the bench.

Then Fafhrd was not shaking, but being shaken by strong hands of flesh on his shoulders, and instead of the dark there was the faintly translucent hide of the Mingols' tent-roof, and in place of his father's face the sallow-cheeked, black-moustached one, somber yet concerned, of Vellix the Venturer.

Fafhrd stared dazedly, then shook his shoulders and head to bring a quicker-tempoed life back into his body and throw off the gripping hands.

But Vellix had already let go and seated himself on the next pile of furs.

'Your pardon, young warrior,' he said gravely. 'You appeared to be having a dream no man would care to continue.'

His manner and the tone of his voice were like the nightmare-Nalgron's. Fafhrd pushed up on an elbow, yawned, and with a shuddery grimace shook himself again.

'You're chilled in body, mind, or both,' Vellix said. 'So we've good excuse for the brandy I promised.'

He brought up from beside him two small silver mugs in one hand and in the other a brown jug of brandy which he now uncorked with that forefinger and thumb.

Fafhrd frowned inwardly at the dark tarnish on the mugs and at the thought of what might be crusted or dusted in their bottoms, or perhaps that of one only. With a troubled twinge, he reminded himself that this man was his rival for Vlana's affections.

'Hold,' he said as Vellix prepared to pour. 'A silver cup played a nasty role in my dream. Zax!' he called to the Mingol looking out the tent door. 'A porcelain mug, if you please!'

'You take the dream as a warning against drinking from silver?' Vellix inquired softly with an ambiguous smile.

'No,' Fafhrd answered, 'but it instilled an antipathy into my flesh, which still crawls.' He wondered a little that the Mingols had so casually let in Vellix to sit beside him. Perhaps the three were old acquaintances from the trading camps. Or perhaps there'd been bribery.

Vellix chuckled and became freer of manner. 'Also, I've fallen into filthy ways, living without a woman or servant. Effendrit! Make that two porcelain mugs, clean as newly-debarked birch!'

It was indeed the other Mingol who had been standing by the door – Vellix knew them better than Fafhrd did. The Venturer immediately handed over one of the gleaming white mugs. He poured a little of the nose-tickling drink into his own porcelain mug, then a generous gush for Fafhrd, then more for himself – as if to demonstrate that Fafhrd's drink could not possibly be poisoned or drugged. And Fafhrd, who had been watching closely, could find no fault in the demonstration. They lightly clinked mugs and when Vellix drank deeply, Fafhrd took a large though carefully slow sip. The stuff burned gently.

'It's my last jug,' Vellix said cheerfully. 'I've traded my whole stock for amber, snow-gems, and other smalls – aye, and my tent and cart too, everything but my two horses and our gear and winter rations.'

'I've heard your horses are the swiftest and hardiest on the Steppes,' Fafhrd remarked.

'That's too large a claim. Here they rank well, no doubt.'

'Here!' Fafhrd said contemptuously.

Vellix eyed him as Nalgron had in all but the last part of the dream. Then he said, 'Fafhrd – I may call you that? Call me Vellix. May I make a suggestion? May I give you advice such as I might give a son of mine?'

'Surely,' Fafhrd answered, feeling not only uncomfortable now but wary.

'You're clearly restless and dissatisfied here. So is any sound young man, anywhere, at your age. The wide world calls you. You've an itching foot. Yet let me say this: it takes more than wit and prudence – aye, and wisdom, too – to cope with civilization and find any comfort. That requires low cunning, a smirching of yourself as civilization is smirched. You cannot climb to success there as you climb a mountain, no matter how icy and treacherous. The latter demands all your best. The former, much of your worst: a calculated self-evil you have yet to experience, and need not. I was born a renegade. My father was a man of the Eight Cities who rode with the Mingols. I wish now I had stuck to the Steppes myself, cruel as they are, nor harkened to the corrupting call of Lankhmar and the Eastern Lands.

'I know, I know, the folk here are narrow-visioned, custom-bound. But matched with the twisted minds of civilization, they're straight as pines. With your natural gifts you'll easily be a chief here – more, in sooth, a chief paramount, weld a dozen clans together, make the Northerners a power for nations to reckon with. Then, if you wish, you can challenge civilization. On your terms, not hers.'

Fafhrd's thoughts and feelings were like choppy water, though he had outwardly become almost preternaturally calm. There was even a current of glee in him, that Vellix rated a youth's chances with Vlana so high that he would ply him with flattery as well as brandy.

But across all other currents, making the chop sharp and high, was the impression, hard to shake, that the Venturer was not altogether dissimulating, that he did feel like a father toward Fafhrd, that he was truly seeking to save him hurt, that what he said of civilization had an honest core. Of course that might be because Vellix felt so sure of Vlana that he could afford to be kind to a rival. Nevertheless . . .

Nevertheless, Fafhrd now once again felt more uncomfortable than anything else.

He drained his mug. 'Your advice is worth thought, sir – Vellix, I mean. I'll ponder it.'

Refusing another drink with a headshake and smile, he stood up and straightened his clothes.

'I had hoped for a longer chat,' Vellix said, not rising.

'I've business to attend,' Fafhrd answered. 'My hearty thanks.'

Vellix smiled thoughtfully as he departed.

The concourse of trodden snow winding amongst the traders' tents was racketty with noise and crowdedly a-bustle. While Fafhrd slept, the men of the Ice Tribe and fully half of the Frost Companions had come in and now many of these were gathered around two sunfires – so called for their bigness, heat, and the height of their leaping flames – quaffing steaming mead and laughing and scuffling together. To either side were oases of buying and bargaining, encroached on by the merry-makers or given careful berth according to the rank of those involved in the business doings. Old comrades spotted one another and shouted and sometimes drove through the press to embrace. Food and drink were spilled, challenges made and accepted, or more often laughed down. Skalds sang and roared.

The tumult irked Fafhrd, who wanted quiet in which to

disentangle Vellix from Nalgron in his feelings, and banish his vague doubts of Vlana, and unsmirch civilization. He walked as a troubled dreamer, frowning yet unmindful of elbowings and other shoves.

Then all at once he was tinglingly alert, for he glimpsed angling toward him through the crowd Hor and Harrax, and he read the purpose in their eyes. Letting an eddy in the crush spin him around, he noted Hrey, one other of Hringorl's creatures, close behind him.

The purpose of the three was clear. Under guise of comradely scuffling, they would give him a vicious beating or worse.

In his moody concern with Vellix, he had forgotten his more certain enemy and rival, the brutally direct yet cunning Hringorl.

Then the three were upon him. In a frozen instant he noted that Hor bore a small bludgeon and that Harrax' fists were overly large, as if they gripped stone or metal to heavy their blows.

He lunged backward, as if he meant to dodge between that couple and Hrey; then as suddenly reversed course and with a shocking bellow raced toward the sunfire ahead. Heads turned at his yell and a startled few dodged from his way. But the Ice Tribesmen and Frost Companions had time to take in what was happening: a tall youth pursued by three huskies. This promised sport. They sprang to either side of the sunfire to block his passage past it. Fafhrd veered first to left, then to right. Jeering, they bunched more closely.

Holding his breath and throwing up an arm to guard his eyes, Fafhrd leaped straight through the flames. They lifted his fur cloak from his back and blew it high. He felt the stab of heat on hand and neck.

He came out with his furs a-smolder, blue flames running up his hair. There was more crowd ahead except for a swept, carpeted, and canopied space between two tents, where chiefs and priests sat intently around a low table where a merchant weighed gold dust in a pair of scales.

He heard bump and yell behind, someone cried, 'Run, coward,' another, 'A fight, a fight'; he saw Mara's face ahead, red and excited.

Then the future chief paramount of Northland – for so he happened at that instant to think of himself – half sprang, half dived a-flame across the canopied table, unavoidably tumbling the merchant and two chiefs, banging aside the scales, and knocking the gold dust to the winds before he landed with a steaming zizzle in the great, soft snowbank beyond.

He swiftly rolled over twice to make sure all his fires were quenched, then scrambled to his feet and ran like a deer into the woods, followed by gusts of curses and gales of laughter.

Fifty big trees later he stopped abruptly in the snowy gloom and held his breath while he listened. Through the soft pounding of his blood, there came not the faintest sound of pursuit. Ruefully he combed with his fingers his stinking, diminished hair and sketchily brushed his now patchy, equally fire-stinking furs.

Then he waited for his breath to quiet and his awareness to expand. It was during this pause that he made a disconcerting discovery. For the first time in his life the forest, which had always been his retreat, his continent-spanning tent, his great private needle-roofed room, seemed hostile to him, as if the very trees and the cold-fleshed, warm-boweled mother-earth in which they were rooted knew of his apostasy, his spurning, jilting and intended divorce of his native land.

It was not the unusual silence, nor the sinister and suspicious quality of the faint sounds he at last began to hear: scratch on bark of small claw, pitter of tiny paw-steps, hoot of a distant owl anticipating night. Those were effects, or at most concomitants. It was something unnameable, intangible, yet profound, like the frown of a god. Or goddess.

He was greatly depressed. At the same time he had never known his heart feel as hard.

When at last he set out again, it was as silently as might be, and not with his unusual relaxed and wide-open awareness, but rather the naked-nerved sensitivity and bent-bow readiness of a scout in enemy territory.

And it was well for him that he did so, since otherwise he might not have dodged the nearly soundless fall of an icicle, sharp, heavy, and long as a siege-catapult's missile, nor the down-clubbing of a huge snow-weighted dead branch that broke with a single thunderous crack, nor the venomous dart of a snow-adder's head from its unaccustomed white coil in the open, nor the sidewise slash of the narrow, cruel claws of a snow-leopard that seemed almost to materialize a-spring in the frigid air and that vanished as strangely when Fafhrd slipped aside from its first attack and faced it with dirk drawn. Nor might he have spotted in time the up-whipping, slip-knotted snare, set against all custom in this home-area of the forest and big enough to strangle not a hare but a bear.

He wondered where Mor was and what she might be muttering or chanting. Had his mistake been simply to dream of Nalgron? Despite yesterday's curse – and others before it – and last night's naked threats, he had never truly and wholly imagined his mother seeking to kill him. But now the hair on his neck was lifted in apprehension and horror, the watchful glare in his eyes was febrile and wild, while a little blood dripped unheeded from the cut in his cheek where the great icicle down-dropping had grazed it.

So intent had he become on spying dangers that it was with a little surprise that he found himself standing in the glade where he and Mara had embraced only yesterday, his feet on the short trail leading to the home tents. He relaxed a little then, sheathing his dirk and pressing a handful of snow to his bleeding cheek – but he relaxed only a little, with the result that he was aware of one coming to meet him before he consciously heard footsteps.

So silently and completely did he then melt into the snowy background that Mara was three paces away before she saw him.

'They hurt you,' she exclaimed.

'No,' he answered curtly, still intent on dangers in the forest.

'But the red snow on your cheek. There was a fight?'

'Only a nick got in the woods. I outran 'em.'

Her look of concern faded. 'First time I saw you run from a quarrel.'

'I had no mind to take on three or more,' he said flatly.

'Why do you look behind? They're trailing you?'

'No.'

Her expression hardened. 'The elders are outraged. The younger men call you scareling. My brothers among them. I didn't know what to say.'

'Your brothers!' Fafhrd exclaimed. 'Let the stinking Snow Clan call me what they will. I care not.'

Mara planted her fists on her hips. 'You've grown very free with your insults of late. I'll not have my family berated, do you hear? Nor myself insulted, now that I think of it.' She was breathing hard. 'Last night you went back to that shriveled old whore of a dancer. You were in her tent for hours.'

'I was not!' Fafhrd denied, thinking *An hour and a half at most*. The bickering was warming his blood and quelling his supernatural dread.

'You lie! The story's all around the camp. Any other girl would have set her brothers on you ere this.'

Fafhrd came back to his schemy self almost with a jerk. On this eve of all eves he must not risk needless trouble – the chance of being crippled, it might even be, or dead.

Tactics, man, tactics, he told himself as he moved eagerly toward Mara, exclaiming in hurt, honeyed tones, 'Mara, my queen, how can you believe such of me, who love you more than—'

'Keep off me, liar and cheat!'

'And you carrying my son,' he persisted, still trying to embrace her. 'How does the bonny babe?'

'Spits at his father. Keep off me, I say.'

'But I yearn to touch your ticklesome skin, than which there is no other balm for me this side of Hell, oh most beauteous made more beautiful by motherhood.'

'Go to Hell, then. And stop these sickening pretenses. Your acting wouldn't deceive a drunken she-scullion. Hamfatter!'

Stung to his blood, which instantly grew hot, Fafhrd retorted, 'And what of your own lies? Yesterday you boasted of how you'd cow and control my mother. Instanter you went sniveling to tell her you were with child by me.'

'Only after I knew you lusted after the actress. And was it anything but the complete truth? Oh, you twister!'

Fafhrd stood back and folded his arms. He pronounced, 'Wife

of mine must be true to me, must trust me, must ask me first before she acts, must comport herself like the mate of a chief paramount to-be. It appears to me that in all of these you fall short.'

'True to you? You're one to talk!' Her fair face grew unpleasantly red and strained with rage. 'Chief paramount! Set your sights merely on being called a man by the Snow Clan, which they've not done yet. Hear me now, sneak and dissembler. You will instantly plead for my pardon on your knees and then come with me to ask my mother and aunts for my hand, or else—'

'I'd sooner kneel to a snake! Or wed a she-bear!' Fafhrd cried out, all thoughts of tactics vanished.

'I'll set my brothers on you,' she screamed back. 'Cowardly boor!'

Fafhrd lifted his fist, dropped it, set his hands to his head and rocked it in a gesture of maniacal desperation, then suddenly ran past her toward the camp.

'I'll set the whole tribe on you! I'll tell it in the Tent of the Women. I'll tell your mother . . .' Mara shrieked after him, her voice fading fast with the intervening boughs, snow, and distance.

Barely pausing to note that none were abroad amongst the Snow Clan's tents, either because they were still at the trading fair or inside preparing supper, Fafhrd bounded up his treasure tree and flipped open the door of his hidey hole. Cursing the fingernail he broke doing so, he got out the sealskin-wrapped bow and arrows and rockets and added thereto his best pair of skis and ski sticks, a somewhat shorter package holding his father's second-best sword well-oiled, and a pouch of smaller gear. Dropping to the snow, he swiftly bound the longer items into a single pack, which he slung over shoulder.

After a moment of indecision, he hurtled inside Mor's tent, snatching from his pouch a small firepot of bubble-stone, and filled it with glowing embers from the hearth, sprinkled ashes over them, laced the pot tight shut, and returned it to his pouch.

Then turning in frantic haste toward the doorway, he stopped dead. Mor stood in it, a tall silhouette white-edged and shadow-faced.

'So you're deserting me and the Waste. Not to return. You think.'

Fafhrd was speechless.

'Yet you will return. If you wish it to be a-crawl on four feet, or blessedly on two, and not stretched lifeless on a litter of spears, weigh soon your duties and your birth.'

Fafhrd framed a bitter answer, but the very words were a gag in his gullet. He stalked toward Mor.

'Make way, Mother,' he managed in a whisper.

She did not move.

His jaws clamped in a horrid grimace of tension, he shot forth his hands, gripped her under the armpits – his flesh crawling – and set her to one side. She seemed as stiff and cold as ice. She made no protest. He could not look her in the face.

Outside, he started at a brisk pace for Godshall, but there were men in his way – four hulking young blond ones flanked by a dozen others.

Mara had brought not only her brothers from the fair, but all her available kinsmen.

Yet now she appeared to have repented of her act, for she was dragging at her eldest brother's arm and talking earnestly to him, to judge by her expression and the movements of her lips.

Her eldest brother marched on as if she weren't there. And now as his gaze hit Fafhrd he gave a joyous shout, jerked from her grasp, and came on a-rush followed by the rest. All waved clubs or their scabbarded swords.

Mara's agonized, 'Fly, my love!' was anticipated by Fafhrd by at least two heartbeats. He turned and raced for the woods, his long, stiff pack banging his back. When the path of his flight joined the trail of footprints he'd made running out of the woods, he took care to set a foot in each without slackening speed.

Behind him they cried, 'Coward!' He ran faster.

When he reached the juttings of granite a short way inside the forest, he turned sharply to the right and leaping from bare rock to rock, making not one additional print, he reached a low cliff of granite and mounted it with only two hand-grabs, then darted on until the cliff's edge hid him from anyone below.

He heard the pursuit enter the woods, angry cries as in veering around trees they bumped each other, then a masterful voice crying for silence.

He carefully lobbed three stones so that they fell along his false trail well ahead of Mara's human hounds. The thud of the stones and the rustle of branches they made falling drew cries of 'There he goes!' and another demand for silence.

Lifting a larger rock, he hurled it two-handed so that it struck solidly the trunk of a stout tree on the nearer side of the trail, jarring down great branchfuls of snow and ice. There were muffled cries of startlement, confusion, and rage from the showered and likely three-quarters buried men. Fafhrd grinned, then his face sobered and his eyes grew dartingly watchful as he set off at a lope through the darkening woods.

But this time he felt no inimical presences and the living and the lifeless, whether rock or ghost, held off their assaults. Perhaps Mor, deeming him sufficiently harried by Mara's kinsmen, had ceased to energize her charms. Or perhaps – Fafhrd left off thinking and devoted all of himself to silent speeding. Vlana and civilization lay ahead. His mother and barbarism behind – but he endeavored not to think of her.

Night was near when Fafhrd left the woods. He had made the fullest possible circuit through them, coming out next to the drop into Trollstep Canyon. The strap of his long pack chafed his shoulder.

There were the lights and sounds of feasting amongst the traders' tents. Godshall and the actors' tents were dark. Still nearer loomed the dark bulk of the stable tent.

He silently crossed the frosty, rutted gravel of the New Road leading south into the canyon.

Then he saw that the stable tent was not altogether dark. A ghostly glow moved inside it. He approached its door cautiously and saw the silhouette of Hor peering in. Still the soul of silence, he came up behind Hor and peered over his shoulder.

Vlana and Vellix were harnessing the latter's two horses to

Essedinex's sleigh, from which Fafhrd had stolen the three rockets.

Hor tipped up his head and lifted a hand to his lips to make some sort of owl or wolf cry.

Fafhrd whipped out his knife and, as he was about to slash Hor's throat, reversed his intent and his knife too, and struck him senseless with a blow of the pommel against the side of his head. As Hor collapsed, Fafhrd hauled him to one side of the doorway.

Vlana and Vellix sprang into the sleigh, the latter touched his horses with the reins, and they came thud-slithering out. Fafhrd gripped his knife fiercely . . . then sheathed it and shrank back into the shadows.

The sleigh went gliding off down the New Road. Fafhrd stared after it, standing tall, his arms as straight down his sides as those of a corpse laid out, but with his fingers and thumbs gripped into tightest fists.

He suddenly turned and fled toward Godshall.

There came an owl-hooting from behind the stable tent. Fafhrd skidded to a stop in the snow and turned around, his hands still fists.

Out of the dark, two forms, one trailing fire, raced toward Trollstep Canyon. The tall form was unmistakably Hringorl's. They stopped at the brink. Hringorl swung his torch in a great circle of flame. The light showed the face of Harrax beside him. Once, twice, thrice, as if in signal to someone far south down the canyon. Then they raced for the stable.

Fafhrd ran for Godshall. There was a harsh cry behind him. He stopped and turned again. Out of the stable galloped a big horse. Hringorl rode it. He dragged by rope a man on skis: Harrax. The pair careened down the New Road in a flaring upswirl of snow.

Fafhrd raced on until he was past Godshall and a quarter way up the slope leading to the Tent of the Women. He cast off his pack, opened it, drew his skis from it and strapped them to his feet. Next he unwrapped his father's sword and belted it to his left side, balancing his pouch on right.

Then he faced Trollstep Canyon where the Old Road had

68

gone. He took up two of his ski sticks, crouched, and dug them in. His face was a skull, the visage of one who casts dice with Death.

At that instant, beyond Godshall, the way he had come, there was a tiny yellow sputtering. He paused for it, counting heartbeats, he knew not why.

Nine, ten, eleven – there was a great flare of flame. The rocket rose, signaling tonight's Show. Twenty-one, twenty-two, twenty-three – and the tail-flame faded and the nine white stars burst out.

Fafhrd dropped his ski sticks, picked up one of the three rockets he'd stolen, and drew its fuse from its end, pulling just hard enough to break the cementing tar without breaking the fuse.

Holding the slender, finger-long, tarry cylinder delicately between his teeth, he took his fire-pot out of his pouch. The bubblestone was barely warm. He unlaced the top and brushed away the ashes below until he saw – and was stung by – a red glow.

He took the fuse from between his teeth and placed it so that one end leaned on the edge of the fire-pot while the other end touched the red glow. There was a sputtering. Seven, eight, nine, ten, eleven, twelve – and the sputtering became a flaring jet, then was done.

Setting his fire-pot on the snow, he took up the two remaining rockets, and hugged their thick bodies under his arms and dug their tails into the snow, testing them against the ground. The tails were truly as stiff and strong as ski sticks.

He held the rockets propped parallel in one hand and blew hard on the glowing fire-patch in his firepot and brought it up toward the two fuses.

Mara ran out of the dark and said, 'Darling, I'm so glad my kin didn't catch you!'

The glow of the fire-pot showed the beauty of her face.

Staring at her across it, Fafhrd said, 'I'm leaving Cold Corner. I'm leaving the Snow Tribe. I'm leaving you.'

Mara said, 'You can't.'

Fafhrd set down the fire-pot and the rockets.

Mara stretched out her hands.

Fafhrd took the silver bracelets off his wrists and put them in Mara's palms.

Mara clenched them and cried, 'I don't ask for these. I don't ask for anything. You're the father of my child. You're mine!'

Fafhrd whipped the heavy silver chain off his neck, laid it across her wrists, and said, 'Yes! You're mine forever, and I'm yours. Your son is mine. I'll never have another Snow-Clan wife. We're married.'

Meanwhile he had taken up the two rockets again and held their fuses to the fire-pot. They sputtered simultaneously. He set them down, thonged shut the fire-pot and thrust it in his pouch. Three, four . . .

Mor looked over Mara's shoulder and said, 'I witness your words, my son. Stop!'

Fafhrd grabbed up the rockets, each by its sputtering body, dug in the stick ends and took off down the slope with a great shove. Six, seven . . .

Mara screamed, 'Fafhrd! Husband!' As Mor shouted, 'No son of mine!'

Fafhrd shoved again with the sputtering rockets. Cold air whipped his face. He barely felt it. The moonlit lip of the jump was close ahead. He felt its up-curve. Beyond it, darkness. Eight, nine . . .

He hugged the rockets fiercely to his sides, under his elbows, and was flying through darkness. Eleven, twelve . . .

The rockets did not fire. The moonlight showed the opposite wall of the canyon rushing toward him. His skis were directed at a point just beneath its top and that point was steadily falling. He tilted the rockets down and hugged them more fiercely still.

They fired. It was as if he were clinging to two great wrists that were dragging him up. His elbows and sides were warm. In the sudden glare the rock wall showed close, but now below. Sixteen, seventeen . . .

He touched down smoothly on the fair crust of snow covering the Old Road and hurled the rockets to either side. There was a double thunderclap and white stars were shooting around him. One smote and stung, then tortured his cheek as it died. There was time for the one great laughing thought, *I depart in a burst of glory*.

Then no time for large thoughts at all, as he gave all his attention to skiing down the steep slope of the Old Road, now bright in the moonlight, now pitchblack as it curved, crags to his right, a precipice to his left. Crouching and keeping his skis locked side to side, he steered by swaying his hips. His face and his hands grew numb. Reality was the Old Road hurled at him. Tiny bumps became great jolts. White rims came close. Black shoulders threatened.

Deep, deep down there were thoughts nevertheless. Even as he strained to keep all his attention on his skiing, they were there. *Idiot, you should have grabbed a pair of sticks with the rockets. But how would you have held them when casting aside the rockets? In your pack? – then they'd be doing you no good now. Will the fire-pot in your pouch prove more worthwhile than sticks? You should have stayed with Mara. Such loveliness you'll never see again. But it's Vlana you want. Or is it? How, with Vellix? If you weren't so cold-hearted and good, you'd have killed Vellix in the stable, instead of speeding to – Did you truly intend killing yourself? What do you intend now? Can Mor's charms out-speed your skiing? Were the rocket wrists really Nalgron's, reaching from Hell? What's that ahead?*

That was a hulking shoulder skidded around. He lay over on his right side as the white edge to his left narrowed. The edge held. Beyond it, on the opposite wall of the widening canyon, he saw a tiny streak of flame. Hringorl still had his torch, as he galloped down the New Road dragging Harrax? Fafhrd lay over again to his right as the Old Road curved farther that way in a tightening turn. The sky reeled. Life demanded that he lay still farther over, braking to a stop. But Death was still an equal player in this game. Ahead was the intersection where Old and New Road met. He must reach it as soon as Vellix and Vlana in their sleigh. Speed was the essence. Why? He was uncertain. New curves ahead.

By infinitesimal stages the slope grew less. Snow-freighted treetops thrust from the sinister depths – to the left – then shot up to either side. He was in a flat black tunnel. His progress became soundless as a ghost's. He coasted to a stop just at the tunnel's end. His numb fingers went up and feather-touched the bulge of the star-born blister on his cheek. Ice needles crackled very faintly inside the blister.

No other sound but the faint tinkle of the crystals growing all around in the still, damp air.

Five paces ahead of him, down a sudden slope, was a bulbous roll bush weighted with snow. Behind it crouched Hringorl's chief lieutenant Hrey – no mistaking that pointed beard, though its red was gray in the moonlight. He held a strung bow in his left hand.

Beyond him, two dozen paces down slope, was the fork where New and Old Road met. The tunnel going south through the trees was blocked by a pair of roll bushes higher than a man's head. Vellix and Vlana's sleigh was stopped short of the pile, its two horses great loomings. Moonlight struck silvery manes and silver bushes. Vlana sat hunched in the sleigh, her head fur-hooded. Vellix had got down and was casting the roll bushes out of the way.

Torchlight came streaking down the New Road from Cold Corner. Vellix gave up his work and drew his sword. Vlana looked over her shoulder.

Hringorl galloped into the clearing with a laughing cry of triumph, and threw his torch high in the air, reined his horse to a stop behind the sleigh. The skier he towed – Harrax – shot past him and halfway up the slope. There Harrax braked to a stop and stooped to unlace his skis. The torch came down and went out sizzling.

Hringorl dropped from his horse, a fighting axe ready in his hand.

Vellix ran toward Hringorl. Clearly he understood that he must dispose of the giant pirate before Harrax got off his skis or he would be fighting two at once. Vlana's face was a small white mask in the moonlight and she half lifted from her seat to stare after him. The hood fell back from her head.

Fafhrd could have helped Vellix, but he still hadn't made a move to unlash his skis. With a pang – or was it relief? – he remembered he'd left his bow and arrows behind. He told himself that he should help Vellix. Hadn't he skied down here at incalculable risk to save the Venturer and Vlana, or at least warn them of the ambush he had suspected ever since he'd seen Hringorl whirl his torch on the precipice's edge? And didn't Vellix look like Nalgron, now more than ever in his moment of bravery? But the phantom Death still stood at Fafhrd's side, inhibiting all action.

Besides, Fafhrd felt there was a spell on the clearing, making all action inside it futile. As if a giant spider, white-furred, had already spun a web around it, shutting it off from the rest of the universe, making it a volume inscribed, 'This space belongs to the White Spider of Death.' No matter that this giant spider spun not silk, but crystals – the result was the same.

Hringorl aimed a great axe swipe at Vellix. The Venturer evaded it and thrust his sword into Hringorl's forearm. With a howl of rage, Hringorl shifted his axe to his left hand, lunged forward and struck again.

Taken by surprise, Vellix barely dodged back out of the way of the hissing curve of steel, bright in the moonlight. Yet he was nimbly on guard again, while Hringorl advanced more warily, axe-head high and a little ahead of him, ready to make short chops.

Vlana stood up in the sleigh, steel flashing in her hand. She made as if to hurl it, then paused uncertainly.

Hrey rose from his bush, an arrow nocked to his bow.

Fafhrd could have killed him, by hurling his sword spearwise if in no other way. But the sense of Death beside him was still paralyzingly strong, and the sense of being in the White Ice Spider's great womblike trap. Besides, what did he really feel toward Vellix, or even Nalgron?

The bowstring twanged. Vellix paused in his fencing, transfixed. The arrow had struck him in the back, to one side of his spine, and protruded from his chest, just below the breastbone.

With a chop of the axe, Hringorl knocked the sword from the dying man's grip as he started to fall. He gave another of his great, harsh laughs. He turned toward the sleigh.

Vlana screamed.

Before he quite realized it, Fafhrd had silently drawn his sword from its well-oiled sheath and, using it as a stick, pushed off down the white slope. His skis sang very faintly, though very high-pitched, against the snow crust.

Death no longer stood at his side. Death had stepped inside him. It was Death's feet that were lashed to the skis. It was Death who felt the White Spider's trap to be home.

Hrey turned, just in convenient time for Fafhrd's blade to open the side of his neck in a deep, slicing thrust that slit gullet as well as jugular. His sword came away almost before the gushing blood, black in the moonlight, had wet it, and certainly before Hrey had lifted his great hands in a futile effort to stop the great choking flow. It all happened very easily. His skis had thrust, Fafhrd told himself, not he. His skis, that had their own life, Death's life, and were carrying him on a most doomful journey.

Harrax, too, as if a very puppet of the gods, finished unlacing his skis and rose and turned just in time for Fafhrd's thrust, made upward from a crouch, to take him high in the guts, just as his arrow had taken Vellix, but in reverse direction.

The sword grated against Harrax's spine, but came out easily. Fafhrd sped downhill with hardly a check. Harrax stared wide-eyed after him. The great brute's mouth was wide open, too, but no sound came from it. Likely the thrust had sliced a lung and his heart as well, or else some of the great vessels springing from it.

And now Fafhrd's sword was pointed straight at the back of Hringorl, who was preparing to mount into the sleigh, and the skis were speeding the bloody blade faster and faster.

Vlana stared at Fafhrd over Hringorl's shoulder, as if she were looking at the approach of Death himself, and she screamed.

Hringorl swung around and instantly raised his axe to strike Fafhrd's sword aside. His wide face had the alert, yet sleepy look of one who has stared at Death many times and is never surprised by the sudden appearance of the Killer of All.

Fafhrd braked and turned so that, his rush slowing, he went past the back end of the sleigh. His sword strained all the while toward Hringorl without quite reaching him. It evaded the chop Hringorl made at it.

Then Fafhrd saw, just ahead, the sprawled body of Vellix. He made a right-angle turn, braking instantly, even thrusting his sword into the snow so that it struck sparks from the rock below, to keep from tumbling over the corpse.

He wrenched his body around then, as far as he could when his feet were still lashed to the skis, just in time to see Hringorl rushing down on him, out of the snow thrown up by the skis, and aiming his axe in a great blow at Fafhrd's neck.

Fafhrd parried the blow with his sword. Held at right angle to the sweep of the axe, the blade would have been shattered, but Fafhrd held his sword at just the proper angle for the axe to be deflected with a screech of steel and go whistling over his head.

Hringorl louted past him, unable to stop his rush.

Fafhrd again wrenched around his body, cursing the skis that now nailed his feet to the earth. His thrust was too late to reach Hringorl.

The thicker man turned and came rushing back, aiming another axe-swipe. This time the only way Fafhrd could dodge it was by falling flat on the ground.

He glimpsed two streakings of moonlit steel. Then he used his sword to thrust himself to his feet, ready for another blow at Hringorl, or another dodge, if there was time.

The big man had dropped his axe and was clawing at his own face.

Lunging by making a clumsy sidewise step with his ski – no place this for style! – Fafhrd ran him through the heart.

Hringorl dropped his hands as his body pitched over backward. From his right eye socket protruded the silver pommel and black grip of a dagger. Fafhrd wrenched out his sword. Hringorl hit with a great soft thud and an outblow of snow around him, writhed violently twice, and was still.

Fafhrd poised his sword and his gaze darted around. He was ready for any other attack, by anyone at all

But not one of the five bodies moved – the two at his feet, the two sprawled on the slope, nor Vlana's erect in the sleigh. With a little surprise he realized that the gasping he heard was his own breath. Otherwise the only sound was a faint, high tinkling, which for the present he ignored. Even Vellix's two horses hitched to the sleigh and Hringorl's big mount, standing a short way up the Old Road, were unaccountably silent.

He leaned back against the sleigh, resting his left arm on the icy tarpaulin covering the rockets and other gear. His right hand still held his sword poised, a little negligently now, but ready.

He inspected the bodies once more, ending at Vlana's. Still none of them had moved. Each of the first four was surrounded by its blotches of blood-blackened snow, huge for Hrey, Harrax, and Hringorl, tiny for the arrow-slain Vellix.

He fixed his gaze on Vlana's staring, whiterimmed eyes. Controlling his breath, he said, 'I owe you thanks for slaying Hringorl. Perhaps. I doubt I could have bested him, he on his feet, I on my back. But was your knife aimed at Hringorl, or at my back? And did I 'scape death simply by falling, while the knife passed over me to strike down another man?'

She answered not a word. Instead her hands flew up to press her cheeks and lips. She continued to stare, now over her fingers, at Fafhrd.

He continued, his voice growing still more casual, 'You chose Vellix over me, after making me a promise. Why not Hringorl then over Vellix – and over me – when Hringorl seemed the likelier man to win? Why didn't you help Vellix with your knife, when he so bravely tackled Hringorl? Why did you scream when you saw me, spoiling my chance to kill Hringorl with one silent thrust?'

He emphasized each question by idly poking his sword in her direction. His breath was coming easily now, weariness departing from his body even as black depression filled his mind.

Vlana slowly took her hands from her lips and swallowed twice. Then she said, her voice harsh, but clear, and not very loud, 'A woman must always keep all ways open, can you understand that? Only by being ready to league with any man, and discard one for another as fortune shifts the plan, can she begin to counter men's great advantage. I chose Vellix over you because his experience was greater and because – believe this or not, as you will – I did not think a partner of mine would have much chance for long life and I wanted you to live. I did not help Vellix here at the roadblock because I thought then that he and I were doomed. The roadblock and from it the knowledge that there must be ambushers around it cowed me – though Vellix seemed not to think so, or to care. As for my screaming when I saw you, I did not recognize you. I thought you were Death himself.'

'Well, it appears I was,' Fafhrd commented softly, looking around for a third time at the scattered corpses. He unlashed his skis. Then, after stamping his feet, he kneeled by Hringorl and jerked the dagger from his eye and wiped in on the dead man's furs.

Vlana continued, 'And I fear death even more than I detested Hringorl. Yes, I would eagerly flee with Hringorl, if it were away from death.'

'This time Hringorl was headed in the wrong direction,' Fafhrd commented, hefting the dagger. It balanced well for thrusting or throwing.

Vlana said, 'Now of course I'm yours. Eagerly and happily – again believe it or not. If you'll have me. Perhaps you still think I tried to kill you.'

Fafhrd turned toward her and tossed the dagger. 'Catch,' he said. She caught.

He laughed and said, 'No, a showgirl who's also been a thief would be apt to be expert at knife-throwing. And I doubt that Hringorl was struck in his brains through his eye by accident. Are you still minded to have revenge on the Thieves' Guild?'

'I am,' she answered.

Fafhrd said, 'Women are horrible. I mean, quite as horrible as men. Oh, is there anyone in the wide world that has aught but ice water in his or her veins?'

And he laughed again, more loudly, as if knowing there could be no answer to that question. Then he wiped his sword on Hringorl's furs, thrust it in his scabbard, and without looking at Vlana strode past her and the silent horses to the pile of roll bushes and began to cast their remainder aside. They were frozen to each other and he had to tug and twist to get them loose, putting more effort into it, fighting the bushes more than he recalled Vellix having to do.

Vlana did not look at him, even as he passed. She was gazing straight up the slope with its sinuous ski track leading to the black tunnel-mouth of the Old Road. Her white gaze was not fixed on Harrax and Hrey, nor on the tunnel mouth. It went higher.

There was a faint tinkling that never stopped.

Then there was a crystal clatter and Fafhrd wrenched loose and hurled aside the last of the ice-weighted roll bushes.

He looked down the road leading south. To civilization, whatever that was worth now.

This road was a tunnel, too, between snow-shouldered pines.

And it was filled, the moonlight showed, with a web of crystals that seemed to go on forever, strands of ice stretching from twig to twig and bough to bough, depth beyond icy depth.

Fafhrd recalled his mother's words, *There is a witchy cold, that can follow you anywhere in Nehwon. Wherever ice once went witchery can send it again. Your father now bitterly regrets . . .*

He thought of a great white spider, spinning its frigid way around this clearing.

He saw Mor's face, beside Mara's, atop the precipice, the other side of the great leap.

He wondered what was being chanted now in the Tent of the Women, and if Mara was chanting too. Somehow he thought not.

Vlana cried out softly, 'Women indeed are horrible. Look. Look. Look!'

At that instant, Hringorl's horse gave a great whinny. There was the pound of hooves as he fled up the Old Road.

An instant later, Vellix's horses reared and screamed.

Fafhrd smote the neck of the nearest horse with the outside of his arm. Then he looked toward the small, big-eyed, triangular white mask of Vlana's face and followed her gaze.

Growing up out of the slope that led to the Old Road were half a dozen tenuous forms high as trees. They looked like hooded women. They got solider and solider as Fafhrd watched.

He crouched down in terror. This movement caught his pouch between his belly and his thigh. He felt a faint warmth.

He sprang up and dashed back the way he had come. He ripped the tarpaulin off the back of the sleigh. He grabbed the eight remaining rockets one by one and thrust the tail of each into the snow so that their heads pointed at the vast, thickening ice-figures.

Then he reached in his pouch, took out his fire-pot, unthonged its top, shook off its gray ashes, shook its red ashes to one side of the bowl, and rapidly touched them to the fuses of the rockets.

Their multiple spluttering in his ears, he sprang into the sleigh.

Vlana did not move as he brushed her. But she chinked. She seemed to have put on a translucent cloak of ice crystals that held her where she stood. Reflected moonlight shone stolidly from the crystals. He felt it would move only as the moon moved.

He grabbed the reins. They stung his fingers like frozen iron. He could not stir them. The ice web ahead had grown around the horses. They were part of it – great equine statues enclosed in a greater crystal. One stood on four legs, one reared on two. The walls of the ice womb were closing in. *There is a witchy cold that can follow you* . . .

The first rocket roared, then the second. He felt their warmth. He heard the mighty tinkling as they struck their up-slope targets.

The reins moved, slapped the backs of the horses. There was a glassy smashing as they plunged forward. He ducked his head and, holding the reins in his left hand, swung up his right and dragged Vlana down into the seat. Her ice-cloak jingled madly and vanished. Four, five . . .

There was a continuous jangling as horses and sleigh shot forward through the ice web. Crystals showered onto and glanced off his ducked head. The jangling grew fainter. Seven, eight . . .

All icy constraints fell away. Hooves pounded. A great north wind sprang up, ending the calm of days. Ahead the sky was faintly pink with dawn. Behind, it was faintly red with fire of pine-needles ignited by the rockets. It seemed to Fafhrd that the north wind brought the roaring of flames.

He shouted, 'Gnamph Nar, Mlurg Nar, great Kvarch Nar –

we'll see them all! All the cities of the Forest Land! All the Land of the Eight Cities.'

Beside him Vlana stirred warm under his embracing arm and took up his cry with, 'Sarheenmar, Ilthmar, Lankhmar! All the cities of the south! Quarmall! Horborixen! Slimspired Tisilinilit! The Rising Land.'

It seemed to Fafhrd that mirages of all those unknown cities and places filled the brightening horizon. 'Travel, love, adventure, the world!' he shouted, hugging Vlana to him with his right arm while his left slapped the horses with the reins.

He wondered why, although his imagination was roaringly aflame like the canyon behind him, his heart was still so cold.

III
THE UNHOLY GRAIL

Three things warned the wizard's apprentice that something was wrong: first the deep-trodden prints of iron-shod hooves along the forest path – he sensed them through his boots before stooping to feel them out in the dark; next, the eerie drone of a bee unnaturally abroad by night; and finally, a faint aromatic odor of burning. Mouse raced ahead, dodging treetrunks and skipping over twisted roots by memory and by a bat's feeling for rebounding whispers of sound. Gray leggings, tunic, peaked hood and streaming cloak made the slight youth, skinny with asceticism, seem like a rushing shadow.

The exaltation Mouse had felt at the successful completion of his long quest and his triumphal return to his sorcerous master, Glavas Rho, now vanished from his mind and gave way to a fear he hardly dared put into thoughts. Harm to the great wizard, whose mere apprentice he was? – 'My Gray Mouse, still midway in his allegiance between white magic and black,' Glavas Rho had once put it – no, it was unthinkable that that great figure of wisdom and spiritual might should come to harm. The great magician . . . (There was something hysterical about the way Mouse insisted on that 'great', for to the world Glavas Rho was but a hedge-wizard, no better than a Mingol necromancer with his second-sighted spotted dog or a conjurer beggar of Quarmall) . . . the great magician and his dwelling were alike protected by strong enchantments no impious outsider could breach – not even (the heart of Mouse skipped a beat) the lord paramount of these forests, Duke Janarrl, who hated all magic, but white worse than black.

And yet the smell of burning was stronger now and Glavas Rho's low cottage was built of resinous wood.

There also vanished from Mouse's mind the vision of a girl's face, perpetually frightened yet sweet – that of Duke Janarrl's daughter Ivrian, who came secretly to study under Glavas Rho, figuratively sipping the milk of his white wisdom side by side with Mouse. Indeed, they had privately come to call each other Mouse and Misling, while under his tunic Mouse carried a plain green glove he had teased from Ivrian when he set forth on his quest, as if he were her armored and beweaponed knight and not a swordless wizardling.

By the time Mouse reached the hilltop clearing he was breathing hard, not from exertion.

There the gathering light showed him at a glance the hoof-hacked garden of magic herbs, the over-turned straw beehive, the great flare of soot sweeping up the smooth surface of the vast granite boulder that sheltered the wizard's tiny house.

But even without the dawn light he would have seen the fire-shrunken beams and fire-gnawed posts a-creep with red ember-worms and the wraithlike green flame where some stubborn sorcerous ointment still burned. He would have smelled the confusion of precious odors of burned drugs and balms and the horribly appetizing kitchen-odor of burned flesh.

His whole lean body winced. Then, like a hound getting the scent, he darted forward.

The wizard lay just inside the buckled door. And he had fared as his house: the beams of his body bared and blackened; the priceless juices and subtle substances boiled, burned, destroyed forever or streamed upward to some cold hell beyond the moon.

From all around came very faintly a low sad hum, as the unhoused bees mourned.

Memories fled horror-stricken through Mouse's mind: these shriveled lips softly chanting incantations, those charred fingers pointing at the stars or stroking a small woodland animal.

Trembling, Mouse drew from the leather pouch at his belt a flat green stone, engraved on the one side with deep-cut alien hieroglyphs, on the other with an armored, many-jointed monster, like a giant ant, that trod among tiny fleeing human figures. That stone had been the object of the quest on which Glavas Rho had sent him. For sake of it, he had rafted across the Lakes of Pleea, tramped the foot-hills of the Mountains of Hunger, hidden from a raiding party of red-bearded pirates, tricked lumpish peasant-fishermen, flattered and flirted with an elderly odorous witch; robbed a tribal shrine, and eluded hounds set on his trail. His winning the green stone without shedding blood meant that he had advanced another grade in his apprenticeship. Now he gazed dully at its ancient surface and then, his trembling controlled, laid it carefully on his master's blackened palm. As he stooped he realized that the soles of his feet were painfully hot, his boots smoking a little at the edges, yet he did not hurry his steps as he moved away.

It was lighter now and he noticed little things, such as the anthill by the threshold. The master had studied the black-armored creatures as intently as he had their cousin bees. Now it was deeply dented by a great heelmark showing a semicircle of pits made by spikes – yet something was moving. Peering closely he saw a tiny heat-maimed warrior struggling over the sand-grains. He remembered the monster on the green stone and shrugged at a thought that led nowhere.

He crossed the clearing through the mourning bees to where pale light showed between the treetrunks and soon was standing, hand resting on a gnarly bole, at a point where the hillside sloped sharply away. In the wooded valley below was a serpent of milky mist, indicating the course of the stream that wound through it. The air was heavy with the dissipating smoke of darkness. The horizon was edged to the right with red from the coming sun. Beyond it, Mouse knew, lay more forest and then the interminable grain fields and marshes of Lankhmar and beyond even those the ancient world-center of Lankhmar city, which Mouse had never seen, yet whose overlord ruled in theory even this far.

But near at hand, outlined by the sunrise red, was a bundle of jagged-topped towers – the stronghold of Duke Janarrl. A wary animation came into Mouse's masklike face. He thought of the spiked heelmark, the hacked turf, the trail of hoofmarks leading down this slope. Everything pointed to the wizard-hating Janarrl as the author of the atrocity behind him, except that, still revering his master's skills as matchless, Mouse did not understand how the Duke had broken through the enchantments, strong enough to dizzy the keenest woodsman, which had protected Glavas Rho's abode for many a year.

He bowed his head . . . and saw, lying lightly on the springing grassblades, a plain green glove. He snatched it up and digging in his tunic drew forth another glove, darkly mottled and streakily bleached by sweat, and held them side by side. They were mates.

His lips writhed back from his teeth and his gaze went again to the distant stronghold. Then he unseated a thick round of scraggy bark from the tree-trunk he'd been touching and delved shoulder-deep in the black cavity revealed. As he did these things with a slow tense automatism, the words came back to him of a reading Glavas Rho had smilingly given him over a meal of milkless gruel.

'Mouse,' the mage had said, firelight dancing on his short white beard, 'when you stare your eyes like that and flare your nostrils, you are too much like a cat for me to credit you will ever be a sheep-dog of the truth. You are a middling dutiful scholar, but secretly you favor swords over wands. You are more tempted by the hot lips of black magic than the chaste slim fingers of white, no matter to how pretty a misling the latter belong – no, do not deny it! You are more drawn to the beguiling sinuosities of the left-hand path than the straight steep road of the right. I fear you will never be mouse in the end but mouser. And never white but gray – oh well, that's better than black. Now, wash up these bowls and go breathe an hour on the newborn ague-plant, for 'tis a chill night, and remember to talk kindly to the thorn bush.'

The remembered words grew faint, but did not fade, as Mouse drew from the hole a leather belt furred green with mold and dangling from it a moldy scabbard. From the latter he drew, seizing it by the thong-wrapped grip, a tapering bronze sword showing more verdigris than metal. His eyes grew wide, but pinpoint-pupiled, and his face yet more mask-like, as he held the pale-green, brown-edged blade against the red hump of the rising sun.

From across the valley came faintly the high, clear, ringing note of a hunting horn, calling men to the chase.

Abruptly Mouse strode off down the slope, cutting over to the trail of the hooves, moving with long hasty strides and a little stiff-leggedly, as if drunk, and buckling around his waist as he went the mold-furred sword-belt.

A dark four-footed shape rushed across the sun-specked forest glade, bearing down the underbrush with its broad low chest and trampling it with its narrow cloven hooves. From behind sounded the notes of a horn and the harsh shouts of men. At the far edge of the glade, the boar turned. Breath whistled through its nostrils and it swayed. Then its half-glazed little eyes fixed on the figure of a man on horseback. It turned toward him and some trick of the sunlight made its pelt grow blacker. Then it charged. But before the terrible up-turning tusks could find flesh to slash, a heavy-bladed spear bent like a bow against the knob of its shoulder and it went crashing over half backward, its blood spattering the greenery.

Huntsmen clad in brown and green appeared in the glade, some surrounding the fallen boar with a wall of spear points, others hurrying up to the man on the horse. He was clad in rich garments of yellow and brown. He laughed, tossed one of his huntsmen the bloodied spear and accepted a silver-worked leather wine flask from another.

A second rider appeared in the glade and the Duke's small yellow eyes clouded under the tangled brows. He drank deep and wiped his lips with the back of his sleeve. The huntsmen were warily closing their spear-wall on the boar, which lay rigid but with head lifted a finger's breadth off the turf, its only movements the darting of its gaze from side to side and the pulse of bright blood from its shoulder. The spearwall was about to close when Janarrl waved the huntsmen to a halt.

'Ivrian!' he called harshly to the newcomer. 'You had two chances at the beast, but you flinched. Your cursed dead mother would already have sliced thin and tasted the beast's raw heart.'

His daughter stared at him miserably. She was dressed as the huntsmen and rode astride with a sword at her side and a spear in her hand, but it only made her seem more the thin-faced, spindle-armed girl.

'You are a milksop, a wizard-loving coward,' Janarrl continued. 'Your abominable mother would have faced the boar a-foot
and laughed when its blood gushed in her face. Look here, this
boar is scotched. It cannot harm you. Drive your spear into it
now! I command you!'

The huntsmen broke their spear-wall and drew back to either
side, making a path between the boar and the girl. They sniggered openly at her and the Duke smiled at them approvingly.
The girl hesitated, sucking at her underlip, staring with fear
and fascination too at the beast which eyed her, head still just
a-lift.

'Drive in your spear!' Janarrl repeated, sucking quickly at the
flask. 'Do so, or I will whip you here and now.'

Then she touched her heels to the horse's flanks and cantered
down the glade, her body bent low, the spear trained at its target.
But at the last instant its point swerved aside and gouged the dirt.
The boar had not moved. The huntsmen laughed raucously.

Janarrl's wide face reddened with anger as he whipped out
suddenly and trapped her wrist, tightened on it. 'Your damned
mother could cut men's throats and not change color. I'll see
you flesh your spear in that carcass, or I'll make you dance, here
and now, as I did last night, when you told me the wizard's spells
and the place of his den.'

He leaned closer and his voice sank to a whisper. 'Know, chit,
that I've long suspected that your mother, fierce as she could be,
was – perhaps ensorceled against her will – a wizard-lover like
yourself . . . and you the whelp of that burned charmer.'

Her eyes widened and she started to pull away from him, but
he drew her closer. 'Have no fear, chit, I'll work the taint out of
your flesh one way or another. For a beginning, prick me that
boar!'

She did not move. Her face was a cream-colored mask of fear.
He raised his hand. But at that moment there was an interruption.

A figure appeared at the edge of the glade at the point where
the boar had turned to make its last charge. It was that of a slim
youth, dressed all in gray. Like one drugged or in a trance, he
walked straight toward Janarrl. The three huntsmen who had

been attending the Duke drew swords and moved leisurely toward him.

The youth's face was white and tensed, his forehead beaded with sweat under the gray hood half thrown back. Jaw muscles made ivory knobs. His eyes, fixed on the Duke, squinted as if they looked at the blinding sun.

His lips parted wide, showing his teeth. 'Slayer of Glavas Rho! Wizard-killer!'

Then his bronze sword was out of its moldy scabbard. Two of the huntsmen moved in his way, one of them crying, 'Beware poison!' at the green of the newcomer's blade. The youth aimed a terrific blow at him, handling his sword as if it were a sledge. The huntsman parried it with ease, so that it whistled over his head, and the youth almost fell with the force of his own blow. The huntsman stepped forward and with a snappy stroke rapped the youth's sword near the hilt to disarm him, and the fight was done before begun – almost. For the glazed look left the youth's eyes and his features twitched like those of a cat and, recovering his grip on his sword, he lunged forward with a twisting motion at the wrist that captured the huntsman's blade in his own green one and whipped it out of its startled owner's grasp. Then he continued his lunge straight toward the heart of the second huntsman, who escaped only by collapsing backward to the turf.

Janarrl leaned forward tensely in his saddle, muttering, 'The whelp has fangs,' but at that instant the third huntsman, who had circled past, struck the youth with sword-pommel on the back of his neck. The youth dropped his sword, swayed and started to fall, but the first huntsman grabbed him by the neck of his tunic and hurled him toward his companions. They received him in their own jocular fashion with cuffs and slaps, slashing his head and ribs with sheathed daggers, eventually letting him fall to the ground, kicking him, worrying him like a pack of hounds.

Janarrl sat motionless, watching his daughter. He had not missed her frightened start of recognition when the youth appeared. Now he saw her lean forward, lips twitching. Twice she started to speak. Her horse moved uneasily and whinnied. Finally she hung her head and cowered back while low retching sobs came from her throat. Then Janarrl gave a satisfied grunt and called out, 'Enough for the present! Bring him here!'

Two huntsmen dragged between them the half-fainting youth clad now in red-spattered gray.

'Coward,' said the Duke. 'This sport will not kill you. They were only gentling you in preparation for other sports. But I forget you are a pawky wizardling, an effeminate creature who babbles spells in the dark and curses behind the back, a craven who fondles animals and would make the forests mawkish places. Faugh! My teeth are on edge. And yet you sought to corrupt my daughter and – Hearken to me, wizardling, I say!' And leaning low from his saddle he caught the youth's sagging head by the hair, tangling in his fingers. The youth's eyes rolled wildly and he gave a convulsive jerk that took the huntsmen by surprise and almost tumbled Janarrl out of the saddle.

Just then there was an ominous crackling of underbrush and the rapid thud of hooves. Someone cried, 'Have a care, master! Oh Gods, guard the Duke!'

The wounded boar had lurched to its feet and was charging the group by Janarrl's horse.

The huntsmen scattered back, snatching for their weapons.

Janarrl's horse shied, further overbalancing its rider. The boar thundered past, like red-smeared midnight. Janarrl almost fell atop it. The boar swung sharply around for a return charge, evading three thrown spears that thudded into the earth just beside it. Janarrl tried to stand, but one of his feet was snagged in a stirrup and his horse, jerking clear, tumbled him again.

The boar came on, but other hooves were thudding now. Another horse swept past Janarrl and a firmly-held spear entered near the boar's shoulder and buried itself deep. The black beast, jarred backward, slashed once at the spear with its tusk, fell heavily on its side and was still.

Then Ivrian let go the spear. The arm with which she had been holding it dangled unnaturally. She slumped in her saddle, catching its pommel with her other hand.

Janarrl scrambled to his feet, eyed his daughter and the boar. Then his gaze traveled slowly around the glade, full circle.

Glavas Rho's apprentice was gone.

'North be south, east be west. Copse be glade and gully crest. Dizziness all paths invest. Leaves and grasses, do the rest.'

Mouse mumbled the chant through swollen lips almost as though he were talking into the ground on which he lay. His fingers arranging themselves into cabalistic symbols, he thumbed a pinch of green powder from a tiny pouch and tossed it into the air with a wrist-flick that made him wince. 'Know it, hound, you are wolf-born, enemy to whip and horn. Horse, think of the unicorn, uncaught since the primal morn. Weave off from me, by the Norn!'

The charm completed, he lay still and the pains in his bruised flesh and bones became more bearable. He listened to the sounds of the hunt trail off in the distance.

His face was pushed close to a patch of grass. He saw an ant laboriously climb a blade, fall to the ground, and then continue on its way. For a moment he felt a bond of kinship between himself and the tiny insect. He remembered the black boar whose unexpected charge had given him a chance to escape and for a strange moment his mind linked it with the ant.

Vaguely he thought of the pirates who had threatened his life in the west. But their gay ruthlessness had been a different thing from the premeditated and presavored brutality of Janarrl's huntsmen.

Gradually anger and hate began to swirl in him. He saw the gods of Glavas Rho, their formerly serene faces white and sneering. He heard the words of the old incantations, but they twanged with a new meaning. Then these visions receded, and he saw only a whirl of grinning faces and cruel hands. Somewhere in it the white, guilt-stricken face of a girl. Swords, sticks, whips. All spinning. And at the center, like the hub of a wheel on which men are broken, the thick form of the Duke.

What was the teaching of Glavas Rho to that wheel? It had rolled over him and crushed him. What was white magic to Janarrl and his henchmen? Only a priceless parchment to be besmirched. Magic gems to be trampled in filth. Thoughts of deep wisdom to be pulped with their encasing brain.

But there was the other magic. The magic Glavas Rho had forbidden, sometimes smilingly but always with an underlying seriousness. The magic Mouse had learned of only by hints and warnings. The magic which stemmed from death and hate and pain and decay, which dealt in poisons and night-shrieks, which trickled down from the black spaces between the stars, which, as Janarrl himself had said, cursed in the dark behind the back.

It was as if all Mouse's former knowledge – of small creatures and stars and beneficial sorceries and Nature's codes of courtesy – burned in one swift sudden holocaust. And the black ashes took life and began to stir, and from them crept a host of night shapes, resembling those which had been burned, but all distorted. Creeping, skulking, scurrying shapes. Heartless, all hate and terror, but as lovely to look on as black spiders swinging along their geometrical webs.

To sound a hunting horn for that pack! To set them on the track of Janarrl!

Deep in his brain an evil voice began to whisper, 'The Duke must die. The Duke must die.' And he knew that he would always hear that voice, until its purpose was fulfilled.

Laboriously he pushed himself up, feeling a stabbing pain that told of broken ribs; he wondered how he had managed to flee this far. Grinding his teeth, he stumbled across a clearing. By the time he had gotten into the shelter of the trees again, the pain had forced him to his hands and knees. He crawled on a little way, then collapsed.

Near evening of the third day after the hunt. Ivrian stole down from her tower room, ordered the smirking groom to fetch her horse, and rode through the valley and across the stream and up the opposite hill until she reached the rock-sheltered house of Glavas Rho. The destruction she saw brought new misery to her white taut face. She dismounted and went close to the fire-gutted ruin, trembling lest she come upon the body of Glavas Rho. But it was not there. She could see that the ashes had been disturbed as though someone had been searching through them and sifting them for any objects that might have escaped the flames. Everything was very quiet.

An inequality in the ground off toward the side of the clearing caught her eye and she walked in that direction. It was a new-made grave, and in place of a headstone, was set around with gray pebbles, a small flat greenish stone with strange carvings on its surface.

A sudden little sound from the forest set her trembling and made her realize that she was very much afraid, only that up to this point her misery had outweighed her terror. She looked up and gave a gasping cry, for a face was peering at her through a hole in the leaves. It was a wild face, smeared with dirt and grass stains, smirched here and there with old patches of dried blood, shadowed by a stubble of beard. Then she recognized it.

'Mouse,' she called haltingly.

She hardly knew the answering voice.

'So you have returned to gloat over the wreckage caused by your treachery.'

'No, Mouse, no!' she cried. 'I did not intend this. You must believe me.'

'Liar! It was your father's men who killed him and burned his house.'

'But I never thought they would!'

'Never thought they would! – as if that's any excuse. You are so afraid of your father that you would tell him anything. You live by fear.'

'Not always, Mouse. In the end I killed the boar.'

'So much the worse – killing the beast the gods had sent to kill your father.'

'But truly I never killed the boar. I was only boasting when I said so – I thought you liked me brave. I have no memory of that killing. My mind went black. I think my dead mother entered me and drove the spear.'

'Liar and changer of lies! But I'll amend my judgment: you live by fear except when your father whips you to courage. I should have realized that and warned Glavas Rho against you. But I had dreams about you.'

'You called me Misling,' she said faintly.

'Aye, we played at being mice, forgetting cats are real. And then while I was away, you were frightened by mere whippings into betraying Glavas Rho to your father!'

'Mouse, do not condemn me.' Ivrian was sobbing. 'I know

that my life has been nothing but fear. Ever since I was a child my father has tried to force me to believe that cruelty and hate are the laws of the universe. He has tortured and tormented me. There was no one to whom I could turn, until I found Glavas Rho and learned that the universe has laws of sympathy and love that shape even death and the seeming hates. But now Glavas Rho is dead and I am more frightened and alone than ever. I need your help, Mouse. You studied under Glavas Rho. You know his teachings. Come and help me.'

His laughter mocked her. 'Come out and be betrayed? Be whipped again while you look on? Listen to your sweet lying voice, while your father's huntsmen creep closer? No, I have other plans.'

'Plans?' she questioned. Her voice was apprehensive. 'Mouse, your life is in danger so long as you lurk here. My father's men are sworn to slay you on sight. I would die, I tell you, if they caught you. Don't delay, get away. Only tell me first that you do not hate me.' And she moved toward him.

Again his laughter mocked her.

'You are beneath my hate,' came the stinging words. 'I feel only contempt for your cowardly weakness. Glavas Rho talked too much of love. There are laws of hate in the universe, shaping even its loves, and it is time I made them work for me. Come no closer! I do not intend to betray my plans to you, or my new hidey holes. But this much I will tell you, and listen well. In seven days your father's torment begins.'

'My father's torment—? Mouse, Mouse, listen to me. I want to question you about more than Glavas Rho's teachings. I want to question you about Glavas Rho. My father hinted to me that he knew my mother, that he was perchance my very father.'

This time there was a pause before the mocking laughter, but when it came, it was doubled. 'Good, good, good! It pleasures me to think that Old Whitebeard enjoyed life a little before he became so wise, wise, wise. I dearly hope he did tumble your mother. That would explain his nobility. Where so much love was – love for each creature ever born – there must have been lust and guilt before. Out of that encounter – and all your mother's evil – his white magic grew. It is true! Guilt and white magic side by side – and the gods never lied! Which leaves you the daughter of Glavas Rho, betraying your true father to his sooty death.'

And then his face was gone and the leaves framed only a dark hole. She blundered into the forest after him, calling out 'Mouse! Mouse!' and trying to follow the receding laughter. But it died away, and she found herself in a gloomy hollow, and she began to realize how evil the apprentice's laughter had sounded, as if he laughed at the death of all love, or even its unbirth. Then panic seized her, and she fled back through the undergrowth, brambles catching at her clothes and twigs stinging her cheeks, until she had regained the clearing and was galloping back through the dusk, a thousand fears besetting her and her heart sick with the thought there was now no one in the wide world who did not hate and despise her.

When she reached the stronghold, it seemed to crouch above her like an ugly jag-crested monster, and when she passed through the great gateway, it seemed to her that the monster had gobbled her up forever.

Come nightfall on the seventh day, when dinner was being served in the great banquet hall, with much loud talk and crunching of rushes and clashing of silver plates, Janarrl stilled a cry of pain and clapped his hand to his heart.

'It is nothing,' he said a moment later to the thin-faced henchman sitting at his side. 'Give me a cup of wine! That will stop it twinging.'

But he continued to look pale and ill at ease, and he ate little of the meat that was served up in great smoking slices. His eyes kept roving about the table, finally settling on his daughter.

'Stop staring at me in that gloomy way, girl!' he called. 'One would think that you had poisoned my wine and were watching to see green spots come out on me. Or red ones edged with black, belike.'

This brought a general guffaw of laughter which seemed to please the Duke, for he tore off the wing of a fowl and gnawed at it hungrily, but the next moment he gave another sudden cry of pain, louder than the first, staggered to his feet, clawed convulsively at his chest, and then pitched over on the table where he lay groaning and writhing in his pain.

'The Duke is stricken,' the thin-faced henchman announced quite unnecessarily and yet most portentously after bending over him. 'Carry him to bed. One of you loosen his shirt. He gasps for air.'

A flurry of whispering went up and down the table. As the great door to his private apartments was opened for the Duke, a heavy gust of chill air made the torches flicker and turn blue, so that shadows crowded into the hall. Then one torch flared white-bright as a star, showing the face of a girl. Ivrian felt the others draw away from her with suspicious glances and mutterings, as if they were certain there had been truth in the Duke's jest. She did not look up. After a while someone came and told her that the Duke commanded her presence. Without a word she rose and followed.

The Duke's face was gray and furrowed with pain, but he had control of himself, though with each breath his hand tightened convulsively on the edge of the bed until his knuckles were like knobs of rock. He was propped up with pillows and a furred robe had been tucked closely about his shoulders and long-legged braziers glowed around the bed. In spite of all he was shivering convulsively.

'Come here, girl,' he ordered in a low, labored voice that hissed against his drawn lips. 'You know what has happened. My heart pains as though there were a fire under it and yet my skin is cased in ice. There is a stabbing in my joints as if long needles pierced clear through the marrow. It is wizard's work.'

'Wizard's work, beyond doubt,' confirmed Giscorl, the thin-faced henchman, who stood at the head of the bed. 'And there is no need to guess who. That young serpent whom you did not kill quickly enough ten days ago! He's been reported skulking in the woods, aye, and talking to . . . certain ones,' he added, eyeing Ivrian narrowly, suspiciously.

A spasm of agony shook the Duke. 'I should have stamped out whelp with sire,' he groaned. Then his eyes shifted back, to Ivrian. 'Look, girl, you've been seen poking about in the forest where the old wizard was killed. It's believed you talked with his cub.'

Ivrian wet her lips, tried to speak, shook her head. She could feel her father's eyes probing into her. Then his fingers reached out and twisted themselves in her hair.

'I believe you're in league with him!' His whisper was like a rusty knife. 'You're helping him do this to me. Admit it! Admit!' And he thrust her cheek against the nearest brazier so that her hair smoked and her 'No!' became a shuddering scream. The brazier swayed and Giscorl steadied it. Through Ivrian's scream the Duke snarled, 'Your mother once held red coals to prove her honor.'

A ghostly blue flame ran up Ivrian's hair. The Duke jerked her from the brazier and fell back against the pillows . . .

'Send her away,' he finally whispered faintly, each word an effort. 'She's a coward and wouldn't dare to hurt even me. Meantime, Giscorl, send out more men to hunt through the woods. They must find his lair before dawn, or I'll rupture my heart withstanding the pain.'

Curtly Giscorl motioned Ivrian toward the door. She cringed, and slunk from the room, fighting down tears. Her cheek pulsed with pain. She was not aware of the strangely speculative smile with which the hawk-faced henchman watched her out.

Ivrian stood at the narrow window of her room watching the little bands of horsemen come and go, their torches glowing like will-o'-the-wisps in the woods. The stronghold was full of mysterious movement. The very stones seemed restlessly alive, as if they shared the torment of their master.

She felt herself drawn toward a certain point out there in the darkness. A memory kept recurring to her of how one day Glavas Rho had showed her a small cavern in the hillside and had warned her that it was an evil place, where much baneful sorcery had been done in the past. Her fingertips moved around the crescent-shaped blister on her cheek and over the rough streak in her hair.

Finally her uneasiness and the pull from the night became too strong for her. She dressed in the dark and edged open the door of her chamber. The corridor seemed for the moment deserted. She hurried along it, keeping close to the wall, and darted down the worn rounded hummocks of the stone stair. The tramp of footsteps sent her hurrying into a niche, where she cowered while two huntsmen strode glum-faced toward the Duke's chamber. They were dust-stained and stiff from riding.

'No one'll find him in all that dark,' one of them muttered. 'It's like hunting an ant in a cellar.'

The other nodded. 'And wizards can change landmarks and make forest paths turn on themselves, so that all searchers are befuddled.'

As soon as they were past Ivrian hastened into the banquet hall, now dark and empty, and through the kitchen with its high brick ovens and its huge copper kettles glinting in the shadows.

Outside in the courtyard torches were flaring and there was a bustle of activity as grooms brought fresh horses or led off spent ones, but she trusted to her huntsman's costume to let her pass unrecognized. Keeping to the shadows, she worked her way around to the stables. Her horse moved restlessly and neighed when she slipped into the stall, but quieted at her low whisper. A few moments and it was saddled, and she was leading it around to the open fields at the back. No searching parties seemed to be near, so she mounted and rode swiftly toward the wood.

Her mind was a storm of anxieties. She could not explain to herself how she had dared come this far, except that the attraction toward that point in the night – the cavern against which Glavas Rho had warned her – possessed a sorcerous insistence not to be denied.

Then, when the forest engulfed her, she suddenly felt that she was committing herself to the arms of darkness and putting behind forever the grim stronghold and its cruel occupants. The ceiling of leaves blotted out most of the stars. She trusted to a light rein on her horse to guide her straight. And in this she was successful, for within a half hour she reached a shallow ravine which led past the cavern she sought.

Now, for the first time, her horse became uneasy. It balked and uttered little whinnying cries of fear and tried repeatedly to turn off as she urged it along the ravine. Its pace slowed to a walk. Finally it refused to move further. Its ears were laid back and it was trembling all over.

Ivrian dismounted and moved on. The forest was portentously quiet, as if all animals and birds – even the insects – had gone. The darkness ahead was almost tangible, as if built of black bricks just beyond her hand.

Then Ivrian became aware of the green glow, vague and faint at first as the ghosts of an aurora. Gradually it grew brighter and acquired a flickering quality, as the leafy curtains between her and it became fewer. Suddenly she found herself staring directly at it – a thick, heavy, soot-edged flame that writhed instead of danced. If green slime could be transmuted to fire, it would have that look. It burned in the mouth of a shallow cavern.

Then, beside the flame, she saw the face of the apprentice of Glavas Rho, and in that instant an agony of horror and sympathy tore at her mind.

The face seemed inhuman – more a green mask of torment than anything alive. The cheeks were drawn in; the eyes were unnaturally wild; it was very pale, and dripping with cold sweat induced by intense inward effort. There was much suffering in it, but also much power – power to control the thick twisting shadows that seemed to crowd around the green flame, power to master the forces of hate that were being marshaled. At regular intervals the cracked lips moved and the arms and hands made set gestures.

It seemed to Ivrian that she heard the mellow voice of Glavas Rho repeating a statement he had once made to Mouse and to her. 'None can use black magic without straining the soul to the uttermost – and staining it into the bargain. None can inflict suffering without enduring the same. None can send death by spells and sorcery without walking on the brink of death's own abyss, aye, and dripping his own blood into it. The forces black magic evokes are like two-edged poisoned swords with grips studded with scorpion stings. Only a strong man, leather-handed, in whom hate and evil are very powerful, can wield them, and he only for a space.'

In Mouse's face Ivrian saw the living example of those words. Step by step she moved toward him, feeling no more power to control her movements than if she were in a nightmare. She became aware of shadowy presences, as if she were pushing her way through cobweb veils. She came so near that she could have reached out her hand and touched him, and still he did not notice her, as if his spirit were out beyond the stars, grappling the blackness there.

Then a twig snapped under her foot and Mouse sprang up with terrifying swiftness, the energy of every taut muscle released. He snatched up his sword and lunged at the intruder. But when the green blade was within a hand's breadth of Ivrian's throat, he checked it with an effort. He glared, lips drawn back from his teeth. Although he had checked his sword, he seemed only half to recognize her.

At that instant Ivrian was buffeted by a mighty gust of wind, which came from the mouth of the cavern, a strange wind, carrying shadows. The green fire burned low, running rapidly along the sticks that were its fuel, and almost snuffing out.

Then the wind ceased and the thick darkness lifted, to be replaced by a wan gray light heralding the dawn. The fire turned from green to yellow. The wizard's apprentice staggered, and the sword dropped from his fingers.

'Why did you come here?' he questioned thickly.

She saw how his face was wasted with hunger and hate, how his clothing bore the signs of many nights spent in the forest like an animal, under no roof. Then suddenly she realized that she knew the answer to his question.

'Oh, Mouse,' she whispered, 'let us go away from this place. Here is only horror.' He swayed, and she caught hold of him. 'Take me with you, Mouse,' she said.

He stared frowningly into her eyes. 'You do not hate me then, for what I have done to your father? Or what I have done to the teachings of Glavas Rho?' he questioned puzzledly. 'You are not afraid of me?'

'I am afraid of everything,' she whispered, clinging to him. 'I am afraid of you, yes, a great deal afraid. But that fear can be unlearned. Oh, Mouse, will you take me away? – to Lankhmar or to Earth's End?'

He took her by the shoulders. 'I have dreamed of that,' he said slowly. 'But you . . . ?'

'Apprentice of Glavas Rho!' thundered a stern, triumphant voice. 'I apprehend you in the name of Duke Janarrl for sorceries practiced on the Duke's body!'

Four huntsmen were springing forward from the undergrowth with swords drawn and Giscorl three paces behind them. Mouse met them halfway. They soon found that this time they were not dealing with a youth blinded by anger, but with a cold and cunning swordsman. There was a kind of magic in his primitive blade. He ripped up the arm of his first assailant with a well-judged thrust, disarmed the second with an unexpected twist, then cooly warded off the blows of the other two, retreating slowly. But other huntsmen followed the first four and circled around. Still fighting with terrible intensity and giving blow for blow, Mouse went down under the sheer weight of their attack. They pinioned his arms and dragged him to his feet. He was bleeding from a cut in the cheek, but he carried his head high, though it was beast-shaggy. His bloodshot eyes sought out Ivrian.

'I should have known,' he said evenly, 'that having betrayed Glavas Rho you would not rest until you had betrayed me. You did your work well, girl. I trust you take much pleasure in my death.'

Giscorl laughed. Like a whip, the words of Mouse stung Ivrian. She could not meet his eyes. Then she became aware that there was a man on horseback behind Giscorl and, looking up, she saw that it was her father. His wide body was bent by pain. His face was a death's mask. It seemed a miracle that he managed to cling to the saddle.

'Quick, Giscorl!' he hissed.

But the thin-faced henchman was already sniffing around in the cavern's mouth like a well trained ferret. He gave a cry of satisfaction and lifted down a little figure from a ledge above the fire, which he next stamped out. He carried the figure as gingerly as if it were made of cobweb. As he passed by her, Ivrian saw that it was a clay doll wide as it was tall and dressed in brown and yellow leaves, and that its features were a grotesque copy of her father's. It was pierced in several places by long bone needles.

'This is the thing, oh Master,' said Giscorl, holding it up, but the Duke only repeated, 'Quick, Giscorl!' The henchman started to withdraw the largest needle which pierced the doll's middle, but the Duke gasped in agony and cried, 'Forget not the balm!' Whereupon Giscorl uncorked with his teeth and poured a large vial of sirupy liquid over the doll's body and the Duke sighed a little with relief. Then Giscorl very carefully withdrew the needles, one by one, and as each needle was withdrawn the Duke's breath whistled and he clapped his hand to his shoulder or thigh, as if it were from his own body that the needles were being drawn. After the last one was out, he sat slumped in his saddle for a long time. When he finally looked up the transformation that had taken place was astonishing. There was color in his face, and the lines of pain had vanished, and his voice was loud and ringing.

'Take the prisoner back to our stronghold to await our judgment,' he cried. 'Let this be a warning to all who would practice wizardry in our domain. Giscorl, you have proved yourself a faithful servant.' His eyes rested on Ivrian. 'You have played with witchcraft too often, girl, and need other instruction. As a beginning you will witness the punishment I shall visit on this foul wizardling.'

'A small boon, oh Duke!' Mouse cried. He had been hoisted onto a saddle and his legs tied under the horse's belly. 'Keep your foul, spying daughter out of my sight. And let her not look at me in my pain.'

'Strike him in the lips, one of you,' the Duke ordered. 'Ivrian, ride close behind him – I command it.'

Slowly the little cavalcade rode off toward the stronghold through the brightening dawn. Ivrian's horse had been brought to her and she took her place as bidden, sunk in a nightmare of misery and defeat. She seemed to see the pattern of her whole life laid out before her – past, present, and future – and it consisted of nothing but fear, loneliness, and pain. Even the memory of her mother, who had died when she was a little girl, was something that still brought a palpitation of panic to her heart: a bold, handsome woman, who always had a whip in her hand, and whom even her father had feared. Ivrian remembered how when the servants had brought word that her mother had broken her neck in a fall from a horse, her only emotion had been fear that they were lying to her, and that this was some new trick of her mother's to put her off guard, and that some new punishment would follow.

Then, from the day of her mother's death, her father had shown her nothing but a strangely perverse cruelty. Perhaps it was his disgust at not having a son that made him treat her like a cowardly boy instead of a girl and encourage his lowliest followers to maltreat her – from the maids who played at ghosts around her bed to the kitchen wenches who put frogs in her milk and nettles in her salad.

Sometimes it seemed to her that anger at not having a son was too weak an explanation for her father's cruelties, and that he was revenging himself through Ivrian on his dead wife, whom he had certainly feared and who still influenced his actions, since he had never married again or openly taken mistresses. Or perhaps there was truth in what he had said of her mother and Glavas Rho – no, surely that must be a wild imagining of his anger. Or perhaps, as he sometimes told her, he was trying to make her live up to her mother's vicious and bloodthirsty example, trying to recreate his hated and adored wife in the person of her daughter, and finding a queer pleasure in the refractoriness of the material on which he worked and the grotesquerie of the whole endeavor.

Then in Glavas Rho Ivrian had found a refuge. When she had first chanced upon the white-bearded old man in her lonely wanderings through the forest, he had been mending the broken leg of a fawn and he had spoken to her softly of the ways of kindness and of the brotherhood of all life, human and animal. And she had come back day after day to hear her own vague intuitions revealed to her as deep truths and to take refuge in his wide sympathy . . . and to explore her timid friendship with his clever little apprentice. But now Glavas Rho was dead and Mouse had taken the spider's way, or the snake's track, or the cat's path, as the old wizard had sometimes referred to bale magic.

She looked up and saw Mouse riding a little ahead and to one side of her, his hands bound behind him, his head and body bowed forward. Conscience smote her, for she knew she had been responsible for his capture. But worse than conscience was the pang of lost opportunity, for there ahead of her rode, doomed, the one man who might have saved her from her life.

A narrowing of the path brought her close beside him. She said hurriedly, ashamedly, 'If there is anything I can do so that you will forgive me a little . . .'

The glance he bent on her, looking sidewise up, was sharp, appraising, and surprisingly alive.

'Perhaps you can,' he murmured softly, so the huntsmen ahead might not hear. 'As you must know, your father will have me tortured to death. You will be asked to watch it. Do just that. Keep your eyes riveted on mine the whole time. Sit close beside your father. Keep your hand on his arm. Aye, kiss him too. Above all, show no sign of fright or revulsion. Be like a statue carved of marble. Watch to the end. One other thing – wear, if you can, a gown of your mother's, or if not a gown, then some article of her clothing.' He smiled at her thinly. 'Do this and I will at least have the consolation of watching you flinch – and flinch – and flinch!'

'No mumbling charms now!' cried the huntsman suddenly, jerking Mouse's horse ahead.

Ivrian reeled as if she had been struck in the face. She had thought her misery could go no deeper, but Mouse's words had beaten it down a final notch. At that instant the cavalcade came into the open, and the stronghold loomed up ahead – a great horned and jag-crested blot on the sunrise. Never before had it seemed so much like a hideous monster. Ivrian felt that its high gates were the iron jaws of death.

Janarrl, striding into the torture chamber deep below his stronghold, experienced a hot wave of exultation, as when he and his huntsmen closed in around an animal for the kill. But atop the wave was a very faint foam of fear. His feelings were a little like those of a ravenously hungry man invited to a sumptuous banquet, but who has been warned by a fortune-teller to fear death by poison. He was haunted by the feverish frightened face of the man arm-wounded by the wizardling's corroded bronze sword. His eyes met those of Glavas Rho's apprentice, whose half-naked body was stretched – though not yet painfully so – upon the rack, and the Duke's sense of fear sharpened. They were too searching, those eyes, too cold and menacing, too suggestive of magical powers.

He told himself angrily that a little pain would soon change their look to one of trapped panic. He told himself that it was natural that he should still be on edge from last night's horrors, when his life had almost been pried from him by dirty sorceries. But deep in his heart he knew that fear was always with him – fear of anything or anyone that some day might be stronger than he and hurt him as he had hurt others – fear of the dead he had harmed and could hurt no longer – fear of his dead wife, who had indeed been stronger and crueler than he and who had humiliated him in a thousand ways that no one but he remembered.

But he also knew that his daughter would soon be here and that he could then shift off his fear on her; by forcing her to fear, he would be able to heal his own courage, as he had done innumerable times in the past.

So he confidently took his place and gave order that the torture begin.

As the great wheel creaked and the leathern wristlets and anklets began to tighten a little, Mouse felt a qualm of helpless panic run over his body. It centered in his joints – those little deep-set hinges of bone normally exempt from danger. There was yet no pain. His body was merely stretched a little, as if he were yawning.

The low ceiling was close to his face. The flickering light of the torches revealed the mortices in the stone and the dusty cobwebs. Toward his feet he could see the upper portion of the wheel, and the two large hands that gripped its spokes, dragging them down effortlessly, very slowly, stopping for twenty heartbeats at a time. By turning his head and eyes to the side he could see the big figure of the Duke – not wide as his doll of him, but wide – sitting in a carven wooden chair, two armed men standing behind him. The Duke's brown hands, their jeweled rings flashing fire, were closed over the knobs on the chair-arms. His feet were firmly planted. His jaw was set. Only his eyes showed any uneasiness or vulnerability. They kept shifting from side to side – rapidly, regularly, like the pivoted ones of a doll.

'My daughter should be here,' he heard the Duke say abruptly in a flat voice. 'Hasten her. She is not to be permitted to delay.'

One of the men hurried away.

Then the twinges of pain commenced, striking at random in the forearm, the back, the knee, the shoulder. With an effort Mouse composed his features. He fixed his attention on the faces around him, surveying them in detail as if they formed a picture, noting the highlights on the cheeks and eyes and beards and the shadows, wavering with the torchflames, that their figures cast upon the low walls.

Then those low walls melted and, as if distance were no longer real, he saw the whole wide world he'd never visited beyond them: great reaches of forest, bright amber desert, and turquoise sea; the Lake of Monsters, the City of Ghouls, magnificent Lankhmar, the Land of the Eight Cities, the Trollstep Mountains, the fabulous Cold Waste and by some chance striding there an open-faced, hulking red-haired youth he'd glimpsed among the pirates and later spoken with – all places and persons he'd never now encounter, but showing in wondrous fine detail, as if carved and tinted by a master miniaturist.

With startling suddenness the pain returned and increased. The twinges became needle stabs – a cunning prying at his insides – fingers of force crawling up his arms and legs toward his spine – an unsettling at the hips. He desperately tensed his muscles against them.

Then he heard the Duke's voice, 'Not so fast. Stop a while.' Mouse thought he recognized the overtones of panic in the voice. He twisted his head despite the pangs it cost him and watched the uneasy eyes. They swung to and fro, like little pendulums.

Suddenly then, as if time were no longer real, Mouse saw another scene in this chamber. The Duke was there and his eyes swinging from side to side, but he was younger and there was open panic and horror in his face. Close beside him was a boldly handsome woman in a dark red dress cut low in the bosom and with slashes inset with yellow silk. Stretched upon the rack itself in Mouse's place was a strappingly beautiful but now pitifully whimpering maid, whom the woman in red was questioning, with great coldness and insistence on detail, about her amorous encounters with the Duke and her attempt on the life of herself, the Duke's wife, by poison.

Footsteps broke that scene, as stones destroy a reflection in water, and brought the present back. Then a voice: 'Your daughter comes, oh Duke.'

Mouse steeled himself. He had not realized how much he dreaded this meeting, even in his pain. He felt bitterly certain that Ivrian would not have heeded his words. She was not evil, he knew, and she had not meant to betray him, but by the same token she was without courage. She would come whimpering, and her anguish would eat at what little self-control he could muster and doom his last wild wishful schemings.

Lighter footsteps were approaching now – hers. There was something curiously measured about them.

It meant added pain for him to turn his head so he could see the doorway; yet he did so, watching her figure define itself as it entered the region of ruddy light cast by the torches.

Then he saw the eyes. They were wide and staring. They were fixed straight on him. And they did not turn away. The face was pale, calm with a deadly serenity.

He saw she was dressed in a gown of dark red, cut low in the bosom and with slashes inset with yellow silk.

And then the soul of Mouse exulted, for he knew that she had done what he had bidden her. Glavas Rho had said, 'The sufferer can hurl his suffering back upon his oppressor, if only his oppressor can be tempted to open a channel for his hate.' Now there was a channel open for him, leading to Janarrl's inmost being.

Hungrily, Mouse fastened his gaze on Ivrian's unblinking eyes, as if they were pools of black magic in a cold moon. Those eyes, he knew, could receive what he could give.

He saw her seat herself by the Duke. He saw the Duke peer sidewise at his daughter and start up as if she were a ghost. But

Ivrian did not look toward him, only her hand stole out and fastened on his wrist, and the Duke sank shuddering back into his chair.

'Proceed!' he heard the Duke call out to the torturers, and this time the panic in the Duke's voice was very close to the surface.

The wheel turned. Mouse heard himself groan piteously. But there was something in him now that could ride on top of the pain and that had no part in the groan. He felt that there was a path between his eyes and Ivrian's – a rock-walled channel through which the forces of human spirit and of more than human spirit could be sent roaring like a mountain torrent. And still she did not turn away. No expression crossed her face when he groaned, only her eyes seemed to darken as she grew still more pale. Mouse sensed a shifting of feelings in his body. Through the scalding waters of pain, his hate rose to the surface, rode atop too. He pushed his hate down the rock-walled channel, saw Ivrian's face grow more deathlike as it struck her, saw her tighten her grip on her father's wrist, sensed the trembling that her father no longer could master.

The wheel turned. From far off Mouse heard a steady, heart-tearing whimpering. But a part of him was outside the room now – high, he felt, in the frosty emptiness above the world. He saw spread out below him a nighted panorama of wooded hills and valleys. Near the summit of one hill was a tight clump of tiny stone towers. But as if he were endowed with a magical vulture's eye, he could see through the walls and roofs of those towers into the very foundations beneath, into a tiny murky room in which men tinier than insects clustered and cowered together. Some were working at a mechanism which inflicted pain on a creature that might have been a bleached and writhing ant. And the pain of that creature, whose tiny thin cries he could faintly hear, had a strange effect on him at this height, strengthening his inward powers and tearing away a veil from his eyes – a veil that had hitherto hidden a whole black universe.

For he began to hear about him a mighty murmuring. The frigid darkness was beaten by wings of stone. The steely light of the stars cut into his brain like painless knives. He felt a wild black whirlpool of evil, like a torrent of black tigers, blast down upon him from above, and he knew that it was his to control. He let it surge through his body and then hurled it down the unbroken path that led to two points of darkness in the tiny room below – the two staring eyes of Ivrian, daughter of Duke Janarrl. He saw the black of the whirlwind's heart spread on her face like an inkblot, seep down her white arms and dye her fingers. He saw her hand tighten convulsively on her father's arm. He saw her reach her other hand toward the Duke and lift her open lips to his cheek.

Then, for one moment while the torch flames whipped low and blue in a physical wind that seemed to blow through the morticed stones of the buried chamber . . . for one moment while the torturers and guards dropped the tools of their trades . . . for one indelible moment of hate fulfilled and revenge accomplished, Mouse saw the strong, square face of Duke Janarrl shake in the agitation of ultimate terror, the features twisted like heavy cloth wrung between invisible hands, then crumpled in defeat and death.

The strand supporting Mouse snapped. His spirit dropped like a plummet toward the buried room.

An agonizing pain filled him, but it promised life, not death. Above him was the low stone ceiling. The hands on the wheel were white and slender. Then he knew that the pain was that of release from the rack.

Slowly Ivrian loosened the rings of leather from his wrists and ankles. Slowly she helped him down, supporting him with all her strength as they dragged their way across the room, from which everyone else had fled in terror save for one crumpled jeweled figure in a carven chair. They paused by that and he surveyed the dead thing with the cool, satisfied, masklike gaze of a cat. Then on and up they went, Ivrian and the Gray Mouser, through corridors emptied by panic, and out into the night.

IV
ILL MET IN LANKHMAR

Silent as specters, the tall and the fat thief edged past the dead, noose-strangled watch-leopard, out the thick, lock-picked door of Jengao the Gem Merchant, and strolled east on Cash Street through the thin black night-smog of Lankhmar, City of Seven-score Thousand Smokes.

East on Cash it had to be, for west at the intersection of Cash and Silver was a police post with unbribed guardsmen in browned-iron cuirasses and helms, restlessly grounding and rattling their pikes, while Jengao's place had no alley entrance or even window in its stone walls three spans thick and the roof and floor almost as strong and without trap doors.

But tall, tight-lipped Slevyas, master thief candidate, and fat, darting-eyed Fissif, thief second class, brevetted first class for this operation, with a rating of talented in double-dealing, were not in the least worried. Everything was proceeding according to plan. Each carried thonged in his pouch a much smaller pouch of jewels of the first water only, for Jengao, now breathing stertorously inside and senseless from the slugging he'd suffered, must be allowed, nay, nursed and encouraged, to build up his business again and so ripen it for another plucking. Almost the first law of the Thieves' Guild was never kill the hen that laid brown eggs with a ruby in the yolk, or white eggs with a diamond in the white.

The two thieves also had the relief of knowing that, with the satisfaction of a job well done, they were going straight home now, not to a wife, Aarth forbid! – or to parents and children, all gods forfend! – but to Thieves' House, headquarters and barracks of the all-mighty Guild which was father to them both and mother too, though no woman was allowed inside its ever-open portal on Cheap Street.

In addition there was the comforting knowledge that although each was armed only with his regulation silver-hilted thief's knife, a weapon seldom used except in rare intramural duels and brawls, in fact more a membership token than a weapon, they were nevertheless most strongly convoyed by three reliable and lethal bravos hired for the evening from the Slayers' Brotherhood, one moving well ahead of them as point, the other two well behind as rear guard and chief striking force, in fact almost out of sight – for it is never wise that such convoying be obvious, or so believed Krovas, Grandmaster of the Thieves' Guild.

And if all that were not enough to make Slevyas and Fissif feel safe and serene, there danced along soundlessly beside them in the shadow of the north curb, a small, malformed or at any rate somewhat large-headed shape that might have been a small dog, a somewhat undersized cat, or a very big rat. Occasionally it scuttled familiarly and even encouragingly a little way toward their snugly felt-slippered feet, though it always scurried swiftly back into the darker dark.

True, this last guard was not an absolutely unalloyed reassurance. At that very moment, scarcely twoscore paces yet from Jengao's, Fissif tautly walked for a bit on tiptoe and strained his pudgy lips upward to whisper softly in Slevyas' long-lobed ear, 'Damned if I like being dogged by that Familiar of Hristomilo, no matter what security he's supposed to afford us. Bad enough that Krovas employs or lets himself be cowed into employing a sorcerer of most dubious, if dire, reputation and aspect, but that—'

'Shut your trap!' Slevyas hissed still more softly.

Fissif obeyed with a shrug and occupied himself even more restlessly and keenly than was his wont in darting his gaze this way and that, but chiefly ahead.

Some distance in that direction, in fact just short of the Gold Street intersection, Cash was bridged by an enclosed second-story passageway connecting the two buildings which made up the premises of the famous stone-masons and sculptors

Rokkermas and Slaarg. The firm's buildings themselves were fronted by very shallow porticos supported by unnecessarily large pillars of varied shape and decoration, advertisements more than structural members.

From just beyond the bridge there came two low, brief whistles, signal from the point bravo that he had inspected that area for ambushes and discovered nothing suspicious and that Gold Street was clear.

Fissif was by no means entirely satisfied by the safety signal. To tell the truth, the fat thief rather enjoyed being apprehensive and even fearful, at least up to a point. A sense of strident panic overlaid with writhing calm made him feel more excitingly alive than the occasional woman he enjoyed. So he scanned most closely through the thin, sooty smog the frontages and over-hangs of Rokkermas and Slaarg as his and Slevyas' leisurely-seeming yet unslow pace brought them steadily closer.

On this side the bridge was pierced by four small windows, between which were three large niches in which stood – another advertisement – three life-size plaster statues, somewhat eroded by years of weather and dyed varyingly tones of dark gray by as many years of smog. Approaching Jengao's before the burglary, Fissif had noted them with a swift but comprehensive over-shoulder glance. Now it seemed to him that the statue to the right had indefinably changed. It was that of a man of medium height wearing cloak and hood, who gazed down with crossed arms and brooding aspect. No, not indefinably quite – the statue was a more uniform dark gray now, he fancied, cloak, hood, and face; it seemed somewhat sharper featured, less eroded; and he would almost swear it had grown shorter!

Just below the niche, moreover, there was a scattering of gray and raw white rubble which he didn't recall having been there earlier. He strained to remember if during the excitement of the burglary, with its lively leopard-slaying and slugging and all, the unsleeping watch-corner of his mind had recorded a distant crash, and now he believed it had. His quick imagination pictured the possibility of a hole or even door behind each statue, through which it might be given a strong push and so tumbled onto passersby, himself and Slevyas specifically, the right-hand statue having been crashed to test the device and then replaced with a near twin.

He would keep close watch on all three statues as he and Slevyas walked under. It would be easy to dodge if he saw one start to overbalance. Should he yank Slevyas out of harm's way when that happened? It was something to think about.

Without pause his restless attention fixed next on the porticos and pillars. The latter, thick and almost three yards tall, were placed at irregular intervals as well as being irregularly shaped and fluted, for Rokkermas and Slaarg were most modern and emphasized the unfinished look, randomness, and the unexpected.

Nevertheless it seemed to Fissif, his wariness wide awake now, that there was an intensification of unexpectedness, specifically that there was one more pillar under the porticos than when he had last passed by. He couldn't be sure which pillar was the newcomer, but he was almost certain there was one.

Share his suspicions with Slevyas? Yes, and get another hissed reproof and flash of contempt from the small, dull-seeming eyes.

The enclosed bridge was close now. Fissif glanced up at the right-hand statue and noted other differences from the one he'd recalled. Although shorter, it seemed to hold itself more strainingly erect, while the frown carved in its dark gray face was not so much one of philosophic brooding as sneering contempt, self-conscious cleverness, and conceit.

Still, none of the three statues toppled forward as he and Slevyas walked under the bridge. However, something else happened to Fissif at that moment.

One of the pillars winked at him.

The Gray Mouser – for so Mouse now named himself to himself and Ivrian – turned around in the right-hand niche, leaped up and caught hold of the cornice, silently vaulted to the flat roof, and crossed it precisely in time to see the two thieves emerge below.

Without hesitation he leaped forward and down, his body straight as a crossbow bolt, the soles of his ratskin boots aimed at the shorter thief's fat-buried shoulder blades, though leading him a little to allow for the yard he'd walk while the Mouser hurtled toward him.

In the instant that he leaped, the tall thief glanced up overshoulder and whipped out a knife, though making no move to push or pull Fissif out of the way of the human projectile speeding toward him. The Mouser shrugged in full flight. He'd just have to deal with the tall thief faster after knocking down the fat one.

More swiftly than one would have thought he could manage, Fissif whirled around then and thinly screamed, 'Slivikin!'

The ratskin boots took him high in the belly. It was like landing on a big cushion. Writhing aside from Slevyas' first thrust, the Mouser somersaulted forward, turning feet over head, and as the fat thief's skull hit a cobble with a dull *bong* he came to his feet with dirk in hand, ready to take on the tall one.

But there was no need. Slevyas, his small eyes glazed, was toppling too.

One of the pillars had sprung forward, trailing a voluminous robe. A big hood had fallen back from a youthful face and long-haired head. Brawny arms had emerged from the long, loose sleeves that had been the pillar's topmost section, while the big fist ending one of the arms had dealt Slevyas a shrewd knockout punch on the chin.

Fafhrd and the Gray Mouser faced each other across the two thieves sprawled senseless. They were poised for attack, yet for the moment neither moved.

Each discerned something inexplicably familiar in the other.

Fafhrd said, 'Our motives for being here seem identical.'

'Seem? Surely must be!' the Mouser answered curtly, fiercely eyeing this potential new foe, who was taller by a head than the tall thief.

'You said?'

'I said, "Seem? Surely must be!"'

'How civilized of you!' Fafhrd commented in pleased tones.

'Civilized?' the Mouser demanded suspiciously, gripping his dirk tighter.

'To care, in the eye of action, exactly what's said,' Fafhrd explained. Without letting the Mouser out of his vision, he glanced down. His gaze traveled from the belt and pouch of one fallen thief, to those of the other. Then he looked up at the Mouser with a broad, ingenuous smile.

'Sixty-sixty?' he suggested.

The Mouser hesitated, sheathed his dirk, and rapped out, 'A deal!' He knelt abruptly, his fingers on the drawstrings of Fissif's pouch. 'Loot you Slivikin,' he directed.

It was natural to suppose that the fat thief had been crying his companion's name at the end.

Without looking up from where he knelt, Fafhrd remarked, 'That . . . ferret they had with them. Where did it go?'

'Ferret?' the Mouser answered briefly. 'It was a marmoset!'

'Marmoset,' Fafhrd mused. 'That's a small tropical monkey, isn't it? Well, might have been, but I got the strange impression that—'

The silent, two-pronged rush which almost overwhelmed them at that instant really surprised neither of them. Each had been expecting it, but the expectation had dropped out of conscious thought with the startlement of their encounter.

The three bravos racing down upon them in concerted attack, two from the west and one from the east, all with swords poised to thrust, had assumed that the two hijackers would be armed at most with knives and as timid or at least cautious in weapons-combat as the general run of thieves and counter-thieves. So it was they who were surprised and thrown into confusion when with the lightning speed of youth the Mouser and Fafhrd sprang up, whipped out fearsomely long swords, and faced them back to back.

The Mouser made a very small parry in carte so that the thrust of the bravo from the east went past his left side only a hair's breadth. He instantly riposted. His adversary, desperately springing back, parried in turn in carte. Hardly slowing, the tip of the Mouser's long, slim sword dropped under that parry with the delicacy of a princess curtsying and then leaped forward and a little upward, the Mouser making an impossibly long-looking lunge for one so small, and went between two scales of the bravo's armored jerkin and between his ribs and through his heart and out his back as if all were angelfood cake.

Meanwhile Fafhrd, facing the two bravos from the west,

swept aside their low thrusts with somewhat larger, down-sweeping parries in seconde and low prime, then flipped up his sword, long as the Mouser's but heavier, so that it slashed through the neck of his right-hand adversary, half decapitating him. Then he, dropping back a swift step, readied a thrust for the other.

But there was no need. A narrow ribbon of bloodied steel, followed by a gray glove and arm, flashed past him from behind and transfixed the last bravo with the identical thrust the Mouser had used on the first.

The two young men wiped and sheathed their swords. Fafhrd brushed the palm of his open right hand down his robe and held it out. The Mouser pulled off right-hand gray glove and shook the other's big hand in his sinewy one. Without word exchanged, they knelt and finished looting the two unconscious thieves, securing the small bags of jewels. With an oily towel and then a dry one, the Mouser sketchily wiped from his face the greasy ash-soot mixture which had darkened it, next swiftly rolled up both towels and returned them to his own pouch. Then, after only a questioning eye-twitch east on the Mouser's part and a nod from Fafhrd, they swiftly walked on in the direction Slevyas and Fissif and their escort had been going.

After reconnoitering Gold Street, they crossed it and continued east on Cash at Fafhrd's gestured proposal.

'My woman's at the Golden Lamprey,' he explained.

'Let's pick her up and take her home to meet my girl,' the Mouser suggested.

'Home?' Fafhrd inquired politely, only the barest hint of question in his voice.

'Dim Lane,' the Mouser volunteered.

'Silver Eel?'

'Behind it. We'll have some drinks.'

'I'll pick up a jug. Never have too much juice.'

'True. I'll let you.'

Several squares farther on Fafhrd, after stealing a number of looks at his new comrade, said with conviction, 'We've met before.'

The Mouser grinned at him. 'Beach by the Mountains of Hunger?'

'Right! When I was a pirate's ship-boy.'

'And I was a wizard's apprentice.'

Fafhrd stopped, again wiped right hand on robe, and held it out. 'Name's Fafhrd. Ef ay ef aitch ar dee.'

Again the Mouser shook it. 'Gray Mouser,' he said defiantly, as if challenging anyone to laugh at the sobriquet. 'Excuse me, but how exactly do you pronounce that? Faf-hrud?'

'Just Faf-erd.'

'Thank you.' They walked on.

'Gray Mouser, eh?' Fafhrd remarked. 'Well, you killed yourself a couple of rats tonight.'

'That I did.' The Mouser's chest swelled and he threw back his head. Then with a comic twitch of his nose and a sidewise half-grin he admitted, 'You'd have got your second man easily enough. I stole him from you to demonstrate my speed. Besides, I was excited.'

Fafhrd chuckled. 'You're telling me? How do you suppose I was feeling?'

Later, as they were crossing Pimp Street, he asked, 'Learn much magic from your wizard?'

Once more the Mouser threw back his head. He flared his nostrils and drew down the corners of his lips, preparing his mouth for boastful, mystifying speech. But once more he found himself twitching his nose and half grinning. What the deuce did this big fellow have that kept him from putting on his usual acts? 'Enough to tell me it's damned dangerous stuff. Though I still fool with it now and then.'

Fafhrd was asking himself a similar question. All his life he'd mistrusted small men, knowing his height awakened their instant jealousy. But this clever little chap was somehow an exception. Quick thinker and brilliant swordsman too, no argument. He prayed to Kos that Vlana would like him.

On the northeast corner of Cash and Whore a slow-burning torch shaded by a broad gilded hoop cast a cone of light up into the thickening black night-smog and another cone down on the cobbles before the tavern door. Out of the shadows into the second cone stepped Vlana, handsome in a narrow black velvet dress and red stockings, her only ornaments a silver-sheathed and -hilted dagger and a silver-worked black pouch, both on a plain black belt.

Fafhrd introduced the Gray Mouser, who behaved with an almost fawning courtesy, obsequiously gallant. Vlana studied him boldly, then gave him a tentative smile.

Fafhrd opened under the torch the small pouch he'd taken off the tall thief. Vlana looked down into it. She put her arms around Fafhrd, hugged him tight, and kissed him soundly. Then she thrust the jewels into the pouch on her belt.

When that was done, he said, 'Look, I'm going to buy a jug. You tell her what happened, Mouser.'

When he came out of the Golden Lamprey he was carrying four jugs in the crook of his left arm and wiping his lips on the back of his right hand. Vlana was frowning. He grinned at her. The Mouser smacked his lips at the jugs. They continued east on Cash. Fafhrd realized that the frown was for more than the jugs and the prospect of stupidly drunken male revelry. The Mouser tactfully walked ahead, ostensibly to lead the way.

When his figure was little more than a blob in the thickening smog, Vlana whispered harshly, 'You had two members of the Thieves' Guild knocked out cold and you didn't cut their throats?'

'We slew three bravos,' Fafhrd protested by way of excuse.

'My quarrel is not with the Slayers' Brotherhood, but that abominable Guild. You swore to me that whenever you had the chance—'

'Vlana! I couldn't have the Gray Mouser thinking I was an amateur counter-thief consumed by hysteria and blood lust.'

'You already set great store by him, don't you?'

'He possibly saved my life tonight.'

'Well, he told me that *he'd* have slit their throats in a wink, if he'd known I wanted it that way.'

'He was only playing up to you from courtesy.'

'Perhaps and perhaps not. But *you* knew and you didn't—'

'Vlana, shut up!'

Her frown became a rageful glare, then suddenly she laughed

wildly, smiled twitchingly as if she were about to cry, mastered herself and smiled more lovingly. 'Pardon me, darling,' she said. 'Sometimes you must think I'm going mad and sometimes I believe I am.'

'Well, don't,' he told her shortly. 'Think of the jewels we've won instead. And behave yourself with our new friends. Get some wine inside you and relax. I mean to enjoy myself tonight. I've earned it.'

She nodded and clutched his arm in agreement and for comfort and sanity. They hurried to catch up with the dim figure ahead.

The Mouser, turning left, led them a half square north on Cheap Street to where a narrower way went east again. The black mist in it looked solid.

'Dim Lane,' the Mouser explained.

Fafhrd nodded that he knew.

Vlana said, 'Dim's too weak – too *transparent* a word for it tonight,' with an uneven laugh in which there were still traces of hysteria and which ended in a fit of strangled coughing. When she could swallow again, she gasped out, 'Damn Lankhmar's night-smog! What a hell of a city!'

'It's the nearness here of the Great Salt Marsh,' Fafhrd explained.

And he did indeed have part of the answer. Lying low betwixt the Marsh, the Inner Sea, the River Hlal, and the flat southern grainfields watered by canals fed by the Hlal, Lankhmar with its innumerable smokes was the prey of fogs and sooty smogs. No wonder the citizens had adopted the black toga as their formal garb. Some averred the toga had originally been white or pale brown, but so swiftly soot-blackened, necessitating endless laundering, that a thrifty overlord had ratified and made official what nature or civilization's arts decreed.

About halfway to Carter Street, a tavern on the north side of the lane emerged from the murk. A gape-jawed serpentine shape of pale metal crested with soot hung high for a sign. Beneath it they passed a door curtained with begrimed leather, the slit in which spilled out noise, pulsing torchlight, and the reek of liquor.

Just beyond the Silver Eel the Mouser led them through an inky passageway outside the tavern's east wall. They had to go single file, feeling their way along rough, slimily bemisted brick and keeping close together.

'Mind the puddle,' the Mouser warned. 'It's deep as the Outer Sea.'

The passageway widened. Reflected torchlight filtering down through the dark mist allowed them to make out only the most general shape of their surroundings. To the right was more windowless, high wall. To the left, crowding close to the back of the Silver Eel, rose a dismal, rickety building of darkened brick and blackened, ancient wood. It looked utterly deserted to Fafhrd and Vlana until they had craned back their heads to gaze at the fourth-story attic under the ragged-guttered roof. There faint lines and points of yellow light shone around and through three tightly-latticed windows. Beyond, crossing the T of the space they were in, was a narrow alley.

'Bones Alley,' the Mouser told them in somewhat lofty tones. 'I call it Ordure Boulevard.'

'I can smell that,' Vlana said.

By now she and Fafhrd could see a long, narrow wooden outside stairway, steep yet sagging and without a rail, leading up to the lighted attic. The Mouser relieved Fafhrd of the jugs and went up it quite swiftly.

'Follow me when I've reached the top,' he called back. 'I think it'll take your weight, Fafhrd, but best one of you at a time.'

Fafhrd gently pushed Vlana ahead. With another hysteria-tinged laugh and a pause midway up for another fit of choked coughing, she mounted to the Mouser where he now stood in an open doorway, from which streamed yellow light that died swiftly in the night-smog. He was lightly resting a hand on a big, empty, wrought-iron lamphook firmly set in a stone section of the outside wall. He bowed aside, and she went in.

Fafhrd followed, placing his feet as close as he could to the wall, his hands ready to grab for support. The whole stairs creaked ominously and each step gave a little as he shifted his weight onto it. Near the top, one gave way with the muted crack of half-rotted wood. Gently as he could, he sprawled himself hand and knee on as many steps as he could reach to distribute his weight, and cursed sulfurously.

'Don't fret, the jugs are safe,' the Mouser called down gayly.

Fafhrd crawled the rest of the way, a somewhat sour look on his face, and did not get to his feet until he was inside the doorway. When he had done so, he almost gasped with surprise.

It was like rubbing the verdigris from a cheap brass ring and finding a rainbow-fired diamond of the first water set in it. Rich drapes, some twinkling with embroidery of silver and gold, covered the walls except where the shuttered windows were – and the shutters of those were gilded. Similar but darker fabrics hid the low ceiling, making a gorgeous canopy in which the flecks of gold and silver were like stars. Scattered about were plump cushions and low tables, on which burned a multitude of candles. On shelves against the walls were neatly stacked like small logs a vast reserve of candles, numerous scrolls, jugs, bottles, and enameled boxes. A low vanity table was backed by a mirror of honed silver and thickly scattered over with jewels and cosmetics. In a large fireplace was set a small metal stove, neatly blacked, with an ornate fire-pot. Also set beside the stove were a tidy pyramid of thin, resinous torches with frayed ends – fire-kindlers – and other pyramids of short-handled brooms and mops, small, short logs, and gleamingly black coal.

On a low dais by the fireplace was a wide, short-legged, high-backed couch covered with a cloth of gold. On it sat a thin, pale-faced, delicately handsome girl clad in a dress of thick violet silk worked with silver and belted with a silver chain. Her slippers were of white snow-serpent fur. Silver pins headed with amethysts held in place her high-piled black hair. Around her shoulders was drawn a white ermine wrap. She was leaning forward with uneasy-seeming graciousness and extending a narrow, white hand which shook a little to Vlana, who knelt before her and now gently took the proffered hand and bowed her head over it, her own glossy, straight, dark-brown hair making a canopy, and pressed the other girl's hand's back to her lips.

Fafhrd was happy to see his woman playing up properly to this definitely odd though delightful situation. Then looking at

Vlana's long, red-stockinged leg stretched far behind her as she knelt on the other, he noted that the floor was everywhere strewn – to the point of double, treble, and quadruple overlaps – with thick-piled, close-woven, many-hued rugs of the finest imported from the Eastern Lands. Before he knew it, his thumb had shot toward the Gray Mouser.

'You're the Rug Robber!' he proclaimed. 'You're the Carpet Crimp! – and the Candle Corsair too!' he continued, referring to two series of unsolved thefts which had been on the lips of all Lankhmar when he and Vlana had arrived a moon ago.

The Mouser shrugged impassive-faced at Fafhrd, then suddenly grinned, his slitted eyes a-twinkle, and broke into an impromptu dance which carried him whirling and jigging around the room and left him behind Fafhrd, where he deftly reached down the hooded and long-sleeved huge robe from the latter's stooping shoulders, shook it out, carefully folded it, and set it on a pillow.

After a long, uncertain pause, the girl in violet nervously patted with her free hand the cloth of gold beside her and Vlana seated herself there, carefully not too close, and the two women spoke together in low voices, Vlana taking the lead, though not obviously.

The Mouser took off his own gray, hooded cloak, folded it almost fussily, and laid it beside Fafhrd's. Then they unbelted their swords, and the Mouser set them atop folded robe and cloak.

Without those weapons and bulking garments, the two men looked suddenly like youths, both with clear, close-shaven faces, both slender despite the swelling muscles of Fafhrd's arms and calves, he with long red-gold hair falling down his back and about his shoulders, the Mouser with dark hair cut in bangs, the one in brown leather tunic worked with copper wire, the other in jerkin of coarsely woven gray silk.

They smiled at each other. The feeling each had of having turned boy all at once made their smiles for the first time a bit embarrassed. The Mouser cleared his throat and, bowing a little but looking still at Fafhrd, extended a loosely spread-fingered arm toward the golden couch and said with a preliminary stammer, though otherwise smoothly enough, 'Fafhrd, my good friend, permit me to introduce you to my princess. Ivrian, my dear, receive Fafhrd graciously if you please, for tonight he and I fought back to back against three and we conquered.'

Fafhrd advanced, stooping a little, the crown of his red-gold hair brushing the bestarred canopy, and knelt before Ivrian exactly as Vlana had. The slender hand extended to him looked steady now, but was still quiveringly a-tremble, he discovered as soon as he touched it. He handled it as if it were silk woven of the white spider's gossamer, barely brushing it with his lips, and still felt nervous as he mumbled some compliments.

He did not sense, at least at the moment, that the Mouser was quite as nervous as he, if not more so, praying hard that Ivrian would not overdo her princess part and snub their guests, or collapse in trembling or tears or run to him or into the next room, for Fafhrd and Vlana were literally the first beings, human or animal, noble, freeman, or slave, that he had brought or allowed into the luxurious nest he had created for his aristocratic beloved – save the two love birds that twittered in a silver cage hanging to the other side of the fireplace from the dais.

Despite his shrewdness and new-found cynicism it never occurred to the Mouser that it was chiefly his charming but preposterous coddling of Ivrian that was keeping doll-like and even making more so the potentially brave and realistic girl who had fled with him from her father's torture chamber four moons ago.

But now as Ivrian smiled at last and Fafhrd gently returned her her hand and cautiously backed off, the Mouser relaxed with relief, fetched two silver cups and two silver mugs, wiped them needlessly with a silken towel, carefully selected a bottle of violet wine, then with a grin at Fafhrd uncorked instead one of the jugs the Northerner had brought, and near-brimmed the four gleaming vessels and served them all four.

With another preliminary clearing of throat, but no trace of stammer this time, he toasted, 'To my greatest theft to date in Lankhmar, which willy-nilly I must share sixty-sixty with' – he couldn't resist the sudden impulse – 'with this great, long-haired, barbarian lout here!' And he downed a quarter of his mug of pleasantly burning wine fortified with brandy.

Fafhrd quaffed off half of his, then toasted back, 'To the most boastful and finical little civilized chap I've ever deigned to share loot with,' quaffed off the rest, and with a great smile that showed white teeth held out his empty mug.

The Mouser gave him a refill, topped off his own, then set that down to go to Ivrian and pour into her lap from their small pouch the gems he'd filched from Fissif. They gleamed in their new, enviable location like a small puddle of rainbow-hued quicksilver.

Ivrian jerked back a-tremble, almost spilling them, but Vlana gently caught her arm, steadying it, and leaned in over the jewels with a throaty gasp of wonder and admiration, slowly turned an envious gaze on the pale girl, and began rather urgently but smilingly to whisper to her. Fafhrd realized that Vlana was acting now, but acting well and effectively, since Ivrian was soon nodding eagerly and not long after that beginning to whisper back. At her direction, Vlana fetched a blue-enameled box inlaid with silver, and the two of them transferred the jewels from Ivrian's lap into its blue velvet interior. Then Ivrian placed the box close beside her and they chatted on.

As he worked through his second mug in smaller gulps, Fafhrd relaxed and began to get a deeper feeling of his surroundings. The dazzling wonder of the first glimpse of this throne room in a slum, its colorful luxury intensified by contrast with the dark and mud and slime and rotten stairs and Ordure Boulevard just outside, faded, and he began to note the rickettiness and rot under the grand overlay.

Black, rotten wood and dry, cracked wood too showed here and there between the drapes and also loosed their sick, ancient stinks. The whole floor sagged under the rugs, as much as a span at the center of the room. A large cockroach was climbing down a gold-worked drape, another toward the couch. Threads of night-smog were coming through the shutters, making evanescent black arabesques against the gilt. The stones of the large fireplace had been scrubbed and varnished, yet most of the mortar was gone from between them; some sagged, others were missing altogether.

The Mouser had been building a fire there in the stove. Now he pushed in all the way the yellow-flaring kindler he'd lit from the fire-pot, hooked the little black door shut over the mounting flames, and turned back into the room. As if he'd read Fafhrd's mind, he took up several cones of incense, set their peaks a-smolder at the fire-pot, and placed them about the room in gleaming, shallow, brass bowls – stepping hard on the one cockroach by the way and surreptitiously catching and crushing the other in the base of his flicked fist. Then he stuffed silken rags in the widest shutter-cracks, took up his silver mug again, and for a moment gave Fafhrd a very hard look, as if daring him to say just one word against the delightful yet faintly ridiculous doll's house he'd prepared for his princess.

Next moment he was smiling and lifting his mug to Fafhrd, who was doing the same. Need of refills brought them close together. Hardly moving his lips, the Mouser explained *sotto voce*, 'Ivrian's father was a duke. I slew him, by black magic, I believe, while he was having me done to death on the torture rack. A most cruel man, cruel to his daughter too, yet a duke, so that Ivrian is wholly unused to fending or caring for herself. I pride myself that I maintain her in grander state than ever her father did with all his serving men and maids.'

Suppressing the instant criticisms he felt of this attitude and program, Fafhrd nodded and said amiably, 'Surely you've thieved together a most charming little palace, quite worthy of Lankhmar's overlord Karstak Ovartamortes, or the King of Kings at Tisilinilit.'

From the couch Vlana called in her husky contralto, 'Gray Mouser, your princess would hear an account of tonight's adventure. And might we have more wine?'

Ivrian called, 'Yes, please, Mouse.'

Wincing almost imperceptibly at that earlier nickname, the Mouser looked to Fafhrd for the go-ahead, got the nod, and launched into his story. But first he served the girls wine. There wasn't enough for their cups, so he opened another jug and after a moment of thought uncorked all three, setting one by the couch, one by Fafhrd where he sprawled now on the pillowy carpets, and reserving one for himself. Ivrian looked wide-eyed apprehensive at this signal of heavy drinking ahead, Vlana cynical with a touch of anger, but neither voiced their criticism.

The Mouser told the tale of counter-thievery well, acting it out in part, and with only the most artistic of embellishments – the ferret-marmoset before escaping ran up his back and tried to scratch out his eyes – and he was interrupted only twice.

When he said, 'And so with a whish and a snick I bared Scalpel –' Fafhrd remarked, 'Oh, so you've nicknamed your sword as well as yourself?'

The Mouser drew himself up. 'Yes, and I call my dirk Cat's Claw. Any objections? Seem childish to you?'

'Not at all. I call my own sword Graywand. All weapons are in a fashion alive, civilized and nameworthy. Pray continue.'

And when he mentioned the beastie of uncertain nature that had gamboled along with the thieves (and attacked his eyes!), Ivrian paled and said with a shudder, 'Mouse! That sounds like a witch's familiar!'

'Wizard's,' Vlana corrected. 'Those gutless Guild-villains have no truck with women, except as fee'd or forced vehicles for their lust. But Krovas, their current king, though super-stitious, is noted for taking *all* precautions, and might well have a warlock in his service.'

'That seems most likely; it harrows me with dread,' the Mouser agreed with ominous gaze and sinister voice. He really didn't believe or feel what he said – he was about as harrowed as virgin prairie – in the least, but he eagerly accepted any and all atmospheric enhancements of his performance.

When he was done, the girls, eyes flashing and fond, toasted him and Fafhrd for their cunning and bravery. The Mouser bowed and eye-twinklingly smiled about, then sprawled him down with a weary sigh, wiping his forehead with a silken cloth and downing a large drink.

After asking Vlana's leave, Fafhrd told the adventurous tale of their escape from Cold Corner – he from his clan, she from an acting troupe – and of their progress to Lankhmar, where they lodged now in an actors' tenement near the Plaza of Dark Delights. Ivrian hugged herself to Vlana and shivered large-eyed at the witchy parts – at least as much in delight as fear of Fafhrd's tale, he thought. He told himself it was natural that a doll-girl should love ghost stories, though he wondered if her pleasure would have been as great if she had known that his ghost stories were truly true. She seemed to live in worlds of imagination – once more at least half the Mouser's doing, he was sure.

The only proper matter he omitted from his account was Vlana's fixed intent to get a monstrous revenge on the Thieves' Guild for torturing to death her accomplices and harrying her out of Lankhmar when she'd tried free-lance thieving in the city, with miming as a cover. Not of course did he mention his own promise – foolish, he thought now – to help her in this bloody business.

After he'd done and got his applause, he found his throat dry despite his skald's training, but when he sought to wet it, he discovered that his mug was empty and his jug too, though he didn't feel in the least drunk; he had talked all the liquor out of him, he told himself, a little of the stuff escaping in each glowing word he'd spoken.

The Mouser was in like plight and not drunk either – though inclined to pause mysteriously and peer toward infinity before answering question or making remark. This time he suggested, after a particularly long infinity-gaze, that Fafhrd accompany him to the Eel while he purchased a fresh supply.

'But we've a lot of wine left in *our* jug,' Ivrian protested. 'Or at least a little,' she amended. It did sound empty when Vlana shook it. 'Besides, you've wine of all sorts here.'

'Not this sort, dearest, and first rule is never mix 'em,' the Mouser explained, wagging a finger. 'That way lies unhealth, aye, and madness.'

'My dear,' Vlana said, sympathetically patting Ivrian's wrist, 'at some time in any good party all the men who are really men simply have to go out. It's extremely stupid, but it's their nature and can't be dodged, believe me.'

'But, Mouse, I'm scared. Fafhrd's tale frightened me. So did yours – I'll hear that big-headed, black ratty familiar a-scratch at the shutters when you're gone, I know I will!'

It seemed to Fafhrd she was not afraid at all, only taking pleasure in frightening herself and in demonstrating her power over her beloved.

'Darlingest,' the Mouser said with a small hiccup, 'there is all the Inner Sea, all the Land of the Eight Cities, and to boot all the Trollstep Mountains in their sky-scraping grandeur between you and Fafhrd's frigid specters or – pardon me, my comrade, but it could be – hallucinations admixed with coincidences. As for familiars, pish! They've never in the world been anything but the loathy, all-too-natural pets of stinking old women and womanish old men.'

'The Eel's but a step, Lady Ivrian,' Fafhrd said, 'and you'll have beside you my dear Vlana, who slew my chiefest enemy with a single cast of that dagger she now wears.'

With a glare at Fafhrd that lasted no longer than a wink, but conveyed 'What a way to reassure a frightened girl!' Vlana said merrily, 'Let the sillies go, my dear. 'Twill give us chance for a private chat, during which we'll take 'em apart from winefumey head to restless foot.'

So Ivrian let herself be persuaded and the Mouser and Fafhrd slipped off, quickly shutting the door behind them to keep out the night-smog. Their rather rapid steps down the stairs could clearly be heard from within. There were faint creakings and groanings of the ancient wood outside the wall, but no sound of another tread breaking or other mishap.

Waiting for the four jugs to be brought up from the cellar, the two newly met comrades ordered a mug each of the same fortified wine, or one near enough, and ensconced themselves at the least noisy end of the long serving counter in the tumultuous tavern. The Mouser deftly kicked a rat that thrust black head and shoulders from his hole.

After each had enthusiastically complimented the other on his girl, Fafhrd said diffidently, 'Just between ourselves, do you think there might be anything to your sweet Ivrian's notion that the small dark creature with Slivikin and the other Guild thief was a wizard's familiar, or at any rate the cunning pet of a sorcerer, trained to act as go-between and report disasters to his master or to Krovas or to both?'

The Mouser laughed lightly. 'You're building bugbears – formless baby ones unlicked by logic – out of nothing, dear barbarian brother, if I may say so. *Imprimis*, we don't really know the beastie was connected with the Guild-thieves at all. May well have been a stray catling or a big bold rat – like this damned one!' He kicked again. 'But, *secundus*, granting it to be the creature of a wizard employed by Krovas, how could it make useful report? I don't believe in animals that talk – except for parrots and such birds, which only . . . parrot – or ones having an elaborate sign language men can share. Or perhaps you envisage the beastie dipping its paddy paw in a jug of ink and writing its report in big on a floor-spread parchment?

'Ho, there, you back of the counter! Where are my jugs? Rats eaten the boy who went for them days ago? Or he simply starved to death while on his cellar quest? Well, tell him to get a swifter move on and meanwhile brim us again!

'No, Fafhrd, even granting the beastie to be directly or indirectly a creature of Krovas, and that it raced back to Thieves' House after our affray, what could it tell them there? Only that something had gone wrong with the burglary at Jengao's. Which they'd soon suspect in any case from the delay in the thieves' and bravos' return.'

Fafhrd frowned and muttered stubbornly, 'The furry slinker might, nevertheless, convey our appearances to the Guild masters, and they might recognize us and come after us and attack us in our homes. Or Slivikin and his fat pal, revived from their bumps, might do likewise.'

'My dear friend,' the Mouser said condolingly, 'once more begging your indulgence, I fear this potent wine is addling your wits. If the Guild knew our looks or where we lodge, they'd have been nastily on our necks days, weeks, nay, months ago. Or conceivably you don't know that their penalty for free-lance or even unassigned thieving within the walls of Lankhmar and for three leagues outside them is nothing less than death, after torture if happily that can be achieved.'

'I know all about that and my plight is worse even than yours,'

Fafhrd retorted, and after pledging the Mouser to secrecy told him the tale of Vlana's vendetta against the Guild and her deadly serious dreams of an all-encompassing revenge.

During the story the four jugs came up from the cellar, but the Mouser only ordered that their earthenware mugs be refilled.

Fafhrd finished, 'And so, in consequence of a promise given by an infatuated and unschooled boy in a southern angle of the Cold Waste, I find myself now as a sober – well, at other times – man being constantly asked to make war on a power as great as that of Karstak Ovartamortes, for as you may know, the Guild has locals in all other cities and major towns of this land, not to mention agreements including powers of extradition with robber and bandit organizations in other countries. I love Vlana dearly, make no mistake about that, and she is an experienced thief herself, without whose guidance I'd hardly have survived my first week in Lankhmar, but on this one topic she has a kink in her brains, a hard knot neither logic nor persuasion can even begin to loosen. And I, well, in the month I've been here I've learned that the only way to survive in civilization is to abide by its unwritten rules – far more important than its laws chiseled in stone – and break them only at peril, in deepest secrecy, and taking all precautions. As I did tonight – not my first hijacking, by the by.'

'Certes t'would be insanity to assault the Guild direct, your wisdom's perfect there,' the Mouser commented. 'If you cannot break your most handsome girl of this mad notion, or coax her from it – and I can see she's a fearless, self-willed one – then you must stoutly refuse e'en her least request in that direction.'

'Certes I must,' Fafhrd agreed, adding somewhat accusingly, 'though I gather you told her you'd have willingly slit the throats of the two we struck senseless.'

'Courtesy merely, man! Would you have had me behave ungraciously to your girl? 'Tis measure of the value I was already setting then on your goodwill. But only a woman's man may cross her. As you must, in this instance.'

'Certes I must,' Fafhrd repeated with great emphasis and conviction. 'I'd be an idiot taking on the Guild. Of course if they should catch me they'd kill me in any case for free-lancing and hijacking. But wantonly to assault the Guild direct, kill one Guild-thief needlessly, only behave as if I might – lunacy entire!'

'You'd not only be a drunken, drooling idiot, you'd question-less be stinking in three nights at most from that emperor of diseases, Death. Malicious attacks on her person, blows directed at the organization, the Guild requires tenfold what she does other rule-breakings. All planned robberies and other thefts would be called off and the entire power of the Guild and its allies mobilized against you alone. I'd count your chances better to take on single-handed the host of the King of Kings rather than the Thieves' Guild's subtle minions. In view of your size, might, and wit you're a squad perhaps, or even a company, but hardly an army. So, no least giving-in to Vlana in this one matter.'

'Agreed!' Fafhrd said loudly, shaking the Mouser's iron-thewed hand in a near crusher grip.

'And now we should be getting back to the girls,' the Mouser said.

'After one more drink while we settle the score. Ho, boy!'

'Suits.' The Mouser dug into his pouch to pay, but Fafhrd protested vehemently. In the end they tossed coin for it, and Fafhrd won and with great satisfaction clinked out his silver smerduks on the stained and dinted counter, also marked with an infinitude of mug circles, as if it had been once the desk of a mad geometer. They pushed themselves to their feet, the Mouser giving the rathole one last light kick for luck.

At this, Fafhrd's thoughts looped back and he said, 'Grant the beastie can't paw-write, or talk by mouth or paw, it still could have followed us at distance, marked down your dwelling, and then returned to Thieves' House to lead its masters down on us like a hound!'

'Now you're speaking shrewd sense again,' the Mouser said. 'Ho, boy, a bucket of small beer to go! On the instant!' Noting Fafhrd's blank look, he explained, 'I'll spill it outside the Eel to kill our scent and all the way down the passageway. Yes, and splash it high on the walls too.'

Fafhrd nodded wisely. 'I thought I'd drunk my way past the addled point.'

Vlana and Ivrian, deep in in excited talk, both started at the pounding rush of footsteps up the stairs. Racing behemoths could hardly have made more noise. The creaking and groaning were prodigious and there were the crashes of two treads breaking, yet the pounding footsteps never faltered. The door flew open and their two men rushed in through a great mushroom top of night-smog which was neatly sliced off its black stem by the slam of the door.

'I told you we'd be back in a wink,' the Mouser cried gayly to Ivrian, while Fafhrd strode forward, unmindful of the creaking floor, crying, 'Dearest heart, I've missed you sorely,' and caught up Vlana despite her voiced protests and pushings-off and kissed and hugged her soundly before setting her back on the couch again.

Oddly, it was Ivrian who appeared to be angry at Fafhrd then, rather than Vlana, who was smiling fondly if somewhat dazedly.

'Fafhrd sir,' she said boldly, her little fists set on her narrow hips, her tapered chin held high, her dark eyes blazing, 'my beloved Vlana has been telling me about the unspeakably atrocious things the Thieves' Guild did to her and to her dearest friends. Pardon my frank speaking to one I've only met, but I think it quite unmanly of you to refuse her the just revenge she desires and fully deserves. And that goes for you too, Mouse, who boasted to Vlana of what you would have done had you but known, who in like case did not scruple to slay my very own father – or reputed father – for his cruelties!'

It was clear to Fafhrd that while he and the Gray Mouser had idly boozed in the Eel, Vlana had been giving Ivrian a doubt-less empurpled account of her grievances against the Guild and playing mercilessly on the naive girl's bookish, romantic sympathies and high concept of knightly honor. It was also clear to him that Ivrian was more than a little drunk. A three-quarters-empty flask of violet wine of far Kiraay sat on the low table next them.

Yet he could think of nothing to do but spread his big hands helplessly and bow his head, more than the low ceiling made necessary, under Ivrian's glare, now reinforced by that of Vlana. After all, they *were* in the right. He *had* promised.

So it was the Mouser who first tried to rebut.

'Come now, pet,' he cried lightly as he danced about the room, silk-stuffing more cracks against the thickening night-smog and stirring up and feeding the fire in the stove, 'and you too, beauteous Lady Vlana. For the past month Fafhrd has been hitting the Guild-thieves where it hurts them most – in their purses a-dangle between their legs. His hijackings of the loot of their robberies have been like so many fierce kicks in their groins. Hurts worse, believe me, than robbing them of life with a swift, near painless sword slash or thrust. And tonight I helped him in his worthy purpose – and will eagerly do so again. Come, drink we up all.' Under his handling, one of the new jugs came uncorked with a pop and he darted about brimming silver cups and mugs.

'A merchant's revenge!' Ivrian retorted with scorn, not one whit appeased, but rather angered anew. 'Ye both are at heart true and gentle knights, I know, despite all current backsliding. At the least you must bring Vlana the head of Krovas!'

'What would she *do* with it? What *good* would it be except to spot the carpets?' the Mouser plaintively inquired, while Fafhrd, gathering his wits at last and going down on one knee, said slowly, 'Most respected Lady Ivrian, it is true I solemnly promised my beloved Vlana I would help her in her revenge, but that was while I was still in barbarous Cold Corner, where blood-feud is a commonplace, sanctioned by custom and accepted by all the clans and tribes and brotherhoods of the savage Northerners of the Cold Waste. In my naivety I thought of Vlana's revenge as being of that sort. But here in civilization's midst, I discover all's different and rules and customs turned upside-down. Yet – Lankhmar or Cold Corner – one must seem to observe rule and custom to survive. Here cash is all-powerful, the idol placed highest, whether one sweat, thieve, grind others down, or scheme for it. Here feud and revenge are outside all rules and punished worse than violent lunacy. Think, Lady Ivrian, if Mouse and I should bring Vlana the head of Krovas, she and I would have to flee Lankhmar on the instant, every man's hand against us; while you infallibly would lose this fairy-land Mouse has created for love of you and be forced to do likewise, be with him a beggar on the run for the rest of your natural lives.'

It was beautifully reasoned and put . . . and no good whatso-ever. While Fafhrd spoke, Ivrian snatched up her new-filled cup and drained it. Now she stood up straight as a soldier, her pale face flushed, and said scathingly to Fafhrd kneeling before her, '*You count the cost!* You speak to me of *things*' – she waved at the many-hued splendor around her – 'of mere property, however costly, when *honor* is at stake. You gave Vlana *your word*. Oh, is knighthood wholly dead? And that applies to you, too, Mouse, who swore you'd slit the miserable throats of two noisome Guild-thieves,'

'I didn't swear *to*,' the Mouser objected feebly, downing a big drink. 'I merely said *I would have*,' while Fafhrd could only shrug again and writhe inside and gulp a little easement from his silver mug. For Ivrian was speaking in the same guilt-showering tones and using the same unfair yet heart-cleaving womanly argu-ments as Mor his mother might have, or Mara, his deserted Snow Clan sweetheart and avowed wife, big-bellied by now with his child.

In a master stroke, Vlana tried gently to draw Ivrian down to her golden seat again. 'Softly, dearest,' she pleaded. 'You have spoken nobly for me and my cause, and believe me, I am most grateful. Your words revived in me great, fine feelings dead these many years. But of us here, only you are truly an aristocrat attuned to the highest proprieties. We other three are naught but thieves. Is it any wonder some of us put safety above honor and word-keeping, and most prudently avoid risking our lives? Yes, we are three thieves and I am outvoted. So please speak no more of honor and rash, dauntless bravery, but sit you down and—'

'You mean they're both *afraid* to challenge the Thieves' Guild, don't you?' Ivrian said, eyes wide and face twisted by loathing. 'I always thought my Mouse was a nobleman first and a thief second. Thieving's nothing. My father lived by cruel thievery done on rich wayfarers and neighbors less powerful than he, yet he was an aristocrat. Oh, you're *cowards*, both of you! *Poltroons!*' she finished, turning her eyes flashing with cold scorn first on the Mouser, then on Fafhrd.

The latter could stand it no longer. He sprang to his feet, face flushed, fists clenched at his sides, quite unmindful of his down-clattered mug and the ominous creak his sudden action drew from the sagging floor.

'*I am not a coward!*' he cried. 'I'll dare Thieves' House and fetch you Krovas' head and toss it with blood a-drip at Vlana's feet. I swear that, witness me, Kos the god of dooms, by the brown bones of Nalgron my father and by his sword Graywand here at my side!'

He slapped his left hip, found nothing there but his tunic, and had to content himself with pointing tremble-armed at his belt and scabbarded sword where they lay atop his neatly folded robe – and then picking up, refilling splashily, and draining his mug.

The Gray Mouser began to laugh in high, delighted, tuneful peals. All stared at him. He came dancing up beside Fafhrd, and still smiling widely, asked, '*Why not?* Who speaks of fearing the Guild-thieves? Who becomes upset at the prospect of this ridiculously easy exploit, when all of us know that all of them, even Krovas and his ruling clique, are but pygmies in mind and skill compared to me or Fafhrd here? A wonderously simple, foolproof scheme has just occurred to me for penetrating Thieves' House, every closet and cranny. Stout Fafhrd and I will put it into effect at once. Are you with me, Northerner?'

'Of course I am,' Fafhrd responded gruffly, at the same time frantically wondering what madness had gripped the little fellow.

'Give me a few heartbeats to gather needed props, and we're off!' the Mouser cried. He snatched from a shelf and unfolded a stout sack, then raced about, thrusting into it coiled ropes, bandage rolls, rags, jars of ointment and unction and unguent, and other oddments.

'But you can't go *tonight*,' Ivrian protested, suddenly grown pale and uncertain-voiced. 'You're both . . . in no condition to.'

'You're both *drunk*,' Vlana said harshly. 'Silly drunk – and that way you'll get naught in Thieves' House but your deaths.

Fafhrd, where's that heartless reason you employed to slay or ice-veined see slain a clutch of mighty rivals and win me at Cold Corner and in the chilly, sorcery-webbed depths of Troll-step Canyon? Revive it! And infuse some into your skipping gray friend.'

'Oh, no,' Fafhrd told her as he buckled on his sword. 'You wanted the head of Krovas heaved at your feet in a great splatter of blood, and that's what you're going to get, like it or not!'

'Softly, Fafhrd,' the Mouser interjected, coming to a sudden stop and drawing tight the sack's mouth by its strings. 'And softly you too, Lady Vlana, and my dear princess. Tonight I intend but a scouting expedition. No risks run, only the information gained needful for planning our murderous strike tomorrow or the day after. So no head-choppings whatsoever tonight, Fafhrd, you hear me? Whatever may hap, hist's the word. And don your hooded robe.'

Fafhrd shrugged, nodded, and obeyed.

Ivrian seemed somewhat relieved. Vlana too, though she said, 'Just the same you're both drunk.'

'All to the good!' the Mouser assured her with a mad smile. 'Drink may slow a man's sword-arm and soften his blows a bit, but it sets his wits ablaze and fires his imagination, and those are the qualities we'll need tonight. Besides,' he hurried on, cutting off some doubt Ivrian was about to voice, 'drunken men are supremely cautious! Have you ever seen a staggering sot pull himself together at sight of the guard and walk circumspectly and softly past?'

'Yes,' Vlana said, 'and fall flat on his face just as he comes abreast 'em.'

'Pish!' the Mouser retorted and, throwing back his head, grandly walked toward her along an imaginary straight line. Instantly he tripped over his own foot, plunged forward, suddenly without touching floor did an incredible forward flip, heels over head, and landed erect and quite softly – toes, ankles, and knees bending just at the right moment to soak up impact – directly in front of the girls. The floor barely complained.

'You see?' he said, straightening up and unexpectedly reeling backward. He tripped over the pillow on which lay his cloak and sword, but by a wrenching twist and a lurch stayed upright and began rapidly to accouter himself.

Under cover of this action Fafhrd made quietly yet swiftly to fill once more his and the Mouser's mugs, but Vlana noted it and gave him such a glare that he set down mugs and uncorked jug so swiftly his robe swirled, then stepped back from the drinks table with a shrug of resignation and toward Vlana a grimacing nod.

The Mouser shouldered his sack and drew open the door. With a casual wave at the girls, but no word spoken, Fafhrd stepped out on the tiny porch. The night-smog had grown so thick he was almost lost to view. The Mouser waved four fingers at Ivrian, softly called, 'Bye-bye, Misling,' then followed Fafhrd.

'Good fortune go with you,' Vlana called heartily.

'Oh, be careful, Mouse,' Ivrian gasped.

The Mouser, his figure slight against the loom of Fafhrd's, silently drew shut the door.

Their arms automatically gone around each other, the girls waited for the inevitable creaking and groaning of the stairs. It delayed and delayed. The night-smog that had entered the room dissipated and still the silence was unbroken.

'What can they be doing out there?' Ivrian whispered. 'Plotting their course?'

Vlana, scowling, impatiently shook her head, then disentangled herself, tiptoed to the door, opened it, descended softly a few steps, which creaked most dolefully, then returned, shutting the door behind her.

'They're gone,' she said in wonder, her eyes wide, her hands spread a little to either side, palms up.

'I'm frightened!' Ivrian breathed and sped across the room to embrace the taller girl.

Vlana hugged her tight, then disengaged an arm to shoot the door's three heavy bolts.

In Bones Alley the Mouser returned to his pouch the knotted line by which they'd descended from the lamp hook. He suggested, 'How about stopping at the Silver Eel?'

'You mean and just *tell* the girls we've been to Thieves' House?' Fafhrd asked, not too indignantly.

'Oh, no,' the Mouser protested. 'But you missed your stirrup cup upstairs and so did I.'

At the word 'stirrup' he looked down at his ratskin boots and then crouching began a little gallop in one place, his boot-soles clopping softly on the cobbles. He flapped imaginary reins – 'Giddap!' – and quickened his gallop, but leaning sharply back pulled to a stop – 'Whoa!' – when with a crafty smile Fafhrd drew from his robe two full jugs.

'Palmed 'em, as 'twere, when I set down the mugs. Vlana sees a lot, but not all.'

'You're a prudent, far-sighted fellow, in addition to having some skill at sword taps,' the Mouser said admiringly. 'I'm proud to call you comrade.'

Each uncorked and drank a hearty slug. Then the Mouser led them west, they veering and stumbling only a little. Not so far as Cheap Street, however, but turning north into an even narrower and more noisome alley.

'Plague Court,' the Mouser said. Fafhrd nodded.

After several preliminary peepings and peerings, they staggered swiftly across wide, empty Crafts Street and into Plague Court again. For a wonder it was growing a little lighter. Looking upward, they saw stars. Yet there was no wind blowing from the north. The air was deathly still.

In their drunken preoccupation with the project at hand and mere locomotion, they did not look behind them. There the night-smog was thicker than ever. A high-circling nighthawk would have seen the stuff converging from all sections of Lankhmar, north, east, south, west – from the Inner Sea, from the Great Salt Marsh, from the many-ditched grainlands, from the River Hlal – in swift-moving black rivers and rivulets, heaping, eddying, swirling, dark and reeking essence of Lankhmar from its branding irons, braziers, bonfires, bonefires, kitchen fires and warmth fires, kilns, forges, breweries, distilleries, junk and garbage fires innumerable, sweating alchemists' and sorcerers' dens, crematoriums, charcoal burners' turfed mounds, all those and many more . . . converging purposefully on Dim Lane and particularly on the Silver Eel and perhaps especially on the rickety house behind it, untenanted except for attic. The closer to that center it got, the more substantial the smog became, eddy-strands and swirl-tatters tearing off and clinging to rough stone corners and scraggly-surfaced brick like black cobwebs.

But the Mouser and Fafhrd merely exclaimed in mild, muted amazement at the stars, muggily mused as to how much the improved visibility would increase the risk of their quest, and cautiously crossing the Street of the Thinkers, called Atheist Avenue by moralists, continued to Plague Court until it forked.

The Mouser chose the left branch, which trended northwest. 'Death Alley.'

Fafhrd nodded.

After a curve and recurve, Cheap Street swung into sight about thirty paces ahead. The Mouser stopped at once and lightly threw his arm against Fafhrd's chest.

Clearly in view across Cheap Street was a wide, low, open doorway, framed by grimy stone blocks. There led up to it two steps hollowed by the treadings of centuries. Orange-yellow light spilled out from bracketed torches inside. They couldn't see very far in because of Death Alley's angle. Yet as far as they *could* see, there was no porter or guard in sight, nor anyone at all, not even a watchdog on a chain. The effect was ominous.

'Now how do we get into the damn place?' Fafhrd demanded in a hoarse whisper. 'Scout Murder Alley for a back window that can be forced? You've pries in that sack, I trow. Or try the roof? You're a roof man, I know already. Teach me the art. I know trees and mountains, snow, ice, and bare rock. See this wall here?' He backed off from it, preparing to up it in a rush.

'Steady on, Fafhrd,' the Mouser said, keeping his hand against the big young man's chest. 'We'll hold the roof in reserve. Likewise all walls. And I'll take it on trust you're a master climber. As to how we get in, we walk straight through that doorway.' He frowned. 'Tap and hobble, rather. Come on, while I prepare us.'

As he drew the skeptically grimacing Fafhrd back down Death Alley until all Cheap Street was again cut off from view, he explained. 'We'll pretend to be beggars, members of *their* guild, which is but a branch of the Thieves' Guild and houses with it, or at any rate reports in to the Beggarmasters at Thieves' House. We'll be new members, who've gone out by day, so it'll not be expected that the Night Beggarmaster and any night watchmen know our looks.'

'But we don't look like beggars,' Fafhrd protested. 'Beggars have awful sores and limbs all a-twist or lacking altogether.'

'That's just what I'm going to take care of now,' the Mouser chuckled, drawing Scalpel. Ignoring Fafhrd's backward step and wary glance, the Mouser gazed puzzledly at the long tapering strip of steel he'd bared, then with a happy nod unclipped from his belt Scalpel's scabbard furbished with ratskin, sheathed the sword and swiftly wrapped it up, hilt and all, in a spiral, with the wide ribbon of a bandage roll dug from his sack.

'There!' he said, knotting the bandage ends. 'Now I've a tapping cane.'

'What's that?' Fafhrd demanded. 'And why?'

'Because I'll be blind, that's why.' He took a few shuffling steps, tapping the cobbles ahead with wrapped sword – gripping it by the quillons, or cross-guard, so that the grip and pommel were up his sleeve – and groping ahead with his other hand. 'That look all right to you?' he asked Fafhrd as he turned back. 'Feels perfect to me. Bat-blind, eh? Oh, don't fret, Fafhrd – the rag's but gauze. I can see through it fairly well. Besides, I don't have to convince anyone inside Thieves' House I'm actually blind. Most Guild-beggars fake it, as you must know. Now what to do with you? Can't have you blind also – too obvious, might wake suspicion.' He uncorked his jug and sucked inspiration. Fafhrd copied this action, on principle.

The Mouser smacked his lips and said, 'I've got it! Fafhrd, stand on your right leg and double up your left behind you at the knee. Hold! Don't fall on me! Avaunt! But steady yourself by my shoulder. That's right. Now get that left foot higher. We'll disguise your sword like mine, for a crutch cane – it's thicker and'll look just right. You can also steady yourself with your other hand on my shoulder as you hop – the halt leading the blind, always good for a tear, always good theater! But higher with that left foot! No, it just doesn't come off – I'll have to rope it. But first unclip your scabbard.'

Soon the Mouser had Graywand and its scabbard in the same state as Scalpel and was tying Fafhrd's left ankle to his thigh, drawing the rope cruelly tight, though Fafhrd's wine-anesthetized nerves hardly registered it. Balancing himself with his steel-corded crutch cane as the Mouser worked, he swigged from his jug and pondered deeply. Ever since joining forces with Vlana, he'd been interested in the theater, and the atmosphere of the actors' tenement had fired that interest further, so that he was delighted at the prospect of acting a part in real life. Yet brilliant as the Mouser's plan undoubtedly was, there did seem to be drawbacks to it. He tried to formulate them.

'Mouser,' he said, 'I don't know as I like having our swords tied up, so we can't draw 'em in emergency.'

'We can still use 'em as clubs,' the Mouser countered, his breath hissing between his teeth as he drew the last knot hard. 'Besides, we'll have our knives. Say, pull your belt around until yours is behind your back, so your robe will hide it sure. I'll do the same with Cat's Claw. Beggars don't carry weapons, at least in view, and we must maintain dramatic consistency in every detail. Stop drinking now; you've had enough. I myself need only a couple swallows more to reach my finest pitch.'

'And I don't know as I like going hobbled into that den of cutthroats. I can hop amazingly fast, it's true, but not as fast as I can run. Is it really wise, think you?'

'You can slash yourself loose in an instant,' the Mouser hissed with a touch of impatience and anger. 'Aren't you willing to make the least sacrifice for art's sake?'

'Oh, very well,' Fafhrd said, draining his jug and tossing it aside. 'Yes, of course I am.'

'Your complexion's too hale,' the Mouser said, inspecting him critically. He touched up Fafhrd's features and hands with pale gray greasepaint, then added wrinkles with dark. 'And your garb's too tidy.' He scooped dirt from between the cobbles and smeared it on Fafhrd's robe, then tried to put a rip in it, but the material resisted. He shrugged and tucked his lightened sack under his belt.

'So's yours,' Fafhrd observed, and stooping on his right leg got a good handful of muck himself, ordure in it by its feel and stink. Heaving himself up with a mighty effort, he wiped the stuff off on the Mouser's cloak and gray silken jerkin too.

The small man got the odor and cursed, but, 'Dramatic consistency,' Fafhrd reminded him. 'It's well we stink. Beggars do – that's one reason folk give 'em coins: to get rid of 'em. And no one at Thieves' House will be eager to inspect us close. Now come on, while our fires are still high.' And grasping hold of the Mouser's shoulder, he propelled himself rapidly toward Cheap Street, setting his bandaged sword between cobbles well ahead and taking mighty hops.

'Slow down, idiot,' the Mouser cried softly, shuffling along with the speed almost of a skater to keep up, while tapping his (sword) cane like mad. 'A cripple's supposed to be *feeble* – that's what draws the sympathy.'

Fafhrd nodded wisely and slowed somewhat. The ominous empty doorway slid again into view. The Mouser tilted his jug to get the last of his wine, swallowed awhile, then choked sputteringly. Fafhrd snatched and drained the jug, then tossed it over shoulder to shatter noisily.

They hop-shuffled into Cheap Street, halting almost at once for a richly clad man and woman to pass. The richness of the man's garb was sober and he was on the fat and oldish side, though hard-featured. A merchant doubtless, and with money in the Thieves' Guild – protection money, at least – to take this route at this hour.

The richness of the woman's garb was garish though not tawdry and she was beautiful and young, and looked still younger. A competent courtesan, almost certainly.

The man started to veer around the noisome and filthy pair, his face averted, but the girl swung toward the Mouser, concern growing in her eyes with hothouse swiftness. 'Oh, you poor boy! Blind. What tragedy,' she said. 'Give us a gift for him, lover.'

'Keep away from those stinkards, Misra, and come along,' he retorted, the last of his speech vibrantly muffled, for he was holding his nose.

She made him no reply, but thrust white hand into his ermine pouch and swiftly pressed a coin against the Mouser's palm and closed his fingers on it, then took his head between her palms and kissed him sweetly on the lips before letting herself be dragged on.

'Take good care of the little fellow, old man,' she called fondly back to Fafhrd while her companion grumbled muffled reproaches at her, of which only 'perverted bitch' was intelligible.

The Mouser stared at the coin in his palm, then sneaked a long look after his benefactress. There was a dazed wonder in his voice as he whispered to Fafhrd, 'Look. *Gold*. A golden coin and a beautiful woman's sympathy. Think you we should give over this rash project and for a profession take up beggary?'

'Buggery even, rather!' Fafhrd answered harsh and low. That 'old man' rankled. 'Onward we, bravely!'

They upped the two worn steps and went through the doorway, noting the exceptional thickness of the wall. Ahead was a long, straight, high-ceilinged corridor ending in stairs and with doors spilling light at intervals and well-set torches adding their flare, but empty all its length.

They had just got through the doorway when cold steel chilled the neck and pricked a shoulder of each of them. From just above, two voices commanded in unison, 'Halt!'

Although fired – and fuddled – by fortified wine, they each had wit enough to freeze and then very cautiously look upward.

Two gaunt, scarred, exceptionally ugly faces, each topped by a gaudy scarf binding back hair, looked down at them from a big, deep niche just above the doorway and helping explain its lowness. Two bent, gnarly arms thrust down the swords that still pricked them.

'Gone out with the noon beggar-batch, eh?' one of them observed. 'Well, you'd better have a high take to justify your tardy return. The Night Beggarmaster's on a Whore Street furlough. Report above to Krovas. Gods, you stink! Better clean up first, or Krovas will have you bathed in live steam. Begone!'

The Mouser and Fafhrd shuffled and hobbled forward at their most authentic. One niche-guard cried after them, 'Relax, boys! You don't have to put it on here.'

'Practice makes perfect,' the Mouser called back in a quavering voice. Fafhrd's finger-ends dug his shoulder warningly.

They moved along somewhat more naturally, so far as Fafhrd's tied-up leg allowed.

'Gods, what an easy life the Guild-beggars have,' the other niche-guard observed to his mate. 'What slack discipline and low standards of skill! Perfect, my sacred butt! You'd think a child could see through those disguises.'

'Doubtless some children do,' his mate retorted. 'But their dear mothers and fathers only drop a tear and a coin or give a kick. Grown folk go blind, lost in their toil and dreams, unless they have a profession such as thieving which keeps them mindful of things as they really are.'

Resisting the impulse to ponder this sage philosophy, and glad they would not have to undergo a Beggarmaster's shrewd inspection – truly, thought Fafhrd, Kos of the Dooms seemed to be leading him direct to Krovas and perhaps head-chopping *would* be the order of the night – he and the Mouser went watchfully and slowly on. And now they began to hear voices, mostly curt and clipped ones, and other noises.

They passed some doorways they'd liked to have paused at, to study the activities inside, yet the most they dared do was slow down a bit more. Fortunately most of the doorways were wide, permitting a fairly long view.

Very interesting were some of those activities. In one room young boys were being trained to pick pouches and slit purses. They'd approach from behind an instructor, and if he heard scuff of bare foot or felt touch of dipping hand – or, worst, heard *clunk* of dropped leaden mock-coin – that boy would be thwacked. Others seemed to be getting training in group-tactics: the jostle in front, the snatch from behind, the swift passing of lifted items from youthful thief to confederate.

In a second room, from which pushed air heavy with the reeks of metal and oil, older student thieves were doing laboratory work in lock picking. One group was being lectured by a grimy-handed graybeard, who was taking apart a most complex lock piece by weighty piece. Others appeared to be having their skill, speed, and ability to work soundlessly tested – they were probing with slender picks the keyholes in a half dozen doors set side-by-side in an otherwise purposeless partition, while a supervisor holding a sandglass watched them keenly.

In a third, thieves were eating at long tables. The odors were tempting, even to men full of booze. The Guild did well by its members.

In a fourth, the floor was padded in part and instruction was going on in slipping, dodging, ducking, tumbling, tripping, and otherwise foiling pursuit. These students were older too. A voice like a sergeant-major's rasped, 'Nah, nah, nah! You couldn't give your crippled grandmother the slip. I said duck, not genuflect to holy Aarth. Now this time—'

'Grif's used grease,' an instructor called.

'He has, eh? To the front, Grif!' the rasping voice replied as the Mouser and Fafhrd moved somewhat regretfully out of sight, for they realized much was to be learned here: tricks that might stand them in good stead even tonight. 'Listen, all of you!' the rasping voice continued, so far-carrying it followed them a surprisingly long way. 'Grease may be very well on a night job – by day its glisten shouts its user's profession to all Nehwon! But in any case it makes a thief overconfident. He comes to depend on it and then in a pinch he finds he's forgot to apply it. Also its aroma can betray him. Here we work always dry-skinned – save for natural sweat! – as all of you were told first night. Bend over, Grif. Grasp your ankles. Straighten your knees.'

More thwacks, followed by yelps of pain, distant now, since the Mouser and Fafhrd were halfway up the end-stairs, Fafhrd vaulting somewhat laboriously as he grasped curving banister and swaddled sword.

The second floor duplicated the first, but was as luxurious as the other had been bare. Down the long corridor lamps and filagreed incense pots pendant from the ceiling alternated, diffusing a mild light and spicy smell. The walls were richly draped, the floor thick-carpeted. Yet this corridor was empty too and, moreover, *completely* silent. After a glance at each other, they started off boldly.

The first door, wide open, showed an untenanted room full of racks of garments, rich and plain, spotless and filthy, also wig stands, shelves of beards and such, and several wall mirrors faced by small tables crowded with cosmetics and with stools before them. A disguising room, clearly.

After a look and listen either way, the Mouser darted in and out to snatch up a large green flask from the nearest table. He unstoppered and sniffed it. A rotten-sweet gardenia-reek contended with the nose-sting of spirits of wine. The Mouser sloshed his and Fafhrd's fronts with this dubious perfume.

'Antidote to ordure,' he explained with the pomp of a physician, stoppering the flask. 'Don't want to be parboiled by Krovas. No, no, no.'

Two figures appeared at the far end of the corridor and came toward them. The Mouser hid the flask under his cloak, holding it between elbow and side, and he and Fafhrd continued onward – to turn back would look suspicious, both drunkenly judged.

The next three doorways they passed were shut by heavy doors. As they neared the fifth, the two approaching figures, coming on arm-in-arm, yet taking long strides, moving more swiftly than the hobble-shuffle, became distinct. Their clothing was that of noblemen, but their faces those of thieves. They were frowning with indignation and suspicion too at the Mouser and Fafhrd.

Just then – from somewhere between the two man-pairs, it sounded – a voice began to speak words in a strange tongue, using the rapid monotone priests employ in a routine service or some sorcerers in their incantations.

The two richly clad thieves slowed at the seventh doorway and looked in. Their progress ceased altogether. Their necks strained, their eyes widened. They visibly paled. Then of a sudden they hastened onward, almost running, and bypassed Fafhrd and the Mouser as if they were furniture. The incantatory voice drummed on without missing a beat.

The fifth doorway was shut, but the sixth was open. The Mouser peeked in with one eye, his nose brushing the jamb. Then he stepped forward and gazed inside with entranced expression, pushing the black rag up onto his forehead for better vision. Fafhrd joined him.

It was a large room, empty so far as could be told of human and animal life, but filled with most interesting things. From knee-height up, the entire far wall was a map of the city of Lankhmar and its immediate surrounds. Every building and street seemed depicted, down to the meanest hovel and narrowest court. There were signs of recent erasure and redrawing at many spots, and here and there little colored hieroglyphs of mysterious import.

The floor was marble, the ceiling blue as lapis lazuli. The side walls were thickly hung, by ring and padlock. One was covered with all manner of thieves' tools, from a huge thick pry-bar that looked as if it could unseat the universe, or at least the door of the overlord's treasure-vault, to a rod so slim it might be an elf-queen's wand and seemingly designed to telescope out and fish from distance for precious gauds on milady's spindle-legged, ivory-topped vanity table; the other wall had on it all sorts of quaint, gold-gleaming and jewel-flashing objects, evidently mementos chosen for their oddity from the spoils of memorable burglaries, from a female mask of thin gold, breathlessly beautiful in its features and contours, but thickly set with rubies simulating the spots of the pox in its fever-stage, to a knife whose blade was wedge-shaped diamonds set side by side and this diamond cutting-edge looking razor-sharp.

All about were tables set chiefly with models of dwelling houses and other buildings, accurate to the last minutia, it looked, of ventilation hole under roof gutter and ground-level drain hole, of creviced wall and smooth. Many were cut away in partial or entire section to show the layout of rooms, closets, strongrooms, doorways, corridors, secret passages, smoke-ways, and air-ways in equal detail.

In the center of the room was a bare round-table of ebony and ivory squares. About it were set seven straight-backed but well-padded chairs, the one facing the map and away from the Mouser and Fafhrd being higher backed and wider armed than the others – a chief's chair, likely that of Krovas.

The Mouser tiptoed forward, irresistibly drawn, but Fafhrd's left hand clamped down on his shoulder like the iron mitten of a Mingol cataphract and drew him irresistibly back.

Scowling his disapproval, the Northerner brushed down the black rag over the Mouser's eyes again, and with his crutch-hand thumbed ahead; then set off in that direction in most carefully calculated, silent hops. With a shrug of disappointment the Mouser followed.

As soon as they had turned away from the doorway, but before they were out of sight, a neatly black-bearded, crop-haired head came like a serpent's around the side of the highest-backed chair and gazed after them from deep-sunken yet glinting eyes. Next a snake-supple, long hand followed the head out, crossed thin lips with ophidian forefinger for silence, and then finger-beckoned the two pairs of dark-tunicked men who were standing to either side of the doorway, their backs to the corridor wall, each of the four gripping a curvy knife in one hand and a dark leather, lead-weighted bludgeon in the other.

When Fafhrd was halfway to the seventh doorway, from which the monotonous yet sinister recitation continued to well, there shot out through it a slender, whey-faced youth, his narrow hands clapped over his mouth, under terror-wide eyes, as if to shut in screams or vomit, and with a broom clamped in an armpit, so that he seemed a bit like a young warlock about to take to the air. He dashed past Fafhrd and the Mouser and away, his racing footsteps sounding rapid-dull on the carpeting and hollow-sharp on the stairs before dying away.

Fafhrd gazed back at the Mouser with a grimace and shrug, then squatting one-legged until the knee of his bound-up leg touched the floor, advanced half his face past the doorjamb. After a bit, without otherwise changing position, he beckoned the Mouser to approach. The latter slowly thrust half his face past the jamb, just above Fafhrd's.

What they saw was a room somewhat smaller than that of the great map and lit by central lamps that burned blue-white instead of customary yellow. The floor was marble, darkly colorful and complexly whorled. The dark walls were hung with astrological and anthropomantic charts and instruments of magic and shelved with cryptically labeled porcelain jars and also with vitreous flasks and glass pipes of the oddest shapes, some filled with colored fluids, but many gleamingly empty. At the foot of the walls, where the shadows were thickest, broken and discarded stuff was irregularly heaped, as if swept out of the way and forgot, and here and there opened a large rathole.

In the center of the room and brightly illuminated by contrast was a long table with thick top and many stout legs. The Mouser thought fleetingly of a centipede and then of the bar at the Eel, for the tabletop was densely stained and scarred by many a spilled elixir and many a deep black burn by fire or acid or both.

In the midst of the table an alembic was working. The lamp's flame – deep blue, this one – kept a-boil in the large crystal cucurbit a dark, viscid fluid with here and there diamond glints. From out of the thick, seething stuff, strands of a darker vapor streamed upward to crowd through the cucurbit's narrow mouth and stain – oddly, with bright scarlet – the transparent head and then, dead black now, flow down the narrow pipe from the head into a spherical crystal receiver, larger even than the cucurbit, and there curl and weave about like so many coils of living black cord – an endless, skinny, ebon serpent.

Behind the left end of the table stood a tall, yet hunchbacked man in black robe and hood, which shadowed more than hid a face of which the most prominent features were a long, thick, pointed nose with out-jutting, almost chinless mouth just below. His complexion was sallow-gray like clay and a short-haired, bristly, gray beard grew high on his wide cheeks. From under a receding forehead and bushy gray brows, wide-set eyes looked intently down at an age-browned scroll, which his disgustingly small clubhands, knuckles big, short backs gray-bristled, ceaselessly unrolled and rolled up again. The only move his eyes ever made, besides the short side-to-side one as he read the lines he was rapidly intoning, was an occasional farther sidewise glance at the alembic.

On the other end of the table, beady eyes darting from the sorcerer to the alembic and back again, crouched a small black beast, the first glimpse of which made Fafhrd dig fingers painfully into the Mouser's shoulder and the latter almost gasp, not from the pain. It was most like a rat, yet it had a higher forehead and closer-set eyes that either had ever seen in a rat, while its forepaws, which it constantly rubbed together in what seemed restless glee, looked like tiny copies of the sorcerer's clubhands.

Simultaneously yet independently, Fafhrd and the Mouser each became certain it was the beast which had gutter-escorted Slivikin and his mate, then fled, and each recalled what Ivrian had said about a witch's familiar and Vlana about the likelihood of Krovas employing a warlock.

What with the ugliness of the clubhanded man and beast and between them the ropy black vapor coiling and twisting in the great receiver and head, like a black umbilical cord, it was a most horrid sight. And the similarities, save for size, between the two creatures were even more disquieting in their implications.

The tempo of the incantation quickened, the blue-white flames brightened and hissed audibly, the fluid in the cucurbit grew thick as lava, great bubbles formed and loudly broke, the black rope in the receiver writhed like a nest of snakes; there was an increasing sense of invisible presences, the supernatural tension grew almost unendurable, and Fafhrd and the Mouser were hard put to keep silent the open-mouthed gasps by which they now breathed, and each feared his heartbeat could be heard cubits away.

Abruptly the incantation peaked and broke off, like a drum struck very hard, then instantly silenced by palm and fingers outspread against the head. With a bright flash and dull explosion, cracks innumerable appeared in the cucurbit; its crystal became white and opaque, yet it did not shatter or drip. The head lifted a span, hung there, fell back. While two black nooses appeared among the coils in the receiver and suddenly narrowed until they were only two big black knots.

The sorcerer grinned, rolling up the end of the parchment with a snap, and shifted his gaze from the receiver to his familiar, while the latter chittered shrilly and bounded up and down in rapture.

'Silence, Slivikin! Comes now your time to race and strain and sweat,' the sorcerer cried, speaking pidgin Lankhmarese now, but so rapidly and in so squeakingly high-pitched a voice that Fafhrd and the Mouser could barely follow him. They did, however, both realize they had been completely mistaken as to the identity of Slivikin. In moment of disaster, the fat thief had called to the witch-beast for help rather than to his human comrade.

'Yes, master,' Slivikin squeaked back no less clearly, in an instant revising the Mouser's opinions about talking animals. He continued in the same fifelike, fawning tones, 'Harkening in obedience, Hristomilo.'

Now they knew the sorcerer's name too.

Hristomilo ordered in whiplash pipings, 'To your appointed work! See to it you summon an ample sufficiency of feasters! I want the bodies stripped to skeletons, so the bruises of the enchanted smog and all evidence of death by suffocation will be vanished utterly. But forget not the loot! On your mission, now – depart!'

Slivikin, who at every command had bobbed his head in a manner reminiscent of his bouncing, now squealed, 'I'll see it done!' and gray-lightninglike leaped a long leap to the floor and down an inky rathole.

Hristomilo, rubbing together his disgusting clubhands much as Slivikin had his, cried chucklingly, 'What Slevyas lost, my magic has rewon!'

Fafhrd and the Mouser drew back out of the doorway, partly with the thought that since neither his incantation and his alembic, nor his familiar now required his unblinking attention, Hristomilo would surely look up and spot them; partly in revulsion from what they had seen and heard; and in poignant if useless pity for Slevyas, whoever he might be, and for the other unknown victims of the rat-like and conceivably rat-related sorcerer's death-spells, poor strangers already dead and due to have their flesh eaten from their bones.

Fafhrd wrested the green bottle from the Mouser and, though almost gagging on the rotten-flowery reek, gulped a large, stinging mouthful. The Mouser couldn't quite bring himself to do the same, but was comforted by the spirits of wine he inhaled during this byplay.

Then he saw, beyond Fafhrd, standing before the doorway to the map room, a richly clad man with gold-hilted knife jewel-scabbarded at his side. His sunken-eyed face was prematurely wrinkled by responsibility, overwork, and authority, and framed by neatly cropped black hair and beard. Smiling, he silently beckoned them.

The Mouser and Fafhrd obeyed, the latter returning the green bottle to the former, who recapped it and thrust it under the left elbow with well-concealed irritation.

Each guessed their summoner was Krovas, the Guild's Grandmaster. Once again Fafhrd marveled, as he hobble-dehoyed along, reeling and belching, how Kos or the Fates were guiding him to his target tonight. The Mouser, more alert and more apprehensive too, was reminding himself that they had been directed by the niche-guards to report to Krovas, so that the situation, if not developing quite in accord with his own misty plans, was still not deviating disastrously.

Yet not even his alertness, nor Fafhrd's primeval instincts, gave him forewarning as they followed Krovas into the map room.

Two steps inside, each of them was shoulder-grabbed and bludgeon-menaced by a pair of ruffians further armed with knives tucked in their belts.

They judged it wise to make no resistance, on this one occasion at least bearing out the Mouser's mouthings about the supreme caution of drunken men.

'All secure, Grandmaster,' one of the ruffians rapped out.

Krovas swung the highest-backed chair around and sat down, eyeing them cooly yet searchingly.

'What brings two stinking, drunken beggar-Guildsmen into the top-restricted precincts of the masters?' he asked quietly.

The Mouser felt the sweat of relief bead his forehead. The disguises he had brilliantly conceived were still working, taking in even the head man, though he had spotted Fafhrd's tipsiness. Resuming his blind-man manner, he quavered, 'We were directed by the guard above the Cheap Street door to report to you in person, great Krovas, the Night Beggarmaster being on furlough for reasons of sexual hygiene. Tonight we've made good haul!' And fumbling in his purse, ignoring as far as possible the tightened grip on his shoulders he brought out the golden coin given him by the sentimental courtesan and displayed it tremble-handed.

'Spare me your inexpert acting,' Krovas said sharply. 'I'm not one of your marks. And take that rag off your eyes.'

The Mouser obeyed and stood to attention again insofar as his pinioning would permit, and smiling the more seeming carefree because of his reawakening uncertainties. Conceivably he wasn't doing quite as brilliantly as he'd thought.

Krovas leaned forward and said placidly yet piercingly, 'Granted you were so ordered – and most improperly so; that door-guard will suffer for his stupidity! – why were you spying into a room beyond this one when I spotted you?'

'We saw brave thieves flee from that room,' the Mouser answered pat. 'Fearing that some danger threatened the Guild, my comrade and I investigated, ready to scotch it.'

'But what we saw and heard only perplexed us, great sir,' Fafhrd appended quite smoothly.

'I didn't ask you, sot. Speak when you're spoken to,' Krovas snapped at him. Then, to the Mouser, 'You're an overweening rogue, most presumptuous for your rank.'

In a flash the Mouser decided that further insolence, rather than fawning, was what the situation required. 'That I am, sir,' he said smugly. 'For example, I have a master plan whereby you and the Guild might gain more wealth and power in three months than your predecessors have in three millennia.'

Krovas' face darkened. 'Boy!' he called. Through the curtains of an inner doorway, a youth, with dark complexion of a Kleshite and clad only in a black loincloth sprang to kneel before Krovas, who ordered, 'Summon first my sorcerer, next the thieves Slevyas and Fissif,' whereupon the dark youth dashed into the corridor.

Then Krovas, his face its normal pale again, leaned back in his great chair, lightly rested his sinewy arms on its great padded ones, and smilingly directed the Mouser, 'Speak your piece. Reveal to us this master plan.'

Forcing his mind *not* to work on the surprising news that Slevyas was not victim but thief and not sorcery-slain but alive and available – why did Krovas want him *now*? – the Mouser threw back his head and, shaping his lips in a faint sneer, began, 'You may laugh merrily at me, Grandmaster, but I'll warrant that in less than a score of heartbeats you'll be straining sober-faced to hear my least word. Like lightning, wit can strike anywhere, and the best of you in Lankhmar have age-honored blind spots for things obvious to us of outland birth. My master plan is but this: let Thieves' Guild under your iron autocracy seize supreme power in Lankhmar City, then in Lankhmar Land, next over all Nehwon, after which who knows what realms undreamt will know your suzerainty!'

The Mouser had spoken true in one respect: Krovas was no longer smiling. He was leaning forward a little and his face was darkening again, but whether from interest or anger it was too soon to say.

The Mouser continued, 'For centuries the Guild's had more than the force and intelligence needed to make a *coup d'état* a nine-finger certainty; today there's not one hair's chance in a bush head of failure. It is the proper state of things that thieves rule other men. All Nature cries out for it. No need slay old Karstak Ovartamortes, merely overmaster, control, and so rule through him. You've already fee'd informers in every noble or wealthy house. Your post's better than the King of Kings'. You've a mercenary striking force permanently mobilized, should you have need of it, in the Slayers' Brotherhood. We Guild-beggars are your foragers. O great Krovas, the multitudes know that thievery rules Nehwon, nay, the universe, nay, more, the highest gods' abode! And the multitudes accept this, they balk only at the hypocrisy of the present arrangement, at the pretense that things are otherwise. Oh, give them their decent desire, great Krovas! Make it all open, honest and aboveboard, with thieves ruling in name as well as fact.'

The Mouser spoke with passion, for the moment believing all he said, even the contradictions. The four ruffians gaped at him with wonder and not a little awe. They slackened their holds on him and on Fafhrd too.

But leaning back in his great chair again and smiling thinly and ominously, Krovas said cooly, 'In *our* Guild intoxication is no excuse for folly, rather grounds for the extremest penalty. But I'm well aware you organized beggars operate under a laxer discipline. So I'll deign to explain to you, you wee drunken dreamer, that we thieves know well that, behind the scenes, we already rule Lankhmar, Nehwon, all life in sooth – for what is life but greed in action? But to make this an open thing would not only force us to take on ten thousand sorts of weary work others now do for us, it would also go against another of life's deep laws: illusion. Does the sweetmeats hawker show you his kitchen? Does a whore let average client watch her enamel-over her wrinkles and hoist her sagging breasts in cunning gauzy slings? Does a conjuror turn out for you his hidden pockets? Nature works by subtle, secret means – man's invisible seed, spider bite, the viewless spores of madness and of death, rocks that are born in earth's unknown bowels, the silent stars a-creep across the sky – and we thieves copy her.'

'That's good enough poetry, sir,' Fafhrd responded with undertone of angry derision, for he had himself been considerably impressed by the Mouser's master plan and was irked that Krovas should do insult to his new friend by disposing of it so lightly. 'Closet kingship may work well enough in easy times. But' – he paused histrionically – 'will it serve when Thieves' Guild is faced with an enemy determined to obliterate it forever, a plot to wipe it entirely from the earth?'

'What drunken babble's this?' Krovas demanded, sitting up straight. '*What* plot?'

''Tis a most *secret* one,' Fafhrd responded grinning, delighted to pay this haughty man in his own coin and thinking it quite just that the thief-king sweat a little before his head was removed for conveyance to Vlana. 'I know naught of it, except that many a master thief is marked down for the knife – and your head doomed to fall!'

Fafhrd merely sneered his face and folded his arms, the still slack grip of his captors readily permitting it, his (sword) crutch hanging against his body from his lightly gripping hand. Then he scowled as there came a sudden shooting pain in his numbed, bound-up left leg, which he had forgotten for a space.

Krovas raised a clenched fist and himself half out of his chair, in prelude to some fearsome command – likely that Fafhrd be tortured. The Mouser cut in hurriedly with, 'The Secret Seven, they're called, are its leaders. None in the outer circles of the conspiracy know their names, though rumor has it that they're secret Guild-thief renegades representing, one for each, the cities of Oool Hrusp, Kvarch Nar, Ilthmar, Horborixen, Tisilinilit, far Kriaay and Lankhmar's very self. It's thought they're moneyed by the merchants of the East, the priests of Wan, the sorcerers of the Steppes and half the Mingol leadership too, legended Quarmall, Aarth's Assassins in Sarheenmar, and also no lesser man than the King of Kings.'

Despite Krovas' contemptuous and then angry remarks, the ruffians holding the Mouser continued to harken to their captive with interest and respect, and they did not retighten their grip on him. His colorful revelations and melodramatic delivery held them, while Krovas' dry, cynical, philosophic observations largely went over their heads.

Hristomilo came gliding into the room then, his feet presumably taking swift, but very short steps, at any rate his black robe hung undisturbed to the marble floor despite his slithering speed.

There was a shock at his entrance. All eyes in the map room followed him, breaths were held, and the Mouser and Fafhrd felt the horny hands that gripped them shake just a little. Even Krovas' all-confident, world-weary expression became tense and guardedly uneasy. Clearly the sorcerer of the Thieves' Guild was more feared than loved by his chief employer and by the beneficiaries of his skills.

Outwardly oblivious to this reaction to his appearance, Hristomilo, smiling thin-lipped, halted close to one side of Krovas' chair and inclined his hood-shadowed rodent face in the ghost of a bow.

Krovas held palm toward the Mouser for silence. Then, wetting his lips, he asked Hristomilo sharply yet nervously, 'Do you know these two?'

Hristomilo nodded decisively. 'They just now peered a befuddled eye each at me,' he said, 'whilst I was about that business we spoke of. I'd have shooed them off, reported them, save such action might have broken my spell, put my words out of time with the alembic's workings. The one's a Northerner, the other's features have a southern cast – from Tovilyis or near, most like. Both younger than their now-looks. Free-lance bravos, I'd judge 'em, the sort the Brotherhood hires as extras when they get at once several big guard and escort jobs. Clumsily disguised now, of course, as beggars.'

Fafhrd by yawning, the Mouser by pitying headshake tried to convey that all this was so much poor guesswork.

'That's all I can tell you without reading their minds,' Hristomilo concluded. 'Shall I fetch my lights and mirrors?'

'Not yet.' Krovas turned face and shot a finger at the Mouser. 'How do you know these things you rant about? – Secret Seven and all. Straight simplest answer now – no rodomontades.'

The Mouser replied most glibly: 'There's a new courtesan dwells on Pimp Street – Tyarya her name, tall, beauteous, but hunchbacked, which oddly delights many of her clients. Now Tyarya loves me 'cause my maimed eyes match her twisted spine, or from simple pity of my blindness – *she* believes it! – and youth, or from some odd itch, like her clients' for her, which that combination arouses in her flesh.

'Now one of her patrons, a trader newly come from Klelg Nar – Mourph, he's called – was impressed by my intelligence, strength, boldness, and closemouthed tact, and those same qualities in my comrade too. Mourph sounded us out, finally asking if we hated the Thieves' Guild for its control of the Beggars' Guild. Sensing a chance to aid the Guild, we played up, and a week ago he recruited us into a cell of three in the outermost strands of the conspiracy web of the Seven.'

'You presumed to do all of this on your own?' Krovas demanded in freezing tones, sitting up straight and gripping hard the chair arms.

'Oh, no,' the Mouser denied guilelessly. 'We reported our every act to the Day Beggarmaster and he approved them, told us to spy our best and gather every scrap of fact and rumor we could about the Seven's conspiracy.'

'And he told me not a word about it!' Krovas rapped out. 'If true, I'll have Bannat's head for this! But you're lying, aren't you?'

As the Mouser gazed with wounded eyes at Krovas, meanwhile preparing a most virtuous denial, a portly man limped past the doorway with help of a gilded staff. He moved with silence and aplomb.

But Krovas saw him. 'Night Beggarmaster!' he called sharply. The limping man stopped, turned, came crippling majestically through the door. Krovas stabbed finger at the Mouser, then Fafhrd. 'Do you know these two, Flim?'

The Night Beggarmaster unhurriedly studied each for a space, then shook his head with its turban of cloth of gold. 'Never seen either before. What are they? Fink beggars?'

'But Flim wouldn't know us,' the Mouser explained desperately, feeling everything collapsing in on him and Fafhrd. 'All our contacts were with Bannat alone.'

Flim said quietly, 'Bannat's been abed with the swamp ague this past ten-day. Meanwhile *I* have been Day Beggarmaster as well as Night.'

At that moment Slevyas and Fissif came hurrying in behind Flim. The tall thief bore on his jaw a bluish lump. The fat thief's head was bandaged above his darting eyes. He pointed quickly at Fafhrd and the Mouser and cried, 'There are the two that slugged us, took our Jengao loot, and slew our escort.'

The Mouser lifted his elbow and the green bottle crashed to shards at his feet on the hard marble. Gardenia-reek sprang swiftly through the air.

But more swiftly still the Mouser, shaking off the careless hold of his startled guards, sprang toward Krovas, clubbing his wrapped-up sword. If he could only overpower the King of Thieves and hold Cat's Claw at his throat, he'd be able to bargain for his and Fafhrd's lives. That is, unless the other thieves wanted their master killed, which wouldn't surprise him at all.

With startling speed Flim thrust out his gilded staff, tripping the Mouser, who went heels over head, midway seeking to change his involuntary somersault into a voluntary one.

Meanwhile Fafhrd lurched heavily against his left-hand captor, at the same time swinging bandaged Graywand strongly upward to strike his right-hand captor under the jaw. Regaining his one-legged balance with a mighty contortion, he hopped for the loot-wall behind him.

Slevyas made for the wall of thieves' tools, and with a muscle-cracking effort wrenched the great pry-bar from its padlocked ring.

Scrambling to his feet after a poor landing in front of Krovas' chair, the Mouser found it empty and the Thief King in a half-crouch behind it, gold-hilted dagger drawn, deep-sunk eyes coldly battle-wild. Spinning around, he saw Fafhrd's guards on the floor, the one sprawled senseless, the other starting to scramble up, while the great Northerner, his back against the wall of weird jewelry, menaced the whole room with wrapped-up Graywand and with his long knife, jerked from its scabbard behind him.

Likewise drawing Cat's Claw, the Mouser cried in trumpet voice of battle, 'Stand aside, all! He's gone mad! I'll hamstring his good leg for you!' And racing through the press and between his own two guards, who still appeared to hold him in some awe, he launched himself with flashing dirk at Fafhrd, praying that the Northerner, drunk now with battle as well as wine and poisonous perfume, would recognize him and guess his strata-gem.

Graywand slashed well above his ducking head. His new friend not only guessed, but was playing up – and not just missing by accident, the Mouser hoped. Stooping low by the wall, he cut the lashings on Fafhrd's left leg. Graywand and Fafhrd's long knife continued to spare him. Springing up, he headed for the corridor, crying over-shoulder to Fafhrd, 'Come on!'

Hristomilo stood well out of his way, quietly observing. Fissif scuttled toward safety. Krovas stayed behind his chair, shouting, 'Stop them! Head them off!'

The three remaining ruffian guards, at last beginning to recover their fighting-wits, gathered to oppose the Mouser. But menacing them with swift feints of his dirk, he slowed them and darted between – and then just in the nick of time knocked aside with a downsweep of wrapped-up Scalpel Flim's gilded staff, thrust once again to trip him.

All this gave Slevyas time to return from the toolswall and aim at the Mouser a great swinging blow with the massive pry-bar. But even as that blow started, a very long, bandaged sword on a very long arm thrust over the Mouser's shoulder and solidly and heavily poked Slevyas high on the chest, jolting him backward, so that the pry-bar's swing was short and whistled past harmlessly.

Then the Mouser found himself in the corridor and Fafhrd beside him, though for some weird reason still only hopping. The Mouser pointed toward the stairs. Fafhrd nodded, but delayed to reach high, still on one leg only, and rip off the nearest wall a dozen cubits of heavy drapes, which he threw across the corridor to baffle pursuit.

They reached the stairs and started up the next flight, the Mouser in advance. There were cries behind, some muffled.

'Stop hopping, Fafhrd!' the Mouser ordered querulously. 'You've got two legs again.'

'Yes, and the other's still dead,' Fafhrd complained. 'Ahh! Now feeling begins to return to it.'

A thrown knife whisked between them and dully clinked as it hit the wall point-first and stone-powder flew. Then they were around the bend.

Two more empty corridors, two more curving flights, and then they saw above them on the last landing a stout ladder mounting to a dark, square hole in the roof. A thief with hair bound back by a colorful handkerchief – it appeared to be a doorguards' identification – menaced the Mouser with drawn sword, but when he saw that there were two of them, both charging him determinedly with shining knives and strange staves of clubs, he turned and ran down the last empty corridor.

The Mouser, followed closely by Fafhrd, rapidly mounted the ladder and without pause vaulted up through the hatch into the star-crusted night.

He found himself near the unrailed edge of a slate roof which slanted enough to have made it look most fearsome to a novice roof-walker, but safe as houses to a veteran.

Crouched on the long peak of the roof was another kerchiefed thief holding a dark lantern. He was rapidly covering and uncovering, presumably in some code, the lantern's bull's eye, whence shot a faint green beam north to where a red point of light winked dimly in reply – as far away as the sea wall, it looked, or perhaps the masthead of a ship beyond, riding in the Inner Sea. Smuggler?

Seeing the Mouser, this one instantly drew sword and, swinging the lantern a little in his other hand, advanced menacingly. The Mouser eyed him warily – the dark lantern with its hot metal, concealed flame, and store of oil would be a tricky weapon.

But then Fafhrd had clambered out and was standing beside the Mouser, on both feet again at last. Their adversary backed slowly away toward the north end of the roof ridge. Fleetingly the Mouser wondered if there was another hatch there.

Turning back at a bumping sound, he saw Fafhrd prudently hoisting the ladder. Just as he got it free, a knife flashed up close past him out of the hatch. While following its flight, the Mouser frowned, involuntarily admiring the skill required to hurl a knife vertically with any accuracy.

It clattered down near them and slid off the roof. The Mouser loped south across the slates and was halfway from the hatch to that end of the roof when the faint chink came of the knife striking the cobbles of Murder Alley.

Fafhrd followed more slowly, in part perhaps from a lesser experience of roofs, in part because he still limped a bit to favor his left leg, and in part because he was carrying the heavy ladder balanced on his right shoulder.

'We won't need that,' the Mouser called back.

Without hesitation Fafhrd heaved it joyously over the edge. By the time it crashed in Murder Alley, the Mouser was leaping down two yards and across a gap of one to the next roof, of opposite and lesser pitch. Fafhrd landed beside him.

The Mouser led them at almost a run through a sooty forest of chimneys, chimney pots, ventilators with tails that made them always face the wind, black-legged cisterns, hatch covers, bird houses, and pigeon traps across five roofs, four progressively a little lower, the fifth regaining a yard of the altitude they'd lost – the spaces between the buildings easy to leap, none more than three yards, no ladder-bridge required, and only one roof with a somewhat greater pitch than that of Thieves' House – until they reached the Street of the Thinkers at a point where it was crossed by a roofed passageway much like the one at Rokkermas and Slaarg's.

While they crossed it at a crouching lope, something hissed close past them and clattered ahead. As they leaped down from the roof of the bridge, three more somethings hissed over their heads to clatter beyond. One rebounded from a square chimney almost to the Mouser's feet. He picked it up, expecting a stone, and was surprised by the greater weight of a leaden ball big as two doubled-up fingers.

'They,' he said, jerking thumb overshoulder, 'lost no time in getting slingers on the roof. When roused, they're good.'

Southeast then through another black chimney-forest to a point on Cheap Street where upper stories overhung the street so much on either side that it was easy to leap the gap. During this roof-traverse, an advancing front of night-smog, dense enough to make them cough and wheeze, had engulfed them and for perhaps sixty heartbeats the Mouser had had to slow to a shuffle and feel his way, Fafhrd's hand on his shoulder. Just short of Cheap Street they had come abruptly and completely out of the smog and seen the stars again, while the black front had rolled off northward behind them.

'Now what the devil was that?' Fafhrd had asked and the Mouser had shrugged.

A nighthawk would have seen a vast thick hoop of black night-smog blowing out in all directions from a center near the Silver Eel, growing ever greater and greater in diameter and circum-ferences.

East of Cheap Street the two comrades soon made their way to the ground, landing back in Plague Court behind the narrow premises of Nattick Nimblefingers the Tailor.

Then at last they looked at each other and their trammeled swords and their filthy faces and clothing made dirtier still by roof-soot, and they laughed and laughed and laughed, Fafhrd roaring still as he bent over to massage his left leg above and below knee. This hooting and wholly unaffected self-mockery continued while they unwrapped their swords – the Mouser as if his were a surprise package – and clipped their scabbards once more to their belts. Their exertions had burned out of them the last mote and atomy of strong wine and even stronger stenchful perfume, but they felt no desire whatever for more drink, only the urge to get home and eat hugely and guzzle hot, bitter gahveh, and tell their lovely girls the tale of the their mad adventure.

They loped on side by side, at intervals glancing at each other and chuckling, though keeping a normally wary eye behind and before for pursuit or interception, despite their expecting neither.

Free of night-smog and drizzled with starlight, their cramped surroundings seemed much less stinking and oppressive than when they had set out. Even Ordure Boulevard had a freshness to it.

Only once for a brief space did they grow serious.

Fafhrd said, 'You were a drunken idiot-genius indeed tonight, even if I was a drunken clodhopper. Lashing up my leg! Tying up our swords so we couldn't use 'em save as clubs!'

The Mouser shrugged. 'Yet that sword-tying doubtless saved us from committing a number of murders tonight.'

Fafhrd retorted, a little hotly, 'Killing in fight isn't murder.'

Again the Mouser shrugged. 'Killing is murder, no matter what nice names you give. Just as eating is devouring, and drinking guzzling. Gods, I'm dry, famished, and fatigued! Come on, soft cushions, food, and steaming gahveh!'

They hastened up the long, creaking, broken-treaded stairs with an easy carefulness and when they were both on the porch, the Mouser shoved at the door to open it with surprise-swiftness.

It did not budge.

'Bolted,' he said to Fafhrd shortly. He noted now there was hardly any light at all coming through the cracks around the door, or noticeable through the lattices – at most, a faint orange-red glow. Then with sentimental grin and in a fond voice in which only the ghost of uneasiness lurked, he said, 'They've gone to sleep, the unworrying wenches!' He knocked loudly thrice and then cupping his lips shouted softly at the door crack, 'Hola, Ivrian! I'm home safe. Hail, Vlana! Your man's done you proud, felling Guide-thieves innumerable with one foot tied behind his back!'

There was no sound whatever from inside – that is, if

one discounted a rustling so faint it was impossible to be sure of it.

Fafhrd was wrinkling his nostrils. 'I smell smoke.'

The Mouser banged on the door again. Still no response.

Fafhrd motioned him out of the way, hunching his big shoulder to crash the portal.

The Mouser shook his head and with a deft tap, slide, and tug removed a brick that a moment before had looked a firm-set part of the wall beside the door. He reached in all his arm. There was the scrape of a bolt being withdrawn, then another, then a third. He swiftly recovered his arm and the door swung fully inward at a touch.

But neither he nor Fafhrd rushed in at once, as both had intended to, for the indefinable scent of danger and the unknown came puffing out along with an increased reek of smoke and a slight sickening sweet scent that though female was no decent female perfume, and a musty-sour animal odor.

They could see the room faintly by the orange glow coming from the small oblong of the open door of the little, well-blacked stove. Yet the oblong did not sit properly upright but was unnaturally a-tilt; clearly the stove had been half overset and now leaned against a side wall of the fireplace, its small door fallen open in that direction.

By itself alone, that unnatural angle conveyed the entire impact of a universe overturned.

The orange glow showed the carpets oddly rucked up with here and there black circles a palm's breadth across, the neatly stacked candles scattered about below their shelves along with some of the jars and enameled boxes, and, above all, two black, low, irregular, longish heaps, the one by the fireplace, the other half on the golden couch, half at its foot.

From each head there stared at the Mouser and Fafhrd innumerable pairs of tiny, rather widely set, furnace-red eyes.

On the thickly carpeted floor on the other side of the fireplace was a silver cobweb – a fallen silver cage, but no love birds sang from it.

There was a faint scrape of metal as Fafhrd made sure Graywand was loose in his scabbard.

As if that tiny sound had beforehand been chosen as the signal for attack, each instantly whipped out sword and they advanced side by side into the room, warily at first, testing the floor with each step.

At the screech of the swords being drawn, the tiny furnace-red eyes had winked and shifted restlessly, and now with the two men's approach they swiftly scattered pattering, pair by red pair, each pair at the forward end of a small, low, slender, hairless-tailed black body, and each making for one of the black circles in the rugs, where they vanished.

Indubitably the black circles were ratholes newly gnawed up through the floor and rugs, while the red-eyed creatures were black rats.

Fafhrd and the Mouser sprang forward, slashing and chopping at them in a frenzy, cursing and human-snarling besides.

They sundered few. The rats fled with preternatural swiftness, most of them disappearing down holes near the walls and the fireplace.

Also Fafhrd's first frantic chop went through the floor and on his third step with an ominous crack and splintering his leg plunged through the floor to his hip. The Mouser darted past him, unmindful of further crackings.

Fafhrd heaved out his trapped leg, not even noting the splinter-scratches it got and as unmindful as the Mouser of the continuing creakings. The rats were gone. He lunged after his comrade, who had thrust a bunch of kindlers into the stove, to make more light.

The horror was that, although the rats were all gone, the two longish heaps remained, although considerably diminished and, as now shown clearly by the yellow flames leaping from the tilted black door, changed in hue – no longer were the heaps red-beaded black, but a mixture of gleaming black and dark brown, a sickening purple-blue, violet and velvet black and ermine white, and the reds of stockings and blood and bloody flesh and bone.

Although hands and feet had been gnawed bone-naked, and bodies tunneled heart-deep, the two faces had been spared. That was not good, for they were the parts purple-blue from death by strangulation, lips drawn back, eyes bulging, all features contorted in agony. Only the black and very dark brown hair gleamed unchanged – that and the white, white teeth.

As each man stared down at his love, unable to look away despite the waves of horror and grief and rage washing higher and higher in him, each saw a tiny black strand uncurl from the black depression ringing each throat and drift off, dissipating, toward the open door behind them – two strands of night-smog.

With a crescendo of crackings the floor sagged fully three spans more in the center before arriving at a new temporary stability.

Edges of centrally tortured minds noted details: that Vlana's silver-hilted dagger skewered to the floor a rat, which, likely enough, overeager had approached too closely before the night-smog had done its magic work. That her belt and pouch were gone. That the blue-enameled box inlaid with silver, in which Ivrian had put the Mouser's share of the hijacked jewels, was gone too.

The Mouser and Fafhrd lifted to each other white, drawn faces which were quite mad, yet completely joined in understanding and purpose. No need to tell each other what must have happened here when the two nooses of black vapor had jerked tight in Hristomilo's receiver, or why Slivikin had bounced and squeaked in glee, or the significance of such phrases as 'an ample sufficiency of feasters', or 'forget not the loot', or 'that business we spoke of'. No need for Fafhrd to explain why he now stripped off his robe and hood, or why he jerked up Vlana's dagger, snapped the rat off it with a wrist-flick, and thrust it in his belt. No need for the Mouser to tell why he searched out a half dozen jars of oil and after smashing three of them in front of the flaming stove, paused, thought, and stuck the other three in the sack at his waist, adding to them the remaining kindlers and the fire-pot, brimmed with red coals, its top lashed down tight.

Then, still without word exchanged, the Mouser muffled his hand with a small rug and reaching into the fireplace deliberately tipped the flaming stove forward, so that it fell door-down on oil-soaked rugs. Yellow flames sprang up around him.

They turned and raced for the door. With louder crackings than any before, the floor collapsed. They desperately scrambled their way up a steep hill of sliding carpets and reached door and porch just before all behind them gave way and the flaming rugs and stove and all the firewood and candles and the golden couch and all the little tables and boxes and jars – and the unthinkably mutilated bodies of their first loves – cascaded into the dry, dusty, cobweb-choked room below, and the great flames of a cleansing or at least obliterating cremation began to flare upward.

They plunged down the stairs, which tore away from the wall and collapsed and dully crashed in the dark just as they reached the ground. They had to fight their way over the wreckage to get to Bones Alley.

By then flames were darting their bright lizard-tongues out of the shuttered attic windows and the boarded-up ones in the story just below. By the time they reached Plague Court, running side by side at top speed, the Silver Eel's fire-alarm was clanging cacophonously behind them.

They were still sprinting when they took the Death Alley fork. Then the Mouser grappled Fafhrd and forced him to a halt. The big man struck out, cursing insanely, and only desisted – his white face still a lunatic's – when the Mouser cried, panting, 'Only ten heartbeats to arm us!'

He pulled the sack from his belt and, keeping tight hold of its neck, crashed it on the cobbles – hard enough to smash not only the bottles of oil, but also the fire-pot, for the sack was soon flaming a little at its base.

Then he drew gleaming Scalpel and Fafhrd Graywand and they raced on, the Mouser swinging his sack in a great circle beside him to fan its flames. It was a veritable ball of fire burning his left hand as they dashed across Cheap Street and into Thieves' House, and the Mouser, leaping high, swung it up into the great niche above the doorway and let go of it.

The niche-guards screeched in surprise and pain at the fiery invader of their hidey-hole and had no time to do anything with their swords, or whatever weapons else they had, against the other two invaders.

Student thieves poured out of the doors ahead at the screeching and foot-pounding, and then poured back as they saw the fierce point of flames and the two demon-faced oncomers brandishing their long, shining swords.

One skinny little apprentice – he could hardly have been ten years old – lingered too long. Graywand thrust him pitilessly through as his big eyes bulged and his small mouth gaped in horror and plea to Fafhrd for mercy.

Now from ahead of them there came a weird, wailing call, hollow and hair-raising, and doors began to thud shut instead of spewing forth the armed guards they almost prayed would appear to be skewered by their swords. Also, despite the long, bracketed torches looking newly renewed, the corridor was dark.

The reason for this last became clear as they plunged up the stairs. Strands of night-smog were appearing in the well, materializing from nothing or the air.

The strands grew longer and more numerous and tangible. They touched and clung nastily. In the corridor above they were forming from wall to wall and from ceiling to floor, like a gigantic cobweb, and were becoming so substantial that the Mouser and Fafhrd had to slash them to get through, or so their two maniac minds believed. The black web muffled a little a repetition of the eerie, wailing call, which came from the seventh door ahead and this time ended in a gleeful chittering and cackling insane as the emotions of the two attackers.

Here too doors were thudding shut. In an ephemeral flash of rationality, it occurred to the Mouser that it was not he and Fafhrd the thieves feared, for they had not been seen yet, but rather Hristomilo and his magic, even though working in defense of Thieves' House.

Even the map room, whence counter-attack would most likely erupt, was closed off by a huge oaken, iron-studded door.

They were now twice slashing black, clinging, rope-thick spiderweb for every single step they drove themselves forward. Midway between the map and magic rooms, there was forming on the inky web, ghostly at first but swiftly growing more substantial, a black spider big as a wolf.

The Mouser slashed heavy cobweb before it, dropped back two steps, then hurled himself at it in a high leap. Scalpel thrust through it, striking amidst its eight new-formed jet eyes, and it collapsed like a daggered bladder, loosing a vile stink.

Then he and Fafhrd were looking into the magic room, the alchemist's chamber. It was much as they had seen it before, except some things were doubled, or multiplied even further.

On the long table two blue-boiled cucurbits bubbled and roiled, their heads shooting out a solid, writhing rope more swiftly than moves the black swamp-cobra, which can run down a man – and not into twin receivers, but into the open air of the room (if any of the air in Thieves' House could have been called open then) to weave a barrier between their swords and Hristomilo, who once more stood tall though hunch-backed over his sorcerous, brown parchment, though this time his exultant gaze was chiefly fixed on Fafhrd and the Mouser, with only an occasional downward glance at the text of the spell he drummingly intoned.

At the other end of the table, in the web-free space, there bounced not only Slivikin, but also a huge rat matching him in size in all members except the head.

From the ratholes at the foot of the walls, red eyes glittered and gleamed in pairs.

With a bellow of rage Fafhrd began slashing at the black barrier, but the ropes were replaced from the cucurbit heads as swiftly as he sliced them, while the cut ends, instead of drooping slackly, now began to strain hungrily toward him like constrictive snakes or strangle-vines.

He suddenly shifted Graywand to his left hand, drew his long knife and hurled it at the sorcerer. Flashing toward its mark, it cut through three strands, was deflected and slowed by a fourth and fifth, almost halted by a sixth, and ended hanging futilely in the curled grip of a seventh.

Hristomilo laughed cacklingly and grinned, showing his huge upper incisors, while Slivikin chittered in ecstasy and bounded the higher.

The Mouser hurled Cat's Claw with no better result – worse, indeed, since his action gave two darting smog-strands time to curl hamperingly around his sword-hand and stranglingly around his neck. Black rats came racing out of the big holes at the cluttered base of the walls.

Meanwhile other strands snaked around Fafhrd's ankles, knees and left arm, almost toppling him. But even as he fought for balance, he jerked Vlana's dagger from his belt and raised it over his shoulder, its silver hilt glowing, its blade brown with dried rat's-blood.

The grin left Hristomilo's face as he saw it. The sorcerer screamed strangely and importuningly then and drew back from his parchment and the table, and raised clawed clubhands to ward off doom.

Vlana's dagger sped unimpeded through the black web – its strands even seemed to part for it – and betwixt the sorcerer's warding hands, to bury itself to the hilt in his right eye.

He screamed thinly in dire agony and clawed at his face.

The black web writhed as if in death spasm.

The cucurbits shattered as one, spilling their lava on the scarred table, putting out the blue flames even as the thick wood of the table began to smoke a little at the lava's edge. Lava dropped with *plops* on the dark marble floor.

With a faint, final scream Hristomilo pitched forward, hands still clutched to his eyes above his jutting nose, silver dagger-hilt still protruding between his fingers.

The web grew faint, like wet ink washed with a gush of clear water.

The Mouser raced forward and transfixed Slivikin and the huge rat with one thrust of Scalpel before the beasts knew what was happening. They too died swiftly with thin screams, while all the other rats turned tail and fled back down their holes swift almost as black lightning.

Then the last trace of night-smog or sorcery-smoke vanished and Fafhrd and the Mouser found themselves standing alone with three dead bodies and a profound silence that seemed to fill not only this room but all Thieves' House. Even the cucurbit-lava had ceased to move, was hardening, and the wood of the table no longer smoked.

Their madness was gone and all their rage too – vented to the last red atomy and glutted to more than satiety. They had no more urge to kill Krovas or any other of the thieves than to swat flies. With horrified inner eye Fafhrd saw the pitiful face of the child-thief he'd skewered in his lunatic anger.

Only their grief remained with them, diminished not one whit, but rather growing greater – that and an ever more swiftly growing revulsion from all that was around them: the dead, the disordered magic room, all Thieves' House, all of the city of Lankhmar to its last stinking alleyway and smog-wreathed spire.

With a hiss of disgust the Mouser jerked Scalpel from the rodent cadavers, wiped it on the nearest cloth, and returned it to its scabbard. Fafhrd likewise sketchily cleansed and sheathed Graywand. Then the two men picked up their knife and dirk from where they'd dropped to the floor when the web had dematerialized, though neither so much as glanced at Vlana's dagger where it was buried. But on the sorcerer's table they did notice Vlana's black velvet, silver-worked pouch and belt, the latter half overrun by the hardened black lava, and Ivrian's blue-enameled box inlaid with silver. From these they took the gems of Jengao.

With no more word than they had exchanged back at the Mouser's burned nest behind the Eel, but with a continuing sense of their unity of purpose, their identity of intent, and of their comradeship, they made their way with shoulders bowed and with slow, weary steps which only very gradually quickened out of the magic room and down the thick-carpeted corridor, past the map room's wide door still barred with oak and iron, and past all the other shut, silent doors – clearly the entire Guild was terrified of Hristomilo, his spells, and his rats; down the echoing stairs, their footsteps speeding a little; down the bare-floored lower corridor past its closed, quiet doors, their footsteps resounding loudly no matter how softly they sought to tread; under the deserted, black-scorched guard-niche, and so out into Cheap Street, turning left and north because that was the nearest way to the Street of the Gods, and there turning right and east – not a waking soul in the wide street except for one skinny, bent-backed apprentice lad unhappily swabbing the flagstones in front of a wine shop in the dim pink light beginning to seep from the east, although there were many forms asleep, a-snore and a-dream in the gutters and under the dark porticos – yes, turning right and east down the Street of the Gods, for that way was the Marsh Gate, leading to Causey Road across the Great Salt Marsh, and the Marsh Gate was the nearest way out of the great and glamorous city that was now loathsome to them, indeed, not to be endured for one more stabbing, leaden heartbeat than was necessary – a city of beloved, unfaceable ghosts.

SWORDS
AGAINST DEATH

CONTENTS

Mouser detest). Of odd disguises and a black kitten. Of a tasty redhead named Ivlis and her maid. Of dust and death.

Of the perils of boredom and of a great challenge and of a very long voyage. One cannot add to the account of these affairs by Ourph the Mingol.

An adventure on Nehwon's western continent, or on the easternmost coast of its eastern continent. No one knows. Showing, by the by, how fear can turn the mildest of men into a foul murderer.

Involving that Atlantis of Nehwon – Simorgya. A tale of the wild Outer Sea. Of fishing for fish – and jewels. Of sheer, blond-haired madness. Vast waves. With some details, though rather few, on how uncomfortable thick, black cloaks can be even for tall, stalwart fighting-men.

Once again blackness, spirit of night, with the Gray Mouser (who strikes a balance between black and white) and russet-headed Fafhrd battling it. The well-known dangers of stealing the eye of an idol, whether the idol be doll-tiny or mountain-huge. Ice, snows, volcanoes, lava – and seven most deadly killers.

Another old theme: the danger of those feathered reptiles, birds. Lankhmar upside-down, with the hawks freed and all her most beautiful women wearing gold and silver cages around their faces. Strange domestic arrangements – and re-arrangements – of the fat merchant Muulsh, his most tantalizing young wife Atya, and her maid.

How the Gray Mouser and Fafhrd were finally most unhappily rid of the ghosts of Ivrian and Vlana, and then became eternal servants, after a fashion and only part-time, of Sheelba of the

Eyeless Face and Ningauble of the Seven Eyes. Of an utter madman with an utterly magnificent project. Of an ill-placed dwelling near Dim Lane, of the Shadowland and its most grim ruler. Also of dust and death. But also of rebirth, or, anyhow, re-lust.

Of one of the earliest services of Fafhrd and the Mouser to their wizardly employers Ningauble and Sheelba. Of a blight on existence. Of the showiest and spiciest shop in any of the many universes. Of the horrid Devourers and their abominable tactics and of how the Gray Mouser and Fafhrd, by sheerest luck, finally bested them. Of how, most delectably and properly, girls are for dessert. But unfortunately spiders too.

I
THE CIRCLE CURSE

A tall swordsman and a small one strode out the Marsh Gate of Lankhmar and east along Causey Road. They were youths by their skin and suppleness, men by their expressions of deep-bitten grief and stony purpose.

The sleepy guardsmen in browned-iron cuirasses did not question them. Only madmen and fools willingly leave the grandest city in the world of Nehwon, especially at dawn and afoot. Besides, these two looked extremely dangerous.

Ahead the sky was bright pink, like the bubbling rim of a great crystal goblet brimmed with effervescent red wine for delight of the gods, while the paler pink glow rising therefrom drove the last stars west. But before the sun could glare one scarlet sliver above the horizon, a black storm came racing out of the north over the Inner Sea – a sea-squall making landfall. It grew almost as dark again as night, except when the lightning stabbed and the thunder shook his great iron shield. The stormwind carried the salty tang of the sea commingled with the foul reek of the marsh. It bent the green swords of the sea grass flat and lashed into writhing the arms of the thorn and seahawk trees. It pushed black swampwater a yard up the northern side of the narrow, serpentine, flat-topped ridge that was Causey Road. Then came pelting rain.

The two swordsmen made no comment to each other and did not alter their movements, except to lift their shoulders and faces a little and slant the latter north, as if they welcomed the storm's cleansing and sting and what tiny distraction it brought to some deep agony of mind and heart.

'Ho, Fafhrd!' a deep voice grated above the thunder's growl and the wind's roar and the rattle of the rain.

The tall swordsman turned his head sharply south.

'Hist, Gray Mouser!'

The small swordsman did likewise.

Close by the southern side of the road a rather large, rounded hut stood on five narrow posts. The posts had to be tall, for Causey Road ran high here yet the floor of the hut's low, rounded doorway looked straight at the tall swordsman's head.

This was nothing very strange, except that all men know that none dwell in the venomous Great Salt Marsh, save for giant worms, poison eels, water cobras, pale spindle-legged swamp rats, and the like.

Blue lightning glared, revealing with great clarity a hooded figure crouched inside the low doorway. Each fold and twist of the figure's draperies stood out as precisely as in an iron engraving closely viewed.

But the lightning showed nothing whatsoever inside the hood, only inky blackness.

Thunder crashed.

Then from the hood the grating voice recited the following lines, harshly and humorlessly hammering out the words, so that what was light verse became a dismal and doomful incantation:

Ho, Fafhrd tall!
Hist, Mouser small!
Why leave you the city
Of marvelous parts?
It were a great pity
To wear out your hearts
And wear out the soles of your feet,
Treading all earth,
Foregoing all mirth,
Before you once more Lankhmar greet.
Now return, now return, now!

This doleful ditty was three-quarters done before the two swordsmen realized that they were striding along steadily all this while and the hut still abreast them. So it must be walking along with them on its posts, or legs rather. And now that they were aware of this, they could see those five thin wooden members swinging and knee-bending.

When the grating voice ceased to speak on that last great 'now', Fafhrd halted.

So did the Mouser.

So did the hut.

The two swordsmen turned toward the low doorway, facing it squarely.

Simultaneously with deafening thunderclap, a great bolt of lightning struck close behind them. It jolted their bodies, shocked their flesh thrillingly and painfully, and it illumined the hut and its dweller brighter than day, yet still revealed nothing inside the dweller's hood.

If the hood had been empty, the draperies at its back would have been shown clearly. But no, there was only that oval of ebon darkness, which even the levinbolt could not illumine.

As unmoved by this prodigy as by the thunder-stroke, Fafhrd bellowed above the storm toward the doorway, his voice sounding tiny to himself in his thunder-smitten ears, 'Hear me, witch, wizard, nightgaunt, whatever you are! I shall never in my life enter again the foul city which has stolen from me my dearest and only love, the incomparable and irreplaceable Vlana, for whom I shall forever grieve and for whose unspeakable death I shall forever feel guilt. The Thieves' Guild slew her for her free-lance thieving – and we slew the slayers, though it profited us nothing at all.'

'Likewise I shall never lift foot toward Lankhmar again,' the Gray Mouser took up from beside him in a voice like an angry trumpet, 'the loathy metropolis which horribly bereft me of my beloved Ivrian, even as Fafhrd was bereft and for similar reason, and left me loaded with an equal weight of sorrow and shame, which I shall bear forever, even past my perishing.' A salt spider big as a platter sailed close by his ear in the grip of the gale, kicking its thick, corpse-white legs, and veered off past the hut, but the Mouser did not start in the least and there was no break whatever in his words as he continued, 'Know, being of black-ness, haunter of the dark, that we slew the foul wizard who murdered our loves and killed his two rodentine familiars and mauled and terrorized his employers at Thieves' House. But revenge is empty. It cannot bring back the dead. It cannot assuage by one atom the grief and guilt we shall feel forever for our darlings.'

'Indeed it cannot,' Fafhrd seconded loudly, 'for we were drunk when our darlings died, and for that there is no forgiveness. We hijacked a small treasure in gems from thieves of the Guild, but we lost the two jewels beyond price and without compare. And we shall never return to Lankhmar!'

Lightning shone from beyond the hut and thunder crackled. The storm was moving inland, south from the road.

The hood that held darkness drew back a little and slowly shook from side to side, once, twice, thrice. The harsh voice intoned, fainter because Fafhrd's and the Mouser's ears were still somewhat deafened and a-ring from that father of thunder-strokes:

Never and forever are neither for men,
You'll be returning again and again.

Then the hut was moving inland too on its five spindly legs. It turned around, so that its door faced away from them, and its speed increased, its legs moving nimbly as those of a cockroach, and was soon lost amongst the tangle of thorn and seahawk trees.

So ended the first encounter of the Mouser and his comrade Fafhrd with Sheelba of the Eyeless Face.

Later that day the two swordsmen waylaid an insufficiently guarded merchant Lankhmar-bound, depriving him of the best two of his four cart-horses – for thieving was first nature to them – and on these clumping mounts made their way out of the Great Salt Marsh and across the Sinking Land to the sinister hub-city of Ilthmar with its treacherous little inns and innumerable statues and bas-reliefs and other depictions of its rat-god. There they changed their clumsy horses for camels and were soon humping south across the desert, following the eastern shore of the turquoise Sea of the East. They crossed the River Tilth in dry season and continued on through the sands, bound for the Eastern Lands, where neither of them had previously traveled. They were searching for distraction in strangeness and intended first to visit Horborixen, citadel of the King of Kings and city second only to Lankhmar in size, antiquity, and baroque splendor.

For the next three years, the Years of Leviathan, the Roc, and the Dragon, they wandered the world of Nehwon south, east, north, and west, seeking forgetfulness of their first great loves and their first great guilts and finding neither. They ventured east past mystic Tisilinilit with its slender, opalescent spires, which always seemed newly crystallized out of its humid, pearly skies, to lands that were legends in Lankhmar and even Horborixen. One amongst many was the skeletally shrunken Empire of Eevamarensee, a country so decadent, so far-grown into the future, that all the rats and men are bald and even the dogs and cats hairless.

Returning by a northerly route through the Great Steppes, they narrowly escaped capture and enslavement by the pitiless Mingols. In the Cold Waste they sought for Fafhrd's Snow Clan, only to discover that it had been last year overwhelmed by a lemming horde of Ice Gnomes and, according to best rumor, massacred to the last person, which would have included Fafhrd's mother Mor, his deserted girl-bride Mara, and his first issue if any.

For a space they served Lithquil, the Mad Duke of Ool Hrusp, devising for him sprightly mock-duels, simulated murders, and other entertainments. Then they coasted south through the Outer Sea aboard a Sarheenmar trader to tropic Klesh, where they adventured a while in the jungle fringes. Then north again, circling past secretest Quarmall, that shadow realm, to the Lakes of Pleea that are the headwaters of the Hlal and to the beggar-city of Tovilyis, where the Gray Mouser believed he had been birthed, but was not sure, and when they left that lowly metropolis he was no surer. Crossing by grain barge the Sea of the East, they prospected for gold a while in the Mountains of the Elder Ones, their last highjacked gems having been long since gambled away or spent. Unsuccessful in this quest, they wended their way west again toward the Inner Sea and Ilthmar.

They lived by thievery, robbery, bodyguarding, brief commissions as couriers and agents – commissions they always, or almost always, fulfilled punctiliously – and by showmanship, the Mouser entertaining by legerdemain, juggling, and buffoonery, while Fafhrd with his gift for tongues and training as a Singing Skald excelled at minstrelsy, translating the legends of his frigid homeland into many languages. They never worked as cooks, clerks, carpenters, tree-fellers, or common servants and they never, never, never enlisted as mercenary soldiers – their service to Lithquil having been of a more personal nature.

They acquired new scars and skills, comprehensions and compassions, cynicisms and secrecies – a laughter that lightly mocked and a cool poise that tightly crusted all inner miseries and most of the time hid the barbarian in Fafhrd and the slum boy in the Mouser. They became outwardly merry, uncaring, and cool, but their grief and guilt stayed with them, the ghosts of Ivrian and Vlana haunting their sleeping and their waking dreams, so that they had little commerce with other girls, and that more a discomfort than a joy. Their comradeship became firmer than a rock, stronger than steel, but all other human relations were fleeting. Melancholy was their commonest mood, though mostly hid even from each other.

Came noon of the Day of the Mouse in the Month of the Lion in the Year of the Dragon. They were taking their siestas in the cool of a cave near Ilthmar. Outside, heat shimmered above hard-baked ground and scanty brown grass, but here was most pleasant. Their horses, a gray mare and a chestnut gelding, found shade in the cavern's mouth. Fafhrd had sketchily inspected the place for serpents, but discovered none. He loathed the cold scaly ones of the south, so different from the hot-blooded, fur-bearing snakes of the Cold Waste. He went a little way into a narrow, rocky corridor leading from the back of the cave under the small mountain in which it was set, but returned when light failed and he had found neither reptiles nor end.

They rested comfortably on their uncurled bedrolls. Sleep would not come to them, so idle talk did. By slow stages this talk became serious. Finally the Gray Mouser summed up the last trinity of years.

'We have searched the wide world over and not found forgetfulness.'

'I dispute that,' Fafhrd countered. 'Not the latter part, for I am still as ghost-locked as you, but we have not crossed the Outer Sea and hunted over the great continent legend will have in the west.'

'I believe we have,' the Mouser disputed. 'Not the former part, I'll agree, and what purpose in searching the sea? But when we went out farthest east and stood on the shore of that great ocean, deafened by its vast surf, I believe we stood on the western coast of the Outer Sea with nothing between us and Lankhmar but wild water.'

'What great ocean?' Fafhrd demanded. 'And what vast surf? It was a lake, a mere puddle with some ripples in it. I could readily see the opposite shore.'

'Then you were seeing mirages, friend of mine, and languishing in one of those moods when all Nehwon seems but a small bubble you could burst with flick of fingernail.'

'Perhaps,' Fafhrd agreed. 'Oh, how weary I am of this life.'

There was a little cough, no more than a clearing of throat, in the dark behind them. They did not otherwise move, but their hair stirred at its roots, so close and intimate had been that tiny noise, and so indicative of intelligence rather than mere animality, because of a measuredly attention-asking quality about it.

Then as one they turned head over shoulder and looked back at the black mouth of the rocky corridor. After a bit it seemed to each of them that he could see seven small, faint green glows swimming in the dark there and lazily changing position, like seven fireflies hovering, but with their light steadier and far more diffuse, as if each firefly wore a cloak made of several layers of gauze.

Then a voice sugary and unctuous, senescent though keen – a voice like a quavering flute – spoke from amidst those dimmest glows, saying, 'Oh my sons, begging the question of that hypothetical western continent, on which I do not propose to enlighten you, there is yet one place in Nehwon you have not searched for forgetfulness since the cruel deaths of your beloved girls.'

'And what place may that be?' the Mouser asked softly after a long moment and with slightest stammer. 'And who are you?'

'The city of Lankhmar, my sons. Who I am, besides your spiritual father, is a private matter.'

'We have sworn a great oath against ever returning to Lankhmar,' Fafhrd growled after a bit, the growl low and just a shade defensive and perhaps even intimidated.

'Oaths are made to be kept only until their purpose be fulfilled,' the fluty voice responded. 'Every geas is lifted at last, every self-set rule repealed. Otherwise orderliness in life becomes a limitation to growth, discipline, chains, integrity, bondage and evil-doing. You have learned what you can from the world. You have graduated from that huge portion of Nehwon. It now remains that you take up your postgraduate studies in Lankhmar, highest university of civilized life here.'

The seven faint glows were growing still dimmer now and drawing together, as if retreating down the corridor.

'We won't go back to Lankhmar,' Fafhrd and the Mouser replied, speaking as one.

The seven glows faded altogether. So faintly the two men could barely hear it – yet hear it each did – the fluty voice inquired. 'Are you afraid?' Then they heard a grating of rock, a very faint sound, yet somehow ponderous.

So ended the first encounter of Fafhrd and his comrade with Ningauble of the Seven Eyes.

After a dozen heartbeats, the Gray Mouser drew his slim, arm-and-a-half-long sword, Scalpel, with which he was accustomed to draw blood with surgical precision, and followed its glittering tip into the rocky corridor. He strode very deliberately, with a measured determination. Fafhrd went after, but more cautiously with many a hesitation, holding the point of his heavier sword Graywand, which he yet handled most nimbly in strife, close to the stony floor and wagging it from side to side. The seven glows in their lazy swayings and bobbings had mightily suggested to him the heads of large cobras raised up to strike. He reasoned that cave cobras, if such existed, might well be phosphorescent like abyssal eels.

They had penetrated somewhat farther under the mountainside than Fafhrd had on his first inspection – their slow pace enabling their eyes to accommodate better to the relative darkness – when with a slight, high-pitched shiver, Scalpel jarred vertical rock. Waiting without a word where they stood, their cave vision improved to the point whcrc it became indisputable, without any more sword-testing at all, that the corridor ended where they were, wanting hole big enough even for a speaking serpent to glide away, let alone a being rightfully capable of speech. The Mouser pressed and then Fafhrd threw his weight against the rock ahead at several points, but it held firm as purest mountain-heart. Nor had they missed any side tracks, even of the narrowest, or any pits or roof-holes on the way – a point they doubly checked going out.

Back at their bedrolls, their horses still tranquilly nibbling brown grass at the cavern's mouth, Fafhrd said abruptly, 'What wc heard speak, it was an echo.'

'How have an echo without a voice?' the Mouser demanded with peevish impatience. 'As well have a tail without a cat. I mean, a living tail.'

'A small snow snake greatly resembles the animated tail of a white house cat,' Fafhrd replied imperturbably. 'Aye, and has just such a high, quavering cry.'

'Are you suggesting—?'

'Of course not. As I imagine you do, I think there was a door somewhere in the rock, fitted so well we could not discern the junctures. We heard it shut. But before that, he – she, it, they – went through it.'

'Then why babble of echoes and snow snakes?'

'It is well to consider all possibilities.'

'He – she and so forth – named us sons,' the Mouser mused.

'Some say the serpent is wisest, oldest, and even father of all,' Fafhrd observed judiciously.

'Snakes again! Well, one thing's certain: all hold it rash folly for a man to take advice of a serpent, let alone seven.'

'Yet he – consider the other pronouns spoken – had a point, Mouser. Mauger the indeterminate western continent, we have traveled all Nehwon in spiderweb wise. What's left but Lankhmar?'

'Damn your pronouns! We swore never to return. Have you forgotten that, Fafhrd?'

'No, but I'm dying of boredom. Times I have sworn never again to drink wine.'

'I would choke to death on Lankhmar! Her day-smokes, her night-smogs, her rats, her filth!'

'At the moment, Mouser, I care little whether I live or die, and where or when or how.'

'Now adverbs and conjunctions! Bah, you need a drink!'

'We seek a deeper forgetfulness. They say to lay a ghost, go where she died.'

'Aye, and be worse haunted!'

'I could not be worse haunted than now.'

'To let a serpent shame us by asking, were we afraid!'

'Are we, perhaps?'

And so the argument went, with the final forseeable result that Fafhrd and the Mouser cantered past Ilthmar to a stony stretch of shore that was a curiously abraded low precipice, and waited there a day and a night for the Sinking Land to emerge with anomalous aqueous convulsions from the waters joining the Sea of the East to the Inner Sea. They swiftly and warily crossed its flinty, steaming expanse – for it was a hot, sunny day – and so again rode Causey Road, but this time back toward Lankhmar.

Distant, twin thunderstorms played to either side – north over the Inner Sea and south above the Great Salt Marsh – as they approached that monstrous city and as its towers, spires, fanes, and great crenelated wall emerged from its huge, customary cap of smoke, being somewhat silhouetted by the light of the setting sun, which was turned to a dull silver disk by the high fog and the smoke.

Once the Mouser and Fafhrd thought they saw a rounded, flat-floored shape on tall, invisible legs moving amongst the seahawk trees and faintly heard a harsh voice crying, 'I told you. I told you. I told you,' but both Sheelba's wizardly hut and voice, if they were those, remained distant as the storms.

In such wise Fafhrd and the Gray Mouser returned flat against their oaths to the city they despised, yet hankered after. They did not find forgetfulness there, the ghosts of Ivrian and Vlana were not laid, yet perhaps solely because of passage of time, the two heroes were a little less troubled by them. Nor were their hates, as of the Thieves' Guild, rekindled, but rather faded. And in any case Lankhmar seemed no worse than any other place in Nehwon and more interesting than most. So they stayed there for a space, making it once more the headquarters of their adventurings.

II
THE JEWELS IN THE FOREST

It was the Year of the Behemoth, the Month of the Hedgehog, the Day of the Toad. A hot, late summer sun was sinking down toward evening over the somber, fertile land of Lankhmar. Peasants toiling in the endless grainfields paused for a moment and lifted their earth-stained faces and noted that it would soon be time to commence lesser chores. Cattle cropping the stubble began to move in the general direction of home. Sweaty merchants and shopkeepers decided to wait a little longer before enjoying the pleasures of the bath. Thieves and astrologers moved restlessly in their sleep, sensing that the hours of night and work were drawing near.

At the southernmost limit of the land of Lankhmar, a day's ride beyond the village of Soreev, where the grainfields give way to rolling forests of maple and oak, two horsemen cantered leisurely along a narrow, dusty road. They presented a sharp contrast. The larger wore a tunic of unbleached linen, drawn tight at the waist by a very broad leather belt. A fold of linen cloak was looped over his head as a protection against the sun. A long sword with a pomegranate-shaped golden pommel was strapped to his side. Behind his right shoulder a quiver of arrows jutted up. Half sheathed in a saddlecase was a thick yew bow, unstrung. His great lean muscles, white skin, copper hair, green eyes, and above all the pleasant yet untamed expression of his massive countenance, all hinted at a land of origin colder, rougher, and more barbarous than that of Lankhmar.

Even as everything about the larger man suggested the wilderness, so the general appearance of the smaller man – and he was considerably smaller – spoke of the city. His dark face was that of a jester. Bright, black eyes, snub nose, and little lines of irony about the mouth. Hands of a conjurer. Something about the set of his wiry frame betokening exceptional competence in street fights and tavern brawls. He was clad from head to foot in garments of gray silk, soft and curiously loose of weave. His slim sword, cased in gray mouseskin, was slightly curved toward the tip. From his belt hung a sling and a pouch of missiles.

Despite their many dissimilarities, it was obvious that the two men were comrades, that they were united by a bond of subtle mutual understanding, woven of melancholy, humor, and many another strand. The smaller rode a dappled gray mare; the larger, a chestnut gelding.

They were nearing a point where the narrow road came to the end of a rise, made of a slight turn, and wound down into the next valley. Green walls of leaves pressed in on either side. The heat was considerable but not oppressive. It brought to mind thoughts of satyrs and centaurs dozing in hidden glades.

Then the gray mare, slightly in the lead, whinnied. The smaller man tightened his hold on the reins, his black eyes darting quick, alert glances, first to one side of the road and then to the other. There was a faint scraping sound, as of wood on wood.

Without warning the two men ducked down, clinging to the side harness of their horses. Simultaneously came the musical twang of bowstrings, like the prelude of some forest concert, and several arrows buzed angrily through the spaces that had just been vacated. Then the mare and the gelding were around the turn and galloping like the wind, their hooves striking up great puffs of dust.

From behind came excited shouts and answers as the pursuit got underway. There seemed to have been fully seven or eight men in the ambuscade – squat, sturdy rogues wearing chain-mail shirts and steel caps. Before the mare and the gelding had gone a stone's throw down the road, they were out and after, a black horse in the lead, a black-bearded rider second.

But those pursued were not wasting time. The larger man rose to a stand in his stirrups, whipping the yew bow from its case. With his left hand he bent it against the stirrup, with his right he drew the upper loop of the string into place. Then his left hand slipped down the bow to the grip and his right reached smoothly back over his shoulder for an arrow. Still guiding his horse with his knees, he rose even higher and turned in his saddle and sent an eagle-feathered shaft whirring. Meanwhile his comrade had placed a small leaden ball in his sling, whirled it twice about his head, so that it hummed stridently, and loosed his cast.

Arrow and missile sped and struck together. The one pierced the shoulder of the leading horseman and the other smote the second on his steel cap and tumbled him from his saddle. The pursuit halted abruptly in a tangle of plunging and rearing horses. The men who had caused this confusion pulled up at the next bend in the road and turned back to watch.

'By the Hedgehog,' said the smaller, grinning wickedly, 'but they will think twice before they play at ambuscades again!'

'Blundering fools,' said the larger. 'Haven't they even learned to shoot from their saddles? I tell you, Gray Mouser, it takes a barbarian to fight his horse properly.'

'Except for myself and a few other people,' replied the one who bore the feline nickname of Gray Mouser. 'But look, Fafhrd, the rogues retreat bearing their wounded, and one gallops far ahead. *Tcha*, but I dinted black beard's pate for him. He hangs over his nag like a bag of meal. If he'd have known who we were, he wouldn't have been so hot on the chase.'

There was some truth to this last boast. The names of the Gray Mouser and the Northerner Fafhrd were not unknown in the lands around Lankhmar and in proud Lankhmar, too. Their taste for strange adventure, their mysterious comings and goings, and their odd sense of humor were matters that puzzled almost all men alike.

Abruptly Fafhrd unstrung his bow and turned forward in his saddle.

'This should be the very valley we are seeking,' he said. 'See, there are the two hills, each with two close-set humps, of which the document speaks. Let's have another look at it, to test my guess.'

The Gray Mouser reached into his capacious leather pouch and withdrew a page of thick vellum, ancient and curiously greenish. Three edges were frayed and worn; the fourth showed a clean and recent cut. It was inscribed with the intricate hieroglyphs of Lankhmarian writing, done in the black ink of the squid. But it was not to these that the Mouser turned his attention, but to several faint lines of diminutive red script, written into the margin. These he read.

'Let kings stack their treasure houses ceiling-high, and merchants burst their vaults with hoarded coin, and fools envy them. I have a treasure that outvalues theirs. A diamond as big as a man's skull. Twelve rubies each as big as the skull of a cat. Seventeen emeralds each as big as the skull of a mole. And certain rods of crystal and bars of orichalcum. Let overlords swagger jewel-bedecked and queens load themselves with gems, and fools adore them. I have a treasure that will outlast theirs. A treasure house have I builded for it in the far southern forest, where the two hills hump double, like sleeping camels, a day's ride beyond the village of Soreev.

'A great treasure house with a high tower, fit for a king's dwelling – yet no king may dwell there. Immediately below the keystone of the chief dome my treasure lies hid, eternal as the glittering stars. It will outlast me and my name, I, Urgaan of Angarngi. It is my hold on the future. Let fools seek it. They shall win it not. For although my treasure house be empty as air, no deadly creature in rocky lair, no sentinel outside anywhere, no pitfall, poison, trap, or snare, above and below the whole place bare, of demon or devil not a hair, no serpent lethal-fanged yet fair, no skull with mortal eye a-glare, yet have I left a guardian there. Let the wise read this riddle and forbear.'

'The man's mind runs to skulls,' muttered the Mouser. 'He must have been a gravedigger or a necromancer.'

'Or an architect,' observed Fafhrd thoughtfully, 'in those past days when graven images of the skulls of men and animals served to bedeck temples.'

'Perhaps,' agreed the Mouser. 'Surely the writing and ink are old enough. They date at least as far back as the Century of the Wars with the East – five long lifespans.'

The Mouser was an accomplished forger, both of handwriting and of objects of art. He knew what he was talking about.

Satisfied that they were near the goal of their quest, the two comrades gazed through a break in the foliage down into the valley. It was shaped like the inside of a pod – shallow, long, and narrow. They were viewing it from one of the narrow ends. The two peculiarly humped hills formed the long sides. The whole of the valley was green with maple and oak, save for a small gap toward the middle. That, thought the Mouser, might mark a peasant's dwelling and the cleared space around it.

Beyond the gap he could make out something dark and squarish rising a little above the treetops. He called his companion's attention to it, but they could not decide whether it was indeed a tower such as the document mentioned, or just a peculiar shadow, or perhaps even the dead, limbless trunk of a gigantic oak. It was too far away.

'Almost sufficient time has passed,' said Fafhrd, after a pause, 'for one of those rogues to have sneaked up through the forest for another shot at us. Evening draws near.'

They spoke to their horses and moved on slowly. They tried to keep their eyes fixed on the thing that looked like a tower, but since they were descending, it almost immediately dropped out of sight below the treetops. There would be no further chance of seeing it until they were quite close at hand.

The Mouser felt a subdued excitement running through his flesh. Soon they would discover if there was a treasure to be had or not. A diamond as big as a man's skull . . . rubies . . . emeralds . . . He found an almost nostalgic delight in prolonging and savoring to the full this last, leisurely stage of their quest. The recent ambuscade served as a necessary spice.

He thought of how he had slit the interesting-looking vellum page from the ancient book on architecture that reposed in the library of the rapacious and overbearing lord Rannarsh. Of how, half in jest, he had sought out and interrogated several peddlers from the South. Of how he had found one who had recently passed through a village named Soreev. Of how that one had told him of a stone structure in the forest south of Soreev, called by the peasants the House of Angarngi and reputed to be long deserted. The peddler had seen a high tower rising above the trees. The Mouser recalled the man's wizened, cunning face and chuckled. And that brought to mind the greedy, sallow face of Lord Rannarsh, and a new thought occurred to him.

'Fafhrd,' he said, 'those rogues we just now put to flight – what did you take them for?'

The Northerner grunted humorous contempt.

'Run-of-the-manger ruffians. Waylayers of fat merchants. Pasture bravos. Bumpkin bandits!'

'Still, they were all well armed, and armed alike – as if they were in some rich man's service. And that one who rode far ahead. Mightn't he have been hastening to report failure to some master?'

'What is your thought?'

The Mouser did not reply for some moments.

'I was thinking,' he said, 'that Lord Rannarsh is a rich man and a greedy one, who slavers at the thought of jewels. And I was wondering if he ever read those faint lines of red lettering and made a copy of them, and if my theft of the original sharpened his interest.'

The Northerner shook his head.

'I doubt it. You are oversubtle. But if he did, and if he seeks to rival us in this treasure quest, he'd best watch each step twice – and choose servitors who can fight on horseback.'

They were moving so slowly that the hooves of the mare and the gelding hardly stirred up the dust. They had no fear of danger from the rear. A well-laid ambuscade might surprise them, but not a man or horse in motion. The narrow road wound along in a purposeless fashion. Leaves brushed their faces, and occasionally they had to swing their bodies out of the way of encroaching branches. The ripe scent of the late summer forest was intensified now that they were below the rim of the valley. Mingled with it were whiffs of wild berries and aromatic shrubs. Shadows imperceptibly lengthened.

'Nine chances out of ten,' murmured the Mouser dreamily, 'the treasure house of Urgaan of Angarngi was looted some hundred years ago, by men whose bodies are already dust.'

'It may be so,' agreed Fafhrd. 'Unlike men, rubies and emeralds do not rest quietly in their graves.'

This possibility, which they had discussed several times

before, did not disturb them now, or make them impatient. Rather did it impart to their quest the pleasant melancholy of a lost hope. They drank in the rich air and let their horses munch random mouthfuls of leaves. A jay called shrilly from overhead and off in the forest a catbird was chattering, their sharp voices breaking in on the low buzzing and droning of the insects. Night was drawing near. The almost-horizontal rays of the sun gilded the treetops. Then Fafhrd's sharp ears caught the hollow lowing of a cow.

A few more turns brought them into the clearing they had spied. In line with their surmise, it proved to contain a peasant's cottage – a neat little low-eaved house of weathered wood, situated in the midst of an acre of grain. To one side was a bean patch; to the other, a woodpile which almost dwarfed the house. In front of the cottage stood a wiry old man, his skin as brown as his homespun tunic. He had evidently just heard the horses and turned around to look.

'Ho, father,' called the Mouser, 'it's a good day to be abroad in, and a good home you have here.'

The peasant considered these statements and then nodded his head in agreement.

'We are two weary travelers,' continued the Mouser.

Again the peasant nodded gravely.

'In return for two silver coins will you give us lodging for the night?'

The peasant rubbed his chin and then held up three fingers.

'Very well, you shall have three silver coins,' said the Mouser, slipping from his horse. Fafhrd followed suit.

Only after giving the old man a coin to seal the bargain did the Mouser question casually, 'Is there not an old, deserted place near your dwelling called the House of Angarngi?'

The peasant nodded.

'What's it like?'

The peasant shrugged his shoulders.

'Don't you know?'

The peasant shook his head.

'But haven't you ever seen the place?' The Mouser's voice carried a note of amazement he did not bother to conceal.

He was answered by another headshake.

'But father, it's only a few minutes' walk from your dwelling, isn't it?'

The peasant nodded tranquilly, as if the whole business were no matter for surprise.

A muscular young man, who had come from behind the cottage to take their horses, offered a suggestion.

'You can see tower from other side the house. I can point her out.'

At this the old man proved he was not completely speechless by saying in a dry, expressionless voice: 'Go ahead. Look at her all you want.'

And he stepped into the cottage. Fafhrd and the Mouser caught a glimpse of a child peering around the door, an old woman stirring a pot, and someone hunched in a big chair before a tiny fire.

The upper part of the tower proved to be barely visible through a break in the trees. The last rays of the sun touched it with deep red. It looked about four or five bowshots distant. And then, even as they watched, the sun dipped under and it became a featureless square of black stone.

'She's an old place,' explained the young man vaguely. 'I been all around her. Father, he's just never bothered to look.'

'You've been inside?' questioned the Mouser.

The young man scratched his head.

'No. She's just an old place. No good for anything.'

'There'll be a fairly long twilight,' said Fafhrd, his wide green eyes drawn to the tower as if by a lodestone. 'Long enough for us to have a closer look.'

'I'd show the way,' said the young man, 'save I got water to fetch.

'No matter,' replied Fafhrd. 'When's supper?'

'When the first stars show.'

They left him holding their horses and walked straight into the woods. Immediately it became much darker, as if twilight were almost over, rather than just begun. The vegetation proved to be somewhat thicker than they had anticipated. There were vines and thorns to be avoided. Irregular, pale patches of sky appeared and disappeared overhead.

The Mouser let Fafhrd lead the way. His mind was occupied with a queer sort of reverie about the peasants. It tickled his fancy to think how they had stolidly lived their toilsome lives, generation after generation, only a few steps from what might be one of the greatest treasure-troves in the world. It seemed incredible. How could people sleep so near jewels and not dream of them? But probably they never dreamed.

So the Gray Mouser was sharply aware of few things during the journey through the woods, save that Fafhrd seemed to be taking a long time – which was strange, since the barbarian was an accomplished woodsman.

Finally a deeper and more solid shadow loomed up through the trees, and in a moment they were standing in the margin of a small, boulder-studded clearing, most of which was occupied by the bulky structure they sought. Abruptly, even before his eyes took in the details of the place, the Mouser's mind was filled with a hundred petty perturbations. Weren't they making a mistake in leaving their horses with those strange peasants? And mightn't those rogues have followed them to the cottage? And wasn't this the Day of the Toad, an unlucky day for entering deserted houses? And shouldn't they have a short spear along, in case they met a leopard? And wasn't that a whippoorwill he heard crying on his left hand, an augury of ill omen?

The treasure house of Urgaan of Angarngi was a peculiar structure. The main feature was a large, shallow dome, resting on walls that formed an octagon. In front, and merging into it, were two lesser domes. Between these gaped a great square doorway. The tower rose asymmetrically from the rear part of the chief dome. The eyes of the Mouser sought hurriedly through the dimming twilight for the cause of the salient peculiarity of the structure, and decided it lay in the utter simplicity. There were no pillars, no outjutting cornices, no friezes, no architectural ornaments of any sort, skull-embellished or otherwise. Save for the doorway and a few tiny windows set in unexpected places, the House of Angarngi was a compact mass of uniformly dark gray stones most closely joined.

But now Fafhrd was striding up the short flight of terraced steps that led toward the open door, and the Mouser followed him, although he would have liked to spy around a little longer. With every step he took forward he sensed an odd reluctance growing within him. His earlier mood of pleasant expectancy vanished as suddenly as if he'd stepped into quicksand. It seemed to him that the black doorway yawned like a toothless mouth. And then a little shudder went through him, for he saw the mouth had a tooth – a bit of ghostly white that jutted up from the floor. Fafhrd was reaching down toward the object.

'I wonder whose skull this may be?' said the Northerner calmly.

The Mouser regarded the thing, and the scattering of bones and fragments of bones beside it. His feeling of uneasiness was fast growing toward a climax, and he had the unpleasant conviction that, once it did reach a climax, something would happen. What was the answer to Fafhrd's question? What form of death had struck down that earlier intruder? It was very dark inside the treasure house. Didn't the manuscript mention something about a guardian? It was hard to think of a flesh-and-blood guardian persisting for three hundred years, but there were things that were immortal or nearly immortal. He could tell that Fafhrd was not in the least affected by any premonitory disquietude, and was quite capable of instituting an immediate search for the treasure. That must be prevented at all costs. He remembered that the Northerner loathed snakes.

'This cold, damp stone,' he observed casually. 'Just the place for scaly, cold-blooded snakes.'

'Nothing of the sort,' replied Fafhrd angrily. 'I'm willing to wager there's not a single serpent inside. Urgaan's note said, "No deadly creature in rocky lair", and to cap that, "no serpent lethal-fanged yet fair".'

'I am not thinking of guardian snakes Urgaan may have left here,' the Mouser explained, 'but only of serpents that may have wandered in for the night. Just as that skull you hold is not one set there by Urgaan "with mortal eye a-glare", but merely the brain-case of some unfortunate wayfarer who chanced to perish here.'

'I don't know,' Fafhrd said, calmly eyeing the skull.

'Its orbits might glow phosphorescently in absolute dark.'

A moment later he was agreeing it would be well to postpone the search until daylight returned, now that the treasure house was located. He carefully replaced the skull.

As they re-entered the woods, the Mouser heard a little inner voice whispering to him, *Just in time. Just in time.* Then the sense of uneasiness departed as suddenly as it had come, and he began to feel somewhat ridiculous. This caused him to sing a bawdy ballad of his own invention, wherein demons and other supernatural agents were ridiculed obscenely. Fafhrd chimed in good-naturedly on the choruses.

It was not as dark as they expected when they reached the cottage. They saw to their horses, found they had been well cared for, and then fell to the savory mess of beans, porridge, and pot herbs that the peasant's wife ladled into oak bowls. Fresh milk to wash it down was provided in quaintly carved oak goblets. The meal was a satisfying one and the interior of the house was neat and clean, despite its stamped earthen floor and low beams, which Fafhrd had to duck.

There turned out to be six in the family, all told. The father, his equally thin and leathery wife, the older son, a young boy, a daughter, and a mumbling grandfather whom extreme age confined to a chair before the fire. The last two were the most interesting of the lot.

The girl was in the gawkish age of mid-adolescence, but there was a wild, coltish grace in the way she moved her lanky legs and slim arms with their prominent elbows. She was very shy, and gave the impression that at any moment she might dart out the door and into the woods.

In order to amuse her and win her confidence, the Mouser began to perform small feats of legerdemain, plucking copper coins out of the ears of the astonished peasant, and bone needles from the nose of his giggling wife. He turned beans into buttons and back again into beans, swallowed a large fork, made a tiny wooden manikin jig on the palm of his hand, and utterly bewildered the cat by pulling what seemed to be a mouse out of its mouth.

The old folks gaped and grinned. The little boy became frantic with excitement. His sister watched everything with concentrated interest, and even smiled warmly when the Mouser presented her with a square of fine, green linen he had conjured from the air, although she was still too shy to speak.

Then Fafhrd roared sea-chanteys that rocked the roof and sang lusty songs that set the old grandfather gurgling with delight. Meanwhile the Mouser fetched a small wineskin from his saddlebags, concealed it under his cloak, and filled the oak goblets as if by magic. These rapidly fuddled the peasants, who were unused to so potent a beverage, and by the time Fafhrd had finished telling a bloodcurdling tale of the frozen north, they were all nodding, save the girl and the grandfather.

The latter looked up at the merry-making adventurers, his watery eyes filled with a kind of impish, senile glee, and mumbled, 'You two be right clever men. Maybe you be beast-dodgers.' But before this remark could be elucidated, his eyes had gone vacant again, and in a few moments he was snoring.

Soon all were asleep, Fafhrd and the Mouser keeping their weapons close at hand, but only variegated snores and occasional snaps from the dying embers disturbed the silence of the cottage.

The Day of the Cat dawned clear and cool. The Mouser stretched himself luxuriously and, catlike, flexed his muscles and sucked in the sweet, dewy air. He felt exceptionally cheerful and eager to be up and doing. Was not this *his* day, the day of the Gray Mouser, a day in which luck could not fail him?

His slight movements awakened Fafhrd and together they stole silently from the cottage so as not to disturb the peasants, who were oversleeping with the wine they had taken. They refreshed their faces and hands in the wet grass and visited their horses. Then they munched some bread, washed it down with drafts of cool well water flavored with wine, and made ready to depart.

This time their preparations were well thought out. The Mouser carried a mallet and a stout iron pry-bar, in case they had to attack masonry, and made certain that candles, flint, wedges, chisels, and several other small tools were in his pouch. Fafhrd borrowed a pick from the peasant's implements and tucked a coil of thin, strong rope in his belt. He also took his bow and quiver of arrows.

The forest was delightful at this early hour. Bird cries and chatterings came from overhead, and once they glimpsed a black, squirrel-like animal scampering along a bough. A couple of chipmunks scurried under a bush dotted with red berries. What had been shadow the evening before was now a variety of green-leafed beauty. The two adventurers trod softly.

They had hardly gone more than a bowshot into the woods when they heard a faint rustling behind them. The rustling came rapidly nearer, and suddenly the peasant girl burst into view. She stood breathless and poised, one hand touching a treetrunk, the other pressing some leaves, ready to fly away at the first sudden move. Fafhrd and the Mouser stood as stock-still as if she were a doe or a dryad. Finally she managed to conquer her shyness and speak.

'You go there?' she questioned, indicating the direction of the treasure house with a quick, ducking nod. Her dark eyes were serious.

'Yes, we go there,' answered Fafhrd, smiling.

'Don't.' This word was accompanied by a rapid headshake.

'But why shouldn't we, girl?' Fafhrd's voice was gentle and sonorous, like an integral part of the forest. It seemed to touch some spring within the girl that enabled her to feel more at ease. She gulped a big breath and began.

'Because I watch it from edge of the forest, but never go close. Never, never, never. I say to myself there be a magic circle I must not cross. And I say to myself there be a giant inside. Queer and fearsome giant.' Her words were coming rapidly now, like an undammed stream. 'All gray he be, like the stone of his house. All gray – eyes and hair and fingernails, too. And he has a stone club as big as a tree. And he be big, bigger than you, twice as big.' Here she nodded at Fafhrd. 'And with his club he kills, kills, kills. But only if you go close. Every day, almost, I play a game with him. I pretend to be going to cross the magic circle. And he watches from inside the door, where I can't see him, and he thinks I'm going to cross. And I dance through the forest all around the house, and he follows me, peering from the little windows. And I get closer and closer to the circle, closer and closer. But I never cross. And he be very angry and gnash his teeth, like rocks rubbing rocks, so that the house shakes. And I run, run, run away. But you mustn't go inside. Oh, you mustn't.'

She paused, as if startled by her own daring. Her eyes were fixed anxiously on Fafhrd. She seemed drawn toward him. The Northerner's reply carried no overtone of patronizing laughter.

'But you've never actually seen the gray giant, have you?'

'Oh, no. He be too cunning. But I say to myself he must be there inside. I know he be inside. And that's the same thing, isn't it? Grandfather knows about him. We used to talk about him, when I was little, Grandfather calls him the beast. But the others laugh at me, so I don't tell.'

Here was another astounding peasant-paradox, thought the Mouser with an inward grin. Imagination was such a rare commodity with them that this girl unhesitatingly took it for reality.

'Don't worry about us, girl. We'll be on the watch for your gray giant,' he started to say, but he had less success than Fafhrd in keeping his voice completely natural or else the cadence of his words didn't chime so well with the forest setting.

The girl uttered one more warning. 'Don't go inside, oh, please,' and turned and darted away.

The two adventurers looked at each other and smiled. Somehow the unexpected fairy tale with its conventional ogre and its charmingly naive narrator added to the delight of the dewy morning. Without a comment they resumed their soft-stepping progress. And it was well that they went quietly for, when they had gotten within a stone's throw of the clearing, they heard low voices that seemed to be in grumbling argument. Immediately they cached the pick and pry-bar and mallet under a clump of bushes, and stole forward, taking advantage of the natural cover and watching where they planted their feet.

On the edge of the clearing stood half a dozen stocky men in black chain-mail shirts, bows on their backs, shortswords at their sides. They were immediately recognizable as the rogues who had laid the ambuscade. Two of them started for the treasure house, only to be recalled by a comrade. Whereupon the argument apparently started afresh.

'That red-haired one,' whispered the Mouser after an unhurried look. 'I can swear I've seen him in the stables of Lord Rannarsh. My guess was right. It seems we have a rival.'

'Why do they wait, and keep pointing at the house?' whispered Fafhrd. 'Is it because some of their comrades are already at work inside?'

The Mouser shook his head. 'That cannot be. See those picks and shovels and levers they have rested on the ground? No, they wait for someone – for a leader. Some of them want to examine the house before he arrives. Others counsel against it. And I will bet my head against a bowling ball that the leader is Rannarsh himself. He is much too greedy and suspicious to entrust a treasure quest to any henchmen.'

'What's to do?' murmured Fafhrd. 'We cannot enter the house unseen, even if it were the wise course, which it isn't. Once in, we'd be trapped.'

'I've half a mind to loose my sling at them right now and teach them something about the art of ambuscade,' replied the Mouser, slitting his eyes grimly. 'Only then the survivors would flee into the house and hold us off until, mayhap, Rannarsh came, and more men with him.'

'We might circle part way around the clearing,' said Fafhrd, after a moment's pause, 'keeping to the woods. Then we can enter the clearing unseen and shelter ourselves behind one of the small domes. In that way we become masters of the doorway, and can prevent their taking cover inside. Thereafter I will address them suddenly and try to frighten them off, you meanwhile staying hid and giving substance to my threats by making enough racket for ten men.'

This seemed the handiest plan to both of them, and they managed the first part of it without a hitch. The Mouser crouched behind the small dome, his sword, sling, daggers, and a couple of sticks of wood laid ready for either noise-making or fight. Then Fafhrd strode briskly forward, his bow held carelessly in front of him, an arrow fitted to the string. It was done so casually that it was a few moments before Rannarsh's henchmen noticed him. Then they quickly reached for their own bows and as quickly desisted when they saw that the huge newcomer had the advantage of them. They scowled in irritated perplexity.

'Ho, rogues!' began Fafhrd. 'We allow you just as much time as it will take you to make yourselves scarce, and no more. Don't think to resist or come skulking back. My men are scattered through the woods. At a sign from me they will feather you with arrows.'

Meanwhile the Mouser had begun a low din and was slowly and artistically working it up in volume. Rapidly varying the pitch and intonation of his voice and making it echo first from some part of the building and then from the forest wall, he created the illusion of a squad of blood-thirsty bow-men. Nasty cries of 'Shall we let fly?' 'You take the redhead,' and 'Try for the belly shot; it's surest,' kept coming now from one point and now another, until it was all Fafhrd could do to refrain from laughing at the woebegone, startled glances the six rogues kept darting around. But his merriment was extinguished when, just as the rogues were starting to slink shamefacedly away, an arrow arched erratically out of the woods, passing a spear's length above his head.

'Curse that branch!' came a deep, guttural voice the Mouser recognized as issuing from the throat of Lord Rannarsh. Immediately after, it began to bark commands.

'At them, you fools! It's all a trick. There are only the two of them. Rush them!'

Fafhrd turned without warning and loosed point-blank at the voice, but did not silence it. Then he dodged back behind the small dome and ran with the Mouser for the woods.

The six rogues, wisely deciding that a charge with drawn swords would be overly heroic, followed suit, unslinging their bows as they went. One of them turned before he had reached sufficient cover, nocking an arrow. It was a mistake. A ball from the Mouser's sling took him low in the forehead, and he toppled forward and was still.

The sound of that hit and fall was the last heard in the clearing for quite a long time, save for the inevitable bird cries, some of which were genuine, and some of which were communications between Fafhrd and the Mouser. The conditions of the death-dealing contest were obvious. Once it had fairly begun, no one dared enter the clearing, since he would become a fatally easy mark; and the Mouser was sure that none of the five remaining rogues had taken shelter in the treasure house. Nor did either side dare withdraw all its men out of sight of the doorway, since that would allow someone to take a commanding position in the top of the tower, providing the tower had a negotiable stair. Therefore it was a case of sneaking about near the edge of the clearing, circling and counter-circling, with a great deal of squatting in a good place and waiting for somebody to come along and be shot.

The Mouser and Fafhrd began by adopting the latter strategy, first moving about twenty paces nearer the point at which the rogues had disappeared. Evidently their patience was a little better than that of their opponents. For after about ten minutes of nerve-racking waiting, during which pointed seed pods had a queer way of looking like arrowheads, Fafhrd got the red-haired henchman full in the throat just as he was bending his bow for a shot at the Mouser. That left four besides Rannarsh him-self. Immediately the two adventurers changed their tactics and separated, the Mouser circling rapidly around the treasure house and Fafhrd drawing as far back from the open space as he dared.

Rannarsh's men must have decided on the same plan, for the Mouser almost bumped into a scar-faced rogue as soft-footed as himself. At such close range, bow and sling were both useless – in their normal function. Scarface attempted to jab the barbed arrow he held into the Mouser's eye. The Mouser weaved his body to one side, swung his sling like a whip, and felled the man senseless with a blow from the horn handle. Then he retreated a few paces, thanked the Day of the Cat that there had not been two of them, and took to the trees as being a safer, though slower method of progress. Keeping to the middle heights, he scurried along with the sure-footedness of a rope walker, swinging from branch to branch only when it was necessary, making sure he always had more than one way of retreat open.

He had completed three quarters of his circuit when he heard the clash of swords a few trees ahead. He increased his speed and was soon looking down on a sweet little combat. Fafhrd, his back to a great oak, had his broadsword out and was holding off two of Rannarsh's henchmen, who were attacking with their shorter weapons. It was a tight spot and the Northerner realized it. He knew that ancient sagas told of heroes who could best four or more men at swordplay. He also knew that such sagas were lies, providing the hero's opponents were reasonably competent.

And Rannarsh's men were veterans. They attacked cautiously but incessantly, keeping their swords well in front of them and never slashing wildly. Their breath whistled through their nostrils, but they were grimly confident, knowing the Northerner dared not lunge strongly at one of them because it would lay him wide open to a thrust by the other. Their game was to get one on each side of him and then attack simultaneously.

Fafhrd's counter was to shift position quickly and attack the nearer one murderously before the other could get back in range. In that way he managed to keep them side by side, where he could hold their blades in check by swift feints and crosswise sweeps. Sweat beaded his face and blood dripped from a scratch on his left thigh. A fearsome grin showed his white teeth, which occasionally parted to let slip a base, primitive insult.

The Mouser took in the situation at a glance, descended rapidly to a lower bough, and poised himself, aiming a dagger at the back of one of Fafhrd's adversaries. He was, however, standing very close to the thick trunk, and around this trunk darted a horny hand tipped with a short sword. The third henchman had also thought it wise to take to the trees. Fortunately for the Mouser, the man was uncertain of his footing and therefore his thrust, although well aimed, came a shade slow. As it was the little gray-clad man only managed to dodge by dropping off.

Thereupon he startled his opponent with a modest acrobatic feat. He did not drop to the ground, knowing that would put everyone at the mercy of the man in the tree. Instead, he grabbed hold of the branch on which he had been standing, swung himself smartly up again, and grappled. Steadying themselves now with one hand, now another, they drove for each other's throats, ramming with knees and elbows whenever they got a chance. At the first onset both dagger and sword were dropped, the latter sticking point-down in the ground directly between the two battling henchmen and startling them so that Fafhrd almost got home an attack.

The Mouser and his man surged and teetered along the branch away from the trunk, inflicting little damage on each other since it was hard to keep balance. Finally they slid off at the same time, but grabbed the branch with their hands. The puffing henchman aimed a vicious kick. The Mouser escaped it by yanking up his body and doubling up his legs. The latter he let fly violently, taking the henchman full in the chest, just where the ribs stop. The unfortunate retainer of Rannarsh fell to the ground, where he had the wind knocked out of him a second time.

At the same moment one of Fafhrd's opponents tried a trick that might have turned out well. When his companion was pressing the Northerner closely, he snatched for the shortsword sticking in the ground, intending to hurl it underhanded as if it were a javelin. But Fafhrd, whose superior endurance was rapidly giving him an advantage in speed, anticipated the movement and simultaneously made a brilliant counterattack against the other man. There were two thrusts, both lightning-like, the first a feint at the belly, the second a slicing stab that sheared through the throat to the spine. Then he whirled around and, with a quick sweep, knocked both weapons out of the hands of the first man, who looked up in bewilderment and promptly collapsed into a sitting position, panting in utter exhaustion, though with enough breath left to cry, 'Mercy!'

To cap the situation, the Mouser dropped lightly down, as if out of the sky. Fafhrd automatically started to raise his sword, for a backhand swipe. Then he stared at the Mouser for as long a time as it took the man sitting on the ground to give three tremendous gasps. Then he began to laugh, first uncontrollable snickers and later thundering peals. It was a laughter in which the battle-begotten madness, completely sated anger, and relief at escape from death were equally mingled.

'Oh, by Glaggerk and by Kos!' he roared. 'By the Behemoth!

Oh, by the Cold Waste and the guts of the Red God! Oh! Oh! Oh!' Again the insane bellowing burst out. 'Oh, by the Killer Whale and the Cold Woman and her spawn!' By degrees the laughter died away, choking in his throat. He rubbed his forehead with the palm of his hand and his face became starkly grave. Then he knelt beside the man he had just slain, and straightened his limbs, and closed his eyes, and began to weep in a dignified way that would have seemed ridiculous and hypocritical in anyone but a barbarian.

Meanwhile the Mouser's reactions were nowhere near as primitive. He felt worried, ironic, and slightly sick. He understood Fafhrd's emotions, but knew that he would not feel the full force of his own for some time yet, and by then they would be deadened and somewhat choked. He peered about anxiously, fearful of an anticlimactic attack that would find his companion helpless. He counted over the tally of their opponents. Yes, the six henchmen were all accounted for. But Rannarsh himself, where was Rannarsh? He fumbled in his pouch to make sure he had not lost his good-luck talismans and amulets. His lips moved rapidly as he murmured two or three prayers and cantrips. But all the while he held his sling ready, and his eyes never once ceased their quick shifting.

From the middle of a thick clump of bushes he heard a series of agonized gasps, as the man he had felled from the tree began to regain his wind. The henchman whom Fafhrd had disarmed, his face ashy pale from exhaustion rather than fright, was slowly edging back into the forest. The Mouser watched him carelessly, noting the comical way in which the steel cap had slipped down over his forehead and rested against the bridge of his nose. Meanwhile the gasps of the man in the bushes were taking on a less agonized quality. At almost the same instant, the two rose to their feet and stumbled off into the forest.

The Mouser listened to their blundering retreat. He was sure that there was nothing more to fear from them. *They* wouldn't come back. And then a little smile stole into his face, for he heard the sounds of a third person joining them in their flight. That would be Rannarsh, thought the Mouser, a man cowardly at heart and incapable of carrying on single-handed. It did not occur to him that the third person might be the man he had stunned with his sling handle.

Mostly just to be doing something, he followed them leisurely for a couple of bowshots into the forest. Their trail was impossible to miss, being marked by trampled bushes and thorns bearing tatters of cloth. It led in a beeline away from the clearing. Satisfied, he returned, going out of his way to regain the mallet, pick, and pry-bar.

He found Fafhrd tying a loose bandage around the scratch on his thigh. The Northerner's emotions had run their gamut and he was himself again. The dead man for whom he had been somberly grieving now meant no more to him than food for beetles and birds. Whereas for the Mouser it continued to be a somewhat frightening and sickening object.

'And now do we proceed with our interrupted business?' the Mouser asked.

Fafhrd nodded in a matter-of-fact manner and rose to his feet. Together they entered the rocky clearing. It came to them as a surprise how little time the fight had taken. True, the sun had moved somewhat higher, but the atmosphere was still that of early morning. The dew had not dried yet. The treasure house of Urgaan of Angarngi stood massive, featureless, grotesquely impressive.

'The peasant girl predicted the truth without knowing it,' said the Mouser with a smile. 'We played her game of "circle-the-clearing and don't-cross-the-magic-circle," didn't we?'

The treasure house had no fears for him today. He recalled his perturbations of the previous evening, but was unable to understand them. The very idea of a guardian seemed somewhat ridiculous. There were a hundred other ways of explaining the skeleton inside the doorway.

So this time it was the Mouser who skipped into the treasure house ahead of Fafhrd. The interior was disappointing, being empty of any furnishings and as bare and unornamented as the outside walls. Just a large, low room. To either side square doorways led to the smaller domes, while to the rear a long hallway was dimly apparent, and the beginnings of a stair leading to the upper part of the main dome.

With only a casual glance at the skull and the broken skeleton, the Mouser made his way toward the stair.

'Our document,' he said to Fafhrd, who was now beside him, 'speaks of the treasure as resting just below the keystone of the chief dome. Therefore we must seek in the room or rooms above.'

'True,' answered the Northerner, glancing around. 'But I wonder, Mouser, just what use this structure served. A man who builds a house solely to hide a treasure is shouting to the world that he *has* a treasure. Do you think it might have been a temple?'

The Mouse suddenly shrank back with a sibilant exclamation. Sprawled a little way up the stair was another skeleton, the major bones hanging together in lifelike fashion. The whole upper half of the skull was smashed to bony shards paler than those of a gray pot. 'Our hosts are overly ancient and indecently naked,' hissed the Mouser, angry with himself for being startled. Then he darted up the stairs to examine the grisly find. His sharp eyes picked out several objects among the bones. A rusty dagger, a tarnished gold ring that looped a knucklebone, a handful of horn buttons, and a slim, green-eaten copper cylinder. The last awakened his curiosity. He picked it up, dislodging hand-bones in the process, so that they fell apart, rattling dryly. He pried off the cap of the cylinder with his dagger point, and shook out a tightly rolled sheet of ancient parchment. This he gingerly unwound. Fafhrd and he scanned the lines of diminutive red lettering by the light from a small window on the landing above.

Mine is a secret treasure. Orichalcum have I, and crystal, and blood-red amber. Rubies and emeralds that demons would war for, and a diamond as big as the skull of a man. Yet none have seen them save I. I, Urgaan of Angarngi, scorn the flattery and the envy of fools. A fittingly lonely treasure house have I built for my jewels. There, hidden under the keystone, they may dream unperturbed until earth and sky wear away. A day's ride beyond the village of Soreev, in the valley of the two double-humped hills, lies that house, trebly-domed and single-towered. It is empty. Any fool may enter. Let him. I care not

'The details differ slightly,' murmured the Mouser, 'but the phrases have the same ring as in our document.'

'The man must have been mad,' asserted Fafhrd, scowling. 'Or else why should he carefully hide a treasure and then, with equal care, leave directions for finding it?'

'We thought *our* document was a memorandum or an oversight,' said the Mouser thoughtfully. 'Such a notion can hardly explain *two* documents.' Lost in speculation, he turned toward the remaining section of the stair, only to find still another skull grinning at him from a shadowy angle. This time he was not startled, yet he experienced the same feeling that a fly must experience when, enmeshed in a spider's web, it sees the dangling, empty corpses of a dozen of its brothers. He began to speak rapidly.

'Nor can such a notion explain *three* or *four* or mayhap a *dozen* such documents. For how came these other questers here, unless each had found a written message? Urgaan of Angarngi may have been mad, but he sought deliberately to lure men here. One thing is certain: this house conceals – or did conceal – some deadly trap. Some guardian. Some giant beast, say. Or perhaps the very stones distill a poison. Perhaps hidden springs release sword blades which stab out through cracks in the walls and then return.'

'That cannot be,' answered Fafhrd. 'These men were killed by great, bashing blows. The ribs and spine of the first were splintered. The second had his skull cracked open. And that third one there. See! The bones of his lower body are smashed.'

The Mouser started to reply. Then his face broke into an unexpected smile. He could see the conclusion to which Fafhrd's arguments were unconsciously leading – and he knew that that conclusion was ridiculous. What thing would kill with great, bashing blows? What thing but the gray giant the peasant girl had told them about? The gray giant twice as tall as a man, with his great stone club – a giant fit only for fairy tales and fantasies.

And Fafhrd returned the Mouser's smile. It seemed to him that they were making a great deal of fuss about nothing. These skeletons were suggestive enough, to be sure, but did they not represent men who had died many, many years ago – centuries ago? What guardian could outlast three centuries? Why, that was a long enough time to weary the patience of a demon! And there were no such things as demons, anyhow. And there was no earthly use in mucking around about ancient fears and horrors that were as dead as dust. The whole matter, thought Fafhrd, boiled down to something very simple. They had come to a deserted house to see if there was a treasure in it.

Agreed upon this point, the two comrades made their way up the remaining section of stair that led to the dimmer regions of the House of Angarngi. Despite their confidence, they moved cautiously and kept sharp watch on the shadows lying ahead. This was wise.

Just as they reached the top, a flash of steel spun out of the darkness. It nicked the Mouser in the shoulder as he twisted to one side. There was a metallic clash as it fell to the stone floor. The Mouser, gripped by a sudden spasm of anger and fright, ducked down and dashed rapidly through the door from which the weapon had come, straight at the danger, whatever it was.

'Dagger-tossing in the dark, eh, you slick-bellied worm?' Fafhrd heard the Mouser cry, and then he, too, had plunged through the door.

Lord Rannarsh cowered against the wall, his rich hunting garb dusty and disordered, his black, wavy hair pushed back from his forehead, his cruelly handsome face a sallow mask of hate and extreme terror. For the moment the latter emotion seemed to predominate and, oddly enough, it did not appear to be directed toward the men he had just assailed, but toward something else, something unapparent.

'O gods!' he cried. 'Let me go from here. The treasure is yours. Let me out of this place. Else I am doomed. The thing has played at cat and mouse with me. I cannot bear it. I cannot bear it!'

'So now we pipe a different tune, do we?' snarled the Mouser. 'First dagger-tossing, then fright and pleas!'

'Filthy coward tricks,' added Fafhrd. 'Skulking here safe while your henchmen died bravely.'

'Safe? Safe, you say? O gods!' Rannarsh almost screamed. Then a subtle change became apparent in his rigid-muscled face. It was not that his terror decreased. If anything, that became greater. But there was added to it, over and above, a consciousness of desperate shame, a realization that he had demeaned himself ineradicably in the eyes of these two ruffians. His lips began to writhe, showing tight-clenched teeth. He extended his left hand in a gesture of supplication.

'Oh, mercy, have mercy,' he cried piteously, and his right hand twitched a second dagger from his belt and hurled it underhand at Fafhrd.

The Northerner knocked aside the weapon with a swift blow of his palm, then said deliberately, 'He is yours, Mouser. Kill the man.'

And now it was cat against cornered rat. Lord Rannarsh whipped a gleaming sword from its gold-worked scabbard and rushed in, cutting, thrusting, stabbing. The Mouser gave ground slightly, his slim blade flickering in a defensive counter-attack that was wavering and elusive, yet deadly. He brought Rannarsh's rush to a standstill. His blade moved so quickly that it seemed to weave a net of steel around the man. Then it leaped forward three times in rapid succession. At the first thrust it bent nearly double against a concealed shirt of chain mail. The second thrust pierced the belly. The third transfixed the throat. Lord Rannarsh fell to the floor, spitting and gagging, his fingers clawing at his neck. There he died.

'An evil end,' said Fafhrd somberly, 'although he had fairer play than he deserved, and handled his sword well. Mouser, I like not this killing, although there was surely more justice to it than the others.'

The Mouser, wiping his weapon against his opponent's thigh, understood what Fafhrd meant. He felt no elation at his victory, only a cold, queasy disgust. A moment before he had been raging, but now there was no anger left in him. He pulled open his gray jerkin and inspected the dagger wound in his left shoulder. A little blood was still welling from it and trickling down his arm.

'Lord Rannarsh was no coward,' he said slowly. 'He killed himself, or at least caused his own death, because we had seen him terrified and heard him cry in fright.'

And at these words, without any warning whatsoever, stark

terror fell like an icy eclipse upon the hearts of the Gray Mouser and Fafhrd. It was as if Lord Rannarsh had left them a legacy of fear, which passed to them immediately upon his death. And the unmanning thing about it was that they had no premonitory apprehension, no hint of its approach. It did not take root and grow gradually greater. It came all at once, paralyzing, overwhelming. Worse still, there was no discernible cause. One moment they were looking down with something of indifference upon the twisted corpse of Lord Rannarsh. The next moment their legs were weak, their guts were cold, their spines were prickling, their teeth clicking, their hearts pounding, their hair lifting at the roots.

Fafhrd felt as if he had walked unsuspecting into the jaws of a gigantic serpent. His barbaric mind was stirred to the deeps. He thought of the grim god Kos brooding alone in the icy silence of the Cold Waste. He thought of the masked powers Fate and Chance, and of the game they play for the blood and brains of men. And he did not will these thoughts. Rather did the freezing fear seem to crystallize them, so that they dropped into his consciousness like snow flakes.

Slowly he regained control over his quaking limbs and twitching muscles. As if in a nightmare, he looked around him slowly, taking in the details of his surroundings. The room they were in was semicircular, forming half of the great dome. Two small windows, high in the curving ceiling, let in light.

An inner voice kept repeating, *Don't make a sudden move. Slowly. Slowly. Above all, don't run. The others did. That was why they died so quickly. Slowly. Slowly.*

He saw the Mouser's face. It reflected his own terror. He wondered how much longer this would last, how much longer he could stand it without running amuck, how much longer he could passively endure this feeling of a great invisible paw reaching out over him, span by span, implacably.

The faint sound of footsteps came from the room below. Regular and unhurried footsteps. Now they were crossing into the rear hallway below. Now they were on the stairs. And now they had reached the landing, and were advancing up the second section of the stairs.

The man who entered the room was tall and frail and old and very gaunt. Scant locks of intensely black hair straggled down over his high-domed forehead. His sunken cheeks showed clearly the outlines of his long jawbone, and waxy skin was pulled tight over his small nose. Fanatical eyes burned in deep, bony sockets. He wore the simple, sleeveless robe of a holy man. A pouch hung from the cord round his waist.

He fixed his eyes upon Fafhrd and the Gray Mouser.

'I greet you, you men of blood,' he said in a hollow voice.

Then his gaze fell with displeasure upon the corpse of Rannarsh.

'More blood has been shed. It is not well.'

And with the bony forefinger of his left hand he traced in the air a curious triple square, the sign sacred to the Great God.

'Do not speak,' his calm, toneless voice continued, 'for I know your purposes. You have come to take treasure from this house. Others have sought to do the same. They have failed. You will fail. As for myself, I have no lust for treasure. For forty years I have lived on crusts and water, devoting my spirit to the Great God.' Again he traced the curious sign. 'The gems and ornaments of this world and the jewels and gauds of the world of demons cannot tempt or corrupt me. My purpose in coming here is to destroy an evil thing.

'I' – and here he touched his chest – 'I am Arvlan of Angarngi, the ninth lineal descendant of Urgaan of Angarngi. This I always knew, and sorrowed for, because Urgaan of Angarngi was a man of evil. But not until fifteen days ago, on the Day of the Spider, did I discover from ancient documents that Urgaan had built this house, and built it to be an eternal trap for the unwise and venturesome. He has left a guardian here, and that guardian has endured.

'Cunning was my accursed ancestor, Urgaan, cunning and evil. The most skillful architect in all Lankhmar was Urgaan, a man wise in the ways of stone and learned in geometrical lore. But he scorned the Great God. He longed for improper powers. He had commerce with demons, and won from them an unnatural treasure. But he had no use for it. For in seeking wealth and knowledge and power, he lost his ability to enjoy any good feeling or pleasure, even simple lust. So he hid his treasure, but hid it in such a way that it would wreak endless evil on the world, even as he felt men and one proud, contemptuous, cruel woman – as heartless as this fane – had wreaked evil upon him. It is my purpose and my right to destroy Urgaan's evil.

'Seek not to dissuade me, lest doom fall upon you. As for me, no harm can befall me. The hand of the Great God is poised above me, ready to ward off any danger that may threaten his faithful servant. His will is my will. Do not speak, men of blood! I go to destroy the treasure of Urgaan of Angarngi.'

And with these words, the gaunt holy man walked calmly on, with measured stride, like an apparition, and disappeared through the narrow doorway that led into the forward part of the great dome.

Fafhrd stared after him, his green eyes wide, feeling no desire to follow or to interfere. His terror had not left him, but it was transmuted. He was still aware of a dreadful threat, but it no longer seemed to be directed against him personally.

Meanwhile, a most curious notion had lodged in the mind of the Mouser. He felt that he had just now seen, not a venerable holy man, but a dim reflection of the centuries-dead Urgaan of Angarngi. Surely Urgaan had that same high-domed forehead, that same secret pride, that same air of command. And those locks of youthfully black hair, which contrasted so ill with the aged face also seemed part of a picture looming from the past. A picture dimmed and distorted by time, but retaining something of the power and individuality of the ancient original.

They heard the footsteps of the holy man proceed a little way into the other room. Then for the space of a dozen heartbeats there was complete silence. Then the floor began to tremble slightly under their feet, as if the earth were quaking, or as if a giant were treading near. Then there came a single quavering cry from the next room, cut off in the middle by a single sickening crash that made them lurch. Then, once again, utter silence.

Fafhrd and the Mouser looked at one another in blank amazement – not so much because of what they had just heard but because, almost at the moment of the crash, the pall of terror had lifted from them completely. They jerked out their swords and hurried into the next room.

It was a duplicate of the one they had quitted, save that instead of two small windows, there were three, one of them near the floor. Also, there was but a single door, the one through which they had just entered. All else was closely morticed stone – floor, walls, and hemi-domed ceiling.

Near the thick center wall, which bisected the dome, lay the body of the holy man. Only 'lay' was not the right word. Left shoulder and chest were mashed against the floor. Life was fled. Blood puddled around.

Fafhrd's and the Mouser's eyes searched wildly for a being other than themselves and the dead man and found none – no, not one gnat hovering amongst the dust motes revealed by the narrow shafts of sunlight shooting down through the windows. Their imaginations searched as wildly and as much in vain for a being that could strike such a man-killing blow and vanish through one of the three tiny orifices of the windows. A giant, striking serpent with a granite head . . .

Set in the wall near the dead man was a stone about two feet square, jutting out a little from the rest. On this was boldly engraved, in antique Lankhmarian hieroglyph: 'Here rests the treasure of Urgaan of Angarngi.'

The sight of that stone was like a blow in the face to the two adventurers. It roused every ounce of obstinacy and reckless determination in them. What matter that an old man sprawled smashed beside it? They had their swords! What matter they now had proof some grim guardian resided in the treasure house? They could take care of themselves! Run away and leave that stone unmoved, with its insultingly provocative inscription? No, by Kos, and the Behemoth! They'd see themselves in Nehwon's hell first!

Fafhrd ran to fetch the pick and the other large tools, which had been dropped on the stairs when Lord Rannarsh tossed his first dagger. The Mouser looked more closely at the jutting stone. The cracks around it were wide and filled with a dark, tarry mixture. It gave out a slightly hollow sound when he tapped it with his sword hilt. He calculated that the wall was about six feet thick at this point – enough to contain a sizable cavity. He tapped experimentally along the wall in both directions, but the hollow ring quickly ceased. Evidently the cavity was a fairly small one. He noted that the crevices between all the other stones were very fine, showing no evidence of any cementing substance whatsoever. In fact, he couldn't be sure that they weren't false crevices, superficial cuts in the surface of solid rock. But that hardly seemed possible. He heard Fafhrd returning, but continued his examination.

The state of the Mouser's mind was peculiar. A dogged determination to get at the treasure overshadowed other emotions. The inexplicably sudden vanishing of his former terror had left certain parts of his mind benumbed. It was as if he had decided to hold his thoughts in leash until he had seen what the treasure cavity contained. He was content to keep his mind occupied with material details, and yet make no deductions from them.

His calmness gave him a feeling of at least temporary safety. His experiences had vaguely convinced him that the guardian, whatever it was, which had smashed the holy man and played cat and mouse with Rannarsh and themselves, did not strike without first inspiring a premonitory terror in its victims.

Fafhrd felt very much the same way, except that he was even more single-minded in his determination to solve the riddle of the inscribed stone.

They attacked the wide crevices with chisel and mallet. The dark tarry mixture came away fairly easily, first in hard lumps, later in slightly rubbery, gouged strips. After they had cleared it away to the depth of a finger, Fafhrd inserted the pick and managed to move the stone slightly. Thus the Mouser was enabled to gouge a little more deeply on that side. Then Fafhrd subjected the other side of the stone to the leverage of the pick. So the work proceeded, with alternate pryings and gougings.

They concentrated on each detail of the job with unnecessary intensity, mainly to keep their imaginations from being haunted by the image of a man more than two hundred years dead. A man with high-domed forehead, sunken cheeks, nose of a skull – that is, if the dead thing on the floor was a true type of the breed of Angarngi. A man who had somehow won a great treasure, and then hid it away from all eyes, seeking to obtain neither glory nor material profit from it. Who said he scorned the envy of fools, and who yet wrote many provocative notes in diminutive red lettering in order to inform fools of his treasure and make them envious. Who seemed to be reaching out across the dusty centuries, like a spider spinning a web to catch a fly on the other side of the world.

And yet, he was a skillful architect, the holy man had said. Could such an architect build a stone automaton twice as tall as a tall man? A gray stone automaton with a great club? Could he make a hiding place from which it could emerge, deal death, and then return? No, no, such notions were childish, not to be entertained! Stick to the job in hand. First find what lay behind the inscribed stone. Leave thoughts until afterward.

The stone was beginning to give more easily to the pressure of the pick. Soon they would be able to get a good purchase on it and pry it out.

Meanwhile an entirely new sensation was growing in the Mouser – not one of terror at all, but of physical revulsion. The air he breathed seemed thick and sickening. He found himself disliking the texture and consistency of the tarry mixture gouged from the cracks, which somehow he could only liken to wholly imaginary substances, such as the dung of dragons or the solidified vomit of the Behemoth. He avoided touching it with his fingers, and he kicked away the litter of chunks and strips that had gathered around his feet. The sensation of queasy loathing became difficult to endure.

He tried to fight it, but had no more success than if it had been seasickness, which in some ways it resembled. He felt unpleasantly dizzy. His mouth kept filling with saliva. The cold sweat of nausea beaded his forehead. He could tell that Fafhrd was unaffected, and he hesitated to mention the matter; it seemed ridiculously out of place, especially as it was unaccompanied by any fear or fright. Finally the stone itself began to have the same effect on him as the tarry mixture, filling him with a seemingly causeless, but none the less sickening revulsion. Then he could bear it no longer. With a vaguely apologetic nod to Fafhrd, he dropped his chisel and went to the low window for a breath of fresh air.

This did not seem to help matters much. He pushed his head through the window and gulped deeply. His mental processes were overshadowed by the general indifference of extreme nausea, and everything seemed very far away. Therefore when he saw that the peasant girl was standing in the middle of the clearing, it was some time before he began to consider the import of the fact. When he did, part of his sickness left him; or at least he was enabled to overpower it sufficiently to stare at her with gathering interest.

Her face was white, her fists were clenched, her arms held rigid at her sides. Even at the distance he could catch something of the mingled terror and determination with which her eyes were fixed on the great doorway. Toward this doorway she was forcing herself to move, one jerking step after another, as if she had to keep screwing her courage to a higher pitch. Suddenly the Mouser began to feel frightened, not for himself at all, but for the girl. Her terror was obviously intense, and yet she must be doing what she was doing – braving her 'queer and fearsome gray giant' – for his sake and Fafhrd's. At all costs, he thought, she must be prevented from coming closer. It was wrong that she be subjected for one moment longer to such a horribly intense terror.

His mind was confused by his abominable nausea, yet he knew what he must do. He hurried toward the stairs with shaky strides, waving Fafhrd another vague gesture. Just as he was going out of the room he chanced to turn up his eyes, and spied something peculiar on the ceiling. What it was he did not fully realize for some moments.

Fafhrd hardly noticed the Mouser's movements, much less his gestures. The block of stone was rapidly yielding to his efforts. He had previously experienced a faint suggestion of the Mouser's nausea, but perhaps because of his greater single-mindedness, it had not become seriously bothersome. And now his attention was wholly concentrated on the stone. Persistent prying had edged it out a palm's breadth from the wall. Seizing it firmly in his two powerful hands, he tugged it from one side to the other, back and forth. The dark, viscous stuff clung to it tenaciously, but with each sidewise jerk it moved forward a little.

The Mouser lurched hastily down the stairs, fighting vertigo. His feet kicked bones and sent them knocking against the walls. What was it he had seen on the ceiling? Somehow, it seemed to mean something. But he must get the girl out of the clearing. She mustn't come any closer to the house. She mustn't enter.

Fafhrd began to feel the weight of the stone, and knew that it was nearly clear. It was damnably heavy – almost a foot thick. Two carefully gauged heaves finished the job. The stone overbalanced. He stepped quickly back. The stone crashed ponderously on the floor. A rainbow glitter came from the cavity that had been revealed. Fafhrd eagerly thrust his head into it.

The Mouser staggered toward the doorway. It was a bloody smear he had seen on the ceiling. And just above the corpse of the holy man. But why should that be? He'd been smashed against the floor, hadn't he? Was it blood splashed up from his lethal clubbing? But then why smeared? No matter. The girl. He must get to the girl. He must. There she was, almost at the doorway. He could see her. He felt the stone floor vibrating slightly beneath his feet. But that was his dizziness, wasn't it?

Fafhrd felt the vibration, too. But any thought he might have had about it was lost in his wonder at what he saw. The cavity was filled to a level just below the surface of the opening, with a heavy metallic liquid that resembled mercury, except that it was night-black. Resting on this liquid was a more astonishing group of gems than Fafhrd had ever dreamed of.

In the center was a titan diamond, cut with a myriad of oddly angled facets. Around it were two irregular circles, the inner formed of twelve rubies, each a decahedron, the outer formed of seventeen emeralds, each an irregular octahedron. Lying between these gems, touching some of them, sometimes connecting them with each other, were thin, fragile-looking bars of crystal, amber, greenish tourmaline, and honey-pale orichalcum. All these objects did not seem to be floating in the metallic liquid so much as resting upon it, their weight pressing down the surface into shallow depressions, some cup-shaped, others trough-like. The rods glowed faintly, while each of the gems glittered with a light that Fafhrd's mind strangely conceived to be refracted starlight.

His gaze shifted to the mercurous heavy fluid, where it bulged up between, and he saw distorted reflections of stars and constellations which he recognized, stars and constellations which would be visible now in the sky overhead, were it not for the concealing brilliance of the sun. An awesome wonder engulfed him. His gaze shifted back to the gems. There was something tremendously meaningful about their complex arrangement, something that seemed to speak of overwhelming truths in an alien symbolism. More, there was a compelling impression of inner movement, or sluggish thought, of inorganic consciousness. It was like what the eyes see when they close at night – not utter blackness, but a shifting, fluid pattern of many-colored points of light. Feeling that he was reaching impiously into the core of a thinking mind, Fafhrd gripped with his right hand for the diamond as big as a man's skull.

The Mouser blundered through the doorway. There could be no mistaking it now. The close-morticed stones were trembling. That bloody smear, as if the ceiling had champed down upon the holy man, crushing him against the floor, or as if the floor had struck upward. But there was the girl, her terror-wide eyes fastened upon him, her mouth open for a scream that did not come. He must drag her away, out of the clearing.

But why should he feel that a fearful threat was now directed at himself as well? Why should he feel that something was poised above him, threatening? As he stumbled down the terraced steps, he looked over his shoulder and up. The tower. The tower! It was falling. It was falling toward him. It was dipping at him over the dome. But there were no fractures along its length. It was not breaking. It was not falling. It was bending.

Fafhrd's hand jerked back, clutching the great, strangely faceted jewel, so heavy that he had difficulty in keeping his hold upon it. Immediately the surface of the metallic, star-reflecting fluid was disturbed. It bobbled and shook. Surely the whole house was shaking, too. The other jewels began to dart about erratically, like water insects on the surface of a puddle.

The various crystalline and metallic bars began to spin, their tips attracted now to one jewel and now to another, as if the jewels were lodestone and the bars iron needles. The whole surface of the fluid was in a whirling, jerking confusion that suggested a mind gone mad because of loss of its chief part.

For an agonizing instant the Mouser stared up in amazement – frozen at the clublike top of the tower, ponderously hurling itself down upon him. Then he ducked and lunged forward at the girl, tackling her, rapidly rolling over and over with her. The tower top struck a sword's length behind them, with a thump that jolted them momentarily off the ground. Then it jerked itself up from the pitlike depression it had made.

Fafhrd tore his gaze away from the incredible, alien beauty of the jewel-confused cavity. His right hand was burning. The diamond was hot. No, it was cold beyond belief. By Kos, the room was changing shape! The ceiling was bulging downward at a point. He made for the door, then stopped dead in his tracks. The door was closing like a stony mouth. He turned and took a few steps over the quaking floor toward the small, low window. It snapped shut, like a sphincter. He tried to drop the diamond. It clung painfully to the inside of his hand. With a snap of his wrist he whipped it away from him. It hit the floor and began to bounce about, glaring like a living star.

The Mouser and the peasant girl rolled toward the edge of the clearing. The tower made two more tremendous bashes at them, but both went yards wide, like the blows of a blind madman. Now they were out of range. The Mouser lay sprawled on his side, watching a stone house that hunched and heaved like a beast, and a tower that bent double as it thumped grave-deep pits into the ground. It crashed into a group of boulders and its top broke off, but the jaggedly fractured end continued to beat the boulders in wanton anger, smashing them into fragments. The Mouser felt a compulsive urge to take out his dagger and stab himself in the heart. A man had to die when he saw something like that.

Fafhrd clung to sanity because he was threatened from a new direction at every minute and because he could say to himself, 'I know. I know. The house is a beast, and the jewels are its mind.

Now that mind is mad. I know. I know.' Walls, ceiling, and floor quaked and heaved, but their movements did not seem to be directed especially at him. Occasional crashes almost deafened him. He staggered over rocky swells, dodging stony advances that were half bulges and half blows, but that lacked the speed and directness of the tower's first smash at the Mouser. The corpse of the holy man was jolted about in grotesque mechanical reanimation.

Only the great diamond seemed aware of Fafhrd. Exhibiting a fretful intelligence, it kept bounding at him viciously, sometimes leaping as high as his head. He involuntarily made for the door as his only hope. It was champing up and down with convulsive regularity. Watching his chance, he dived at it just as it was opening, and writhed through. The diamond followed him, striking at his legs. The carcass of Rannarsh was flung sprawling in his path. He jumped over it, then slid, lurched, stumbled, fell down stairs in earthquake, where dry bones danced. Surely the beast must die, the house must crash and crush him flat. The diamond leaped for his skull, missed, hurtled through the air, and struck a wall. Thereupon it burst into a great puff of iridescent dust.

Immediately the rhythm of the shaking of the house began to increase. Fafhrd raced across the heaving floor, escaped by inches the killing embrace of the great doorway, plunged across the clearing – passing a dozen feet from the spot where the tower was beating boulders into crushed rock – and then leaped over two pits in the ground. His face was rigid and white. His eyes were vacant. He blundered bull-like into two or three trees, and only came to a halt because he knocked himself flat against one of them.

The house had ceased most of its random movements, and the whole of it was shaking like a huge dark jelly. Suddenly its forward part heaved up like a behemoth in death agony. The two smaller domes were jerked ponderously a dozen feet off the ground, as if they were the paws. The tower whipped into convulsive rigidity. The main dome contracted sharply, like a stupendous lung. For a moment it hung there, poised. Then it crashed to the ground in a heap of gigantic stone shards. The earth shook. The forest resounded. Battered atmosphere whipped branches and leaves. Then all was still. Only from the fractures in the stone a tarry, black liquid was slowing oozing, and here and there iridescent puffs of air suggested jewel-dust.

Along a narrow, dusty road two horsemen were cantering slowly toward the village of Soreev in the southernmost limits of the land of Lankhmar. They presented a somewhat battered appearance. The limbs of the larger, who was mounted on a chestnut gelding showed several bruises, and there was a bandage around his thigh and another around the palm of his right hand. The smaller man, the one mounted on a gray mare, seemed to have suffered an equal number of injuries.

'Do you know where we're headed?' said the latter, breaking a long silence. 'We're headed for a city. And in that city are endless houses of stone, stone towers without numbers, streets paved with stone, domes, arches, stairs. *Tcha*, if I feel then as I feel now, I'll never go within a bowshot of Lankhmar's walls.'

His large companion smiled.

'What now, little man? Don't tell me you're afraid of – earthquakes?'

III
THIEVES' HOUSE

'What's the use of knowing the name of a skull? One would never have occasion to talk to it,' said the fat thief loudly. 'What interests me is that it has rubies for eyes.'

'Yet it is written here that its name is Ohmphal,' replied the black-bearded thief in the quieter tones of authority.

'Let me see,' said the bold, red-haired wench, leaning over his shoulder. She needed to be bold; all women were immemorially forbidden to enter Thieves' House. Together the three of them read the tiny hieroglyphs.

ITEM: *the skull Ohmphal, of the Master Thief Ohmphal, with great ruby eyes, and one pair of jeweled hands.* HISTORY OF ITEM: *the skull Ohmphal was stolen from the Thieves' Guild by the priests of Votishal and placed by them in the crypt of their accursed temple.* INSTRUCTIONS: *the skull Ohmphal is to be recovered at the earliest opportunity, that it may be given proper veneration in the Thieves' Sepulcher.* DIFFICULTIES: *the lock of the door leading to the crypt is reputed to be beyond the cunning of any thief to pick.* WARNINGS: *within the crypt is rumored to be a guardian beast of terrible ferocity.*

'Those crabbed letters are devilish hard to read,' said the red-haired wench, frowning.

'And no wonder, for they were written centuries ago,' said the black-bearded thief.

The fat thief said, 'I never heard tell of a Thieves' Sepulcher, save the junkyard, the incinerator, and the Inner Sea.'

'Times and customs change,' the black-bearded thief

philosophized. 'Periods of reverence alternate with periods of realism.'

'Why is it called the skull Ohmphal?' the fat thief wondered. 'Why not the skull *of* Ohmphal?'

The black-bearded thief shrugged.

'Where did you find this parchment?' the red-haired wench asked him.

'Beneath the false bottom of a moldering chest in our store-rooms,' he replied.

'By the gods who are not,' chuckled the fat thief, still poring over the parchment, 'the Thieves' Guild must have been superstitious in those ancient days. To think of wasting jewels on a mere skull. If we ever get hold of Master Ohmphal, we'll venerate him – by changing his ruby eyes into good hard money.'

'Aye!' said the black-bearded thief. 'And it was just that matter I wanted to talk to you about, Fissif – the getting hold of Ohmphal.'

'Oh, but there are – difficulties, as you, Krovas our master, must surely know,' said the fat thief, quickly singing another tune. 'Even today, after the passage of centuries, men still shudder when they speak of the crypt of Votishal, with its lock and its beast. There is no one in the Thieves' Guild who can—'

'No one in the Thieves' Guild, that's true!' interrupted the black-bearded thief sharply. 'But' – and here his voice began to go low – 'there are those outside the Thieves' Guild who can. Have you heard that there is recently returned here to Lankhmar a certain rogue and picklock known as the Gray Mouser? And with him a huge barbarian who goes by the name of Fafhrd, but is sometimes called the Beast-Slayer? We have a score as you well know, to settle with both of them. They slew our sorcerer, Hristomilo. That pair commonly hunts alone – yet if you were to approach them with this tempting suggestion . . .'

'But, Master,' interposed the fat thief, 'in that case, they would demand at least two-thirds of the profits.'

'Exactly!' said the black-bearded thief, with a sudden flash of cold humor. The red-haired wench caught his meaning, and laughed aloud. 'Exactly! And that is just the reason why I have chosen you, Fissif, the smoothest of double-crossers, to undertake this business.'

The ten remaining days of the Month of the Serpent had passed, and the first fifteen days of the Month of the Owl, since those three had conferred. And the fifteenth day had darkened into night. Chill fog, like a dark shroud, hugged ancient stony Lankhmar, chief city of the land of Lankhmar. This night the fog had come earlier than usual, flowing down the twisting streets and mazy alleyways. And it was getting thicker.

In one street rather narrower and more silent than the rest – Cheap Street, its name – a square yellow torchlight shone from a wide doorway in a vast and rambling house of stone. There was something ominous in a single open door in a street where all other doors were barred against the darkness and the damp. People avoided this street at night. And there was reason for their fear. The house had a bad reputation. People said it was the den in which the thieves of Lankhmar gathered to plot and palaver and settle their private bickerings, the headquarters from which Krovas, the reputed Master Thief, issued his orders – in short, the home of the formidable Thieves' Guild of Lankhmar.

But now a man came hurrying along this street, every now and then looking apprehensively over his shoulder. He was a fat man, and he hobbled a little, as if he had recently ridden hard and far. He carried a tarnished and ancient-looking copper box of about the size to contain a human head. He paused in the doorway and uttered a certain password – seemingly to the empty air, for the long hall ahead of him was empty. But a voice from a point inside and above the doorway answered, 'Pass, Fissif. Krovas awaits you in his room.' And the fat one said, 'They follow me close – you know the two I mean.' And the voice replied, 'We are ready for them.' And the fat one hurried down the hall.

For a considerable time, then, there was nothing but silence and the thickening fog. Finally a faint warning whistle came from somewhere down the street. It was repeated closer by and answered from inside the doorway.

Then, from the same direction as the first whistle, came the tread of feet, growing louder. It sounded as if there were only one person, but the effulgence of the light from the door showed that there was also a little man, who walked softly, a little man clad in close-fitting garments of gray – tunic, jerkin, mouseskin cap and cloak.

His companion was rangy and copper-haired, obviously a northern barbarian from the distant lands of the Cold Waste. His tunic was rich brown, his cloak green. There was considerable leather about him – wrist-bands, headband, boots, and a wide tight-laced belt. Fog had wet the leather and misted the brass studding it. As they entered the square of light before the doorway, a frown furrowed his broad wide forehead. His green eyes glanced quickly from side to side. Putting his hand on the little man's shoulder, he whispered:

'I don't like the looks of this, Gray Mouser.'

'*Tcha!* The place always looks like this, as you well know,' retorted the Gray Mouser sharply, his mobile lips sneering and dark eyes blazing. 'They just do it to scare the populace. Come on, Fafhrd! We're not going to let that misbegotten, double-dealing Fissif escape after the way he cheated us.'

'I know all that, my angry little weasel,' the barbarian replied, tugging the Mouser back. 'And the idea of Fissif escaping displeases me. But putting my bare neck in a trap displeases me more. Remember, they whistled.'

'*Tcha!* They always whistle. They like to be mysterious. I know these thieves. Fafhrd. I know them well. And you yourself have twice entered Thieves' House and escaped. Come on!'

'But I don't know *all* of Thieves' House,' Fafhrd protested. 'There's a modicum of danger.'

'Modicum! *They* don't know all of Thieves' House, their own place. It's a maze of the unknown, a labyrinth of forgotten history. *Come on!*'

'I don't know. It awakens evil memories of my lost Vlana.'

'And of my lost Ivrian! But must we let them win because of that?'

The big man shrugged his shoulders and started forward.

'On second thought,' whispered the Mouser, 'there may be

something to what you say.' And he slipped a dirk from his belt.

Fafhrd showed white teeth in grin and slowly pulled a big-pommeled longsword from its well-oiled scabbard.

'A rotten weapon for infighting,' murmured the Mouser in a comradely sardonical way.

Warily now they approached the door, each taking a side and sticking close to the wall. Holding the grip of his sword low, the point high, ready to strike in any direction, Fafhrd entered. The Mouser was a little ahead of him. Out of the corner of his eye Fafhrd saw something snakelike dropping down at the Mouser's head from above, and struck at it quickly with his sword. This flipped it toward him and he caught it with his free hand. It was a strangler's noose. He gave it a sudden sidewise heave and the man gripping the other end toppled out from a ledge above. For an instant he seemed to hang suspended in the air, a dark-skinned rogue with long black hair and a greasy tunic of red leather worked with gold thread. As Fafhrd deliberately raised his sword, he saw that the Mouser was lunging across the corridor at him, dirk in hand. For a moment he thought the Mouser had gone mad. But the Mouser's dirk missed him by a hairbreadth and another blade whipped past his back.

The Mouser had seen a trapdoor open in the floor beside Fafhrd and a bald-headed thief shoot up, sword in hand. After deflecting the blow aimed at his companion, the Mouse slammed the trapdoor back and had the satisfaction of catching with it the blade of the sword and two left-hand fingers of the ducking thief. All three were broken and the muted yowl from below was impressive. Fafhrd's man, spitted on the longsword, was quite dead.

From the street came several whistles and the sound of men moving in.

'They've cut us off!' snapped the Mouser. 'Our best chance lies ahead. We'll make for Krovas' room. Fissif may be there. Follow me!'

And he darted down the corridor and up a winding stair, Fafhrd behind him. At the second level they left the stair and raced for a doorway from which yellow light shone.

It puzzled the Mouser that they had met with no interference. His sharp ears no longer caught sounds of pursuit. On the threshold he pulled up quickly, so that Fafhrd collided with him.

It was a large room with several alcoves. Like the rest of the building, the floor and walls were of smooth dark stone, unembellished. It was lit by four earthenware lamps set at random on a heavy cyprus table. Behind the table sat a richly robed, black-bearded man, seemingly staring down in extreme astonishment at a copper box and a litter of smaller objects, his hands gripping the table edge. But they had no time to consider his odd motionlessness and still odder complexion, for their attention was immediately riveted on the red-haired wench who stood beside him.

As she sprang back like a startled cat, Fafhrd pointed at what she held under one arm and cried, 'Look, Mouser, the skull! The skull and the hands!'

Clasped in her slim arm was indeed a brownish, ancient-looking skull, curiously banded with gold from whose eye sockets great rubies sparkled and whose teeth were diamonds and blackened pearls. And in her white hand were gripped two neat packets of brown bones, tipped with a golden gleam and reddish sparkle. Even as Fafhrd spoke she turned and ran toward the largest alcove, her lithe legs outlined against silken garments. Fafhrd and the Mouser rushed after her. They saw she was heading for a small low doorway. Entering the alcove her free hand shot out and gripped a cord hanging from the ceiling. Not pausing, swinging at the hips, she gave it a tug. Folds of thick, weighted velvet fell down behind her. The Mouser and Fafhrd plunged into them and floundered. It was the Mouser who got through first, wriggling under. He saw an oblong of faint light narrowing ahead of him, sprang for it, grabbed at the block of stone sinking into the low doorway, then jerked his hand back with a curse and sucked at bruised fingers. The stone panel closed with a slight grating noise.

Fafhrd lifted the thick folds of velvet on his broad shoulders as if they were a great cloak. Light from the main rooms flooded into the alcove and revealed a closely mortised stone wall of uniform appearance. The Mouser started to dig the point of his dirk into a crack, then desisted.

'Pah! I know these doors! They're either worked from the other side or else by distant levers. She's gotten clear away and the skull with her.'

He continued to suck the fingers that had come so near to being crushed, wondering superstitiously if his breaking of the trapdoor thief's fingers had been a kind of omen.

'We forget Krovas,' said Fafhrd suddenly, lifting the drapes with his hand and looking back over his shoulder.

But the black-bearded man had not taken any notice of the commotion. As they approached him slowly they saw that his face was bluish-purple under the swarthy skin, and that his eyes bulged not from astonishment, but from strangulation. Fafhrd lifted the oily, well-combed beard and saw cruel indentations on the throat, seeming more like those of claws than fingers. The Mouser examined the things on the table. There were a number of jeweler's instruments, their ivory handles stained deep yellow from long use. He scooped up some small objects.

'Krovas had already pried three of the finger-jewels loose and several of the teeth,' he remarked, showing Fafhrd three rubies and a number of pearls and diamonds, which glittered on his palm.

Fafhrd nodded and again lifted Krovas' beard, frowning at the indentations, which were beginning to deepen in color.

'I wonder who the woman is?' said the Mouser. 'No thief is permitted to bring a woman here on pain of death. But the Master Thief has special powers and perhaps can take chances.'

'He has taken one too many,' muttered Fafhrd.

Then the Mouser awoke to their situation. He had half-formulated a plan of effecting an escape from the Thieves' House by capturing and threatening Krovas. But a dead man cannot be effectively intimidated. As he started to speak to Fafhrd they caught the murmur of several voices and the sound of approaching footsteps. Without deliberation they retired into the alcove, the Mouser cutting a small slit in the drapes at eye level and Fafhrd doing the same.

They heard someone say, 'Yes, the two of them got clean away, damn their luck! We found the alley door open.'

The first thief to enter was paunchy, white-faced, and obviously frightened. The Gray Mouser and Fafhrd immediately recognized him as Fissif. Pushing him along roughly was a tall, expressionless fellow with heavy arms and big hands. The Mouser knew him, too – Slevyas the Tight-lipped, recently promoted to be Krovas' chief lieutenant. About a dozen others filed into the room and took up positions near the walls. Veteran thieves all, with a considerable sprinkling of scars, pockmarks, and other mutilations, including two black-patched eye sockets. They were somewhat wary and ill at ease, held daggers and shortswords ready, and all stared intently at the strangled man.

'So Krovas is truly dead,' said Slevyas, shoving Fissif forward. 'At least that much of your story is true.'

'Dead as a fish,' echoed a thief who had moved closer to the table. 'Now we've got us a better master. We'll have no more of black-beard and his red-haired wench.'

'Hide your teeth, rat, before I break them!' Slevyas whipped out the words coldly.

'But you are our master now,' replied the thief in a surprised voice.

'Yes, I'm the master of all of you, unquestioned master, and my first piece of advice is this: to criticize a dead thief may not be irreverent – but it is certainly a waste of time. Now, Fissif, where's the jeweled skull? We all know it's more valuable than a year's pickpocketing, and that the Thieves' Guild needs gold. So, no nonsense!'

The Mouser peering cautiously from his slit, grinned at the look of fear on Fissif's fat-jowled face.

'The skull, Master?' said Fissif in a quavering sepulchral tone. 'Why, it's flown back to the grave from which we three filched it. Surely if those bony hands could strangle Krovas, as I saw with my own eyes, the skull could fly.'

Slevyas slapped Fissif across the face.

'You lie, you quaking bag of mush! I will tell you what happened. You plotted with those two rogues, the Gray Mouser and Fafhrd. You thought no one would suspect you because you double-crossed them according to instructions. But you planned a double-double-cross. You helped them escape the trap we had set, let them kill Krovas, and then assured their escape by starting a panic with your tale of dead fingers killing Krovas. You thought you could brazen it out.'

'But Master,' Fissif pleaded, 'with my own eyes I saw the skeletal fingers leap to his throat. They were angry with him because he had pried forth some of the jewels that were their nails and—'

Another slap changed his statement to a whining grunt.

'A fool's story,' sneered a scrawny thief. 'How could the bones hold together?'

'They were laced on brass wires,' returned Fissif in meek tones.

'Nah! And I suppose the hands, after strangling Krovas, picked up the skull and carried it away with them?' suggested another thief. Several sniggered. Slevyas silenced them with a look, then indicated Fissif with his thumb.

'Pinion him,' he ordered.

Two thieves sidled up to Fissif, who offered no resistance. They twisted his arms behind his back.

'We'll do this thing decently,' said Slevyas, seating himself on the table. 'Thieves' trial. Everything in order. Briefly this is a matter for the Thieves' Jury to consider. Fissif, cut-purse of the first rank, was commissioned to loot the sacred grave at the temple of Votishal of one skull and one pair of hands. Because of certain unusual difficulties involved, Fissif was ordered to league himself with two outsiders of special talent, to wit, the northern barbarian Fafhrd and the notorious Gray Mouser.'

The Mouser made a courteous and formal bow behind the drapes, then glued his eye once more to the slit.

'The loot obtained, Fissif was to steal it from the two others – and at the earliest possible moment, to avoid their stealing it from him.'

The Mouser thought he heard Fafhrd smother a curse and grit his teeth.

'If possible, Fissif was to slay them,' concluded Slevyas. 'In any case he was to bring the loot direct to Krovas. So much for Fissif's instructions, as detailed to me by Krovas. Now tell your story, Fissif, but – mind you – no old-wives' tales.'

'Brother thieves,' began Fissif in a heavy mournful voice. This was greeted by several derisive cries. Slevyas rapped carelessly for order.

'I followed out those instructions just as they were given me,' continued Fissif. 'I sought out Fafhrd and the Gray Mouser, and interested them in the plan. I agreed to share the loot equally with them, a third to each man.'

Fafhrd, squinting at Fissif through the drape, nodded his head solemnly. Fissif then made several uncomplimentary remarks about Fafhrd and the Mouser, evidently hoping thereby to convince his listeners that he had not plotted with them. The other thieves only smiled grimly.

'And when it came to the actual filching of the loot from the temple,' Fissif went on, gaining confidence from the sound of his own voice, 'it turned out I had little need of their help.'

Again Fafhrd smothered a curse. He could hardly endure listening in silence to such outrageous lies. But the Mouser enjoyed it after a fashion.

'This is an unwise time to brag,' interjected Slevyas. 'You know very well that the Mouser's cunning was needed in picking the great triple lock, and that the guardian beast could not easily have been slain but for the Northerner.'

Fafhrd was somewhat mollified by this. Fissif became humble again and bowed his head in assent. The thieves began gradually to close in on him.

'And so,' he finished in a kind of panic, 'I took up the loot while they slept, and spurred on to Lankhmar. I dared not slay them, for fear the killing of one would awaken the other. I brought the loot direct to Krovas, who complimented me and began to pry out the gems. There lies the copper box which held the skull and hands.' He pointed at the table. 'And as for what happened afterward—' He paused, wet his lips, looked around fearfully, then added in a small despairing voice, 'It happened just as I told you before.'

The thieves, snarling disbelief, closed in, but Slevyas halted them with a peremptory rap. He seemed to be considering something.

Another thief darted into the room, saluted Slevyas. 'Master,' he panted, 'Moolsh, stationed on the roof opposite the alley door, has just reported that, though open all night, no one either entered or left. The two intruders may still be here!'

Slevyas' start as he received the news was almost imperceptible. He stared at his informant. Then slowly and as if drawn by instinct, his impassive face turned until his pale, small eyes rested upon the heavy drapes curtaining the alcove. As he was about to give an order, the drapes bellied out as if with a great gust of wind. They swung forward and up until almost level with the ceiling, and he glimpsed two figures racing forward. The tall, copper-haired barbarian was aiming a blow at him.

With a suppleness which belied his large frame, Slevyas half-ducked, half-dropped, and the great longsword bit deep into the table against which he had been resting. From the floor he saw his underlings springing back in confusion, one staggered by a blow. Fissif, quicker-nerved than the rest because he knew his life was at stake in more ways than one, snatched and hurled a dagger. It was an imperfect throw, traveling pommel-forward. But it was accurate. Slevyas saw it take the tall barbarian on the side of the head as he rushed through the doorway, seeming to stagger him. Then Slevyas was on his feet, sword drawn and organizing pursuit. In a few moments the room was empty, save for dead Krovas staring at an empty copper box in a cruel mockery of astonishment.

The Gray Mouser knew the layout of the Thieves' House – not as well as the palm of his hand, but well enough – and he led Fafhrd around stony angles, sprang up and down small sets of steps, two or three each, which made it difficult to determine which level they were on. The Mouser had drawn his slim sword Scalpel for the first time and used it to knock over the candles they passed, and to make swipes at the wall torches, hoping thereby to confuse the pursuit, whose whistles sounded sharply from behind them. Twice Fafhrd stumbled and recovered himself.

Two half-dressed apprentice thieves stuck their heads out of a door. The Mouser slammed it in their inquiring excited faces, then sprang down a curving stairway. He was heading for a third exit he surmised would be poorly guarded.

'If we are separated, let our rendezvous be the Silver Eel,' he said in a quick aside to Fafhrd, mentioning a tavern they frequented.

The Northerner nodded. His head was beginning to feel less dizzy now, though it still pained him considerably. He did not, however, gauge accurately the height of the low arch under which the Mouser sped after descending the equivalent of two levels, and it gave his head as hard a clip as had the dagger. Everything went dark and whirling before his eyes. He heard the Mouser saying, 'This way now! We follow the left-hand wall,' and trying to keep a tight hold on his consciousness, he plunged into the narrow corridor down which the Mouser was pointing. He thought the Mouser was following him.

But the Mouser had waited a moment too long. True, the main pursuit was still out of sight, but a watchman whose duty it was to patrol this passage, hearing the whistles, had returned hurriedly from a friendly game of dice. The Mouser ducked as the artfully-cast noose settled around his neck, but not quite soon enough. It tightened cruelly against ear, cheek, and jaw-bone, and brought him down. In the next instant Scalpel severed the cord, but that gave the watchman time to get out his sword. For a few perilous moments the Mouser fought him from the floor, warding off a flashing point that came close enough to his nose to make him cross-eyed. Watching his chance, he scrambled to his feet, rushed his man back a dozen paces with a whirlwind attack in which Scalpel seemed to become three or four swords, and ended the man's cries for help with a slicing thrust through the neck.

The delay was sufficient. As the Mouser wrenched away the noose from his cheek and mouth, where it had gagged him during the fight, he saw the first of Slevyas' crowd dart out under the archway. Abruptly the Mouser made off down the main corridor, away from the path of escape Fafhrd had taken. A half dozen plans flashed through his mind. There came a triumphant outcry as Slevyas' crowd sighted him, then a number of whistles from ahead. He decided his best chance was to make for the roof, and whirled into a cross corridor. He was hopeful that Fafhrd had escaped, though the Northerner's behavior bothered him. He was supremely confident that he, the Gray Mouser could elude ten times as many thieves as now careened and skidded through the mazy corridors of the Thieves' House. He lengthened his skipping stride, and his soft-shod feet fairly flew over the well-worn stone.

Fafhrd, lost in pitch darkness for he didn't know how long, steadied himself against what felt like a table and tried to remember how he had gotten so grievously far astray. But his skull throbbed and kept tightening with pain, and the incidents he recalled were jumbled up, with gaps in between. There was a matter of sprawling down a stair and of pushing against a wall of carven stone which had given way silently and let him tumble through. At one point he had been violently sick and at another he must have been unconscious for some time, for he recalled pushing himself up from a prone position and crawling for some distance on hands and knees through a jumble of casks and bales of rotten cloth. That he had banged his head at least once more he was certain; pushing his fingers through his tangled, sweaty locks he could detect as many as three distinct lumps in his scalp. His chief emotion was a dull and persistent anger directed at the heavy masses of stone around him. His primitive imagination half-invested them with a conscious intent to oppose him and block him off whichever way he moved. He knew that he had somehow confused the Mouser's simple directions. Just which wall was it the little gray man had told him to follow? And just where was the Mouser? In some fearful mix-up likely.

If only the air weren't so hot and dry, he felt he'd be able to think things out better. Nothing seemed to agree. Even the quality of the air didn't fit with his impression that he had been descending most of the way, as if into a deep cellar. It should have been cold and damp, but it wasn't. It was dry and warm. He slid his hand along the wooden surface on which it was resting, and soft dust piled up between his fingers. That, along with the impenetrable darkness and total silence, would seem to indicate he was in a region of the Thieves' House long disused. He brooded for a moment over his memories of the stone crypt from which he and the Mouser and Fissif had filched the jeweled skull. The fine dust, rising to his nostrils, made him sneeze, and that started him moving again. His groping hand found a wall. He tried to recall the direction from which he had originally approached the table, but was unable to, and so started out at random. He moved along slowly, feeling his way, hand and foot.

His caution saved him. One of the stones seemed to give slightly under his exploring foot and he jerked back. Abruptly there came a rasping sound followed by a clank and two muffled thuds. The air in front of his face was disturbed. He waited a moment, then groped forward cautiously through the blackness. His hand encountered a strip of rusty metal at shoulder level. Feeling along it gingerly he found it protruded from a crevice in the left wall, and ended in a point a few inches from a wall he now discovered to be on his right. Further groping revealed a similar blade below the first. He now realized that the thudding sounds had been caused by counterweights, which, released by pressure on the stone, had automatically propelled the blades through the crevice. Another step forward and he would have been spitted. He reached for his longsword, found it was not in the scabbard, so took the scabbard instead and with it broke off the two blades close to the wall. Then he turned and retraced his steps to the dust-covered table.

But a slow tracing of the wall beyond the table led him back to the corridor of the sword blades. He shook his aching head and cursed angrily because he had no light nor way of making fire. How then? Had he originally entered this blind alley by way of the corridor, missing the deadly stone by pure luck? That seemed to be the only answer, so with a growl he started off again down the corridor of the sword blades, arms outstretched and hands brushing the two walls, so that he might know when he came to an intersection, and footing it most gingerly. After a little it occurred to him that he might have fallen into the chamber behind from some entrance partway up the wall, but stubbornness kept him from turning back a second time.

The next thing his exploring foot encountered was an emptiness, which turned out to be the beginning of a flight of stone steps leading down. At that point he gave up trying to remember just how he had gotten where he was. About twenty steps down his nostrils caught a musty, arid odor welling up from below. Another twenty steps and he began comparing it to the odor found in certain ancient desert tombs of the Eastern Lands. There was an almost imperceptible spiciness to it, a dead spiciness. His skin felt hot and dry. He drew his long knife from his belt and moved silently, slowly.

At the fifty-third step the stair ended and the side walls retreated. From the feel of the air, he thought he must be in a large chamber. He advanced a little way, his boots scuffling a thick carpet of fine dust. There was a dry flapping and faint rattling in the air above his head. Twice something small and hard brushed his cheek. He remembered bat-infested caves into which he had previously ventured. But these tiny noises, though in many ways similar, were not quite like those of bats. The short hairs prickled on the back of his neck. He strained his eyes, but saw only the meaningless pattern of points of light that comes with inky darkness.

Again one of the things brushed his face and this time he was ready for it. His big hands grabbed swiftly – and then nearly dropped what they clutched, for it was dry and weightless, a mere framework of tiny brittle bones which cracked under his fingers. His finger and thumb encountered a minute animal skull.

His mind fought down the idea of bats which were skeletons and yet flapped to and fro in a great tomb-like chamber. Surely this creature must have died hanging to the roof above his head, and his entrance dislodged it. But he did not grasp again at the faint rattling noises in the air.

Then he began to sense sounds of another sort – diminutive shrill squeaks almost too high for the ear to catch. Whatever they were, real or imagined, there was that about them which bred panic, and Fafhrd found himself shouting: 'Speak to me! What are you whining and tittering about? Reveal your-selves!'

At this, echoes cried faintly back to him, and he knew for certain he was in a large chamber. Then there was silence, even the sounds in the air receding. And after the silence had endured for twenty or more beats of Fafhrd's pounding heart, it was broken in a way Fafhrd did not like.

A faint, high, listless voice came from somewhere ahead of him, saying, 'The man is a Northerner, brothers, a longhaired, uncouth barbarian from the Cold Waste.'

From a spot a little way to one side a similar voice responded, 'In our days we met many of his breed at the docks. We soused them with drink, and stole gold dust from their pouches. We were mighty thieves in our day, matchless in craft and cunning.'

And a third – 'See, he has lost his sword, and look brothers, he has crushed a bat and holds it in his hand.'

Fafhrd's shout to the effect that this was all nonsense and mummery died before it reached his lips, for it suddenly occurred to him to wonder how these creatures could tell his appearance and even see what he held in his hand, when it was pitch dark. Fafhrd knew well that even the cat and the owl are blind in complete darkness. A crawling terror took hold of him.

'But the skull of a bat is not the skull of a man,' came what seemed to be the first voice. 'He is one of the three who recovered our brother's skull from the temple of Votishal. Yet he has not brought the skull with him.'

'For centuries our brother's bejeweled head has languished lonely under the accursed fane of Vitishal,' spoke a fourth. 'And now that those above have stolen him back, they do not mean to return him to us. They would tear out his glittering eyes and sell them for greasy coins. They are puny thieves, godless and greedy. They have forgotten us, their ancient brothers, and are evil entirely.'

There was something horribly dead and far away about the voices, as if they formed in a void. Something emotionless and yet strangely sad and strangely menacing, halfway between a faint, hopeless sigh and a fainter, icy laugh. Fafhrd clenched his hands tight, so that the tiny skeleton crackled to splinters, which he brushed away spasmodically. He tried to rally his courage and move forward, but could not.

'It is not fitting that such ignoble fate befall our brother,' came the first voice, which held the barest suggestion of authority over the others. 'Hearken now, Northerner, to our words, and hearken well.'

'See, brothers,' broke in the second, 'the Northerner is afraid, and wipes his mouth with his great hand, and gnaws his knuckle in uncertainty and fear.'

Fafhrd began to tremble at hearing his actions so minutely described. Long-buried terrors arose in his mind. He remembered his earliest thoughts of death, how as a boy he had first witnessed the terrible funeral rites of the Cold Waste and joined in muted prayers to Kos and the nameless god of doom. Then, for the first time, he thought he could distinguish something in the darkness. It might only have been a peculiar formation of the meaningless patter of dimly glittering points of light, but he distinguished a number of tiny sparklings on a level with his own head, all in pairs about a thumb's-length apart. Some were deep red, and some green, and some pale-blue like sapphires. He vividly recalled the ruby eyes of the skull stolen from Votishal, the skull Fissif averred had strangled Krovas with bony hands. The points of light were gathering together and moving toward him, very slowly.

'Northerner,' continued the first voice, 'know that we are the ancient master thieves of Lankhmar, and that we needs must have the lost brain, which is his skull, of our brother Ohmphal. You must bring it to us before the stars of midnight next shine overhead. Else you will be sought out and your life drawn from you.'

The pairs of colored lights were still closing in, and now Fafhrd thought he could hear the sound of dry, grating footsteps in the dust. He recalled the deep purple indentations on the throat of Krovas.

'You must bring the skull without fail,' echoed the second voice.

'Before next midnight,' came another.

'The jewels must be in the skull; not one must be held back from us.'

'Ohmphal our brother shall return.'

'If you fail us,' whispered the first voice, 'we shall come for the skull – and for you.'

And then they seemed to be all around him, crying out 'Ohmphal – Ohmphal,' in those detestable voices which were still not one whit louder or less far away. Fafhrd thrust out his hands convulsively, touched something hard and smooth and dry. And with that he shook and started like a frightened horse, turned and ran off at full speed, came to a painful, stumbling stop against the stone steps, and raced up them three at a time, stumbling and bruising his elbows against the walls.

The fat thief Fissif wandered about disconsolately in a large low cellar-chamber dimly lighted, littered with odds and ends and piled with empty casks and bales of rotten cloth. He chewed a mildly soporific nut which stained his lips blue and dribbled down his flabby jaws; at regular intervals he sighed in self-pity. He realized his prospects in the Thieves' Guild were rather dubious, even though Slevyas had granted him a kind of reprieve. He recalled the fishy look in Slevyas' eye and shivered. He did not like the loneliness of the cellar-chamber, but anything was preferable to the contemptuous, threatening glances of his brother thieves.

The sound of dragging footsteps caused him to swallow one of his monotonous sighs – his chew along with it – and duck behind a table. There appeared from the shadows a startling apparition. Fissif recognized it as the Northerner, Fafhrd, but it was a very sorry-looking Fafhrd, face pale and grimy, clothes and hair bedraggled and smeared with a grayish dust. He moved like a man bewildered or deep in thought. Fissif, realizing that here indeed was a golden opportunity, picked up a sizable tapestry-weight that was lying at hand, and stole softly after the brooding figure.

Fafhrd had just about convinced himself that the strange voices from which he had fled were only the figments of his brain, fostered by fever and headache. After all, he reasoned, a blow on the head often made a person see colored lights and hear ringing noises; he must have been almost witless to get lost in the dark so readily – the ease with which he'd retraced his path this time proved that. The thing to do now was concentrate on escaping from this musty den. He mustn't dream. There was a houseful of thieves on the lookout for him, and he might expect to meet one at any turn.

As he shook his head to clear it, and gazed up alertly, there descended on his thick skull the sixth blow it had received that night. But this one was harder.

Slevyas' reaction to the news of Fafhrd's capture was not exactly what Fissif had expected. He did not smile. He did not look up from the platter of cold meats set before him. He merely took a small swallow of pale-yellow wine and went on eating.

'The jeweled skull?' he questioned curtly, between mouthfuls.

Fissif explained that it was possible the Northerner had hidden or lost it somewhere in the lower reaches of the cellars. A careful search would answer the question. 'Perhaps the Gray Mouser was carrying it . . .'

'You killed the Northerner?' asked Slevyas after a pause.

'Not quite,' answered Fissif proudly. 'But I joggled his brains for him.'

Fissif expected a compliment at this, or at least a friendly nod, but received instead a cold, appraising stare, the import of which was difficult to determine. Slevyas thoroughly masticated a mouthful of meat, swallowed it, then took a deliberate swallow of wine. All the while his eyes did not leave Fissif.

Finally he said, 'Had you killed him, you would at this instant be put to torture. Understand, fat-belly, that I do not trust you. Too many things point to your complicity. If you had plotted with him, you would have killed him to prevent your treason being revealed. Perhaps you did try to kill him. Fortunate for you his skull is thick.'

The matter-of-fact tone stifled Fissif's protest. Slevyas drained the last of his cup, leaned back, and signed for the apprentices to take the dishes away.

'Has the Northerner regained his senses?' he asked abruptly.

Fissif nodded, and added, 'He seemed to be in a fever. Struggled against his bonds and muttered words. Something about "next midnight". He repeated that three times. The rest was in an outlandish tongue.'

A scrawny, rat-eared thief entered. 'Master,' he said, bowing obsequiously, 'we have found the Gray Mouser. He sits at the Silver Eel Tavern. Several of ours watch the place. Shall he be captured or slain?'

'Has he the skull with him? Or a box that might hide it?'

'No, Master,' responded the thief lugubriously, bowing even lower than before.

Slevyas sat for a moment in thought, then motioned an apprentice to bring parchment and the black ink of the squid. He wrote a few lines, then threw a question to Fissif.

'What were the words the Northerner muttered?'

'"Next midnight", Master,' answered Fissif, becoming obsequious himself.

'They will fit nicely,' said Slevyas, smiling thinly as if at an irony only he could perceive. His pen moved on over the stiff parchment.

The Gray Mouser sat with his back to the wall behind a tankard-dented, wine-stained table at the Silver Eel, nervously rolling between finger and thumb one of the rubies he had taken from under the eyes of dead Krovas. His small cup of wine spiced with bitter herbs was still half full. His glance flitted restlessly around the almost empty rooms and back and forth between the four small window spaces, high in the wall, that let in the chill fog. He gazed narrowly at the fat, leather-aproned innkeeper who snored dismally on a stool beside the short stair leading up to the door. He listened with half an ear to the disjointed, somnolent mumbling of the two soldiers across the room, who clutched large tankards and, heads leaned together in drunken confidentialness, tried to tell each other of ancient stratagems and mighty marches.

Why didn't Fafhrd come? This was no time for the huge fellow to be late, yet since the Mouser's arrival at the Silver Eel the candles had melted down half an inch. The Mouser no longer found pleasure in recalling the perilous stages of his escape from Thieves' House – the dash up the stairs, the leaping from roof to roof, the short fight among the chimneys. By the Gods of Trouble! Would he have to go back to that den, now filled with ready knives and open eyes, to begin search for his companion? He snapped his fingers so that the jewel between them shot high toward the sooty ceiling, a little track of sparkling red which his other hand snatched back as it descended, like a lizard trapping a fly. Again he stared suspiciously at the slumped, open-mouthed innkeeper.

From the corner of his eye he saw the small steel messenger streaking down toward him from a fog-dim rectangle of window. Instinctively he jerked to one side. But there was no need. The dagger buried its point in the tabletop an arm's length to one side. For what seemed a long time the Mouser stood ready to jump again. The hollow *chunking* noise of the impact had not awakened the innkeeper nor disturbed the soldiers, one of whom now snored, too. Then the Mouser's left hand reached out and rocked the dagger loose. He slipped the small roll of parchment from the forte of the blade and, his gaze still walking guard on the windows, read in snatches the harshly drawn runes of Lankhmar.

Their import was this: *If you do not bring the jeweled skull to what was Krovas' and is now Slevyas' chamber by next midnight, we will begin to kill the Northerner.*

Again next night the fog crept into Lankhmar. Sounds were muffled and torches ringed with smoky halos. But it was not yet late, although midnight was nearing and the streets were filled with hurrying shopkeepers and craftsmen, and drinkers happily laughing from their first cups, and sailors new on leave ogling the shopgirls.

In the street next that on which stood Thieves' House – the Street of the Silk Merchants, it was called – the crowd was thinning. The merchants were shutting shop. Occasionally they exchanged the noisy greetings of business rivals and plied shrewd questions pertaining to the state of trade. Several of them looked curiously at a narrow stone building, overshadowed by the dark mass of Thieves' House, and from whose slitlike upper windows warm light shone. There dwelt, with servants and hired bodyguard, one Ivlis, a handsome red-haired wench who sometimes danced for the overlord, and who was treated with respect, not so much for that reason, but because it was said that she was the mistress of the master of the Thieves' Guild, to whom the silk merchants paid tribute. But that very day rumor had whispered that the old master was dead and a new one taken his place. There was speculation among the silk merchants as to whether Ivlis was now out of favor and had shut herself up in fear.

A little old woman came hobbling along, her crooked cane feeling for the cracks between the slick cobblestones. Because she had a black cloak huddled around her and a black cowl over her head – and so seemed a part of the dark fog – one of the merchants almost collided with her in the shadows. He helped her around a slimy puddle and grinned commiseratingly when she complained in a quavering voice about the condition of the street and the manifold dangers to which an old woman was exposed. She went off mumbling to herself in a rather senile fashion, 'Come on now, it's just a little farther, just a little farther. But take care. Old bones are brittle, brittle.'

A loutish apprentice dyer came ambling along, bumped into her rudely, and walked on without looking back to see whether she had fallen. But he had not taken two steps before a well-planted kick jarred his spine. He whirled around clumsily but he saw only the bent old form tottering off, cane tapping uncertainly. Eyes and mouth wide open, he moved back several steps, scratching his head in bewilderment not unmixed with superstitious wonder. Later that night he gave half his wages to his old mother.

The old woman paused before the house of Ivlis, peered up at the lighted windows several times as if she were in doubt and her eyesight bad, then climbed up laboriously to the door and feebly waggled her cane against it. After a pause she rapped again, and cried out in a fretful, high voice: 'Let me in. Let me in. I bear news from the gods to the dweller in this house. You inside there, let me in!'

Finally a wicket opened and a gruff, deep voice said. 'Go on your way, old witch. None enters here tonight.'

But the old woman took no notice of this and repeated stubbornly, 'Let me in, I say. I read the future. It's cold in the street and the fog freezes my old throat. Let me in. This noon a bat came flapping and told me portentously of events destined for the dweller in this house. My old eyes can see the shadows of things which are not yet. Let me in, I say.'

The slim figure of a woman was silhouetted in the window above the door. After a little it moved away.

The interchange of words between the old woman and the

guard went on for some time. Then a soft, husky voice called down the stairwell, 'Let the wise woman in. She's alone, isn't she? Then I will talk with her.'

The door opened, though not very wide, and the black-cloaked form tottered in. The door was immediately closed and barred.

The Gray Mouser looked around at the three bodyguards standing in the darkened hall, strapping fellows with two shortswords each. They were certainly not of the Thieves' Guild. They seemed ill at ease. He did not forget to wheeze asthmatically, holding his bent side, and thank with a simpering, senile leer the one who had opened the door.

The guard drew back with an ill-concealed expression of disgust. The Mouser was not a pretty sight, his face covered with cunningly blended grease and gray ashes, studded with hideous warts of putty, and half covered with wispy gray hair straggling down from the dried scalp of a real witch – so Laavyan the wig-seller had averred – that covered his pate.

Slowly the Mouser began to ascend the stair, leaning heavily on the cane and stopping every few steps as if to recover his breath. It was not easy for him to go at such a snail-like pace, with midnight so near. But he had already failed three times in attempts to enter this well-guarded house, and he knew that the slightest unnatural action might betray him. Before he was halfway up, the husky voice gave a command and a dark-haired serving woman, in a black silk tunic, hurried down, her bare feet making little noise on the stone.

'You're very kind to an old woman,' he wheezed, patting the smooth hand which gripped his elbow. They began to move up a little faster. The Mouser's inner core of thought was concentrated on the jeweled skull. He could almost see it wavering in the darkness of the stairwell, a pale brown ovoid. That skull was the key to the Thieves' House and Fafhrd's safety. Not that Slevyas would be likely to release Fafhrd, even if the skull was brought. But having the skull, the Mouser knew he would be in a position to bargain. Without it, he would have to storm Slevyas' lair with every thief forewarned and ready for him. Last night luck and circumstance had fought on his side. It would not happen again. As these thoughts were passing through the Mouser's mind he grumbled and whined vaguely about the height of the stair and the stiffness of old joints.

The maid led him into a room strewn with thick-piled rugs and hung with silken tapestry. From the ceiling depended on heavy brassy chains a large-bowled copper lamp, intricately engraved, unlighted. A soft illumination and a pleasant aromatic odor came from pale-green candles set on little tables which also held jars of perfume, small fat-bellied pots of unguent, and the like.

Standing in the center of the room was the red-haired wench he had seen take the skull from Krovas' chamber. Her robe was of white silk. Her gleaming hair, redder than auburn, was held high with golden-headed pins. He had time now to study her face, noting the hardness of her yellow-green eyes and tight jaw, contrasted with her full soft lips and pale creamy skin. He recognized anxiety in the tense lines of her body.

'You read the future, hag?' Her question was more like a command.

'By hand and hair I read it,' replied the Mouser, putting an eerie note into his quavering falsetto. 'By palm and heart and eye.' He tottered toward her. 'Yes, and small creatures talk to me and tell me secrets.' With that he suddenly drew from under his cloak a small black kitten and almost thrust it into her face. She recoiled in surprise and cried out, but he could see that the action had, in her estimation, established him as a genuine witch.

Ivlis dismissed the maid and the Mouser hastened to follow up his advantage before Ivlis' mood of awe vanished. He spoke of doom and destiny, of omens and portents, of money and love and voyages over water. He played upon the superstitions he knew to be current among the dancing girls of Lankhmar. He impressed her by speaking of 'a dark man with a black beard, either recently dead or at death's door,' not mentioning the name of Krovas for fear too much accuracy would awaken her suspicion. He wove facts, guesses, and impressive generalities into an intricate web.

The morbid fascination of staring into the forbidden future

took hold of her and she leaned forward, breathing rapidly, twisting her slim fingers together, sucking her under lip. Her hurried questions mainly concerned 'a cruel, cold-faced, large man,' in whom the Mouser recognized Slevyas, and whether or not she should leave Lankhmar.

The Mouser kept up a steady stream of words, only pausing occasionally to cough, wheeze, or cackle for added realism. At times he almost believed that he was indeed a witch, and that the things he spoke were dark unholy truths.

But thoughts of Fafhrd and the skull were uppermost in his mind, and he knew that midnight was close at hand. He learned much of Ivlis: for one thing, that she hated Slevyas almost more than she feared him. But the information he most wanted eluded him.

Then the Mouser saw something which stirred him on to greater efforts. Behind Ivlis a gap in the silken hangings showed the wall, and he noted that one of the large paneling stones seemed to be out of place. Suddenly he realized that the stone was of the same size, shape, and quality as that in Krovas' room. This, then, must be, he thought optimistically, the other end of the passage down which Ivlis had escaped. He determined that it would be his means of entry to the Thieves' House, whether he brought the skull or not.

Fearing to waste more time, the Mouser sprang his trick. He paused abruptly, pinched the kitten's tail to make it mew, then sniffed several times, made a hideous face, and said, 'Bones! I smell a dead man's bones!'

Ivlis caught her breath and looked up quickly at the large lamp hanging from the ceiling, the lamp which was unlit. The Mouser guessed what that glance meant.

But either his own satisfaction betrayed him or else Ivlis guessed she had been tricked into betraying herself, for she gazed at him sharply. The superstitious excitement drained from her face and the hardness came back into her eyes.

'You're a man!' she spat at him suddenly. Then with fury, 'Slevyas sent you!'

With that she jerked one of the dagger-long pins from her hair and flung herself at him, striking at his eyes as he dodged.

He caught her wrist with his left hand, clapped his right over her mouth. The struggle was brief and almost completely noiseless because of the thick carpeting on which they rolled. When she had been carefully trussed and gagged with strips torn from the silken hangings, the Mouser first closed the door to the stair, then pulled open the stone panel, finding the narrow passageway he had expected. Ivlis glared at him, every look a vituperation, and struggled futilely. But he knew there was no time for explanations. Hitching up his incongruous garments, he sprang nimbly for the lamp, caught the upper edge. The chains held and he raised himself until his eyes could see over the edge. Cradled inside were the dull brown gem-glittering skull and the jewel-tipped bones.

The upper bowl of the crystal water clock was almost empty. Fafhrd stolidly watched the twinkling drops form and fall into the lower bowl. He was on the floor with his back to the wall. His legs were tied from knee to ankle, his arms laced behind him with an equally unnecessary amount of cordage, so that he felt quite numb. To either side of him squatted an armed thief.

When the upper bowl emptied it would be midnight.

Occasionally his gaze shifted to the dark, disfigured faces which ringed the table on which the clock and certain curious instruments of torture rested. The faces were those of the aristocrats of the Thieves' Guild, men with crafty eyes and lean cheeks, who vied with one another as to the richness and greasiness of their finery. Flickering torches threw highlights of soiled reds and purples, tarnished cloth of silver and gold. But behind their masklike expressions Fafhrd sensed uncertainty. Only Slevyas, sitting in the chair of dead Krovas, seemed truly calm and self-possessed. His voice was almost casual as he interrogated a lesser thief who knelt abjectly before him.

'Are you indeed as great a coward as you would make us think?' he asked. 'Would you have us believe you were afraid of an empty cellar?'

'Master, I am no coward,' pleaded the thief. 'I followed the Northerner's footprints in the dust along the narrow corridor and almost to the bottom of the ancient stair, forgotten until today. But no man alive could hear without terror those strange, high voices, those bony rattlings. The dry air choked my throat, a wind blew out my torch. Things tittered at me. Master, I would attempt to filch a jewel from inside a wakeful cobra's coil if you should command it. But down into that place of darkness I could not force myself.'

Fafhrd saw Slevyas' lips tighten and waited for him to pronounce sentence on the miserable thief, but remarks by the notables sitting around the table interrupted.

'There may be some truth to his tale,' said one. 'After all, who knows what may be in these cellars the Northerner's blundering discovered?'

'Until last night we never knew they existed,' echoed another. 'In the trackless dust of centuries strange things may lurk.[3]

'Last night,' added a third, 'we scoffed at Fissif's tale. Yet on the throat of Krovas we found the marks of claws or of naked bone.'

It was as if a miasma of fear had welled up from the cellars far below. Voices were solemn. The lesser thieves who stood near the walls, bearing torches and weapons, were obviously gripped by superstitious dread. Again Slevyas hesitated, although unlike the others he seemed perplexed rather than frightened. In the hush the monotonous splashes of the falling drops sounded loudly. Fafhrd decided to fish in troubled waters.

'I will tell you myself of what I found in the cellars,' he said in a deep voice. 'But first tell me where you thieves bury your dead.'

Appraising eyes turned upon him. This was the first time he had spoken since he came to his senses. His question was not answered, but he was allowed to speak. Even Slevyas, although he frowned at Fafhrd's words and fingered a thumbscrew, did not object. And Fafhrd's words were something to hear. They had a cavernous quality which suggested the northland and the Cold Waste, a dramatic ring like that in the voice of a skald. He told in detail of his descent into the dark regions below. Indeed, he added new details for effect, and made the whole experience seem like some frightening epic. The lesser thieves, unused to this kind of talk, gaped at him. Those around the table sat very still. He spun out his story as long as he dared, playing for time.

During the pauses in his speech the dripping of the water clock was no longer to be heard. Then Fafhrd's ear caught a small grating sound, as of stone on stone. His listeners did not seem to notice it, but Fafhrd recognized it as the opening of the stone panel in the alcove, before which the black drapes still hung.

He had reached the climax of his revelations.

'There, in those forgotten cellars,' his voice told, going a note deeper, 'are the living bones of the ancient Thieves of Lankhmar. Long have they lain there, hating you who have forgotten them. The jeweled skull was that of their brother, Ohmphal. Did not Krovas tell you that the plans for stealing the skull were handed down from the dim past? It was intended that Ohmphal be restored to his brothers. Instead, Krovas desecrated the skull, tearing out the jewels. Because of that indignity, the bony hands found supernatural power with which to slay him. I know not where the skull is now. But if it has not already returned to them, those below will come for it even now, tonight. And they will not be merciful.'

And then Fafhrd's words froze in his throat. His final argument, which had to do with his own release, remained unspoken. For, suspended in the air immediately in front of the black draperies of the alcove, was the skull of Ohmphal, its jeweled eyes glittering with light that was more than reflection. The eyes of the thieves followed those of Fafhrd, and the air whistled with intaken breaths of fear, fear so intense that it momentarily precluded panic. A fear such as they felt toward their living master, but magnified many times.

And then a high wailing voice spoke from the skull, 'Move not, oh you craven thieves of today! Tremble and be silent. It is your ancient master who speaks. Behold, I am Ohmphal!'

The effect of that voice was peculiar. Most of the thieves shrank back, gritting their teeth and clenching their hands to control trembling. But the sweat of relief trickled down Fafhrd's head, for he recognized the Mouser. And in fat Fissif's face puzzlement mingled with fear.

'First,' continued the voice from the skull, 'I shall strangle the Northman as an example to you. Cut his bonds and bring him to me. Be quick, lest I and my brothers slay you all.'

With twitching hands the thieves to the right and left of Fafhrd slit his lashings. He tensed his great muscles, trying to work out the paralyzing numbness. They pulled him to his feet and pushed him forward, stumbling, toward the skull.

Abruptly the black draperies were shaken by a commotion behind them. There came a shrill, almost animal scream of rage. The skull of Ohmphal slid down the black velvet and rolled out into the room, the thieves leaping out of its way and squealing as if for fear it came to bite their ankles with poisoned teeth. From the hole in its base fell a candle which flickered out. The draperies swung to one side and two struggling figures reeled into the room. For a moment even Fafhrd thought he was going mad at such an utterly unexpected sight as a fight between an old hag in black, with skirts tucked above her sturdy knees, and a red-haired wench with a dagger. Then the hag's cowl and wig were torn off and he recognized, under a complexion of grease and ashes, the Mouser's face. Fissif sprang forward past Fafhrd, his dagger out. The Northerner, awakening to action, caught him by the shoulder, hurled him against the wall, then snatched a sword from the fingers of a nerveless thief and staggered forward himself, muscles still numb.

Meanwhile Ivlis, becoming aware of the assembled thieves, suddenly stopped trying to skewer the Mouser. Fafhrd and the Mouser turned toward the alcove, where escape lay, and were almost bowled over by the sudden outrush of Ivlis' three bodyguards, come to rescue their mistress. The bodyguards immediately attacked Fafhrd and the Mouser, since they were nearest, chasing them back across the room, striking also at the thieves with their short heavy swords.

This incident further startled the thieves, yet gave them time to recover a little from their supernatural fear. Slevyas, sensing the essentials of the situation, fairly drove a group of underlings to block the alcove, galvanizing them into action with flat-edged thwacks of his sword blade. Then came chaos and pandemonium. Swords clashed and skirled together. Daggers flashed. Men were knocked down by panicky, meaningless rushes. Heads were thumped and blood flowed. Torches were swung and hurled like clubs, fell to the floor and singed the fallen, making them howl. Thief fought thief in the confusion, the notables who had sat at the table forming a unit for self-protection. Slevyas mustered a small body of followers and rushed Fafhrd. The Mouser tripped Slevyas, but the latter whirled around on his knees and ripped the black cloak with his longsword, almost skewering the small man. Fafhrd laid around him with a chair, bowling over those who opposed him; then spilled the table over on its side, the water clock crashing to splinters.

Gradually Slevyas regained control of the thieves. He knew they were at a disadvantage in the confusion, so his first move was to call them off, mustering them in two groups, one in the alcove, from which the drapes had been torn away, the other around the door. Fafhrd and the Mouser crouched behind the overturned table in the opposite angle of the room, its thick top serving as a barricade. The Mouser was somewhat surprised to find Ivlis crouching beside him.

'I saw you try to kill Slevyas,' she whispered grimly. 'In any case we are compelled to join forces.'

With Ivlis was one of the bodyguards. The other two lay dead or insensible, along with the dozen thieves who were scattered around the floor among the fallen torches which cast a faint flickering eerie light on the scene. Wounded thieves moaned, and crawled or were dragged out into the corridor by their comrades. Slevyas was shouting for mannets and more torches.

'We'll have to make a rush,' whispered Fafhrd through closed teeth with which he was knotting a bandage around a gash in his arm. And then he suddenly raised his head and sniffed. Somehow, through that confusion and the faint sweetish smell of blood had come an odor that made his flesh prickle and creep, an odor at once alien and familiar; a fainter odor, hot, dry and dusty. For a moment the thieves fell silent and Fafhrd thought he heard the sound of distant marching, the clicking of bony feet.

Then a thief cried, 'Master, Master, the skull, the skull! It moves! It clamps its teeth!'

There was a confused sound of men drawing back, then Slevyas' curse. The Mouser, peering around the tabletop, saw Slevyas kick the jeweled skull toward the center of the room.

'Fools,' he cried to his cowering followers, 'do you still believe those lies, those old-wives' whispers? Do you think dead bones can walk? I and no other am your master! And may all dead thieves be damned eternally!'

With that he brought his sword down whistling. The skull of Ohmphal shattered like an eggshell. A whining cry of fear came from the thieves. The room grew darker as though it were filling with dust.

'Now follow me!' cried Slevyas. 'Death to the intruders!'

But the thieves shrank back, darker shadows in the gloom. Fafhrd, sensing opportunity and mastering his growing fear, rushed out at Slevyas. The Mouser followed him. Fafhrd intended to kill him with his third blow. First a swipe at Slevyas' longer sword to deflect it, next a quick blow at the side to bring him off guard, then finally a back-handed slash at the head.

But Slevyas was a better swordsman than that. He parried the third cut so that it whistled harmlessly over his head, then thrust at the Northerner's throat. That thrust brought Fafhrd's supple muscles to full life; true, the blade grazed his neck, but his parry, striking Slevyas' sword near the hilt, numbed the master thief's hand. Fafhrd knew he had him then and drove him back with a mercilessly intense onslaught. He did not notice how the room was darkening. He did not wonder why Slevyas' desperate calls for assistance went unanswered; why the thieves were crowding toward the alcove, and why the wounded were crawling back into the room from the corridor. Toward that doorway he drove Slevyas, so that the man was silhouetted against it. Finally as Slevyas reached the doorway, he disarmed him with a blow which sent the thief's sword spinning, and put his own point to Slevyas' throat.

'Yield!' he cried.

Only then he realized the hateful dusty odor was thick in his nostrils, that the room was in utter silence, that from the corridor came a hot wind and the sound of marching bones clicking against the stone pavement. He saw Slevyas look over his shoulder, and he saw a fear like death in Slevyas' face. Then came a sudden intense darkness, like a puff of inky smoke. But before it came he saw bony arms clasp Slevyas' throat, and, as the Mouser dragged him back, he saw the doorway crowded with black skeletal forms whose eyes glittered green and red and sapphire. Then utter darkness, hideous with the screams of the thieves as they fought to crowd into the narrow tunnel in the alcove. And over and above the screams sounded thin high voices, like those of bats, cold as eternity. One cry he heard clearly.

'Slayer of Ohmphal, this is the vengeance of Ohmphal's brothers.'

Then Fafhrd felt the Mouser dragging him forward again, toward the corridor door. When he could see properly, he found they were fleeing through an empty Thieves' House – he, the Mouser, Ivlis, and the lone bodyguard.

Ivlis' maidservant, having barred the other end of the corridor in terror at the approaching sounds, crouched trembling in the rugs on the other side, listening in unwilling, sick horror – unable to flee – to the muffled screams and pleas and to the faint moaning sounds which bore a note of terrible triumph. The small black kitten arched its back, hair on end, and spat and hissed. Presently all sounds ceased.

Thereafter it was noted in Lankhmar that thieves were fewer. And it was rumored that the Thieves' Guild conducted strange rites at full moon, descending into deep cellars and worshipping some sort of ancient gods. It was even said that they gave these gods, whoever they were, one-third of all they stole.

But Fafhrd, drinking with the Mouser and Ivlis and a wench from Tovilyis in an upper room at the Silver Eel, complained that the fates were unfair.

'All that trouble and nothing to show for it! The gods have a lasting grudge against us.'

The Mouser smiled, reached into his pouch, and laid three rubies on the table.

'Ohmphal's fingertips,' he said briefly.

'How can you dare keep them?' questioned Ivlis. 'Are you not afraid of brown bones at midnight?' She shuddered and eyed the Mouser with a certain solicitude.

He returned her gaze and replied, though the ghost of his Ivrian rebuked him, 'My taste runs to pink bones, fittingly clothed.'

IV
THE BLEAK SHORE

'So you think a man can cheat death and outwit doom?' said the small, pale man, whose bulging forehead was shadowed by a black cowl.

The Gray Mouser, holding the dice box ready for a throw, paused and quickly looked sideways at the questioner.

'I said that a cunning man can cheat death for a long time.'

The Silver Eel bustled with pleasantly raucous excitement. Fighting men predominated and the clank of swordsmen's harness mingled with the thump of tankards, providing a deep obbligato to the shrill laughter of the women. Swaggering guardsmen elbowed the insolent bravos of the young lords. Grinning slaves bearing open wine jars dodged nimbly between. In one corner a slave girl was dancing, the jingle of her silver anklet bells inaudible in the din. Outside the small, tight-shuttered windows a dry, whistling wind from the south filled the air with dust that eddied between the cobblestones and hazed the stars. But here all was jovial confusion.

The Gray Mouser was one of a dozen at the gaming table. He was dressed all in gray – jerkin, silken shirt, and mouseskin cap – but his dark, flashing eyes and cryptic smile made him seem more alive than any of the others, save for the huge copper-haired barbarian next to him, who laughed immoderately and drank tankards of the sour wine of Lankhmar as if it were beer.

'They say you're a skilled swordsman and have come close to death many times,' continued the small, pale man in the black robe, his thin lips barely parting as he spoke the words.

But the Mouser had made his throw, and the odd dice of Lankhmar had stopped with the matching symbols of the eel and serpent uppermost, and he was raking in triangular golden coins. The barbarian answered for him.

'Yes, the gray one handles a sword daintily enough – almost as well as myself. He's also a great cheat at dice.'

'Are you, then, Fafhrd?' asked the other. 'And do you, too, truly think a man can cheat death, be he ever so cunning a cheat at dice?'

The barbarian showed his white teeth in a grin and peered puzzledly at the small, pale man whose somber appearance and manner contrasted so strangely with the revelers thronging the low-ceilinged tavern fumy with wine.

'You guess right again,' he said in a bantering tone. 'I am Fafhrd, a Northerner, ready to pit my wits against any doom.' He nudged his companion. 'Look, Mouser, what do you think of this little black-coated mouse who's sneaked in through a crack in the floor and wants to talk with you and me about death?'

The man in black did not seem to notice the jesting insult. Again his bloodless lips hardly moved, yet his words were unaffected by the surrounding clamor, and impinged on the ears of Fafhrd and the Gray Mouser with peculiar clarity.

'It is said you two came close to death in the Forbidden City of the Black Idols, and in the stone trap of Angarngi, and on the misty island in the Sea of Monsters. It is also said that you have walked with doom on the Cold Waste and through the Mazes of Klesh. But who may be sure of these things, and whether death and doom were truly near? Who knows but what you are both braggarts who have boasted once too often? Now I have heard tell that death sometimes calls to a man in a voice only he can hear. Then he must rise and leave his friends and go to whatever place death shall bid him, and there meet his doom. Has death ever called to you in such a fashion?'

Fafhrd might have laughed, but did not. The Mouser had a witty rejoinder on the tip of his tongue, but instead he heard himself saying: 'In what words might death call?'

'That would depend,' said the small man. 'He might look at two such as you and say the Bleak Shore. Nothing more than that. The Bleak Shore. And when he said it three times you would have to go.'

This time Fafhrd tried to laugh, but the laugh never came. Both of them could only meet the gaze of the small man with the white, bulging forehead, stare stupidly into his cold, cavernous eyes. Around them the tavern roared with mirth at some jest. A drunken guardsman was bellowing a song. The gamblers called impatiently to the Mouser to stake his next wager. A giggling woman in red and gold stumbled past the small, pale man, almost brushing away the black cowl that covered his pate. But he did not move. And Fafhrd and the Gray Mouser continued to stare – fascinatedly, helplessly – into his chill, black eyes, which now seemed to them twin tunnels leading into a far and evil distance. Something deeper than fear gripped them in iron paralysis. The tavern became faint and soundless, as if viewed through many thicknesses of glass. They saw only the eyes and what lay beyond the eyes, something desolate, dreary, and deadly.

'The Bleak Shore,' he repeated.

Then those in the tavern saw Fafhrd and the Gray Mouser rise and without sign or word of leave-taking walk together to the low oaken door. A guardsman cursed as the huge Northerner blindly shoved him out of the way. There were a few shouted questions and mocking comments – the Mouser had been winning – but these were quickly hushed, for all perceived something strange and alien in the manner of the two. Of the small, pale, black-robed man none took notice. They saw the door open. They heard the dry moaning of the wind and a hollow flapping that probably came from the awnings. They saw an eddy of dust swirl up from the threshold. Then the door was closed and Fafhrd and the Mouser were gone.

No one saw them on their way to the great stone docks that bank the east side of the River Hlal from one end of Lankhmar to the other. No one saw Fafhrd's north-rigged, red-sailed sloop cast off and slip out into the current that slides down to the squally Inner Sea. The night was dark and the dust kept men indoors. But the next day they were gone, and the ship with them, and its Mingol crew of four – these being slave prisoners, sworn to life service, whom Fafhrd and the Mouser had brought back from an otherwise unsuccessful foray against the Forbidden City of the Black Idols.

About a fortnight later a tale came back to Lankhmar from Earth's End, the little harbor town that lies farthest of all towns to the west, on the very margin of the shipless Outer Sea; a tale of how a north-rigged sloop had come into port to take on an unusually large amount of food and water – unusually large because there were only six in the crew: a sullen, white-skinned Northern barbarian; an unsmiling little man in gray; and four squat, stolid, black-haired Mingols. Afterward the sloop had sailed straight into the sunset. The people of Earth's End had watched the red sail until nightfall, shaking their heads at its audacious progress. When this tale was repeated in Lankhmar, there were others who shook their heads, and some who spoke significantly of the peculiar behavior of the two companions on the night of their departure. And as the weeks dragged on into months and the months slowly succeeded one another, there were many who talked of Fafhrd and the Gray Mouser as two dead men.

Then Ourph the Mingol appeared and told his curious story to the dockmen of Lankhmar. There was some difference of opinion as to the validity of the story, for although Ourph spoke the soft language of Lankhmar moderately well, he was an outsider, and, after he was gone, no one could prove that he was or was not one of the four Mingols who had sailed with the north-rigged sloop. Moreover, his story did not answer several puzzling questions, which is one of the reasons that many thought it untrue.

'They were mad,' said Ourph, 'or else under a curse, those two men, the great one and the small one. I suspected it when they spared our lives under the very walls of the Forbidden City. I knew it for certain when they sailed west and west and west, never reefing, never changing course, always keeping the star of the ice fields on our right hand. They talked little, they slept little, they laughed not at all. Ola, they were cursed! As for us four – Teevs, Larlt, Ouwenyis, and I – we were ignored but not abused. We had our amulets to keep off evil magics. We were sworn slaves to the death. We were men of the Forbidden City. We made no mutiny.

'For many days we sailed. The sea was stormless and empty

around us, and small, very small; it looked as if it bent down out of sight to the north and the south and the awful west, as if the sea ended an hour's sail from where we were. And then it began to look that way to the east, too. But the great Northerner's hand rested on the steering oar like a curse, and the small gray one's hand was as firm. We four sat mostly in the bow, for there was little enough sail-tending, and diced our destinies at night and morning, and gambled for our amulets and clothes – we would have played for our hides and bones, were we not slaves.

'To keep track of the days, I tied a cord around my right thumb and moved it over a finger each day until it passed from right little finger to left little finger and came to my left thumb. Then I put it on Teev's right thumb. When it came to his left thumb he gave it to Larlt. So we numbered the days and knew them. And each day the sky became emptier and the sea smaller, until it seemed that the end of the sea was but a bowshot away from our stem and sides and stern. Teevs said that we were upon an enchanted patch of water that was being drawn through the air toward the red star that is Hell. Surely Teevs may have been right. There cannot be so much water to the west. I have crossed the Inner Sea and the Sea of Monsters – and I say so.

'It was when the cord was around Larlt's left ring finger that the great storm came at us from the southwest. For three days it blew stronger and stronger, smiting the water into great seething waves; crags and gullies piled mast-high with foam. No other men have seen such waves nor should see them; they are not churned for us or for our oceans. Then I had further proof that our masters were under a curse. They took no notice of the storm; they let it reef their sails for them. They took no notice when Teevs was washed overboard, when we were half swamped and filled to the gunwales with spume, our bailing buckets foaming like tankards of beer. They stood in the stern, both braced against the steering oar, both drenched by the following waves, staring straight ahead, seeming to hold converse with creatures that only the bewitched can hear. Ola! They were accursed! Some evil demon was preserving their lives for a dark reason of his own. How else came we safe through the storm?

'For when the cord was on Larlt's left thumb, the towering

waves and briny foam gave way to a great black sea swell that the whistling wind rippled but did not whiten. When the dawn came and we first saw it, Ouwenyis cried out that we were riding by magics upon a sea of black sand; and Larlt averred that we were fallen during the storm into the ocean of sulfurous oil that some say lies under the earth – for Larlt has seen the black, bubbling lakes of the Far East; and I remembered what Teevs had said and wondered if our patch of water had not been carried through the thin air and plunged into a wholly different sea on a wholly different world. But the small gray one heard our talk and dipped a bucket over the side and soused us with it, so that we knew our hull was still in water and that the water was salt – wherever that water might be.

'And then he bid us patch the sails and make the sloop shipshape. By midday we were flying west at a speed even greater than we had made during the storm, but so long were the swells and so swift did they move with us that we could only climb five or six in a whole day. By the Black Idols, but they were long!

'And so the cord moved across Ouwenyis' fingers. But the clouds were as leaden dark above us as was the strange sea heavy around our hull, and we knew not if the light that came through them was that of the sun or of some wizard moon, and when we caught sight of the stars they seemed strange. And still the white hand of the Northerner lay heavy on the steering oar, and still he and the gray one stared straight ahead. But on the third day of our flight across that black expanse the Northerner broke silence. A mirthless, terrible smile twisted his lips, and I heard him mutter "the Bleak Shore". Nothing more than that. The gray one nodded, as if there were some portentous magic in the words. Four times I heard the words pass the Northerner's lips, so that they were imprinted on my memory.

'The days grew darker and colder, and the clouds slid lower and lower, threatening, like the roof of a great cavern. And when the cord was on Ouwenyis' pointing finger we saw a leaden and motionless extent ahead of us, looking like the swells, but rising above them, and we knew that we were come to the Bleak Shore.

'Higher and higher that shore rose, until we could distinguish the towering basalt crags, rounded like the sea swell, studded here and there with gray boulders, whitened in spots as if by the droppings of gigantic birds – yet we saw no birds, large or small. Above the cliffs were dark clouds, and below them was a strip of pale sand, nothing more. Then the Northerner bent the steering oar and sent us straight in, as though he intended our destruction; but at the last moment he passed us at mast length by a rounded reef that hardly rose above the crest of the swell and found us harbor room. We sent the anchor over and rode safe.

'Then the Northerner and the gray one, moving like men in a dream, accoutered themselves, a shirt of light chain mail and a rounded, uncrested helmet for each – both helmets and shirts white with salt from the foam and spray of the storm. And they bound their swords to their sides, and wrapped great cloaks about them, and took a little food and a little water, and bade us unship the small boat. And I rowed them ashore and they stepped out onto the beach and walked toward the cliffs. Then, although I was much frightened, I cried out after them, "Where are you going? Shall we follow? What shall we do?" For several moments there was no reply. Then, without turning his head, the gray one answered, his voice a low, hoarse, yet far-carrying whisper. And he said, "Do not follow. We are dead men. Go back if you can."

'And I shuddered and bowed my head to his words and rowed out to the ship. Ouwenyis and Larlt and I watched them climb the high, rounded crags. The two figures grew smaller and smaller, until the Northerner was no more than a tiny, slim beetle and his gray companion almost invisible, save when they crossed a whitened space. Then a wind came down from the crags and blew the swell away from the shore, and we knew we could make sail. But we stayed – for were we not sworn slaves? And am I not a Mingol?

'As evening darkened, the wind blew stronger, and our desire to depart – if only to drown in the unknown sea – became greater. For we did not like the strangely rounded basalt crags of the Bleak Shore; we did not like it that we saw no gulls or hawks or birds of any kind in the leaden air, no seaweed on the beach. And we all three began to catch glimpses of something shimmering at the summit of the cliffs. Yet it was not until the third hour of night that we upped anchor and left the Bleak Shore behind.

'There was another great storm after we were out several days, and perhaps it hurled us back into the seas we know. Ouwenyis was washed overboard and Larlt went mad from thirst, and toward the end I knew not myself what was happening. Only I was cast up on the southern coast near Quarmall and, after many difficulties, am come here to Lankhmar. But my dreams are haunted by those black cliffs and by visions of the whitening bones of my masters, and their grinning skulls staring empty-eyed at something strange and deadly.'

Unconscious of the fatigue that stiffened his muscles, the Gray Mouser wormed his way past the last boulder, finding shallow handholds and footholds at the juncture of the granite and black basalt, and finally stood erect on the top of the rounded crags that walled the Bleak Shore. He was aware that Fafhrd stood at his side, a vague, hulking figure in whitened chain-mail vest and helmet. But he saw Fafhrd vaguely, as if through many thicknesses of glass. The only things he saw clearly – and it seemed he had been looking at them for an eternity – were two cavernous, tunnel-like black eyes, and beyond them something desolate and deadly, which had once been across the Outer Sea but was now close at hand. So it had been, ever since he had risen from the gaming table in the low-ceilinged tavern in Lankhmar. Vaguely he remembered the staring people of Earth's End, the foam, and fury of the storm, the curve of the black sea swell, and the look of terror on the face of Ourph the Mingol; these memories, too, came to him as if through many thicknesses of glass. Dimly he realized that he and his companion were under a curse, and that they were now come to the source of that curse.

For the flat landscape that spread out before them was without sign of life. In front of them the basalt dipped down to form a large hollow of black sand – tiny particles of iron ore. In the sand were half embedded more than two score of what seemed to the Gray Mouser to be inky-black, oval boulders of various sizes. But they were too perfectly rounded, too regular in form to be boulders, and slowly it was borne in on the Mouser's consciousness that they were not boulders, but monstrous black eggs, a few small, some so large that a man could not have clasped his arms around them, one big as a tent.

Scattered over the sand were bones, large and small. The Mouser recognized the tusked skull of a boar, and two smaller ones – wolves. There was the skeleton of some great predatory cat. Beside it lay the bones of a horse, and beyond them the rib case of a man or ape. The bones lay all around the huge black eggs – a whitely gleaming circle.

From somewhere a toneless voice sounded, thin but clear, in accents of command, saying: 'For warriors, a warrior's doom.'

The Mouser knew the voice, for it had been echoing in his ears for weeks, ever since it had first come from the lips of a pale little man with a bulging forehead, wearing a black robe and sitting near him in a tavern in Lankhmar. And a more whispering voice came to him from within, saying. *He seeks always to repeat past experience, which has always been in his favor.*

Then he saw that what lay before him was not utterly lifeless. Movement of a sort had come to the Bleak Shore. A crack had appeared in one of the great black eggs, and then in another, and the cracks were branching, widening as bits of shell fell to the black, sandy floor.

The Mouser knew that this was happening in answer to the first voice, the thin one. He knew this was the end to which the thin voice had called him across the Outer Sea. Powerless to move farther, he dully watched the slow progress of this monstrous birth. Under the darkening leaden sky he watched twin deaths hatching out for him and his companion.

The first hint of their nature came in the form of a long, swordlike claw which struck out through a crack, widening it farther. Fragments of shell fell more swiftly.

The two creatures which emerged in the gathering dusk held enormity even for the Mouser's drugged mind. Shambling things, erect like men but taller, with reptilian heads boned and crested like helmets, feet clawed like a lizard's, shoulders topped with bony spikes, forelimbs each terminating in a single yard-

266

long claw. In the semidarkness they seemed like hideous caricatures of fighting men, armored and bearing swords. Dusk did not hide the yellow of their blinking eyes.

Then the voice called again: 'For warriors, a warrior's doom.'

At those words the bonds of paralysis dropped from the Mouser. For an instant he thought he was waking from a dream. But then he saw the new-hatched creatures racing toward them, a shrill, eager screeching issuing from their long muzzles. From beside him he heard a quick, rasping sound as Fafhrd's sword whipped from its scabbard. Then the Mouser drew his own blade, and a moment later it crashed against a steel-like claw which thrust at his throat. Simultaneously, Fafhrd parried a like blow from the other monster.

What followed was nightmare. Claws that were swords slashed and stabbed. Not so swiftly that they could not be parried, though there were four against two. Counter-thrusts glanced off impenetrable bony armor. Both creatures suddenly wheeled, striking at the Mouser. Fafhrd drove in from the side, saving him. Slowly the two companions were driven back toward where the crag sheered off. The beasts seemed tireless, creatures of bone and metal rather than flesh. The Mouser foresaw the end. He and Fafhrd might hold them off for a while longer, but eventually fatigue would supervene; their parries would become slower, weaker; the beasts would have them.

As if in anticipation of this, the Mouser felt a claw nick his wrist. It was then that he remembered the dark, cavernous eyes that had drawn them across the Outer Sea, the voice that had loosed doom upon them. He was gripped with a strange, mad rage – not against the beasts but their master. He seemed to see the black, dead eyes staring at him from the black sand. Then he lost control of his actions. When the two monsters next attempted a double attack on Fafhrd he did not turn to help, but instead dodged past and dashed down into the hollow, toward the embedded eggs.

Left to face the monsters alone. Fafhrd fought like a madman himself, his great sword whistling as his last resources of energy jolted his muscles. He hardly noticed when one of the beasts turned back to pursue his comrade.

The Mouser stood among the eggs, facing one of a glossier hue and smaller than most. Vindictively he brought his sword crashing down upon it. The blow numbed his hand, but the egg shattered.

Then the Mouser knew the source of the evil of the Bleak Shore, lying here and sending its spirit abroad, lying here and calling men to doom. Behind him he heard the scrabbling steps and eager screeching of the monster chosen for his destruction. But he did not turn. Instead, he raised his sword and brought it down whirring on the half-embryonic creature gloating in secret over the creatures he had called to death, down on the bulging forehead of the small pale man with the thin lips.

Then he waited for the finishing blow of the claw. It did not come. Turning, he saw the monster sprawled on the black sand. Around him, the deadly eggs were crumbling to dust. Silhouetted against the lesser darkness of the sky, he saw Fafhrd stumbling toward him, sobbing out vague words of relief and wonder in a deep, throaty voice. Death was gone from the Bleak Shore, the curse cut off at the root. From out of the night sounded the exultant cry of a sea bird, and Fafhrd and the Mouser thought of the long, trackless road leading back to Lankhmar.

V
THE HOWLING TOWER

The sound was not loud, yet it seemed to fill the whole vast, darkening plain, and the palely luminous, hollow sky: a wailing and howling, so faint and monotonous that it might have been inaudible save for the pulsing rise and fall; an ancient, ominous sound that was somehow in harmony with the wild, sparsely vegetated landscape and the barbaric garb of the three men who sheltered in a little dip in the ground, lying close to a dying fire.

'Wolves, perhaps,' Fafhrd said. 'I have heard them howl that way on the Cold Waste when they hunted me down. But a whole ocean sunders us from the Cold Waste and there's a difference between the sounds, Gray Mouser.'

The Mouser pulled his gray woolen cloak closer around him. Then he and Fafhrd looked at the third man, who had not spoken. The third man was meanly clad, and his cloak was ragged and the scabbard of his shortsword was frayed. With surprise, they saw that his eyes stared, white circled, from his pinched, leathery face and that he trembled.

'You've been over these plains many times before,' Fafhrd said to him, speaking the guttural language of the guide. 'That's why we've asked you to show us the way. You must know this country well.' The last words pointed the question.

The guide gulped, nodded jerkily. 'I've heard it before, not so loud,' he said in a quick, vague voice. 'Not at this time of year. Men have been known to vanish. There are stories. They say men hear it in their dreams and are lured away – not a good sound.'

'No wolf's a good wolf,' rumbled Fafhrd amusedly.

It was still light enough for the Mouser to catch the obstinate guarded look on the guide's face as he went on talking.

'I never saw a wolf in these parts, nor spoke with a man who killed one.' He paused, then rambled off abstractedly. 'They tell of an old tower somewhere out on the plains. They say the sound is strongest there. I have not seen it. They say—'

Abruptly he stopped. He was not trembling now, seemed withdrawn into himself. The Mouser prodded him with a few tempting questions, but the answers were little more than mouth noises, neither affirmative nor negative.

The fire glowed through white ashes, died. A little wind rustled the scant grasses. The sound had ceased now, or else it had sunk so deeply into their minds that it was no longer audible. The Mouser, peering sleepily over the humped horizon of Fafhrd's great cloaked body, turned his thoughts to faroff, many-taverned Lankhmar, leagues and leagues away across alien lands and a whole uncharted ocean. The limitless darkness pressed down.

Next morning the guide was gone. Fafhrd laughed and made light of the occurrence as he stood stretching and snuffing the cool, clear air.

'Foh! I could tell these plains were not to his liking, for all his talk of having crossed them seven times. A bundle of super-stitious fears! You saw how he quaked when the little wolves began to howl. My word on it, he's run back to his friends we left at the last water.'

The Mouser, fruitlessly scanning the empty horizon, nodded without conviction. He felt through his pouch.

'Well, at least he's not robbed us – except for the two gold pieces we gave him to bind the bargain.'

Fafhrd's laughter pealed and he thumped the Mouser be-tween the shoulder blades. The Mouser caught him by the wrist, threw him with a twist and a roll, and they wrestled on the ground until the Mouser was pinned.

'Come on,' grinned Fafhrd, springing up. 'It won't be the first time we've traveled strange country alone.'

They tramped far that day. The springiness of the Mouser's wiry body enabled him to keep up with Fafhrd's long strides. Toward evening a whirring arrow from Fafhrd's bow brought down a sort of small antelope with delicately ridged horns. A little earlier they had found an unsullied waterhole and filled their skin bags. When the late summer sunset came, they made camp and munched carefully broiled lion and crisped bits of fat.

The Mouser sucked his lips and fingers clean, then strolled to the top of a nearby hummock to survey the line of their next day's march. The haze that had curtailed vision during the afternoon was gone now, and he could peer far over the rolling, swelling grasslands through the cool, tangy air. At that moment the road to Lankhmar did not seem so long, or so weary. Then his sharp eyes spied an irregularity in the horizon toward which they were tending. Too distinct for trees, too evenly shaped for rock; and he had seen no trees or rock in this country. It stood out sharp and tiny against the pale sky. No, it was built by man; a tower of some sort.

At that moment the sound returned. It seemed to come from everywhere at once; as if the sky itself were wailing faintly, as if the wide, solid ground were baying mournfully. It was louder this time, and there was in it a strange confusion of sadness and threat, grief and menace.

Fafhrd jumped to his feet and waved his arms strongly, and the Mouser heard him bellow out in a great, jovial voice, 'Come, little wolves, come and share our fire and singe your cold noses. I will send my bronze-beaked birds winging to welcome you, and my friend will show you how a slung stone can buzz like a bee. We will teach you the mysteries of sword and axe. Come, little wolves, and be guests of Fafhrd and the Gray Mouser! Come, little wolves – or biggest of them all!'

The huge laugh with which he ended this challenge drowned out the alien sound and it seemed slow in reasserting itself, as though laughter were a stronger thing. The Mouser felt cheered and it was with a light heart that he told Fafhrd of what he had seen, and reminded him of what the guide had said about the noise and the tower.

Fafhrd only laughed again and guessed, 'Perhaps the sad, furry ones have a den there. We shall find out tomorrow, since we go that way. I would like to kill a wolf.'

The big man was in a jolly mood and would not talk with the Mouser about serious or melancholy things. Instead, he sang drinking songs and repeated old tavern jokes, chuckling hugely and claiming that they made him feel as drunk as wine. He kept up such an incessant clamor that the Mouser could not tell whether the strange howling had ceased, though he rather imagined he heard it once or twice. Certainly it was gone by the time they wrapped themselves up for sleep in the wraithlike starlight.

Next morning Fafhrd was gone. Even before the Mouser had halooed for him and scanned the nearby terrain, he knew that his foolish, self-ridiculed fears had become certainties. He could still see the tower, although in the flat, yellow light of morning it seemed to have receded, as though it were seeking to evade him. He even fancied he saw a tiny moving figure nearer to the tower than to him. That, he knew, was only imagination. The distance was too great. Nevertheless, he wasted little time in chewing and swallowing some cold meat, which still had a savory taste, in wrapping up some more for his pouch, and in taking a gulp of water. Then he set out at a long, springy lope, a pace he knew he could hold for hours.

At the bottom of the next swell in the plain he found slightly softer ground, cast up and down it for Fafhrd's footprints and found them. They were wide-spaced, made by a man running.

Toward midday he found a waterhole, lay down to drink and rest a little. A short way back he had again seen Fafhrd's prints. Now he noted another set in the soft earth; not Fafhrd's, but roughly parallel to his. They were at least a day older, wide-spaced, too, but a little wobbly. From their size and shape they might very well have been made by the guide's sandals; the middle of the print showed faintly the mark of thongs such as he had worn about the instep.

The Mouser loped doggedly on. His pouch, rolled cloak, water bag, and weapons were beginning to feel a burden. The tower was appreciably closer, although the sun haze masked any details. He calculated he had covered almost half the distance.

The slight successive swells in the prairieland seemed as endless as those in a dream. He noticed them not so much by sight as by the infinitesimal hindrance and easing they gave his lope. The little low clumps of bush and brush by which he measured his progress were all the same. The infrequent gullies were no wider than could be taken in a stride. Once a coiled greenish serpent raised its flat head from the rock on which it was sunning and observed his passing. Occasionally grass-hoppers whirred out of his path. He ran with his feet close to the ground to conserve energy, yet there was a strong, forward leap to his stride, for he was used to matching that of a taller man. His nostrils flared wide, sucking and expelling air. The wide mouth was set. There was a grim, fixed look to the black eyes above the browned cheeks. He knew that even at his best he would be hard put to equal the speed in Fafhrd's rangy, long-muscled frame.

Clouds sailed in from the north, casting great, hurrying shadows over the landscape, finally blotting out the sun altogether. He could see the tower better now. It was of a dark color, with black specks that might be small windows.

It was while he was pausing atop a rise for a breathing spell that the sound re-commenced, taking him unaware, sending a shiver over his flesh. It might have been the low clouds that gave it greater power and an eerie, echoing quality. It might have been his being alone that made it seem less sorrowful and more menacing. But it was undeniably louder, and its rhythmic swells came like great gusts of wind.

The Mouser had counted on reaching the tower by sunset. But the early appearance of the sound upset his calculations and did not bode well for Fafhrd. His judgment told him he could cover the rest of the distance at something like top speed. Instantly he came to a decision. He tossed his big pouch, waterskin, bundled cloak, sword, and harness into a clump of bushes; kept only his light inner jerkin, long dagger, and sling. Thus lightened, he spurted ahead, feet flying. The low clouds darkened. A few drops of rain spattered. He kept his eyes on the ground, watching for inequalities and slippery spots. The sound seemed to intensify and gain new unearthliness of timbre with every bounding stride he took forward.

Away from the tower the plain had been empty and vast, but here it was desolate. The sagging or tumbled wooden out-buildings, the domestic grains and herbs run wild and dying out, the lines of stunted and toppled trees, the suggestion of fences and paths and ruts – all combined to give the impression that human life had once been here but had long since departed. Only the great stone tower, with its obstinate solidity, and with sound pouring from it or seeming to pour from it, was alive.

The Mouser, pretty well winded though not shaky, now changed his course and ran in an oblique direction to take advantage of the cover provided by a thin line of trees and wind-blown scrub. Such caution was second nature with him. All his instincts clamored against the possibility of meeting a wolf or hound pack on open ground.

He had worked his way past and partway around the tower before he came to the conclusion that there was no line of concealment leading all the way up to the base. It stood a little aloof from the ruins around it.

The Mouser paused in the shelter afforded by a weather-silvered, buckled outbuilding; automatically searched about until he found a couple of small stones whose weight suited his sling. His sturdy chest still worked like a bellows, drinking air. Then he peered around a corner at the tower and stood there crouched a little, frowning.

It was not as high as he had thought; five stories or perhaps six. The narrow windows were irregularly placed, and did not give any clear idea of inner configuration. The stones were large and rudely hewn; seemed firmly set, save for those of the battlement, which had shifted somewhat. Almost facing him was the dark, uninformative rectangle of a doorway.

There was no rushing such a place, was the Mouser's thought; no sense in rushing a place that had no sign of defenders. There was no way of getting at it unseen; a watcher on the battlements would have noted his approach long ago. One could only walk up to it, tensely alert for unexpected attacks. And so the Mouser did that.

Before he had covered half the distance his sinews were taut and straining. He was mortally certain that he was being watched by something more than unfriendly. A day's running had made him a little light-headed, and his senses were abnormally clear. Against the unending hypnotic background of the howling he heard the splatters of the separate raindrops, not yet become a shower. He noted the size and shape of each dark stone around the darker doorway. He smelled the characteristic odor of stone, wood, soil, but yet no heavy animal smell. For the thousandth time he tried to picture some possible source for the sound. A dozen hound packs in a cavern underground? That was close, but not close enough. Something eluded him. And now the dark walls were very near, and he strained his eyes to penetrate the gloom of the doorway.

The remote grating sound might not have been enough of a warning, for he was almost in a trance. It may have been the sudden, very slight increase of darkness over his head that twanged the taut bowstrings of his muscles and sent him lunging with cat-like rapidity into the tower – instinctively, without pausing to glance up. Certainly he had not an instant to spare, for he felt an unyielding surface graze his escaping body and flick his heels. A spurt of wind rushed past him from behind, and the jar of a mighty impact staggered him. He spun around to see a great square of stone half obscuring the doorway. A few moments before it had formed part of the battlement.

Looking at it as it lay there denting the ground, he grinned for the first time that day and almost laughed in relief.

The silence was profound, startling. It occurred to the Mouser that the howling had ceased utterly. He glanced around the barren, circular interior, then started up the curving stone stair that hugged the wall. His grin was dangerous now, businesslike. On the first level above he found Fafhrd and – after a fashion – the guide. But he found a puzzle, too.

Like that below, the room occupied the full circumference of the tower. Light from the scattered, slit-like windows dimly revealed the chests lining the walls and the dried herbs and desiccated birds, small mammals, and reptiles hanging from the ceiling, suggesting an apothecary's shop. There was litter everywhere, but it was a tidy litter, seeming to have a tortuously logical arrangement all its own. On a table was a hodge-podge of stoppered bottles and jars, mortars and pestles, odd instruments of horn, glass, and bone, and a brazier in which charcoal smoldered. There was also a plate of gnawed bones and beside it a brass-bound book of parchment, spread open by a dagger set across the pages.

Fafhrd lay face-up on a bed of skins laced to a low wooden framework. He was pale and breathed heavily, looked as if he had been drugged. He did not respond when the Mouser shook him gently and whispered his name, then shook him hard and shouted it. But the thing that baffled the Mouser was the multitude of linen bandages wound around Fafhrd's limbs and chest and throat, for they were unstained and, when he parted them, there were no wounds beneath. They were obviously not bonds.

And lying beside Fafhrd, so close that his big hand touched the hilt, was Fafhrd's great sword, unsheathed.

It was only then that the Mouser saw the guide, huddled in a dark corner behind the couch. He was similarly bandaged. But the bandages were stiff with rusty stains, and it was easy to see that he was dead.

The Mouser tried again to wake Fafhrd, but the big man's face stayed a marble mask. The Mouser did not feel that Fafhrd was actually there, and the feeling frightened and angered him.

As he stood nervously puzzling he became aware of slow steps descending the stone stair. Slowly they circled the tower. The sound of heavy breathing was heard, coming in regular spaced gasps. The Mouser crouched behind the tables, his eyes glued on the black hole in the ceiling through which the stair vanished.

The man who emerged was old and small and bent, dressed in garments as tattered and uncouth and musty-looking as the contents of the room. He was partly bald, with a matted tangle of gray hair around his large ears. When the Mouser sprang up and menaced him with a drawn dagger he did not attempt to flee, but went into what seemed an ecstasy of fear – trembling, babbling throaty sounds, and darting his arms about meaninglessly.

The Mouser thrust a stubby candle into the brazier, held it to the old man's face. He had never seen eyes so wide with terror – they jutted out like little white balls – nor lips so thin and unfeelingly cruel.

The first intelligible words that issued from the lips were

hoarse and choked; the voice of a man who has not spoken for a long time.

'You are dead. You are dead!' he cackled at the Mouser, pointing a shaky finger. 'You should not be here. I killed you. Why else have I kept the great stone cunningly balanced, so that a touch would send it over? I knew you did not come because the sound lured you. You came to hurt me and to help your friend. So I killed you. I saw the stone fall. I saw you under the stone. You could not have escaped it. You are dead.'

And he tottered toward the Mouser, brushing at him as though he could dissipate the Mouser like smoke. But when his hands touched solid flesh he squealed and stumbled away.

The Mouser followed him, moving his knife suggestively. 'You are right as to why I came,' he said. 'Give me back my friend. Rouse him.'

To his surprise, the old man did not cringe, but abruptly stood his ground. The look of terror in the unblinking eyes underwent a subtle change. The terror was still there, but there was something more. Bewilderment vanished and something else took its place. He walked past the Mouser and sat down on a stool by the table.

'I am not much afraid of you,' he muttered, looking sideways. 'But there are those of whom I am very much afraid. And I fear you only because you will try to hinder me from protecting myself against them or taking the measures I know I must take.' He became plaintive. 'You must not hinder me. You must not.'

The Mouser frowned. The ghastly look of terror – and something more – that warped the old man's face seemed a permanent thing, and the strange words he spoke did not sound like lies.

'Nevertheless, you must rouse my friend.'

The old man did not answer this. Instead, after one quick glance at the Mouser, he stared vacantly at the wall, shaking his head, and began to talk.

'I do not fear you. Yet I know the depths of fear. You do not. Have you lived alone with *that sound* for years on years, knowing what it meant? I have.

'Fear was born into me. It was in my mother's bones and

blood. And in my father's and in my brothers'. There was too much magic and loneliness in this, our home, and in my people. When I was a child they all feared and hated me – even the slaves and the great hounds that before me slavered and growled and snapped.

'But my fears were stronger than theirs, for did they not die one by one in such a way that no suspicion fell upon me until the end? I knew it was one against many, and I took no chances. When it began, they always thought I would be the next to go!' He cackled at this. 'They thought I was small and weak and foolish. But did not my brothers die as if strangled by their own hands? Did not my mother sicken and languish? Did not my father give a great cry and leap from the tower's top?

'The hounds were the last to go. They hated me most – even more than my father hated me – and the smallest of them could have torn out my throat. They were hungry because there was no one left to feed them. But I lured them into the deep cellar, pretending to flee from them; and when they were all inside I slipped out and barred the door. For many a night thereafter they bayed and howled at me, but I knew I was safe. Gradually the baying grew less and less as they killed each other, but the survivors gained new life from the bodies of the slain. They lasted a long time. Eventually there was only one single thin voice left to howl vengefully at me. Each night I went to sleep, telling myself, "Tomorrow there will be silence." But each morning I was awakened by the cry. Then I forced myself to take a torch and go down and peer through the wicket in the door of the cellar. But though I watched for a long time there was no movement, save that of the flickering shadows, and I saw nothing but white bones and tatters of skin. And I told myself that the sound would soon go away.'

The old man's thin lips were twisted into a pitiful and miserable expression that sent a chill over the Mouser.

'But the sound lived on, and after a long while it began to grow louder again. Then I knew that my cunning had been in vain. I had killed their bodies, but not their ghosts, and soon they would gain enough power to return and slay me, as they had always intended. So I studied more carefully my father's books of magic and sought to destroy their ghosts utterly or to curse them to such faroff places that they could never reach me. For a while I seemed to be succeeding, but the scales turned and they began to get the better of me. Closer and closer they came, and sometimes I seemed to catch my father's and brothers' voices, almost lost among the howling.

'It was on a night when they must have been very close that an exhausted traveller came running to the tower. There was a strange look in his eyes, and I thanked the beneficent god who had sent him to my door, for I knew what I must do. I gave him food and drink, and in his drink I mingled a liquid that enforced sleep and sent his naked ghost winging out of his body. *They* must have captured and torn it, for presently the man bled and died. But it satisfied them somewhat, for their howling went a long way off, and it was a long time before it began to creep back. Thereafter the gods were good and always sent me a guest before the sound came too close. I learned to bandage those I drugged so that they would last longer, and their deaths would satisfy the howling ones more fully.'

The old man paused then, and shook his head queerly and made a vague, reproachful, clucking noise with his tongue.

'But what troubles me now,' he said, 'is that they have become greedier, or perhaps they have seen through my cunning. For they are less easy to satisfy, and press at me closely and never go far away. Sometimes I wake in the night, hearing them snuffing about, and feeling their muzzles at my throat. I must have more men to fight them for me. I must. He' – pointing at the stiff body of the guide – 'was nothing to them. They took no more notice of him than a dry bone. That one' – his finger wavered over to Fafhrd – 'is big and strong. He should hold them back for a long time.'

It was dark outside now, and the only light came from the guttering candle. The Mouser glared at the old man where he sat perched on the stool like some ungainly plucked fowl. Then he looked to where Fafhrd lay, watched the great chest rise and fall, saw the strong, pallid jaw jutting up over high wrappings. And at that, a terrible anger and an unnerving, boundless irritation took hold of him and he hurled himself upon the old man.

But at the instant he started his long dagger on the downward stroke the sound gushed back. It seemed to overflow from some pit of darkness, and to inundate the tower and plain so that the walls vibrated and dust puffed out from the dead things hanging from the ceiling.

The Mouser stopped the blade a hand's breadth from the throat of the old man, whose head, twisted back, jiggled in terror. For the return of the sound forcibly set the question: Could anyone but the old man save Fafhrd now? The Mouser wavered between alternatives, pushed the old man away, knelt by Fafhrd's side, shook him, spoke to him. There was no response. Then he heard the voice of the old man. It was shaky and half drowned by the sound, but it carried an almost gloating note of confidence.

'Your friend's body is poised on the brink of life. If you handle it roughly it may overbalance. If you strip off the bandages he will only die the quicker. You cannot help him.' Then, reading the Mouser's question, 'No, there is no antidote.' Then hastily, as if he feared to take away all hope, 'But he will not be defenseless against them. He is strong. His ghost may be strong, too. He may be able to weary them out. If he lives until midnight he may return.'

The Mouser turned and looked up at him. Again the old man seemed to read something in the Mouser's merciless eyes, for he said, 'My death by your hand will not satisfy those who howl. If you kill me, you will not save your friend, but doom him. Being cheated of my ghost, they will rend his utterly.'

The wizened body trembled in an ecstasy of excitement and terror. The hands fluttered. The head bobbed back and forth, as if with the palsy. It was hard to read anything in that twitching, saucer-eyed face. The Mouser slowly got to his feet.

'Perhaps not,' said the Mouser. 'Perhaps as you say, your death will doom him.' He spoke slowly and in a loud, measured tone. 'Nevertheless, I shall take the chance of killing you right now unless you suggest something better.'

'Wait,' said the old man, pushing at the Mouser's dagger and drawing a pricked hand away. 'Wait. There is a way you could help him. Somewhere out there' – he made a sweeping, upward gesture with his hand – 'your friend's ghost is battling them. I have more of the drug left. I will give you some. Then you can fight them side by side. Together you may defeat them. But you must be quick. Look! Even now they are at him!'

The old man pointed at Fafhrd. The bandage on the barbarian's left arm was no longer unstained. There was a growing splotch of red on the left wrist – the very place where a hound might take hold. Watching it, the Mouser felt his insides grow sick and cold. The old man was pushing something into his hand. 'Drink this. Drink this now,' he was saying.

The Mouser looked down. It was a small glass vial. The deep purple of the liquid corresponded with the hue of a dried trickle he had seen at the corner of Fafhrd's mouth. Like a man bewitched, he plucked out the stopper, raised it slowly to his lips, paused.

'Swiftly! Swiftly!' urged the old man, almost dancing with impatience. 'About half is enough to take you to your friend. The time is short. Drink! Drink!'

But the Mouser did not. Struck by a sudden, new thought, he eyed the old man over his upraised hand. And the old man must have instantly read the import of that thought, for he snatched up the dagger lying on the book and lunged at the Mouser with unexpected rapidity. Almost the thrust went home, but the Mouser recovered his wits and struck sideways with his free fist at the old man's hand so that the dagger clattered across the floor. Then, with a rapid, careful movement, the Mouser set the vial on the table. The old man darted after him, snatching at it, seeking to upset it, but the Mouser's iron grip closed on his wrists. He was forced to the floor, his arms pinioned, his head pushed back.

'Yes,' said the Mouser, 'I shall drink. Have no fear on that score. But you shall drink, too.'

The old man gave a strangled scream and struggled convulsively. 'No! No!' he cried. 'Kill me! Kill me with your knife! But not the drink! Not the drink!' The Mouser, kneeling on his arms to pinion them, pried at his jaw. Suddenly he became quiet and stared up, a peculiar lucidity in his white-circled, pinpoint-pupiled eyes. 'It's no use. I sought to trick you,' he said. 'I gave the last of the drug to your friend. The stuff you hold is poison. We shall both die miserably, and your friend will be irrevocably doomed.'

But when he saw that the Mouser did not heed this, he began once more to struggle like a maniac. The Mouser was inexorable. Although the base of his thumb was bitten deep, he forced the old man's jaws apart, held his nose and poured the thick purple liquor down. The face of the old man grew red and the veins stood out. When the gulp came it was like a death rattle. Then the Mouser drank off the rest – it was salty like blood and had a sickeningly sweet odor – and waited.

He was torn with revulsion at what he had done. Never had he inflicted such terror on man or woman before. He would much rather have killed. The look on the old man's face was grotesquely similar to that of a child under torture. Only that poor aged wretch, thought the Mouser, knew the full meaning of the howling that even now dinned menacingly in their ears. The Mouser almost let him reach the dagger toward which he was weakly squirming. But he thought of Fafhrd and gripped the old man tight.

Gradually the room filled with haze and began to swing and slowly spin. The Mouser grew dizzy. It was as if the sound were dissolving the walls. Something was wrenching at his body and prying at his mind. Then came utter blackness, whirled and shaken by a pandemonium of howling.

But there was no sound at all on the vast alien plain to which the blackness suddenly gave way. Only sight and a sense of great cold. A cloudless, sourceless moonlight revealed endless sweeps of smooth black rock and sharply edged the featureless horizon.

He was conscious of a thing that stood by him and seemed to be trying to hide behind him. Then, at a small distance, he noted a pale form which he instinctively knew to be Fafhrd. And around the pale form seethed a pack of black, shadowy animal shapes, leaping and retreating, worrying at the pale form, their eyes glowing like the moonlight, but brighter, their long muzzles soundlessly snarling. The thing beside him seemed to shrink closer. And then the Mouser rushed forward toward his friend.

The shadow pack turned on him and he braced himself to meet their onslaught. But the leader leaped past his shoulder, and the rest divided and flowed by him like a turbulent black stream. Then he realized that the thing which had sought to hide behind him was no longer there. He turned and saw that the black shapes pursued another small pale form.

It fled fast, but they followed faster. Over sweep after sweep of rock the hunt continued. He seemed to see taller, man-shaped figures among the pack. Slowly they dwindled in size, became tiny, vague. And still the Mouser felt the horrible hate and fear that flowed from them.

Then the sourceless moonlight faded, and only the cold remained, and that, too, dissipated, leaving nothing.

When he awoke, Fafhrd's face was looking down at him, and Fafhrd was saying, 'Lie still, little man. Lie still. No, I'm not badly hurt. A torn hand. Not bad. No worse than your own.'

But the Mouser shook his head impatiently and pushed his aching shoulder off the couch. Sunlight was knifing in through the narrow windows, revealing the dustiness of the air. Then he saw the body of the old man.

'Yes,' Fafhrd said as the Mouser lay back weakly. 'His fears are ended now. They've done with him. I should hate him. But who can hate such tattered flesh? When I came to the tower he gave me the drink. There was something wrong in my head. I believed what he said. He told me it would make me a god. I drank, and it sent me to a cold waste in hell. But now it's done with and we're still in Nehwon.'

The Mouser, eyeing the thoroughly and unmistakably dead things that dangled from the ceiling, felt content.

VI
THE SUNKEN LAND

'I was born with luck as a twin!' roared Fafhrd jovially, leaping up so swiftly that the cranky sloop rocked a little in spite of its outriggers. 'I catch a fish in the middle of the ocean. I rip up its belly. And look, little man, what I find!'

The Gray Mouser drew back from the fish-bloodied hand thrust almost into his face, wrinkled his nose with sneering fastidiousness, raised his left eyebrow and peered. The object did not seem very small even on Fafhrd's broad palm, and although slimed-over a little, was indubitably gold. It was both a ring and a key, the key part set at a right angle, so that it would lie along the finger when worn. There were carvings of some sort. Instinctively the Gray Mouser did not like the object. It somehow focused the vague uneasiness he had felt now for several days.

To begin with, he did not like the huge, salty Outer Sea, and only Fafhrd's bold enthusiasm and his own longing for the land of Lankhmar had impelled him to embark on this long, admittedly risky voyage across uncharted deeps. He did not like the fact that a school of fish was making the water boil at such a great distance from any land. Even the uniformly storm-less weather and favorable winds disturbed him, seeming to indicate correspondingly great misfortunes held in store, like a growing thundercloud in quiet air. Too much good luck was always dangerous. And now this ring, acquired without effort by an astonishingly lucky chance.

They peered at it more closely, Fafhrd slowly turning it around. The carving on the ring part, as far as one could make out, represented a sea monster dragging down a ship. It was highly stylized, however, and there was little detail. One might be mistaken. What puzzled the Mouser most, since he had traveled to far places and knew much of the world, was that he did not recognize the style.

But in Fafhrd it roused strange memories. Recollections of certain legends told around flickering driftwood fires through the long Northern nights; tales of great seafarings and distant raids made in ancient days; firelight glimpses of certain bits of loot taken by some unaccountably distant ancestor and considered too traditionally significant to barter or sell or even give away; ominously vague warnings used to frighten little boys who were inclined to swim or sail too far out. For a moment his green eyes clouded and his wind-burned face became serious, but only for a moment.

'A pretty enough thing, you'll agree,' he said, laughing. 'Whose door do you think it unlocks? Some king's mistress, I'd say. It's big enough for a king's finger.' He tossed it up, caught it, and wiped it on the rough cloth of his tunic.

'I wouldn't wear it,' said the Mouser. 'It was probably eaten from a drowned man's hand and sucked poison from the sea ooze. Throw it back.'

'And fish for a bigger one?' asked Fafhrd, grinning. 'No, I'm content with this.' He thrust it down on the middle finger of his left hand, doubled up his fist, and surveyed it critically. 'Good for bashing people with, too,' he remarked.

Then, seeing a big fish flash out of the water and almost flop into the cockpit, he snatched up his bow, fitted to the string a featherless arrow whose head was barbed and heavily weighted, and stared down over the side, one foot extended along the outrigger. A light, waxed line was attached to the arrow.

The Mouser watched him, not without envy. Fafhrd, big rangy man that he was, seemed to acquire an altogether new litheness and sureness of movement whenever they were on shipboard. He became as nimble as the Mouser was on shore. The Mouser was no landlubber and could swim as well as Fafhrd, but he always felt a trifle uneasy when there was only water in sight, day in and day out, just as Fafhrd felt uneasy in cities, though relishing taverns and street fights. On shipboard the Mouser became cautious and apprehensive; he made a point of watching for slow leaks, creeping fires, tainted food and rotten cordage. He disapproved of Fafhrd's constant trying out of new rigs and waiting until the last moment before reefing sail. It irked him a little that he couldn't quite call it foolhardy.

Fafhrd continued to scan intently the swelling, sliding waters. His long, copper-red hair was shoved back over his ears and knotted securely. He was clothed in rough brownish tunic and trousers. Light leather slippers, easily kicked off, were on his feet. Belt, longsword, and other weapons were, of course, wrapped away in oiled cloth against corrosion and rust. And there were no jewels or ornaments, save for the ring.

The Mouser's gaze shifted past him to where clouds were piling up a little on the horizon off the bow to starboard. He wondered, almost with relief, whether this mightn't be the dirty weather due them. He pulled his thin gray tunic closer at his throat and shifted the tiller a little. The sun, near setting, projected his crouching shadow against the brownish sail.

Fafhrd's bow twanged and the arrow plummeted. Line hissed from the reel he held in his arrow hand. He checked it with his thumb. It slackened a trifle, then jerked off toward the stern. Fafhrd's foot slid along the outrigger until it stopped against the pontoon, a good three arm's-lengths from the side. He let the other foot slide after it and lay there effortlessly braced, sea drenching his legs, playing the fish carefully, laughing and grunting satisfiedly.

'And what was your luck this time?' the Mouser asked afterward, as Fafhrd served them smoking-hot, white tender flesh boiled over the firebox in the snug cabin forward. 'Did you get a bracelet and necklace to match the ring?'

Fafhrd grinned with his mouth full and did not answer, as if there were nothing in the world to do but eat. But when they stretched themselves out later in the starry, cloud-broken darkness alive with a racing wind from starboard that drove their craft along at an increasing speed, he began to talk.

'I think they called the land Simorgya. It sank under the sea ages ago. Yet even then my people had gone raiding against it, though it was a long sail out and a weary beat homeward. My memory is uncertain. I only heard scraps of talk about it when I was a little child. But I did see a few trinkets carved somewhat like this ring; just a very few. The legends, I think, told that the men of far Simorgya were mighty magicians, claiming power over wind and waves and the creatures below. Yet the sea gulped them down for all that. Now they're there.' He rotated his hand until his thumb pointed at the bottom of the boat. 'My people, the legends say, went raiding against them one summer, and none of the boats returned, save one, which came back after hope had been lost, its men almost dead from thirst. They told of sailing on and on, and never reaching Simorgya, never sighting its rocky coast and squat, many-windowed towers. Only the empty sea. More raiders went out the next summer and the next, yet none ever found Simorgya.'

'But in that case,' questioned the Mouser sharply, 'may we not even now be sailing over that sunken land? May not that very fish you caught have swum in and out of the windows of those towers?'

'Who can say?' answered Fafhrd, a little dreamily. 'The ocean's big. If we're where we think we are – that is, almost home – it might be the case. Or not. I do not know if there ever really was a Simorgya. The legend-makers are great liars. In any case, that fish could hardly have been so ancient as to have eaten the flesh of a man of Simorgya.'

'Nevertheless,' said the Mouser in a small, flat voice, 'I'd throw the ring away.'

Fafhrd chuckled. His imagination was stirred, so that he saw the fabled land of Simorgya, not lightless and covered with great drifts of sea ooze, but as it once might have been, alive with ancient industry and commerce, strong with alien wizardry. Then the picture changed and he saw a long, narrow, twenty-oared galley, such as his people made, driving ahead into a stormy sea. There was the glint of gold and steel about the captain on the poop, and the muscles of the steersman cracked as he strained at the steering oar. The faces of the warrior-rowers were exultantly eager, dominated by the urge to rape the unknown. The whole ship was like a thirsty spearhead. He marveled at the vividness of the picture. Old longings vibrated faintly in his flesh. He felt the ring, ran his finger over the carving of the ship and monster, and again chuckled.

The Mouser fetched a stubby, heavy-wicked candle from the cabin and fixed it in a small horn lantern that was proof against the wind. Hanging at the stern it pushed back the darkness a little, not much. Until midnight it was the Mouser's watch. After a while Fafhrd slumbered.

He awoke with the feeling that the weather had changed and quick work was wanted. The Mouser was calling him. The sloop had heeled over so that the starboard pontoon rode the crests of the waves. There was chilly spray in the wind. The lantern swung wildly. Only astern were stars visible. The Mouser brought the sloop into the wind, and Fafhrd took a triple reef in the sail, while waves hammered the bow, an occasional light crest breaking over.

When they were on their course again, he did not immediately join the Mouser, but stood wondering, for almost the first time, how the sloop would stand heavy seas. It was not the sort of boat he would have built in his Northern homeland, but it was the best that could be gotten under the circumstances. He had caulked and tarred it meticulously, replaced any wood that looked too weak, substituted a triangular sail for the square one, and increased the height of the bow a trifle. To offset a tendency to capsize, he had added outriggers a little astern of the mast, getting the strongest, truest wood for the long crosspieces, carefully steaming them into the proper shape. It was a good job, he knew, but that didn't change the fact that the boat had a clumsy skeleton and many hidden weaknesses. He sniffed the raw, salt air and peered to windward through narrowed eyes, trying to gauge the weather. The Mouser was saying something, he realized and he turned his head to listen.

'Throw the ring away before she blows a hurricane!'

He smiled and made a wide gesture that meant 'No.' Then he turned back to gaze at the wild glimmering chaos of darkness and waves to windward. Thoughts of the boat and the weather dropped away, and he was content to drink in the awesome, age-old scene, swaying to keep balance, feeling each movement of the boat and at the same time sensing, almost as if it were something akin to himself, the godless force of the elements.

It was then the thing happened that took away his power to

react and held him, as it were, in a spell. Out of the surging wall of darkness emerged the dragon-headed prow of a galley. He saw the black wood of the sides, the light wood of the oars, the glint of wet metal. It was so like the ship of his imaginings that he was struck dumb with wonder as to whether it was only another vision, or whether he had had a foreglimpse of it by second sight, or whether he had actually summoned it across the deeps by his thoughts. It loomed higher, higher, higher.

The Mouser cried out and pushed over the tiller, his body arched with the mighty effort. Almost too late the sloop came out of the path of the dragon-headed prow. And still Fafhrd stared as at an apparition. He did not hear the Mouser's warning shout as the sloop's sail filled from the other side and slammed across with a rush. The boom caught him in the back of the knees and hurled him outward, but not into the sea, for his feet found the narrow pontoon and he balanced there precariously. In that instant an oar of the galley swung down at him and he toppled sideways, instinctively grasping the blade as he fell. The sea drenched him and wrenched at him, but he clung tightly and began to pull himself up the oar, hand over hand.

His legs were numb from the blows; he feared he would be unable to swim. And he was still bewitched by what he saw. For the moment he forgot the Mouser and the sloop entirely. He shook off the greedy waves, reached the side of the galley, caught hold of the oar-hole. Then he looked back and saw, in a kind of stupid surprise, the disappearing stern of the sloop and the Mouser's gray-capped face, revealed by a close swing of the lantern, staring at him in blank helplessness.

What happened next ended whatever spell had held him. A hand that carried steel struck. He twisted to one side and caught the wrist, then grasped the side of the galley, got his foot in the oarhole, on top of the oar, and heaved. The man dropped the knife too late, clawed at the side, failed to get a secure hold, and was dragged overboard, spitting and snapping his jaws in futile panic. Fafhrd, instinctively taking the offensive, sprang down onto the oarbench, which was the last of ten and half under the poop deck. His questioning eyes spied a rack of swords and he whirled one out, menacing the two shadowy figures hastening toward him, one from the forward oar-benches, one from the poop. They attacked with a rush, but silently, which was strange. The spray-wet weapons sparkled as they clashed.

Fafhrd fought warily, on guard for a blow from above, timing his lunges to the roll of the galley. He dodged a swashing blow and parried an unexpected back-handed slash from the same weapon. Stale, sour wine fumes puffed into his face. Someone dragged out an oar and thrust it like a huge lance; it came between Fafhrd and the two swordsmen, crashing heavily into the sword rack. Fafhrd glimpsed a rat-like, beady-eyed, toothy face peering up at him from the deeper darkness under the poop. One of the swordsmen lunged wildly, slipped and fell. The other gave ground, then gathered himself for a rush. But he paused with his sword in midair, looking over Fafhrd's head as if at a new adversary. The crest of a great wave struck him in the chest, obscuring him.

Fafhrd felt the weight of the water on his shoulders and clutched at the poop for support. The deck was at a perilous tilt. Water gushed up through the opposite oarholes. In the confusion, he realized, the galley had gotten into the troughs, and was beginning to take the seas broadside. She wasn't built to stand that. He vaulted up out of another breaking wave onto the poop and added his strength to that of the lone struggling steersman. Together they strained at the great oar, which seemed to be set in stone instead of water. Inch by inch, they fought their way across the narrow deck. None the less, the galley seemed doomed.

Then something – a momentary lessening of the wind and waves or perhaps a lucky pull by a forward oarsman – decided the issue. As slowly and laboriously as a waterlogged hulk the galley lifted and began to edge back into the proper course. Fafhrd and steersman strained prodigiously to hold each foot gained. Only when the galley was riding safe before the wind did they look up. Fafhrd saw two swords leveled steadily at his chest. He calculated his chances and did not move.

It was not easy to believe that fire had been preserved through that tremendous wetting, but one of the swordsmen nevertheless carried a sputtering tarry torch. By its light Fafhrd saw that they were Northerners akin to himself. Big raw-boned fellows, so blond they seemed almost to lack eyebrows. They wore metal-studded war gear and close-fitting bronze helmets. Their expressions were frozen halfway between a glare and a grin. Again he smelled stale wine. His glance strayed forward. Three oarsmen were bailing with bucket and hand crane.

Somebody was striding toward the poop – the leader, if one could guess from gold and jewels and an air of assurance. He sprang up the short ladder, his limbs supple as a cat's. He seemed younger than the rest and his features were almost delicate. Fine, silky blond hair was plastered wetly against his cheeks. But there was feline rapacity in his tight, smiling lips, and there was craziness in his jewel-blue eyes. Fafhrd hardened his own face against their inspection. One question kept nagging him. Why, even at the height of the confusion, had there been no cries, no shout, no bellowed orders? Since he had come aboard, there had not been a word uttered.

The young leader seemed to come to a conclusion about Fafhrd, for his thin smile widened a trifle and he motioned toward the oar deck. Then Fafhrd broke silence and said in a voice that sounded unnatural and hoarse, 'What do you intend? Weight well the fact that I saved your ship.'

He tensed himself, noting with some satisfaction that the steersman stayed close beside him, as if their shared task had forged a bond between them. The smile left the leader's face. He laid his finger to his lips and then impatiently repeated his first gesture. This time Fafhrd understood. He was to replace the oarsman he had pulled overboard. He could not but admit there was a certain ironic justice to the idea. It was borne in on him that swift death would be his lot if he renewed the fight at such a disadvantage; slow death, if he leaped overboard in the mad hope of finding the sloop in the howling, heaving darkness. The arms holding the swords became taut. He curtly nodded his head in submission. At least they were his own people.

With his first feel of the heavy, rebellious water against the blade of his oar, a new feeling took hold of Fafhrd – a feeling with which he was not unfamiliar. He seemed to become part of the ship, to share its purposes, whatever they might be. It was the age-old spirit of the oarbench. When his muscles had warmed to the task and his nerves became accustomed to the rhythm, he found himself stealing glances at the men around him, as if he had known them before; trying to penetrate and share the eager, set look on their faces.

Something huddled in many folds of ragged cloth shuffled out from the little cabin far back under the poop and held a leather flask to the lips of the opposite oarsman. The creature looked absurdly squat among such tall men. When it turned Fafhrd recognized the beady eyes he had glimpsed before and, as it came nearer, distinguished under the heavy cowl the wrinkled, subtle, ocher face of an aged Mingol.

'So you're the new one,' the Mingol croaked jeeringly. 'I liked your swordplay. Drink deep now, for Lavas Laerk may decide to sacrifice you to the sea gods before morning. But mind you, don't dribble any.'

Fafhrd sucked greedily, then almost coughed and spat when a rush of strong wine seared his throat. After a while the Mingol jerked the flask away.

'Now you know what Lavas Laerk feeds his oarsmen. There are few crews in this world or the next that row on wine.' He chuckled, then said, 'But you're wondering why I talk aloud. Well, young Lavas Laerk may put a vow of silence on all his men, but he may not do the same to me, who is only a slave. For I tend the fire – how carefully you know – and serve out the wine and cook the meat, and recite incantations for the good of the ship. There are certain things that neither Lavas Laerk nor any other man, nor any other demon, may demand of me.'

'But what does Lavas Laerk—'

The Mingol's leathery palm clapped over Fafhrd's mouth and shut off the whispered question.

'Sh! Do you care so little for life? Remember, you are Lavas Laerk's henchman. But I will tell you what you would know.' He sat down on the wet bench beside Fafhrd, looking like a bundle of black rags someone had dropped there. 'Lavas Laerk has sworn to raid far Simorgya, and he has put a vow of silence upon himself and his men until they sight the coast. Sh! Sh! I know they say Simorgya is under the waves, or that there never was such a place. But Lavas Laerk swore a great oath before his mother, whom he hates worse than he hates his friends, and he killed a man who thought to question his decision. So it's Simorgya we seek, if only to steal pearls from the oysters and ravish the fishes. Lean down and row more easily for a space, and I will tell you a secret that's no secret and make a prophecy that's no prophecy.' He crowded closer. 'Lavas Laerk hates all men who are sober, for he believes – and rightly – that only drunken men are even a little like himself. Tonight the crew will row well, though it's a day since they've had meat. Tonight the wine will make them see at least the glow of the visions that Lavas Laerk sees. But next morning there will be aching backs and sick guts and pain-hammered skulls. And then there will be mutiny and not even Lavas Laerk's madness will save him.'

Fafhrd wondered why the Mingol shuddered, coughed weakly and made a gargling sound. He reached over and a warm fluid drenched his naked hand. Then Lavas Laerk pulled his dirk from the Mingol's neck and the Mingol rolled forward off the bench.

No word was spoken, but knowledge that some abominable deed had been committed passed from oarsman to oarsman through the stormy darkness until it reached the bench in the bow. Then gradually there began a kind of pent-up commotion, which increased markedly as there slowly percolated forward an awareness of the specially heinous nature of the deed – the murder of the slave who tended the fire and whose magical powers, though often scoffed at, were entwined with the destiny of the ship itself. Still no completely intelligible words, but low grunts and snarls and mutterings, the scrape of oars being drawn in and rested, a growing murmur in which consternation and fear and danger were mixed, and which washed back and forth between bow and poop like a wave in a tub. Half caught up by it, Fafhrd readied himself for a spring, though whether at the apprehensively motionless figure of Lavas Laerk or back toward the comparative safety of the poop cabin, he could not say. Certainly Lavas Laerk was doomed; or rather he would have been doomed, had not the steersman screamed from the poop in a great shaky voice, 'Land ho! Simorgya! Simorgya!'

That wild cry, like a clawed skeletal hand, seized upon the agitation of the crew and wrenched it to an almost unbearable climax. A shuddering inhalation of breath swept the ship. Then came shouts of wonder, cries of fear, curses that were half prayers. Two oarsmen started to fight together for no other reason than that the sudden, painful upgush of feeling demanded action of some sort, any sort. Another pushed wildly at his oar, screeching at the rest to follow his example and reverse the galley's course and so escape. Fafhrd vaulted up on his bench and stared ahead.

It loomed up vast as a mountain and perilously close. A great black blot vaguely outlined by the lesser darkness of the night, partly obscured by trailings of mist and scud, yet showing in various places and at varying distances squares of dim light which by their regular arrangement could be nothing but windows. And with each pounding heartbeat the roar of surf and the thunder of breaking waves grew louder.

All at once it was upon them. Fafhrd saw a great overhanging crag slide by, so close it snapped the last oar on the opposite side. As the galley lifted on a wave he looked awestruck into three windows in the crag – if it was a crag and not a half submerged tower – but saw nothing save a ghostly yellow luminescence. Then he heard Lavas Laerk bellowing commands in a harsh, high-pitched voice. A few of the men worked frantically at the oars, but it was too late for that, although the galley seemed to have gotten behind some protecting wall of rock into slightly calmer water. A terrible rasping noise went the length of the keel. Timbers groaned and cracked. A last wave lifted them and a great grinding crash sent men reeling and tumbling. Then the galley stopped moving altogether and the only sound was the roar of the surf, until Lavas Laerk cried exultantly, 'Serve out weapons and wine! Make ready for a raid!'

The words seemed incredible in this more than dangerous situation, with the galley broken beyond repair, gutted by the rocks. Yet the men rallied and seemed even to catch something of the wild eagerness of their master, who had proved to them that the world was no more sane then he.

Fafhrd watched them fetch torch after torch from the poop

cabin, until the whole stern of the wreck smoked and flared. He watched them snatch and suck at the wineskins and heft the swords and dirks given out, comparing them and cleaving at the air to get the feel. Then some of them grabbed hold of him and hustled him to the sword rack, saying, 'Here, Red Hair, you must have a weapon, too.' Fafhrd went along unresisting, yet he felt that something would prevent them from arming one who so late had been their enemy. And he was right in this, for Lavas Laerk stopped the lieutenant who was about to hand Fafhrd a sword, and stared with growing intentness at Fafhrd's left hand.

Puzzled, Fafhrd raised it, and Lavas Laerk cried, 'Seize him!' and at the same instant jerked something from Fafhrd's middle finger. Then Fafhrd remembered. It was the ring.

'There can be no doubt about the workmanship,' said Lavas Laerk, peering cunningly at Fafhrd, his bright blue eyes giving the impression of being out of focus or slightly crossed. 'This man is a Simorgyan spy, or perhaps a Simorgyan demon who has taken the form of a Northerner to allay our suspicions. He climbed out of the sea in the teeth of a roaring storm, did he not? What man among you saw any boat?'

'I saw a boat,' ventured the steersman hurriedly. 'A queer sloop with a triangular sail—' But Lavas Laerk shut him up with a sideways glance.

Fafhrd felt the point of a dirk at his back and checked his tightening muscles.

'Shall we kill him?' The question came from close behind Fafhrd's ear.

Lavas Laerk smiled crookedly up at the darkness and paused, as if listening to the advice of some invisible storm wraith. Then he shook his head. 'Let him live for the present. He can show us where loot is hid. Guard him with naked swords.'

Whereupon they all left the galley, clambering down ropes hung from the prow onto rocks which the surf alternately covered and uncovered. One or two laughed and jumped. A dropped torch hissed out in the brine. There was much shouting. Someone began to sing in a drunken voice that had an edge like a rusty knife. Then Lavas Laerk got them into a sort of order and they marched away, half of them carrying torches, a few still hugging wineskins, sliding and slipping, cursing the sharp rocks and barnacles which cut them when they fell, hurling exaggerated threats at the darkness ahead, where strange windows glowed. Behind them the long galley lay like a dead beetle, the oars sprawled out all askew from the ports.

They had marched for some little distance, and the sound of the breakers was less thunderous, when their torchlight helped reveal a portal in a great wall of black rock that might or might not have been a castle rather than a caverned cliff. The portal was square and high as an oar. Three worn stone steps drifted with wet sand led up to it. Dimly they could discern on the pillars, and on the heavy lintel overhead, carvings partly obliterated by slime and incrustations of some sort, but unmistakably Simorgyan in their obscure symbolism.

The crew, staring silently now, drew closer together. The ragged procession became a tight knot. Then Lavas Laerk called mockingly, 'Where are your guards, Simorgya? Where are your fighting men?' and walked straight up the stone steps. After a moment of uncertainty, the knot broke and the men followed him.

On the massive threshold Fafhrd involuntarily halted, dumbstruck by realization of the source of the faint yellow light he had earlier noticed in the high windows. For the source was everywhere: ceiling, walls, and slimy floor all glowed with a wavering phosphorescence. Even the carvings glimmered. Mixed awe and repugnance gripped him. But the men pressed around and against him, and carried him forward. Wine and leadership had dulled their sensibilities and as they strode down the long corridor they seemed little aware of the abysmal scene.

At first some held their weapons ready to meet a possible foray or ambush, but soon they lowered them negligently, and even sucked at the wineskins and jested. A hulking oarsman, whose blond beard was patched with yellow scud from the surf, struck up a chantey and others joined in, until the dank walls roared. Deeper and deeper they penetrated into the cave or castle, along the wide, winding, ooze-carpeted corridor.

Fafhrd was carried along by a current. When he moved too slowly, the others jostled him and he quickened his pace, but it was all involuntary. Only his eyes responded to his will, turning from side to side, drinking in details with fearful curiosity: the endless series of vague carvings, wherein sea monsters and unwholesome manlike figures and vaguely anthropomorphic giant skates or rays seemed to come alive and stir as the phosphorescence fluctuated; a group of highest windows or openings of some sort, from which dark slippery weeds trailed down; the pools of water here and there; the still-alive, gasping fish which the others trod or kicked aside; the clumps of bearded shells clinging to the corners; the impression of things scuttling out of the way ahead. Louder and louder the thought drummed in his skull: surely the others must realize where they were. Surely they must know the phosphorescence was that of the sea. Surely they must know that this was the retreat of the more secret creatures of the deep. Surely, surely they must know that Simorgya had indeed sunk under the sea and only risen up yesterday – or yester-hour.

But on they marched after Lavas Laerk, and still sang and shouted and swilled wine in quick gulps, throwing back their heads and lifting up the sacks as they strode. And Fafhrd could not speak. His shoulder muscles were contracted as if the weight of the sea were already pressing them down. His mind was engulfed and oppressed by the ominous presence of sunken Simorgya. Memories of the legends. Thoughts of the black centuries during which sea life had slowly crept and wriggled and swum through the mazes of rooms and corridors until it had a lair in every crack and cranny and Simorgya was one with the mysteries of the ocean. In a deep grotto that opened on the corridor he made out a thick table of stone, with a great stone chair behind it; and though he could not be sure, he thought he distinguished an octopus shape slouched there in a travesty of a human occupant, tentacles coiling the chair, unblinking eyes staring glisteningly.

Gradually the flare of the smoky torches paled, as the phosphorescence grew stronger. And when the men broke off singing, the sound of the surf was no longer audible.

Then Lavas Laerk, from around a sharp turn in the corridor, uttered a triumphant cry. The others hastened after, stumbling, lurching, calling out eagerly.

'Oh, Simorgya!' cried Lavas Laerk. 'We have found your treasure house!'

The room in which the corridor ended was square and considerably lower-ceilinged than the corridor. Standing here and there were a number of black, soggy-looking, heavily-bound chests. The stuff underfoot was muckier. There were more pools of water. The phosphorescence was stronger.

A blond-bearded oarsman leaped ahead as the others hesitated. He wrenched at the cover of the nearest chest. A corner came away in his hands, the wood soft as cheese, the seeming metal a black, smeary ooze. He grasped at it again and pulled off most of the top, revealing a layer of dully-gleaming gold and slime-misted gems. Over that jeweled surface a crablike creature scuttled, escaping through a hole in the back.

With a great, greedy shout, the others rushed at the chests, jerking, gouging, even smiting with their swords at the spongy wood. Two, fighting as to which should break open a chest, fell against it and it went to pieces under them, leaving them struggling in jewels and muck.

All this while Lavas Laerk stood on the same spot from which he had uttered his first taunting cry. To Fafhrd, who stood forgotten beside him, it seemed that Lavas Laerk was distraught that his quest should come to any end, that Lavas Laerk was desperately searching for something further, something more than jewels and gold to sate his mad willfulness. Then he noted that Lavas Laerk was looking at something intently – a square, slime-filmed, but apparently golden door across the room from the mouth of the corridor; upon it was the carving of some strange, undulant blanket-like sea monster. He heard Lavas Laerk laugh throatily and watched him stride unswervingly toward the door. He saw that Lavas Laerk had something in his hand. With a shock of surprise he recognized it as the ring Lavas Laerk had taken from him. He saw Lavas Laerk shove at the door without budging it. He saw Lavas Laerk fumble with the ring and fit the key part into the golden door and turn it. He saw the door give a little to Lavas Laerk's next push.

Then he realized – and the realization came with an impact like a rushing wall of water – that nothing had happened accidentally, that everything from the moment his arrow struck the fish had been intended by someone or something – something that wanted a door unlocked – and he turned and fled down the corridor as if a tidal wave were sucking at his heels.

The corridor, without torchlight, was pale and shifty as a nightmare. The phosphorescence seemed to crawl as if alive, revealing previously unspied creatures in every niche. Fafhrd stumbled, sprawled at full length, raced on. His fastest bursts of speed seemed slow, as in a bad dream. He tried to look only ahead, but still glimpsed from the corners of his eyes every detail he had seen before: the trailing weeds, the monstrous carvings, the bearded shells, the somberly staring octopus eyes. He noted without surprise that his feet and body glowed wherever the slime had splashed or smeared. He saw a small square of darkness in the omnipresent phosphorescence and sprinted toward it. It grew in size. It was the cavern's portal. He plunged across the threshold into the night. He heard a voice calling his name.

It was the Gray Mouser's voice. It came from the opposite direction to the wrecked galley. He ran toward it across treacherous ledges. Starlight, now come back, showed a black gulf before his feet. He leaped, landed with a shaking impact on another rock surface, dashed forward without falling. He saw the top of a mast above an edge of darkness and almost bowled over the small figure that was staring raptly in the direction from which he had just fled. The Mouser seized him by the shoulder, dragged him to the edge, pulled him over. They clove the water together and swam out to the sloop anchored in the rock-sheltered lee. The Mouser started to heave at the anchor but Fafhrd slashed the line with a knife snatched from the Mouser's belt and jerked up the sail in swift, swishing rushes.

Slowly the sloop began to move. Gradually the ripples became wavelets, the wavelets became smacking waves. Then they slipped past a black, foam-edged sword of rock and were in the open sea. Still Fafhrd did not speak, but crowded on all canvas and did all else possible to coax speed from the storm-battered sloop. Resigned to mystification, the Mouser helped him.

They had not been long underway when the blow fell. The Mouser, looking sternward, gave a hoarse incredulous cry. The wave swiftly overtaking them was higher than the mast. And something was sucking the sloop back. The Mouser raised his arms shieldingly. Then the sloop began to climb; up, up, up until it reached the top, overbalanced, and plummeted down on the opposite side. The first wave was followed by a second and a third, and a fourth, each almost as high. A larger boat would surely have been swamped. Finally the waves gave way to a choppy, foaming, unpredictable chaos, in which every ounce of effort and a thousand quick decisions were needed to keep the sloop afloat.

When the pale foredawn came, they were back on the homeward course again, a small improvised sail taking the place of the one ripped in the aftermath of the storm, enough water bailed from the hold to make the sloop seaworthy. Fafhrd, dazedly watching for the sunrise, felt weak as a woman. He only half heard the Mouser tell, in snatches, of how he had lost the galley in the storm, but followed what he guessed to be its general course until the storm cleared, and had sighted the strange island and landed there, mistakenly believing it to be the galley's home port.

The Mouser then brought thin, bitter wine and salt fish, but Fafhrd pushed them away and said, 'One thing I must know. I never looked back. You were staring earnestly at something behind me. What was it?'

The Mouser shrugged his shoulders. 'I don't know. The distance was too great and the light was queer. What I thought I saw was rather foolish. I'd have given a good deal to have been closer.' He frowned, shrugged his shoulders again. 'Well, what I thought I saw was this: a crowd of men wearing big black cloaks – they looked like Northerners – came rushing out of an opening of some sort. There was something odd about them: the light by which I saw them didn't seem to have any source. Then they waved the big black cloaks around as if they were fighting with them or doing some sort of dance . . . I told you it was very foolish . . . and then they got down on their hands and knees and covered themselves up with the cloaks and crawled back into the place from which they had come. Now tell me I'm a liar.'

Fafhrd shook his head. 'Only those weren't cloaks,' he said.

The Mouser began to sense that there was much more to it than he had even guessed. 'What were they, then?' he asked.

'I don't know,' said Fafhrd.

'But then what was the place, I mean the island that almost sucked us down when it sank?'

'Simorgya,' said Fafhrd and lifted his head and began to grin in a cruel, chilly, wild-eyed way that took the Mouser aback. 'Simorgya,' repeated Fafhrd, and pulled himself to the side of the boat and glared down at the rushing water. 'Simorgya. And now it's sunk again. And may it soak there forever and rot in its own corruption, till all's muck!' He trembled spasmodically with the passion of his curse, then sank back. Along the rim of the east a ruddy smudge began to show.

VII
THE SEVEN BLACK PRIESTS

Eyes like red lava peered from a face black as dead lava down the sheer mountainside at the snowy ledge that narrowed off into chilly darkness barely touched by dawn. The black priest's heart pounded its rib cage. Never in his life nor his priest-father's before him had intruders come by this narrow way that led from the Outer Sea across the mountains known as the Bones of the Old Ones. Never in three long returns of the Year of the Monsters, never in four sailings of the ship to tropic Klesh to get them wives, had any but he and his fellow-priests trod the way below. Yet he had always guarded it as faithfully and warily as if it were the nightly assault-route of blasphemy-bent spearmen and bowmen.

There it came again – and unmistakably! – the rumble of singing. To judge from the tone, the man must have a chest like a bear's. As if he had drilled for this nightly (and he had) the black priest laid aside his conical hat and stepped out of his fur-lined shoes and slipped off his fur-lined robe, revealing his skinny-limbed, sag-bellied, well-greased frame.

Moving back in the stony niche, he selected a narrow stick from a closely-shielded fire and laid it across a pit in the rock. Its unsputtering flame revealed that the pit was filled to a hand's breadth of the top with a powder that glittered like smashed jewels. He judged it would take some thirty slow breaths for the stick to burn through at the middle.

He silently returned to the edge of the niche, which was the height of three tall men – seven times his own height – above the snowy ledge. And now, far along that ledge, he could dimly distinguish a figure – no, two. He drew a long knife from his loincloth and, crouching forward, poised himself on his hands and toes. He breathed a prayer to his strange and improbable god. Somewhere above, ice or rocks creaked and snapped faintly, as if the mountain too were flexing its muscles in murderous anticipation.

'Give us the next verse, Fafhrd,' merrily called the foremost of the two snow-treaders. 'You've had thirty paces to compose it, and our adventure took no longer. Or is the poetic hoot owl frozen at last in your throat?'

The Mouser grinned as he strode along with seeming recklessness, the sword Scalpel swinging at his side. His high-collared gray cloak and hood, pulled close around him, shadowed his swart features but could not conceal their impudence.

Fafhrd's garments, salvaged from their sloop wrecked on the chilly coast, were all wools and furs. A great golden clasp gleamed dully on his chest and a golden band, tilted awry, confined his snarled reddish hair. His white-skinned face, with green eyes wide set, had a calm bold look to it, though the brow was furrowed in thought. From over his right shoulder protruded a bow, while from over his left shoulder gleamed the sapphire eyes of a brazen dragon-head that was the pommel of a longsword slung on his back.

His brow cleared and, as if some more genial mountain than the frozen one they traveled along had given tongue, he sang:

> Oh, Lavas Laerk
> Had a face like a dirk
> And of swordsmen twenty-and-three,
> And his greased black ship
> Through the waves did slip—
> 'Twas the sleekest craft at sea;
> Yet it helped him naught
> When he was caught
> By magic, the Mouser, and me.
> And now he feeds fishes
> The daintiest dishes,
> But—

The words broke off and the Gray Mouser heard the hissing scuff of leather on snow. Whirling around, he saw Fafhrd hurtled over the side of the cliff and he had a moment to wonder whether the huge Northerner, maddened by his own doggerel, had decided to illustrate dramatically Lavas Laerk's plunge to the bottomless deeps.

The next moment Fafhrd caught himself with elbows and hands on the margin of the ledge. Simultaneously, a black and gleaming form hit the spot he had just desperately vacated, broke its fall with bent arms and hunched shoulders, spun over in a somersault, and lunged at the Mouser with a knife that flashed like a splinter of the moon. The knife was about to take the Mouser in the belly when Fafhrd, supporting his weight on one forearm, twitched the attacker back by an ankle. At this the small black one hissed low and horribly, turned again, and lunged at Fafhrd. But now the Mouser was roused at last from the shocked daze that he assured himself could never grip him in a less hatefully cold country. He dove forward at the small black one, diverting his thrust – there were sparks as the weapon struck stone within a finger's width of Fafhrd's arm – and skidding his greased form off the ledge beyond Fafhrd. The small black one swooped out of sight as silently as a bat.

Fafhrd, dangling his great frame over the abyss, finished his verse:

But the daintiest dish is he.

'Hush, Fafhrd,' the Mouser hissed, stooped as he listened intently. 'I think I heard him hit.'

Fafhrd absentmindedly eased himself up to a seat. 'Not if that chasm is half as deep as the last time we saw its bottom, you didn't,' he assured his comrade.

'But what was he?' the Mouser asked frowningly. 'He looked like a man of Klesh.'

'Yes, with the jungle of Klesh as far from here as the moon,' Fafhrd reminded him with a chuckle. 'Some maddened hermit frostbitten black, no doubt. There are strange skulkers in these little hills, they say.'

The Mouser peered up the dizzy mile-high cliff and spotted the nearby niche. 'I wonder if there are more of him?' he questioned uneasily.

'Madmen commonly go alone,' Fafhrd asserted, getting up. 'Come, small nagger, we'd best be on our way if you want a hot breakfast. If the old tales are true, we should be reaching the Cold Waste by sunup – and there we'll find a little wood at least.'

At that instant a great glow sprang from the niche from which the small attacker had dropped. It pulsed, turning from violet to green to yellow to red.

'What makes that?' Fafhrd mused, his interest roused at last. 'The old tales say nothing of firevents in the Bones of the Old Ones. Now if I were to give you a boost, Mouser, I think you could reach that knob and then make your own way—'

'Oh no,' the Mouser interrupted, tugging at the big man and silently cursing himself for starting the question-asking. 'I want my breakfast cooked over more wholesome flames. And I would be well away from here before other eyes see the glow.'

'None will see it, small dodger of mysteries,' Fafhrd said chucklingly, letting himself be urged away along the path. 'Look, even now it dies.'

But at least one other eye had seen the pulsing glow – an eye as large as a squid's and bright as the Dog Star.

'Ha, Fafhrd!' the Gray Mouser cried gaily some hours later in the full-broken dawn. 'There's an omen to warm our frozen hearts! A green hill winks at us frosty men – gives us the glad eye like a malachite-smeared dusky courtesan of Klesh!'

'She's as hot as a courtesan of Klesh, too,' the huge Northerner supplemented, rounding the brown crag's bulging shoulder in his turn, 'for she's melted all the snow.'

It was true. Although the far horizon shone white and green with the snows and glacial ice of the Cold Waste, the saucer-like depression in the foreground held a small unfrozen lake. And while the air was still chilly around them, so that their breath drifted away in small white clouds, the brown ledge they trod was bare.

Up from the nearer shore of the lake rose the hill to which the

Mouser had referred, the hill from which one star-small point still reflected the new-risen sun's rays at them blindingly.

'That is, if it is a hill,' Fafhrd added softly. 'And in any case, whether a courtesan of Klesh or hill, she has several faces.'

The point was well taken. The hill's green flanks were formed of crags and hummocks which the imagination could shape into monstrous faces – all the eyes closed save the one that twinkled at them. The faces melted downward like wax into huge stony rivulets – or might they be elephantine trunks? – that plunged into the unruffled acid-seeming water. Here and there among the green were patches of dark red rock that might be blood, or mouths. Clashing nastily in color, the hill's rounded summit seemed to be composed of a fleshily pink marble. It too persisted in resembling a face – that of a sleeping ogre. It was crossed by a stretch of vividly red rock that might be the ogre's lips. From a slit in the red rock, a faint vapor rose.

The hill had more than a volcanic look. It seemed like an upwelling from a more savage, primal, fiercer consciousness than any that even Fafhrd and the Gray Mouser knew, an upwelling frozen in the act of invading a younger, weaker world – frozen yet eternally watchful and waiting and yearning.

And then the illusion was gone – or four-faces-out-of-five gone and the fifth wavering. The hill was just a hill again – an odd volcanic freak of the Cold Waste – a green hill with a glitter.

Fafhrd let out a gusty sigh. He surveyed the farther shore of the lake. It was hillocky and matted with a dark vegetation that unpleasantly resembled fur. At one point there rose from it a stubby pillar of rock almost like an altar. Beyond the hairy bushes, which were here and there flecked with red-leafed ones, stretched the ice and snow, broken only occasionally by great rocks and rare clumps of dwarfed trees.

But something else was foremost in the Mouser's thoughts.

'The eye, Fafhrd. The glad, glittering eye!' he whispered, dropping his voice as though they were in a crowded street and some informer or rival thief might overhear. 'Only once before have I seen such a gleam, and that was by moonlight, across a king's treasure chamber. That time I did not come away with a huge diamond. A guardian serpent prevented it. I killed the wriggler, but its hiss brought other guards.

'But this time there's only a little hill to climb. And if at this distance the gem gleams so bright, Fafhrd' – his hand dropped and gripped his companion's leg, at the sensitive point just above the knee, for emphasis – 'think how big!'

The Northerner, frowning faintly at the violent squeeze as well as at his doubts and misgivings, nevertheless sucked an icy breath in appreciative greed.

'And we poor shipwrecked marauders,' continued the Mouser raptly, 'will be able to tell the gaping and envious thieves of Lankhmar that we not only crossed the Bones of the Old Ones, but picked them on the way.'

And he went skipping gaily down the skimpy ledge that merged into the narrow, lake-edged, rocky saddle that joined this greater mountain with the green one. Fafhrd followed more slowly, gazing steadily at the green hill, waiting for it to turn back into faces again, or to turn to no faces at all. It did neither. It occurred to him that it might have been partly shaped by human hands and, after that, the notion of a diamond-eyed idol seemed less implausible. At the far end of the saddle, just at the base of the green hill, he caught up with the Mouser, who was studying a flat, dark rock covered with gashes which a moment's glance told Fafhrd must be artificial.

'The runes of tropic Klesh!' the Northerner muttered. 'What should such hieroglyphs be doing so far from their jungle?'

'Chiseled, no doubt, by some hermit frostbitten black, whose madness taught him the Kleshic language,' the Mouser observed sardonically. 'Or have you already forgotten last night's knifer?'

Fafhrd shook his head curtly. Together they pored over the deep-chopped letters, bringing to bear knowledge gained from the perusing of ancient treasure-maps and the deciphering of code-messages carried by intercepted spies.

'The seven black . . .' Fafhrd read laboriously.

' . . . priests,' the Mouser finished for him. 'They're in it, whoever they may be. And a god or beast or devil – that writhing hieroglyph means any one of the three, depending on the surrounding words, which I don't understand. It's very ancient writing. And the seven black priests are to serve the writhing hieroglyph, or to bind it – again either might be meant, or both.'

'And so long as the priesthood endures,' Fafhrd took up, 'that long will the god-beast-devil lie quietly . . . or sleep . . . or stay dead . . . or not come up . . .'

Abruptly the Mouser bounded straight into the air, fanning his feet. 'This rock is hot,' he complained.

Fafhrd understood. Even through the thick walrus-soles of his boots he was beginning to feel the unnatural warmth.

'Hotter than the floor of hell,' the Mouser observed, hopping first on one foot and then the other. 'Well, what now, Fafhrd? Shall we go up, or not?'

Fafhrd answered him with a sudden shout of laughter. 'You decided that, little man, long ago! Was it *I* who started to talk about huge diamonds?'

So up they went, choosing that point where a gigantic trunk, or tentacle, or melted chin strained from the encasing granite. It was not an easy climb, even at the beginning, for the green stone was everywhere rounded off, showing no marks of chisel or axe – which rather dampened Fafhrd's vague theory that this was a hill half-formed by human-wielded tools.

Upward the two of them edged and strained, their breath blowing out in bigger white clouds although the rock was uncomfortably hot under their hands. After an inch-by-inch climb up a slippery surface, where hands and feet and elbows and knees and even toasted chin must all help, they stood at last on the lower lip of one of the green hill's mouths. Here it seemed their ascent must end, for the great cheek above was smooth and sloped outward a spear's length above them.

But Fafhrd took from the Mouser's back a rope that had once guyed the mast of their shipwrecked sloop, made a noose in it, and cast it up toward the forehead above, where a stubby horn or feeler projected. It caught and held. Fafhrd put his weight on it to test it, then looked inquiringly at his companion.

'What have you in mind?' the Mouser asked, clinging affectionately to the rock-face. 'This whole climb begins to seem mere foolishness.'

'But what of the jewel?' Fafhrd replied in pleasant mockery. 'So big, Mouser, so big!'

'Likely just a bit of quartz,' the Mouser said sourly. 'I have lost my hunger for it.'

'But as for me,' Fafhrd cried, 'I have only now worked up a good appetite.'

And he swung out into emptiness, around the green cheek and into thin, brilliant sunlight.

It seemed to him as if the still lake and the green hill were rocking, instead of himself. He came to rest below the face's monstrously pouchy eyelid. He climbed up hand over hand, found good footing on the ledge that was the eyelid pouch, and twitched the end of the rope back to the Mouser, whom he could no longer see. On the third cast it did not swing back. He squatted on the ledge, bracing himself securely to guy the rope. It went tight in his hands. Very soon the Mouser stepped onto the ledge beside him.

The gaiety was back in the small thief's face, but it was a fragile gaiety, as though he wanted to get this done with quickly. They edged their way along the great eye-pouch until they were directly below the fancied pupil. It was rather above Fafhrd's head, but the Mouser, nimbly hitching himself up on Fafhrd's shoulders peered in readily.

Fafhrd, bracing himself against the green wall, waited impatiently. It seemed as if the Mouser would never speak. 'Well?' he asked finally, when his shoulders had begun to ache from the Mouser's weight.

'Oh, it's a diamond, all right.' The Mouser sounded oddly uninterested. 'Yes, it's big. My fingers can just about span it. And it's cut like a smooth sphere – a sort of diamond eye. But I don't know about getting it out. It's set very deep. Should I try? Don't bellow so, Fafhrd, you'll blow us both off! I suppose we might as well take it, since we've come so far. But it won't be easy. My knife can't . . . yes, it can! I thought it was rock around the gem. But it's tarry stuff. Squidgy. There! I'm coming down.'

Fafhrd had a glimpse of something smooth, globular and dazzling, with an ugly, ragged, tarry circlet clinging to it. Then it seemed that someone flicked his elbow lightly. He looked down. Momentarily he had the strangest feeling of being in the green steamy jungle of Klesh. For protruding from the brown fur of his cloak was a wickedly barbed little dart, thickly smeared with a substance as black and tarry as that disfiguring the diamond eye.

He quickly dropped flat on the ledge, crying out to the Mouser to do the same. Then he carefully tugged loose the dart, finding to his relief that, although it had nicked the thick hide of his cloak beneath the fur, it had not touched flesh.

'I think I see him,' called the Mouser, peering down cautiously over the protected ledge. 'A little fellow with a very long blowgun and dressed in furs and a conical hat. Crouching there in those dark bushes across the lake. Black, I think, like our knifer last night. A Kleshian, I'd say, unless he's one more of your frostbitten hermits. Now he lifts the gun to his lips. Watch yourself!'

A second dart pinged against the rock above them, then dropped down close by Fafhrd's hand. He jerked it away sharply.

There was a whirring sound, ending in a muted snap. The Mouser had decided to get a blow in. It is not easy to swing a sling while lying prone on a ledge, but the Mouser's missile crackled into the furry bushes close to the black blowgunner, who immediately ducked out of sight.

It was easy enough then to decide on a plan of action, for few were available. While the Mouser raked the bushes across the lake with sling shots, Fafhrd went down the rope. Despite the Mouser's protection, he fervently prayed that his cloak be thick enough. He knew from experience that the darts of Klesh are nasty things. At irregular intervals came the whirr of the Mouser's casts, cheering him on.

Reaching the green hill's base, he strung his bow and called up to the Mouser that he was ready in his turn to cover the retreat. His eyes searched the furry cliffs across the lake, and twice when he saw movement he sent an arrow from his precious store of twenty. Then the Mouser was beside him and they were racing off along the hot mountain edge toward where the cryptically ancient glacial ice gleamed green. Often they looked back across the lake at the dubious furry bushes spotted here and there with blood-red ones, and twice or thrice they thought they saw movement in them – movement coming their way. Whenever this happened, they sent an arrow or a stone whirring, though with what effect they could not tell.

'The seven black priests—' Fafhrd muttered.

'The six,' the Mouser corrected. 'We killed one of them last night.'

'Well, the six then,' Fafhrd conceded. 'They seem angry with us.'

'As why shouldn't they be?' the Mouser demanded. 'We stole their idol's only eye. Such an act annoys priests tremendously.'

'It seemed to have more eyes than that one,' Fafhrd asserted thoughtfully, 'if only it had opened them.'

'Thank Aarth it didn't!' the Mouser hissed. 'And 'ware that dart!'

Fafhrd hit the dirt – or rather the rock – instantly, and the black dart skirred on the ice ahead.

'I think they're unreasonably angry,' Fafhrd asserted, scrambling to his feet.

'Priests always are,' the Mouser said philosophically, with a sidewise shudder at the dart's black-crusted point.

'At any rate, we're rid of them,' Fafhrd said with relief, as he and the Mouser loped onto the ice. The Mouser leered at him sardonically, but Fafhrd didn't notice.

All day they trudged rapidly across the green ice, seeking their way southward by the sun, which got hardly a hand's breadth above the horizon. Toward night the Mouser brought down two low-winging arctic birds with three casts of his sling, while Fafhrd's long-seeing eyes spied a black cave-mouth in an outcropping of rock under a great snowy slope. Luckily there was a clump of dwarfed trees, uprooted and killed by moving ice, near the cave's mouth, and soon the two adventurers were gnawing tough, close-grained brown bird and watching the flickering little fire in the cave's entrance.

Fafhrd stretched hugely and said, 'Farewell to all black priests! That's another bother done with.' He reached out a large, long-fingered hand. 'Mouser, let me see that glass eye you dug from the green hill.'

The Mouser without comment reached into his pouch and handed Fafhrd the brilliant tar-circled globule. Fafhrd held it between his big hands and viewed it thoughtfully. The fire-light shone through it and spread from it, highlighting the cave with red, baleful beams. Fafhrd stared unblinkingly at the gem, until the Mouser became very conscious of the great silence around them, broken only by the tiny but frequent crackling of the fire and the large but infrequent cracking of the ice outside. He felt weary to death, yet somehow couldn't consider sleep.

Finally Fafhrd said, in a faint unnatural voice, 'The earth we walk on once lived – a great hot beast, breathing out fire and spewing molten rock. Its constant yearning was to spit red-hot stuff at the stars. This was before all men.'

'What's that?' the Mouser queried, stirring from his half-trance.

'Now men have come, the earth has gone to sleep,' Fafhrd continued in the same hollow voice, not looking at the Mouser. 'But in its dream it thinks of life, and stirs, and tries to shape itself into the form of men.'

'What's that, Fafhrd?' the Mouser repeated uneasily. But Fafhrd answered him with sudden snores. The Mouser carefully teased the gem from his comrade's fingers. Its tarry rim was soft and slippery – repugnantly so, almost as if it were a kind of black tissue. The Mouser put the thing back in his pouch. A long time passed. Then the Mouser touched his companion's fur-clad shoulder. Fafhrd woke with a swift shudder. 'What is it, small one?' he demanded.

'Morning,' the Mouser told him briefly, pointing over the ashes of the fire at the lightening sky.

As they stooped their way out of the cave, there was a faint roaring sound. Looking over the snow-rim and up the slope, Fafhrd saw hurtling down toward them a vast white globe that grew in size in the very brief time while he watched. He and the Mouser barely managed to dive back into the cavern before the earth shook and the noise became ear-splitting and everything went momentarily dark as the huge snowball thundered over the cave-mouth. They both smelled the cold sour ashes blown into their faces from the dead fire by the globe's passing, and the Mouser coughed.

But Fafhrd instantly lunged out of the cave, swiftly stringing his great bow and fitting to it an arrow long as his arm. He sighted up the slope. At the slope's summit, tiny as bugs beyond the wickedly-barbed arrowhead, were a half dozen conical-hatted figures, sharply silhouetted against the yellow-purple dawn.

They seemed busy as bugs too, fussing furiously with a white globe as tall as themselves.

Fafhrd let out half a breath, paused, and loosed his arrow. The tiny figures continued for several breaths to worry the stubborn globe. Then the one nearest it sprang convulsively and sprawled atop it. The globe began to roll down the slope, carrying the arrow-pierced black priest with it and gathering snow as it went. Soon he was hidden in the ever-thickening crust, but not before his flailing limbs had changed the globe's course, so that it missed the cave-mouth by a spear's length.

As the thundering died, the Mouser peered out cautiously.

'I shot the second avalanche aside,' Fafhrd remarked casually. 'Let's be moving.'

The Mouser would have led the way around the hill – a long and winding course looking treacherous with snow and slippery rock – but Fafhrd said, 'No, straight over the top, where their snowballs have cleared a path for us. They're much too cunning to expect us to take that path.'

However, he kept an arrow nocked to his bow as they made their way up the rocky slope, and moved quite cautiously as they surmounted the naked crest. A white landscape green-spotted with glacial ice opened before them, but no dark specks moved upon it and there were no hiding places nearby. Fafhrd unstrung his bow and laughed.

'They seem to have scampered off,' he said. 'Doubtless they're running back to their little green hill to warm themselves. At any rate, we're rid of them.'

'Yes, just as we were yesterday,' the Mouser commented dryly. 'The fall of the knifer didn't seem to worry them at all, but doubtless they're scared witless because you put an arrow into another of their party.'

'Well, at all events,' Fafhrd said curtly, 'granting that there were seven black priests to begin with, there are now but five.'

And he led the way down the other side of the hill, taking big reckless strides. The Mouser followed slowly, a stone rocking in his dangled sling and his gaze questing restlessly to every side. When they came to snow, he studied it, but there were no tracks as far as he could see to either side. By the time he reached the foot of the hill, Fafhrd was a sling's cast ahead. To make up the distance, the Mouser began a soft-footed, easy lope, yet he did not desist from his watchfulness. His attention was attracted by a squat hummock of snow just ahead of Fafhrd. Shadows might have told him whether there was anything crouched behind it, but the yellow-purple haze hid the sun, so he kept on watching the hummock, meanwhile speeding up his pace. He reached the hummock and saw there was no one behind it almost at the moment he caught up with Fafhrd.

The hummock exploded into a scatter of snow-chunks and a black sag-bellied figure erupted out of it at Fafhrd, ebony arm extended for a knife-slash at the Northerner's neck. Almost simultaneously the Mouser lunged forward, whirling his sling backhanded. The stone, still in the leather loop, caught the slasher high in the face. The curved knife missed by inches. The slasher fell. Fafhrd looked around with mild interest.

The attacker's forehead was so deeply indented that there could be no question of his condition, yet the Mouser stared down at him for a long time. 'A man of Klesh, all right,' he said broodingly, 'but fatter. Armored against the cold. Strange they should have come so far to serve their god.' He looked up and without raising his arm from his side, sharply twirled his sling – much as a bravo might in some alley as a warning to skulkers.

'Four to go,' he said and Fafhrd nodded slowly and soberly.

All day they trod across the Cold Waste – watchfully, but without further incident. A wind came up and the cold bit. The Mouser pulled in his hood so that it covered his mouth and nose, while even Fafhrd hugged his cloak closer around him.

As the sky was darkening to umber and indigo, Fafhrd suddenly stopped and strung his bow and let fly. For a moment the Mouser, who was a bit bothered by his comrade's bemused air, thought that the Northerner was shooting at mere snow. Then the snow leaped, kicking four gray hooves, and the Mouser realized Fafhrd had brought down white-furred meat. He licked his numb lips greedily as Fafhrd swiftly bled and gutted the animal and slung it over his shoulder.

A little way ahead was an outcropping of black rock. Fafhrd studied it for a moment, then took an axe from his belt and struck the rock a careful blow with the back of the head. The Mouser eagerly gathered in the corner of his cloak the large and small chunks that flaked off. He could feel their oiliness and he felt warmed by the mere thought of the rich flame they would make.

Just beyond the outcropping was a low cliff and at its base a cave-mouth slightly sheltered by a tall rock perhaps two spears' lengths in front of it. The Mouser felt a great glow of antici-pated content as he followed Fafhrd toward the inviting dark orifice. He had greatly feared, being numb with cold, aching with fatigue, famished, that they might have to camp out and content themselves with the bones of yesternight's birds. Now in an astonishingly short space they had found food, fuel, shelter. So wonderfully convenient . . .

And then, as Fafhrd rounded the sheltering rock and strode toward the cave-mouth, the thought came to the Mouser: *Much too convenient*. Without further thought, he dropped the coal and sprang at his comrade, hurling the huge fellow flat on his face.

A dart hissed close over him and clicked faintly against the sheltering rock. Again without pause the Mouser darted into the cave-mouth, whipping his sword Scalpel from its sheath. As he entered the cave he zigged a bit to the left, then zagged suddenly to the right and flattened himself against the rocky wall there, slashing prudently at the darkness as he tried to pierce it with his gaze.

Across from him, on the other side of the mouth, the cave bent back in an elbow, the end of which, to the Mouser's amazement, was not dark but dimly lit by a pulsing light that seemed neither that of fire nor the outer twilight. If anything, it resembled the unnatural glow they had seen back in the Bones of the Old Ones.

But unnatural or not, it had the advantage of silhouetting the Mouser's antagonist. The squat fellow was now gripping a curved knife rather than a blowgun. As the Mouser sprang at him, he scuttled back along the elbow and dodged around the corner from behind which the pulsing glow came. To the Mouser's further amazement, he felt not only a growing warmth as he pursued but also moistness in the air. He rounded the corner. The black priest, who'd stopped just beyond it, lunged at him. But the Mouser was prepared for this and Scalpel took his adversary neatly in the chest, just off center, transfixing him, while the curved knife slashed only steamy air.

For a moment the fanatic priest tried to work his way up along the thin blade and so get within striking distance of the Mouser. Then the nefarious glare died in the priest's eyes and he slumped, while the Mouser distastefully whipped out the blade.

The priest tottered back into the steamy glow, which the Mouser now saw came from a small pit just beyond. With a blood-choking gargling moan the black one stepped back into the pit and vanished. There was a scuff of flesh against rock, a pause, and then a faint splash, and then no sound at all, except for the soft, distant bubbling and seething that the Mouser now realized came steadily from the pit – that is, until Fafhrd came clumping up belatedly.

'Three to go,' the Mouser informed him casually. 'The fourth is cooking at the bottom of that pit. But I want broiled dinner tonight, not boiled, and besides, I haven't a long enough fork. So fetch in the black stones I dropped.'

Fafhrd objected at first, eyeing the steam-and-fire vent almost superstitiously, and urged that they seek other lodging. But the Mouser argued that to spend the night in the now-empty, easily scanned cave was far better than to risk ambush in the outer dark. To the Mouser's relief Fafhrd agreed after peering down the pit for possible handholds that might help a live or boiled attacker. The small man had no desire to leave this pleasantly steamy spot.

The fire was built against the outer wall of the cave and near the mouth, so that no one could creep in without being revealed by its flames. After they had polished off some grilled liver and a number of tough, seared chops and had tossed the bones into the hot fire, where they sputtered merrily, Fafhrd settled back against the rocky wall and asked the Mouser to let him look at the diamond eye.

The Mouser complied with some reluctance, once again experiencing repugnance for the frostily-gleaming stone's tarry circlet. He had the feeling that Fafhrd was going to do something unwise with the stone – what, he didn't know. But the Northerner merely glanced at it for a moment, almost puzzledly, and then thrust it away in *his* pouch. The Mouser started to object, but Fafhrd curtly replied that it was their common property. The Mouser could not but agree.

They had decided to stand watch by turns, Fafhrd first. The Mouser snuggled his cloak around him, and tucked under his head a pillow made of pouch and folded hood. The coal fire flamed, the strange glow from the pit pulsed wanly. The Mouser found it decidedly pleasant to be between the dry heat of the former and the moist warmth of the latter, both spiced by the chill air from outside. He watched the play of shadows through half-closed eyes. Fafhrd, sitting between the Mouser and the flames, bulked reassuringly large, wide-eyed, and alert. The Mouser's last thought as he drowsed off was that he was rather glad that Fafhrd had the diamond. It made his own pillow that much less bumpy.

He woke hearing an odd soft voice. The fire had burned low. For a frightening moment he thought that a stranger had somehow come into the cave – perhaps muttering hypnotic words to put a sleepspell on his comrade. Then he realized that the voice was the one Fafhrd had used last night, and that the Northerner was staring into the diamond eye as if he were seeing limitless visions there, and rocking it slowly to and fro. The rocking made the glittering beams from the gem synchronize with the pulsing glow in a way the Mouser didn't like.

'Nehwon's blood,' Fafhrd was murmuring, his voice almost a chant, 'still pulses strongly under its wrinkled rocky skin, and still bleeds hot and raw from wounds in the mountains. But it needs the blood of heroes before it can shape itself into the form of men.'

The Mouser jumped up, grabbed Fafhrd by the shoulder and shook him gently.

'Those who truly worship Nehwon,' Fafhrd went on entrancedly, as if nothing had happened, 'guard its mountain-wounds and wait and pray for the great day of fulfillment when Nehwon shall wake again, this time in man's form, and rid itself of the vermin called men.'

The Mouser's shaking became violent and Fafhrd woke with a start – only to assert that he had been awake all the time and that the Mouser had been having a nightmare. He laughed at the Mouser's counter-assertions and would not budge from his own. Nor would he give up the diamond, but tucked it deep in his pouch, gave two huge yawns and fell asleep while the Mouser was still expostulating.

The Mouser did not find his watch a pleasant one. In place of his former trust in this rocky nook, he now scented danger in every direction and peered as often at the steamy pit as at the black entrance beyond the glowing coals, entertaining himself with vivid visions of a cooked priest somehow writhing his way up. Meanwhile the more logical part of his mind dwelled on an unpleasantly consistent theory that the hot inner layer of Nehwon was indeed jealous of man, and that the green hill was one of those spots where inner Nehwon was seeking to escape its rocky jacket and form itself into all-conquering man-shaped giants of living stone. The black Kleshite priests would be Nehwon-worshippers eager for the destruction of all other men. And the diamond eye, far from being a bit of valuable and harmless loot, was somehow alive and seeking to enchant Fafhrd with its glittering gaze, and lead him to an obscure doom.

Three times the Mouser tried to get the gem away from his comrade, the third time by slitting the bottom of the Northerner's pouch. But though the Mouser knew himself the most cunning cutpurse in Lankhmar, though perhaps a trifle out of practice, Fafhrd each time hugged the pouch tighter to him and muttered peevishly in his sleep and unerringly brushed away the Mouser's questing hand. The Mouser thought of taking the diamond eye by force, but was stopped by the unreasoning conviction that this would touch off murderous resistance in the

Northerner. Indeed, he had strong misgivings as to the state in which his comrade would awake.

But when the cave-mouth finally lightened, Fafhrd roused himself with a shake and a morning yawn-and-growl as stentorian and genial as any the Mouser had ever winced at. Fafhrd acted with such chipper, clear-headed enthusiasm that the Mouser's fears were quite blown away, or at least driven deep into the back of his mind. The two adventurers had a cold-meat breakfast, and carefully wrapped up and packed away the legs and shoulders that had been roasted during the night.

Then while Fafhrd covered him with arrow nocked to taut bowstring, the Mouser darted out and sprang to cover behind the outside of the stone sheltering the entrance. Bobbing up here and there for quick glances over its top, he scanned the cliff above the cave for any sign of ambushers. Holding his sling at the ready, he covered Fafhrd while the latter rushed forth. After a bit they satisfied themselves that there were at least no nearby lurkers in the pale dawn, and Fafhrd led off with a swinging stride. The Mouser followed briskly enough, but after a little while became possessed with a doubt. It seemed to him that Fafhrd was not leading them straight along their course, but swinging rather sharply off toward the left. It was hard to be at all sure, for the sun had still not broken through and the sky was filled with purplish and yellowish scarf-like clouds, while the Mouser could not tell for certain just which way they had come yesterday, since things are very different looking back than looking forward.

Nevertheless he voiced his doubts after a while, but Fafhrd replied with such good-humored assurance, 'The Cold Waste was my childhood playground, as familiar to me as Lankhmar's mazy alleys or the swampways of the Great Salt Marsh to you,' that the Mouser was almost completely satisfied. Besides, the day was windless, which pleased the Mouser no end, because of his worship of warmth.

After a good half-day's trudging they mounted a snowy rise and the Mouser's eyebrows rose incredulously at the landscape ahead: a tilted plain of green ice smooth as glass. Its upper edge, which lay somewhat to their right, was broken by jagged pinnacles, like the crest of a great smooth wave. Its lower slope stretched down for a vast distance to their left, finally losing itself in what looked like a white mist, while straight ahead there seemed to be no end.

The plain was so green that it looked like a giddily enchanted ocean, tilted at the command of some mighty magician. The Mouser felt sure it would reflect the stars on a clear night.

He was somewhat horrified, though hardly surprised, when his comrade coolly proposed that they walk straight across it. The Northerner's shrewd gaze had spotted a section just ahead of them where the slope leveled off briefly before sweeping down again. Along this level ribbon, Fafhrd asserted, they could walk with ease – and then the Northerner set out without waiting for a reply.

With a fatalistic shrug the Mouser followed, walking at first as if on eggs and with many an uneasy glance at the great downward slope. He wished he had bronze-cleated boots – even ones worn flat like Fafhrd's – or some sort of spurs to fix to his own slippery shoes, so that he'd have a better chance of stopping himself if he did start to slide. After a while he grew more confident and took longer and swifter, if still most gingerly steps, and the gap Fafhrd had put between them was closed.

They had walked for perhaps three bowshots across the plain, and still had no sight of an end to it, when a flicker of movement in the corner of his right eye made the Mouser look around.

Swiftly and silently sliding down toward them from some hiding place in the ragged crest, came the remaining black priests, three abreast. They kept their footing like expert skiers – and indeed they seemed to be wearing skis of some sort. Two of them carried spears improvised by thrusting dagger grips into the muzzles of their long blowguns, while the midmost had as lance a narrow, needle-sharp icicle or ice-shard at least eight feet long.

No time now for slings and arrows, and of what use to sword-skewer one who has already spear-skewered you? Besides, an icy slope is no place for dainty near-stationary maneuvering. Without a word to Fafhrd, so certain he was that the Northerner would do the same, the Mouser took off down the dreaded leftward slope.

It was as if he had cast himself into the arms of a demon of speed. Ice whirred softly under his boots; quiet air became cold wind whipping his garments and chilling his cheeks.

But not enough speed. The skiing black priests had a head-start. The Mouser hoped the level stretch would wreck them, but they merely sailed out from it with squat majesty and came down without losing footing – and hardly two spears' lengths behind. Daggers and ice-lance gleamed wickedly.

The Mouser drew Scalpel and after trying fruitlessly to pole himself along to greater velocity with it, squatted down so as to offer the least resistance to the air. Still the black priests gained. Fafhrd beside him dug in his dragon-pommeled long-sword so that ice-dust spouted up fountain-wise, and shot off in a great swing sideward. The priest bearing the ice-lance swerved after him.

Meanwhile the two other priests caught up with the Mouser. He arched his hurtling body away from the spear-thrust of the first and knocked that of the second aside with Scalpel, and for the next few moments there was fought the strangest sort of duel – almost as if they weren't moving at all, since they were all moving at the same speed. At one point the Mouser was sliding down backward, parrying the nasty blowgun-spears with his shorter weapon.

But two against one always helps, and this time might have proved fatal, if Fafhrd had not just then caromed back from his great sideward swing full of speed from some slope he alone had seen, and whirled his sword. He passed just behind the two priests and then their heads were skidding along separately from their bodies, though all at the same speed.

Yet it would have been all up with Fafhrd, for the last black priest, perhaps helped by the weight of his ice-lance, came hurtling after Fafhrd at even greater speed and would have skewered him except the Mouser deflected the ice-lance upward, with Scalpel held in two hands, and the icy point merely ruffled Fafhrd's streaming red hair.

The next moment they all plunged into the white-icy mist. The last glimpse the Mouser had of Fafhrd was of his speeding head alone, cutting a wake in the neck-high mist. Then the Mouser's eyes were beneath the mist's surface.

It was most strange to the Mouser to skim swiftly through milky stuff, ice-crystals stinging his cheeks, not knowing each instant if an unknown barrier might wreck him. He heard a grunt that sounded like Fafhrd's, and on top of that a tingling crash, which might have been the ice-spear shattering, followed by a sighing, tortured moan. Next came the feeling of reaching bottom, followed by an upward swoop, and then the Mouser broke out of the mist into the purple-yellow day and skidded into a soft snowbank and began to laugh wildly with relief. It was some moments before he noticed that Fafhrd, also shaking with laughter, was likewise half buried in the snow beside him.

When Fafhrd looked at the Mouser, the latter shrugged inquiringly at the mist behind them. The Northerner nodded confirmingly.

'The last priest dead. None to go!' the Mouser proclaimed happily, stretching in the snow as if it were a featherbed. His chief idea was to find the nearest cave – he was sure there would be one – and enjoy a great rest.

But Fafhrd turned out to be full of other ideas and a seething energy. Nothing would do but they must press on swiftly until dusk, and he presented to the Mouser such alluring pictures of getting out of the Cold Waste by tomorrow, or even nightfall, that the small man soon found himself trotting along after the big one, though he couldn't help wondering from time to time how Fafhrd could be so supremely sure of his direction in this chaos of ice, snow, and churning, unpleasantly-tinted clouds. The whole Cold Waste couldn't have been his playground, surely, the Mouser told himself, with an inward shudder at child Fafhrd's notion of proper places to play.

Twilight overtook them before they reached the forests Fafhrd had promised, and at the Mouser's urgent insistence they began to hunt for a place to pass the night. This time a cave wasn't so easily come by. It was quite dark before Fafhrd spotted a rocky notch with a clump of stunted trees growing in front of it that promised at least fuel and passable shelter.

However, it appeared that the wood would hardly be needed, for just short of the tree-clump was a black rock outcropping resembling the one that had given them coal last night.

But just as Fafhrd joyfully lifted his axe, the outcropping came to life and lunged at his belly with a dagger.

Only Fafhrd's exuberant and undiminished energy saved his life. He arched his belly aside with a supple swiftness that amazed even the Mouser, and drove the axe deep into his attacker's head. The squat black body thrashed its limbs convulsively and swiftly grew stiff. Fafhrd's deep laughter rumbled like thunder. 'Shall we call him the none black priest, Mouser?' he inquired.

But the Mouser saw no cause for amusement. All his uneasiness returned. If they had missed their count on one of the black priests – say the one who had spun down in the snowball or the one supposedly slain in the mist – why mightn't they have missed their count on another? Besides, how could they have been so convinced, simply from an ancient inscription, that there had been only seven black priests? And once you admitted there might have been eight, why mightn't there be nine, or ten, or twenty?

However, Fafhrd merely chuckled at these worries and chopped wood and built a roaring fire in the rocky notch. And although the Mouser knew the fire would advertise their presence for miles around, he was so grateful for its warmth that he found himself unable to criticize Fafhrd at all severely. And when they had warmed and eaten their roast meat from the morning, such a delicious tiredness came over the Mouser that he tucked his cloak around him and headed straight for sleep. However, Fafhrd chose that moment to drag out and inspect by firelight the diamond eye, which made the Mouser open his own a slit.

This time Fafhrd did not seem inclined to go into a trance. He grinned in a lively and greedy fashion as he turned the gem this way and that, as though to admire the beams flashing from it while mentally appraising its value in square Lankhmarian goldpieces.

Although reassured, the Mouser was annoyed. 'Put it away, Fafhrd,' he snapped sleepily.

Fafhrd stopped turning the gem and one of its beams blinked directly at the Mouser. The latter shivered, for he had for a moment the sharp conviction that the gem was looking at him with evil intelligence.

But Fafhrd obediently tucked the gem away with a laugh-and-a-yawn and cloaked himself up for sleep. Gradually the Mouser's eerie feelings and realistic fears were both lulled as he watched the dancing flames, and he drowsed off.

The Mouser's next conscious sensations were of being tossed roughly down onto thick grass that felt unpleasantly like fur. His head ached splittingly and there was a pulsing yellow-purple glow, shot through with blinding gleams. It was a few moments before he realized that all these lights were outside his skull rather than inside it.

He lifted his head to look around and agonizing pain shot through it. However, he persisted and shortly found out where he was.

He was lying on the hillocky, dark-vegetated shore across the acid-seeming lake from the green hill. The night sky was live with northern lights, while from the mouthlike slit – now open wider – in the green hill's pinkish top, a red smoke came in puffs like a man eagerly panting and heaving. All the hill's green flank-faces seemed monstrously alive in the mixed lights, their mouths twitching and their eyes flashing – as if every one of them held an eye-diamond. Only a few feet away from the Mouser, Fafhrd stood stiffly behind the stubby pillar of rock, which was indeed a carved altar of some sort topped by a great bowl. The Northerner was chanting something in a grunty language the Mouser didn't know and had never heard Fafhrd use.

The Mouser struggled to a sitting position. Gingerly feeling his skull, he found a large lump over his right ear. At the same time Fafhrd struck sparks – apparently with stone and steel – above the bowl, and a pillar of purple flame shot up from it, and the Mouser saw that Fafhrd's eyes were tight shut and that in his hand he held the diamond eye.

Then the Mouser realized that the diamond eye had been far

wiser than the black priests who had served its mountain idol. They, like many priests, had been much too fanatical and not nearly as clever as the god they served. While they had sought to rescue the filched eye and destroy the blasphemous thieves who had stolen it, the eye had taken care of itself very nicely. It had enchanted Fafhrd and deceived him into taking a circling course that would lead him and the Mouser back to the vengeful green hill. It had even speeded up the last stage of the journey, forcing Fafhrd to move by night, carrying the Mouser with him after stunning him in his sleep with a dangerously heavy blow.

Also, the diamond eye must have been more foresighted and purposeful than its priests. It must have some important end in view, over and beyond that of getting itself returned to its mountain-idol. Otherwise, why should it have instructed Fafhrd to preserve the Mouser carefully and bring him along? The diamond eye must have some use for both of them. Through the Mouser's aching brain reverberated the phrase he remembered Fafhrd muttering two nights before: 'But it needs the blood of heroes before it can shape itself into the form of man.'

As all these thoughts were seething painfully in the Mouser's brain, he saw Fafhrd coming toward him with diamond eye in one hand and drawn longsword in the other, but a winning smile on his blind face.

'Come, Mouser,' Fafhrd said gently, 'it is time we crossed the lake and climbed the hill and received the kiss and sweet suck of the topmost lips and mingled our blood with the hot blood of Nehwon. In that way we will live on in the stony rock-giants about to be born, and know with them the joy of crushing cities and trampling armies and stamping on all cultivated fields.'

These mad phrases stung the Mouser into action, unintimidated by the pulsing lights of sky and hill. He jerked Scalpel from its scabbard and sprang at Fafhrd, engaging the longsword and making a particularly clever disarming thrust-and-twist guaranteed to send the longsword spinning from Fafhrd's hand – especially since the Northerner still had his eyes closed tight.

Instead, Fafhrd's heavy blade evaded the Mouser's swift one as easily as one avoids a baby's slap, and, smiling sorrowfully, sent a rippling thrust at the Mouser's throat that the latter could escape only with the most fantastic and frantic of backward leaps.

The leap took him in the direction of the lake. Instantly Fafhrd closed in, attacking with scornful poise. His large face was a mask of blond contempt. His far heavier sword moved as deftly as Scalpel, weaving a gleaming arabesque of attack that forced the Mouser back, back, back.

And all the while Fafhrd's eyes stayed tight shut. Only when driven to the brink of the lake did the Mouser realize the reason. The diamond eye in Fafhrd's left hand was doing all the seeing for the Northerner. It followed every movement of Scalpel with a snaky intentness.

So, as he danced on the slippery black rim above the wildly-reflecting lake, with the skies throbbing yellow-purple above him and the green hill panting behind, the Mouser suddenly ignored Fafhrd's threatening blade and ducked and slashed unexpectedly at the diamond eye.

Fafhrd's cut whistled a finger's breadth above the Mouser's head.

The diamond eye, struck by Scalpel, exploded in a white burst.

The black furry ground beneath their feet heaved as if in despairing torment.

The green hill erupted with a vindictive red blast that sent the Mouser staggering and that shot a gush of molten rock twice the hill's height toward the bruised night-sky.

The Mouser grabbed hold of his bewilderedly-staring companion and rushed him away from the green hill and the lake.

A dozen heartbeats after they left the spot, the erupting molten rock drenched the altar and splashed wide. Some of the red gouts came even as far as the Mouser and Fafhrd, shooting fiery darts over their shoulders as they scampered. One or two gouts hit and the Mouser had to beat out a small fire they started in Fafhrd's cloak.

Looking back as he ran, the Mouser got a last glimpse of the green hill. Although still spouting fire and dribbling red streams, it seemed otherwise very solid and still, as though all its potentialities for life were vanished for a time, or forever.

When they finally stopped running, Fafhrd looked stupidly down at his left hand and said, 'Mouser, I've cut my thumb. It's bleeding.'

'So's the green hill,' the Mouser commented, looking back. 'And bleeding to death, I'm happy to say.'

VIII
CLAWS FROM THE NIGHT

Fear hovered in the moonlight over Lankhmar. Fear flowed like mist through the twisting thoroughfares and mazy alleyways, trickling even into that most intricately curved and crevice-like street where a sootily flickering lantern marked the doorway to the tavern of the Silver Eel.

It was a subtle fear, not the sort inspired by a besieging army, or warring nobles, or revolting slaves, or a mad overlord bent on wanton slaughter, or an enemy fleet sailing from the Inner Sea into the estuary of the Hlal. But it was none the less potent. It clutched the soft throats of the chattering women now entering the low doorway of the Silver Eel, making their laughter more sudden and shrill. It touched the women's escorts too, making them speak louder and rattle their swords more than necessary.

This was a party of young aristocrats seeking excitement in a place known to be disreputable and somewhat dangerous. Their garments were rich and fantastic, after the fashion of the decadent Lankhmar nobility. But there was one thing that seemed almost too crazily faddish even in exotic Lankhmar. The head of each woman was enclosed in a small, delicately-wrought silver bird cage.

Again the door opened, this time to emit two men who swiftly walked away. The one was tall and hulking, and seemed to be concealing some object under his great cloak. The other was small and lithe, clad from crown to toe in a soft gray that merged with the diffused moonlight. He was carrying a fishpole over his shoulder.

'I wonder what Fafhrd and the Gray Mouser are up to now,' murmured a hanger-on, peering curiously over his shoulder. The landlord shrugged.

'No good, I'll warrant,' pressed the hanger-on. 'I saw the thing under Fafhrd's cloak move, as if alive. Today, in Lankhmar, that is most suspicious. You see what I mean? And then the fishpole.'

'Peace,' said the landlord. 'They are two honest rogues, even though much in need of money, if what they owe me for wine is any indication. Say nothing against them.'

But he looked a trifle puzzled and perturbed as he went inside again, impatiently pushing the hanger-on ahead of him.

It was three months since the fear had come to Lankhmar, and at the beginning it had been a very different sort of thing – hardly fear at all. Just an overly numerous series of thefts of cheap trinkets and costly gems, with women the chief sufferers. Bright and shining objects, no matter what their nature, were given the preference.

Gossip had it that a band of exceptionally light-fingered and haphazard pilferers was making a speciality of the tiring rooms of great ladies, though the whipping of maids and body-slaves failed to uncover any of the expected confederates. Then someone advanced the theory that it was the work of cunning children too young to judge well the value of objects.

But gradually the character of the thefts began to change. Fewer worthless baubles were taken. More and more often, valuable gems were plucked from a jumble of glass and gilt, giving the odd impression that the marauders were only by practice developing a sense of discrimination.

At about this time people began to suspect that the ancient and almost reputable Thieves' Guild of Lankhmar had invented a new stratagem, and there was talk of torturing a few suspected leaders or waiting for a west wind and burning the Street of the Silk Merchants.

But since the Thieves' Guild was a conservative and hide-bound organization wedded to traditional methods of thievery, suspicion shifted somewhat when it became increasingly evident that a mentality of incredible daring and ingenuity was at work.

Valuables disappeared in broad daylight, even from chambers locked and carefully guarded, or from sheer-walled roof-gardens. A lady secure in her home chanced to lay a bracelet on an inaccessible windowledge; it vanished while she chatted with a friend. A lord's daughter, walking in a private garden, felt someone reach down from a thickly-leafed tree and snatch a diamond pin from her hair; the tree was immediately climbed by nimble servitors, but nothing was found.

Then a hysterical maid ran to her mistress with the information that she had just seen a large bird, black in colour, making off through a window with an emerald ring clutched securely in its talons.

This story at first met with angry disbelief. It was concluded that the girl herself must have stolen the ring. She was whipped almost to death amid general approval.

The next day a large black bird swooped down on the niece of the Overlord and ripped a jewel from her ear.

Much supporting evidence was immediately forthcoming. People told of seeing birds of unusual appearance at odd times and places. It was recalled that in each of the thefts an aerial route had been left open. The victims began to remember things that had seemed inconsequential at the time – the beat of wings, the rustle of feathers, bird tracks and droppings, hovering shadows and the like.

All Lankhmar buzzed with amazed speculation. It was believed, however, that the thefts would cease, now that the authors were known and suitable precautions taken. No special significance was attached to the injured ear of the Overlord's niece. Both these judgments proved wrong.

Two days later, the notorious courtesan Lessnya was beset by a large black bird while crossing a wide square. Forewarned, Lessnya struck at the bird with a gilt wand she was carrying, shouting to scare it off.

To the horror of the onlookers, the bird eluded the wild blows, set its talons in her white shoulder, and pecked her right eye viciously. Thereupon it gave a shuddering squawk, flapped its wings, and took off amid a flurry of black feathers, gripping a jade brooch in its claws.

Within the next three days, five more women were robbed in the same way; three of these were mutilated.

Lankhmar was frightened. Such unwholesomely purposeful

behavior on the part of birds roused all sorts of superstitious fear. Bowmen armed with triple-pronged fowling-arrows were stationed on the roofs. Timid women stayed indoors, or wore cloaks to hide their jewels. Shutters were kept closed at night despite the summer heat. Considerable numbers of innocent pigeons and gulls were shot or poisoned. Cocky young nobles summoned their falconers and went hawking after the marauders.

But they had difficulty in locating any; and on the few occasions they did, their falcons found themselves opposed by adversaries who flew swiftly and fought back successfully. More than one mews mourned the death of a favorite fighting bird. All efforts to trace the winged thieves failed.

These activities did have one tangible result: most of the attacks and thefts thereafter occurred during the hours of darkness.

Then a woman died painfully three hours after having been clawed around the neck, and black robed physicians averred that there must have been a virulent poison in the wounding talons.

Panic grew and wild theories were advanced. The priests of the Great God maintained that it was a divine rebuke to feminine vanity, and made dire prophecies about an imminent revolt of all animals against sinful man. Astrologers dropped dark and disturbing hints. A frantic mob burned a rookery belonging to a wealthy grain merchant, and then milled through the streets, stoning all birds and killing three of the sacred black swans before being dispersed.

Still the attacks continued. And Lankhmar, with her usual resiliency, began to adjust herself somewhat to this bizarre and inexplicable siege from the sky. Rich women made a fashion of their fear by adopting silver networks to protect their features. Several wits made jokes about how, in a topsy-turvy world, the birds were loose and the women wore the cages. The courtesan Lessnya had her jeweler contrive a lustrous eye of hollow gold, which men said added to her exotic beauty.

Then Fafhrd and the Gray Mouser appeared in Lankhmar. Few guessed where the huge Northern barbarian and his small, dexterous companion had been or why they had returned at this particular time. Nor did Fafhrd or the Gray Mouser offer any explanations.

They busied themselves with inquiries at the Silver Eel and elsewhere, drinking much wine but avoiding brawls. Through certain devious channels of information the Mouser learned that the fabulously wealthy but socially unacceptable moneylender Muulsh had bought a famous ruby from the King of the East – then hard-pressed for cash – and was going to give it to his wife. Whereupon the Mouser and Fafhrd made further inquiries and certain secret preparations, and slipped away together from the tavern of the Silver Eel on a moonlit night, bearing objects of a mysterious nature which awakened doubts and suspicions in the mind of the landlord and others.

For there was no denying that the thing Fafhrd carried under his great cloak moved as if alive and was the size of a large bird.

Moonlight did not soften the harsh angular lines of the great stone house of Muulsh, the moneylender. Square, flat-roofed, small-windowed, three stories high, it stood a little distance from the similar houses of the wealthy grain merchants like a rejected hanger-on.

Close to it flowed the waters of the Hlal, angrily churning past this portion of the city, which thrust out like an elbow into the mighty stream. Abutting and o'ertopping it on the side nearest the river loomed a lightless, tower-like structure, one of the several accursed and abandoned temples of Lankhmar, shut up in ancient times for reasons now known only to certain priests and necromancers.

Crowding close on the other side were the dark, solid forms of warehouses. There was an impression of tight-lipped power about this house of Muulsh – of great wealth and weighty secrets closely guarded.

But the Gray Mouser, peering down through one of the usual Lankhmar roof-windows into the tiring room of Muulsh's wife, was seeing a very different aspect of Muulsh's character. The notoriously heartless moneylender, quailing under a connubial tongue-lashing, looked like nothing so much as a fawning lapdog – except perhaps an anxious and solicitous hen.

'You worm! You slug! You gross, fat beast!' his slender young wife railed at him, almost chanting the words. 'You've ruined my life with your stinking money-grubbing! Not one noblewoman will even speak to me. Not one lord or grain merchant so much as dares flirt with me. Everywhere I am ostracized. And all because your fingers are greasy and vile from handling coins!'

'But, Atya,' he murmured timidly, 'I've always thought you had friends to visit. Almost every day you go off for hours on end – though without telling me where you've been.'

'You insensitive clod!' she cried. 'Is it any wonder that I slip away to some lonely nook to weep and seek bitter consolation in private? You will never understand the delicacy of my emotions. Why did I ever marry you? I wouldn't have, you may be sure – except that you forced my poor father into it when he was in difficulties. You bought me! It's the only way you know of getting anything.

'And then when my poor father died, you had the effrontery to buy this house, his house, the house I was born in. You did it to complete my humiliation. To take me back where everybody knew me and could say, "There goes the wife of that utterly impossible moneylender" – if they use such a polite word as wife! All you want is to torture and degrade me, drag me down to your own unutterable level. Oh, you obscene pig!'

And she made a tattoo with her gilded heels on the gleaming parquetry of the floor. Clad in yellow silk tunic and pantaloons, she was very pretty in a small, slight way. Her small-chinned, bright-eyed face was oddly attractive under its canopy of gleamingly smooth black hair. Her swift movements had the quality of restless fluttering. At the moment her every gesture conveyed anger and unbearable irritation, but there was also a kind of studied ease about her manner that suggested to the Mouser, who was hugely enjoying everything, a scene that had been played and replayed many times.

The room suited her well, with its silken hangings and fragile furniture. Low tables, scattered about, were crowded with jars of cosmetics, bowls of sweetmeats, and all sorts of frivolous bric-a-brac. The flames of slim tapers swayed in the warm breeze from the open windows.

On delicate chains were suspended a full dozen cages of

canaries, nightingales, love birds, and other tiny warblers, some drowsing, others chirruping sleepily. Here and there were strewn small fluffy rugs. All in all, a very downy nest amidst the stoniness of Lankhmar.

Muulsh was somewhat as she had described him – fat, ugly, and perhaps twenty years older than she. His gaudy tunic fitted him like a sack. The look of mingled apprehension and desire he fixed upon his wife was irresistibly comic.

'Oh, Atya, my little dove, do not be angry with me. I try so hard to please you, and I love you so very much,' he cried, and tried to lay his hand on her arm. She eluded him. He hurried clumsily after her, immediately bumping into one of the bird cages, which hung at an inconvenient height. She turned on him in a miniature fury.

'Disturb my pets, will you, you brute! There, there, my dears, don't be frightened. It's just the old she-elephant.'

'Damn your pets!' he cursed impulsively, holding his forehead. Then he recollected himself and dodged backward, as if in fear of being thwacked with a slipper.

'Oh! So in addition to all your other crude affronts, we are also to be damned?' she said, her voice suddenly icy.

'No, no, my beloved Atya. I forgot myself. I love you very much, and your feathered pets as well. I meant no harm.'

'Of course you meant no harm! You merely want to torment us to death. You want to degrade and—'

'But, Atya,' he interrupted placatingly, 'I don't think I've really degraded you. Remember, even before I married you, your family never mingled with Lankhmar society.'

That remark was a mistake, as the eavesdropping Mouser, choking back his laughter, could plainly see. Muulsh must have realized it too, for as Atya went white and reached for a heavy crystal bottle, he retreated and cried out, 'I've brought you a present.'

'I can imagine what it's like,' she sneered disdainfully, relaxing a trifle but still holding the bottle poised. 'Some trinket a lady would give her maid. Or flashy rags fit only for a harlot.'

'Oh, no, my dear. This is a gift for an empress.'

'I don't believe you. It's because of your foul taste and filthy manners that Lankhmar won't accept me.' Her fine, decadently weak features contracted in a pout, her charming bosom still rising and falling from anger. '"She's the concubine of Muulsh the moneylender," they say, and snigger at me. Snigger!'

'They've no right to. I can buy the lot of them! Just wait until they see you wearing my gift. It's a jewel that the wife of the Overlord would give her eyeteeth to possess!'

At mention of the word 'jewel' the Mouser sensed a subtle shiver of anticipation run through the room. More than that, he saw one of the silken hangings stir in a way that the lazy breeze could hardly account for.

He edged cautiously forward, craning his neck and peered down sideways into the space between the hangings and the wall. Then slowly a smile of elfish amusement appeared on his compact, snub-nosed face.

Crouched in the faintly amber luminescence that filtered through the draperies were two scrawny men, naked except for dark breechcloths. Each carried a bag big enough to fit loosely over a human head. From these bags leaked a faint soporific scent that the Mouser had noticed before without being able to place.

The Mouser's smile deepened. Noiselessly he drew forward the slim fishpole at his side and inspected the line and the stickily-smeared claws that served for a hook.

'Show me the jewel!' said Atya.

'I shall, my dear. At once,' answered Muulsh. 'But don't you think we'd first best close the sky-window and the other ones?'

'We'll do nothing of the kind!' snapped Atya. 'Must I stifle just because a lot of old women have given way to a silly fear?'

'But, my dove, it's not a silly fear. All Lankhmar is afraid. And rightly.'

He moved as though to call a slave. Atya stamped her foot pettishly. 'Stop, you fat coward! I refuse to give way to childish frights. I won't believe any of those fantastic stories, no matter how many great ladies swear to them. Don't you dare have the windows closed. Show me the jewel at once, or – or I'll never be nice to you again.'

She seemed close to hysteria. Muulsh sighed and resigned himself.

'Very well, my sweet.'

He walked over to an inlaid table by the door, clumsily ducking past several bird cages, and fumbled at a small casket. Four pairs of eyes followed him intently. When he returned there was something in his hand that glittered. He set it down on the center of the table.

'There,' he said, stepping back. 'I told you it was fit for an empress, and it is.'

For a space there was breathless silence in the room. The two thieves behind the draperies edged forward hungrily, quietly loosening the drawstrings of the bags, their feet caressing the polished floor like cats' paws.

The Mouser slid the slim fishing rod through the sky-window, avoiding the silver chains of the cages, until the pendant claw was poised directly above the center of the table, like a spider preparing to drop on an unsuspecting large red beetle.

Atya stared. A new dignity and self-respect crept into Muulsh's expression. The jewel gleamed like a fat, lucent, quivering drop of blood.

The two thieves crouched to spring. The Mouser joggled the rod slightly, gauging his aim before he dropped the claw. Atya reached out an eager hand and moved toward the table.

But all these intended actions were simultaneously interrupted.

There was a beat and whirr of powerful wings. An inky bird a little larger than a crow flapped through a side window and skidded down into the room, like a fragment of blackness detached from the outer night. Its talons made arm-long scratches as it hit the table. Then it arched its neck, gave a loud, shuddering squawk, and launched itself toward Atya.

The room whirled with chaotic movements. The gummed claw halted midway in its drop. The two thieves fought ungracefully to keep their balance and avoid being seen. Muulsh waved his arms and shouted, 'Shoo! Shoo!' Atya collapsed.

The black bird swept close past Atya, its wings brushing and striking the silver cages, and beat out into the night.

Again there was momentary silence in the room. The gentle

songbirds had been quite stilled by the incursion of their raptorial brother. The rod vanished through the sky-window. The two thieves scuttled behind the draperies and noiselessly edged toward a door. Their looks of bafflement and fright were giving way to professional chagrin.

Atya rose to her knees, dainty hands pressed to her face. A shudder tightened around Muulsh's fleshy neck and he moved toward her.

'Did it – did it hurt you? Your face. It struck at you.'

Atya dropped her hands, revealing an unmaimed countenance. She stared at her husband. Then all at once the stare changed to a glare, like a pot suddenly come to a boil.

'You big useless hen!' she cried out. 'For all you cared, it might have pecked out both my eyes! Why didn't you do something? Yelling "Shoo! Shoo!" when it struck at me! And the jewel gone forever now! Oh, you miserable capon!'

She rose to her feet, taking off one of her slippers with a wildly determined air. Muulsh retreated, protesting and bumped into a whole cluster of bird cages.

Only Fafhrd's tossed-aside cloak marked the spot where the Gray Mouser had left him. Hastening to the roof-edge, he made out Fafhrd's large form some distance away across the roofs of the adjoining warehouses. The barbarian was staring at the moonlit sky. The Mouser gathered up the cloak, leaped the narrow gap, and followed.

When the Mouser reached him, Fafhrd was grinning with great satisfaction so that his big white teeth showed. The size of his supple, brawny frame and the amount of metal-studded leather he wore in the form of armbands and broad belt were as much out of tune with civilized Lankhmar as were his long, copper hair, handsomely rugged features, and pale Northern skin, ghostly in the moonlight. Firmly clutching his heavy hawking-glove at the wrist was a white-capped eagle, which ruffled its feathers and made a disagreeable gargling noise in its throat at the Mouser's approach.

'Now tell me I can't hawk by full moon!' he cried out in great good humor. 'I don't know what happened in the room, or what luck you had, but as for the black bird that went in and came out – Lo! It is here!'

He pushed at a limp bundle of black feathers with his foot.

The Mouser hissed the names of several gods in quick succession, then asked, 'But the jewel?'

'I don't know about that,' said Fafhrd, brushing the matter aside. 'Ah, but you should have seen it, little man! A wondrous fight!' His voice regained its enthusiasm. 'The other one flew swift and cunningly but Kooskra here rose like the north wind up a mountain pass. For a while I lost them in the fray. There seemed to be something of a fight. Then Kooskra brought him down.'

The Mouser had dropped to his knees and was gingerly examining Kooskra's quarry. He slipped a small knife from his belt.

'And to think,' continued Fafhrd, as he adjusted a leather hood over the eagle's head, 'that they told me these birds were demons or fierce phantasms of darkness! Faugh! They're only ungainly, night-flying crows.'

'You talk too loudly,' said the Mouser. Then he looked up. 'But there's no gainsaying that tonight the eagle beat the fishpole. See what I found in this one's gullet. He kept it to the end.'

Fafhrd snatched the ruby from the Mouser with his free hand and held it up to the moon.

'King's ransom!' he cried. 'Mouser, our fortune's made! I see it all. We shall follow these birds as they rob and let Kooskra rape them of their booty.' He laughed aloud.

This time there was no warning beat of wings – only a gliding shadow which grazed Fafhrd's upraised hand and slid silently away. It almost came to rest on the roof, then flapped powerfully upward.

'Blood of Kos!' cursed Fafhrd, waking from his dumb-founded amazement. 'Mouser, he's taken it!' Then, 'At him, Kooskra! At him!' as he swiftly unhooded the eagle.

But this time it was apparent from the first that something was wrong. The beat of the eagle's wings was slow, and he seemed to have difficulty gaining height. Nevertheless he drew near the quarry. The black bird veered suddenly, swooped, and rose again. The eagle followed closely, though his flight was still unsteady.

Wordlessly Fafhrd and the Mouser watched the birds approach the massive, high-reared tower of the deserted temple, until their feathered forms were silhouetted against its palely glowing, ancient surface.

Kooskra seemed then to recover full power. He gained a superior position, hovered while his quarry frantically darted and wheeled, then plummeted down.

'Got him, by Kos!' breathed Fafhrd, thumping his knee with his fist.

But it was not so. Kooskra struck at thin air. At the last moment the black bird had slipped aside and taken cover in one of the high-set windows of the tower.

And now it was certain beyond doubt that something was wrong with Kooskra. He sought to beat about the embrasure sheltering his quarry, but lost height. Abruptly he turned and flew out from the wall. His wings moved in an irregular and convulsive way. Fafhrd's fingers tightened apprehensively on the Mouser's shoulder.

As Kooskra reached a point above them, he gave a great wild scream that shook the soft Lankhmar night. Then he fell, like a dead leaf, circling and spinning. Only once again did he seem to make an effort to command his wings, and then to no avail.

He landed heavily a short distance from them. When Fafhrd reached the spot, Kooskra was dead.

The barbarian knelt there, absently smoothing the feathers, staring up at the tower. Puzzlement, anger, and some sorrow lined his face.

'Fly north, old bird,' he murmured in a deep, small voice. 'Fly into nothingness, Kooskra.' Then he spoke to the Mouser. 'I find no wounds. Nothing touched him on this flight, I'll swear.'

'It happened when he brought down the other,' said the Mouser soberly. 'You did not look at the talons of that ugly fowl. They were smeared with a greenish stuff. Through some small gouge it entered him. Death was in him while he sat on your wrist, and it worked faster when he flew at the black bird.'

Fafhrd nodded, still staring at the tower. 'We've lost a fortune and a faithful killer tonight. But the night's not done. I have a curiosity about these death-dealing shadows.'

'What are you thinking?' asked the Mouser.

'That a man might easily hurl a grapnel and a line over a corner of that tower, and that I have such a line wound around my waist. We used it to mount Muulsh's roof, and I shall use it again. Don't waste your words, little man. Muulsh? What have we to fear from him? He saw a bird take the jewel. Why should he send guards to search the roofs?

'Yes, I know the bird will fly away when I go after him. But he may drop the jewel, or you may get in a lucky cast with your sling. Besides, I have a special notion about these matters. Poison claws? I'll wear my gloves and cloak, and carry a naked dagger. Come on, little man. We'll not argue. That corner away from Muulsh's and the river should do the trick. The one where the tiny broken spire rises. We come, oh tower!' And he shook his fist.

The Mouser hummed a fragment of song under his breath and kept glancing around apprehensively, as he steadied the line by which Fafhrd was mounting the wall of the tower-temple. He felt decidedly ill at ease, what with Fafhrd on a fool's errand, and the night's luck probably run out, and the ancient temple silent and desolate.

It was forbidden on pain of death to enter such places, and no man knew what evil things might lurk there, fattening on loneliness. Besides all that, the moonlight was too revealing; he winced at the thought of what excellent targets he and Fafhrd made against the wall.

In his ears droned the low but mighty clamor of the waters of the Hlal, which swished and eddied past the base of the opposite wall. Once it seemed to him that the temple itself vibrated as though the Hlal were gnawing at its vitals.

Before his feet yawned the dark, six-foot chasm separating the warehouse from the temple. It allowed a sidewise glimpse of the walled temple-garden, overgrown with pale weeds and clogged with decay.

And now as he glanced in that direction he saw something

that made him raise his eyebrows and sent a shiver crawling over his scalp. For across the moonlit space stole a manlike but unwholesomely bulky figure.

The Mouser's impression was that the strange body lacked the characteristic human curves and taperings of limb, that its face lacked features, that it was unpleasantly froglike. It seemed to be colored a uniform dull brown.

It vanished in the direction of the temple. What was it, the Mouser could not for the moment conjecture.

Intent on warning Fafhrd, he looked up, but the barbarian was already swinging into the embrasure at a dizzy height above. Disliking to shout, he paused undecided, half of a mind to shin up the line and join his comrade. All the while he kept humming a fragment of song – one used by thieves and supposed to enforce slumber on the inmates of a house being robbed. He wished fervently that the moon would get under a cloud.

Then, as if his fear had fathered a reality, something roughly grazed his ear and hit with a deadened thump against the temple wall. He knew what that meant – a ball of wet clay projected by a sling.

As he let his body collapse, two similar missiles followed the first. Close range, he could tell from the impact, and designed to kill rather than stun. He scanned the moonlit roof, but could see nothing. Before his knees touched the roof he had decided what he must do if he were to help Fafhrd at all. There was one quick way of retreat and he took it.

He grasped the long slack of the rope and dove into the chasm between the buildings, as three more balls of clay flattened against the wall.

As Fafhrd warily swung into the embrasure and found solid footing, he realized what had been bothering him about the character of the weatherworn carvings on the ancient wall: in one way or another they all seemed to be concerned with birds – raptorial birds in particular – and with human beings having grotesque avian features: beaked heads, batlike wings, and taloned limbs.

There was a whole border of such creatures around the embrasure, and the projecting stone ornament over which the grapnel was caught represented the head of a hawk. This unpleasant coincidence loosened the stout gates of fear within him and a faint sense of awe and horror trickled into his mind, extinguishing a part of his anger at Kooskra's repellent death. But at the same time it served to confirm certain vague notions that had come to him earlier.

He looked around. The black bird seemed to have retreated into the interior of the tower, where tenuous moonlight revealed an obscurely littered stone floor and a door half open on a rectangle of blackness. Whipping out a long knife, he trod softly inward, shifting his weight slowly from one foot to the other to feel for possible weaknesses in the centuries-old masonry.

It grew darker and then a little lighter, as his straining eyes accustomed themselves to the dimness. The stone beneath his feet became slippery. And in stronger and stronger waves there was borne to his nostrils the pungent, musty smell of a mews.

There was an intermittent soft rustling, too. He told himself it was only natural that birds of some sort – perhaps pigeons – should nest in this deserted structure, but a darker train of reasoning insisted that his previous speculations were right.

He passed a projecting panel of stone and came into the chief upper chamber of the tower.

Moonlight striking through two gaps in the ceiling high above vaguely revealed alcoved walls, which widened away from him toward the left. The sound of the Hlal was muted and deepened here, as though it rose up more through the stones than through the air. He was very close, now, to the half-open door.

He noted a tiny grilled opening in it, like that of a cell. Rising against the wall at the broad end of the room was what seemed to be an altar of some sort, embellished by indistinct sculptures. And on either side of it, in regular terraces like those of the altar itself, were tier on tier of small black blots.

Then he heard a raucous, falsetto cry, 'Man! Man! Kill! Kill!' and saw a portion of the black blots launch themselves from the tiers, expanding in size as they spread their wings and converged upon him.

And largely because his fear had been expecting this, he jerked up his cloak to protect his naked head and whirled his knife at them in sweeping strokes. This close he could see them better: inky-feathered, cruelly taloned birds, each a brother to the two Kooskra had fought, squawking, squawking, striking at him like fighting cocks able to fly.

At first he thought he could readily beat them off, but it was like fighting an eddying storm of shadows. Perhaps he struck two or three. He could not tell. And it made no difference. He felt talons grasp and prick his left wrist.

Then, because it seemed the only thing to do, he leaped through the half-open door, slammed it behind him, knifed off the bird that clung like death to his wrist, found the pricks by touch, nicked them with his knife, and sucked the poison that might have been on the talons.

His shoulder pressed against the door, he listened to their baffled flapping and angry croaking. From here escape would be difficult; this inner room was indeed nothing but a cell, lightless save for the trace of moonlight that filtered through the grilled hole in the door. He could conjecture no ready way of regaining the embrasure and descending – they would have him completely at their mercy as he clung to the line.

He wanted to bellow a warning to the Mouser, but was afraid that his shouts, probably unintelligible at the distance, would only summon the Mouser into the same trap. In a rage of uncertainty he stamped vindictively the body of the bird he had slain.

Gradually his fears and anger calmed somewhat. The birds seemed to have retreated. No longer did they swoop futilely against the door or cling screaming to the grillwork in the opening.

Through this aperture he could gain a fair view of the shadowy altar and the ladder-like perches. The black occupants were restless, edging back and forth, crowding one another, flurrying excitedly from perch to perch. The air was heavy with their smell.

And then he heard again the raucous, falsetto voice, only this time there was more than one.

'Jewels, jewels. Bright, bright.'

'Sparkling ones. Shining ones.'

'Ear to tear. Eye to peck.'

'Cheek to scratch. Neck to claw.'

And this time there was no doubting that it was the birds themselves who spoke. Fafhrd stared, fascinated. He had heard birds talk before – cursing parrots and slit-tongued ravens. Here there was the same monotony of tone and impression of mindlessness, the same vituperative repetitions. Indeed he had known parrots able to mimic human voices much more accurately.

But the phrases themselves were so devilishly apt that he momentarily feared they would cease to be mere isolated chatterings and become an intelligent discourse, with question and answer fitting. And he could not forget that undeniably purposeful command, 'Man! Man! Kill! Kill!'

As he listened spellbound to their cruel chorus, a figure stole past the grilled opening toward the altar. It was manlike only in its general form, featureless, with a uniform, leathery brown surface, like a heavy-hided, hairless bear. He saw the birds launch themselves at this strange figure too, and swarm around it, squawking and striking.

But it paid them no attention whatever, as though it were immune to beaks and poisoned claws. It strode unhurriedly with upraised head toward the altar. There the shifting moonlight from a gap above now struck almost vertically, making a pallid puddle on the floor before the altar itself, and Fafhrd saw the creature fumble at a large casket and begin to lift out small things that gleamed and glittered, unmindful of the birds which swirled around in ever greater number.

Then the creature moved so that the moonlight fell full upon it, and Fafhrd saw that it was a man clad in an ungainly suit of thick leather, with two long thin slits for eyeholes. He was clumsily but methodically transferring the contents of the casket to a leather bag he carried. And Fafhrd realized that the casket had been the cache for the many jewels and trinkets the birds had stolen.

The leather-armored form completed its task and strode off the way it had come, still surrounded by the small black storm-cloud of perplexedly squawking birds.

But as the figure came opposite Fafhrd the birds suddenly dropped away from it and flew back toward the altar, as if in obedience to a command that had come to them through the general din. The leather-armored form stopped dead and glanced searchingly around, the long eye-slits giving it an appearance of cryptic menace.

Then it started forward again. But simultaneously a noose dropped and tightened like a drawstring around the leather bag that formed its head.

The figure began to struggle and to stagger erratically, pawing at its neck with its leather-cased hand. Then it flailed both arms around in a ponderous, desperate way, so that the bag it still held came open and spurted jewels and jeweled metal. Finally a cunning jerk of the lasso sprawled it on the floor.

Fafhrd chose this moment to make a break for freedom. He relied on confusion and surprise. But in this he was not wise. Perhaps a trace of poison in his veins had touched his mind a little.

He almost reached the passage leading to the embrasure before a second noose tightened cruelly around his own throat. His running feet went out from under him and his skull thumped the floor as he fell. The noose tightened further until he felt he was suffocating in a sea of black feathers wherein all the jewels of the world flashed blindingly.

As consciousness painfully pounded its way back into his skull, he heard a voice crying out frightenedly and jerkily:

'In the name of the Great God, who are you? What are you?'

Then a second voice answering – high, sweet, swift, bird-like, imperious, icy: 'I am the winged priestess, mistress of the hawks. I am the clawed queen, the feathered princess, incarnation of She who has ruled here forever, despite priests' interdict and Overlord's command. I am she who visits suitable injury on the haughty and voluptuous women of Lankhmar. I am she who sends messengers to take the tribute that was once laid freely though tremblingly upon my altar.'

Then the first voice spoke, in great apprehension, though not weakly: 'But you cannot mean to doom me in so hideous a way. I will keep your secrets well. I am only a thief.'

Then the second voice again, 'You are indeed a thief, for you sought to ravish the altar-treasure of Winged Tyaa, and for that crime the birds of Tyaa mete out punishment as they see fit. If they think you deserve mercy they will not kill; only peck out an eye – or, perhaps, two.'

There was a trilling and chirruping quality to the voice so that Fafhrd's tortured brain kept picturing some impossibly monstrous songbird. He sought to struggle to his feet, but found he was bound tightly to a chair. His arms and legs were numb, his left arm in addition ached and burned.

Then the soft moonlight ceased to be so much of a shooting pain, and he saw he was still in the same chamber, near the grilled door, facing the altar. Beside him was another chair, and in it sat the leather-armored man, similarly bound. But the leather hood had been removed, revealing the shaven skull and pockmarked, heavy-featured face of a man whom Fafhrd recognized – Stravas, a well-known cutpurse.

'Tyaa, Tyaa,' squawked the birds. 'Eyes to peck. Nose to rip.'

The eyes of Stravas were dark creases of fear between his shaved brows and thick cheeks. He spoke again toward the altar.

'I am a thief. Yes. But so are you. The gods of this temple are banned and forbidden. The Great God himself cursed them. Centuries ago they left this place. Whatever else you may be, you are an interloper. Somehow, perhaps by magic, you taught the birds to steal, knowing that many of them by nature like to pilfer shining things. What they steal, you take.

'You are no better than I, who guessed your secret and contrived a way to rob you in turn. You are no priestess, meting out death for sacrilege. Where are your worshippers? Where is your priesthood? Where are your benefactions? You are a thief!'

He strained tautly forward against his bonds, as if wanting to hurl himself toward the doom that might answer his reckless speech. Then Fafhrd saw, standing behind Stravas, a figure that made him doubt if his senses had rightly returned. For it was that of another leather-masked man.

But, as he blinked hard and peered again, he saw that the mask was only a small visor and that otherwise the man was clothed as a falconer, with heavy jerkin and huge gauntlets. From the broad leather belt hung a shortsword and a coiled lasso. Twisting around, Fafhrd glimpsed the outlines of a similar figure beside his own chair.

Then the voice from the altar answered, somewhat more strident and shrill, but still musical and horribly birdlike. And as it answered, the birds chorused, 'Tyaa! Tyaa!'

'Now indeed you will die, and in tatters. And that one beside you, whose impious eagle slew Kivies and was by him slain, shall die too. But you will die knowing that Tyaa is Tyaa, and that her priestess and incarnate self is no interloper.'

And now Fafhrd looked straight at the altar – an action which he had unconsciously avoided up until this moment because of an overpowering superstitious awe and a queer revulsion.

The downward-striking shaft of moonlight had moved a little further toward the altar, revealing two stone figures which jutted out from it on either side, like gargoyles. Their carved faces were the faces of women but the menacingly bent arms ended in claws, and folded wings thrust over the shoulders. Whatever ancient craftsman had formed them, he had worked with devilish skill, for they gave the impression of being about to spread their stony wings and launch forward into the air.

On the altar itself, between the winged women, but further back and out of the moonlight, perched a large black shape with pendant crescents of blackness that might have been wings. Fafhrd stared at it, licking his lips, his poison-dulled mind unable to cope with the possibilities it conjured up.

But at the same time, although he was hardly aware of what they were doing, his long-fingered supple hands were beginning to work at the tight lashings that confined his wrists.

'Know, fool,' came the voice from the black shape, 'that gods do not cease to be when banned by false priests, or flee when cursed by a false and presumptuous god. Though priest and worshipper depart, they linger. I was small and I had no wings when I first climbed to this place, yet I felt their presence in the very stones. And I knew that my heart was sister to them.'

At that moment Fafhrd heard the Mouser calling his name, faintly and muffledly, but unmistakably. It seemed to come from the lower interior regions of the temple, mingling with the faint, deep-throated roar of the Hlal. The shape on the altar gave a trilling call and made a gesture, so that one of the pendant crescents moved.

A single black bird skimmed down to perch on the wrist of the falconer behind Stravas. Then the falconer moved away. His footsteps sounded as though he were descending a stair. The other falconer hastened to the embrasure through which Fafhrd had entered, and there was the sound of knife sawing rope. Then he returned.

'It seems that Tyaa does not lack worshippers tonight,' chittered the shape on the altar. 'And some day all the luxurious women of Lankhmar will mount terrified but unresisting to this place, to sacrifice portions of their beauty to Tyaa.'

It appeared to Fafhrd's sharpening eyesight that the blackness of the shape was too smooth for feathers, yet he could not be sure. He continued to work at the lashings, feeling those on his right wrist loosen.

'Beauty to spoil. Beauty to spoil,' hoarsely chanted the birds. 'Kiss with beak. Pet with claw.'

'When I was small,' continued the voice, 'I only dreamed of such things, stealing away secretly when I could from my father's house to this holy place. Yet even at that time the spirit of Tyaa was in me, making me feared and avoided by others.

'Then one day I found a young wounded bird hiding here, and I nursed it back to health. It was a descendant of one of the ancient birds of Tyaa, who, when the temple was defiled and shut up, flew away to the Mountains of Darkness to await the time when Tyaa would call them back. Sensing by occult means that Tyaa had been reborn in me, it had returned. It knew me, and slowly – because we were small and alone – we remembered some of the ancient rituals and regained the power of conversing together.

'Then as year followed year, the others straggled back from the Mountains of Darkness, one by one. And these mated. And our ceremonies grew in perfection. It became difficult for me to be a priestess of Tyaa, without the outer world uncovering my secret. There was food to get, blood and flesh. There were long hours of instruction.

348

'Yet I persevered. And all the while those of my station in the outer world hated me more and more, sensing my power, and they affronted me and sought to humiliate me.

'A thousand times a day the honor of Tyaa was trampled in the dust. I was cheated of the privileges of my birth and station, and forced to consort with the uncouth and vulgar. Yet I submitted, and acted as if I were one of them, mocking their witlessness and frivolity and vanity. I bided my time, feeling within me the ever-strengthening spirit of Tyaa.'

'Tyaa! Tyaa!' echoed the birds.

'And then I searched for and found helpers in my quest: two descendants of the ancient Falconers of Tyaa, whose families had cherished the old worship and the old traditions. They knew me and did me homage. They are my priesthood.'

Fafhrd sensed the falconer beside him bow reverently low. He felt as if he were witnessing some malign shadow-show. Apprehension for the Mouser was like a lead weight pressing down on his confused thoughts. Irrelevantly, he noted a pearl-crusted brooch and a sapphire bracelet on the dirtied floor a little way from his chair. The jewels still lay where they had spilled from Stravas' bag.

'Four months ago,' persisted the voice, 'in the waning of the Moon of the Owl, I felt that Tyaa had grown to full stature in me, and that the time had come for Tyaa's reckoning with Lankhmar.

'So I sent the birds forth to take the old tribute, bidding them punish when tribute was refused, or when the woman was notorious for vanity and pride. Swiftly they regained all their old cunning. Tyaa's altar was fittingly decked. And Lankhmar learned to fear, though not knowing they feared Tyaa. It shall not be so for long!' Here the voice became piercingly shrill.

'Soon I shall proclaim Tyaa openly. The doors of the temple will be opened to worshipper and tribute-bringer. The idols of the Great God will be cast down, and his temples broken. The rich and insolent women who despised Tyaa in me will be summoned here. And this altar will feel again the sweetness of sacrifice.' The voice rose to a screech. 'Even now it begins! Even now two interlopers will feel Tyaa's vengeance!'

Sound of a shuddering inhalation came from Stravas' throat, and he rocked futilely from side to side against his bonds. Fafhrd pried frantically at the loosening lashing of his right hand. A portion of the black birds rose at command from their perches – but then settled uncertainly back, for the trilling command was not completed.

The other falconer had returned and was advancing toward the altar, his right hand raised in solemn salute. There was no bird on his wrist now. In his left hand he carried a bloody shortsword.

The shape on the altar eagerly edged forward into the moonlight, so that Fafhrd saw it clearly for the first time. It was no giant bird or monstrous hybrid, but a woman muffled in black draperies with long, pendant sleeves. Her black hood fallen back revealed, white in the moonlight though stranded with gleaming black hair, a triangular face, whose glassily bright eyes and predatory aspect were suggestive of a bird, but also of an evil, oddly beautiful child. She moved in a crouching, short-stepped, fluttering way.

'Three in a night,' she cried. 'You have killed the third. It is well, falconer.'

Stravas could be heard saying in a gasping voice, 'I know you. I know you.'

Still the falconer advanced, until she said quietly, 'What is it? What do you want?' Then the falconer leaped at her with catlike swiftness and advanced the bloody sword so that it glittered redly against the black fabric covering her bosom.

And Fafhrd heard the Mouser say, 'Move not, Atya. Nor command your birds to any evil action. Or you will die in a wink, as your falconer and his black pet died.'

For five choking heartbeats there was dead silence. Then the woman on the altar began to breathe in a dry, strangled way, and utter short, broken cries that were almost croakings.

Some of the black birds rose from their perches and beat about uncertainly, dipping in and out of the shafts of moonlight, though keeping clear of the altar. The woman began to sway and rock from side to side. The sword followed her unalterably, like a pendulum.

Fafhrd noted the second falconer move up beside him, raising his shortsword for a throw. Putting all his strength into one mighty leverage of wrist and forearm, Fafhrd snapped the last of the lashings, ponderously heaved himself and the chair up and forward, caught the falconer's wrist as it started to whip the shortsword forward, and hurtled down with him to the floor. The falconer squealed in pain and a bone snapped. Fafhrd lay heavily atop him, staring at the leather-masked, gauntleted Mouser and the woman.

'Two falconers in a night,' said the Mouser, mimicking the woman. 'It is well, Fafhrd.' Then he continued pitilessly, 'The masquerade is over, Atya, Your vengeance on the highborn women of Lankhmar has come to an end. Ah, but fat Muulsh will be surprised at his little dove! To steal even your own jewels! Almost too cunning, Atya!'

A cry of bitter anguish and utter defeat came from the woman, in which her humiliation and weakness showed naked. But then she ceased to sway and a look of utter desperation tightened her decadent face.

'To the Mountains of Darkness!' she cried out wildly. 'To the Mountains of Darkness! Bear Tyaa's tribute to Tyaa's last stronghold!' And she followed this with a series of strange whistles and trillings and screams.

At this all the birds rose together, though still keeping clear of the altar. They milled wildly, giving vent to varied squawkings, which the woman seemed to answer.

'No tricks now, Atya!' said the Mouser. 'Death is close.'

Then one of the black fowls dipped to the floor, clutched an emerald-studded bracelet, rose again, and beat with it through a deep embrasure in that wall of the temple which overlooked the River Hlal. One after another, the other birds followed its example.

As if in some grotesque ritual procession, they sailed out into the night, bearing a fortune in their claws: necklaces, brooches, rings and pins of gold, silver, and electrum set with all colors of jewels, palely rich in the moonlight.

After the last three for whom no jewels were left vanished, Atya raised her black-draped arms toward the two outjutting sculptures of winged women, as if imploring a miracle, gave voice to a mad lonely wail, recklessly sprang from the altar, and ran after the birds.

The Mouser did not strike, but followed her, his sword dangerously close. Together they plunged into the embrasure. There was another cry, and after a little the Mouser returned alone and came over to Fafhrd. He cut Fafhrd's bonds, and pulled away the chair, helping him up. The injured falconer did not move, but lay whimpering softly.

'She sprang into the Hlal?' asked Fafhrd, his throat dry. The Mouser nodded.

Fafhrd dazedly rubbed his forehead. But his mind was clearing, as the effects of the poison waned.

'Even as the names were the same,' he mumbled softly. 'Atya and Tyaa!'

The Mouser went toward the altar and began to saw at the lashings of the cutpurse. 'Some of your men tried to pepper me tonight, Stravas,' he said lightly. 'I had no easy time eluding them and finding my way up the choked stairs.'

'I am sorry for that – now,' said Stravas.

'They were your men too, I suppose, who went jewel-stealing to Muulsh's house tonight?'

Stravas nodded, uncramping loosened limbs. 'But I hope we're allies now,' he answered, 'though there's no loot to share, except for some worthless glass and gew-gaws.' He laughed grimly. 'Was there no way to get rid of those black demons without losing all?'

'For a man plucked from the beak of death, you are very greedy, Stravas,' said the Mouser. 'But I suppose it's your professional training. No, I for one am glad the birds have fled. Most of all I feared they would get out of hand – as would surely have happened had I killed Atya. Only she could control them. Then we'd have died surely. Observe how Fafhrd's arm is swollen.'

'Perhaps the birds will bring the treasure back,' said Stravas hopefully.

'I do not think so,' answered the Mouser.

*

Two nights later, Muulsh, the money-lender, having learned something of these matters from a broken-armed falconer who had long been employed to care for his wife's songbirds, sprawled comfortably on the luxurious bed in his wife's room. One pudgy hand clasped a goblet of wine, the other that of a pretty maid who had been his wife's hairdresser.

'I never really loved her,' he said, pulling the demurely smiling wench toward him. 'It was only that she used to goad and frighten me.'

The maid gently disengaged her hand.

'I just want to hang the coverings on those cages,' she explained. 'Their eyes remind me of hers.' And she shivered delicately under her thin tunic.

When the last songbird was shrouded and silent, she came back and sat on his knee.

Gradually the fear left Lankhmar. But many wealthy women continued to wear silver cages over their features, considering it a most enchanting fashion. Gradually style altered the cages to soft masks of silver network.

And some time afterward the Mouser said to Fafhrd, 'There is a thing I have not told you. When Atya leaped into the Hlal, it was full moonlight. Yet somehow my eyes lost her as she fell, and I saw no splash whatever, although I peered closely. Then, as I lifted my head, I saw the end of that ragged procession of birds across the moon. Behind them came, I thought, a very much larger bird, flapping strongly.'

'And you think . . .' asked Fafhrd.

'Why, I think Atya drowned in the Hlal,' said the Mouser.

IX
THE PRICE OF PAIN-EASE

The big barbarian Fafhrd, outcast of the World of Nehwon's Cold Waste and forever a foreigner in the land and city of Lankhmar, Nehwon's most notable area, and the small but deadly swordsman the Gray Mouser, a stateless person even in careless, unbureaucratic Nehwon, and man without a country (that he knew of), were fast friends and comrades from the moment they met in Lankhmar City near the intersection of Gold and Cash Streets. But they never shared a home. For one obvious thing, they were by nature, except for their companionship, loners; and such are almost certain to be homeless. For another, they were almost always adventuring, tramping, or exploring, or escaping from the deadly consequences of past misdeeds and misjudgments. For a third, their first and only true loves – Fafhrd's Vlana and the Mouser's Ivrian – were foully murdered (and bloodily though comfortlessly revenged) the first night the two young men met, and any home without a best-loved woman is a chilly place. For a fourth, they habitually stole all their possessions, even their swords and daggers, which they always named Graywand and Heartseeker and Scalpel and Cat's Claw, no matter how often they lost them and pilfered replacements – and homes are remarkably difficult to steal. Here, of course, one does not count tents, inn-lodgings, caves, palaces in which one happens to be employed or perhaps the guest of a princess or queen, or even shacks one rents for a while, as the Mouser and Fafhrd briefly and later did in an alley near the Plaza of Dark Delights.

Yet after their first trampings and gallopings of Nehwon, after their second, mostly womanless, adventures in and about Lankhmar – for the memories of Ivrian and Vlana haunted them for years – and after their ensorceled voyage across the Outer Sea and back, and after their encounters with the Seven Black Priests and with Atya and Tyaa, and their second return to Lankhmar, they did for a few brief moons share a house and home, although it was a rather small and, naturally, stolen one, and the two women in it ghosts only, and its location – because of the morbid mood they also shared – most dubious and dire.

Coming one night half drunk by way of Plague Court and Bones Alley from the tavern at Cash and Whore named the Golden Lamprey to an inn of most merry yet most evil recollection called the Silver Eel – on Dim Lane, this, halfway between Cheap and Carter – they spied behind it the still uncleared cinders and blackened, tumbled stones of the tenement where their first loves Ivrian and Vlana had, after many torments, been burned to white ashes, some atomies of whom they might even now be seeing by the murky moonlight.

Much later that night and much more drunk, they wandered north beyond the Street of the Gods to the section of the aristocrats by the Sea Wall and east of the Rainbow Palace of Lankhmar's Overlord Karstak Ovartamortes. In the estate of Duke Danius, the Mouser spied through the spiked wall and now by brighter moonlight – the air there being cleansed of night smog by the gentle north seawind – a snug, trim, well-polished, natural wooden garden house with curvingly horned ridgepole and beam-ends, to which abode he took a sudden extreme fancy and which he even persuaded Fafhrd to admire. It rested on six short cedar posts which in turn rested on flat rock. Nothing then would do but rush to Wall Street and the Marsh Gate, hire a brawny two-score of the inevitable night-long idlers there with a silver coin and big drink apiece and promise of a gold coin and bigger drink to come, lead them to Danius' dark abode, pick the iron gate-lock, lead them warily in, order them heave up the garden house and carry it out – providentially without any great creakings and with no guards or watchmen appearing. In fact, the Mouser and Fafhrd were able to finish another jug of wine during their supervising. Next tightly blindfold the two score carriers – this was the only difficult part of the operation, requiring all the Mouser's adroit, confident cajoling and Fafhrd's easy though somewhat ominous and demanding friendliness – and guide and goad the forty of the impromptu porters as they pantingly and sweatingly carried the house. They went south down empty Carter Street and west up Bones Alley (the garden house fortunately being rather narrow, three smallish rooms in a row) to the empty lot behind the Silver Eel, where after Fafhrd had hurled aside three stone blocks there was space to ease it down. Then it only remained to guide the still-blindfolded carriers back to the Marsh Gate, give them their gold and buy them their wine – a big jug apiece seemed wisest to blot out memory – then rush back in the pinkening dawn to buy from Braggi, the tavern-master, the worthless lot behind the Silver Eel, reluctantly chop off with Fafhrd's fighting axe the garden house's ridgepole and beam-horns, throw water and then disguising ashes onto the roof and walls (without thought of what evil omen this was, recalling Vlana and Ivrian), finally stagger inside and collapse into sleep on the naked floor before even looking around.

When they woke next evening, the place turned out to be quite nice inside, the two end-rooms each a thick-carpeted bedroom with highly erotic murals filling the walls. The Mouser puzzled as to whether Duke Danius shared his garden-concubines with a friend or else rushed back and forth between the two bedrooms all by himself. The central room was a most couth and sedate living room with several shelves of expensively bound stimulating books and a fine larder of rare jugged foods and wines. One of the bedrooms even had a copper bathtub – the Mouser appropriated that one at once – and both bedrooms had privies easily cleaned out below by a part-time and out-dwelling houseboy they hired that night from the Eel.

The theft was highly successful, they had no trouble from Lankhmar's brown-cuirassed and generally lazy guardsmen, no trouble from Duke Danius – if he hired house-spies, they botched their not-too-easy job. And for several days the Gray Mouser and Fafhrd were very happy in their new domicile, eating and drinking up Danius' fine provender, making the quick run to the Eel for extra wine, the Mouser taking two or three perfumed, soapy, oily, slow baths a day, Fafhrd going every two days to the nearest public steam-bath and putting in a lot of time on the books, sharpening his already considerable knowledge of High Lankhmarese, Ilthmarish, and Quarmallian.

By slow degrees, Fafhrd's bedroom became comfortably sloppy, the Mouser's quite fussily tidy and neat – it was simply their real natures expressing themselves.

After a few days Fafhrd discovered a second library, most cunningly concealed, of books dealing with nothing but death, books at complete variance with the other supremely erotic volumes. Fafhrd found them equally educational, while the Gray Mouser amused himself by picturing Duke Danius pausing to scan a few paragraphs about strangulation or Kleshite jungle-poisons while dashing back and forth between his two bedrooms and their two or more girls.

However, they didn't invite any girls to their charming new home and perhaps for a very good reason, because after half a moon or so the ghost of slim Ivrian began to appear to the Mouser and the ghost of tall Vlana to Fafhrd, both spirits perhaps raised from their remaining mineral dust drifting around-about, and even plastered on the outer walls. The girl-ghosts never spoke, even in faintest whisper; they never touched, even so much as by the brush of a single hair; Fafhrd never spoke of Vlana to the Mouser, nor the Mouser to Fafhrd of Ivrian. The two girls were invariably invisible, inaudible, intangible, *yet they were there*.

Secretly from each other, each man consulted witches, witch doctors, astrologers, wizards, necromancers, fortune tellers, reputable physicians, priests even, seeking a cure for their ills (each desiring to see more of his dead girl or nothing at all), yet finding none.

Within three moons the Mouser and Fafhrd – very easy-amiable to each other, very tolerant on all matters, very quick to crack jokes, smiling far more than was their wont – were both rapidly going mad. The Mouser realized this one gray dawn when the instant he opened his eyes a pale, two-dimensional Ivrian at last appeared and gazed sadly at him one moment from the ceiling and then utterly vanished.

Big drops of sweat beaded his entire face and head from hairline down on all sides; his throat was acid, and he gagged and retched. Then with one fling of his right arm, he threw off all his bedclothes and raced naked out of his bedroom and across the living room into Fafhrd's.

The Northerner wasn't there.

He stared at the tousled, empty bed for a long time. Then he drank at one swallow half a bottle of fortified wine. Then he brewed himself a pot of burningly hot, triple-strength gahveh. As he gulped it down, he found himself violently shivering and shaking. He threw on a wool robe and belted it tightly around him, drew on his wool boots, then still shivered and shook as he finished his still steaming gahveh.

All day long he paced the living room or sprawled in one of its big chairs, alternating fortified wine and hot gahveh, awaiting Fafhrd's return, still shaking from time to time and pulling his warm robe tighter around him.

But the Northerner never appeared.

When the windows of thin and ash-dusty horn yellowed and darkened in the late afternoon, the Mouser began to think in a more practical fashion of his plight. It occurred to him that the one sorcerer he had *not* consulted about his horrible Ivrian hang-up – just conceivably because that was the one sorcerer he believed might not be a faker and quack – was Sheelba of the Eyeless Face, who dwelt in a five-legged hut in the Great Salt Marsh immediately east of Lankhmar.

He whipped off his woolen stuff and speedily donned his gray tunic of coarsely woven silk, his ratskin boots, belted on his slim sword Scalpel and his dagger Cat's Claw (he'd early noted that Fafhrd's ordinary clothes and sword Graywand and dagger Heartseeker were gone), caught up his hooded cloak of the same material as his tunic, and fled from the dreadful little house in vast, sudden fear that Ivrian's sad ghost would appear to him again and then, without talking or touching, again vanish.

It was sunset. The houseboy from the Eel was cleaning out the privies. The Mouser asked, rather wildly and fiercely, 'Seen Fafhrd today?'

The lad started back. 'Yes,' he said. 'He rode off at dawn on a big white horse.'

'Fafhrd doesn't own a horse,' the Mouser said harshly and dangerously.

Again the lad started back. 'It was the biggest horse I've ever seen. It had a brown saddle and harness, studded with gold.'

The Mouser snarled and half drew Scalpel from her mousekin scabbard. Then, beyond the lad, he saw, twinkling and gleaming in the gloom, a huge, jet-black horse with black saddle and harness, studded with silver.

He raced past the lad, who threw himself sidewise into the dirt, vaulted up onto the saddle, grasped the reins, thrust his feet into the stirrups – which hung exactly at the right height for him – and booted the horse, which instantly took off down Dim Lane, galloped north on Carter and west on the Street of the Gods – the crowd scampering out of the way – and was through the open Marsh Gate before the guards could draw back their ragged-edged pikes for a thrust or advance them as a formal barrier.

The sunset was behind, the night was ahead, damp wind was on his cheeks, and the Mouser found all of these things good.

The black horse galloped down Causey Road for sixty or so bowshots, or eighteen score spear-casts, and then plunged off the road inland and south, so suddenly the Mouser was almost unsaddled. But he managed to keep his seat, dodging as best he could the weaponed branches of the thorn and seahawk trees. After not more than a hundred gasping breaths, the horse came to a halt, and there facing them was Sheelba's hut, and a little above the Mouser's head the low, dark doorway and a black-robed and black-hooded figure crouched in it.

The Mouser said loudly, 'What are you up to, you wizardly trickster? I know you must have sent this horse for me.'

Sheelba said not a word and moved not a whit, even though his crouching position looked most uncomfortable, at least for a being with legs rather than, say, tentacles.

After a bit the Mouser demanded still more loudly, 'Did you send for Fafhrd this morning? Send for him a huge white horse with a gold-studded brown harness?'

This time Sheelba started a little, though he settled himself quickly again and still spoke no word, while of course the space that should have held his face remained blacker even than his draperies.

Dusk deepened. After a much longer bit, the Mouser said in a low, broken voice, 'O Sheelba, great magician, grant me a boon or else I shall go mad. Give me back my beloved Ivrian, give me her entire, or else rid me of her altogether, as if she had never been. Do either of those and I will pay any price you set.'

In a grating voice like the clank of small boulders moved by a sullen surf, Sheelba said from his doorway, 'Will you faithfully serve me as long as you live? Do my every lawful command? On my part, I promise not to call on you more than once a year, or at most twice, nor demand more than three moons out of thirteen of your time. You must swear to me by Fafhrd's bones and your own that, one, you will use any strategem, no matter how shameful and degrading, to get me the Mask of Death from the Shadowland, and that, two, you will slay any being who seeks to thwart you, whether it be your unknown mother or the Great God himself.'

After a still longer pause the Mouser said in a still smaller voice, 'I promise.'

Sheelba said, 'Very well. Keep the horse. Ride it east past Ilthmar, the City of Ghouls, the Sea of Monsters, and the Parched Mountains until you come to the Shadowland. There search out the Blue Flame and from the seat of the throne before it, fetch me the Mask of Death. Or snatch it off Death's face, if he's at home. By the way, in the Shadowland, you will find your Ivrian. In particular, beware a certain Duke Danius, whose garden house you recently purloined, not altogether by chance, and whose death library I imagine you have discovered and perused. This Danius person fears death more than any creature has ever in history, as recorded or recollected by man, demon, or god, and he is planning a foray into the Shadowland with no less a purpose than to slay Death himself (or herself or itself, for there even my knowledge stops) and destroy all Death's possessions, including the Mask you promised to procure me. Now, do my errand. That is all.'

The numb, astounded, yet still unhappy and suspicious Mouser watched the dark doorway for as long as it took the moon to rise and silhouette herself behind the sharply angled branches of a dead seahawk tree, but Sheelba said not another word, nor made a move, while the Mouser could think of not a single sensible question to ask further. So at last he touched his heels against the flanks of the black horse and it instantly turned around, carefully single-footed to Causey Road, and there cantered east.

Meanwhile, at almost exactly the same time, since it is a good day's ride from Lankhmar across the Great Salt Marsh and the Sinking Land to the mountains behind Ilthmar, city of evil reputation, Fafhrd was having the same identical conversation and making exactly the same deal with Ningauble of the Seven Eyes in his vast and mazy cave, except that Ningauble, as was his gossipy wont, talked a thousand words to Sheelba's one, yet in the end said nothing more than Sheelba.

So the two disreputable and mostly unprincipled heroes set out for the Shadowland, the Mouser prudently following the coast road north to Sarheenmar and there cutting inland, Fafhrd recklessly riding straight northwest across the Poisoned Desert. Yet both had good luck and crossed the Parched Mountains on the same day, the Mouser taking the Northern Pass, Fafhrd the Southern.

The heavy overcast, which began at the watershed of the Parched Mountains, thickened, though not a drop of rain or atom of mist fell. The air was cool and moist and, nourished perhaps by underground water of most distant source, thick green grass grew and an open forest of black cedars sprang up. Herds of black antelopes and black reindeer nibbled the endless grass to a lawn, yet there were no herdsmen or human folk at all. The sky grew darker yet, almost a perpetual night, odd low hills topped by congeries of black rock appeared, there were distant fires of many hues, though none blue, and each vanished if you approached it, and you found no ash or other sign of it at its site. So the Mouser and Fafhrd well knew they had entered the Shadowland, death-feared by the merciless Mingols to the north, by the bone-proud, invisible-fleshed ivory Ghouls to the west, to the east by the hairless folk and bald beasts of the shrunken yet diplomatically subtle and long-enduring Empire of Eevarensee, and to the south by the King of Kings himself, who had a standing rule that instant death be the lot of any person, even his own vizier or most-beloved son or favoritest queen, who so much as whispered the name 'Shadowland', let alone discussed the dark area in any wise.

Eventually the Mouser sighted a black pavilion and rode toward it and dismounted from his black horse and parted the silken drapes of the doorway and there behind an ebony table, listlessly sipping white wine from a crystal goblet, in her and his favoritest robe of violet silk, sat his beloved Ivrian, with an ermine wrap about her shoulders.

But her small, slender hands were death blue, the color of slate, and her face of like hue and vacant-eyed. Only her hair was as livingly glossy black as ever, though longer than the Mouser recalled, as were her fingernails.

She stared her eyes, which the Mouser now saw were faintly filmed by grainy white, and parted her black lips and said in monotone, 'It delights me beyond my powers of expression to see you, Mouser, ever-beloved, who now have risked even the horrors of the Shadowland for sake of me, yet you are alive and I am dead. Come never again to trouble me, my darlingest love. Enjoy. Enjoy.'

And even as the Mouser hurled himself forward toward her, smashing to one side the frail black table, her figure grew somewhat faint and she sank swiftly into the ground as if it were diaphanous, gentle, unfeared quicksand – though solid turf when the Mouser clawed at it.

Meantime, a few Lankhmar leagues to the south, Fafhrd was suffering exactly the same experience with his dearly-beloved Vlana, slate-faced and slate-handed – those dear, long, strong fingers – actress-clad in black tunic and red stockings with dark brown hair agleam, except that before she too sank into the ground, she ended, being a rather rougher woman than Ivrian, by intoning in a voice that was most strange for being a lifeless monotone rather than the spirited accents the words implied, 'And now exit fast, you beloved booby, sweetest man in live world or Shadowland. Do Ningauble's idiot job, which will almost certainly be your death, stupid boy, for you've most unwisely promised him. Then gallop like Hell southwest. If you do die by the way and join me in the Shadowland, I'll spit in your face, never speak you a single word, and never once share your black mossy bed. That's what death's like.'

As Fafhrd and the Mouser, though leagues apart, simultaneously tore like terrified mice from the two black pavilions, they each sighted to the east a steel-blue flame rising like the longest and gleamingest of stilettos, far higher than any other flame they'd seen in the Shadowland, a most narrow, bright-blue flame deeply stabbing the black overcast. The Mouser saw it a bit to the south, Fafhrd a bit to the north. Each frantically dug heels in his horse and galloped on, their paths slowly converging. At that moment, their interviews with their beloveds huge in their memories, to encounter Death seemed the best thing in the world to them, the most to be desired, whether to kill life's awfulest creature, or by him be killed.

Yet as they galloped along, Fafhrd couldn't help thinking of how Vlana was ten years older than he, and had looked all of that and more in the Shadowland, while the Mouser's mind couldn't avoid touching the topic of Ivrian's basic silliness and snobbery.

Yet they both galloped on willfully, wildly, joyfully, toward the blue flame, which grew ever thicker and brighter, until they saw it came from the huge central chimney of an open-gated, open-doored, low, vast black castle on a low long hill.

They trotted into the palace side by side, the gate and doorway both being wide and neither man recognizing the presence of the other. The black granite wall before them was indented by a wide fireplace in which blue flame shone almost as blindingly as the naked sun and shot its fiercest flame up the chimney, to make the flame they had noted from afar. Before the fireplace stood an ebony chair, cushioned with black velvet, and on that most graceful of seats rested a shining black mask, full-faced, with wide-open eyeholes.

The eight iron-shod hooves of the white horse and the black one sounded a dead clank on the black flagstones.

Fafhrd and the Mouser dismounted and moved, respectively,

to the north and south sides of the ebony chair, upholstered with black velvet, on which rested the spangled mask of Death. Perhaps fortunately, at that time Death himself was away, on business or vacation.

At that instant, both Fafhrd and the Mouser realized he was promise-bound by oath to Ningauble and Sheelba, to slay his comrade. The Mouser whisked out Scalpel. Quite as swiftly Fafhrd whipped out Graywand. They stood face to face, ready to kill each other.

At that instant a long, glittering scimitar came down between them, swift as light, and the black, glittering mask of death was cloven precisely in two, black forehead to black chin.

Then the swift sword of Duke Danius went licking right at Fafhrd. The Northerner barely parried the blow of the mad-eyed aristocrat. The gleaming blade swept back toward the Mouser, who also barely shoved aside the slice.

Both heroes likely would have been slain – for who in the long run has might to master the insane? – except that at that instant Death himself returned to his customary abode in his black castle in the Shadowland and with his black hands seized Duke Danius by the neck and strangled him dead within seventeen of Fafhrd's heartbeats and twenty-one of the Mouser's – and some hundreds of Danius'.

Neither of the two heroes dared look at Death. Before that most remarkable and horrid being was a third finished with Danius, his foolish foe, they snatched up a gleaming half of a black mask each, sprang each on his horse, and galloped side-by-side like twin lunatics of the frantickest sort, ridden even harder than they rode their powerful white and black horses by that cosmically champion jockey Fear, out of the Shadowland south-west by the straightest path possible.

Lankhmar and her environs, to which they swiftly returned, were no great good to them. Ningauble and Sheelba were both most angry at getting only half a mask apiece, even though it was the mask of the most potent being in all universes known and unknown. The two rather self-centered and somewhat irrational archimages, intent on and vastly enamored of their private war – though they were undoubtedly the cunningest and wisest sorcerers ever to exist in the world of Nehwon – were entirely adamant against the very sound four arguments Fafhrd and the Gray Mouser advanced in their self-defense: one, that they had stuck to the magician-set rules by first making certain to get the Mask of Death (or as much as they could of it) out of the Shadowland at whatever personal cost to themselves and diminishment of their self-respect. For, if they had fought each other, as Rule Two required, they would most likely have simultaneously slain each other, and so not even a sliver of a mask get to Sheel or Ning, while who in his sane senses would take on Death as an opponent? – Danius being a most crushing, present argument here. Two, that half a magical mask is better than none. Three, that each magician having half the mask, both would be forced to quit their stupid war, cooperate in future, and so double their already considerable powers. And, four, that the two sorcerers had neither returned Vlana and Ivrian in their lovely, living flesh to Fafhrd and the Mouser, nor vanished them utterly from time, so that there was no memory of them anywhere, as promised, but only tortured the two heroes – and likely the two girls also – by a final horrid encounter. In pets most undignified for great wizards, Ningauble magicked all objects whatsoever out of the home Fafhrd and the Mouser had stolen, while Sheelba burned it to ashes indistinguishable from those of the earlier tenement in which Vlana and Ivrian had perished.

Which was probably all to the good, since the whole idea of the two heroes dwelling in a house behind the Silver Eel – right in the midst of the graveyard of their great beloveds – had undoubtedly been most morbid from the start.

Thereafter Sheelba and Ningauble, showing no gratitude whatever, or remorse for their childish revenges, insisted on exacting from the Mouser and Fafhrd the utmost service established by the bargain they had set with the two heroes.

But Fafhrd and the Gray Mouser were never once again haunted by those two admirable and grand girls Ivrian and Vlana, nor even thought of them except with heart-easing and painless gratitude. In fact, within a few days the Mouser began the hottest sort of love affair with a slightly underage and most winsome niece of Karstak Ovartamortes, while Fafhrd took on the identical twin daughters, most beauteous and wealthy and yet on the verge of turning to prostitution for the excitement it promised, of Duke Danius.

What Vlana and Ivrian thought of all this in their eternal dwelling in the Shadowland is entirely their business and that of Death, on whose horrid visage they now could look with no fear whatever.

X
BAZAAR OF THE BIZARRE

The strange stars of the World of Nehwon glinted thickly above the black-roofed city of Lankhmar, where swords clink almost as often as coins. For once there was no fog.

In the Plaza of Dark Delights, which lies seven blocks south of the Marsh Gate and extends from the Fountain of Dark Abundance to the Shrine of the Black Virgin, the shop-lights glinted upward no more brightly than the stars glinted down. For there the vendors of drugs and the peddlers of curiosa and the hawkers of assignations light their stalls and crouching places with foxfire, glowworms, and firepots with tiny single windows, and they conduct their business almost as silently as the stars conduct theirs.

There are plenty of raucous spots a-glare with torches in nocturnal Lankhmar, but by immemorial tradition soft whispers and a pleasant dimness are the rule in the Plaza of Dark Delights. Philosophers often go there solely to meditate, students to dream, and fanatic-eyed theologians to spin like spiders abstruse new theories of the Devil and of the other dark forces ruling the universe. And if any of these find a little illicit fun by the way, their theories and dreams and theologies and demonologies are undoubtedly the better for it.

Tonight, however, there was a glaring exception to the darkness rule. From a low doorway with a trefoil arch new-struck through an ancient wall, light spilled into the Plaza. Rising above the horizon of the pavement like some monstrous moon a-shine with the ray of a murderous sun, the new doorway dimmed almost to extinction the stars of the other merchants of mystery.

Eerie and unearthly objects for sale spilled out of the doorway a little way with the light, while beside the doorway crouched an avid-faced figure clad in garments never before seen on land or sea . . . in the World of Nehwon. He wore a hat like a small red pail, baggy trousers, and outlandish red boots with upturned toes. His eyes were as predatory as a hawk's, but his smile as cynically and lasciviously cajoling as an ancient satyr's.

Now and again he sprang up and pranced about, sweeping and re-sweeping with a rough long broom the flagstones as if to clean path for the entry of some fantastic emperor, and he often paused in his dance to bow low and loutingly, but always with upglancing eyes, to the crowd gathering in the darkness across from the doorway and to swing his hand from them toward the interior of the new shop in a gesture of invitation at once servile and sinister.

No one of the crowd had yet plucked up courage to step forward into the glare and enter the shop, or even inspect the rarities set out so carelessly yet temptingly before it. But the number of fascinated peerers increased momently. There were mutterings of censure at the dazzling new method of merchandising – the infraction of the Plaza's custom of darkness – but on the whole the complaints were outweighed by the gasps and murmurings of wonder, admiration and curiosity kindling ever hotter.

The Gray Mouser slipped into the Plaza at the Fountain end as silently as if he had come to slit a throat or spy on the spies of the Overlord. His ratskin moccasins were soundless. His sword Scalpel in its mouseskin sheath did not swish ever so faintly against either his tunic or cloak, both of gray silk curiously coarse of weave. The glances he shot about him from under his gray silk hood half thrown back were freighted with menace and a freezing sense of superiority.

Inwardly the Mouser was feeling very much like a schoolboy – a schoolboy in dread of rebuke and a crushing assignment of homework. For in the Mouser's pouch of ratskin was a note scrawled in dark brown squid-ink on silvery fish-skin by Sheelba of the Eyeless Face, inviting the Mouser to be at this spot at this time.

Sheelba was the Mouser's supernatural tutor and – when the whim struck Sheelba – guardian, and it never did to ignore his invitations, for Sheelba had eyes to track down the unsociable though he did not carry them between his cheeks and forehead.

But the tasks Sheelba would set the Mouser at times like these were apt to be peculiarly onerous and even noisome – such as procuring nine white cats with never a black hair among them, or stealing five copies of the same book of magic runes from five widely separated sorcerous libraries or obtaining specimens of the dung of four kings living or dead – so the Mouser had come early, to get the bad news as soon as possible, and he had come alone, for he certainly did not want his comrade Fafhrd to stand snickering by while Sheelba delivered his little wizardly homilies to a dutiful Mouser . . . and perchance thought of extra assignments.

Sheelba's note, invisibly graven somewhere inside the Mouser's skull, read merely, *When the star Akul bedizens the Spire of Rhan, be you by the Fountain of Dark Abundance*, and the note was signed only with the little featureless oval which is Sheelba's sigil.

The Mouser glided now through the darkness to the Fountain, which was a squat black pillar from the rough rounded top of which a single black drop welled and dripped every twenty elephant's heartbeats.

The Mouser stood beside the Fountain and, extending a bent hand, measured the altitude of the green star Akul. It had still to drop down the sky seven finger widths more before it would touch the needle-point of the slim star-silhouetted distant minaret of Rhan.

The Mouser crouched doubled-up by the black pillar and then vaulted lightly atop it to see if that would make any great difference in Akul's attitude. It did not.

He scanned the nearby darkness for motionless figures . . . especially that of one robed and cowled like a monk – cowled so deeply that one might wonder how he saw to walk. There were no figures at all.

The Mouser's mood changed. If Sheelba chose not to come courteously beforehand, why he could be boorish too! He strode off to investigate the new bright archdoored shop, of whose infractious glow he had become inquisitively aware at least a block before he had entered the Plaza of Dark Delights.

Fafhrd the Northerner opened one wine-heavy eye and without moving his head scanned half the small firelit room in which he slept naked. He shut that eye, opened the other, and scanned the other half.

There was no sign of the Mouser anywhere. So far so good! If his luck held, he would be able to get through tonight's embarrassing business without being jeered at by the small gray rogue.

He drew from under his stubbly cheek a square of violet serpent-hide pocked with tiny pores so that when he held it between his eyes and the dancing fire it made stars. Studied for a time, these stars spelled out obscurely the message: *When Rhandagger stabs the darkness in Akul-heart, seek you the Source of the Black Drops.*

Drawn boldly across the prickholes in an orange-brown like dried blood – in fact spanning the violet square – was a seven-armed swastika, which is one of the sigils of Ningauble of the Seven Eyes.

Fafhrd had no difficulty in interpreting the Source of the Black Drops as the Fountain of Dark Abundance. He had become wearily familiar with such cryptic poetic language during his boyhood as a scholar of the singing skalds.

Ningauble stood to Fafhrd very much as Sheelba stood to the Mouser except that the Seven-Eyed One was a somewhat more pretentious archimage, whose taste in the thaumaturgical tasks he set Fafhrd ran in larger directions, such as the slaying of dragons, the sinking of four-masted magic ships, and the kidnapping of ogre-guarded enchanted queens.

Also, Ningauble was given to quiet realistic boasting, especially about the grandeur of his vast cavern-home, whose stony serpent-twisting back corridors led, he often averred, to all spots in space and time – provided Ningauble instructed one beforehand exactly how to step those rocky crooked low-ceilinged passageways.

Fafhrd was driven by no great desire to learn Ningauble's formulas and enchantments, as the Mouser was driven to learn Sheelba's, but the Septinocular One had enough holds on the Northerner, based on the latter's weaknesses and past misdeeds, so that Fafhrd had always to listen patiently to Ningauble's wizardly admonishments and vaunting sorcerous chitchat – but *not*, if humanly or inhumanly possible, while the Gray Mouser was present to snigger and grin.

Meanwhile, Fafhrd, standing before the fire, had been whipping, slapping, and belting various garments and weapons and ornaments onto his huge brawny body with its generous stretches of thick short curling red-gold hairs. When he opened the outer door and, also booted and helmeted now, glanced down the darkling alleyway preparatory to leaving and noted only the hunch-backed chestnut vendor a-squat by his brazier at the next corner, one would have sworn that when he did stride forth toward the Plaza of Dark Delights it would be with the clankings and thunderous tread of a siege-tower approaching a thick-walled city.

Instead the lynx-eared old chestnut vendor, who was also a spy of the Overlord, had to swallow down his heart when it came sliding crookedly up his throat as Fafhrd rushed past him tall as a pine tree, swift as the wind, and silent as a ghost.

The Mouser elbowed aside two gawkers with shrewd taps on the floating rib and strode across the dark flagstones toward the garishly bright shop with its doorway like an upended heart. It occurred to him they must have had masons working like fiends to have cut and plastered that archway so swiftly. He had been past here this afternoon and noted nothing but blank wall.

The outlandish porter with the red cylinder hat and twisty red shoe-toes came frisking out to the Mouser with his broom and then went curtsying back as he re-swept a path for this first customer with many an obsequious bow and smirk.

But the Mouser's visage was set in an expression of grim and all-skeptical disdain. He paused at the heaping of objects in front of the door and scanned it with disapproval. He drew Scalpel from its thin gray sheath and with the tip of the long blade flipped back the cover on the topmost of a pile of musty books. Without going any closer he briefly scanned the first page, shook his head, rapidly turned a half dozen more pages with Scalpel's tip, using the sword as if it were a teacher's wand to point out words here and there – because they were ill-chosen, to judge from his expression – and then abruptly closed the book with another sword-flip.

Next he used Scalpel's tip to lift a red cloth hanging from a table behind the books and peer under it suspiciously, to rap contemptuously a glass jar with a human head floating in it, to touch disparagingly several other objects and to waggle reprovingly at a foot-chained owl which hooted at him solemnly from its high perch.

He sheathed Scalpel and turned toward the porter with a sour, lifted-eyebrow look which said – nay, shouted – plainly, 'Is *this* all you have to offer? Is this garbage your excuse for defiling the Dark Plaza with glare?'

Actually the Mouser was mightily interested by every least item which he had glimpsed. The book, incidentally, had been in a script which he not only did not understand, but did not even recognize.

Three things were very clear to the Mouser: first, that this stuff offered here for sale did not come from anywhere in the World of Nehwon, no, not even from Nehwon's farthest outback; second, that all this stuff was, in some way which he could not yet define, extremely dangerous; third, that all this stuff was monstrously fascinating and that he, the Mouser, did not intend to stir from this place until he had personally scanned, studied, and if need be tested, every last intriguing item and scrap.

At the Mouser's sour grimace, the porter went into a convulsion of wheedling and fawning caperings, seemingly torn between a desire to kiss the Mouser's foot and to point out with flamboyant caressing gestures every object in his shop.

He ended by bowing so low that his chin brushed the pavement, sweeping an ape-long arm toward the interior of the shop, and gibbering in atrocious Lankhmarese, 'Every object to pleasure the flesh and senses and imagination of man. Wonders undreamed. Very cheap, very cheap! Yours for a penny! The Bazaar of the Bizarre. Please to inspect, oh king!'

The Mouser yawned a very long yawn with the back of his hand to his mouth, next he looked around him again with the patient, worldly smile of a duke who knows he must put up with many boredoms to encourage business in his demesne, finally he shrugged faintly and entered the shop.

Behind him the porter went into a jigging delirium of glee and began to re-sweep the flagstones like a man maddened with delight.

Inside, the first thing the Mouser saw was a stack of slim books bound in gold-lined fine-grained red and violet leather.

The second was a rack of gleaming lenses and slim brass tubes calling to be peered through.

The third was a slim dark-haired girl smiling at him mysteriously from a gold-barred cage that swung from the ceiling.

Beyond that cage hung others with bars of silver and strange green, ruby, orange, ultramarine, and purple metals.

Fafhrd saw the Mouser vanish into the shop just as his left hand touched the rough chill pate of the Fountain of Dark Abundance and as Akul pointed precisely on Rhan-top as if it were that needle-spire's green-lensed pinnacle-lantern.

He might have followed the Mouser, he might have done no such thing, he certainly would have pondered the briefly glimpsed event, but just then there came from behind him a long low 'Hssssst!'

Fafhrd turned like a giant dancer and his longsword Graywand came out of its sheath swiftly and rather more silently than a snake emerges from its hole.

Ten arm lengths behind him, in the mouth of an alleyway darker than the Dark Plaza would have been without its new commercial moon, Fafhrd dimly made out two robed and deeply cowled figures poised side by side.

One cowl held darkness absolute. Even the face of a Negro of Klesh might have been expected to shoot ghostly bronze gleams. But here there were none.

In the other cowl there nested seven very faint pale greenish glows. They moved about restlessly, sometimes circling each other, swinging mazily. Sometimes one of the seven horizontally oval gleams would grow a little brighter, seemingly as it moved forward toward the mouth of the cowl – or a little darker, as it drew back.

Fafhrd sheathed Graywand and advanced toward the figures. Still facing him, they retreated slowly and silently down the alley.

Fafhrd followed as they receded. He felt a stirring of interest . . . and of other feelings. To meet his own supernatural mentor alone might be only a bore and a mild nervous strain; but it would be hard for anyone entirely to repress a shiver of awe at encountering at one and the same time both Ningauble of the Seven Eyes and Sheelba of the Eyeless Face.

Moreover, that those two bitter wizardly rivals would have joined forces, that they should apparently be operating together in amity . . . Something of great note must be afoot! There was no doubting that.

The Mouser meantime was experiencing the smuggest, most mind-teasing, most exotic enjoyments imaginable. The sleekly leather-bound gold-stamped books turned out to contain scripts stranger far than that in the book whose pages he had flipped outside – scripts that looked like skeletal beasts, cloud swirls, and twisty-branched bushes and trees – but for a wonder he could read them all without the least difficulty.

The books dealt in the fullest detail with such matters as the private life of devils, the secret histories of murderous cults, and – these were illustrated – the proper dueling techniques to employ against sword-armed demons and the erotic tricks of lamias, succubi, bacchantes, and hamadryads.

The lenses and brass tubes, some of the latter of which were as fantastically crooked as if they were periscopes for seeing over the walls and through the barred windows of other universes, showed at first only delightful jeweled patterns, but after a bit the Mouser was able to see through them into all sorts of interesting places: the treasure-rooms of dead kings, the bed-chambers of living queens, council-crypts of rebel angels, and the closets in which the gods hid plans for worlds too frighteningly fantastic to risk creating.

As for the quaintly clad slim girls in their playfully widely-barred cages, well, they were pleasant pillows on which to rest eyes momentarily fatigued by book-scanning and tube-peering.

Ever and anon one of the girls would whistle softly at the Mouser and then point cajolingly or imploringly or with languorous hintings at a jeweled crank set in the wall whereby her cage, suspended on a gleaming chain running through gleaming pulleys, could be lowered to the floor.

At these invitations the Mouser would smile with a bland amorousness and nod and softly wave a hand from the finger-hinge as if to whisper, 'Later . . . later. Be patient.'

After all, girls had a way of blotting out all lesser, but not thereby despicable, delights. Girls were for dessert.

Ningauble and Sheelba receded down the dark alleyway with Fafhrd following them until the latter lost patience and, somewhat conquering his unwilling awe, called out nervously, 'Well, are you going to keep on fleeing me backward until we all pitch into the Great Salt Marsh? What do you want of me? What's it all about?'

But the two cowled figures had already stopped, as he could perceive by the starlight and the glow of a few high windows, and now it seemed to Fafhrd that they had stopped a moment before he had called out. A typical sorcerers' trick for making one feel awkward! He gnawed his lip in the darkness. It was ever thus!

'Oh My Gentle Son . . .' Ningauble began in his most sugary-priestly tones, the dim puffs of his seven eyes now hanging in his cowl as steadily and glowing as mildly as the Pleiades seen late on a summer night through a greenish mist rising from a lake freighted with blue vitriol and corrosive gas of salt.

'I asked what it's all about!' Fafhrd interrupted harshly. Already convicted of impatience, he might as well go the whole hog.

'Let me put it as a hypothetical case,' Ningauble replied imperturbably. 'Let us suppose, My Gentle Son, that there is a man in a universe and that a most evil force comes to this universe from another universe, or perhaps from a congeries of universes, and that this man is a brave man who wants to defend his universe and who counts his life as a trifle and that moreover he has to counsel him a very wise and prudent and public-spirited uncle who knows all about these matters which I have been hypothecating—'

'The Devourers menace Lankhmar!' Sheelba rapped out in a voice as harsh as a tree cracking and so suddenly that Fafhrd almost started – and for all we know, Ningauble too.

Fafhrd waited a moment to avoid giving false impressions and then switched his gaze to Sheelba. His eyes had been growing accustomed to the darkness and he saw much more now than he had seen at the alley's mouth, yet he still saw not one jot more than absolute blackness inside Sheelba's cowl.

'Who are the Devourers?' he asked.

It was Ningauble, however, who replied, 'The Devourers are the most accomplished merchants in all the many universes – so accomplished, indeed, that they sell only trash. There is a deep necessity in this, for the Devourers must occupy all their cunning in perfecting their methods of selling and so have not an instant to spare in considering the worth of what they sell. Indeed, they dare not concern themselves with such matters for a moment, for fear of losing their golden touch – and yet such are their skills that their wares are utterly irresistible, indeed the finest wares in all the many universes – if you follow me?'

Fafhrd looked hopefully toward Sheelba, but since the latter did not this time interrupt with some pithy summation, he nodded to Ningauble.

Ningauble continued, his seven eyes beginning to weave a bit, judging from the movements of the seven green glows, 'As you might readily deduce, the Devourers possess all the mightiest magics garnered from the many universes, whilst their assault groups are led by the most aggressive wizards imaginable, supremely skilled in all methods of battling, whether it be with the wits, or the feelings, or with the beweaponed body.

'The method of the Devourers is to set up shop in a new world and first entice the bravest and the most adventuresome and the supplest-minded of its people – who have so much imagination that with just a touch of suggestion they themselves do most of the work of selling themselves.

'When these are safely ensnared, the Devourers proceed to deal with the remainder of the population: meaning simply that they sell and sell and sell! – sell trash and take good money and even finer things in exchange.'

Ningauble sighed windily and a shade piously. 'All this is very bad, My Gentle Son,' he continued, his eye-glows weaving hypnotically in his cowl, 'but natural enough in universes administered by such gods as we have – natural enough and perhaps endurable. However' – he paused – 'there is worse to come! The Devourers want not only the patronage of all beings in all universes, but – doubtless because they are afraid someone will some day raise the ever-unpleasant question of the true worth of things – they want all their customers reduced to a state of slavish and submissive suggestibility, so that they are fit for nothing whatever but to gawk at and buy the trash the Devourers offer for sale. This means of course that eventually the Devourers' customers will have nothing wherewith to pay the Devourers for their trash, but the Devourers do not seem to be concerned with this eventuality. Perhaps they feel that there is always a new universe to exploit. And perhaps there is!'

'Monstrous!' Fafhrd commented. 'But what do the Devourers gain from all these furious commercial sorties, all this mad merchandising? What do they really want?'

Ningauble replied, 'The Devourers want only to amass cash and to raise little ones like themselves to amass more cash and they want to compete with each other at cash-amassing. (Is that coincidentally a city, do you think, Fafhrd? Cashamash?) And the Devourers want to brood about their great service to the many universes – it is their claim that servile customers make the most obedient subjects for the gods – and to complain about how the work of amassing cash tortures their minds and upsets their digestions. Beyond this, each of the Devourers also secretly collects and hides away forever, to delight no eyes but his own, all the finest objects and thoughts created by true men and women (and true wizards and true demons) and bought by the

Devourers at bankruptcy prices and paid for with trash or – this is their ultimate preference – with nothing at all.'

'Monstrous indeed!' Fafhrd repeated. 'Merchants are ever an evil mystery and these sound the worst. But what has all this to do with me?'

'Oh My Gentle Son,' Ningauble responded, the piety in his voice now tinged with a certain clement disappointment, 'you force me once again to resort to hypothecating. Let us return to the supposition of this brave man whose whole universe is direly menaced and who counts his life a trifle and to the related supposition of this brave man's wise uncle, whose advice the brave man invariably follows—'

'The Devourers have set up shop in the Plaza of Dark Delights!' Sheelba interjected so abruptly and in such iron-harsh syllables that this time Fafhrd actually did start. 'You must obliterate this outpost tonight!'

Fafhrd considered that for a bit, then said, in a tentative sort of voice, 'You will both accompany me, I presume, to aid me with your wizardly sendings and castings in what I can see must be a most perilous operation, to serve me as a sort of sorcerous artillery and archery corps while I play assault battalion—'

'Oh My Gentle Son . . .' Ningauble interrupted in tones of deepest disappointment, shaking his head so that his eye-glows jogged in his cowl.

'You must do it alone!' Sheelba rasped.

'Without any help at all?' Fafhrd demanded. 'No! Get someone else. Get this doltish brave man who always follows his scheming uncle's advice as slavishly as you tell me the Devourers' customers respond to their merchandising. Get *him!* But as for me – No, I say!'

'Then leave us, coward!' Sheelba decreed dourly, but Ningauble only sighed and said quite apologetically, 'It was intended that you have a comrade in this quest, a fellow soldier against noisome evil – to wit, the Gray Mouser. But unfortunately he came early to his appointment with my colleague here and was enticed into the shop of the Devourers and is doubtless now deep in their snares, if not already extinct. So you can see that we do take thought for your welfare and have no wish to overburden you with solo quests. However, My Gentle Son, if it still be your firm resolve . . .'

Fafhrd let out a sigh more profound than Ningauble's. 'Very well,' he said in gruff tones admitting defeat, 'I'll do it for you. Someone will have to pull that poor little gray fool out of the pretty-pretty fire – or the twinkly-twinkly water! – that tempted him. But how do I go about it?' He shook a big finger at Ningauble. 'And no more Gentle-Sonning!'

Ningauble paused. Then he said only, 'Use your own judgment.'

Sheelba said, 'Beware the Black Wall!'

Ningauble said to Fafhrd, 'Hold, I have a gift for you,' and held out to him a ragged ribbon a yard long, pinched between the cloth of the wizard's long sleeve so that it was impossible to see the manner of hand that pinched. Fafhrd took the tatter with a snort, crumpled it into a ball, and thrust it into his pouch.

'Have a greater care with it,' Ningauble warned. 'It is the Cloak of Invisibility, somewhat worn by many magic usings. Do not put it on until you near the Bazaar of the Devourers. It has two minor weaknesses: it will not make you altogether invisible to a master sorcerer if he senses your presence and takes certain steps. Also, see to it that you do not bleed during this exploit, for the cloak will not hide blood.'

'I've a gift too!' Sheelba said, drawing from out of his black cowl-hole – with sleeve-masked hand, as Ningauble had done – something that shimmered faintly in the dark like . . .

Like a spiderweb.

Sheelba shook it, as if to dislodge a spider, or perhaps two.

'The Blindfold of True Seeing,' he said as he reached it toward Fafhrd. 'It shows all things as they really are! Do not lay it across your eyes until you enter the Bazaar. On no account, as you value your life or your sanity, wear it now!'

Fafhrd took it from him most gingerly, the flesh of his fingers crawling. He was inclined to obey the taciturn wizard's instructions. At this moment he truly did not much care to see the true visage of Sheelba of the Eyeless Face.

*

The Gray Mouser was reading the most interesting book of them all, a great compendium of secret knowledge written in a script of astrologic and geomantic signs, the meanings of which fairly leaped off the page into his mind.

To rest his eyes from that – or rather to keep from gobbling the book too fast – he peered through a nine-elbowed brass tube at a scene that could only be the blue heaven-pinnacle of the universe where angels flew shimmeringly like dragonflies and where a few choice heroes rested from their great mountain-climb and spied down critically on the antlike labors of the gods many levels below.

To rest his eye from *that*, he looked up between the scarlet (bloodmetal?) bars of the inmost cage at the most winsome, slim, fair, jet-eyed girl of them all. She knelt, sitting on her heels, with her upper body leaned back a little. She wore a red velvet tunic and had a mop of golden hair so thick and pliant that she could sweep it in a neat curtain over her upper face, down almost to her pouting lips. With the slim fingers of one hand she would slightly part these silky golden drapes to peer at the Mouser playfully, while with those of the other she rattled golden castanets in a most languorously slow rhythm, though with occasional swift staccato bursts.

The Mouser was considering whether it might not be as well to try a turn or two on the ruby-crusted golden crank next to his elbow, when he spied for the first time the glimmering wall at the back of the shop. What could its material be? he asked himself. Tiny diamonds countless as the sand set in smoky glass? Black opal? Black pearl? Black moonshine?

Whatever it was, it was wholly fascinating, for the Mouser quickly set down his book, using the nine-crooked spy-tube to mark his place – a most engrossing pair of pages on dueling where were revealed the Universal Parry and its five false variants and also the three true forms of the Secret Thrust – and with only a finger-wave to the ensorceling blonde in red velvet he walked quickly toward the back of the shop.

As he approached the Black Wall he thought for an instant that he glimpsed a silver wraith, or perhaps a silver skeleton, walking toward him out of it, but then he saw that it was only his own darkly handsome reflection, pleasantly flattered by the lustrous material. What had momentarily suggested silver ribs was the reflection of the silver lacings on his tunic.

He smirked at his image and reached out a finger to touch *its* lustrous finger when – Lo, a wonder! – his hand went into the wall with never a sensation at all save a faint tingling coolth promising comfort like the sheets of a fresh-made bed.

He looked at his hand inside the wall and – Lo, another wonder – it was all a beautiful silver faintly patterned with tiny scales. And though his own hand indubitably, as he could tell by clenching it, it was scarless now and a mite slimmer and longer fingered – altogether a more handsome hand than it had been a moment ago.

He wriggled his fingers and it was like watching small silver fish dart about – fingerlings!

What a droll conceit, he thought, to have a dark fishpond or rather swimming pool set on its side indoors, so that one could walk into the fracious erect fluid quietly and gracefully, instead of all the noisy, bouncingly athletic business of diving!

And how charming that the pool should be filled not with wet soppy cold water, but with a sort of moon-dark essence of sleep! An essence with beautifying cosmetic properties too – a sort of mudbath without the mud. The Mouser decided he must have a swim in this wonder pool at once, but just then his gaze lit on a long high black couch toward the other end of the dark liquid wall, and beyond the couch a small high table set with viands and a crystal pitcher and goblet.

He walked along the wall to inspect these, his handsome reflection taking step for step with him.

He trailed his hand in the wall for a space and then withdrew it, the scales instantly vanishing and the familiar old scars returning.

The couch turned out to be a narrow high-sided black coffin lined with quilted black satin and piled at one end with little black satin pillows. It looked most invitingly comfortable and restful – not quite as inviting as the Black Wall, but very attractive just the same; there was even a rack of tiny black books nested in the black satin for the occupant's diversion and also a black candle, unlit.

The collation on the little ebony table beyond the coffin consisted entirely of black foods. By sight and then by nibbling and sipping the Mouser discovered their nature: thin slices of a very dark rye bread crusted with poppy seeds and dripped with black butter; slivers of charcoal-seared steak; similarly broiled tiny thin slices of calf's liver sprinkled with dark spices and liberally pricked with capers; the darkest grape jellies; truffles cut paper thin and mushrooms fried black; pickled chestnuts; and of course, ripe olives and black fish eggs – caviar. The black drink, which foamed when he poured it, turned out to be stout laced with the bubbly wine of Ilthmar.

He decided to refresh the inner Mouser – the Mouser who lived a sort of blind soft greedy undulating surface-life between his lips and his belly – before taking a dip in the Black Wall.

Fafhrd re-entered the Plaza of Dark Delights walking warily and with the long tatter that was the Cloak of Invisibility trailing from between left forefinger and thumb and with the glimmering cobweb that was the Blindfold of True Seeing pinched even more delicately by its edge between the same digits of his right hand. He was not yet altogether certain that the trailing gossamer hexagon was completely free of spiders.

Across the Plaza he spotted the bright-mouthed shop – the shop he had been told was an outpost of the deadly Devourers – through a ragged gather of folk moving about restlessly and commenting and speculating to one another in harsh excited undertones.

The only feature of the shop Fafhrd could make out at all clearly at this distance was the red-capped red-footed baggy-trousered porter, not capering now but leaning on his long broom beside the trefoil-arched doorway.

With a looping swing of his left arm Fafhrd hung the Cloak of Invisibility around his neck. The ragged ribband hung to either side down his chest in its wolfskin jerkin only halfway to his wide belt which supported longsword and short-axe. It did not vanish his body to the slightest degree that he could see and he doubted it worked at all. Like many another thaumaturge, Ningauble never hesitated to give one useless charms, not for any treacherous reason, necessarily, but simply to improve one's morale. Fafhrd strode boldly toward the shop.

The Northerner was a tall, broad-shouldered, formidable-looking man – doubly formidable by his barbaric dress and weaponing in supercivilized Lankhmar – and so he took it for granted that the ordinary run of city folk stepped out of his way; indeed it had never occurred to him that they should not.

He got a shock. All the clerks, seedy bravos, scullery folk, students, slaves, second-rate merchants and second-class courtesans who would automatically have moved aside for him (though the last with a saucy swing of the hips) now came straight at him, so that he had to dodge and twist and stop and even sometimes dart back to avoid being toe-tramped and bumped. Indeed one fat pushy proud-stomached fellow almost carried away his cobweb, which he could see now by the light of the shop was free of spiders – or if there were any spiders still on it, they must be very small.

He had so much to do dodging Fafhrd-blind Lankhmarians that he could not spare one more glance for the shop until he was almost at the door. And then before he took his first close look, he found that he was tilting his head so that his left ear touched the shoulder below it and that he was laying Sheelba's spiderweb across his eyes.

The touch of it was simply like the touch of any cobweb when one runs face into it walking between close-set bushes at dawn. Everything shimmered a bit as if seen through a fine crystal grating. Then the least shimmering vanished, and with it the delicate clinging sensation, and Fafhrd's vision returned to normal – as far as he could tell.

It turned out that the doorway to the Devourers' shop was piled with garbage – garbage of a particularly offensive sort: old bones, dead fish, butcher's offal, moldering gravecloths folded in uneven squares like badly bound uncut books, broken glass and potsherds, splintered boxes, large stinking dead leaves orange-spotted with blight, bloody rags, tattered discarded loincloths, large worms nosing about, centipedes a-scuttle, cockroaches a-stagger, maggots a-crawl – and less agreeable things.

Atop all perched a vulture which had lost most of its feathers and seemed to have expired of some avian eczema. At least Fafhrd took it for dead, but then it opened one white-filmed eye.

The only conceivably salable object outside the shop – but it was a most notable exception – was the tall black iron statue, somewhat larger than life-size, of a lean swordsman of dire yet melancholy visage. Standing on its square pedestal beside the door, the statue leaned forward just a little on its long two-handed sword and regarded the Plaza dolefully.

The statue almost teased awake a recollection in Fafhrd's mind – a recent recollection, he fancied – but then there was a blank in his thoughts and he instantly dropped the puzzle. On raids like this one, relentlessly swift action was paramount. He loosened his axe in its loop, noiselessly whipped out Graywand and, shrinking away from the piled and crawling garbage just a little, entered the Bazaar of the Bizarre.

The Mouser, pleasantly replete with tasty black food and heady black drink, drifted to the Black Wall and thrust in his right arm to the shoulder. He waved it about, luxuriating in the softly flowing coolth and balm – admiring its fine silver scales and more than human handsomeness. He did the same with his right leg, swinging it like a dancer exercising at the bar. Then he took a gently deep breath and drifted farther in.

Fafhrd on entering the Bazaar saw the same piles of gloriously bound books and racks of gleaming brass spy-tubes and crystal lenses as had the Mouser – a circumstance which seemed to overset Ningauble's theory that the Devourers sold only trash.

He also saw the eight beautiful cages of jewel-gleaming metals and the gleaming chains that hung them from the ceiling and went to the jeweled wall cranks.

Each cage held a gleaming, gloriously hued, black- or light-haired spider big as a rather small person and occasionally waving a long jointed claw-handed leg, or softly opening a little and then closing a pair of fanged down-swinging mandibles, while staring steadily at Fafhrd with eight watchful eyes set in two jewel-like rows of four.

Set a spider to catch a spider, Fafhrd thought, thinking of his cobweb, and then wondered what the thought meant.

He quickly switched to more practical questions then, but he had barely asked himself whether before proceeding further he should kill the very expensive-looking spiders, fit to be the coursing beasts of some jungle empress – another count against Ning's trash-theory! – when he heard a faint splashing from the back of the shop. It reminded him of the Mouser taking a bath – the Mouser loved baths, slow luxurious ones in hot soapy scented oil-dripped water, the small gray sybarite! – and so Fafhrd hurried off in that direction with many a swift upward overshoulder glance.

He was detouring the last cage, a scarlet-metaled one holding the handsomest spider yet, when he noted a book set down with a crooked spy-tube in it – exactly as the Mouser would keep his place in a book by closing it on a dagger.

Fafhrd paused to open the book. Its lustrous white pages were blank. He put his impalpably cobwebbed eye to the spy-tube. He glimpsed a scene that could only be the smoky red hell-nadir of the universe, where dark devils scuttled about like centipedes and where chained folk gazing yearningly upward and the damned writhed in the grip of black serpents whose eyes shone and whose fangs dripped and whose nostrils breathed fire.

As he dropped tube and book, he heard the faint sonorous quick dull report of bubbles being expelled from a fluid at its surface. Staring instantly toward the dim back of the shop, he saw at last the pearl-shimmering Black Wall and a silver skeleton eyed with great diamonds receding into it. However, this costly bone-man – once more Ning's trash-theory disproved! – still had one arm sticking partway out of the wall and this arm was not bone, whether silver, white, brownish or pink, but live-looking flesh covered with proper skin.

As the arm sank into the wall, Fafhrd sprang forward as fast as he ever had in his life and grabbed the hand just before it vanished. He knew then he had hold of his friend, for he would recognize anywhere the Mouser's grip, no matter how enfeebled. He tugged, but it was as if the Mouser were mired in black quicksand. He laid Graywand down and grasped the

Mouser by the wrist too and braced his feet against the rough black flags and gave a tremendous heave.

The silver skeleton came out of the wall with a black splash, metamorphosing as it did into a vacant-eyed Gray Mouser who without a look at his friend and rescuer went staggering off in a curve and pitched head over heels into the black coffin.

But before Fafhrd could hoist his comrade from this new gloomy predicament, there was a swift clash of footsteps and there came racing into the shop, somewhat to Fafhrd's surprise, the tall black iron statue. It had forgotten or simply stepped off its pedestal, but it had remembered its two-handed sword, which it brandished about most fiercely while shooting searching black glances like iron darts at every shadow and corner and nook.

The black gaze passed Fafhrd without pausing, but halted at Graywand lying on the floor. At the sight of that longsword the statue started visibly, snarled its iron lips, narrowed its black eyes. It shot glances more ironly stabbing than before, and it began to move about the shop in sudden zigzag rushes, sweeping its darkly flashing sword in low scythe-strokes.

At that moment the Mouser peeped moon-eyed over the edge of the coffin, lifted a limp hand and waved it at the statue, and in a soft sly foolish voice cried, 'Yoo-hoo!'

The statue paused in its searchings and scythings to glare at the Mouser in mixed contempt and puzzlement.

The Mouser rose to his feet in the black coffin, swaying drunkenly, and dug in his pouch.

'Ho, slave!' he cried to the statue with maudlin gaiety, 'your wares are passing passable. I'll take the girl in red velvet.' He pulled a coin from his pouch, goggled at it closely, then pitched it at the statue. 'That's one penny. And the nine-crooked spytube. That's another penny.' He pitched it. 'And *Gron's Grand Compendium of Exotic Lore* – another penny for you! Yes, and here's one more for supper – very tasty, 'twas. Oh and I almost forgot – here's for tonight's lodging!' He pitched a fifth large copper coin at the demonic black statue and, smiling blissfully, flopped back out of sight. The black quilted satin could be heard to sigh as he sank in it.

Four-fifths of the way through the Mouser's penny-pitching Fafhrd decided it was useless to try to unriddle his comrade's nonsensical behavior and that it would be far more to the point to make use of this diversion to snatch up Graywand. He did so on the instant, but by that time the black statue was fully alert again, if it had ever been otherwise. Its gaze switched to Graywand the instant Fafhrd touched the longsword and it stamped its foot, which rang against the stone, and cried a harsh metallic 'Ha!'

Apparently the sword became invisible as Fafhrd grasped it, for the black statue did not follow him with its iron eyes as he shifted position across the room. Instead it swiftly laid down its own mighty blade and caught up a long narrow silver trumpet and set it to its lips.

Fafhrd thought it wise to attack before the statue summoned reinforcements. He rushed straight at the thing, swinging back Graywand for a great stroke at the neck – and steeling himself for an arm-numbing impact.

The statue blew and instead of the alarm blare Fafhrd had expected, there silently puffed out straight at him a great cloud of white powder that momentarily blotted out everything, as if it were the thickest of fogs from Hlal the River.

Fafhrd retreated, choking and coughing. The demon-blown fog cleared quickly, the white powder falling to the stony floor with unnatural swiftness, and he could see again to attack, but now the statue apparently could see him too, for it squinted straight at him and cried its metallic 'Ha!' again and whirled its sword around its iron head preparatory to the charge – rather as if winding itself up.

Fafhrd saw that his own hands and arms were thickly filmed with the white powder, which apparently clung to him everywhere except his eyes, doubtless protected by Sheelba's cobweb.

The iron statue came thrusting and slashing in. Fafhrd took the great sword on his, chopped back, and was parried in return. And now the combat assumed the noisy deadly aspects of a conventional longsword duel, except that Graywand was notched whenever it caught the chief force of a stroke, while the statue's somewhat longer weapon remained unmarked. Also, whenever Fafhrd got through the other's guard with a thrust – it was almost impossible to reach him with a slash – it turned out that the other had slipped his lean body or head aside with unbelievably swift and infallible anticipations.

It seemed to Fafhrd – at least at the time – the most fell, frustrating, and certainly the most wearisome combat in which he had ever engaged, so he suffered some feelings of hurt and irritation when the Mouser reeled up in his coffin again and leaned an elbow on the black-satin-quilted side and rested chin on fist and grinned hugely at the battlers and from time to time laughed wildly and shouted such enraging nonsense as, 'Use Secret Thrust Two-and-a-Half, Fafhrd – it's all in the book!' or 'Jump in the oven! – there'd be a master stroke of strategy!' or – this to the statue – 'Remember to sweep under his feet, you rogue!'

Backing away from one of Fafhrd's sudden attacks, the statue bumped the table holding the remains of the Mouser's repast – evidently its anticipatory abilities did not extend to its rear – and scraps of black food and white potsherds and jags of crystal scattered across the floor.

The Mouser leaned out of his coffin and waved a finger waggishly. 'You'll have to sweep that up!' he cried and went off into a gale of laughter.

Backing away again, the statue bumped the black coffin. The Mouser only clapped the demonic figure comradely on the shoulder and called, 'Set to it again, clown! Brush him down! Dust him off!'

But the worst was perhaps when, during a brief pause while the combatants gasped and eyed each other dizzily, the Mouser waved coyly to the nearest giant spider and called his inane 'Yoo-hoo!' again, following it with, 'I'll see you, dear, after the circus.'

Fafhrd, parrying with weary desperation a fifteenth or a fiftieth cut at his head, thought bitterly, *This comes of trying to rescue small heartless madmen who would howl at their grandmothers hugged by bears. Sheelba's cobweb has shown me the Gray One in his true idiot nature.*

The Mouser had first been furious when the sword-skirling

clashed him awake from his black satin dreams, but as soon as he saw what was going on he became enchanted at the wildly comic scene.

For, lacking Sheelba's cobweb, what the Mouser saw was only the zany red-capped porter prancing about in his tip-curled red shoes and aiming with his broom great strokes at Fafhrd, who looked exactly as if he had climbed a moment ago out of a barrel of meal. The only part of the Northerner not whitely dusted was a mask-like stretch across his eyes.

What made the whole thing fantastically droll was that miller-white Fafhrd was going through all the motions – and emotions! – of a genuine combat with excruciating precision, parrying the broom as if it were some great jolting scimitar or two-handed broadsword even. The broom would go sweeping up and Fafhrd would gawk at it, giving a marvelous interpretation of apprehensive goggling despite his strangely shadowed eyes. Then the broom would come sweeping down and Fafhrd would brace himself and seem to catch it on his sword only with the most prodigious effort – and then pretend to be jolted back by it!

The Mouser had never suspected Fafhrd had such a perfected theatric talent, even if it were acting of a rather mechanical sort, lacking the broad sweeps of true dramatic genius, and he whooped with laughter.

Then the broom brushed Fafhrd's shoulder and blood sprang out.

Fafhrd, wounded at last and thereby knowing himself unlikely to outendure the black statue – although the latter's iron chest was working now like a bellows – decided on swifter measures. He loosened his hand-axe again in its loop and at the next pause in the fight, both battlers having outguessed each other by retreating simultaneously, whipped it up and hurled it at his adversary's face.

Instead of seeking to dodge or ward off the missile, the black statue lowered its sword and merely wove its head in a tiny circle.

The axe closely circled the lean black head, like a silver wood-tailed comet whipping around a black sun, and came back straight at Fafhrd like a boomerang – and rather more swiftly than Fafhrd had sent it.

But time slowed for Fafhrd then and he half ducked and caught it left-handed as it went whizzing past his cheek.

His thoughts too went for a moment fast as his actions. He thought of how his adversary, able to dodge every frontal attack, had not avoided the table or the coffin behind him. He thought of how the Mouser had not laughed now for a dozen clashes and he looked at him and saw him, though still dazed-seeming, strangely pale and sober-faced, appearing to stare with horror at the blood running down Fafhrd's arm.

So crying as heartily and merrily as he could, 'Amuse yourself! Join in the fun, clown! – here's your slap-stick,' Fafhrd tossed the axe toward the Mouser.

Without waiting to see the result of that toss – perhaps not daring to – he summoned up his last reserves of speed and rushed at the black statue in a circling advance that drove it back toward the coffin.

Without shifting his stupid horrified gaze, the Mouser stuck out a hand at the last possible moment and caught the axe by the handle as it spun lazily down.

As the black statue retreated near the coffin and poised for what promised to be a stupendous counter-attack, the Mouser leaned out and, now grinning foolishly again, sharply rapped its black pate with the axe.

The iron head split like a coconut, but did not come apart. Fafhrd's hand-axe, wedged in it deeply, seemed to turn all at once to iron like the statue and its black haft was wrenched out of the Mouser's hand as the statue stiffened up straight and tall.

The Mouser stared at the split head woefully, like a child who hadn't known knives cut.

The statue brought its great sword flat against its chest, like a staff on which it might lean but did not, and it fell rigidly forward and hit the floor with a ponderous clank.

At that stony-metallic thundering, white wildfire ran across the Black Wall, lightening the whole shop like a distant levin-bolt, and iron-basalt thundering echoed from deep within it.

Fafhrd sheathed Graywand, dragged the Mouser out of the black coffin – the fight hadn't left him the strength to lift even his small friend – and shouted in his ear, 'Come on! Run!'

The Mouser ran for the Black Wall.

Fafhrd snagged his wrist as he went by and plunged toward the arched door, dragging the Mouser after him.

The thunder faded out and there came a low whistle, cajolingly sweet.

Wildfire raced again across the Black Wall behind them – much more brightly this time, as if a lightning storm were racing toward them.

The white glare striking ahead imprinted one vision indelibly on Fafhrd's brain: the giant spider in the inmost cage pressed against the bloodred bars to gaze down at them. It had pale legs and a velvet red body and a mask of sleek thick golden hair from which eight jet eyes peered, while its fanged jaws hanging down in the manner of the wide blades of a pair of golden scissors rattled together in a wild staccato rhythm like castanets.

That moment the cajoling whistle was repeated. It too seemed to be coming from the red and golden spider.

But strangest of all to Fafhrd was to hear the Mouser, dragged unwillingly along behind him, cry out in answer to the whistling, 'Yes, darling, I'm coming. Let me go, Fafhrd! Let me climb to her! Just one kiss! Sweetheart!'

'Stop it, Mouser,' Fafhrd growled, his flesh crawling in mid-plunge. 'It's a giant spider!'

'Wipe the cobwebs out of your eyes, Fafhrd,' the Mouser retorted pleadingly and most unwittingly to the point. 'It's a gorgeous girl! I'll never see her ticklesome like – and I've paid for her! *Sweetheart!*'

Then the booming thunder drowned his voice and any more whistling there might have been, and the wildfire came again, brighter than day, and another great thunderclap right on its heels, and the floor shuddered and the whole shop shook, and Fafhrd dragged the Mouser through the trefoil-arched doorway, and there was another great flash and clap.

The flash showed a semicircle of Lankhmarians peering ashen-faced overshoulder as they retreated across the Plaza of Dark Delights from the remarkable indoor thunderstorm that threatened to come out after them.

Fafhrd spun around. The archway had turned to blank wall.

The Bazaar of the Bizarre was gone from the World of Nehwon.

The Mouser, sitting on the dank flags where Fafhrd had dragged him, babbled wailfully, 'The secrets of time and space! The lore of the gods! The mysteries of Hell! Black nirvana! Red and gold Heaven! Five pennies gone forever!'

Fafhrd set his teeth. A mighty resolve, rising from his many recent angers and bewilderments, crystallized in him.

Thus far he had used Sheelba's cobweb – and Ningauble's tatter too – only to serve others. Now he would use them for himself! He would peer at the Mouser more closely and at every person he knew. He would study even his own reflection! But most of all, he would stare Sheelba and Ning to their wizardly cores!

There came from overhead a low 'Hssst!'

As he glanced up he felt something snatched from around his neck and, with the faintest tingling sensation, from off his eyes.

For a moment there was a shimmer traveling upward and through it he seemed to glimpse distortedly, as through thick glass, a black face with a cobwebby skin that entirely covered mouth and nostrils and eyes.

Then that dubious flash was gone and there were only two cowled heads peering down at him from over the wall top. There was chuckling laughter.

Then both cowled heads drew back out of sight and there was only the edge of the roof and the sky and the stars and the blank wall

SWORDS IN
THE MIST

CONTENTS

all the world's waters. Of land tunnels and sea tunnels, of water wells in earth and air wells in water, of cliffs paper-thin and oceans at war. Of the Triple Goddess at work in Nehwon, or at play. Of a masked black sea-witch and her magical toys. Of two luscious sea-queens and their outre harem guard. Together with a compendium of practical information useful to those who must walk, not on water, but – without diving garb – down, through, and under the aqueous element.

The devious workings of the Sea-King's curse. A swimming race between men and sharks and how it was betted on. Of noisome Ilthmar. Of Doors between distant worlds. A warning to all to avoid side-paths when visiting Ningauble of the Seven Eyes in his caverns, and of how this wise rule was broken upon one occasion.

In his gambits, a chess-player sacrifices pawn or piece to checkmate his adversary. But in *his* games, a black magician, in order to triumph, may sacrifice living pieces and even himself the player.

1. *Tyre* Of a humiliating enchantment which robbed Fafhrd and the Gray Mouser of all girls, except Chloe the cross-eyed Greek. And of how the Mouser fell into love, though not with Chloe.

2. *Ningauble* Of a visit by the two heroes to the Gossiper of the Gods, to find a cure for their girl-denying enchantment. Of a word-war of maneuver between Ningauble and the Mouser, with mention of four infamous handmaidens of Ishtar and a dwarf who was richly compensated for his deformity, of the Friday concubine of the satrap Philip, and of like matters.

3. *The Woman Who Came* How on Ningauble's advice and to make a magic to restore them, Fafhrd and the Mouser went on a multiple quest to procure the Shroud of Ahriman, aphrodisiacal mummy of the Demon Pharaoh, the Cup from which

Socrates drank the hemlock, a sprig from the primal Tree of Life, and The Woman Who Would Come When She Was Ready.

4. *The Lost City* Of the heroes' cautious courting of shy, sly Ahura. Of the rift she naughtily digged between them. Of the journey they made, all three together. Of the Mouser's theory of Ahura's sex, and of how he felt it disproved in the moment of proving it. Of a saving gale, a messenger-bat, and the making of a great magic.

5. *Anra Devadoris* Of a fastidious stranger named the Dark Gift of Demons. Of the most taxing sword fight in the Gray Mouser's duel-starred life. Of the stranger's filthy bed.

6. *The Mountain* Of a demon peak that preyed on its countryside, and of a demon castle atop that peak. Of the follies of heroes and of a quest resumed.

7. *Ahura Devadoris* The spoken story of the Bright Gift of Demons. Of a tyranny more intimate and absolute than that of a wizard over his concubine-acolyte. Of the mixings of magics and whoredoms. Of a Tyrian orgy and its frightful close.

8. *The Old Man Without a Beard* Ahura's weird tale concluded. Of a sorcerer, his student, and their evil curriculum. Of an especially close confinement suffered by Ahura.

9. *The Castle Called Mist* Of a vast edifice alive or stretching into other dimensions. Horrors innumerable. End of Ahura's tale. Fate of the Old Man. A final duel and a final revelation. Lankhmar once more in view.

I
THE CLOUD OF HATE

Muffled drums beat out a nerve-scratching rhythm and red lights flickered hypnotically in the underground Temple of Hates, where five thousand ragged worshipers knelt and abased themselves and ecstatically pressed foreheads against the cold and gritty cobbles as the trance took hold and the human venom rose in them.

The drumbeat was low. And save for snarls and mewlings, the inner pulsing was inaudible. Yet together they made a hellish vibration which threatened to shake the city and land of Lankhmar and the whole world of Nehwon.

Lankhmar had been at peace for many moons and so the hates were greater. Tonight, furthermore, at a spot halfway across the city, Lankhmar's black-togaed nobility celebrated with merriment and feasting and twinkling dance the betrothal of their Overlord's daughter to the Prince of Ilthmar, and so the hates were redoubled.

The single-halled subterranean temple was so long and wide and at the same time so irregularly planted with thick pillars that at no point could a person see more than a third of the way across it. Yet it had a ceiling so low that at any point a man standing tall could have brushed it with his fingertips – except that here all groveled. The air was swooningly fetid. The dark bent backs of the hate-ensorceled worshipers made a kind of hummocky dark ground, from which the nitre-crusted stone pillars rose like gray tree trunks.

The masked Archpriest of the Hates lifted a skinny finger. Parchment-thin iron cymbals began to clash in unison with the drums and the furnace-red flickerings, wringing to an unendurable pitch the malices and envies of the blackly en-raptured communicants.

Then in the gloom of that great slit-like hall, dim pale tendrils began to rise from the dark hummocky ground of the bent backs, as though a white, swift-growing ghost-grass had been seeded there. The tendrils, which in another world might have been described as ectoplasmic, quickly multiplied, thickened, lengthened, and then coalesced into questing white serpentine shapes, so that it seemed as if tongues of thick river-fog had come licking down into this sub-cellar from the broad-flowing river Hlal.

The white serpents coiled past the pillars, brushed the low ceiling, moistly caressed the backs of their devotees and source, and then in turn coalesced to pour up the curving black hole of a narrow spiral stairway, the stone steps of which were worn almost to chute-like smoothness – a sinuously billowing white cylinder in which a redness lurked.

And all the while the drums and cymbals did not falter for a single beat, nor did the Hell-light tenders cease to crank the wooden wheels on which shielded, red-burning candles were affixed, nor did the eyes of the Archpriest flicker once sideways in their wooden mask, nor did one mesmerized bent soul look up.

Along a misted alley overhead there was hurrying home to the thieves' quarter a beggar girl, skinny-frail of limb and with eyes big as a lemur's peering fearfully from a tiny face of elfin beauty. She saw the white pillar, slug-flat now, pouring out between the bars of a window-slit level with the pavement, and although there were thick chilly tendrils of river-fog already following her, she knew that this was different.

She tried to run around the thing, but swift almost as a serpent striking it whipped across to the opposite wall, barring her way. She ran back, but it outraced her and made a U, penning her against the unyielding wall. Then she only stood still and shook as the fog-serpent narrowed and grew denser and came wreathing around her. Its tip swayed like the head of a poisonous snake preparing to strike and then suddenly dipped toward her breast. She stopped shaking then and her head fell back and the pupils rolled up in her lemur-like eyes so that they showed only great whites, and she dropped to the pavement limp as a rag.

The fog-serpent nosed at her for a few moments, then as though irked at finding no life remaining, flipped her over on her face, and went swiftly questing in the same direction the river-fog itself was taking: across city towards the homes of the nobles and the lantern-jeweled palace of the Overlord.

Save for an occasional fleeting red glint in the one, the two sorts of fog were identical.

Beside a dry stone horse-trough at the juncture of five alleys, two men curled close to either side of a squat brazier in which a little charcoal glowed. The spot was so near the quarter of the nobles that the sounds of music and laughter came at intervals, faintly, along with a dim rainbow-glow of light. The two men might have been a hulking beggar and a small one, except that their tunics and leggings and cloaks, though threadbare, were of good stuff, and scabbarded weapons lay close to the hand of each.

The larger said, 'There'll be fog tonight. I smell it coming from the Hlal.' This was Fafhrd, brawny-armed, pale and serene of face, reddish gold of hair.

For reply the smaller shivered and fed the brazier two small goblets of charcoal and said sardonically, 'Next predict glaciers! – advancing down the Street of the Gods, by preference.' That was the Mouser, eyes wary, lips quirking, cheeks muffled by gray hood drawn close.

Fafhrd grinned. As a tinkling gust of distant song came by, he asked the dark air that carried it, 'Now why aren't we warmly cushioned somewhere inside tonight, well drunk and sweetly embraced?'

For answer the Gray Mouser drew from his belt a ratskin pouch and slapped it by its drawstrings against his palm. It flattened as it hit and nothing chinked. For good measure he writhed at Fafhrd the backs of his ten fingers, all ringless.

Fafhrd grinned again and said to the dusky space around them, which was now filled with the finest mist, the fog's forerunner, 'Now that's a strange thing. We've won I know not how many jewels and oddments of gold and electrum in our adventurings – and even letters of credit on the Guild of the Grain Merchants. Where have they all flown to? – the credit-letters on parchment wings, the jewels jetting fire like tiny red and green pearly cuttlefish. Why aren't we rich?'

The Mouser snorted, 'Because you dribble away our get on worthless drabs, or oftener still pour it out for some noble whim – some plot of bogus angels to storm the walls of Hell. Meantime I stay poor nursemaiding you.'

Fafhrd laughed and retorted, 'You overlook your own whimsical imprudences, such as slitting the Overlord's purse and picking his pocket too the selfsame night you rescued and returned him his lost crown. No, Mouser, I think we're poor because—' Suddenly he lifted an elbow and flared his nostrils as he snuffed the chill moist air. 'There's a taint in the fog tonight,' he announced.

The Mouser said dryly, 'I already smell dead fish, burnt fat, horse dung, tickly lint, Lankhmar sausage gone stale, cheap temple incense burnt by the ten-pound cake, rancid oil, moldy grain, slaves' barracks, embalmers' tanks crowded to the black brim, and the stink of a cathedral full of unwashed carters and trulls celebrating orgiastic rites – and now you tell me of a taint!'

'It is something different from all those,' Fafhrd said, peering successively down the five alleys. 'Perhaps the last . . .' His voice trailed off doubtfully and he shrugged.

Strands of fog came questing through small high-set street-level windows into the tavern called the Rats' Nest, interlacing curiously with the soot-trail from a failing torch, but unnoticed except by an old harlot who pulled her patchy fur cloak closer to her throat.

All eyes were on the wrist game being played across an ancient oaken table by the famed bravo Gnarlag and a dark-skinned mercenary almost as big-thewed as he. Right elbows firmly planted and right hands bone-squeezingly gripped, each strained to force the back of the other's wrist down against the ringed and scarred and carved and knife-stuck wood. Gnarlag, who scowled sneeringly, had the advantage by a thumb's length.

One of the fog-strands, as though itself a devotee of the wrist game and curious about the bout, drifted over Gnarlag's shoulder. To the old harlot the inquisitive fog-strand looked redly-veined – a reflection from the torches, no doubt, but she prayed it brought fresh blood to Gnarlag.

The fog finger touched the taut arm. Gnarlag's sneering look turned to one of pure hate and the muscles of his forearm seemed to double in thickness as he rotated it more than a half turn. There was a muffled snap and a gasp of anguish. The mercenary's wrist had been broken.

Gnarlag stood up. He knocked to the wall a wine cup offered him and cuffed aside a girl who would have embraced him. Then grabbing up his two swords on their thick belt from the bench beside him, he strode to the brick stairs and up out of the Rats' Nest. By some trick of air currents, perhaps, it seemed that a fog-strand rested across his shoulders like a comradely arm.

When he was gone, someone said, 'Gnarlag was ever a cold and ungrateful winner.' The dark mercenary stared at his dangling hand and bit back groans.

'So tell me, giant philosopher, why we're not dukes,' the Gray Mouser demanded, unrolling a forefinger from the fist on his knee so that it pointed across the brazier at Fafhrd. 'Or emperors, for that matter, or demigods.'

'We are not dukes because we're no man's man,' Fafhrd replied smugly, settling his shoulders against the stone horse-trough. 'Even a duke must butter up a king, and demigods the gods. We butter no one. We go our own way, choosing our own adventures – and our own follies! Better freedom and a chilly road than a warm hearth and servitude.'

'There speaks the hound turned out by his last master and not yet found new boots to slaver on,' the Mouser retorted with comradely sardonic impudence. 'Look you, you noble liar, we've labored for a dozen lords and kings and merchants fat. You've served Movarl across the Inner Sea. I've served the bandit Harsel. We've both served this Glipkerio, whose girl is tied to Ilthmar this same night.'

'Those are exceptions,' Fafhrd protested grandly. 'And even

403

when we serve, we make the rules. We bow to no man's ultimate command, dance to no wizard's drumming, join no mob, hark to no wildering hate-call. When we draw sword, it's for ourselves alone. *What's that?'*

He had lifted his sword for emphasis, gripping it by the scabbard just below the guard, but now he held it still with the hilt near his ear.

'It hums a warning!' he said tersely after a moment. 'The steel twangs softly in its sheath!'

Chuckling tolerantly at this show of superstition, the Mouser drew his slimmer sword from its light scabbard, sighted along the blade's oiled length at the red embers, spotted a couple of dark flecks and began to rub at them with a rag.

When nothing more happened, Fafhrd said grudgingly as he laid down his undrawn sword, 'Perchance only a dragon walked across the cave where the blade was forged. Still, I don't like this tainted mist.'

Gis the cutthroat and the courtesan Tres had watched the fog coming across the fantastically peaked roofs of Lankhmar until it obscured the low-swinging yellow crescent of the moon and the rainbow glow from the palace. Then they had lit the cressets and drawn the blue drapes and were playing at throw-knife to sharpen their appetites for a more intimate but hardly kinder game.

Tres was not unskillful, but Gis could somersault the weapon a dozen or thirteen times before it stuck in wood and throw as truly between his legs as back over his shoulder without mirror. Whenever he threw the knife so it struck very near Tres, he smiled. She had to remind herself that he was not much more evil than most evil men.

A frond of fog came wreathing between the blue drapes and touched Gis on the temple as he prepared to throw. 'The blood in the fog's in your eye-whites!' Tres cried, staring at him weirdly. He seized the girl by the ear and, smiling hugely, slashed her neck just below her dainty jaw. Then, dancing out of the way of the gushing blood, he delicately snatched up his belt of daggers and darted down the curving stairs to the street, where he plunged into a warmhearted fog that was somehow as full of rage as the strong wine of Tovilysis is of sugar, a veritable cistern of wrath. His whole being was bathed in sensations as ecstatic as those strong but fleeting ones the tendril's touch on his temple had loosed from his brain. Visions of daggered princesses and skewered serving maids danced in his head. He stepped along happily, agog with delicious anticipations, beside Gnarlag of the Two Swords, knowing him at once for a hate-brother, sacrosanct, another slave of the blessed fog.

Fafhrd cupped his big hands over the brazier and whistled the gay tune sifting from the remotely twinkling palace. The Mouser, now re-oiling the blade of Scalpel against the mist, observed, 'For one beset by taunts and danger-hums, you're very jolly.'

'I like it here,' the Northerner asserted. 'A fig for courts and beds and inside fires! The edge of life is keener in the street – as on the mountaintop. Is not imagined wine sweeter than wine?' ('Ho!' the Mouser laughed, most sardonically.) 'And is not a crust of bread tastier to one an-hungered than lark's tongues to an epicure? Adversity makes the keenest appetite, the clearest vision.'

'There spoke the ape who could not reach the apple,' the Mouser told him. 'If a door to paradise opened in that wall there, you'd dive through.'

'Only because I've never been to paradise,' Fafhrd swept on. 'Is it not sweeter now to hear the music of Innesgay's betrothal from afar than mingle with the feasters, jig with them, be cramped and blinkered by their social rituals?'

'There's many a one in Lankhmar gnawn fleshless with envy by those sounds tonight,' the Mouser said darkly. 'I am not gnawn so much as those stupid ones. I am more intelligently jealous. Still, the answer to your question: no!'

'Sweeter by far tonight to be Glipkerio's watchman than his pampered guest,' Fafhrd insisted, caught up by his own poetry and hardly hearing the Mouser.

'You mean we serve Glipkerio *free?*' the latter demanded loudly. 'Aye, there's the bitter core of all freedom: no pay!'

Fafhrd laughed, came to himself, and said almost abashedly,

'Still, there is something in the keenness and the watchman part. We're watchmen not for pay, but solely for the watching's sake! Indoors and warm and comforted, a man is blind. Out here we see the city and the stars, we hear the rustle and the tramp of life, we crouch like hunters in a stony blind, straining our senses for—'

'Please, Fafhrd, no more danger signs,' the Mouser protested. 'Next you'll be telling me there's a monster a-drool and a-stalk in the streets, all slavering for Innesgay and her betrothal-maids, no doubt. And perchance a sword-garnished princeling or two, for appetizer.'

Fafhrd gazed at him soberly and said, peering around through the thickening mist, 'When I am *quite* sure of that, I'll let you know.'

The twin brothers Kreshmar and Skel, assassins and alley-bashers by trade, were menacing a miser in his hovel when the red-veined fog came in after them. As swiftly as ambitious men take last bite and wine-swig at a family dinner when unexpectedly summoned to the emperor's banquet board, the two finished their business. Kreshmar neatly bludgeoned a crater in the miser's skull while Skel thrust into his belt the one small purse of gold they had thus far extorted from the ancient man now turning to corpse. They stepped briskly outside, their swords a-swing at their hips, and into the fog, where they marched side-by-side with Gnarlag and Gis in the midst of the compact pale mass that moved almost indistinguishably with the river-fog and yet intoxicated them as surely as if it were a clouded white wine of murder and destruction, zestfully sluicing away all natural cautions and fears, promising an infinitude of thrilling and most profitable victims.

Behind the four marchers, the false fog thinned to a single glimmering thread, red as an artery, silver as a nerve, that led back unbroken around many a stony corner to the Temple of the Hates. A pulsing went ceaselessly along the thread, as nourishment and purpose were carried from the temple to the marauding fog mass and to the four killers, now doubly hate-enslaved, marching along with it. The fog mass moved purposefully as a snow tiger toward the quarter of the nobles and Glipkerio's rainbow-lanterned palace above the breakwater of the Inner Sea.

Three black-clad police of Lankhmar, armed with metal-capped cudgels and weighted wickedly-barbed darts, saw the thicker fog masses coming and the marchers in it. The impression to them was of four men frozen in a sort of pliant ice. Their flesh crawled. They felt paralyzed. The fog fingered them, but almost instantly passed them by as inferior material for its purpose.

Knives and swords licked out of the fog mass. With never a cry the three police fell, their black tunics glistening with a fluid that showed red only on their sallow slack limbs. The fog mass thickened, as if it had fed instantly and richly on its victims. The four marchers became almost invisible from the outside, though from the inside they saw clearly enough.

Far down the longest and most landward of the five alleyways, the Mouser saw by the palace-glimmer behind him the white mass coming, shooting questing tendrils before it, and cried gayly, 'Look, Fafhrd, we've company! The fog comes all the twisty way from Hlal to warm its paddy paws at our little fire.'

Fafhrd, frowning his eyes, said mistrustfully, 'I think it masks other guests.'

'Don't be a scareling,' the Mouser reproved him in a fey voice. 'I've a droll thought, Fafhrd: what if it be not fog, but the smoke of all the poppy-gum and hemp-resin in Lankhmar burning at once? What joys we'll have once we are sniffing it! What dreams we'll have tonight!'

'I think it brings nightmares,' Fafhrd asserted softly, rising in a half crouch. Then, 'Mouser, the taint! And my sword tingles to the touch!'

The questingmost of the swiftly-advancing fog tendrils fingered them both then and seized on them joyously, as if here were the two captains it had been seeking, the slave-leadership which would render it invincible.

The two blood-brothers tall and small felt to the full then the intoxication of the fog, its surging bittersweet touchsong of hate, its hot promises of all bloodlusts forever fulfilled, an uninhibited eternity of murder-madness.

Fafhrd, wineless tonight, intoxicated only by his own idealisms and the thought of watchmanship, was hardly touched by the sensations, did not feel them as temptations at all.

The Mouser, much of whose nature was built on hates and envies, had a harder time, but he too in the end rejected the fog's masterful lures – if only, to put the worst interpretation on it, because he wanted always to be the source of his own evil and would never accept it from another, not even as a gift from the archfiend himself.

The fog shrank back a dozen paces then, cat-quick, like a vixenishly proud woman rebuffed, revealing the four marchers in it and simultaneously pointing tendrils straight at the Mouser and Fafhrd.

It was well for the Mouser then that he knew the membership of Lankhmar's underworld to the last semiprofessional murderer and that his intuitions and reflexes were both arrow-swift. He recognized the smallest of the four – Gis with his belt of knives – as also the most immediately dangerous. Without hesitation he whipped Cat's Claw from its sheath, poised, aimed, and threw it. At the same instant Gis, equally knowledgeable and swift of thought and speedy of reaction, hurled one of his knives.

But the Mouser, forever cautious and wisely fearful, snatched his head to one side the moment he'd made his throw, so that Gis's knife only sliced his ear flap as it hummed past.

Gis, trusting too supremely in his own speed, made no similar evasive movement – with the result that the hilt of Cat's Claw stood out from his right eye socket an instant later. For a long moment he peered with shock and surprise from his other eye, then slumped to the cobbles, his features contorted in the ultimate agony.

Kreshmar and Skel swiftly drew their swords and Gnarlag his two, not one whit intimidated by the winged death that had bitten into their comrade's brain.

Fafhrd, with a fine feeling for tactics on a broad front, did not draw sword at first but snatched up the brazier by one of its three burningly hot short legs and whirled its meager red-glowing contents in the attackers' faces.

This stopped them long enough for the Mouser to draw Scalpel and Fafhrd his heavier cave-forged sword. He wished he could do without the brazier – it was much too hot, but seeing himself opposed to Gnarlag of the Two Swords, he contented himself with shifting it jugglingly to his left hand.

Thereafter the fight was one swift sudden crisis. The three attackers, daunted only a moment by the spray of hot coals and quite uninjured by them, raced forward surefootedly. Four truly-aimed blades thrust at the Mouser and Fafhrd.

The Northerner parried Gnarlag's right-hand sword with the brazier and his left-hand sword with the guard of his own weapon, which he managed simultaneously to thrust through the bravo's neck.

The shock of that death-stroke was so great that Gnarlag's two swords, bypassing Fafhrd one to each side, made no second stroke in their wielder's death-spasm. Fafhrd, conscious now chiefly of an agonizing pain in his left hand, chucked the brazier away in the nearest useful direction – which happened to be at Skel's head, spoiling that one's thrust at the Mouser, who was skipping nimbly back at the moment, though not more swiftly than Kreshmar and Skel were attacking.

The Mouser ducked under Kreshmar's blade and thrust Scalpel up through the assassin's ribs – the easy way to the heart – then quickly whipped it out and gave the same measured dose of thin steel to the dazedly staggering Skel. Then he danced away, looking around him dartingly and holding his sword high and menacing.

'All down and dead,' Fafhrd, who'd had longer to look, assured him. 'Ow, Mouser, I've burnt my fingers!'

'And I've a dissected ear,' that one reported, exploring cautiously with little pats. He grinned. 'Just at the edge, though.' Then, having digested Fafhrd's remark, 'Serve you right for fighting with a kitchen boy's weapon!'

Fafhrd retorted, 'Bah! If you weren't such a miser with the charcoal, I'd have blinded them all with my embercast!'

'And burnt your fingers even worse,' the Mouser countered

pleasantly. Then, still more happy-voiced, 'Methought I heard gold chink at the belt of the one you brazier-bashed. Skel . . . yes, alley-basher Skel. When I've recovered Cat's Claw—'

He broke off because of an ugly little sucking sound that ended in a tiny *plop*. In the hazy glow from the nobles' quarter they saw a horridly supernatural sight: the Mouser's bloody dagger poised above Gis's punctured eye socket, supported only by a coiling white tentacle of the fog which had masked their attackers and which had now grown still more dense, as if it had sucked supreme nutriment – as indeed it had – from its dead servitors in their dying.

Eldritch dreads woke in the Mouser and Fafhrd: dreads of the lightning that slays from the storm-cloud, of the giant sea-serpent that strikes from the sea, of the shadows that coalesce in the forest to suffocate the mighty man lost, of the black smoke-snake that comes questing from the wizard's fire to strangle.

All around them was a faint clattering of steel against cobble: other fog tentacles were lifting the four dropped swords and Gis's knife, while yet others were groping at that dead cut-throat's belt for his undrawn weapons.

It was as if some great ghost squid from the depths of the Inner Sea were arming itself for combat.

And four yards above the ground, at the rooting point of the tentacles in the thickened fog, a red disk was forming in the center of the fog's body, as it were – a reddish disk that looked moment by moment more like a single eye large as a face.

There was the inescapable thought that as soon as that eye could see, some ten beweaponed tentacles would thrust or slash at once, unerringly.

Fafhrd stood terror-bemused between the swiftly-forming eye and the Mouser. The latter, suddenly inspired, gripped Scalpel firmly, readied himself for a dash, and cried to the tall northerner, 'Make a stirrup!'

Guessing the Mouser's stratagem, Fafhrd shook his horrors and laced his fingers together and went into a half crouch. The Mouser raced forward and planted his right foot in the stirrup Fafhrd had made of his hands and kicked off from it just as the latter helped his jump with a great heave – and a simultaneous 'Ow!' of extreme pain.

The Mouser, preceded by his exactly aimed sword, went straight through the reddish ectoplasmic eye disk, dispersing it entirely. Then he vanished from Fafhrd's view as suddenly and completely as if he had been swallowed up by a snowbank.

An instant later the armed tentacles began to thrust and slash about, at random and erratically, as blind swordsmen might. But since there were a full ten of them, some of the strokes came perilously close to Fafhrd and he had to dodge and duck to keep out of the way. At the rutch of his shoes on the cobbles the tentacle-wielded swords and knives began to aim themselves a little better, again as blind swordsmen might, and he had to dodge more nimbly – not the easiest or safest work for a man so big. A dispassionate observer, if such had been conceivable and available, might have decided the ghost squid was trying to make Fafhrd dance.

Meanwhile on the other side of the white monster, the Mouser had caught sight of the pinkishly silver thread and, leaping high as it lifted to evade him, slashed it with the tip of Scalpel. It offered more resistance to his sword than the whole fog-body had and parted with a most unnatural and unexpected *twang* as he cut it through.

Immediately the fog-body collapsed and far more swiftly than any punctured bladder – rather it fell apart like a giant white puffball kicked by a giant boot – and the tentacles fell to pieces too and the swords and knives came clattering down harmlessly on the cobbles and there was a swift fleeting rush of stench that made both Fafhrd and the Mouser clap hand to nose and mouth.

After sniffing cautiously and finding the air breathable again, the Mouser called brightly, 'Hola there, dear comrade! I think I cut the thing's thin throat, or heart string, or vital nerve, or silver tether, or birth cord, or whatever the strand was.'

'Where did the strand lead back to?' Fafhrd demanded.

'I have no intention of trying to find that out,' the Mouser assured him, gazing warily over his shoulder in the direction from which the fog had come. 'You try threading the Lankhmar labyrinth if you want to. But the strand seems as gone as the thing.'

'Ow!' Fafhrd cried out suddenly and began to flap his hands. 'Oh you small villain, to trick me into making a stirrup of my burnt hands!'

The Mouser grinned as he poked about with his gaze at the nastily slimed cobbles and the dead bodies and the scattered hardware. 'Cat's Claw must be here somewhere,' he muttered, 'and I did hear the chink of gold . . .'

'You'd feel a penny under the tongue of a man you were strangling!' Fafhrd told him angrily.

At the Temple of the Hates, five thousand worshipers began to rise up weakly and groaningly, each lighter of weight by some few ounces than when he had first bowed down. The drummers slumped over their drums, the lantern-crankers over their extinguished red candles, and the lank Archpriest wearily and grimly lowered his head and rested the wooden mask in his clawlike hands.

At the alley-juncture, the Mouser dangled before Fafhrd's face the small purse he had just slipped from Skel's belt.

'My noble comrade, shall we make a betrothal gift of it to sweet Innesgay?' he asked liltingly. 'And rekindle the dear little brazier and end this night as we began it, savoring all the matchless joys of watchmanship and all the manifold wonders of—'

'Give it here, idiot boy!' Fafhrd snarled, snatching the chinking thing for all his burnt fingers. 'I know a place where they've soothing salves – and needles too, to stitch up the notched ears of thieves – and where both the wine and the girls are sharp and clean!'

II
LEAN TIMES IN LANKHMAR

Once upon a time in Lankhmar, City of the Black Toga, in the world of Nehwon, two years after the Year of the Feathered Death, Fafhrd and the Gray Mouser parted their ways.

Exactly what caused the tall brawling barbarian and the slim elusive Prince of Thieves to fall out, and the mighty adventuring partnership to be broken, is uncertainly known and was at the time the subject of much speculation. Some said they had quarreled over a girl. Others maintained, with even greater unlikelihood, that they had disagreed over the proper division of a loot of jewels raped from Muulsh the Moneylender. Srith of the Scrolls suggests that their mutual cooling off was largely the reflection of a supernatural enmity existing at the time between Sheelba of the Eyeless Face, the Mouser's demonic mentor, and Ningauble of the Seven Eyes, Fafhrd's alien and multi-serpentine patron.

The likeliest explanation, which runs directly counter to the Muulsh Hypothesis, is simply that times were hard in Lankhmar, adventures few and uninviting, and that the two heroes had reached that point in life when hard-pressed men desire to admix even the rarest quests and pleasurings with certain prudent activities, leading either to financial or to spiritual security, though seldom if ever to both.

This theory – that boredom and insecurity, and a difference of opinion as to how these dismal feelings might best be dealt with, chiefly underlay the estrangement of the twain . . . this theory may account for and perhaps even subsume the otherwise ridiculous suggestion that the two comrades fell out over the proper spelling of Fafhrd's name, the Mouser perversely favoring a simple Lankhmarian equivalent of 'Faferd' while the name's owner insisted that only the original mouth-filling agglomeration of consonants could continue to satisfy his ear and eye and his semi-literate, barbarous sense of the fitness of things. Bored and insecure men will loose arrows at dust motes.

Certain it is that their friendship, though not utterly fractured, grew very cold and that their life-ways, though both continuing in Lankhmar, diverged remarkably.

The Gray Mouser entered the service of one Pulg, a rising racketeer of small religions, a lord of Lankhmar's dark underworld who levied tribute from the priests of all godlets seeking to become gods – on pain of various unpleasant, disturbing and revolting things happening at future services of the defaulting godlet. If a priest didn't pay Pulg, his miracles were sure to misfire, his congregation and collection would fall off sharply, and it was quite possible that a bruised skin and broken bones would be his lot.

Accompanied by three or four of Pulg's bullies and frequently a slim dancing girl or two, the Mouser became a familiar and newly-ominous sight in Lankhmar's Street of the Gods, which leads from the Marsh Gate to the distant docks and the Citadel. He still wore gray, went close-hooded, and carried Cat's Claw and Scalpel at his side, but the dagger and slim curving sword kept in their sheaths. Knowing from of old that a threat is generally more effective than its execution, he limited his activities to the handling of conversations and cash. 'I speak for Pulg – Pulg with a *guh!*' was his usual opening. Later, if holy men grew recalcitrant or overly keen in their bargaining and it became necessary to maul saintlets and break up services, he would sign the bullies to take these disciplinary measures while he himself stood idly by, generally in slow sardonic converse with the attendant girl or girls and often munching sweetmeats. As the months passed, the Mouser grew fat and the dancing girls successively more child-slim and submissive-eyed.

Fafhrd, on the other hand, broke his longsword across his knee (cutting himself badly in the act), tore from his garments the few remaining ornaments (dull worthless scraps of base metal) and bits of ratty fur, forswore strong drink and all allied pleasures (he had been on small beer and womanless for some time), and became the sole acolyte of Bwadres, the sole priest of Issek of the Jug. Fafhrd let his beard grow until it was as long as his shoulder-brushing hair, he became lean and hollow-cheeked and cavern-eyed, and his voice changed from bass to tenor, though *not* as a result of the distressing mutilation which some whispered he had inflicted upon himself – these last knew he had cut himself but lied wildly as to where.

The gods *in* Lankhmar (that is, the gods and candidates for divinity who dwell or camp, it may be said, in the Imperishable City, not the gods *of* Lankhmar – a very different and most secret and dire matter) . . . the gods *in* Lankhmar sometimes seem as if they must be as numberless as the grains of sand in the Great Eastern Desert. The vast majority of them began as men, or more strictly the memories of men who led ascetic, vision-haunted lives and died painful, messy deaths. One gets the impression that since the beginning of time an unending horde of their priests and apostles (or even the gods themselves, it makes little difference) have been crippling across that same desert, the Sinking Land, and the Great Salt Marsh to converge on Lankhmar's low, heavy-arched Marsh Gate – meanwhile suffering by the way various inevitable tortures, castrations, blindings and stonings, impalements, crucifixions, quarterings and so forth at the hands of eastern brigands and Mingol unbelievers who, one is tempted to think, were created solely for the purpose of seeing to the running of that cruel gauntlet. Among the tormented holy throng are a few warlocks and witches seeking infernal immortality for their dark satanic would-be deities and a very few proto-goddesses – generally maidens reputed to have been enslaved for decades by sadistic magicians and ravished by whole tribes of Mingols.

Lankhmar itself and especially the earlier-mentioned street serves as the theatre or more precisely the intellectual and artistic testing-ground of the proto-gods after their more material but no more cruel sifting at the hands of the brigands and Mingols. A new god (his priest or priests, that is) will begin at the Marsh Gate and more or less slowly work his way up the Street of the Gods, renting a temple or preempting a few yards of cobbled pavement here and there, until he has found his proper level. A very few win their way to the region adjoining the Citadel and join the aristocracy of the gods in Lankhmar – transients still, though resident there for centuries and even millennia (the gods *of* Lankhmar are as jealous as they are secret). Far more godlets, it can justly be said, play a one-night stand near the Marsh Gate and then abruptly disappear, perhaps to seek cities where the audiences are less critical. The majority work their way about halfway up the Street of the Gods and then slowly work their way down again, resisting bitterly every inch and yard, until they once more reach the Marsh Gate and vanish forever from Lankhmar and the memories of men.

Now Issek of the Jug, whom Fafhrd chose to serve, was once of the most lowly and unsuccessful of the gods, godlets rather, in Lankhmar. He had dwelt there for about thirteen years, during which time he had traveled only two squares up the Street of the Gods and was now back again, ready for oblivion. He is not to be confused with Issek the Armless, Issek of the Burnt Legs, Flayed Issek, or any other of the numerous and colorfully mutilated divinities of that name. Indeed, his unpopularity may have been due in part to the fact that the manner of his death – racking – was not deemed particularly spectacular. A few scholars have confused him with Jugged Issek, an entirely different saintlet whose claim to immortality lay in his confinement for seventeen years in a not overly roomy earthenware jar. The Jug (Issek of the Jug's Jug) was supposed to contain Waters of Peace from the Cistern of Cillivat – but none apparently thirsted for them. Indeed, had you sought for a good example of a has-been god who had never really been anything, you could hardly have hit on a better choice than Issek of the Jug, while Bwadres was the very type of the failed priest – sere, senile, apologetic and mumbling. The reason that Fafhrd attached himself to Bwadres, rather than to any one of a vast number of livelier holy men with better prospects, was that he had once seen Bwadres pat a deaf-and-dumb child on the head *while* (so far as Bwadres could have known) *no one was looking* and the incident (possibly unique in Lankhmar) had stuck in the mind of the barbarian. But otherwise Bwadres was a most unexceptional old dodderer.

However, after Fafhrd became his acolyte, things somehow began to change.

In the first place, and even if he had contributed nothing else, Fafhrd made a very impressive one-man congregation from the very first day when he turned up so ragged-looking and bloody (from the cuts breaking his longsword). His near seven-foot height and still warlike carriage stood out mountainously among the old women, children and assorted riffraff who made up the odorous, noisy, and vastly fickle crowd of worshipers at the Marsh Gate end of the street of the Gods. One could not help thinking that if Issek of the Jug could attract one such worshiper the godlet must have unsuspected virtues. Fafhrd's formidable height, shoulder breadth and bearing had one other advantage: he could maintain claim to a very respectable area of cobbles for Bwardes and Issek merely by stretching himself out to sleep on them after the night's services were over.

It was at this time that oafs and ruffians stopped elbowing Bwadres and spitting on him. Fafhrd was not pacific in his new personality – after all, Issek of the Jug was notably a godlet of peace – but Fafhrd had a fine barbaric feeling for the proprieties. If anyone took liberties with Bwadres or disturbed the various rituals of Issek-worship, he would find himself lifted up and sat down somewhere else, with an admonitory *thud* if that seemed called for – a sort of informal one-stroke bastinado.

Bwadres himself brightened amazingly as a result of this wholly unexpected respite granted him and his divinity on the very brink of oblivion. He began to eat more often than twice a week and to comb his long skimpy beard. Soon his senility dropped away from him like an old cloak, leaving of itself only a mad stubborn gleam deep in his yellowly crust-edged eyes, and he began to preach the gospel of Issek of the Jug with a fervor and confidence that he had never known before.

Meanwhile Fafhrd, in the second place, fairly soon began to contribute more to the promotion of the Issek of the Jug cult than his size, presence, and notable talents as a chucker-out. After two months of self-imposed absolute silence, which he refused to break even to answer the simplest questions of Bwadres, who was at first considerably puzzled by his gigantic convert, Fafhrd procured a small broken lyre, repaired it, and began regularly to chant the Creed and History of Issek of the Jug at all services. He competed in no way with Bwadres, never chanted any of the litanies or presumed to bless in Issek's name; in fact he always kneeled and resumed silence while serving Bwadres as acolyte, but seated on the cobbles at the foot of the service area while Bwadres meditated between rituals at the head, he would strike melodious chords from his tiny lyre and chant away in a rather high-pitched, pleasing, romantically vibrant voice.

Now as a Northerner boy in the Cold Waste, far poleward of Lankhmar across the Inner Sea, the forested Land of the Eight Cities and the Trollstep Mountains, Fafhrd had been trained in the School of the Singing Skalds (so called, although they chanted rather than sang, because they pitched their voices tenor) rather than in the School of the Roaring Skalds (who pitched their voices bass). This resumption of a childhood-inculcated style of elocution, which he also used in answering the few questions his humility would permit him to notice, was the real and sole reason for the change in Fafhrd's voice that was made the subject of gossip by those who had known him as the Gray Mouser's deep-voiced swordmate.

As delivered over and over by Fafhrd, the History of Issek of the Jug gradually altered, by small steps which even Bwadres could hardly cavil at had he wished, into something considerably more like the saga of a Northern hero, though toned down in some respects. Issek had not slain dragons and other monsters as a child – that would have been against his Creed – he had only sported with them, swimming with leviathan, frisking with behemoth, and flying through the trackless spaces of air on the backs of wivern, griffin and hippogryph. Nor had Issek as a man scattered kings and emperors in battle, he had merely dumb-founded them and their quaking ministers by striding about on fields of poisoned sword-points, standing at attention in fiery furnaces, and treading water in tanks of boiling oil – the while delivering majestic sermons on brotherly love in perfect, intricately rhymed stanzas.

Bwadres' Issek had expired quite quickly, though with some

kindly parting admonitions, after being disjointed on the rack. Fafhrd's Issek (now *the* Issek) had broken seven racks before he began seriously to weaken. Even when, supposedly dead, he had been loosed and had got his hands on the chief torturer's throat there had been enough strength remaining in them alone so that he had been able to strangle the wicked man with ease, although the latter was a champion of wrestlers among his people. However, Fafhrd's Issek had not done so – again it would have been quite against his Creed – he had merely broken the torturer's thick brass band of office from around his trembling neck and twisted it into an exquisitely beautiful symbol of the Jug before finally permitting his own ghost to escape from him into the eternal realms of spirit, there to continue its wildly wonderful adventurings.

Now, since the vast majority of the gods *in* Lankhmar, arising from the Eastern Lands or at least from the kindredly decadent southern country around Quarmall, had been in their earthly incarnations rather effete types unable to bear more than a few minutes of hanging or a few hours of impalement, and with relatively little resistance to molten lead or showers of barbed darts, also not given overly to composing romantic poetry or to dashing exploits with strange beasts, it is hardly to be wondered that Issek of the Jug, as interpreted by Fafhrd, swiftly won and held the attention and soon thereafter also the devotion of a growing section of the usually unstable, gods-dazzled mob. In particular, the vision of Issek of the Jug rising up with his rack, striding about with it on his back, breaking it, and then calmly waiting with arms voluntarily stretched above his head until another rack could be readied and attached to him . . . that vision, in particular, came to occupy a place of prime import- ance in the dreams and daydreams of many a porter, beggar, drab scullion, and the brats and aged dependants of such.

As a result of this popularity, Issek of the Jug was soon not only moving up the Street of the Gods for a second time – a rare enough feat in itself – but also moving at a greater velocity than any god had been known to attain in the modern era. Almost every service saw Bwadres and Fafhrd able to move their simple altar a few more yards toward the Citadel end as their swelling congregations overflowed areas temporarily sacred to gods of less drawing power, and frequently late-coming and tireless worshipers enabled them to keep up services until the sky was reddening with the dawn – ten or twelve repetitions of the ritual (and the yardage gain) in one night. Before long the makeup of their congregations had begun to change. Pursed and then fatter-pursed types showed up: mercenaries and merchants, sleek thieves and minor officials, jeweled courtesans and slumming aristocrats, shaven philosophers who scoffed lightly at Bwadres' tangled arguments and Issek's irrational Creed but were secretly awed by the apparent sincerity of the ancient man and his giant poetical acolyte . . . and with these monied newcomers came, inevitably, the iron-tough hirelings of Pulg and other such hawks circling over the fowl yards of religion.

Naturally enough, this threatened to pose a considerable problem for the Gray Mouser.

So long as Issek, Bwadres and Fafhrd stayed within hooting range of the Marsh Gate, there was nothing to worry about. There when collection time came and Fafhrd circled the congregation with cupped hands, the take, if any, was in the form of moldy crusts, common vegetables past their prime, rags, twigs, bits of charcoal, and – very rarely, giving rise to shouts of wonder – bent and dinted greenish coins of brass. Such truck was below the notice of even lesser racketeers than Pulg, and Fafhrd had no trouble whatever in dealing with the puny and dull-witted types who sought to play Robber King in the Marsh Gate's shadow. More than once the Mouser managed to advise Fafhrd that this was an ideal state of affairs and that any considerable further progress of Issek up the Street of the Gods could lead only to great unpleasantness. The Mouser was nothing if not cautious and most prescient to boot. He liked, or firmly believed he liked, his newly-achieved security almost better than he liked himself. He knew that, as a recent hireling of Pulg, he was still being watched closely by the Great Man and that any appearance of continuing friendship with Fafhrd (for most outsiders thought they had quarreled irrevocably) might some day be counted against him. So on the occasions when he drifted down the Street of the Gods during off-hours – that is, by daylight, for religion is largely a nocturnal, torch-lit business in Lankhmar – he would never seem to speak to Fafhrd directly. Nevertheless he would by seeming accident end up near Fafhrd and, while apparently engaged in some very different private business or pleasure (or perhaps come secretly to gloat over his large enemy's fallen estate – that was the Mouser's second line of defense against conceivable accusations by Pulg) he would manage considerable conversations out of the corner of his mouth, which Fafhrd would answer, if at all, in the same way – though in his case presumably from abstraction rather than policy.

'Look, Fafhrd,' the Mouser said on the third of such occasions, meanwhile pretending to study a skinny-limbed pot-bellied beggar girl, as if trying to decide whether a diet of lean meat and certain calisthenics would bring out in her a rare gaminesque beauty. 'Look, Fafhrd, right here you have what you want, whatever that is – *I* think it's a chance to patch up poetry and squeak it at fools – but whatever it is, you must have it here near the Marsh Gate, for the only thing in the world that is not near the Marsh Gate is money, and you tell me you don't want that – the more fool you! – but let me tell you something: if you let Bwadres get any nearer the Citadel, yes even a pebble's toss, you will get money whether you want it or not, and with that money you and Bwadres will buy something, also willy-nilly and no matter how tightly you close your purse and shut your ears to the cries of the hawkers. That thing which you and Bwadres will buy is trouble.'

Fafhrd answered only with a faint grunt that was the equivalent of a shoulder shrug. He was looking steadily down past his bushy beard with almost cross-eyed concentration at something his long fingers were manipulating powerfully yet delicately, but that the large backs of his hands concealed from the Mouser's view.

'How is the old fool, by the by, since he's eating regularly?' the Mouser continued, leaning a hair closer in an effort to see what Fafhrd was handling. 'Still stubborn as ever, eh? Still set on taking Issek to the Citadel? Still as unreasonable about . . . er . . . business matters?'

'Bwadres is a good man,' Fafhrd said quietly.

'More and more that appears to be the heart of the trouble,' the Mouser answered with a certain sardonic exasperation. 'But look, Fafhrd, it's not necessary to change Bwadres' mind – I'm beginning to doubt whether even Sheelba and Ning, working together, could achieve that cosmic revolution. You can do by yourself all that needs to be done. Just give your poetry a little downbeat, add a little defeatism to Issek's Creed – even you must be tired by now of all this ridiculous mating of northern stoicism to southern masochism, and wanting a change. One theme's good as another to a true artist. Or, simpler still, merely refrain from moving Issek's altar up the street on your big night . . . or even move it down a little! – Bwadres gets so excited when you have big crowds that the old fool doesn't know which direction you're going, anyhow. You could progress like the well-frog. Or, wisest of all, merely prepare yourself to split the take before you hand over the collection to Bwadres. I could teach you the necessary legerdermain in the space of one dawn, though you really don't need it – with those huge hands you can palm anything.'

'No,' said Fafhrd.

'Suit yourself,' the Mouser said very very lightly, though not quite unfeelingly. 'Buy trouble if you will, death if you must. Fafhrd, what *is* that thing you're fiddling with? No, don't hand it to me, you idiot! Just let me glimpse it. By the Black Toga! – what *is* that?'

Without looking up or otherwise moving, Fafhrd had cupped his hands sideways, much as if he were displaying in the Mouser's direction a captive butterfly or beetle – and indeed it did seem at first glimpse as if it were a rare large beetle he was cautiously baring to view, one with a carapace of softly burnished gold.

'It is an offering to Issek,' Fafhrd droned. 'An offering made last night by a devout lady who is wed in spirit to the god.'

'Yes, and to half the young aristos of Lankhmar too and not all in spirit,' the Mouser hissed. 'I know one of Lessnya's double-spiral bracelets when I see it. Reputedly given her by the Twin Dukes of Ilthmar, by the by. What did you have to do to her to get it? – stop, don't answer. I know . . . recite poetry! Fafhrd, things are far worse than I dreamed. If Pulg knew you were already getting gold . . .' He let his whisper trail off. 'But what have you *done* with it?'

'Fashioned it into a representation of the Holy Jug,' Fafhrd answered, bowing his head a shade farther and opening his hands a bit wider and tipping them a trifle.

'So I see,' the Mouser hissed. The soft gold had been twisted into a remarkably smooth strange knot. 'And not a bad job at all. Fafhrd, how you keep such a delicate feeling for curves when for six months you've slept without them against you is quite beyond me. Doubtless such things go by opposites. Don't speak for a moment now, I'm getting an idea. And by the Black Scapula! – a good one! Fafhrd, you must give me that trinket so that I may give it to Pulg. No – please hear me out and then think this through! – not for the gold in it, not as a bribe or as part of a first split – I'm not asking that of you or Bwadres – but simply as a keepsake, a presentation piece. Fafhrd, I've been getting to know Pulg lately and I find he has a strange sentimental streak in him – he likes to get little gifts, little trophies, from his . . . er . . . customers, we sometimes call them. These curios must always be items relating to the god in question – chalices, censors, bones in silver filigree, jeweled amulets, that sort of thing. He likes to sit looking at his shelves of them and dream. Sometimes I think the man is getting religion without realizing it. If I should bring him this bauble he would – I know! – develop an affection for Issek. He would tell me to go easy on Bwadres. It would probably even be possible to put off the question of tribute money for . . . well, for three more squares at least.'

'No,' said Fafhrd.

'So be it, my friend. Come with me, my dear, I am going to buy you a steak.' This second remark was in the Mouser's regular speaking voice and directed, of course, at the beggar girl, who reacted with a look of already practiced and rather languorous affright. 'Not a fish steak either, puss. Did you know there were other kinds? Toss this coin to your mother, dear, and come. The steak stall is four squares up. No, we won't take a litter – you need the exercise. *Farewell – Death-seeker!*'

Despite the wash-my-hands-of-you-tone of this last whisper,

the Gray Mouser did what he could to put off the evil night of reckoning, devising more pressing tasks for Pulg's bullies and alleging that this or that omen was against the immediate settling of the Bwadres account – for Pulg, alongside his pink streak of sentimentality, had recently taken to sporting a gray one of superstition.

There would have been no insurmountable problem at all, of course, if Bwadres had only had that touch of realism about money matters that, when a true crisis arises, is almost invariably shown by even the fattest, greediest priest or the skinniest, most unworldly holy man. But Bwadres was stubborn – it was probably, as we have hinted, the sole remaining symptom, though a most inconvenient one, of his only seemingly cast-off senility. Not one rusty iron *tik* (the smallest coin of Lankhmar) would he pay to extortioners – such was Bwadres' boast. To make matters worse, if that were possible, he would not even *spend* money renting gaudy furniture or temple space for Issek, as was practically mandatory for gods progressing up the central stretch of the Street. Instead he averred that every tik collected, every bronze agol, every silver smerduk, every gold rilk, yes every diamond-in-amber gluditch! – would be saved to *buy* for Issek the finest temple at the Citadel end, in fact the temple of Aarth the Invisible All-Listener, accounted one of the most ancient and powerful of all the gods *in* Lankhmar.

Naturally, this insane challenge, thrown out for all to hear, had the effect of still further increasing Issek's popularity and swelled his congregations with all sorts of folk who came, at first at least, purely as curiosity seekers. The odds on how far Issek would get up the Street how soon (for they regularly bet on such things in Lankhmar) began to switch wildly up and down as the affair got quite beyond the shrewd but essentially limited imaginations of bookmakers. Bwadres took to sleeping curled in the gutter around Issek's coffer (first an old garlic bag, later a small stout cask with a slit in the top for coins) and with Fafhrd curled around him. Only one of them slept at a time, the other rested but kept watch.

At one point the Mouser almost decided to slit Bwadres' throat as the only possible way out of his dilemma. But he knew that such an act would be the one unforgivable crime against his new profession – it would be *bad for business* – and certain to ruin him forever with Pulg and all other extortioners if ever traced to him even in faintest suspicion. Bwadres must be roughed up if necessary, yes even tortured, but at the same time he must be treated in all ways as a goose who laid golden eggs. Moreover, the Mouser had a presentiment that putting Bwadres out of the way would not stop Issek. Not while Issek had Fafhrd.

What finally brought the affair to a head, or rather to its first head, and forced the Mouser's hand was the inescapable realization that if he held off any longer from putting the bite on Bwadres for Pulg, then rival extortioners – one Basharat in particular – would do it on their own account. As the Number One Racketeer of Religions in Lankhmar, Pulg certainly had first grab, but if he delayed for an unreasonable length of time in making it (no matter on what grounds of omens or arguments about flattening the sacrifice) then Bwadres was anybody's victim – Basharat's in particular, as Pulg's chief rival.

So it came about, as it so often does, that the Mouser's efforts to avert the evil nightfall only made it darker and stormier when it finally came down.

When at last that penultimate evening did arrive, signalized by a final warning sent Pulg by Basharat, the Mouser, who had been hoping all along for some wonderful last-minute inspiration that never came, took what may seem to some a coward's way out. Making use of the beggar girl, whom he had named Lilyblack, and certain other of his creatures, he circulated a rumor that the Treasurer of the Temple of Aarth was preparing to decamp in a rented black sloop across the Inner Sea, taking with him all funds and temple-valuables, including a set of black-pearl-crusted altar furnishings, gift of the wife of the High Overlord, on which the split had not yet been made with Pulg. He timed the rumor so that it would return to him, by unimpeachable channels, just after he had set out for Issek's spot with four well-armed bullies.

It may be noted, in passing, that Aarth's Treasurer actually was in monetary hot waters and really had rented a black sloop.

Which proved not only that the Mouser used good sound fabric for his fabrications, but also that Bwadres had by landlords' and bankers' standards made a very sound choice in selecting Issek's temple-to-be – whether by chance or by some strange shrewdness co-dwelling with his senile stubbornness.

The Mouser could not divert his whole expeditionary force, for Bwadres must be saved from Basharat. However, he was able to split it with the almost certain knowledge that Pulg would consider his action the best strategy available at the moment. Three of the bullies he sent on with firm instructions to bring Bwadres to account, while he himself raced off with minimum guard to intercept the supposedly fleeing and loot-encumbered treasurer.

Of course the Mouser *could* have made himself part of the Bwadres-party, but that would have meant he would have had personally to best Fafhrd or he be bested by him, and while the Mouser wanted to do everything possible for his friend he wanted to do just a little bit more than that (he thought) for his own security.

Some, as we have suggested, may think that in taking this way out the Gray Mouser was throwing his friend to the wolves. However, it must always be remembered that the Mouser knew Fafhrd.

The three bullies, who did *not* know Fafhrd (the Mouser had selected them for that reason), were pleased with the turn of events. An independent commission always meant the chance of some brilliant achievement and so perhaps of promotion. They waited for the first break between services, when there was inevitably considerable passing about and jostling. Then one, who had a small ax in his belt, went straight for Bwadres and his cask, which the holy man also used as altar, draping it for the purpose with the sacred garlic bag. Another drew sword and menaced Fafhrd, keeping sound distance from and careful watch on the giant. The third, adopting the jesting, rough-and-ready manner of the master of the show in a bawdy house, spoke ringing warnings to the crowd and kept a reasonably watchful eye on *them*. The folk of Lankhmar are so bound by tradition that it was unthinkable that they would interfere with any activities as legitimate as those of an extortioner – the Number One Extortioner, too – even in defense of a most favored priest, but there are occasional foreigners and madmen to be dealt with (though in Lankhmar even the madmen generally respect the traditions).

No one in the congregation saw the crucial thing that happened next, for their eyes were all on the first bully, who was lightly choking Bwadres with one hand while pointing his ax at the cask with the other. There was a cry of surprise and a clatter. The second bully, lunged forward toward Fafhrd, had dropped his sword and was shaking his hand as if it pained him. Without haste Fafhrd picked him up by the slack of his garments between his shoulder blades, reached the first bully in two giant strides, slapped the ax from his hand, and picked him up likewise.

It was an impressive sight: the giant, gaunt-cheeked, bearded acolyte wearing his long robe of undyed camel's hair (recent gift of a votary) and standing with knees bent and feet wide-planted as he held aloft to either side a squirming bully.

But although indeed a most impressive tableau, it presented a made-to-order opening for the third bully, who instantly unsheathed his scimitar and, with an acrobat's smile and wave to the crowd, lunged toward the apex of the obtuse angle formed by the juncture of Fafhrd's legs.

The crowd shuddered and squealed with the thought of the poignancy of the blow.

There was a muffled *thud*. The third bully dropped *his* sword. Without changing his stance Fafhrd swept together the two bullies he was holding so that their heads met with a loud *thunk*. With an equally measured movement he swept them apart again and sent them sprawling to either side, unconscious, among the onlookers. Then stepping forward, still without seeming haste, he picked up the third bully by neck and crotch and pitched him a considerably greater distance into the crowd, where he bowled over two of Basharat's henchmen who had been watching the proceedings with great interest.

There was absolute silence for three heartbeats, then the crowd applauded rapturously. While the tradition-bound

Lankhmarians thought it highly proper for extortioners to extort, they also considered it completely in character for a strange acolyte to work miracles, and they never omitted to clap a good performance.

Bwadres, fingering his throat and still gasping a little, smiled with simple pleasure and when Fafhrd finally acknowledged the applause by dropping down cross-legged to the cobbles and bowing his head, the old priest launched instantly into a sermon in which he further electrified the crowd by several times hinting that, in his celestial realms, *Issek was preparing to visit Lankhmar in person.* His acolyte's routing of the three evil men Bwadres attributed to the inspiration of Issek's might – to be interpreted as a sort of foretaste of the god's approaching reincarnation.

The most significant consequence of this victory of the doves over the hawks was a little midnight conference in the back room of the Inn of the Silver Eel, where Pulg first warmly praised and then coolly castigated the Gray Mouser.

He praised the Mouser for intercepting the Treasurer of Aarth, who it turned out *had* just been embarking on the black sloop, not to flee Lankhmar, though, but only to spend a water-guarded weekend with several riotous companions and one Ilala, High Priestess of the goddess of the same name. However, he *had* actually taken along several of the black-pearl-crusted altar furnishings, apparently as a gift for the High Priestess, and the Mouser very properly confiscated them before wishing the holy band the most exquisite of pleasures on their holiday. Pulg judged that the Mouser's loot amounted to just about twice the usual cut, which seemed a reasonable figure to cover the Treasurer's irregularity.

He rebuked the Mouser for failing to warn the three bullies about Fafhrd and omitting to instruct them in detail on how to deal with the giant.

'They're your boys, son, and I judge you by their perform-ance,' Pulg told the Mouser in fatherly matter-of-fact tones. 'To me, if they stumble, you flop. You know this Northerner well, son; you should have had them trained to meet his sleights. You solved your main problem well, but you slipped on an important detail. I expect good strategy from my lieutenants, but I demand flawless tactics.'

The Mouser bowed his head.

'You and this Northerner were comrades once,' Pulg continued. He leaned forward across the dinted table and drew down his lower lip. 'You're not still soft on him, are you, son?'

The Mouser arched his eyebrows, flared his nostrils and slowly swung his face from side to side.

Pulg thoughtfully scratched his nose. 'So we come tomorrow night,' he said. 'Must make an example of Bwadres – an example that will stick like Mingol glue. I'd suggest having Grilli hamstring the Northerner at the first onset. Can't kill him – he's the one that brings in the money. But with ankle tendons cut he could still stump around on his hands and knees and be in some ways an even better drawing card. How's that sound to you?'

The Mouser slitted his eyes in thought for three breaths. Then, 'Bad,' he said boldly. 'It gripes me to admit it, but this Northerner sometimes conjures up battle-sleights that even I can't be sure of countering – crazy berserk tricks born of sudden whim that no civilized man can anticipate. Chances are Grilli could nick him, but what if he didn't? Here's my reed – it lets you rightly think that I may still be soft on the man, but I give it because it's my best reed: let me get him drunk at nightfall. Dead drunk. Then he's out of the way for certain.'

Pulg growled. 'Sure you can deliver on that, son? They say he's forsworn booze. And he sticks to Bwadres like a giant squid.'

'I can detach him,' the Mouser said. 'And this way we don't risk spoiling him for Bwadres' show. Battle's always uncertain. You may plan to hock a man and then have to cut his throat.'

Pulg shook his head. 'We also leave him fit to tangle with our collectors the next time they come for the cash. Can't get him drunk every time we pick up the split. Too complicated. And looks very weak.'

'No need to,' the Mouser said confidently. 'Once Bwadres starts paying, the Northerner will go along.'

Pulg continued to shake his head. 'You're guessing, son,' he said. 'Oh, to the best of your ability, but still guessing. I want this deal bagged up strongly. An example that will stick, I said. Remember, son, the man we're really putting on this show for tomorrow night is Basharat. He'll be there, you can bet on it, though standing in the last row, I imagine – did you hear how your Northerner dumped two of his boys? I liked that.' He grinned widely, then instantly grew serious again.

'So we'll do it my way, eh? Grilli's very sure.'

The Mouser shrugged once, deadpan. 'If you say so. Of course, some Northerners suicide when crippled. I don't think *he* would, but he might. Still, even allowing for that, I'd say your plan has four chances in five of working out perfectly. Four in five.'

Pulg frowned furiously, his rather piggy red-rimmed eyes fixed on the Mouser. Finally he said, '*Sure* you can get him drunk, son? Five in five?'

'I can do it,' the Mouser said. He had thought of a half dozen additional arguments in favor of his plan, but he did not utter them. He did not even add, 'Six in six,' as he was tempted to. He was learning.

Pulg suddenly leaned back in his chair and laughed, signing that the business part of their conference was over. He tweaked the naked girl standing beside him. 'Wine!' he ordered. 'No, not that sugary slop I keep for customers – didn't Zizzi instruct you? – but the real stuff from behind the green idol. Come, son, pledge me a cup, and then tell me a little about this Issek. I'm interested in him. I'm interested in 'em all.' He waved loosely at the darkly gleaming shelves of religious curios in the handsomely carved traveling case rising beyond the end of the table. He frowned a very different frown from his business one. 'There are more things in this world than we understand,' he said sententiously. 'Did you know that, son?' The Great Man shook his head, again very differently. He was swiftly sinking into his most deeply metaphysical mood. 'Makes me wonder, sometimes. You and I, son, know that these' – He waved again at the case – 'are toys. But the feelings that men have toward them . . . they're real, eh? – and they can be strange. Easy to understand part of those feelings – brats shivering at bogies, fools gawking at a show and hoping for blood or a bit of undressing – but there's another part that's strange. The priests bray nonsense, the people groan and pray, and then *something* comes into existence. I don't know what that something is – I wish I did, I think – but it's strange.' He shook his head. 'Makes any man wonder. So drink your wine, son – watch his cup, girl, and don't let it empty – and talk to me about Issek. I'm interested in 'em all, but right now I'd like to hear about him.'

He did not in any way hint that for the past two months he had been watching the services of Issek for at least five nights a week from behind a veiled window in various lightless rooms along the Street of the Gods. And that was something that not even the Mouser knew about Pulg.

So as a pinkly opalescent, rose-ribboned dawn surged up the sky from the black and stinking Marsh, the Mouser sought out Fafhrd. Bwadres was still snoring in the gutter, embracing Issek's cask, but the big barbarian was awake and sitting on the curb, hand grasping his chin under his beard. Already a few children had gathered at a respectful distance, though no one else was abroad.

'That the one they can't stab or cut?' the Mouser heard one of the children whisper.

'That's him,' another answered.

'I'd like to sneak up behind him and stick him with this pin.'

'I'll bet you would!'

'I guess he's got iron skin,' said a tiny girl with large eyes.

The Mouser smothered a guffaw, patted that last child on the head, and then advanced straight to Fafhrd and, with a grimace at the stained refuse between the cobbles, squatted fastidiously on his hams. He still could do it easily, though his new belly made a considerable pillow in his lap.

He said without preamble, speaking too low for the children to hear, 'Some say the strength of Issek lies in love, some say in honesty, some say in courage, some say in stinking hypocrisy. I believe I have guessed the one true answer. If I am right, you will drink wine with me. If I am wrong, I will strip to my loincloth, declare Issek my god and master, and serve as acolyte's acolyte. Is it a wager?'

Fafhrd studied him. 'It is done,' he said.

The Mouser advanced his right hand and lightly rapped Fafhrd's body twice through the soiled camel's hair – once on the chest, once between the legs.

Each time there was a faint *thud* with just the hint of a *clank*.

'The cuirass of Mingsward and the groin-piece of Gortch,' the Mouser pronounced. 'Each heavily padded to keep them from ringing. Therein lie Issek's strength and invulnerability. They wouldn't have fit you six months ago.'

Fafhrd sat as one bemused. Then his face broke into a large grin. 'You win,' he said. 'When do I pay?'

'This very afternoon,' the Mouser whispered, 'when Bwadres eats and takes his forty winks.' He rose with a light grunt and made off, stepping daintily from cobble to cobble.

Soon the Street of the Gods grew moderately busy and for a while Fafhrd was surrounded by a scattering of the curious, but it was a very hot day for Lankhmar. By midafternoon the Street was deserted, even the children had sought shade. Bwadres droned through the Acolyte's Litany twice with Fafhrd, then called for food by touching his hand to his mouth – it was his ascetic custom always to eat at this uncomfortable time rather than in the cool of the evening.

Fafhrd went off and shortly returned with a large bowl of fish stew. Bwadres blinked at the size of it, but tucked it away, belched, and curled around the cask after an admonition to Fafhrd. He was snoring almost immediately.

A hiss sounded from the low wide archway behind them. Fafhrd stood up and quietly moved into the shadows of the portico. The Mouser gripped his arm and guided him toward one of several curtained doorways.

'Your sweat's a flood, my friend,' he said softly. 'Tell me, do you really wear the armor from prudence, or is it a kind of metal hair-shirt?'

Fafhrd did not answer. He blinked at the curtain the Mouser drew aside. 'I don't like this,' he said. 'It's a house of assignation. I may be seen and then what will dirty-minded people think?'

'Hung for the kid, hung for the goat,' the Mouser said lightly. 'Besides, you haven't been seen – yet. In with you!'

Fafhrd complied. The heavy curtains swung to behind them, leaving the room in which they stood lit only by high louvers. As Fafhrd squinted into the semi-darkness, the Mouser said, 'I've paid the evening's rent on this place. It's private, it's near. None will know. What more could you ask?'

'I guess you're right,' Fafhrd said uneasily. 'But you've spent too much rent money. Understand, my little man, I can have only one drink with you. You tricked me into that – after a fashion you did – but I pay. But only one cup of wine, little man. We're friends, but we have our separate paths to tread. So only one cup. Or at most two.'

'Naturally,' purred the Mouser.

The objects in the room grew in the swimming gray blank of Fafhrd's vision. There was an inner door (also curtained), a narrow bed, a basin, a low table and stool, and on the floor beside the stool several portly short-necked large-eared shapes. Fafhrd counted them and once again his face broke into a large grin.

'Hung for a kid, you said,' he rumbled softly in his old bass voice, continuing to eye the stone bottles of vintage. 'I see four kids, Mouser.'

The Mouser echoed himself. 'Naturally.'

By the time the candle the Mouser had fetched was guttering in a little pool, Fafhrd was draining the third 'kid'. He held it upended above his head and caught the last drop, then batted it lightly away like a large feather-stuffed ball. As its shards exploded from the floor, he bent over from where he was sitting on the bed, bent so low that his beard brushed the floor, and clasped the last 'kid' with both hands and lifted it with exaggerated care onto the table. Then taking up a very short-bladed knife and keeping his eyes so close to his work that they were inevitably crossed, he picked every last bit of resin out of the neck, flake by tiny flake.

Fafhrd no longer looked at all like an acolyte, even a misbehaving one. After finishing the first 'kid' he had stripped for action. His camel's hair robe was flung into one corner of the room, the pieces of padded armor into another. Wearing only a once-white loincloth, he looked like some lean doomful berserk, or a barbaric king in a bath-house.

For some time no light had been coming through the louvers. Now there was a little – the red glow of torches. The noises of night had started and were on the increase – thin laughter, hawkers' cries, various summonses to prayer . . . and Bwadres calling 'Fafhrd!' again and again in his raspy long-carrying voice. But that last had stopped some time ago.

Fafhrd took so long with the resin, handling it like gold leaf, that the Mouser had to fight down several groans of impatience. But he was smiling his soft smile of victory. He did move once – to light a fresh taper from the expiring one. Fafhrd did not seem to notice the change in illumination. By now, it occurred to the Mouser, his friend was doubtless seeing everything by that brilliant light of spirits of wine which illumines the way of all brave drunkards.

Without any warning the Northerner lifted the short knife high and stabbed it into the center of the cork.

'Die, false Mingol!' he cried, withdrawing the knife with a twist, the cork on its point. 'I drink your blood!' And he lifted the stone bottle to his lips.

After he had gulped about a third of its contents, by the Mouser's calculation, he set it down rather suddenly on the table. His eyeballs rolled upward, all the muscles of his body quivered with the passing of a beatific spasm, and he sank back majestically, like a tree that falls with care. The frail bed creaked ominously but did not collapse under its burden.

Yet this was not quite the end. An anxious crease appeared between Fafhrd's shaggy eyebrows, his head tilted up and his bloodshot eyes peered out menacingly from their eagle's nest of hair, searching the room.

Their gaze finally settled on the last stone bottle. A long rigidly-muscled arm shot out, a great hand shut on the top of the bottle and placed it under the edge of the bed and did not leave it. Then Fafhrd's eyes closed, his head dropped back with finality and, smiling, he began to snore.

The Mouser stood up and came over. He rolled back one of Fafhrd's eyelids, gave a satisfied nod, then gave another after feeling Fafhrd's pulse, which was surging with as slow and strong a rhythm as the breakers of the Outer Sea. Meanwhile the

Mouser's other hand, operating with an habitual deftness and artistry unnecessary under the circumstances, abstracted from a fold in Fafhrd's loincloth a gleaming gold object he had earlier glimpsed there. He tucked it away in a secret pocket in the skirt of his gray tunic.

Someone coughed behind him.

It was such a deliberate-sounding cough that the Mouser did not leap or start, but only turned around without changing the planting of his feet in a movement slow and sinuous as that of a ceremonial dancer in the Temple of the Snake.

Pulg was standing in the inner doorway, wearing the black-and-silver striped robe and cowl of a masker and holding a black, jewel-spangled vizard a little aside from his face. He was looking at the Mouser enigmatically.

'I didn't think you could do it, son, but you did,' he said softly. 'You patch your credit with me at a wise time. Ho, Wiggin, Quatch! Ho, Grilli!'

The three henchmen glided into the room behind Pulg, all garbed in garments as somberly gay as their master's. The first two were stocky men, but the third was slim as a weasel and shorter than the Mouser, at whom he glared with guarded and rivalrous venom. The first two were armed with small crossbows and shortswords, but the third had no weapon in view.

'You have the cords, Quatch?' Pulg continued. He pointed at Fafhrd. 'Then bind me this man to the bed. See that you secure well his brawny arms.'

'He's safer unbound,' the Mouser started to say, but Pulg cut in on him with, 'Easy, son. You're still running this job, but I'm going to be looking over your shoulder; yes, and I'm going to be revising your plan as you go along, changing any detail I choose. Good training for you. Any competent lieutenant should be able to operate under the eyes of his general, yes, even when other subordinates are listening in on the reprimands. We'll call it a test.'

The Mouser was alarmed and puzzled. There was something about Pulg's behavior that he did not at all understand. Something discordant, as if a secret struggle were going on inside the master extortioner. He was not obviously drunk, yet his piggy eyes had a strange gleam. He seemed almost fey.

'How have I forfeited your trust?' the Mouser asked sharply.

Pulg grinned skewily. 'Son, I'm ashamed of you,' he said. 'High Priestess Ilala told me the *full* story of the black sloop – how you sublet it from the treasurer in return for allowing him to keep the pearl tiara and stomacher. How you had Ourph the Mingol sail it to another dock. Ilala got mad at the treasurer because he went cold on her or scared and wouldn't give her the black gewgaws. That's why she came to me. To cap it, your Lilyblack spilled the same story to Grilli here, whom she favors. Well, son?'

The Mouser folded his arms and threw back his head. 'You said yourself the split was sufficient,' he told Pulg. 'We can always use another sloop.'

Pulg laughed low and rather long. 'Don't get me wrong, son,' he said at last. 'I *like* my lieutenants to be the sort of men who'd want a bolt-hole handy – I'd suspect their brains if they didn't. I *want* them to be sort of men who worry a lot about their precious skins, but only after worrying about *my* hide first! Don't fret, son. We'll get along – I think. Quatch! Is he bound yet?'

The two burlier henchmen, who had hooked their cross-bows to their belts, were well along with their job. Tight loops of rope at chest, waist and knees bound Fafhrd to the bed, while his wrists had been drawn up level with the top of his head and tightly laced to the sides of the bed. Fafhrd still snored peacefully on his back. He had stirred a little and groaned when his hand had been drawn away from the bottle under the bed, but that was all. Wiggin was preparing to bind the Northerner's ankles, but Pulg signed it was enough.

'Grilli!' Pulg called. 'Your razor!'

The weasel-like henchman seemed merely to wave his hand past his chest and – lo! – there was a gleaming square-headed blade in it. He smiled as he moved toward Fafhrd's naked ankles. He caressed the thick tendons under them and looked pleadingly at Pulg.

Pulg was watching the Mouser narrowly.

The Mouser felt an unbearable tension stiffening him. He must do something! He raised the back of his hand to his mouth and yawned.

Pulg pointed at Fafhrd's other end. 'Grilli,' he repeated, 'shave me this man! Debeard and demane him! Shave him like an egg!' Then he leaned toward the Mouser and said in a sort of slack-mouthed confidential way, 'I've heard of these barbs that it draws their strength. Think you so? No matter, we'll see.'

Slashing of a lusty man's head-and-face hair and then shaving him close takes considerable time, even when the barber is as shudderingly swift as Grilli and as heedless of the dim and flickering light. Time enough for the Mouser to assess the situation seventeen different ways and still not find its ultimate key. One thing shone through from every angle: the irrationality of Pulg's behaviour. Spilling secrets . . . accusing a lieutenant in front of henchmen . . . proposing an idiot 'test' . . . wearing grotesque holiday clothes . . . binding a man dead drunk . . . and now this superstitious nonsense of shaving Fafhrd – why, it was as if Pulg were fey indeed and performing some eerie ritual under the demented guise of shrewd tactics.

And there was one thing the Mouser was certain of: that when Pulg got through being fey or drugged or whatever it was, he would never again trust any of the men who had been through the experience with him, including – most particularly! – the Mouser. It was a sad conclusion – to admit that his hard-bought security was now worthless – yet it was a realistic one and the Mouser perforce came to it. So even while he continued to puzzle, the small man in gray congratulated himself on having bargained himself so disastrously into possession of the black sloop. A bolt-hole might soon be handy indeed, and he doubted whether Pulg had discovered where Ourph had concealed the craft. Meanwhile he must expect treachery from Pulg at any step and death from Pulg's henchmen at their master's unpredictable whim. So the Mouser decided that the less *they* (Grilli in particular) were in a position to do the Mouser or anyone else damage, the better.

Pulg was laughing again. 'Why, he looks like a new-hatched babe!' the master extortioner exclaimed. 'Good work, Grilli!'

Fafhrd did indeed look startlingly youthful without any hair above that on his chest, and in a way far more like what most people think an acolyte should look. He might even have appeared romantically handsome except that Grilli, in perhaps an excess of zeal, had also shorn naked his eyebrows – which had the effect of making Fafhrd's head, very pale under the vanished hair, seem like a marble bust set atop a living body.

Pulg continued to chuckle. 'And no spot of blood – no, not one! That is the best of omens! Grilli, I love you!'

That was true enough too – in spite of his demonic speed, Grilli had not once nicked Fafhrd's face or head. Doubtless a man thwarted of the opportunity to hamstring another would scorn any lesser cutting – indeed, consider it a blot on his own character. Or so the Mouser guessed.

Gazing at his shorn friend, the Mouser felt almost inclined to laugh himself. Yet this impulse – and along with it his lively fear for his own and Fafhrd's safety – was momentarily swallowed up in the feeling that something about this whole business was very *wrong* – wrong not only by any ordinary standards, but also in a deeply occult sense. This stripping of Fafhrd, this shaving of him, this binding of him to the rickety narrow bed . . . wrong, wrong, wrong! Once again it occurred to him, more strongly this time, that Pulg was unknowingly performing an eldritch ritual.

'Hist!' Pulg cried, raising a finger. The Mouser obediently listened along with the three henchmen and their master. The ordinary noises outside had diminished, for a moment almost ceased. Then through the curtained doorway and the red-lit louvers came the raspy high voice of Bwadres beginning the Long Litany and the mumbling sigh of the crowd's response.

Pulg clapped the Mouser hard on the shoulder. 'He is about it! 'Tis time!' he cried. 'Command us! We will see, son, how well you have planned. Remember, I will be watching over your shoulder and that it is my desire that you strike at the end of Bwadres' sermon when the collection is taken.' He frowned at Grilli, Wiggin and Quatch. 'Obey this, my lieutenant!' he warned sternly. 'Jump at his least command! – save when I countermand. Come on, son, hurry it up, start giving orders!'

The Mouser would have liked to punch Pulg in the middle of the jeweled vizard which the extortioner was just now again lifting to his face – punch his fat nose and fly this madhouse of commanded commandings. But there was Fafhrd to be considered – stripped, shaved, bound, dead drunk, immeasurably helpless. The Mouser contented himself with starting through the outer door and motioning the henchmen and Pulg too to follow him. Hardly to his surprise – for it was difficult to decide *what* behavior would have been surprising under the circumstances – they obeyed him.

He signed Grilli to hold the curtain aside for the others. Glancing back over the smaller man's shoulder, he saw Quatch, last to leave, dip to blow out the taper and under cover of that movement snag the two-thirds-full bottle of wine from under the edge of the bed and lug it along with him. And for some reason that innocently thievish act struck the Mouser as being the most occultly wrong thing of all the supernally off-key events that had been occurring recently. He wished there were some god in whom he had real trust so that he could pray to him for enlightenment and guidance in the ocean of inexplicably strange intuitions engulfing him. But unfortunately for the Mouser there was no such divinity. So there was nothing for it but to plunge all by himself into that strange ocean and take his chances – do without calculation whatever the inspiration of the moment moved him to do.

So while Bwadres keened and rasped through the Long Litany against the sighing responses of the crowd (and an uncommonly large number of cat-calls and boos), the Mouser was very busy indeed, helping prepare the setting and place the characters for a drama of which he did not know more than scraps of the plot. The many shadows were his friends in this – he could slip almost invisibly from one shielding darkness to another – and he had the trays of half the hawkers in Lankhmar as a source of stage properties.

Among other things, he insisted on personally inspecting the weapons of Quatch and Wiggin – the shortswords and their sheaths, the small crossbows and the quivers of tiny quarrels that were their ammunition – most wicked-looking short arrows. By the time the Long Litany had reached its wailing conclusion, the stage was set, though exactly when and where and how the curtain would rise – and who would be the audience and who the players – remained uncertain.

At all events it was an impressive scene: the long Street of Gods stretching off toward a colorful torchlit dolls' world of distance in either direction, low clouds racing overhead, faint ribbons of mist gliding in from the Great Salt Marsh, the rumble of far distant thunder, bleat and growl of priests of gods other than Issek, squealing laughter of women and children, leather-lunged calling of hawkers and news-slaves, odor of incense curling from temples mingling with the oily aroma of fried foods on hawkers' trays, the reek of smoking torches, and the musk and flower smells of gaudy ladies.

Issek's audience, augmented by the many drawn by the tale of last night's doings of the demon acolyte and the wild predictions of Bwadres, blocked the Street from curb to curb, leaving only difficult gangway through the roofed porticos to either side. All levels of Lankhmarian society were represented – rags and ermine, bare feet and jeweled sandals, mercenaries' steel and philosophers' wands, faces painted with rare cosmetics and faces powdered only with dust, eyes of hunger, eyes of satiety, eyes of mad belief and eyes of a skepticism that hid fear.

Bwadres, panting a little after the Long Litany, stood on the curb across the Street from the low archway of the house where the drunken Fafhrd slept bound. His shaking hand rested on the cask that, draped now with the garlic bag, was both Issek's coffer and altar. Crowded so close as to leave him almost no striding space were the inner circles of the congregation – devotees sitting cross-legged, crouched on knees, or squatting on hams.

The Mouser had stationed Wiggin and Quatch by an overset fishmonger's cart in the center of the Street. They passed back and forth the stone bottle Quatch had snared, doubtless in part to make their odorous post more bearable, though every time the Mouser noted their bibbing he had a return of the feeling of occult wrongness.

Pulg had picked for his post a side of the low archway in front of Fafhrd's house, to call it that. He kept Grilli beside him, while Mouser crouched nearby after his preparations were complete. Pulg's jeweled mask was hardly exceptional in the setting; several women were vizarded and a few of the other men – colorful blank spots in the sea of faces.

It was certainly not a calm sea. Not a few of the audience seemed greatly annoyed at the absence of the giant acolyte (and had been responsible for the boos and cat-calls during the Litany). While even the regulars missed the acolyte's lute and his sweet tenor tale-telling and were exchanging anxious questions and speculations. All it took was someone to shout, 'Where's the acolyte?' and in a few moments half the audience was chanting, 'We want the acolyte! We want the acolyte!'

Bwadres silenced them by looking earnestly up the Street with shaded eyes, pretending he saw one coming, and then suddenly pointing dramatically in that direction, as if to signal the approach of the man for whom they were calling. While the crowd craned their necks and shoved about, trying to see what Bwadres was pretending to – and incidentally left off chanting – the ancient priest launched into his sermon.

'I will tell you what has happened to my acolyte!' he cried. 'Lankhmar has swallowed him. Lankhmar has gobbled him up – Lankhmar the evil city, the city of drunkenness and lechery and all corruption – Lankhmar, the city of the stinking black bones!'

This last blasphemous reference to the gods *of* Lankhmar (whom it can be death to mention, though the gods *in* Lankhmar may be insulted without limit) further shocked the crowd into silence.

Bwadres raised his hands and face to the low racing clouds.

'Oh, Issek, compassionate mighty Issek, pity thy humble servitor who now stands friendless and alone. I had one acolyte, strong in thy defense, but they took him from me. You told him, Issek, much of your life and your secrets, he had ears to hear it and lips to sing it, but now the black devils have got him! Oh, Issek, have pity!'

Bwadres spread his hands toward the mob and looked them around.

'Issek was a young god when he walked the earth, a young god speaking only of love, yet they bound him to the rack of torture. He brought Waters of Peace for all in his Holy Jug, but they broke it.' And here Bwadres described at great length and with far more vividness than his usual wont (perhaps he felt he had to make up for the absence of his skald-turned-acolyte) the life and

441

especially the torments and death of Issek of the Jug, until there was hardly one among the listeners who did not have vividly in mind the vision of Issek on his rack (succession of racks, rather) and who did not feel at least sympathetic twinges in his joints at the thought of the god's suffering.

Women and strong men wept unashamedly, beggars and scullions howled, philosophers covered their ears.

Bwadres wailed on toward a shuddering climax. 'As you yielded up your precious ghost on the eighth rack, oh, Issek, as your broken hands fashioned even your torturer's collar into a Jug of surpassing beauty, you thought only of us, oh, Holy Youth. You thought only of making beautiful the lives of the most tormented and deformed of us, thy miserable slaves.'

At those words Pulg took several staggering steps forward from the side of the archway, dragging Grilli with him, and dropped to his knees on the filthy cobbles. His black-and-silver striped cowl fell back on his shoulders and his jeweled black vizard slipped from his face, which was thus revealed as unashamedly coursing with tears.

'I renounce all other gods,' the boss extortioner gasped between sobs. 'Hereafter I serve only gentle Issek of the Jug.'

The weasely Grilli, crouching contortedly in his efforts to avoid being smirched by the nasty pavement, gazed at his master as to one demented, yet could not or still dared not break Pulg's hold on his wrist.

Pulg's action attracted no particular attention – conversions were a smerduck a score at the moment – but the Mouser took note of it, especially since Pulg's advance had brought him so close that the Mouser could have reached out and patted Pulg's bald pate. The small man in gray felt a certain satisfaction or rather relief – if Pulg had for some time been a secret Issek-worshiper, then his feyness might be explained. At the same time a gust of emotion akin to pity went through him. Looking down at his left hand the Mouser discovered that he had taken out of its secret pocket the gold bauble he had filched from Fafhrd. He was tempted to put it softly in Pulg's palm. How fitting, how soul-shaking, how *nice* it would be, he thought, if at the moment the floodgates of religious emotion burst in him, Pulg were to receive this truly beautiful memento of the god of his choice. But gold is gold, and a black sloop requires as much upkeep as any other color yacht, so the Mouser resisted the temptation.

Bwadres threw wide his hands and continued, 'With dry throats, oh, Issek, we thirst for thy Waters. With gullets burning and cracked, thy slaves beg for a single sip from thy Jug. We would ransom our souls for one drop of it to cool us in this evil city, damned by black bones. Oh, Issek, descend to us! Bring us thy Waters of Peace! We need you, we want you. Oh, Issek, come!'

Such was the power and yearning in that last appeal that the whole crowd of kneeling worshipers gradually took it up, chanting with all reverence, louder and louder, in an unendingly repeated, self-hypnotizing response: 'We want Issek! We want Issek!'

It was that mighty rhythmic shouting which finally penetrated to the small conscious core of Fafhrd's wine-deadened brain where he lay drunk in the dark, though Bwadres' remarks about dry throats and burning gullets and healing drops and sips may have opened the way. At any rate, Fafhrd came suddenly and shudderingly awake with the one thought in his mind: another drink – and the one sure memory: that there was some wine left.

It disturbed him a little that his hand was not still on the stone bottle under the edge of the bed, but for some dubious reason up near his ear.

He reached for the bottle and was outraged to find that he could not move his arm. Something or someone was holding it.

Wasting no time on petty measures, the large barbarian rolled his whole body over mightily, with the idea of at once wrenching free from whatever was holding him and getting under the bed where the wine was.

He succeeded in tipping the bed on its side and himself with it. But *that* didn't bother him, it didn't shake up his numb body at all. What *did* bother him was that he couldn't sense any wine nearby – smell it, see it squintily, bump his head into it . . . certainly not the quart or more he remembered having safeguarded for just such an emergency as this.

At about the same time he became dimly aware that he was

somehow *attached* to whatever he'd been sleeping on – especially his wrists and shoulders and chest.

However, his legs seemed reasonably free, though somewhat hampered at the knees, and since the bed happened to have fallen partly on the low table and with its head braced against the wall, the blind twist-and-heave he gave now actually brought him to his feet and the bed with him.

He squinted around. The curtained outer doorway was an oblong of lesser darkness. He immediately headed for it. The bed foiled his first efforts to get through, bringing him up short in a most exasperating manner, but by ducking and by turning edgewise he finally managed it, pushing the curtain ahead of him with his face. He wondered muddily if he were paralyzed, the wine he'd drunk all gone into his arms, or if some warlock had put a spell on him. It was certainly degrading to have to go about with one's wrists up about one's ears. Also his head and cheeks and chin felt unaccountably chilly – possibly another evidence of black magic.

The curtain dragged off his head finally and he saw ahead of him a rather low archway and – vaguely and without being at all impressed by them – crowds of people kneeling and swaying.

Ducking down again, he lumbered through the archway and straightened up. Torchlight almost blinded him. He stopped and stood there blinking. After a bit his vision cleared a little and the first person he saw that meant anything to him was the Gray Mouser.

He remembered now that the last person he had been drinking with was the Mouser. By the same token – in this matter Fafhrd's maggoty mind worked very fast indeed – the Mouser must be the person who had made away with his quart or more of midnight medicine. A great righteous anger flamed in him and he took a very deep breath.

So much for Fafhrd and what *he* saw.

What the *crowd* saw – the god-intoxicated, chanting, weeping crowd – was very different indeed.

They saw a man of divine stature strapped with hands high to a framework of some sort. A mightily muscled man, naked save for a loincloth, with a shorn head and face that, marble white, looked startlingly youthful. Yet with the expression on that marble face of one who is being tortured.

And if anything else were needed (truly, it hardly was) to convince them that here was the god, the divine Issek, they had summoned with their passionately insistent cries, then it was supplied when that nearly seven-foot-tall apparition called out in a deep voice of thunder:

'*Where is the jug?* WHERE IS THE JUG?'

The few people in the crowd who were still standing dropped instantly to their knees at that point or prostrated themselves. Those kneeling in the opposite direction switched around like startled crabs. Two score persons, including Bwadres, fainted, and of these the hearts of five stopped beating forever. At least a dozen individuals went permanently mad, though at the moment they seemed no different from the rest – including (among the twelve) seven philosophers and a niece of Lankhmar's High Overlord. As one, the members of the mob abased themselves in terror and ecstasy – groveling, writhing, beating breasts or temples, clapping hands to eyes and peering fearfully through hardly parted fingers as if at an unbearably bright light.

It may be objected that at least a few of the mob should have recognized the figure before them as that of Bwadres' giant acolyte. After all, the height was right. But consider the differences: The acolyte was full-bearded and shaggy-maned; the apparition was beardless and bald – and strangely so, lacking even eyebrows. The acolyte had always gone robed; the apparition was nearly naked. The acolyte had always used a sweetly high voice; the apparition roared harshly in a voice almost two octaves lower.

Finally, the apparition was bound – to a torture rack, surely – and calling in the voice of one being tortured for his Jug.

As one, the members of the mob abased themselves.

With the exception of the Gray Mouser, Grilli, Wiggin, and Quatch. They knew well enough who faced them. (Pulg knew too, of course, but he, most subtle-brained in some ways and now firmly converted to Issekianity, merely assumed that Issek had chosen to manifest himself in the body of Fafhrd and that he, Pulg, had been divinely guided to prepare that body for the purpose. He humbly swelled with the full realization of the importance of his own position in the scheme of Issek's reincarnation.)

His three henchmen, however, were quite untouched by religious emotions. Grilli for the moment could do nothing as Pulg was still holding his wrist in a grip of fervid strength.

But Wiggin and Quatch were free. Although somewhat dull-brained and little used to acting on their own initiative, they were not long in realizing that the giant had appeared who was supposed to be kept out of the way so that he would not queer the game of their strangely-behaving master and his tricky gray-clad lieutenant. Moreover, they well knew what jug Fafhrd was shouting for so angrily, and since they also knew they had stolen and drunken it empty, they likely also were moved by guilty fears that Fafhrd might soon see them, break loose, and visit vengeance upon them.

They cranked up their crossbows with furious haste, slapped in quarrels, knelt, aimed, and discharged the bolts straight at Fafhrd's naked chest. Several persons in the mob noted their action and shrieked at its wickedness.

The two bolts struck Fafhrd's chest, bounced off, and dropped to the cobbles – quite naturally enough, as they were two of the fowling quarrels (headed merely with little knobs of wood and used for knocking down small birds) with which the Mouser had topped off their quivers.

The crowd gasped at Issek's invulnerability and cried for joy and amazement.

However, although fowling quarrels will hardly break a man's skin, even when discharged at close range, they nevertheless sting mightily even the rather numb body of a man who has recently drunk numerous quarts of wine. Fafhrd roared in agony, punched out his arms convulsively, *and broke the framework to which he was attached.*

The crowd cheered hysterically at this further proper action in the drama of Issek which his acolyte had so often chanted.

Quatch and Wiggin, realizing that their missile weapons had somehow been rendered innocuous, but too dull-witted or wine-fuddled to see anything either occult or suspicious in the manner of that rendering, grabbed at their shortswords and rushed forward at Fafhrd to cut him down before he could finish detaching himself from the fragments of the broken bed which he was now trying to do in a puzzled way.

Yes, Quatch and Wiggin rushed forward, but almost immediately came to a halt – in the very strange posture of men who are trying to lift themselves into the air by heaving at their own belts.

The shortswords would not come out of their scabbards. Mingol glue is indeed a powerful adhesive and the Mouser had been most determined that, however little else he accomplished, Pulg's henchmen should be put in a position where they could harm no one.

However, he had been able to do nothing in the way of pulling Grilli's fangs, as the tiny man was most sharp-witted himself and Pulg had kept him closely at his side. Now almost foaming at the mouth in vulpine rage and disgust, Grilli broke loose from his god-besotted master, whisked out his razor, and sprang at Fafhrd, who at last had clearly realized what was encumbering him and was having a fine time breaking the last pesky fragments of the bed over his knee or by the leverage of foot against cobble – to the accompaniment of the continuing wild cheers of the mob.

But the Mouser sprang rather more swiftly. Grilli saw him coming, shifted his attack to the gray-clad man, feinted twice and loosed one slash that narrowly missed. Thereafter he lost blood too quickly to be interested in attempting any further fencing. Cat's Claw is narrow but it cuts throats as well as any other dagger (though it does not have a sharply curved or barbed tip, as some literal-minded scholars have claimed).

The bout with Grilli left the Mouser standing very close to Fafhrd. The little man realized he still held in his left hand the golden representation of the Jug fashioned by Fafhrd, and that object now touched off in the Mouser's mind a series of inspirations leading to actions that followed one another very much like the successive figures of a dance.

He slapped Fafhrd back-handed on the cheek to attract the giant's attention. Then he sprang to Pulg, sweeping his left hand in a dramatic arc as if conveying something from the naked god to the extortioner, and lightly placed the golden bauble in the supplicating fingers of the latter. (One of those times had come when all ordinary scales of value fail – even for the Mouser – and gold is – however briefly – of no worth.) Recognizing the holy object, Pulg almost expired in ecstasy.

But the Mouser had already skipped on across the Street. Reaching Issek's coffer-altar, beside which Bwadres was stretched unconscious but smiling, he twitched off the garlic bag and sprang upon the small cask and danced upon it, hooting to further attract Fafhrd's attention and then pointing at his own feet.

Fafhrd saw the cask, all right, as the Mouser had intended he should, and the giant did not see it as anything to do with Issek's collections (the thought of all such matters was still wiped from his mind) but simply as a likely source of the liquor he craved. With a glad cry he hastened toward it across the Street, his worshipers scuttling out of his way or moaning in beatific ecstasy when he trod on them with his naked feet. He caught up the cask and lifted it to his lips.

To the crowd it seemed that Issek was drinking his own coffer – an unusual yet undeniably picturesque way for a god to absorb his worshipers' cask offerings.

With a roar of baffled disgust Fafhrd raised the cask to smash it on the cobbles, whether from pure frustration or with some idea of getting at the liquor he thought it held is hard to say, but just then the Mouser caught his attention again. The small man had snatched two tankards of ale from an abandoned tray and was pouring the heady liquid back and forth between them until the high-piled foam trailed down the sides.

Tucking the cask under his left arm – for many drunkards have a curious prudent habit of absentmindedly hanging onto things, especially if they may contain liquor – Fafhrd set out again after the Mouser, who ducked into the darkness of the nearest portico and then danced out again and led Fafhrd in a great circle all the way around the roiling congregation.

Literally viewed it was hardly an edifying spectacle – a large god stumbling after a small gray demon and grasping at a tankard of beer that just kept eluding him – but the Lankhmarians were already viewing it under the guise of two dozen different allegories and symbolisms, several of which were later written up in learned scrolls.

The second time through the portico Issek and the small gray demon did not come out again. A large chorus of mixed voices kept up expectant and fearful cries for some time, but the two supernatural beings did not reappear.

Lankhmar is full of mazy alleyways and this stretch of the Street of the Gods is particularly rich in them, some of them leading by dark and circuitous routes to localities as distant as the docks.

But the Issekians – old-timers and new converts alike – largely did not even consider such mundane avenues in analyzing their god's disappearance. Gods have their own doorways into and out of space and time and it is their nature to vanish suddenly and inexplicably. Brief reappearances are all we can hope for from a god whose chief life-drama on earth has already been played, and indeed it might prove uncomfortable if he hung around very long, protracting a Second Coming – too great a strain on everybody's nerves for one thing.

The large crowd of those who had been granted the vision of Issek was slow in dispersing, as might well have been expected – they had much to tell each other, much about which to speculate and, inevitably, to argue.

The blasphemous attack of Quatch and Wiggin on the god was belatedly recalled and avenged, though some already viewed the incident as part of a general allegory. The two bullies were lucky to escape with their lives after an extensive mauling.

Grilli's corpse was unceremoniously picked up and tossed in next morning's Death Cart. End of *his* story.

Bwadres came out of his faint with Pulg bending solicitously over him – and it was largely these two persons who shaped the subsequent history of Issekianity.

To make a long or, rather, complex story simple and short, Pulg became what can best be described as Issek's grand vizier and worked tirelessly for Issek's greater glory – always wearing on his chest the god-created golden emblem of the Jug as the sign of his office. He did not upon his conversion to the gentle god give up his old profession, as some moralists might expect, but carried it on with even greater zeal than before, extorting mercilessly from the priests of all gods other than Issek and grinding them down. At the height of its success, Issekianity boasted five large temples in Lankhmar, numerous minor shrines in the same city, and a swelling priesthood under the nominal leadership of Bwadres, who was lapsing once more into general senility.

Issekianity flourished for exactly three years under Pulg's viziership. But when it became known (due to some incautious babblings of Bwadres) that Pulg was not only conducting under the guise of extortion a holy war on all other gods *in* Lankhmar, with the ultimate aim of driving them from the city and if possible from the world, but that he even entertained murky designs of overthrowing the gods *of* Lankhmar or at least forcing them to recognize Issek's overlordship . . . when all this became apparent, the doom of Issekianity was sealed. On the third anniversary of Issek's Second Coming, the night descended ominous and thickly foggy, the sort of night when all wise Lankhmarians hug their indoor fires. About midnight awful screams and piteous howlings were heard throughout the city, along with the rending of thick doors and the breaking of heavy masonry – preceded and followed, some tremulously maintained, by the clicking tread of bones on the march. One youth who peered out through an attic window lived long enough before he expired in gibbering madness to report that he had seen striding through the streets a multitude of black-togaed figures, sooty of hand, foot and feature and skeletally lean.

Next morning the five temples of Issek were empty and defiled and his minor shrines all thrown down, while his numerous clergy, including his ancient high priest and overweeningly ambitious grand vizier, had vanished to the last member and were gone beyond human ken.

Turning back to a dawn exactly three years earlier we find the Gray Mouser and Fafhrd clambering from a cranky, leaky skiff into the cockpit of a black sloop moored beyond the Great Mole that juts out from Lankhmar and the east bank of the River Hlal into the Inner Sea. Before coming aboard, Fafhrd first handed up Issek's cask to the impassive and sallow-faced Ourph and then with considerable satisfaction pushed the skiff wholly under water.

The cross-city run the Mouser had led him, followed by a brisk spell of galley-slave work at the oars of the skiff (for which he indeed looked the part in his lean near-nakedness) had quite cleared Fafhrd's head of the fumes of wine, though it now ached villainously. The Mouser still looked a bit sick from his share in the running – he was truly in woefully bad trim from his months of lazy gluttony.

Nevertheless the twain joined with Ourph in the work of upping anchor and making sail. Soon a salty, coldly refreshing wind on their starboard beam was driving them directly away from the land and Lankhmar. Then while Ourph fussed over Fafhrd and bundled a thick cloak about him, the Mouser turned quickly in the morning dusk to Issek's cask, determined to get at the loot before Fafhrd had opportunity to develop any silly religious or Northernly-noble qualms and perhaps toss the cask overboard.

The Mouser's fingers did not find the coin-slit in the top – it was still quite dark – so he upended the pleasantly heavy object, crammed so full it did not even jingle. No coin-slit in that end either, seemingly, though there was what looked like a burned inscription in Lankhmarian hieroglyphs. But it was still too dark for easy reading and Fafhrd was coming up behind him, so the Mouser hurriedly raised the heavy hatchet he had taken from the sloop's tool rack and bashed in a section of wood.

There was a spray of stingingly aromatic fluid of most familiar odor. *The cask was filled with brandy – to the absolute top, so that it had not gurgled.*

A little later they were able to read the burnt inscription. It was most succinct: 'Dear Pulg – Drown your sorrows in this – Basharat.'

It was only too easy to realize how yesterday afternoon the Number Two Extortioner had had a perfect opportunity to effect the substitution – the Street of the Gods deserted, Bwadres almost druggedly asleep from the unaccustomedly large fish dinner, Fafhrd gone from his post to guzzle with the Mouser.

'That explains why Basharat was not on hand last night,' the Mouser said thoughtfully.

Fafhrd was for throwing the cask overboard, not from any disappointment at losing loot, but because of a revulsion at its contents, but the Mouser set aside the cask for Ourph to close and store away – he knew that such revulsions pass. Fafhrd, however, extorted the promise that the fiery fluid only be used in direst emergency – as for burning enemy ships.

The red dome of the sun pushed above the eastern waves. By its ruddy light Fafhrd and the Mouser really looked at each other for the first time in months. The wide sea was around them, Ourph had taken the lines and tiller, and at last nothing pressed. There was an odd shyness in both their gazes – each had the sudden thought that he had taken his friend away from the life-path he had chosen in Lankhmar, perhaps the life-path best suited to his treading.

'Your eyebrows will grow back – I suppose,' the Mouser said at last, quite inanely.

'They will indeed,' Fafhrd rumbled. 'I'll have a fine shock of hair by the time you've worked off that belly.'

'Thank you, Egg-Top,' the Mouser replied. Then he gave a small laugh. 'I have no regrets for Lankhmar,' he said, lying mightily, though not entirely. 'I can see now that if I'd stayed I'd have gone the way of Pulg and all such Great Men – fat, power-racked, lieutenant-plagued, smothered with false-hearted dancing girls, and finally falling into the arms of religion. At least I'm saved that last chronic ailment, which is worse than the dropsy.' He looked at Fafhrd narrowly. 'But how of you, old friend? Will you miss Bwadres and your cobbled bed and your nightly tale-weaving?'

Fafhrd frowned as the sloop plunged on northward and the salt spray dashed him.

'Not I,' he said at last. 'There are always other tales to be woven. I served a god well, I dressed him in new clothes, and then I did a third thing. Who'd go back to being an acolyte after being so much more? You see, old friend, I really *was* Issek.'

The Mouser arched his eyebrows. 'You were?'

Fafhrd nodded twice, most gravely.

III
THEIR MISTRESS, THE SEA

The next few days were not kind to the Mouser and Fafhrd. To begin with, both got seasick from their many months ashore. Between gargantuan groaning retches, Fafhrd monotonously berated the Mouser for having tricked him out of asceticism and stolen from him his religious vocation. While in the intervals of his vomiting, the Gray Mouser cursed Fafhrd back, but chiefly excoriated himself for having been such a fool as to give up the soft life in Lankhmar for sake of a friend.

During this period – brief in reality, an eternity to the sufferers – Ourph the Mingol managed sails and tiller. His impassive, wrinkle-netted face forever threatened to break into a grin, yet never did, though from time to time his jet eyes twinkled.

Fafhrd, first to recover, took back command from Ourph and immediately started ordering an endless series of seaman-like exercises: reefings, furlings, raisings, and changing of sails; shiftings of ballast; inspection of crawl-spaces for rats and roaches; luffings, tackings, jibings, and the like.

The Mouser swore feebly yet bitterly as these exercises sent both Ourph and Fafhrd clumping all over the deck, often across his prone body, and changed the steady pitch and roll of the *Black Treasurer*, to which he'd been getting accustomed, into unpredictable jitterbuggings which awakened nausea anew.

Whenever Fafhrd left off this slave-driving, he would sit cross-legged, deaf to the Mouser's sultry swearing, and silently meditate, his gaze directed at first always toward Lankhmar, but later more and more toward the north.

When the Mouser at last recovered, he forswore all food save watery gruel in small measures, and scorning Fafhrd's nautical exercises, began grimly to put himself through a variety of gymnastical ones until he collapsed sweating and panting – yet only waiting until he had his breath back to begin again.

It was an odd sight to see the Mouser walking about on his hands while Ourph raced forward to change the set of the jib and Fafhrd threw his weight on the tiller and bellowed, 'Hard a-lee!'

Yet at odd moments now and then, chiefly at sunset, when they each sipped a measure of water tinted with sweet wine – the brandy being still under interdict – they began to reminisce and yarn together, only a little at first, then for longer and longer periods.

They spoke of piratings, both inflicted and suffered. They recalled notable storms and calms, sighting of mysterious ships which vanished in fog or distance, never more to be seen. They talked of sea monsters, mermaids, and oceanic devils. They relived the adventure of their crossing of the Outer Sea to the fabled Western Continent, which of all Lankhmarts only Fafhrd, the Mouser, and Ourph knew to be more than legend.

Gradually the Mouser's belly melted and a bristly lawn of hair grew on Fafhrd's pate, cheeks, and chin, and around his mouth. Life became happenings rather than afflictions. They lived as well as saw sunsets and dawns. The stars became friendly. Above all, they began to match their rhythms to those of the sea, as if she were someone they lived and voyaged with, rather than sailed upon.

But their water and stores began to run low, the wine ran out, and they lacked even suitable clothing – Fafhrd in particular.

Their first piratical foray ended in near disaster. The small and lubberly-sailing merchant ship they approached most subtly at dawn suddenly bristled with brown-helmeted pikemen and slingers. It was a Lankhmar bait-ship, designed to trap pirates.

They escaped only because the trap was sprung too soon and the *Black Treasurer* was able to out-sail the bait-ship, transformed into a speedy goer by proper handling. At that, Ourph was struck senseless by a slung stone and Fafhrd had two ribs cracked by another.

Their next sea-raid was only a most qualified success. The

cutter they conquered turned out to be manned by five elderly Mingol witches by profession, they said, and bound on a fortune-telling and trading voyage to the southern settlements around Quarmall.

The Mouser and Fafhrd exacted from them a modest supply of water, food, and wine, and Fafhrd took several silk and fur tunics, some silver-plated jewelry, a longsword and ax which he fancied, and leather to make him boots. However, they left the surly women by no means destitute and forcibly prevented Ourph from raping even one of them, let alone all five as he had boastfully threatened.

They departed then, somewhat ashamed, to the tune of the witchwomen's chanting curses – most venomous ones, calling down on Fafhrd and the Mouser all the worst evils of air and earth, fire and water. Their failure to curse Ourph also, made the Mouser wonder whether the witchwomen were not angriest because Ourph had been prevented in his most lascivious designs.

Now that the *Black Treasurer* was somewhat better provisioned, Fafhrd began to talk airily about voyaging once again across the Outer Sea, or toward the Frozen Sea north of No-Ombrulsk, there to hunt the polar tiger and white-furred giant worm.

That was the last straw to Ourph, who was a most even-tempered, sweet old man – for a Mingol. Overworked, skull-bashed, thwarted of a truly unusual amorous opportunity for one of his age, and now threatened with idiot-far-voyagings, he demanded to be set ashore.

The Mouser and Fafhrd complied. All this while the *Black Treasurer* had been southwesting along Lankhmar's northwestern coast. So it was near the small village of Earth's End that they put landside the old Mingol, who was still cursing them grumblingly, despite the gifts with which they had loaded him.

After consultation, the two heroes decided to set course straight north, which would land them in the forested Land of the Eight Cities at the city of Ool Plerns, whose Mad Duke had once been their patron.

The voyage was uneventful. No ships were sighted. Fafhrd

cut, sewed, and nailed himself boots, which he footed with spikes, perhaps from some dream of mountaineering. The Mouser continued his calisthenics and read *The Book of Aarth*, *The Book of Lesser Gods*, *The Management of Miracles*, and a scroll titled *Sea Monsters* from the sloop's small but select library.

Nights they would lazily talk for hours, feeling nearest then to the stars, the sea, and each other. They argued as to whether the stars had existed forever or been launched by the gods from Nehwon's highest mountain – or whether, as current metaphysics asserted, the stars were vast firelit gems set in islands at the opposite end of the great bubble (in the waters of eternity) that was Nehwon. They disputed as to who was the world's worst warlock: Fafhrd's Ningauble, the Mouser's Sheelba, or – barely conceivably – some other sorcerer.

But chiefly they talked of their mistress, the sea, whose curving motions they loved again, and to whose moods they now felt preternaturally attuned, particularly in darkness. They spoke of her rages and caressings, her coolths and unending dancings, sometimes lightly footing a minuet, sometimes furiously a-stamp, and her infinitude of secret parts.

The west wind gradually lessened, then shifted to a fluky east wind. Stores were once more depleted. At last they admitted to each other that they couldn't fetch Ool Plerns on this reach and they contented themselves with sailing to intercept the Claws – the narrow but mountainously rocky end of the Eastern Continent's great western-thrusting northern peninsula, comprised of the Land of the Eight Cities, the Cold Waste, and numerous grim and great mountain ranges. The east wind died entire one midnight. The *Black Treasurer* floated in a calm so complete it was as if their aqueous mistress had fallen into a trance. Not a breath stirred. They wondered what the morrow would show, or bring.

IV
WHEN THE SEA-KING'S AWAY

Stripped to his loincloth, underbelt, and with amulet pouch a-dangle under his chin, the Gray Mouser stretched lizard-like along the bowed sprit of the sloop *Black Treasurer* and stared straight down into the hole in the sea. Sunlight unstrained by slightest wisp of cloud beat hotly on his deep-tanned back, but his belly was cold with the magic of the thing.

All around about, the Inner Sea lay calm as a lake of mercury in the cellar of a wizard's castle. No ripple came from the unbounded horizon to south, east and north, nor rebounded from the endless vertically-fluted curtain of creamy rock that rose a bowshot to the west and was a good three bowshots high, which the Mouser and Fafhrd had only yesterday climbed and atop which they had made a frightening discovery. The Mouser could have thought of those matters, or of the dismal fact that they were becalmed with little food and less water (and a tabooed cask of brandy) a weary sail west from Ool Hrusp, the last civilized port on this coast – or uncivilized either. He could have wondered about the seductive singing that had seemed to come from the sea last night, as of female voices softly improvising on the themes of waves hissing against sand, gurgling melodiously among rocks, and screaming wind-driven against icy coasts. Or he could perhaps best have pondered on Fafhrd's madness of yesterday afternoon, when the large Northerner had suddenly started to babble dogmatically about finding for himself and the Mouser 'girls under the sea' and had even begun to trim his beard and brush out his brown otterskin tunic and polish his best male costume jewelry so as to be properly attired to receive the submarine girls and arouse their desires. There was an old Simorgyan legend, Fafhrd had insisted, according to which on the seventh day of the seventh moon of the seventh year of the Sevens-Cycle the king of the sea journeyed to the other end of the earth, leaving his opalescently beautiful green wives and faintly silver-scaled slim concubines free to find them lovers if they could . . . and this, Fafhrd had stridently asserted he knew by the spectral calm and other occult tokens, was the place of the sea-king's home and the eve of the day!

In vain had the Mouser pointed out to him that they had not sighted an even faintly feminine-looking fish in days, that there were absolutely no islets or beaches in view suitable for commerce with mermaids or for the sunbathing and primping of loreleis, that there were no black hulks whatever or wrecked pirate ships drifting about that might conceivably have fair captives imprisoned below decks and so technically 'under the sea', that the region beyond the deceptive curtain-wall of creamy rock was the last from which one could expect girls to come, that – to sum it up – the *Black Treasurer* had not fetched the faintest sort of girl-blink either to starboard or larboard for weeks. Fafhrd had simply replied with crushing conviction that the sea-king's girls were there down below, that they were now preparing a magic channel or passageway whereby air-breathers might visit them, and that the Mouser had better be ready like himself to hasten when the summons came.

The Mouser had thought that the heat and dazzle of the unremitting sun – together with the sudden intense yearnings normal to all sailormen long at sea – must have deranged Fafhrd and he had dug up from the hold and unsuccessfully coaxed the Northerner to wear a wide-brimmed hat and slitted ice-goggles. It had been a great relief to the Mouser when Fafhrd had fallen into a profound sleep with the coming of night, though then the illusion – or reality – of the sweet siren-singing had returned to trouble his own tranquility.

Yes, the Mouser might well have thought of any of these matters, Fafhrd's prophetic utterances in particular, while he lay poised but unsweating in the hot sun along the stout bowsprit of the *Black Treasurer*, yet the fact is that he had mind only for the jade marvel so close that he could almost reach down a hand and touch the beginning of it.

It is well to approach all miracles and wonders by gradual stages or degrees and we can do this by examining another aspect of the glassy seascape of which the Mouser also might well have been thinking – but wasn't.

Although untroubled by swell, wavelet or faintest ripple or quiver, the Inner Sea around the sloop was not perfectly flat. Here and there, scatteredly, it was dimpled with small depressions about the size and shape of shallow saucers, as if giant invisible featherweight water-beetles were standing about on it – though the dimples were not arranged in any six-legged or four-legged or even tripod patterns. Moreover, a slim stalk of air seemed to go down from the center of each dimple for an indefinite distance into the water, quite like the tiny whirlpool that sometimes forms when the turquoise plug is pulled in the brimful golden bathtub of the Queen of the East (or the drain unstoppered in a bathtub of any humbler material belonging to any lowlier person) – except that there was no whirling of water in this case and the airstalks were not twisted and knotted but straight, as though scores of slim-bladed rapiers with guards like shallow saucers but all as invisible as air had been plunged at random into the motionless waters around the *Black Treasurer*. Or as though a sparse forest of invisible lily pads with straight invisible stems had sprung up around the sloop.

Imagine such an air-stalked dimple magnified so that the saucer was not a palm's breadth but a good spearcast across and the rodlike sword-straight stalk not a fingernail's width but a good four feet, imagine the sloop slid prow-foremost down into that shallow depression but stopping just short of the center and floating motionless there, imagine the bowsprit of the slightly tilted ship projecting over the exact center of the central tube or well of air, imagine a small, stalwart, nut-brown man in a gray loincloth lying along the bowsprit, his feet braced against the foredeck rails, and looking straight down the tube . . . and you have the Gray Mouser's situation exactly!

To be *in* the Mouser's situation and peering down the tube was very fascinating indeed, an experience calculated to drive other thoughts out of any man's mind – or even any woman's! The water here, a bowshot from the creamy rock-wall, was green, remarkably clear, but too deep to allow a view of the bottom – soundings taken yesterday had shown it to vary between six score and seven score feet. Through this water the well-size tube went down as perfectly circular and as smooth as if it were walled with glass; and indeed the Mouser would have believed that it was so walled – that the water immediately around it had been somehow frozen or hardened without altering in transparency – except that at the slightest noise, such as the Mouser's coughing, little quiverings would run up and down it in the form of series of ring-shaped waves.

What power prevented the tremendous weight of the sea from collapsing the tube in an instant, the Mouser could not begin to imagine.

Yet it was endlessly fascinating to peer down it. Sunlight transmitted through the sea water illuminated it to a considerable depth brightly if greenishly and the circular wall played odd tricks with distance. For instance, at this moment the Mouser, peering down slantwise through the side of the tube, saw a thick fish as long as his arm swimming around it and nosing up to it. The shape of the fish was very familiar yet he could not at once name it. Then thrusting his head out to one side and peering down at the same fish through the clear water alongside the tube, he saw that the fish was three times the length of his body – in fact, a shark. The Mouser shivered and told himself that the curved wall of the tube must act like the reducing lenses used by a few artists in Lankhmar.

On the whole, though, the Mouser might well have decided in the end that the vertical tunnel in the water was an illusion born of sun-glare and suggestion and have put on the ice-goggles and stuffed his ears with wax against any more siren-singing and then perhaps swigged at the forbidden brandy and gone to sleep, except for certain other circumstances footing the whole affair much more firmly in reality. For instance, there was a knotted rope securely tied to the bowsprit and hanging down the center of the tube and this rope creaked from time to time with the weight on it, and also there were threads of black smoke coming out of the watery hole (these were what made the Mouser cough), and last but not least was a torch burning redly far down in the hole – so far down its flame looked no bigger than a candle's – and just beside the flame, somewhat obscured by its smoke and much tinied by distance, was the upward-peering face of Fafhrd!

The Mouser was inclined to take on faith the reality of anything Fafhrd got mixed up with, certainly anything that Fafhrd got physically into – the near-seven-foot Northerner was much too huge a hulk of solid matter to be picturable as strolling arm-in-arm with illusions.

The events leading up to the reality-footing facts of the rope, the smoke, and Fafhrd down the air-well had been quite simple. At dawn the sloop had begun to drift mysteriously among the water dimples, there being no perceptible wind or current. Shortly afterwards it had bumped over the lip of the large saucer-shaped depression and slid to its present position with a little rush and then frozen there, as though the sloop's bowsprit and the hole were mutually desirous magnetic poles coupled together. Thereafter, while the Mouser had watched with eyes goggling and teeth a-chatter, Fafhrd had sighted down the hole, grunted with stolid satisfaction, slung the knotted rope down it, and then proceeded to array himself, seemingly with both war and love in mind – pomading his bushy hair and beard, perfuming his hairy chest and armpits, putting on a blue silk tunic under the gleaming one of otterskin and all his silver-plated necklaces, armbands, brooches and rings as well, but also strapping longsword and ax to his sides and lacing on his spiked boots. Then he had lit a long thin torch of resinous pine in the galley firebox and when it was flaming bravely he had, despite the Mouser's solicitous cries and tugging protests, gone out on the bowsprit and lowered himself into the hole, using thumb and forefinger of his right hand to grip the torch and the other three fingers of that hand, along with his left hand, to grip the rope. Only then had he spoken, calling on the Mouser to make ready and follow him if the Mouser were more hot-blooded man than cold-blooded lizard.

The Mouser had made ready to the extent of stripping off most of his clothing – it had occurred to him it would be necessary to dive for Fafhrd when the hole became aware of its own impossibility and collapsed – and he had fetched to the foredeck his own sword Scalpel and dagger Cat's Claw in their case of oiled sealskin with the notion they might be needed against sharks. Thereafter he had simply poised on the bowsprit, as we have seen, observing Fafhrd's slow descent and letting the fascination of it all take hold of him.

At last he dipped his head and called softly down the hole, 'Fafhrd, have you reached bottom yet?' frowning at the ring-shaped ripples even this gentle calling sent traveling down the hole and up again by reflection.

'WHAT DID YOU SAY?'

Fafhrd's answering bellow, concentrated by the tube and coming out of it like a solid projectile, almost blasted the Mouser off the bowsprit. Far more terrifying, the ring-ripples accompanying the bellow were so huge they almost seemed to close off the tube – narrowing it from four to two or three feet at any rate and dashing a spray of drops up into the Mouser's face as they reached the surface, lifting the rim upward as if the water were elastic, and then were reflected down the tube again.

The Mouser closed his eyes in a wince of horror, but when he opened them the hole was still there and the giant ring-ripples were beginning to abate.

Only a shade more loudly than the first time, but much more poignantly, the Mouser called down, 'Fafhrd, don't do that again!'

'WHAT?'

This time the Mouser was prepared for it – just the same it was most horrid to watch those huge rings traveling up and down the tube in an arrow-swift green peristalsis. He firmly resolved to do no more calling, but just then Fafhrd started to speak up the tube in a voice of more rational volume – the rings produced were hardly thicker than a man's wrist.

'COME ON, MOUSER! IT'S EASY! YOU ONLY HAVE TO DROP THE LAST SIX FEET!'

'Don't drop it, Fafhrd!' the Mouser instantly replied. 'Climb back up!'

'I ALREADY HAVE! DROPPED, I MEAN. I'M ON THE BOTTOM. OH, MOUSER . . . !'

The last part of Fafhrd's call was in a voice so infused with a mingled awe and excitement that the Mouser immediately asked back down, 'What? "Oh, Mouser" – what?'

'IT'S WONDERFUL, IT'S AMAZING, IT'S FANTASTIC!' the reply came back from below – but this time very faintly all of a sudden, as if Fafhrd had somehow gone around an impossible bend or two in the tube.

'*What* is, Fafhrd?' the Mouser demanded – and this time his own voice raised moderate rings. 'Don't go away, Fafhrd. But what *is* down there?'

'EVERYTHING!' the answer came back, not quite so faint this time.

'Are there girls?' the Mouser queried.

'A WHOLE WORLD!'

The Mouser sighed. The moment had come, he knew, as it always did, when outward circumstances and inner urges commanded an act, when curiosity and fascination tipped the scale of caution, when the lure of a vision and an adventure became so great and deep-hooking that he must respond to it or have his inmost self-respect eaten away.

Besides, he knew from long experience that the only way to extricate Fafhrd from the predicament into which he got himself was to go fetch the perfumed and be-sworded lout!

So the Mouser sprang up lightly, clipped to his underbelt his sealskin-cased weapons, hung beside them in loops a short length of knotted line with a slip-noose tied in one end, made sure that the sloop's hatches were securely covered and even that the galley fire was tighly boxed, rattled off a short scornful prayer to the gods *of* Lankhmar, and lowered himself off the bowsprit and down into the green hole.

The hole was chilly and it smelled of fish, smoke, and Fafhrd's pomade. The Mouser's main concern as soon as he got in it, he discovered to his surprise, was not to touch its glassy sides. He had the feeling that if he so much as lightly brushed it, the water's miraculous 'skin' would rupture and he would be engulfed – rather as an oiled needle floating on a bowl of water in its tiny hammock of 'water skin' is engulfed and sinks when one pinks it. He descended rapidly knot by knot, supporting himself by his hands, barely touching his toes to the rope below, praying there would be no sway and that he would be able to check it if it started. It occurred to him that he should have told Fafhrd to guy the rope at the bottom if he possibly could and above all have warned him not to shout up the tube while the Mouser descended – the thought of being squeezed by those dread water-rings was almost too much to bear. Too late now! – any word now would only too surely bring a bellow from the Northerner in reply.

First fears having been thus inspected, though by no means banished, the Mouser began to take some note of his surroundings. The luminous green world was not just one emerald blank as it had seemed at first. There was life in it, though not in the greatest abundance: thin strands of scalloped maroon seaweed, near-invisible jellyfish trailing their opalescent fringes, tiny dark skates hovering like bats, small silvery backboned fish gliding and darting – some of them, a blue-and-yellow-ringed and black-spotted school, even contesting lazily over the *Black Treasurer's* morning garbage, which the Mouser recognized by a large pallid beef-bone Fafhrd had gnawed briefly before tossing overside.

Looking up, he was hard put not to grasp in horror. The hull of the sloop, pressing down darkly, though pearled with bubbles, looked seven times higher above him than the distance he had descended by his count of the knots. Looking straight up the tube, however, he saw that the circle of deep blue sky had not shrunk correspondingly while the bowsprit bisecting it was still reassuringly thick. The curve of the tube had shrunk the sloop as it had the shark. The illusion was most weird and foreboding, nonetheless.

And now as the Mouser continued his swift descent, the circle overhead did grow smaller and more deeply blue, becoming a cobalt platter, a peacock saucer, and finally no more than a strange ultramarine coin that was the converging point of the tube and rope and in which the Mouser thought he saw a star flash. The Gray One puffed a few rapid kisses toward it, thinking how like they were to a drowning man's last bubbles. The light dimmed. The colours around him faded, the maroon seaweed turned gray, the fish lost their yellow rings, and the Mouser's own hands became blue as those of a corpse. And now he began to make out dimly the sea bottom, at the same extravagant distance below as the sloop was above, though immediately under him the bottom was oddly veiled or blanketed and only far off could he make out rocks and ridged stretches of sand.

His arms and shoulders ached. His palms burned. A monstrously fat grouper swam up to the tube and followed him down it, circling. The Mouser glared at it menacingly and it turned on its side and opened an impossibly large moon-crescent of mouth. The Mouser saw the razor teeth and realized it was the shark he'd seen or another like it, tinied by the lens of the tube. The teeth clashed, some of them inside the tube, only inches from his side. The water's 'skin' did not rupture disastrously, although the Mouser got the eerie impression that the 'bite' was bleeding a little water into the tube. The shark swam off to continue its circling at a moderate distance and the Mouser refrained from any more menacing looks.

Meanwhile the fishy smell had grown stronger and the smoke must have been getting thicker too, for now the Mouser coughed in spite of himself, setting the water rings shooting up and down. He fought to suppress an anguished curse – and at that moment his toes no longer touched rope. He unloosed the extra coil from his belt, went down three more knots, tightened the slip-noose above the second knot from the bottom, and continued on his way.

Five handholds later his feet found a footing in cold muck. He gratefully unclenched his hands, working his cramped fingers, at the same time calling 'Fafhrd!' softly but angrily. Then he looked around.

He was standing in the center of a large low tent of air, which was floored by the velvety sea-muck in which he had sunk to his ankles and roofed by the leadenly gleaming under-surface of the water – not evenly though, but in swells and hollows with ominous downward bulges here and there. The air-tent was about ten feet high at the foot of the tube. Its diameter seemed at least twenty times that, though exactly how far the edges extended it was impossible to judge for several reasons: the great irregularity of the tent's roof, the difficulty of even guessing at the extent of some outer areas where the distance between water-roof and muck-floor was measurable in inches, the fact that the gray light transmitted from above hardly permitted decent vision for more than two dozen yards, and finally the circumstance that there was considerable torch-smoke in the way here and there, writhing in thick coils along the ceiling, collecting in topsy-turvy pockets, though eventually gliding sluggishly up the tube.

What fabulous invisible 'tent-poles' propped up the oceans-heavy roof the Mouser could no more conceive than the force that kept the tube open.

Writhing his nostrils distastefully, both at the smoke and the augmented fishy smell, the Mouser squinted fiercely around the tent's full circumference. Eventually he saw a dull red glow in the black smudge where it was thickest and a little later Fafhrd emerged. The reeking flame of the pine torch, which was still no more than half consumed, showed the Northerner bemired with sea-muck to his thighs and hugging gently to his side with his bent left arm a dripping mess of variously gleaming objects. He was stooped over somewhat, for the roof bulged down where he stood.

'Blubber brain!' the Mouser greeted him. 'Put out that torch before we smother! We can see better without it. Oh, oaf, to blind yourself with smoke for the sake of light!'

To the Mouser there was obviously only one sane way to extinguish the torch – jab it in the wet muck underfoot – but Fafhrd, though evidently most agreeable to the Mouser's suggestion in a vacantly smiling way, had another idea. Despite the Mouser's anguished cry of warning, he casually thrust the flaming stick into the watery roof.

There was a loud hissing and a large downward puff of steam and for a moment the Mouser thought his worst dreads had been realized, for an angry squirt of water from the quenching point struck Fafhrd in the neck. But when the steam cleared it became evident that the rest of the sea was not going to follow the squirt, at least not at once, though now there was an

467

ominous lump, like a rounded tumor, in the roof where Fafhrd had thrust the torch and from it water ran steadily in a stream thick as a quill, digging a tiny crater where it struck the muck below.

'Don't do that!' the Mouser commanded in unwise fury.

'This?' Fafhrd asked gently, poking a finger through the ceiling next to the dripping bulge. Again came the angry squirt, diminishing at once to a trickle, and now there were two bulges closely side by side, quite like breasts.

'Yes, *that* – not again,' the Mouser managed to reply, his voice distant and high because of the self-control it took him not to rage at Fafhrd and so perhaps provoke even more reckless probings.

'Very well, I won't,' the Northerner assured him. 'Though,' he added, gazing thoughtfully at the twin streams, 'it would take those dribblings years to fill up this cavity.'

'Who speaks of years down here?' the Mouser snarled at him. 'Dolt! Iron Skull! What made you lie to me? "Everything" was down here, you said – "a whole world". And what do I find? Nothing! A miserable little cramp-roofed field of stinking mud!' And the Mouser stamped a foot in rage, which only splashed him foully, while a puffed, phosphorescent-whiskered fish expiring on the mire looked up at him reproachfully.

'That rude treading,' Fafhrd said softly, 'may have burst the silver-filigreed skull of a princess. "Nothing," say you? Look you then, Mouser, what treasure I have digged from your stinking field.'

And as he came toward the Mouser, his big feet gliding gently through the top of the muck for all the spikes on his boots, he gently rocked the gleaming things cradled in his left arm and let the fingers of his right hand drift gently among them.

'Aye,' he said, 'jewels and gauds undreamed by those who sail above, yet all teased by me from the ooze while I sought another thing.'

'What other thing, Gristle Dome?' the Mouser demanded harshly, though eyeing the gleaming things hungrily.

'The path,' Fafhrd said a little querulously, as if the Mouser must know what he meant. 'The path that leads from some

468

corner or fold of this tent of air to the sea-king's girls. These things are a sure promise of it. Look you, here, Mouser.' And he opened his bent left arm a little and lifted out most delicately with thumb and fingertips a life-size metallic mask.

Impossible to tell in that drained gray light whether the metal were gold or silver or tin or even bronze and whether the wide wavy streaks down it, like the tracks of blue-green sweat and tears, were verdigris or slime. Yet it was clear that it was female, patrician, all-knowing yet alluring, loving yet cruel, hauntingly beautiful. The Mouser snatched it eagerly yet angrily and the whole lower face crumpled in his hand, leaving only the proud forehead and the eyeholes staring at him more tragically than eyes.

The Mouser flinched back, expecting Fafhrd to strike him, but in the same instant he saw the Northerner turning away and lifting his straight right arm, index finger a-point, like a slow semaphor.

'You were right, oh Mouser!' Fafhrd cried joyously. 'Not only my torch's smoke but its very light blinded me. See! See the path!'

The Mouser's gaze followed Fafhrd's pointing. Now that the smoke was somewhat abated and the torch-flame no longer shot out its orange rays, the patchy phosphorescence of the muck and of the dying sea-things scattered about had become clearly visible despite the muted light filtering from above.

The phosphorescence was not altogether patchy, however. Beginning at the hole from which the knotted rope hung, a path of unbroken greenish-yellow witch-fire a long stride in width led across the muck toward an unpromising-looking corner of the tent of air where it seemed to disappear.

'Don't follow it, Fafhrd,' the Mouser automatically enjoined, but the Northerner was already moving past him, taking long dreamlike strides. By degrees his cradling arm unbent and one by one his ooze-won treasures began to slip from it into the muck. He reached the path and started along it, placing his spike-soled feet in the very center.

'Don't follow it, Fafhrd,' the Mouser repeated – a little hopelessly, almost whiningly, it must be admitted. 'Don't follow it, I say. It leads only to squidgy death. We can still go back up the rope, aye, and take your loot with us . . .'

But meanwhile he himself was following Fafhrd and snatching up, though more cautiously than he had the mask, the objects his comrade let slip. It was not worth the effort, the Mouser told himself as he continued to do it: though they gleamed enticingly, the various necklaces, tiaras, filigreed breast-cups and great-pinned brooches weighed no more and were no thicker than plaitings of dead ferns. He could not equal Fafhrd's delicacy and they fell apart at his touch.

Fafhrd turned back to him a face radiant as one who dreams sleeping of ultimate ecstasies. As the last ghost-gaud slipped from his arm, he said, 'They are nothing – no more than the mask – mere sea-gnawed wraiths of treasure. But oh, the promise of them, Mouser! Oh, the promise!'

And with that he turned forward again and stooped under a large downward bulge in the low leaden-hued roof.

The Mouser took one look back along the glowing path to the small circular patch of sky-light with the knotted rope falling in the center of it. The twin streams of water coming from the two 'wounds' in the ceiling seemed to be running more strongly – where they hit, the muck was splashing. Then he followed Fafhrd.

On the other side of the bulge the ceiling rose again to more than head-height, but the walls of the tent narrowed in sharply. Soon they were treading along a veritable tunnel in the water, a leaden arch-roofed passageway no wider than the phosphorescently yellow-green path that floored it. The tunnel curved just enough now to left, now right, so that there was no seeing any long distance ahead. From time to time the Mouser thought he heard faint whistlings and moanings echoing along it. He stepped over a large crab that was backing feebly and saw beside it a dead man's hand emerging from the glowing muck, one shred-fleshed finger pointing the way they were taking.

Fafhrd half turned his head and muttered gravely, 'Mark me, Mouser, there's magic in this somewhere!'

The Mouser thought he had never in his life heard a less necessary remark. He felt considerably depressed. He had long given up his puerile pleadings with Fafhrd to turn back – he knew there was no way of stopping Fafhrd short of grappling with him, and a tussle that would invariably send them crashing through one of the watery walls of the tunnel was by no means to his liking. Of course, he could always turn back alone. Still . . .

With the monotony of the tunnel and of just putting one foot after the other into the clinging muck and withdrawing it with a soft *plop*, the Mouser found time to become oppressed too with the thought of the weight of the water overhead. It was as though he walked with all the ships of the world on his back. His imagination would picture nothing but the tunnel's instant collapse. He hunched his head into his shoulders and it was all he could do not to drop to his elbows and knees and then stretch himself face down in the muck with the mere anticipation of the event.

The sea seemed to grow a little whiter ahead and the Mouser realized the tunnel was approaching the underreaches of the curtain-wall of creamy rock he and Fafhrd had climbed yesterday. The memory of that climb let his imagination escape at last, perhaps because it fitted with the urge that he and Fafhrd somehow lift themselves out of their present predicament.

It had been a difficult ascent, although the pale rock had proved hard and reliable, for footholds and ledges had been few and they had had to rope up and go by way of a branching chimney, often driving pitons into cracks to create a support where none was – but they had had high hopes of finding fresh water and game, too, likely enough, so far west of Ool Hrusp and its hunters. At last they had reached the top, aching and a little blown from their climb and quite ready to throw themselves down and rest while they surveyed the landscape of grassland and stunted trees that they knew to be characteristic of other parts of this most lonely peninsula stretching south-westward between the Inner and Outer Seas.

Instead they had found . . . nothing. Worse than nothing, in a way, if that were possible. The longed-for top proved to be the merest edge of rock, three feet wide at the most and narrower some places, while on the other side the rock descended even more precipitously than on the side which they had climbed – indeed it was deeply undercut in large areas – and for an equal or rather somewhat greater distance. From the foot of this dizzying drop a wilderness of waves, foam and rocks extended to the horizon.

They had found themselves clinging a-straddle to a veritable rock curtain, paper-thin in respect to its height and horizontal extent, between the Inner and what they realized must be the Outer Sea, which had eaten its way across the unexplored peninsula in this region but not yet quite broken through. As far as eye could see in either direction the same situation obtained, though the Mouser fancied he could make out a thickening of the wall in the direction of Ool Hrusp.

Fafhrd had laughed at the surprise of the thing – gargantuan bellows of mirth that had made the Mouser curse him silently for fear mere vibrations of his voice might shatter and tumble down the knife-edged saddle on which they perched. Indeed the Mouser had grown so angry with Fafhrd's laughter that he had sprung up and nimbly danced a jig of rage on the rock-ribbon, thinking meanwhile of wise Sheelba's saying: 'Know it or not, man treads between twin abysses a tightrope that has neither beginning nor end.'

Having thus expressed their feeling of horrified shock, each in his way, they had surveyed the yeasty sea below more rationally. The amount of surf and the numbers of emergent rocks showed it to be more shallow for some distance out – even likely, Fafhrd had opined, to drain itself at low tide, for his moon-lore told him that tides in this region of the world must at the moment be near high. Of the emergent rocks, one in particular stood out: a thick pillar two bowshots from the curtain wall and as high as a four-story house. The pillar was spiraled by ledges that looked as if they were in part of human cutting, while set in its thicker base and emerging from the foam there appeared an oddly criss-crossed weed-fringed rectangle that looked mightily like a large stout door – though where such a door might lead and who would use it were perplexing questions indeed.

Then, since there was no answering that question or others and since there was clearly no fresh water or game to be had from this literal shell of a coast, they had descended back to the Inner Sea and the *Black Treasurer*, though now each time they had driven a piton it had been with the fear that the whole wall might split and collapse . . .

'Ware rocks!'

Fafhrd's warning cry pulled the Mouser out of his waking memory-dream – dropped him in a split instant as if it were from the upper reaches of the creamy curtain-wall to a spot almost an equal distance below its sea-gnarled base. Just ahead of him three thick lumpy daggers of rock thrust down inexplicably through the gray watery ceiling of the tunnel. The Mouser shudderingly wove his head past them, as Fafhrd must have, and then looking beyond his comrade he saw more rocky protuberances encroaching on the tunnel from all sides – saw, in fact, as he strode on, that the tunnel was changing from one of water and muck to one roofed, walled and floored with solid rock. The water-born light faded away behind them, but the increasing phosphorescence natural to the animal life of a sea cavern almost compensated for it, boldly outlining their wet stony way and here and there glowing with especial brilliance and variety of color from the bands, portholes, feelers and eye-rings of many a dying fish and crawler.

The Mouser realized they must be passing far under the curtain-wall he and Fafhrd had climbed yesterday and that the tunnel ahead must be leading under the Outer Sea they had seen tossing with billows. There was no longer that immediate oppressive sense of a crushing weight of ocean overhead or of brushing elbows with magic. Yet the thought that if the tube, tent and tunnel behind them should collapse, then a great gush of solid water would rush into the rock-tunnel and engulf them, was in some ways even worse. Back under the water roof he'd had the feeling that even if it should collapse he might reach the surface alive by bold swimming and conceivably drag the cumbered Fafhrd up with him. But here they'd be hopelessly trapped.

True, the tunnel seemed to be ascending, but not enough or swiftly enough to please the Mouser. Moreover, if it did finally emerge, it would be to that shattering welter of foam they'd

peered down at yesterday. Truly, the Mouser found it hard to
pick between his druthers, or even to have any druthers at all.
His feelings of depression and doom gradually sank to a new and
perhaps ultimate nadir, and in a desperate effort to wrench them
up he deliberately imagined to himself the zestiest tavern he
knew in Lankhmar – a great gray cellar all a-flare with torches,
wine streaming and spilling, tankards and coins a-clink, voices
braying and roaring, poppy fumes a-twirl, naked girls writhing
in lascivious dances . . .

'*Oh, Mouser . . . !*'

Fafhrd's deep and feelingful whisper and the Northerner's
large hand against his chest halted the Mouser's plodding, but
whether it fetched his spirit back below the Outer Sea or simply
produced a fantastic alteration in its escapist imagining, the
Gray One could not at once be sure.

They were standing in the entrance to a vast submarine grotto
that rose in multiple steps and terraces toward an indefinite
ceiling from which cascaded down like silver mist a glow about
thrice the strength of moonlight. The grotto reeked of the sea
like the tunnel behind them; it was likewise scattered with
expiring fish and eels and small octopuses; mollusks tiny and
huge clustered on its walls and corners between weedy draperies
and silver-green veils; while its various niches and dark circular
doorways and even the stepped and terraced floor seemed
shaped in part at least by the action of rushing waters and
grinding sand.

The silver mist did not fall evenly but concentrated itself in
swirls and waves of light on three terraces. The first of these was
placed centrally and only a level stretch separated it from the
tunnel's mouth. Upon this terrace was set a great stone table
with weed-fringed sides and mollusk-crusted legs. A great
golden basin stood on one end of this table and two golden
goblets beside the basin.

Beyond the first terrace rose a second uneven flight of steps
with areas of menacing shadow pressing upon it from either
side. Behind the areas of darkness were a second and third
terrace that the silvery light favored. The one on the right –
Fafhrd's side, to call it that, for he stood to the right in the

474

tunnel mouth – was walled and arched with mother-of-pearl, almost as if it were one gigantic shell, and pearly swells rose from its floor like heaped satin pillows. The one on the Mouser's side, slightly below, was backed by an arras of maroon seaweed that fell in wide scalloped strands and billowed on the floor. From between these twin terraces the flight of irregular steps or ledges continued upward into a third area of darkness.

Shifting shadows and dark wavings and odd gleamings hinted that the three areas of darkness might be occupied; there was no doubt that the three bright terraces were. On the upper terrace on Fafhrd's side stood a tall and opulently beautiful woman whose golden hair rose in spiral masses like a shell and whose dress of golden fishnet clung to her pale greenish flesh. Her fingers showed greenish webs between them and on the side of her neck as she turned were faint scorings like a fish's gills.

On the Mouser's side was a slimmer yet exquisitely feminine creature whose silver flesh seemed to merge into silver scales on shoulders, back and flanks under her robe of filmy violet and whose short dark hair was split back from her low forehead's center by a scalloped silver crest a hand's breadth high. She too showed the faint neck-scorings and finger-webs.

The third figure, standing a-crouch behind the table, was sexlessly scrawny, with an effect of wiry old age, and either gowned or clad closely in jet black. A shock of rope-thick hairs dark red as iron rust covered her head while her gills and finger-webs were starkly apparent.

Each of these women wore a metal mask resembling in form and expression the eaten-away one Fafhrd had found in the muck. That of the first figure was gold; of the second, silver; of the third, green-splotched sea-darkened bronze.

The first two women were still, not as if they were part of a show but as though they were observing one. The scrawny black sea-witch was vibrantly active, although she hardly moved on her black-webbed toes except to shift position abruptly and ever so slightly now and then. She held a short whip in either hand, the webs folded outside her bent knuckles, and with these whips she maintained and directed the swift spinning of a half dozen objects on the polished table top. What these objects were it was

475

impossible to say, except that they were roughly oval. Some by their semi-transparency as they spun might have been large rings or saucers, others actual tops by their opacity. They gleamed silver and green and golden and they spun so swiftly and moved in such swift intersecting orbits as they spun that they seemed to leave gleaming wakes of spin in the misty air behind them. Whenever one would flag in its spinning and its true form begin to blink into visibility, she'd bring it back up to speed again with two or three rapid whip slashes; or should one veer too close to the table's edge or the golden basin, or threaten to collide with another, she'd redirect its orbit with deft lashings; now and again, with incredible skill, she'd flick one so that it jumped high in the air and then flick it again at landing so that it went on spinning without a break, leaving above it an evanescent loop of silvery air-spin.

These whirring objects made the pulsing moans and whistles the Mouser had heard along the tunnel.

As he watched them now and listened to them, the Gray One became convinced – partly because the silvery curving tubes of spin made him think of the air shaft he'd rope-climbed and the air-tunnel he'd plodded – that these spinning things were a cruel part of the magic that had created and held open the path through the Inner Sea behind them, and that once they should cease whirring then the shaft and tent and tunnel would collapse and the waters of the Inner Sea speed through the rock-tunnel into this grotto.

And indeed the scrawny black sea-witch looked to the Mouser as though she'd been whipping her tops for hours and – more to the point – would be able to keep on whipping them for hours more. She showed no signs of her exertion save the rhythmic rise and fall of her breastless chest and the extra whistle of breath through the mouth-slit of her mask and the gape and close of her gills.

Now she seemed for the first time to see him and Fafhrd, for without leaving off her whipping she thrust her bronze mask toward them, red ropes a-spill across its green-blotched forehead, and glared at them – hungrily, it seemed. Yet she made them no other menace, but after a searching scrutiny jerked back her head twice, to left and to right, as if for a sign that they should go past her. At the same time the green and silver queens beckoned to them languorously.

This woke the Mouser and Fafhrd from their dazed watching and they complied eagerly enough, though in passing the table the Mouser sniffed wine and paused to take up the two golden goblets, handing one to his comrade. They drained them despite the green hue of the drink, for the stuff smelled right and was fiery sweet yet tart. The black witch took no note of them, but went on whipping her gleaming, mist-waked tops.

As he drank, the Mouser noted that the table top was of purple-splotched, creamy marble polished to an exquisite smoothness. He also saw into the golden bowl. It held no store of green wine, but was filled almost to the brim with a crystal fluid that might or might not have been water. On the fluid floated a model, hardly a finger long, of the hull of a black boat. A tiny tube of air seemed to go down from its prow.

But there was no time for closer looking, for Fafhrd was moving on. The Mouser stepped up into his area of shadow to the left as Fafhrd had done to the right . . . and as he so stepped, there sidled from the shadows before him two bluely pallid men armed each with a pair of wave-edged knives. They were sailors, he judged from their pigtails and shuffling gait, although they were both naked, and they were indisputably dead – by token of their unhealthy color, their carelessness of thick slime streaking them, the way their bulging eyes showed only whites and the bottom crescent of the irises, and the fact that their hair, ears and other portions of their anatomies looked somewhat fish-chewed. Behind them waddled a scimitar-wielding dwarf with short spindle legs and monstrous head and gills – a veritable walking embryo. His great saucer eyes too were the upturned ones of a dead thing, which did not make the Mouser feel any easier as he whisked Scalpel and Cat's Claw out of their sealskin case, for the three converged on him confidently where he stood and rapidly shifted to block his way as he sought to circle behind them.

It was probably just as well that the Mouser had at that moment no attention to spare for his comrade's predicament.

Fafhrd's area of shadow was black as ink toward the wall, and as the Northerner strode through the margin of it past a ridged and man-sized knob of rock rising from the ledges and between him and the Mouser, there lifted from the further blackness – like eight giant serpents rearing from their lair – the thick, sinuous, crater-studded arms of a monstrous octopus. The sea-beast's movement must have struck internal sparks, for it simultaneously flashed into a yellow-streaked purplish iridescence, showing Fafhrd its baleful eyes large as plates, its cruel beak big as the prow of an overturned skiff, and the rather unlikely circumstance that the end of each mighty tentacle wrapped powerfully around the hilt of a gleaming broadsword.

Snatching at his own sword and ax, Fafhrd backed away from the be-weaponed squid against the rigid knob of rock. Two of the ridges, being the vertical shell-edges of a mollusk four feet across, instantly closed on the slack of his otterskin tunic, firmly holding him there.

Greatly daunted but determined to live nevertheless, the Northerner swung his sword in a great figure eight, the lower loop of which almost nicked the floor while the upper loop rose above his head like a tall arching shield. This double-petaled flower of steel baffled the four blades or so with which the octopus first came chopping at him rather cautiously, and as the sea monster drew back his arms for another volley of slashes, Fafhrd's left arm licked out with his ax and chopped through the nearest tentacle.

His adversary hooted loudly then and struck repeatedly with all his swords, and for a space it looked as though Fafhrd's universal parry must surely be pierced, but then the ax licked out again from the center of the sword-shield, once, twice, and two more tentacle tips fell and the swords they gripped with them. The octopus drew back then out of reach and sprayed a great mist-cloud of stinking black ink from its tube, under cover of which it might work its will unseen on the pinned Northerner, but even as the blinding mist billowed toward him Fafhrd hurled his ax at the huge central head. And although the black fog hid the ax almost as soon as it left his hand, the heavy weapon must have reached a vital spot for immediately the octopus hurled its remaining swords about the grotto at random (fortunately striking no one although they made a fine clatter) as its tentacles thrashed in dying convulsions.

Fafhrd drew a small knife, slashed his otterskin tunic down the front and across the shoulders, stepped out of it with a contemptuous wave to the mollusk as if to say, 'Have it for supper if you will,' and turned to see how his comrade fared. The Mouser, bleeding greenly from two trivial wounds in ribs and shoulder, had just finished severing the major tendons of his three hideous opponents – this having proved the only way to immobilize them when various mortal wounds had slowed them in no way at all nor caused them to bleed one drop of blood of any color.

He smiled sickishly at Fafhrd and turned with him toward the upper terraces. And now it became clear that the Green and Silver Ones were at least in one respect true queens, for they had not fled the prodigious battles as lesser women might, but abided them and now waited with arms lightly outstretched. Their gold and silver masks could not smile, but their bodies did, and as the two adventurers mounted toward them from the shadow into the light (the Mouser's little wounds changing from green to red, but Fafhrd's blue tunic staying pretty inky) it seemed to them that veily finger-webs and light neck-scorings were the highest points of female beauty. The lights faded somewhat on the upper terraces, though not on the lower where the monotonous six-toned music of the tops kept reassuringly on, and the two heroes entered each into the dark lustrous realm where all thoughts of wounds are forgotten and all memories of even the zestiest Lankhmar wine-cellar grow flat, and the Sea, our cruel mother and moving mistress, repays all debts.

A great soundless jar, as of the rock-solid earth moving, recalled the Mouser to his surroundings. Almost simultaneously the whir of one of the tops mounted to a high-pitched whine ending in a tinkly crash. The silver light began to pulse and flicker wildly throughout the grotto. Springing to his feet and looking down the steps, the Mouser saw a memory-etching sight: the rust-topped black sea-witch whipping wildly at her rebellious tops, which leaped and bounded about the table like fierce silver weasels, while through the air around her from all sides but chiefly from the tunnel there converged an arrow-swift flight of flying fish, skates, and ribbon-edged eels, all inky black and with tiny jaws agape.

At that instant Fafhrd seized him by the shoulder and jerked him fully around, pointing up the ledges. A silver lightning flash showed a great cross-beamed, weed-fringed door at the head of the rocky stairs. The Mouser nodded violently – meaning he understood it resembled and must be the door they had yesterday seen from the ribbony cliff-summit – and Fafhrd, satisfied his comrade would follow him, dashed toward it up the ledges.

But the Mouser had a different thought and darted in the opposite direction in the face of an ominous wet reeking wind. Returning a dozen lightning-flashes later, he saw the green and silver queens disappearing into round black tunnel mouths in the rock to either side of the terrace and then they were gone.

As he joined Fafhrd in the work of unsettling the crossbars of the great weedy door and drawing its massive rusty bolts, it quivered under a portentous triple knocking as though someone had smote it thrice with a long-skirted cloak of chain mail. Water squirted under it and through the lower third of the central vertical crack. The Mouser looked behind him then, with the thought that they might yet have to seek another avenue of escape . . . and saw a great white-headed pillar of water jetting more than half the height of the grotto from the mouth of the tunnel connecting with the Inner Sea. Just then the silver cavern-light went out, but almost immediately other light spilled from above. Fafhrd had heaved open half of the great door. Green water foamed about their knees and subsided. They fought their way through and as the great door slammed behind them under a fresh surge of water, they found themselves sloshing about on a wild beach blown with foam, swimming with surf, and floored chiefly with large flat water-worn oval rocks like giants' skipping stones. The Mouser, turned shoreward, squinted desperately at the creamy cliff two bow-shots away, wondering if they could possibly reach it through the mounting tide and climb it if they did.

But Fafhrd was looking seaward. The Mouser again felt himself shoulder-grabbed, spun around, and this time dragged up a curving ledge of the great tower-rock in the base of which was set the door through which they had just emerged. He stumbled, cutting his knees, but was jerked ruthlessly on. He decided that Fafhrd must have some very good reason for so rudely enjoining haste and thereafter did his best to hurry without assistance at Fafhrd's heels up the spiraling ramp-like ledge. On the second circling he stole a seaward look, gasped, and increased the speed of his mad dizzy scramble.

The stony beach below was drained and only here and there patched with huge gouts of spume, but roaring toward them from outer ocean was a giant wave that looked almost half as high as the pillar they were mounting – a great white wall of water flecked with green and brown and studded with rocks – a wave such as distant earthquakes send charging across the sea like a massed cavalry of monsters. Behind that wave came a taller one, and behind that a third taller still.

The Mouser and Fafhrd were three gasping circles higher when the stout tower shuddered and shook to the crashing impact of the first giant wave. Simultaneously the landward door at its base burst open from within and the cavern-traveling water from the Inner Sea gushed out creamily to be instantly engulfed. The crest of the wave caught at Fafhrd's and the Mouser's ankles without quite tripping them or much slowing their progress. The second and third did likewise, although they had gained another circle before each impact. There was a fourth wave and a fifth, but no higher than the third. The adventurers reached the stumpy summit and cast themselves down on it, clutching at the still-shaking rock and slewing around to watch the shore – Fafhrd noting the astonishing minor circumstance that the Mouser was gripping, between his teeth in the corner of his mouth a small black cigar.

The creamy curtain wall shuddered at the impact of the first wave and great cracks ran across it. The second wave shattered it and it fell into the third with an explosion of spray, displacing so much salt water that the return wave almost swamped the tower, its dirty crest tugging at the Mouser's and Fafhrd's fingers and licking along their sides. Again the tower shook and rocked beneath them but did not fall and that was the last of the great waves. Fafhrd and the Mouser circled down the spiraling ledges until they caught up with the declining sea, which still deeply covered the door at the tower's base. Then they looked landward again, where the mist raised by the catastrophe was dissipating.

A full half mile of the curtain wall had collapsed from base to crest, its shards vanishing totally beneath the waves, and through that gap the higher waters of the Inner Sea were pouring in a flat sullen tide that was swiftly obliterating the choppy aftermath of the earthquake waves from the Outer Sea.

On this wide river in the sea the *Black Treasurer* appeared from the mist riding straight toward their refuge rock.

Fafhrd cursed superstitiously. Sorcery working against him he could always accept, but magic operating in his favor he invariably found disturbing.

As the sloop drew near, they dove together into the sea, reached it with a few brisk strokes, scrambled aboard, steered it past the rock, and then lost no time in toweling and dressing their nakedness and preparing hot drinks. Soon they were looking at each over steaming mugs of grog. The brandy keg had been broached at last.

'Now that we've changed oceans,' Fafhrd said, 'we'll raise No-Ombrulsk in a day with this wet wind.'

The Mouser nodded and then smiled steadily at his comrade for a space. Finally he said, 'Well, old friend, are you sure that is all you have to say?'

Fafhrd frowned. 'Well, there's one thing,' he replied somewhat uncomfortably after a bit. 'Tell me, Mouser, did your girl ever take off her mask?'

'Did yours?' the Mouser asked back, eyeing him quizzically.

Fafhrd frowned. 'Well, more to the point,' he said gruffly, 'did any of it really happen? We lost our swords and duds but we have nothing to show for it.'

The Mouser grinned and took the black cigar from the corner of his mouth and handed it to Fafhrd.

'This is what I went back for,' he said, sipping his grog. 'I thought we needed it to get our ship back, and perhaps we did.'

It was a tiny replica, carved in jet with the Mouser's teeth marks deeply indenting it near the stern, of the *Black Treasurer*.

V
THE WRONG BRANCH

It is rumored by the wise-brained rats which burrow the citied earth and by the knowledgeable cats that stalk its shadows and by the sagacious bats that wing its night and by the sapient zats which soar through airless space, slanting their metal wings to winds of light, that those two swordsmen and blood-brothers, Fafhrd and the Gray Mouser, have adventured not only in the World of Nehwon with its great empire of Lankhmar, but also in many other worlds and times and dimensions, arriving at these through certain secret doors far inside the mazy caverns of Ningauble of the Seven Eyes – whose great cave, in this sense, exists simultaneously in many worlds and times. It is a Door, while Ningauble glibly speaks the languages of many worlds and universes, loving the gossip of all times and places.

In each new world, the rumor goes, the Mouser and Fafhrd awaken with knowledge and speaking skills and personal memories suitable to it, and Lankhmar then seems to them only a dream and they know not its languages, though it is ever their primal homeland.

It is even whispered that on one occasion they lived a life in the strangest of worlds variously called Gaia, Midgard, Terra, and Earth, swashbuckling there along the eastern shore of an inner sea in kingdoms that were great fragments of a vasty empire carved out a century before by one called Alexander the Great.

So much Srith of the Scrolls has to tell us. What we know from informants closer to the source is as follows:

After Fafhrd and the Gray Mouser escaped from the sea-king's wrath, they set a course for chilly No-Ombrulsk, but by midnight the favoring west wind had shifted around into a blustering northeaster. It was Fafhrd's judgment, at which the Mouser sneered, that this thwarting was the beginning of the sea-king's revenge on them. They perforce turned tail (or stern, as finicky sailormen would have us say) and ran south under jib alone, always keeping the grim mountainous coast in view to larboard, so they would not be driven into the trackless Outer Sea, which they had crossed only once in their lives before, and then in dire circumstance, much farther south.

Next day they reentered the Inner Sea by way of the new strait that had been created by the fall of the curtain rocks. That they were able to make this perilous and uncharted passage without holing the *Black Treasurer*, or even scraping her keel, was cited by the Mouser as proof that they had been forgiven or forgotten by the sea-king, if such a formidable being indeed existed. Fafhrd, contrariwise, murkily asserted that the sea-queen's weedy and polygynous husband was only playing cat and mouse with them, letting them escape one danger so as to raise their hopes and then dash them even more devilishly at some unknown future time.

Their adventurings in the Inner Sea, which they knew almost as well as a queen of the east her turquoise and golden bathing pool, tended more and more to substantiate Fafhrd's pessimistic hypothesis. They were becalmed a score of times and hit by three-score sudden squalls. They had thrice to outsail pirates and once best them in bloody hand-to-hand encounter. Seeking to reprovision in Ool Hrusp, they were themselves accused of piracy by the Mad Duke's harbor patrol, and only the moonless night and some very clever tacking – and a generous measure of luck – allowed the *Black Treasurer* to escape, its side bepricked and its sails transfixed with arrows enough to make it resemble a slim aquatic ebon hedgehog, or a black needlefish.

Near Kvarch Nar they did manage to reprovision, though only with coarse food and muddy river water. Shortly thereafter the seams of the *Black Treasurer* were badly strained and two opened by glancing collision with an underwater reef which never should have been where it was. The only possible point where they could careen and mend their ship was the tiny beach on the southwest side of the Dragon Rocks, and it took them two days of nip-and-tuck sailing and bailing to get them there with deck above water. Whereupon while one patched or napped, the other must stand guard against inquisitive two- and three-headed dragons and even an occasional monocephalic. When they got a cauldron of pitch seething for final repairs, the dragons all deserted them, put off by the black stuff's stink – a circumstance which irked rather than pleased the two adventurers, since they hadn't had the wit to keep a pot of pitch a-boil from the start. (They were most touchy and thin-skinned now from their long run of ill fortune.)

A-sail once more, the Mouser at long last agreed with Fafhrd that they truly had the sea-king's curse on them and must seek sorcerous aid in getting it removed – because if they merely forsook sea for land, the sea-king might well pursue them through his allies the Rivers and the Rainstorms, and they would still be under the full curse whenever they again took to ocean.

It was a close question as to whether they should consult Sheelba of the Eyeless Face, or Ningauble of the Seven Eyes. But since Sheelba laired in the Salt Marsh next to the city of Lankhmar, where their recent close connection with Pulg and Issekianity might get them into more trouble, they decided to consult Ningauble in his caverns in the low mountains behind Ilthmar.

Even the sail to Ilthmar was not without dangers. They were attacked by giant squids and by flying fish of the poison-spined variety. They also had to use all their sailor skill and expend all the arrows which the Ool Hruspians had given them, in order to stand off yet one more pirate attack. The brandy was all drunk.

As they were anchoring in Ilthmar harbor, the *Black Treasurer* literally fell apart like a joke-box, starboard side parting from larboard like two quarters of a split melon, while the mast and cabin, weighted by the keel, sank speedily as a rock.

Fafhrd and Mouser saved only the clothes they were in, their swords, dirk, and ax. And it was well they hung onto the latter, for while swimming ashore they were attacked by a school of sharks, and each man had to defend self and comrade while swimming encumbered. Ilthmarts lining the quays and moles cheered the heroes and the sharks impartially, or rather as to how they had laid their money, the odds being mostly three-to-one against both heroes surviving, with various shorter odds on the big man, the little man, or one or the other turning the trick.

Ilthmarts are a somewhat heartless people and much given to gambling. Besides, they welcome sharks into their harbor, since it makes for an easy way of disposing of common criminals, robbed and drunken strangers, slaves grown senile or otherwise useless, and also assures that the shark-god's chosen victims will always be spectacularly received.

When Fafhrd and the Mouser finally staggered ashore panting, they were cheered by such Ilthmarts as had won money on them. A larger number were busy booing the sharks.

The cash they got by selling the wreckage of the *Black Treasurer* was not enough to buy or hire them horses, though sufficient to provide food, wine, and water for one drunk and a few subsequent days of living.

During the drunk they more than once toasted the *Black Treasurer*, a faithful ship which had literally given its all for them, worked to death by storms, pirate attacks, the gnawing of sea-things, and other sacraments of the sea-king's rage. The Mouser drank curses on the sea-king, while Fafhrd crossed his fingers. They also had more or less courteously to fight off the attentions of numerous dancing girls, most of them fat and retired. .

It was a poor drunk, on the whole. Ilthmar is a city in which even a minimally prudent man dare not sleep soused, while the endless repetitions of its rat-god, more powerful even than its shark-god, in sculptures, murals, and smaller decor (and in large live rats silent in the shadows or a-dance in the alleys) make for a certain nervousness in newcomers after a few hours.

Thereafter it was a dusty two-day trudge to the caverns of Ningauble, especially for men untrained to tramping by many months a-sea and with the land becoming sandy desert toward the end.

The coolth of the hidden-mouthed rocky tunnel leading to Ningauble's deep abode was most welcome to men weary, dry, and powdered with fine sand. Fafhrd, being the more knowledgeable of Ningauble and his mazy lair, led the way, hands groping above and before him for stalactites and sharp rock edges which might inflict grievous head-bashings and other wounds. Ningauble did not approve the use by others of torch or candle in his realm.

After avoiding numerous side passages they came to a Y-shaped branching. Here the Mouser, pressing ahead, made out a pale glow far along the left-hand branch and insisted they explore that tunnel.

'After all,' he said, 'if we find we've chosen wrong, we can always come back.'

'But the right-hand branch is the one leading to Ningauble's auditorium,' Fafhrd protested. 'That is, I'm almost certain it is. That desert sun curdled my brain.'

'A plague on you for a pudding-head and a know-not-know,' the Mouser snapped, himself irritable still from the heat and dryness of their tramping, and strode confidently a-crouch down the left-hand branch. After two heartbeats, Fafhrd shrugged and followed.

The light grew ever more cooly bright ahead. Each experienced a brief spell of dizziness and a momentary unsettling of the rock underfoot, as if there were a very slight earthquake.

'Let's go back,' Fafhrd said.

'Let's at least *see*,' the Mouser retorted. 'We're already there.'

A few steps more and they were looking down another slope of desert. Just outside the entrance arch there stood with preternatural calm a richly-caparisoned white horse, a smaller black one with silver harness buckles and rings, and a sturdy mule laden with water-bags, pots, and parcels looking as though they contained provender for man and four-foot beast. By each of the saddles hung a bow and quiver of arrows, while to the white horse's saddle was affixed a most succinct note on a scrap of parchment:

Poseidon's curse is lifted, Ning.

There was something very strange about the writing, though neither could wholly define wherein the strangeness lay.

Perhaps it was that Ningauble had written down the sea-king as Poseidon, but that seemed a most acceptable alternate. And yet . . .

'It is most peculiar of Ningauble,' Fafhrd said, his voice sounding subtly odd to the Mouser and to himself too, '– most peculiar to do favors without demanding much information and even service in return.'

'Let us not look gift-steeds in the mouth,' the Mouser advised. 'Nor even a gift mule, for that matter.'

The wind had changed while they had been in the tunnels, so that it was not now blowing sultry from the east, but cool from the west. Both men felt greatly refreshed, and when they discovered that one of the mule's bags contained not branch water, but delicious strong water, their minds were made up. They mounted, Fafhrd the white, the Mouser the black, and single-footed confidently west, the mule tramping after.

A day told them that something unusual had happened, for they did not fetch Ilthmar or even the Inner Sea.

Also, they continued to be bothered by something strange about the words they were using, though each understood the other clearly enough.

In addition, both realized that something was happening to his memories and even common knowledge, though they did not at first reveal to each other this fear. Desert game was plentiful, and delicious when broiled, enough to quiet wonderings about an indefinable difference in the shape and coloration of the animals. And they found a rarely sweet desert spring.

It took a week, and also an encounter with a peaceful caravan of silk-and-spice merchants, before they realized that they were speaking to each other not in Lankhmarese, pidgin Mingol, and Forest Tongue, but in Phoenician, Aramaic, and Greek; and that Fafhrd's childhood memories were not of the Cold Waste, but of lands around a sea called Baltic; the Mouser's not of Tovilyis, but Tyre; and that here the greatest city was not called Lankhmar, but Alexandria.

And even with those thoughts, the memory of Lankhmar and the whole world of Nehwon began to fade in their minds, become a remembered dream or series of dreams.

489

Only the memory of Ningauble and his caverns stayed sharp and clear. But the exact nature of the trick he had played on them became cloudy.

No matter, the air here was sharp and clean, the food good, the wine sweet and addling, the men built nicely enough to promise interesting women. What if the names and the new words seemed initially weird? Such feelings diminished even as one thought about them.

Here was a new world, promising unheard-of adventures. Though even as one thought 'new', it became a world more familiar.

They cantered down the white sandy track of their new, yet foreordained, destiny.

VI
ADEPT'S GAMBIT

1. *Tyre*

It happened that while Fafhrd and the Gray Mouser were dallying in a wine shop near the Sidonian Harbor of Tyre, where all wine shops are of doubtful repute, a long-limbed yellow-haired Galatian girl lolling in Fafhrd's lap turned suddenly into a wallopingly large sow. It was a singular occurrence, even in Tyre. The Mouser's eyebrows arched as the Galatian's breasts, exposed by the Cretan dress that was the style revival of the hour, became the uppermost pair of slack white dugs, and he watched the whole proceeding with unfeigned interest.

The next day four camel traders, who drank only water disinfected with sour wine, and two purple-armed dyers, who were cousins of the host, swore that no transformation took place and that they saw nothing, or very little out of the ordinary. But three drunken soldiers of King Antiochus and four women with them, as well as a completely sober Armenian juggler, attested the event in all its details. An Egyptian mummy-smuggler won brief attention with the claim that the oddly garbed sow was only a semblance, or phantom, and made dark references to visions vouchsafed men by the animal gods of his native land, but since it was hardly a year since the Seleucids had beaten the Ptolomies out of Tyre, he was quickly shouted down. An impecunious traveling lecturer from Jerusalem took up an even more attenuated position, maintaining that the sow was not a sow, or even a semblance, but only the semblance of a semblance of a sow.

Fafhrd, however, had no time for such metaphysical niceties.

When, with a roar of disgust not unmingled with terror, he had shoved the squealing monstrosity halfway across the room so that it fell with a great splash into the water tank, it turned back again into a long-limbed Galatian girl and a very angry one, for the stale water in which the sow had floundered drenched her garments and plastered down her yellow hair (the Mouser murmured, 'Aphrodite!') and the sow's uncorsetable bulk had split the tight Cretan waist. The stars of midnight were peeping through the skylight above the tank, and the wine cups had been many times refilled, before her anger was dissipated. Then, just as Fafhrd was impressing a reintroductory kiss upon her melting lips, he felt them once again become slobbering and tusky. This time she picked herself up from between two wine casks and, ignoring the shrieks, excited comments, and befuddled stares as merely part of a rude mystification that had been carried much too far, she walked with Amazonian dignity from the room. She paused only once, on the dark and deep-worn threshold, and then but to hurl at Fafhrd a small dagger, which he absentmindedly deflected upward with his copper goblet, so that it struck full in the mouth a wooden satyr on the wall, giving that deity the appearance of introspectively picking his teeth.

Fafhrd's sea-green eyes became likewise thoughtful as he wondered what magician had tampered with his love life. He slowly scanned the wine shop patrons, face by sly-eyed face, pausing doubtfully when he came to a tall, dark-haired girl beyond the water tank, finally returning to the Mouser. There he stopped, and a certain suspiciousness became apparent in his gaze.

The Mouser folded his arms, flared his snub nose, and returned the stare with all the sneering suavity of a Parthian ambassador. Abruptly he turned, embraced and kissed the cross-eyed Greek girl sitting beside him, grinned wordlessly at Fafhrd, dusted from his coarse-woven gray silk robe the antimony that had fallen from her eyelids, and folded his arms again.

Fafhrd began softly to beat the base of his goblet against the butt of his palm. His wide, tight-laced leather belt, wet with the sweat that stained his white linen tunic, creaked faintly.

Meanwhile murmured speculation as to the person responsible for casting a spell on Fafhrd's Galatian eddied around the tables and settled uncertainly on the tall, dark-haired girl, probably because she was sitting alone and therefore could not join in the suspicious whispering.

'She's an odd one,' Chloe, the cross-eyed Greek, confided to the Mouser. 'Silent Salmacis they call her, but I happen to know that her real name is Ahura.'

'A Persian?' asked the Mouser.

Chloe shrugged. 'She's been around for years, though no one knows exactly where she lives or what she does. She used to be a gay, gossipy little thing, though she never would go with men. Once she gave me an amulet, to protect me from someone, she said – I still wear it. But then she was away for a while,' Chloe continued garrulously, 'and when she came back she was just like you see her now – shy, and tight-mouthed as a clam, with a look in her eyes of someone peering through a crack in a brothel wall.'

'Ah,' said the Mouser. He looked at the dark-haired girl, and continued to look, appreciatively, even when Chloe tugged at his sleeve. Chloe gave herself a mental bastinado for having been so foolish as to call a man's attention to another girl.

Fafhrd was not distracted by this byplay. He continued to stare at the Mouser with the stony intentness of a whole avenue of Egyptian colossi. The cauldron of his anger came to a boil.

'Scum of wit-weighted culture,' he said, 'I consider it the nadir of base perfidy that you should try out on me your puking sorcery.'

'Softly, man of strange loves,' purred the Mouser. 'This unfortunate mishap has befallen several others besides yourself, among them an ardent Assyrian warlord whose paramour was changed into a spider between the sheets, and an impetuous Ethiop who found himself hoisted several yards into the air and kissing a giraffe. Truly, to one who knows the literature, there is nothing new in the annals of magic and thaumaturgy.'

'Moreover,' continued Fafhrd, his low-pitched voice loud in the silence, 'I regard it an additional treachery that you should practice your pig-trickery on me in an unsuspecting moment of pleasure.'

'And even if I should choose sorcerously to discommode your lechery,' hypothesized the Mouser, 'I do not think it would be the woman that I would metamorphose.'

'Furthermore,' pursed Fafhrd, leaning forward and laying his hand on the large sheathed dirk beside him on the bench, 'I judge it an intolerable and direct affront to myself that you should pick a Galatian girl, member of a race that is cousin to my own.'

'It would not be the first time,' observed the Mouser portentously, slipping his fingers inside his robe, 'that I have had to fight you over a woman.'

'But it would be the first time,' asserted Fafhrd, with an even greater portentousness, 'that you had to fight me over a pig!'

For a moment he maintained his belligerent posture, head lowered, jaw outthrust, eyes slitted. Then he began to laugh.

It was something, Fafhrd's laughter. It began with windy snickers through the nostrils, next spewed out between clenched teeth, then became a series of jolting chortles, swiftly grew into a roar against which the barbarian had to brace himself, legs spread wide, head thrown back, as if against a gale. It was a laughter of the storm-lashed forest or the sea, a laughter that conjured up wide visions, that seemed to blow from a more primeval, heartier, lusher time. It was the laughter of the Elder Gods observing their creature man and noting their omissions, miscalculations and mistakes.

The Mouser's lips began to twitch. He grimaced wryly, seeking to avoid the infection. Then he joined in.

Fafhrd paused, panted, snatched up the wine pitcher, drained it.

'Pig-trickery!' he bellowed, and began to laugh all over again.

The Tyrian riffraff gawked at them in wonder – astounded, awestruck, their imagination cloudily stirred.

Among them, however, was one whose response was noteworthy. The dark-haired girl was staring at Fafhrd avidly, drinking in the sound, the oddest sort of hunger and baffled curiosity – and calculation – in her eyes.

The Mouser noticed her and stopped his laughter to watch. Mentally Chloe gave herself an especially heavy swipe on the soles of her bound, naked feet.

Fafhrd's laughter trailed off. He blew out the last of it soundlessly, sucked in a normal breath, hooked his thumbs in his belt.

'The dawn stars are peeping,' he commented to the Mouser, ducking his head for a look through the skylight. 'It's time we were about the business.'

And without more ado he and Mouser left the shop, pushing out of their way a newly arrived and very drunken merchant of Pergamum, who looked after them bewilderedly, as if he were trying to decide whether they were a tall god and his dwarfish servitor, or a small sorceror and the great-thewed automaton who did his bidding.

Had it ended there, two weeks would have seen Fafhrd claiming that the incident of the wine shop was merely a drunken dream that had been dreamed by more than one – a kind of coincidence with which he was by no means unfamiliar. But it did not. After 'the business' (which turned out to be much more complicated than had been anticipated, evolving from a fairly simple affair of Sidonian smugglers into a glittering intrigue studded with Cilician pirates, a kidnaped Cappadocian princess, a forged letter of credit on a Syracusan financier, a bargain with a female Cyprian slave-dealer, rendezvous that turned into an ambush, some priceless tomb-filched Egyptian jewels that no one ever saw, and a band of Idumean brigands who came galloping out of the desert to upset everyone's calculations) and after Fafhrd and the Gray Mouser had returned to the soft embraces and sweet polyglot of the seaport ladies, pig-trickery befell Fafhrd once more, this time ending in a dagger brawl with some men who thought they were rescuing a pretty Bithynian girl from death by salty and odorous drowning at the hands of a murderous red-haired giant – Fafhrd had insisted on dipping the girl, while still metamorphosed, into a hogshead of brine remaining from pickled pork. This incident suggested to the Mouser a scheme he never told Fafhrd: namely, to engage an amiable girl, have Fafhrd turn her into a pig, immediately sell her to a butcher, next sell her to an amorous merchant when she had escaped the bewildered butcher as a furious girl, have Fafhrd sneak after the merchant and turn her back into a pig (by this time he ought to be able to do it merely by making eyes at her), then sell her to another butcher and begin all over again. Low prices, quick profits.

For a while Fafhrd stubbornly continued to suspect the Mouser, who was forever dabbling in black magic and carried a gray leather case of bizarre instruments picked from the pockets of wizards and recondite books looted from Chaldean libraries – even though long experience had taught Fafhrd that the Mouser seldom read systematically beyond the prefaces in the majority of his books (though he often unrolled the latter portions to the accompaniment of penetrating glances and trenchant criticisms) and that he was never able to evoke the same results two times running with his enchantments. That he could manage to transform two of Fafhrd's lights of love was barely possible; that he should get a sow each time was unthinkable. Besides, the thing happened more than twice; in fact, there never was a time when it did not happen. Moreover, Fafhrd did not really believe in magic, least of all the Mouser's. And if there was any doubt left in his mind, it was dispelled when a dark and satiny-skinned Egyptian beauty in the Mouser's close embrace was transformed into a giant snail. The Gray One's disgust at the slimy tracks on his silken garments was not to be mistaken, and was not lessened when two witnesses, traveling horse doctors, claimed that they had seen no snail, giant or ordinary, and agreed that the Mouser was suffering from an obscure kind of wet rot that induced hallucinations in its victim, and for which they were prepared to offer a rare Median remedy at the bargain price of nineteen drachmas a jar.

Fafhrd's glee at his friend's discomfiture was short-lived, for after a night of desperate and far-flung experimentation, which, some said, blazed from the Sidonian harbor to the Temple of Melkarth a trail of snail tracks that next morning baffled all the madams and half the husbands in Tyre, the Mouser discovered something he had suspected all the time, but had hoped was not the whole truth: namely, that Chloe alone was immune to the strange plague his kisses carried.

Needless to say, this pleased Chloe immensely. An arrogant self-esteem gleamed like two clashing swords from her crossed eyes and she applied nothing but costly scented oil to her poor, mentally bruised feet – and not only mental oil, for she quickly made capital of her position by extorting enough gold from the Mouser to buy a slave whose duty it was to do very little else. She no longer sought to avoid calling the Mouser's attention to other women, in fact she rather enjoyed doing so, and the next time they encountered the dark-haired girl variously called Ahura and Silent Salmacis, as they were entering a tavern known as the Murex Shell, she volunteered more information.

'Ahura's not so innocent, you know, in spite of the way she sticks to herself. Once she went off with some old man – that was before she gave me the charm – and once I heard a primped-up Persian lady scream at her, "What have you done with your brother?" Ahura didn't answer, just looked at the woman coldly as a snake, and after a while the woman ran out. Brr! You should have seen her eyes!'

But the Mouser pretended not to be interested.

Fafhrd could undoubtedly have had Chloe for the polite asking, and Chloe was more than eager to extend and cement in this fashion her control over the twain. But Fafhrd's pride would not allow him to accept such a favor from his friend, and he had frequently in past days, moreover, railed against Chloe as a decadent and unappetizing contemplater of her own nose.

So he perforce led a monastic life and endured contemptuous feminine glares across the drinking table and fended off painted boys who misinterpreted his misogyny and was much irritated by a growing rumor to the effect that he had become a secret eunuch priest of Cybele. Gossip and speculation had already fantastically distorted the truer accounts of what had happened, and it did not help when the girls who had been transformed denied it for fear of hurting their business. Some people got the idea that Fafhrd had committed the nasty sin of bestiality and they urged his prosecution in the public courts. Others accounted him a fortunate man who had been visited by an amorous goddess in the guise of a swine, and who thereafter scorned all earthly girls. While still others whispered that he was a brother of Circe and that he customarily dwelt on a floating island in the Tyrrhenian Sea, where he kept cruelly transformed into pigs a whole herd of beautiful shipwrecked maidens. His laughter was heard no more and dark circles appeared in the white skin around his eyes and he began to make guarded inquiries among magicians in hopes of finding some remedial charm.

'I think I've hit on a cure for your embarrassing ailment,' said the Mouser carelessly one night, laying aside a raggedy brown papyrus. 'Came across it in this obscure treatise, "The Demonology of Isaiah ben Elshaz". It seems that whatever change takes place in the form of the woman you love, you should continue to make love to her, trusting to the power of your passion to transform her back to her original shape.'

Fafhrd left off honing his great sword and asked, 'Then why don't you try kissing snails?'

'It would be disagreeable and, for one free of barbarian prejudices, there is always Chloe.'

'Pah! You're just going with her to keep your self-respect. I know you. For seven days now you'd had thoughts for no one but that Ahura wench.'

'A pretty chit, but not to my liking,' said the Mouser icily. 'It must be your eye she's the apple of. However, you really should try my remedy; I'm sure you'd prove so good at it that the shes of all the swine in the world would come squealing after you.'

Whereupon Fafhrd did go so far as to hold firmly at arm's length the next sow his pent passion created, and feed it slops in the hope of accomplishing something by kindness. But in the end he had once again to admit defeat and assuage with owl-stamped Athenian silver didrachmas an hysterically angry Scythian girl who was sick at the stomach. It was then that an ill-advised curious young Greek philosopher suggested to the Northman that the soul or inward form of the thing loved is alone of importance, the outward form having no ultimate significance.

'You belong to the Socratic school?' Fafhrd questioned gently.

The Greek nodded.

'Socrates was the philosopher who was able to drink unlimited quantities of wine without blinking?'

Again the quick nod.

'That was because his rational soul dominated his animal soul?'

'You are learned,' replied the Greek, with a more respectful but equally quick nod.

'I am not through. Do you consider yourself in all ways a true follower of your master?'

This time the Greek's quickness undid him. He nodded, and two days later he was carried out of the wine shop by friends, who found him cradled in a broken wine barrel, as if new-born in no common manner. For days he remained drunk, time enough for a small sect to spring up who believed him a reincarnation of Dionysus and as such worshiped him. The sect was dissolved when he became half sober and delivered his first oracular address, which had as its subject the evils of drunkenness.

The morning after the deification of the rash philosopher, Fafhrd awoke when the first sunbeams struck the flat roof on which he and the Mouser had chosen to pass the night. Without sound or movement, suppressing the urge to groan out for someone to buy him a bag of snow from the white-capped Lebanons (over which the sun was even now peeping) to cool his aching head, he opened an eye on the sight that he in his wisdom had expected: the Mouser sitting on his heels and looking at the sea.

'Son of a wizard and a witch,' he said, 'it seems that once again we must fall back upon our last resource.'

The Mouser did not turn his head, but he nodded it once, deliberately.

'The first time we did not come away with our lives,' Fafhrd went on.

'The second time we lost our souls to the Other Creatures,' the Mouser chimed in, as if they were singing a dawn chant to Isis.

'And the last time we were snatched away from the bright dream of Lankhmar.'

'He may trick us into drinking the drink, and we not awake for another five hundred years.'

'He may send us to our deaths and we not to be reincarnated for another two thousand,' Fafhrd continued.

'He may show us Pan, or offer us to the Elder Gods, or whisk us beyond the stars, or send us into the underworld of Quarmall,' the Mouser concluded.

There was a pause of several moments.

Then the Gray Mouser whispered, 'Nevertheless, we must visit Ningauble of the Seven Eyes.'

And he spoke truly, for as Fafhrd had guessed, his soul was hovering over the sea dreaming of dark-haired Ahura.

2. Ningauble

So they crossed the snowy Lebanons and stole three camels, virtuously choosing to rob a rich landlord who made his tenants milk rocks and sow the shores of the Dead Sea, for it was unwise to approach the Gossiper of the Gods with an overly dirty conscience. After seven days of pitching and tossing across the desert, furnace days that made Fafhrd curse Muspelheim's fire gods, in whom he did not believe, they reached the Sand Combers and the Great Sand Whirlpools, and warily slipping past them while they were only lazily twirling, climbed the Rocky Islet. The city-loving Mouser ranted at Ningauble's preference for 'a godforsaken hole in the desert', although he suspected that the Newsmonger and his agents came and went by a more hospitable road than the one provided for visitors, and although he knew as well as Fafhrd that the Snarer of Rumors (especially the false, which are the more valuable) must live as close to India and the infinite garden lands of the Yellow Men as to barbaric Britain and marching Rome, as close to the heaven-steaming trans-Ethiopian jungle as to the mystery of lonely tablelands and star-scraping mountains beyond the Caspian Sea.

With high expectations they tethered their camels, took torches, and fearlessly entered the Bottomless Caves, for it was not so much in the visiting of Ningauble that danger lay as in the tantalizing charm of his advice, which was so great that one had to follow wherever it led.

Nevertheless Fafhrd said, 'An earthquake swallowed Ningauble's house and it stuck in his throat. May he not hiccup.'

As they were passing over the Trembling Bridge spanning the Pit of Ultimate Truth, which could have devoured the light of ten thousand torches without becoming any less black, they met and edged wordlessly past a helmeted, impassive fellow whom they recognized as a far-journeying Mongol. They speculated as to whether he too were a visitor of the Gossiper, or a spy – Fafhrd had no faith in the clairvoyant power of the seven eyes, averring that they were merely a sham to awe fools and that Ningauble's information was gathered by a corps of peddlers, panders, slaves, urchins, eunuchs, and midwives, which outnumbered the grand armies of a dozen kings.

They reached the other side with relief and passed a score of tunnel mouths, which the Mouser eyed most wistfully.

'Mayhap we should choose one at random,' he muttered, 'and seek yet another world. Ahura's not Aphrodite, nor yet Astarte – quite.'

'Without Ning's guidance?' Fafhrd retorted. 'And carrying our curses with us? Press on!'

Presently they saw a faint light flickering on the stalactited roof, reflected from a level above them. Soon they were struggling toward it up the Staircase of Error, an agglomeration of great rough rocks. Fafhrd stretched his long legs; the Mouser leaped catlike. The little creatures that scurried about their feet, brushed their shoulders in slow flight, or merely showed their yellow, insatiably curious eyes from crevice and rocky perch, multiplied in number; for they were nearing the Arch-eavesdropper.

A little later, having wasted no time in reconnoitering, they stood before the Great Gate, whose iron-studded upper reaches disdained the illumination of the tiny fire. It was not the gate, however, that interested them, but its keeper, a monstrously paunched creature sitting on the floor beside a vast heap of potsherds, and whose only movement was a rubbing of what seemed to be his hands. He kept them under the shabby but voluminous cloak which also completely hooded his head. A third of the way down the cloak, two large bats clung.

Fafhrd cleared his throat.

The movement ceased under the cloak.

Then out of the top of it sinuously writhed something that seemed to be a serpent, only in place of a head it bore an opalescent jewel with a dark central speck. Nevertheless, one might finally have judged it a serpent, were it not that it also resembled a thick-stalked exotic bloom. It restlessly turned this way and that until it pointed at the two strangers. Then it went rigid and the bulbous extremity seemed to glow more brightly. There came a low purring and five similar stalks twisted rapidly from under the hood and aligned themselves with their companion. Then the six black pupils dilated.

'Fat-bellied rumor monger!' hailed the Mouser nervously. 'Must you forever play at peep show?'

For one could never quite get over the faint initial uneasiness that came with meeting Ningauble of the Seven Eyes.

'That is an incivility, Mouser,' a voice from under the hood quavered thinly. 'It is not well for men who come seeking sage counsel to cast fleers before them. Nevertheless, I am today in a merry humor and will give ear to your problem. Let me see, now, what world do you and Fafhrd come from?'

'Earth, as you very well know, you king of shreds of lies and patches of hypocrisy,' the Mouser retorted thinly, stepping nearer. Three of the eyes closely followed his advance, while a fourth kept watch on Fafhrd.

At the same time, 'Further incivilities,' Ningauble murmured sadly, shaking his head so that his eye-stalks jogged. 'You think it easy to keep track of the times and spaces and of the worlds manifold? And speaking of time, is it not time indeed that you ceased to impose on me, because you once got me an unborn ghoul that I might question it of its parentage? The service to me was slight, accepted only to humor you; and I, by the name of the Spoorless God, have repaid it twenty times over.'

'Nonsense, Midwife of Secrets,' retorted the Mouser, stepping forward familiarly, his gay impudence almost restored. 'You know as well as I that deep in your great paunch you are trembling with delight at having a chance to mouth your knowledge to two such appreciative listeners as we.'

'That is as far from the truth as I am from the Secret of the Sphinx,' commented Ningauble, four of his eyes following the Mouser's advance, one keeping watch on Fafhrd, while the sixth looped back around the hood to reappear on the other side and gaze suspiciously behind them.

'But, Ancient Tale-bearer, I am sure you have been closer to the Sphinx than any of her stony lovers. Very likely she first received her paltry riddle from your great store.'

Ningauble quivered like jelly at this tickling flattery.

'Nevertheless,' he piped, 'today I am in a merry humor and will give ear to your question. But remember that it will almost certainly be too difficult for me.'

'We know your great ingenuity in the face of insurmountable obstacles,' rejoined the Mouser in the properly soothing tones.

'Why doesn't your friend come forward?' asked Ningauble, suddenly querulous again.

Fafhrd had been waiting for that question. It always went against his grain to have to behave congenially toward one who called himself the Mightiest Magician as well as the Gossiper of the Gods. But that Ningauble should let hang from his shoulders two bats whom he called Hugin and Munin in open burlesque of Odin's ravens, was too much for him. It was more a patriotic than religious matter with Fafhrd. He believed in Odin only during moments of sentimental weakness.

'Slay the bats or send them slithering and I'll come, but not before,' he dogmatized.

'Now I'll tell you nothing,' said Ningauble pettishly, 'for, as all know, my health will not permit bickering.'

'But, Schoolmaster of Falsehood,' purred the Mouser, darting a murderous glance at Fafhrd, 'that is indeed to be regretted, especially since I was looking forward to regaling you with the intricate scandal that the Friday concubine of the satrap Philip withheld even from her body slave.'

'Ah well,' conceded the Many-Eyed One, 'it is time for Hugin and Munin to feed.'

The bats reluctantly unfurled their wings and flew lazily into the darkness.

Fafhrd stirred himself and moved forward, sustaining the

scrutiny of the majority of the eyes, all six of which the Northman considered artfully manipulated puppet-orbs. The seventh no man had seen, or boasted of having seen, save the Mouser, who claimed it was Odin's other eye, stolen from sagacious Mimer – this not because he believed it, but to irk his Northern comrade.

'Greetings, Snake Eyes,' Fafhrd boomed.

'Oh, is it you, Hulk?' said Ningauble carelessly. 'Sit down, both, and share my humble fire.'

'Are we not to be invited beyond the Great Gate and share your fabulous comforts too?'

'Do not mock me, Gray One. As all know, I am poor, penurious Ningauble.'

So with a sigh the Mouser settled himself on his heels, for he well knew that the Gossiper prized above all else a reputation for poverty, chastity, humility, and thrift, therefore playing his own doorkeeper, except on certain days when the Great Gate muted the tinkle of impious sistrum and the lascivious wail of flute and the giggles of those who postured in the shadow shows.

But now Ningauble coughed piteously and seemed to shiver and warmed his cloaked members at the fire. And the shadows flickered weakly against iron and stone, and the little creatures crept rustling in, making their eyes wide to see and their ears cupped to hear; and upon their rhythmically swinging, weaving stalks pulsated the six eyes. At intervals, too, Ningauble would pick up, seemingly at random, a potsherd from the great pile and rapidly scan the memorandum scribbled on it, without breaking the rhythm of the eyestalks or, apparently, the thread of his attention.

The Mouser and Fafhrd crouched on their hams.

As Fafhrd started to speak, Ningauble questioned rapidly, 'And now, my children, you had something to tell me concerning the Friday concubine—'

'Ah, yes, Artist of Untruth,' the Mouser cut in hastily. 'Concerning not so much the concubine as three eunuch priests of Cybele and a slave-girl from Samos – a tasty affair of wondrous complexity, which you must give me leave to let simmer in my mind so that I may serve it up to you skimmed of the slightest fat of exaggeration and with all the spice of true detail.'

'And while we wait for the Mouser's mind-pot to boil,' said Fafhrd casually, at last catching the spirit of the thing, 'you may the more merrily pass the time by advising us as to a trifling difficulty,' And he gave a succinct account of their tantalizing bedevilment by sow- and snail-changed maidens.

'And you say that Chloe alone proved immune to the spell?' queried Ningauble thoughtfully, tossing a potsherd to the far side of the pile. 'Now that brings to my mind—'

'The exceedingly peculiar remark at the end of Diotima's fourth epistle to Socrates?' interrupted the Mouser brightly. 'Am I not right, Father?'

'You are not,' replied Ningauble coldly. 'As I was about to observe, when this tick of the intellect sought to burrow the skin of my mind, there must be something that throws a protective influence around Chloe. Do you know of any god or demon in whose special favor she stands, or any incantation or rune she habitually mumbles, or any notable talisman, charm, or amulet she customarily wears or inscribes on her body?'

'She did mention one thing,' the Mouser admitted diffidently after a moment. 'An amulet given her years ago by some Persian, or Greco-Persian girl. Doubtless a trifle of no consequence.'

'Doubtless. Now, when the first sow-change occurred, did Fafhrd laugh the laugh? He did? That was unwise, as I have many times warned you. Advertise often enough your connection with the Elder Gods and you may be sure that some greedy searcher from the pit . . .'

'But what *is* our connection with the Elder Gods?' asked the Mouser, eagerly, though not hopefully. Fafhrd grunted derisively.

'Those are matters best not spoken of,' Ningauble ordained. 'Was there anyone who showed a particular interest in Fafhrd's laughter?'

The Mouser hesitated. Fafhrd coughed. Thus prodded, the Mouser confessed, 'Oh, there was a girl who was perhaps a trifle more attentive than the others to his bellowing. A Persian girl. In fact, as I recall, the same one who gave Chloe the amulet.'

'Her name is Ahura,' said Fafhrd. 'The Mouser's in love with her.'

'A fable!' the Mouser denied laughingly, double-daggering Fafhrd with a superstitious glare. 'I can assure you, Father, that she is a very shy, stupid girl, who cannot possibly be concerned in any way with our troubles.'

'Of course, since you say so,' Ningauble observed, his voice icily rebuking. 'However, I can tell you this much: the one who has placed the ignominious spell upon you is, insofar as he partakes of humanity, a man . . .'

(The Mouser was relieved. It was unpleasant to think of dark-haired, lithe Ahura being subjected to certain methods of questioning which Ningauble was reputed to employ. He was irked at his own clumsiness in trying to lead Ningauble's attention away from Ahura. Where she was concerned, his wit failed him.)

' . . . and an adept,' Ningauble concluded. 'Yes, my sons, an adept – a master practitioner of blackest magic without faintest blink of light.'

The Mouser started. Fafhrd groaned, 'Again?'

'Again,' Ningauble affirmed. 'Though why, save for your connection with the Elder Gods, you should interest those most recondite of creatures, I cannot guess. They are not men who wittingly will stand in the glaringly illuminated foreground of history. They seek—'

'But who is it?' Fafhrd interjected.

'Be quiet, Mutilator of Rhetoric. They seek the shadows, and surely for good reason. They are the glorious amateurs of high magic, disdaining practical ends, caring only for the satisfaction of their insatiable curiosities, and therefore doubly dangerous. They are . . .'

'But what's his name?'

'Silence, Trampler of Beautiful Phrases. They are in their fashion fearless, irreligiously considering themselves the co-equals of destiny and having only contempt for the Demigoddess of Chance, the Imp of Luck, and the Demon of Improbability.

In short, they are adversaries before whom you should certainly tremble and to whose will you should unquestionably bow.'

'But his name, Father, his name!' Fafhrd burst out, and the Mouser, his impudence again in the ascendant, remarked, 'It is he of the Sabihoon, is it not, Father?'

'It is not. The Sabihoon are an ignorant fisher folk who inhabit the hither shore of the far lake and worship the beast god Wheen, denying all others,' a reply that tickled the Mouser, for to the best of his knowledge he had just invented the Sabihoon.

'No, his name is . . .' Ningauble paused and began to chuckle. 'I was forgetting that I must under no circumstances tell you his name.'

Fafhrd jumped up angrily. 'What?'

'Yes, children,' said Ningauble, suddenly making his eyestalks staringly rigid, stern and uncompromising. 'And I must furthermore tell you that I can in no way help you in this matter . . .' (Fafhrd clenched his fists) ' . . . and I am very glad of it too . . .' (Fafhrd swore) ' . . . for it seems to me that no more fitting punishment could have been devised for your abominable lecheries, which I have so often bemoaned . . .' (Fafhrd's hand went to his sword hilt) ' . . . in fact, if it had been up to me to chastise you for your manifold vices, I would have chosen the very same enchantment . . .' (But now he had gone too far; Fafhrd growled, 'Oh, so it is you who are behind it!' ripped out his sword and began to advance slowly on the hooded figure) ' . . . Yes, my children, you must accept your lot without rebellion or bitterness . . .' (Fafhrd continued to advance) ' . . . Far better that you should retire from the world as I have and give yourselves to meditation and repentance . . .' (The sword, flickering with firelight, was only a yard away) ' . . . Far better that you should live out the rest of this incarnation in solitude, each surrounded by his faithful band of sows or snails . . .' (The sword touched the ragged robe) ' . . . devoting your remaining years to the promotion of a better understanding between mankind and the lower animals. However—' (Ningauble sighed and the sword hesitated) ' . . . if it is still your firm and foolhardy intention to challenge this adept, I suppose I must aid you with what little advice I can give, though warning you that it will plunge you into maelstroms of trouble and lay upon you geases you will grow gray in fulfilling, and incidentally be the means of your deaths.'

Fafhrd lowered his sword. The silence in the black cave grew heavy and ominous. Then, in a voice that was distant yet resonant, like the sound that came from the statue of Memnon at Thebes when the first rays of the morning sun fell upon it, Ningauble began to speak.

'It comes to me, confusedly, like a scene in a rusted mirror; nevertheless, it comes, and thus: You must first possess yourselves of certain trifles. The shroud of Ahriman, from the secret shrine near Persepolis—'

'But what about the accursed swordsmen of Ahriman, Father?' put in the Mouser. 'There are twelve of them. Twelve, Father, and all very accursed and hard to persuade.'

'Do you think I am setting toss-and-fetch problems for puppy dogs?' wheezed Ningauble angrily. 'To proceed: You must secondly obtain powdered mummy from the Demon Pharaoh, who reigned for three horrid and unhistoried midnights after the death of Ikhnaton—'

'But, Father,' Fafhrd protested, blushing a little, 'you know who owns that powdered mummy, and what she demands of any two men who visit her.'

'Shh! I'm your elder, Fafhrd, by eons. Thirdly, you must get the cup from which Socrates drank the hemlock; fourthly, a sprig from the original Tree of Life, and lastly . . .' He hesitated as if his memory had failed him, dipped up a potsherd from the pile, and read from it: 'And lastly, you must procure the woman who will come when she is ready.'

'What woman?'

'The woman who will come when she is ready.' Ningauble tossed back the fragment, starting a small landslide of shards.

'Corrode Loki's bones!' cursed Fafhrd, and the Mouser said, 'But, Father, no woman comes when she's ready. She always waits.'

Ningauble sighed merrily and said, 'Do not be downcast,

508

children. Is it ever the custom of your good friend the Gossiper to give simple advice?'

'It is not,' said Fafhrd.

'Well, having all these things, you must go to the Lost City of Ahriman that lies east of Armenia – whisper not its name—'

'Is it Khatti?' whispered the Mouser.

'No, Blowfly. And furthermore, why are you interrupting me when you are supposed to be hard at work recalling all the details of the scandal of the Friday concubine, the three eunuch priests, and the slave girl from Samos?'

'Oh truly, Spy of the Unmentionable, I labor at that until my mind becomes a weariness and a wandering, and all for love of you.' The Mouser was glad of Ningauble's question, for he had forgotten the three eunuch priests, which would have been most unwise, as no one in his senses sought to cheat the Gossiper of even a pinch of misinformation promised.

Ningauble continued, 'Arriving at the Lost City, you must seek out the ruined black shrine, and place the woman before the great tomb, and wrap the shroud of Ahriman around her, and let her drink the powdered mummy from the hemlock cup, diluting it with a wine you will find where you find the mummy, and place in her hand the sprig from the Tree of Life, and wait for the dawn.'

'And then?' rumbled Fafhrd.

'And then the mirror becomes all red with rust. I can see no further, except that someone will return from a place which it is unlawful to leave, and that you must be wary of the woman.'

'But, Father, all this scavenging of magical trumpery is a great bother,' Fafhrd objected. 'Why shouldn't we go at once to the Lost City?'

'Without the map on the shroud of Ahriman?' murmured Ningauble.

'And you still can't tell us the name of the adept we seek?' the Mouser ventured. 'Or even the name of the woman? Puppy dog problems indeed! We give you a bitch, Father, and by the time you return her, she's dropped a litter.'

Ningauble shook his head ever so slightly, the six eyes

retreated under the hood to become an ominous multiple gleam, and the Mouser felt a shiver crawl on his spine.

'Why is it, Riddle-Vendor, that you always give us half knowledge?' Fafhrd pressed angrily. 'Is it that at the last moment our blades may strike with half force?'

Ningauble chuckled.

'It is because I know you too well, children. If I said one word more, Hulk, you could be cleaving with your great sword – at the wrong person. And your cat-comrade would be brewing his child's magic – the wrong child's magic. It is no simple creature you foolhardily seek, but a mystery, no single identity but a mirage, a stony thing that has stolen the blood and substance of life, a nightmare crept out of dream.'

For a moment it was as if, in the far reaches of that nighted cavern, something that waited stirred. Then it was gone.

Ningauble purred complacently, 'And now I have an idle moment, which, to please you, I will pass in giving ear to the story that the Mouser has been impatiently waiting to tell me.'

So, there being no escape, the Mouser began, first explaining that only the surface of the story had to do with the concubine, the three priests, and the slave girl; the deeper portion touching mostly, though not entirely, on four infamous hand-maidens of Ishtar and a dwarf who was richly compensated for his deformity. The fire grew low and a little, lemurlike creature came edging in to replenish it, and the hours stretched on, for the Mouser always warmed to his own tales. There came a place where Fafhrd's eyes bugged with astonishment, and another where Ningauble's paunch shook like a small mountain in earthquake, but eventually the tale came to an end, suddenly and seemingly in the middle, like a piece of foreign music.

Then farewells were said and final questions refused answer, and the two seekers started back the way they had come. And Ningauble began to sort in his mind the details of the Mouser's story, treasuring it the more because he knew it was an improvisation, his favorite proverb being, 'He who lies artistically, treads closer to the truth than ever he knows.'

Fafhrd and the Mouser had almost reached the bottom of the boulder stair when they heard a faint tapping and turned to see

Ningauble peering down from the verge, supporting himself with what looked like a cane and rapping with another.

'Children,' he called, and his voice was tiny as the note of the lone flute in the Temple of Baal, 'it comes to me that something in the distant spaces lusts for something in you. You must guard closely what commonly needs no guarding.'

'Yes, Godfather of Mystification.'

'You will take care?' came the elfin note. 'Your beings depend on it.'

'Yes, Father.'

And Ningauble waved once and hobbled out of sight. The little creatures of his great darkness followed him, but whether to report and receive orders or only to pleasure him with their gentle antics, no man could be sure. Some said that Ningauble had been created by the Elder Gods for men to guess about and so sharpen their imaginations for even tougher riddles. None knew whether he had the gift of foresight, or whether he merely set the stage for future events with such a bewildering cunning that only an efreet or an adept could evade acting the part given him.

3. *The Woman Who Came*

After Fafhrd and the Gray Mouser emerged from the Bottomless Caves into the blinding upper sunlight, their trail for a space becomes dim. Material relating to them has, on the whole, been scanted by annalists, since they were heroes too disreputable for classic myth, too cryptically independent ever to let themselves be tied to a folk, too shifty and improbable in their adventurings to please the historian, too often involved with a riffraff of dubious demons, unfrocked sorcerors, and discredited deities – a veritable underworld of the supernatural. And it becomes doubly difficult to piece together their actions during a period when they were engaged in thefts requiring stealth, secrecy, and bold misdirection. Occasionally, however, one comes across the marks they left upon the year.

For instance, a century later the priests of Ahriman were

chanting, although they were too intelligent to believe it themselves, the miracle of Ahriman's snatching of his own hallowed shroud. One night the twelve accursed swordsmen saw the blackly scribbled shroud rise like a pillar of cobwebs from the altar, rise higher than mortal man, although the form within seemed anthropoid. Then Ahriman spoke from the shroud, and they worshiped him, and he replied with obscure parables and finally strode giantlike from the secret shrine.

The shrewdest of the century-later priests remarked, 'I'd say a man on stilts, or else –' (happy surmise!) '– one man on the shoulders of another.'

Then there were things that Nikri, body slave to the infamous False Laodice, told the cook while she anointed the bruises of her latest beating. Things concerning two strangers who visited her mistress, and the carousal her mistress proposed to them, and how they escaped the black eunuch scimitarmen she had set to slay them when the carousal was done.

'They were magicians, both of them,' Nikri averred, for at the peak of the doings they transformed my lady into a hideous, wiggly-horned sow, a horrid chimera of snail and swine. But that wasn't the worst, for they stole her chest of aphrodisiac wines. When she discovered that the demon mummy was gone with which she'd hoped to stir the lusts of Ptolemy, she screamed in rage and took her back-scratcher to me. Ow, but that hurts!'

The cook chuckled.

But as to who visited Hieronymus, the greedy tax farmer and connoisseur of Antioch, or in what guise, we cannot be sure. One morning he was found in his treasure room with his limbs stiff and chill, as if from hemlock, and there was a look of terror on his fat face, and the famous cup from which he had often caroused was missing, although there were circular stains on the table before him. He recovered, but would never tell what had happened.

The priests who tended the Tree of Life in Babylon were a little more communicative. One evening just after sunset they saw the topmost branches shake in the gloaming and heard the snick of a pruning knife. All around them, without other sound or movement, stretched the desolate city, from which the inhabitants had been herded to nearby Seleucia three quarters of a century before and to which the priests crept back only in a great fear to fulfill their sacred duties. They instantly prepared, some of them to climb the Tree armed with tempered golden sickles, others to shoot down with gold-tipped arrows whatever blasphemer was driven forth, when suddenly a large gray batlike shape swooped from the Tree and vanished behind a jagged wall. Of course, it might conceivably have been a gray-cloaked man swinging on a thin, tough, rope, but there were too many things whispered about the creatures that flapped by night through the ruins of Babylon for the priests to dare pursuit.

Finally Fafhrd and the Gray Mouser reappeared in Tyre, and a week later they were ready to depart on the ultimate stage of their quest. Indeed, they were already outside the gates, lingering at the landward end of Alexander's mole, spine of an ever-growing isthmus. Gazing at it, Fafhrd remembered how once an unintroduced stranger had told him a tale about two fabulous adventurers who had aided mightily in the foredoomed defense of Tyre against Alexander the Great more than a hundred years ago. The larger had heaved heavy stone blocks on the attacking ships, the smaller had dove to file through the chains with which they were anchored. Their names, the stranger had said, were Fafhrd and the Gray Mouser. Fafhrd had made no comment.

It was near evening, a good time to pause in adventurings, to recall past escapades, to hazard misty, wild, rosy speculations concerning what lay ahead.

'I think any woman would do,' insisted the Mouser bickering. 'Ningauble was just trying to be obscure. Let's take Chloe.'

'If only she'll come when she's ready,' said Fafhrd, half smiling.

The sun was dipping ruddy-golden into the rippling sea. The merchants who had pitched shop on the landward side in order to get first crack at the farmers and inland traders on market day were packing up wares and taking down canopies.

'Any woman will eventually come when she's ready, even Chloe,' retorted the Mouser. 'We'd only have to take along a silk tent for her and a few pretty conveniences. No trouble at all.'

'Yes,' said Fafhrd. 'We could probably manage it without more than one elephant.'

Most of Tyre was darkly silhouetted against the sunset, although there were gleams from the roofs here and there, and the gilded peak of the Temple of Melkarth sent a little water-borne glitter track angling in toward the greater one of the sun. The fading Phoenician port seemed entranced, dreaming of past glories, only half listening to today's news of Rome's implacable eastward advance, and Philip of Macedon's loss of the first round at the Battle of the Dogs' Heads, and now Antiochus preparing for the second, with Hannibal come to help him from Tyre's great fallen sister Carthage across the sea.

'I'm sure Chloe will come if we wait until tomorrow,' the Mouser continued. 'We'll have to wait in any case, because Ningauble said the woman wouldn't come until she was ready.'

A cool little wind came out of the wasteland that was Old Tyre. The merchants hurried; a few of them were already going home along the mole, their slaves looking like hunch-backs and otherwise misshapen monsters because of the packs on their shoulders and heads.

'No,' said Fafhrd, 'we'll start. And if the woman doesn't come when she's ready, then she isn't the woman who will come when she's ready, or if she is, she'll have to hump herself to catch up.'

The three horses of the adventurers moved restlessly and the Mouser's whinnied. Only the great camel, on which were slung the wine-sacks, various small chests, and snugly-wrapped weapons, stood sullenly still. Fafhrd and the Mouser casually watched the one figure on the mole that moved against the homing stream; they were not exactly suspicious, but after the year's doings they could not overlook the possibility of death-dealing pursuers, taking the form either of accursed swordsmen, black eunuch scimitarmen, gold-weaponed Babylonian priests, or such agents as Hieronymus of Antioch might favor.

'Chloe would have come on time, if only you'd helped me persuade her,' argued the Mouser. 'She likes you, and I'm sure she must have been the one Ningauble meant, because she has that amulet which works against the adept.'

The sun was a blinding sliver on the sea's rim, then went under. All the little glares and glitters on the roofs of Tyre winked out. The Temple of Melkarth loomed black against the fading sky. The last canopy was being taken down and most of the merchants were more than halfway across the mole. There was still only one figure moving shoreward.

'Weren't seven nights with Chloe enough for you?' asked Fafhrd. 'Besides, it isn't she you'll be wanting when we kill the adept and get this spell off us.'

'That's as it may be,' retorted the Mouser. 'But remember we have to catch our adept first. And it's not only I whom Chloe's company could benefit.'

A faint shout drew their attention across the darkling water to where a lateen-rigged trader was edging into the Egyptian Harbor. For a moment they thought the landward end of the mole had been emptied. Then the figure moving away from the city came out sharp and black against the sea, a slight figure, not burdened like the slaves.

'Another fool leaves sweet Tyre at the wrong time,' observed the Mouser. 'Just think what a woman will mean in those cold mountains we're going to, Fafhrd, a woman to prepare dainties and stroke your forehead.'

Fafhrd said, 'It isn't your forehead, little man, you're thinking of.'

The cool wind came again and the packed sand moaned at its passing. Tyre seemed to crouch like a beast against the threats of darkness. A last merchant searched the ground hurriedly for some lost article.

Fafhrd put his hand on his horse's shoulder and said, 'Come on.'

The Mouser made a last point. 'I don't think Chloe would insist on taking the slave girl to oil her feet, that is, if we handled it properly.'

Then they saw that the other fool leaving sweet Tyre was coming toward them, and that it was a woman, tall and slender, dressed in stuffs that seemed to melt into the waning light, so that Fafhrd found himself wondering whether she truly came from Tyre or from some aerial realm whose inhabitants may venture to earth only at sunset. Then, as she continued to approach at an easy, swinging stride, they saw that her face was fair and that her hair was raven; and the Mouser's heart gave a great leap and he felt that this was the perfect consummation of their waiting, that he was witnessing the birth of an Aphrodite, not from the foam but the dusk; for it was indeed his dark-haired Ahura of the wine shops, no longer staring with cold, shy curiosity, but eagerly smiling.

Fafhrd, not altogether untouched by similar feelings, said slowly, 'So you are the woman who came when she was ready?'

'Yes,' added the Mouser gaily, 'and did you know that in a minute more you'd have been too late?'

4. *The Lost City*

During the next week, one of steady northward journeying along the fringe of the desert, they learned little more of the motives or history of their mysterious companion than the dubious scraps of information Chloe had provided. When asked why she had come, Ahura replied that Ningauble had sent her, that Ningauble had nothing to do with it and that it was all an accident, that certain dead Elder Gods had dreamed her a vision, that she sought a brother lost in a search for the Lost City of Ahriman; and often her only answer was silence, a silence that seemed sometimes sly and sometimes mystical. However, she stood up well to hardship, proved a tireless rider, and did not complain at sleeping on the ground with only a large cloak snuggled around her. Like some especially sensitive migratory bird, she seemed possessed of an even greater urge than their own to get on with the journey.

Whenever opportunity offered, the Mouser paid assiduous court to her, limited only by the fear of working a snail-change. But after a few days of this tantalizing pleasure, he noticed that Fafhrd was vying for it. Very swiftly the two comrades became rivals, contesting as to who should be the first to offer Ahura assistance on those rare occasions when she needed it, striving to top each other's brazenly boastful accounts of incredible adventures, constantly on the alert lest the other steal a moment alone. Such a spate of gallantry had never before been known on their adventurings. They remained good friends – and they were aware of that – but very surly friends – and they were aware of that too. And Ahura's shy, or sly, silence encouraged them both.

They forded the Euphrates south of the ruins of Carchemish, and struck out for the headwaters of the Tigris, intersecting but swinging east away from the route of Xenophon and the Ten Thousand. It was then that their surliness came to a head. Ahura had roamed off a little, letting her horse crop the dry herbage, while the two sat on a boulder, and expostulated in whispers, Fafhrd proposing that they both agree to cease paying court to the girl until their quest was over, the Mouser doggedly advancing his prior claim. Their whispers became so heated that they did not notice a white pigeon swooping toward them until it landed with a downward beat of wings on an arm Fafhrd had flung wide to emphasize his willingness to renounce the girl temporarily – if only the Mouser would.

Fafhrd blinked, then detached a scrap of parchment from the pigeon's leg, and read, 'There is danger in the girl. You must both forgo her.'

The tiny seal was an impression of seven tangled eyes.

'Just *seven* eyes!' remarked the Mouser. 'Pah, he is modest!' And for a moment he was silent, trying to picture the gigantic web of unknown strands by which the Gossiper gathered his information and conducted his business.

But this unsuspected seconding of Fafhrd's argument finally won from him a sulky consent, and they solemnly pledged not to lay hand on the girl, or each in any way to further his cause, until they had found and dealt with the adept.

They were now in townless land that caravans avoided, a land like Xenophon's, full of chill misty mornings, dazzling noons, and treacherous twilights, with hints of shy, murderous, mountain-dwelling tribes recalling the omnipresent legends of 'little people' as unlike men as cats are unlike dogs. Ahura

517

seemed unaware of the sudden cessation of the attentions paid her, remaining as provocatively shy and indefinite as ever.

The Mouser's attitude toward Ahura, however, began to undergo a gradual but profound change. Whether it was the souring of his inhibited passion, or the shrewder insight of a mind no longer a-bubble with the fashioning of compliments and witticisms, he began to feel more and more that the Ahura he loved was only a faint spark almost lost in the darkness of a stranger who daily became more riddlesome, dubious, and even, in the end, repellent. He remembered the other name Chloe had given Ahura, and found himself brooding oddly over the legend of Hermaphroditus bathing in the Carian fountain and becoming joined in one body with the nymph Salmacis. Now when he looked at Ahura he could see only avid eyes that peered secretly at the world through a crevice. He began to think of her chuckling soundlessly at night at the mortifying spell that had been laid upon himself and Fafhrd. He became obsessed with Ahura in a very different way, and took to spying on her and studying her expression when she was not looking, as if hoping in that way to penetrate her mystery.

Fafhrd noticed it and instantly suspected that the Mouser was contemplating going back on his pledge. He restrained his indignation with difficulty and took to watching the Mouser as closely as the Mouser watched Ahura. No longer when it became necessary to procure provisions was either willing to hunt alone. The easy amicability of their friendship deteriorated. Then, late one afternoon while they were traversing a shadowy ravine east of Armenia, a hawk dove suddenly and sank its talons in Fafhrd's shoulder. The Northerner killed the creature in a flurry of reddish feathers before he noticed that it too carried a message.

'Watch out for the Mouser,' was all it said, but coupled with the smart of the talon-pricks, that was quite enough for Fafhrd. Drawing up beside the Mouser while Ahura's horse pranced skittishly away from the disturbance, he told the Mouser his full suspicions and warned him that any violation of their agreement would at once end their friendship and bring them into deadly collision.

518

The Mouser listened like a man in a dream, still moodily watching Ahura. He would have liked to have told Fafhrd his real motives, but was doubtful whether he could make them intelligible. Moreover, he was piqued at being misjudged. So when Fafhrd's direful outburst was finished he made no comment. Fafhrd interpreted this as an admission of guilt and cantered on in a rage.

They were now nearing that rugged vantage-land from which the Medes and the Persians had swooped down on Assyria and Chaldea, and where, if they could believe Ningauble's geography, they would find the forgotten lair of the Lord of Eternal Evil. At first the archaic map on the shroud of Ahriman proved more maddening than helpful, but after a while, clarified in part by a curiously erudite suggestion of Ahura, it began to make disturbing sense, showing them a deep gorge where the foregoing terrain led one to expect a saddle-backed crest, and a valley where there ought to have been a mountain. If the map held true, they would reach the Lost City in a very few days.

All the while, the Mouser's obsession deepened, and at last took definite and startling form. He believed that Ahura was a man.

It was very strange that the intimacy of camp life and the Mouser's own zealous spying should not long ago have turned up concrete proof or disproof of this clear-cut supposition. Nevertheless, as the Mouser wonderingly realized on reviewing events, they had not. Granted, Ahura's form and movements, all her least little actions were those of a woman, but he recalled painted and padded minions, sweet not simpering, who had aped femininity almost as well. Preposterous – but there it was. From that moment his obsessive curiosity became a compulsive sweat and he redoubled his moody peering, much to the anger of Fafhrd, who took to slapping his sword hilt at unexpected intervals, though without ever startling the Mouser into looking away. Each in his way stayed as surly sullen as the camel that displayed a more and more dour balkiness at this preposterous excursion from the healthy desert.

Those were nightmare days for the Gray One, as they advanced ever closer through gloomy gorges and over craggy crests toward Ahriman's primeval shrine. Fafhrd seemed an ominous, white-faced giant reminding him of someone he had known in waking life, and their whole quest a blind treading of the more subterranean routes of dream. He still wanted to tell the giant his suspicions, but could not bring himself to it, because of their monstrousness and because the giant loved Ahura. And all the while Ahura eluded him, a phantom fluttering just beyond reach; though, when he forced his mind to make the comparison, he realized that her behaviour had in no way altered, except for an intensification of the urge to press onward, like a vessel nearing its home port.

Finally there came a night when he could bear his torturing curiosity no longer. He writhed from under a mountain of oppressive unremembered dreams and, propped on an elbow, looked around him, quiet as the creature for which he was named.

It would have been cold if it had not been so still. The fire had burned to embers. It was rather the moonlight that showed him Fafhrd's tousled head and elbow outthrust from shaggy bearskin cloak. And it was the moonlight that struck full on Ahura stretched beyond the embers, her lidded, tranquil face fixed on the zenith, seeming hardly to breathe.

He waited a long time. Then, without making a sound, he laid back his gray cloak, picked up his sword, went around the fire, and kneeled beside her. Then, for another space, he dispassionately scrutinized her face. But it remained the hermaphroditic mask that had tormented his waking hours – if he were still sure of the distinction between waking and dream. Suddenly his hands grasped at her – and as abruptly checked. Again he stayed motionless for a long time. Then, with movements as deliberate and rehearsed-seeming as a sleep-walker's, but more silent, he drew back her woollen cloak, took a small knife from his pouch, lifted her gown at the neck, careful not to touch her skin, slit it to her knee, treating her chiton the same.

The breasts, white as ivory, that he had known would not be there, were there. And yet, instead of his nightmare lifting, it deepened.

It was something too profound for surprise, this wholly

unexpected further insight. For as he knelt there, somberly studying, he knew for a certainty that this ivory flesh too was a mask, as cunningly fashioned as the face and for as frighteningly incomprehensible a purpose.

The ivory eyelids did not flicker, but the edges of the teeth showed in what he fancied was a deliberate, flickery smile.

He was never more certain than at this moment that Ahura was a man.

The embers crunched behind him.

Turning, the Mouser saw only the streak of gleaming steel poised above Fafhrd's head, motionless for a moment, as if with superhuman forbearance a god should give his creature a chance before loosing the thunderbolt.

The Mouser ripped out his own slim sword in time to ward the titan blow. From hilt to point, the two blades screamed.

And in answer to the scream, melting into, continuing, and augmenting it, there came from the absolute calm of the west a gargantuan gust of wind that sent the Mouser staggering forward and Fafhrd reeling back, and rolled Ahura across the place where the embers had been.

Almost as suddenly the gale died. As it died, something whipped batlike toward the Mouser's face and he grabbed at it. But it was not a bat, or even a large leaf. It felt like papyrus.

The embers, blown into a clump of dry grass, had perversely started a blaze. To its flaring light he held the thin scrap that had fluttered out of the infinite west.

He motioned frantically to Fafhrd, who was clawing his way out of a scrub pine.

There was squid-black writing on the scrap, in large characters, above the tangled seal.

'By whatever gods you revere, give up this quarrel. Press onward at once. Follow the woman.'

They became aware that Ahura was peering over their abutting shoulders. The moon came gleamingly from behind the small black tatter of cloud that had briefly obscured it. She looked at them, pulled together chiton and gown, belted them with her cloak. They collected their horses, extricated the fallen camel from the cluster of thorn bushes in which it was satisfiedly tormenting itself, and set out.

After that the Lost City was found almost too quickly; it seemed like a trap or the work of an illusionist. One moment Ahura was pointing out to them a boulder-studded crag; the next, they were looking down a narrow valley choked with crazily-leaning, moonsilvered monoliths and their accomplice shadows.

From the first it was obvious that 'city' was a misnomer. Surely men had never dwelt in those massive stone tents and huts, though they may have worshiped there. It was a habitation for Egyptian colossi, for stone automata. But Fafhrd and the Mouser had little time to survey its entirety, for without warning Ahura sent her horse clattering and sliding down the slope.

Thereafter it was a harebrained, drunken gallop, their horses plunging shadows, the camel a lurching ghost, through forests of crude-hewn pillars, past teetering single slabs big enough for palace walls, under lintels for elephants, always following the elusive hoofbeat, never catching it, until they suddenly emerged into clear moonlight and drew up in an open space between a great sarcophagus-like block or box with steps leading up to it, and a huge, crudely man-shaped monolith.

But they had hardly begun to puzzle out the things around them before they became aware that Ahura was gesturing impatiently. They recalled Ningauble's instructions, and realized that it was almost dawn. So they unloaded various bundles and boxes from the shivering, snapping camel, and Fafhrd unfolded the dark, cobwebby shroud of Ahriman and wrapped it around Ahura as she stood wordlessly facing the tomb, her face a marble portrait of eagerness, as if she sprang from the stone around her.

While Fafhrd busied himself with other things, the Mouser opened the ebony chest they had stolen from the False Laodice. A fey mood came upon him and, dancing cumbrously in imitation of a eunuch serving man, he tastefully arrayed a flat stone with all the little jugs and jars and tiny amphorae that the chest contained. And in an appropriate falsetto he sang:

'I laid a board for the Great Seleuce,
I decked it pretty and abstruse;
And he must have been pleased,
For when stuffed, he wheezed,
"As punishment castrate the man."

'You thee, Fafhwd,' he lisped, 'the man had been cathtwated ath a boy, and tho it wath no punithment at all. Becauthe of pweviouth cathwathion—'

'I'll castrate your wit-engorged top end,' Fafhrd cried, raising the next implement of magic, but thought better of it.

Then Fafhrd handed him Socrates' cup and, still prancing and piping, the Mouser measured into it the mummy powder and added the wine and stirred them together and, dancing fantastically toward Ahura, offered it to her. When she made no movement, he held it to her lips and she greedily gulped it without taking her eyes from the tomb.

Then Fafhrd came with the sprig from the Babylonian Tree of Life, which still felt marvelously fresh and firm-leafed to his touch, as if the Mouser had only snipped it a moment ago. And he gently pried open her clenched fingers and placed the sprig inside them and folded them again.

Thus ready, they waited. The sky reddened at the edge and seemed for a moment to grow darker, the stars fading and the moon turning dull. The outspread aphrodisiacs chilled, refusing the night breeze their savor. And the woman continued to watch the tomb, and behind her, seeming to watch the tomb too, as if it were her fantastic shadow, loomed the man-shaped monolith, which the Mouser now and then scrutinized uneasily over his shoulder; being unable to tell whether it were of primevally crude workmanship or something that men had laboriously defaced because of its evil.

The sky paled until the Mouser could begin to make out some monstrous carvings on the side of the sarcophagus – of men like stone pillars and animals like mountains – and until Fafhrd could see the green of the leaves in Ahura's hand.

Then he saw something astounding. In an instant the leaves withered and the sprig became a curled and blackened stick. In the same instant Ahura trembled and grew paler still, snow pale, and to the Mouser it seemed that there was a tenuous black cloud forming around her head, that the riddlesome stranger he hated was pouring upward like a smoky jinni from her body, the bottle.

The thick stone cover of the sarcophagus groaned and began to rise.

Ahura began to move toward the sarcophagus. To the Mouser it seemed that the cloud was drawing her along like a black sail.

The cover was moving more swiftly, as if it were the upper jaw of a stone crocodile. The black cloud seemed to the Mouser to strain triumphantly toward the widening slit, dragging the white wisp behind it. The cover opened wide. Ahura reached the top and then either peered down inside or, as the Mouser saw it, was almost sucked in along with the black cloud. She shook violently. Then her body collapsed like an empty dress.

Fafhrd gritted his teeth, a joint cracked in the Mouser's wrist. The hilts of their swords, unconsciously drawn, bruised their palms.

Then, like an idler from a day of bowered rest, an Indian prince from the tedium of the court, a philosopher from quizzical discourse, a slim figure rose from the tomb. His limbs were clad in black, his body in silver metal, his hair and beard raven and silky. But what first claimed the sight, like an ensign on a masked man's shield, was a chatoyant quality of his youthful olive skin, a silvery gleaming that turned one's thoughts to fishes' bellies and leprosy – that, and a certain familiarity.

For the face of this black and silver stranger bore an unmistakable resemblance to Ahura.

5. *Anra Devadoris*

Resting his long hands on the edge of the tomb, the newcomer surveyed them pleasantly and nodded as if they were intimates. Then he vaulted lightly over and came striding down the steps, treading on the shroud of Ahriman without so much as a glance at Ahura.

He eyed their swords. 'You anticipate danger?' he asked, politely stroking the beard which, it seemed to the Mouser, could never have grown so bushily silky except in a tomb.

'You are an adept?' Fafhrd retorted, stumbling over the words a little.

The stranger disregarded the question and stooped to study amusedly the zany array of aphrodisiacs.

'Dear Ningauble,' he murmured, 'is surely the father of all seven-eyed Lechers. I suppose you know him well enough to guess that he had you fetch these toys because he wants them for himself. Even in his duel with me, he cannot resist the temptation of a profit on the side. But perhaps this time the old pander had curtsied to destiny unwittingly. At least, let us hope so.'

And with that he unbuckled his sword belt and carelessly laid it by, along with the wondrously slim, silver-hilted sword.

The Mouser shrugged and sheathed his own weapon, but Fafhrd only grunted.

'I do not like you,' he said. 'Are you the one who put the swine-curse on us?'

The stranger regarded him quizzically.

'You are looking for a cause,' he said. 'You wish to know the name of an agent you feel has injured you. You plan to unleash your rage as soon as you know. But behind every cause is another cause, and behind the last agent is yet another agent. An immortal could not slay a fraction of them. Believe me, who have followed that trail further than most and who have had some experience of the special obstacles that are placed in the way of one who seeks to live beyond the confines of his skull and the meager present – the traps that are set for him, the titanic enmities he awakens. I beseech you to wait a while before warring, as I shall wait before answering your second question. That I am an adept I freely admit.'

At this last statement the Mouser felt another light-headed impulse to behave fantastically, this time in mimicry of a magician. Here was the rare creature on whom he could test the rune against adepts in his pouch! He wanted to hum a death spell between his teeth, to flap his arms in an incantational gesture, to spit at the adept and spin widder-shins on his left heel thrice. But he too chose to wait.

'There is always a simple way of saying things,' said Fafhrd ominously.

'But there is where I differ with you,' returned the adept, almost animatedly. 'There are no ways of saying certain things, and others are so difficult that a man pines and dies before the right words are found. One must borrow phrases from the sky, words from beyond the stars. Else were all an ignorant, imprisoning mockery.'

The Mouser stared at the adept, suddenly conscious of a monstrous incongruity about him – as if one should glimpse a hint of double-dealing in the curl of Solon's lips, or cowardice in the eyes of Alexander, or imbecility in the face of Aristotle. For although the adept was obviously erudite, confident, and powerful, the Mouser could not help thinking of a child morbidly avid for experience, a timid, painfully curious small boy. And the Mouser had the further bewildering feeling that this was the secret for which he had spied so long on Ahura.

Fafhrd's sword-arm bulged and he seemed about to make an even pithier rejoinder. But instead he sheathed his sword, walked over to the woman, held his fingers to her wrists for a moment, then tucked his bearskin cloak around her.

'Her ghost has gone only a little way,' he said. 'It will soon return. What did you do to her, you black and silver popinjay?'

'What matters what I've done to her or you, or me?' retorted the adept, almost peevishly. 'You are here, and I have business with you.' He paused. 'This, in brief, is my proposal: that I make you adepts like myself, sharing with you all knowledge of which your minds are capable, on condition only that you continue to submit to such spells as I have put upon you and may put upon you in future, to further our knowledge. What do you say to that?'

'Wait, Fafhrd!' implored the Mouser, grabbing his comrade's arm. 'Don't strike yet. Let's look at the statue from all sides. Why, magnanimous magician, have you chosen to make this offer to us, and why have you brought us out here to make it, instead of getting your yes or no in Tyre?'

'An adept,' roared Fafhrd, dragging the Mouser along. 'Offers to make me an adept! And for that I should go on kissing swine! Go spit down Fenris' throat!'

'As to why I have brought you here,' said the adept coolly, 'there are certain limitations on my powers of movement, or at least on my powers of satisfactory communication. There is, moreover, a special reason, which I will reveal to you as soon as we have concluded our agreement – though I may tell you that, unknown to yourselves, you have already aided me.'

'But why pick on *us*? Why?' persisted the Mouser, bracing himself against Fafhrd's tugging.

'Some whys, if you follow them far enough, lead over the rim of reality,' replied the black and silver one. 'I have sought knowledge beyond the dreams of ordinary men; I have ventured far into the darkness that encircles minds and stars. But now, midmost of the pitchy windings of that fearsome labyrinth, I find myself suddenly at my skein's end. The tyrant powers who ignorantly guard the secret of the universe, without knowing what it is, have scented me. Those vile wardens, of whom Ningauble is the merest agent and even Ormadz a cloudy symbol, have laid their traps and built their barricades. And my best torches have snuffed out, or proved too flickery-feeble. I need new avenues of knowledge.'

He turned upon them eyes that seemed to be changing to twin holes in a curtain. 'There is something in the inmost core of you, something that you, or others before you, have close-guarded down the ages. Something that lets you laugh in a way that only the Elder Gods ever laughed. Something that makes you see a kind of jest in horror and disillusionment and death. There is much wisdom to be gained by the unraveling of that something.'

'Do you think us pretty woven scarves for your slick fingers to fray,' snarled Fafhrd. 'So you can piece out that rope you're at the end of, and climb all the way down to Niflheim?'

'Each adept must fray himself, before he may fray others,' the stranger intoned unsmilingly. 'You do not know the treasure you keep virgin and useless within you, or spill in senseless laughter. There is much richness in it, many complexities,

destiny-threads that lead beyond the sky to realms undreamt.'
His voice became swift and invoking.

'Have you no itch to understand, no urge for greater
adventuring than schoolboy rambles? I'll give you gods for
foes, stars for your treasure-trove, if only you will do as I command. All men will be your animals; the best, your hunting pack.
Kiss snails and swine? That's but an overture. Greater than Pan,
you'll frighten nations, rape the world. The universe will
tremble at your lust, but you will master it and force it down.
That ancient laughter will give you the might—'

'Filth-spewing pimp! Scabby-lipped pander! Cease!' bellowed
Fafhrd.

'Only submit to me and to my will,' the adept continued
rapturously, his lips working so that his black beard twitched
rhythmically. 'All things we'll twist and torture, know their
cause. The lechery of gods will pave the way we'll tramp
through windy darkness 'til we find the one who lurks in
senseless Odin's skull twitching the strings that move your lives
and mine. All knowledge will be ours, all for us three. Only give
up your wills, submit to me!'

For a moment the Mouser was hypnotized by the glint of
ghastly wonders. Then he felt Fafhrd's biceps, which had
slackened under his grasp – as if the Northerner were yielding
too – suddenly tighten, and from his own lips he heard words
projected coldly into the echoing silence.

'Do you think a rhyme is enough to win us over to your
nauseous titillations? Do you think we care a jot for your high-
flown muck-peering? Fafhrd, this slobberer offends me, past ills
that he has done us aside. It only remains to determine which
one of us disposes of him. I long to unravel him, beginning with
the ribs.'

'Do you not understand what I have offered you, the
magnitude of the boon? Have we no common ground?'

'Only to fight on. Call up your demons, sorcerer, or else look
to your weapon.'

An unearthly lust receded, rippling from the adept's eyes,
leaving behind only a deadliness. Fafhrd snatched up the cup of
Socrates and dropped it for a lot, swore as it rolled toward the

Mouser, whose cat-quick hand went softly to the hilt of the slim sword called Scalpel. Stooping, the adept groped blindly behind him and regained his belt and scabbard, drawing from it a blade that looked as delicate and responsive as a needle. He stood, a lank and icy indolence, in the red of the risen sun, the black anthropomorphic monolith looming behind him for his second.

The Mouser drew Scalpel silently from its sheath, ran a finger caressingly down the side of the blade, and in so doing noticed an inscription in black crayon which read, 'I do not approve of this step you are taking. Ningauble.' With a hiss of annoyance the Mouser wiped it off on his thigh and concentrated his gaze on the adept – so preoccupiedly that he did not observe the eyes of the fallen Ahura quiver open.

'And now, Dead Sorcerer,' said the Gray One lightly, 'my name is the Gray Mouser.'

'And mine is Anra Devadoris.'

Instantly the Mouser put into action his carefully weighed plan: to take two rapid skips forward and launch his blade-tipped body at the adept's sword, which was to be deflected, and at the adept's throat, which was to be sliced. He was already seeing the blood spurt when, in the middle of the second skip, he saw, whirring like an arrow toward his eyes, the adept's blade. With a belly-contorted effort he twisted to one side and parried blindly. The adept's blade whipped in greedily around Scalpel, but only far enough to snag and tear the skin at the side of the Mouser's neck. The Mouser recovered balance crouching, his guard wide open, and only a backward leap saved him from Anra Devadoris' second serpentlike strike. As he gathered himself to meet the next attack, he gaped amazedly, for never before in his life had he been faced by superior speed. Fafhrd's face was white. Ahura, however, her head raised a little from the furry cloak, smiled with a weak and incredulous but evil joy – a frankly vicious joy wholly unlike her former sly, intangible intimations of cruelty.

But Anra Devadoris smiled wider and nodded with a patronizing gratefulness at the Mouser, before gliding in. And now it was the blade Needle that darted in unhurried lightning attack, and Scalpel that whirred in frenzied defense.

529

The Mouser retreated in jerky, circling stages, his face sweaty, his throat hot, but his heart exulting, for never before had he fought this well – not even on that stifling morning when, his head in a sack, he had disposed of a whimsically cruel Egyptian kidnapper.

Inexplicably, he had the feeling that his days spent in spying on Ahura were now paying off.

Needle came slipping in and for the moment the Mouser could not tell upon which side of Scalpel it skirred and so sprang backward, but not swiftly enough to escape a prick in the side. He cut viciously at the adept's withdrawing arm – and barely managed to jerk his own arm out of the way of a stop thrust.

In a nasty voice so low that Fafhrd hardly heard her, and the Mouser heard not at all, Ahura called, 'The spiders tickled your flesh ever so lightly as they ran, Anra.'

Perhaps the adept hesitated almost imperceptibly, or perhaps it was only that his eyes grew a shade emptier. At all events, the Mouser was not given that opportunity, for which he was desperately searching, to initiate a counterattack and escape the deadly whirligig of his circling retreat. No matter how intently he peered, he could spy no gap in the sword-woven steel net his adversary was tirelessly casting toward him, nor could he discern in the face behind the net any betraying grimace, any flicker of eye hinting at the next point of attack, any flaring of nostrils or distension of lips telling of gasping fatigue similar to his own. It was inhuman, unalive, the mask of a machine built by some Daedalus, or of a leprously silver automaton stepped out of myth. And like a machine, Devadoris seemed to be gaining strength and speed from the very rhythm that was sapping his own.

The Mouser realized that he must interrupt that rhythm by a counterattack, any counterattack, or fall victim to a swiftness become blinding.

And then he further realized that the proper opportunity for that counterattack would never come, that he would wait in vain for any faltering in his adversary's attack, that he must risk everything on a guess.

His throat burned, his heart pounded on his ribs for air, a stinging, numbing poison seeped through his limbs.

Devadoris started a feint, or a deadly thrust, at his face.

Simultaneously, the Mouser heard Ahura jeer, 'They hung their webs on your beard and the worms knew your secret parts, Anra.'

He guessed – and cut at the adept's knee.

Either he guessed right, or else something halted the adept's deadly thrust.

The adept easily parried the Mouser's cut, but the rhythm was broken and his speed slackened.

Again he developed speed, again at the last possible moment the Mouser guessed. Again Ahura eerily jeered, 'The maggots made you a necklace, and each marching beetle paused to peer into your eye, Anra.'

Over and over it happened, speed, guess, macabre jeer, but each time the Mouser gained only momentary respite, never the opportunity to start an extended counterattack. His circling retreat continued so uninterruptedly that he felt as if he had been caught in a whirlpool. With each revolution, certain fixed landmarks swept into view: Fafhrd's blanched agonized face; the hulking tomb; Ahura's hate-contorted, mocking visage; the red stab of the risen sun; the gouged black, somber monolith, with its attendant stony soldiers and their gigantic stone tents; Fafhrd again . . .

And now the Mouser knew his strength was failing for good and all. Each guessed counterattack brought him less respite, was less of a check to the adept's speed. The landmarks whirled dizzily, darkened. It was as if he had been sucked to the maelstrom's center, as if the black cloud which he had fancied pouring from Ahura were enveloping him vampirously, choking off his breath.

He knew that he would be able to make only one more counter-cut, and must therefore stake all on a thrust at the heart.

He readied himself.

But he had waited too long. He could not gather the necessary strength, summon the speed.

He saw the adept preparing the lightning death-stroke.

His own thrust was like the gesture of a paralyzed man seeking to rise from his bed.

Then Ahura began to laugh.

It was a horrible, hysterical laugh; a giggling, snickering laugh; a laugh that made him dully wonder why she should find such joy in his death; and yet, for all the difference, a laugh that sounded like a shrill, distorted echo of Fafhrd's or his own.

Puzzledly, he noted that Needle had not yet transfixed him, that Devadoris' lightning thrust was slowing, slowing, as if the hateful laughter were falling in cumbering swathes around the adept, as if each horrid peal dropped a chain around his limbs.

The Mouser leaned on his own sword and collapsed, rather than lunged, forward.

He heard Fafhrd's shuddering sigh.

Then he realized that he was trying to pull Scalpel from the adept's chest and that it was an almost insuperably difficult task, although the blade had gone in as easily as if Anra Devadoris had been a hollow man. Again he tugged, and Scalpel came clear, fell from his nerveless fingers. His knees shook, his head sagged, and darkness flooded everything.

Fafhrd, sweat-drenched, watched the adept. Anra Devadoris' rigid body teetered like a stone pillar, slim cousin to the monolith behind him. His lips were fixed in a frozen, foreknowing smile. The teetering increased, yet for a while, as if he were an incarnation of death's ghastly pendulum, he did not fall. Then he swayed too far forward and fell like a pillar, without collapse. There was a horrid, hollow crash as his head struck the black pavement.

Ahura's hysterical laughter burst out afresh.

Fafhrd ran forward calling to the Mouser, anxiously shook the slumped form. Snores answered him. Like some spent Theban phalanx-man drowsing over his pike in the twilight of the battle, the Mouser was sleeping the sleep of complete exhaustion. Fafhrd found the Mouser's gray cloak, wrapped it around him, and gently laid him down.

Ahura was shaking convulsively.

Fafhrd looked at the fallen adept, lying there so formally outstretched, like a tomb-statue rolled over. Devadoris' lankness was skeletal. He had bled hardly at all from the wound given him by Scalpel, but his forehead was crushed like an eggshell. Fafhrd touched him. The skin was cold, the muscles hard as stone.

Fafhrd had seen men go rigid immediately upon death – Macedonians who had fought too desperately and too long. But they had become weak and staggering toward the end. Anra Devadoris had maintained the appearance of ease and perfect control up to the last moment, despite the poisons that must have been coursing through his veins almost to the exclusion of blood. All through the duel, his chest had hardly heaved.

'By Odin crucified!' Fafhrd muttered. 'He was something of a man, even though he was an adept.'

A hand was laid on his arm. He jerked around. It was Ahura come behind him. The whites showed around her eyes. She smiled at him crookedly, then lifted a knowing eyebrow, put her finger to her lips, and dropped suddenly to her knees beside the adept's corpse. Gingerly she touched the satin smooth surface of the tiny blood-clot on the adept's breast. Fafhrd, noting afresh the resemblance between the dead and the crazy face, sucked in his breath. Ahura scurried off like a startled cat.

Suddenly she froze like a dancer and looked back at him, and a gloating, transcendent vindictiveness came into her face. She beckoned to Fafhrd. Then she ran lightly up the steps to the tomb and pointed into it and beckoned again. Doubtfully the Northerner approached, his eyes on her strained and unearthly face, beautiful as an efreet's. Slowly he mounted the steps.

Then he looked down.

Looked down to feel that the wholesome world was only a film on primary abominations. He realized that what Ahura was showing him had somehow been her ultimate degradation and the ultimate degradation of the thing that had named itself Anra Devadoris. He remembered the bizarre taunts that Ahura had thrown at the adept during the duel. He remembered her laughter, and his mind eddied along the edge of suspicions of pit-spawned improprieties and obscene intimacies. He hardly noticed that Ahura had slumped over the wall of the tomb, her white arms hanging down as if pointing all ten slender fingers in limp horror. He did not know that the blackly puzzled eyes of the suddenly awakened Mouser were peering up at him.

Thinking back, he realized that Devadoris' fastidiousness and exquisitely groomed appearance had made him think of the tomb as an eccentric entrance to some luxurious underground palace.

But now he saw that there were no doors in that cramping cell into which he peered, nor cracks indicating where hidden doors might be. Whatever had come from there, had lived there, where the dry corners were thick with webs and the floor swarmed with maggots, dung beetles, and furry black spiders.

6. *The Mountain*

Perhaps some chuckling demon, or Ningauble himself, planned it that way. At all events, as Fafhrd stepped down from the tomb, he got his feet tangled in the shroud of Ahriman and bellowed wildly (the Mouser called it 'bleating') before he noticed the cause, which was by that time ripped to tatters.

Next Ahura, aroused by the tumult, set them into a brief panic by screaming that the black monolith and its soldiery were marching toward them to grind them under stony feet.

Almost immediately afterwards the cup of Socrates momentarily froze their blood by rolling around in a semicircle, as if its learned owner were invisibly pawing for it, perhaps to wet his throat after a spell of dusty disputation in the underworld. Of the withered sprig from the Tree of Life there was no sign, although the Mouser jumped as far and as skittishly as one of his namesakes when he saw a large black walking-stick insect crawling away from where the sprig might have fallen.

But it was the camel that caused the biggest commotion, by suddenly beginning to prance about clumsily in a most uncharacteristically ecstatic fashion, finally cavorting up eagerly on two legs to the mare, which fled in squealing dismay. Afterwards it became apparent that the camel must have gotten into the aphrodisiacs, for one of the bottles was pashed as if by a hoof, with only a scummy licked patch showing where its leaked contents had been, and two of the small clay jars were vanished entirely. Fafhrd set out after the two beasts on one of the remaining horses, hallooing crazily.

The Mouser, left alone with Ahura, found his glibness put to the test in saving her sanity by a barrage of small talk, mostly well-spiced Tyrian gossip, but including a wholly apocryphal tale of how he and Fafhrd and five small Ethiopian boys once played Maypole with the eye-stalks of a drunken Ningauble, leaving him peering about in the oddest directions. (The Mouser was wondering why they had not heard from their seven-eyed mentor. After victories Ningauble was always particularly prompt in getting in his demands for payment; and very exacting too – he would insist on a strict accounting for the three missing aphrodisiac containers.)

The Mouser might have been expected to take advantage of this opportunity to press his suit with Ahura, and if possible assure himself that he was now wholly free of the snail-curse. But, her hysterical condition aside, he felt strangely shy with her, as if, although this was the Ahura he loved, he were now meeting her for the first time. Certainly this was a wholly different Ahura from the one with whom they had journeyed to the Lost City, and the memory of how he had treated that other Ahura put a restraint on him. So he cajoled and comforted her as he might have some lonely Tyrian waif, finally bringing two funny little hand-puppets from his pouch and letting them amuse her for him.

And Ahura sobbed and stared and shivered, and hardly seemed to hear what nonsense the Mouser was saying, yet grew quiet and sane-eyed and appeared to be comforted.

When Fafhrd eventually returned with the still giddy camel and the outraged mare, he did not interrupt, but listened gravely, his gaze occasionally straying to the dead adept, the black monolith, the stone city, or the valley's downward slope to the north. High over their heads a flock of birds was flying in the same direction. Suddenly they scattered wildly, as if an eagle had dropped among them. Fafhrd frowned. A moment later he heard a whirring in the air. The Mouser and Ahura looked up too, momentarily glimpsed something slim hurtling downward. They cringed. There was a thud as a long whitish arrow buried itself in a crack in the pavement hardly a foot from Fafhrd and stuck there vibrating.

After a moment Fafhrd touched it with shaking hand. The shaft was crusted with ice, the feathers stiff, as if, incredibly, it had sped for a long time through frigid supramundane air. There was something tied snugly around the shaft. He detached and unrolled an ice-brittle sheet of papyrus, which softened under his touch, and read, 'You must go farther. Your quest is not ended. Trust in omens. Ningauble.'

Still trembling, Fafhrd began to curse thunderously. He crumpled the papyrus, jerked up the arrow, broke it in two, threw the parts blindly away. 'Misbegotten spawn of a eunuch, an owl, and an octopus!' he finished. 'First he tries to skewer us from the skies, then he tells us our quest is not ended – when we've just ended it!'

The Mouser, well-knowing these rages into which Fafhrd was apt to fall after battle, especially a battle in which he had not been able to participate, started to comment coolly. Then he saw the anger abruptly drain from Fafhrd's eyes, leaving a wild twinkle which he did not like.

'Mouser!' said Fafhrd eagerly. 'Which way did I throw the arrow?'

'Why, north,' said the Mouser without thinking.

'Yes, and the birds were flying north, and the arrow was coated with ice!' The wild twinkle in Fafhrd's eyes became a berserk brilliance. 'Omens, he said? We'll trust in omens all right! We'll go north, north, and still north!'

The Mouser's heart sank. Now would be a particularly difficult time to combat Fafhrd's long-standing desire to take him to 'that wonderously cold land where only brawny, hot-blooded men may live and they but by the killing of fierce, furry animals' – a prospect poignantly disheartening to a lover of hot baths, the sun, and southern nights.

'This is the chance of all chances,' Fafhrd continued, intoning like a skald. 'Ah, to rub one's naked hide with snow, to plunge like walrus into ice-garnished water. Around the Caspian and over greater mountains than these goes a way that men of my race have taken. Thor's gut, but you will love it! No wine, only hot mead and savory smoking carcasses, skin-toughening furs to wear, cold air at night to keep dreams clear and sharp, and great strong-hipped women. Then to raise sail on a winter ship and laugh at the frozen spray. Why have we so long delayed? Come! By the icy member that begot Odin, we must start at once!'

The Mouser stifled a groan. 'All, blood-brother,' he intoned, not a whit less brazen-voiced, 'my heart leaps even more than yours at the thought of nerve-quickening snow and all the other niceties of the manly life I have long yearned to taste. But' – here his voice broke sadly – 'we forget this good woman, whom in any case, even if we disregard Ningauble's injunction, we must take safely back to Tyre.'

He smiled inwardly.

'But I don't want to go back to Tyre,' interrupted Ahura, looking up from the puppets with an impishness so like a child's that the Mouser cursed himself for ever having treated her as one. 'This lonely spot seems equally far from all builded places. North is as good a way as any.'

'Flesh of Freya!' bellowed Fafhrd, throwing his arms wide. 'Do you hear what she says, Mouser? By Idun, that was spoken like a true snow-land woman! Not one moment must be wasted now. We shall smell mead before a year is out. By Frigg, a woman! Mouser, you good for one so small, did you not notice the pretty way she put it?'

So it was bustle about and pack and (for the present, at least, the Mouser conceded) no way out of it. The chest of aphrodisiacs, the cup, and the tattered shroud were bundled back onto the camel, which was still busy ogling the mare and smacking its great leathery lips. And Fafhrd leaped and shouted and clapped the Mouser's back as if there were not an eon-old dead stone city around them and a lifeless adept warming in the sun.

In a matter of moments they were jogging off down the valley, with Fafhrd singing tales of snowstorms and hunting and monsters big as icebergs and giants as tall as frost mountains, and the Mouser dourly amusing himself by picturing his own death at the hands of some overly affectionate 'great strong-hipped' woman.

Soon the way became less barren. Scrub trees and the valley's downward trend hid the city behind them. A surge of relief which the Mouser hardly noticed went through him as the last stony sentinel dipped out of sight, particularly the black monolith left to brood over the adept. He turned his attention to what lay ahead – a conical mountain barring the valley's mouth and wearing a high cap of mist, a lonely thunderhead which his imagination shaped into incredible towers and spires.

Suddenly his sleepy thoughts snapped awake. Fafhrd and Ahura had stopped and were staring at something wholly unexpected – a low wooden windowless house pressed back among the scrubby trees, with a couple of tilled fields behind it. The rudely carved guardian spirits at the four corners of the roof and topping the kingposts seemed Persian, but Persian purged of all southern influence – ancient Persian.

And ancient Persian too appeared the thin features, straight nose, and black-streaked beard of the aged man watching them circumspectly from the low doorway. It seemed to be Ahura's face he scanned most intently – or tried to scan, since Fafhrd mostly hid her.

'Greetings, Father,' called the Mouser. 'Is this not a merry day for riding, and yours good lands to pass?'

'Yes,' replied the aged man dubiously, using a rusty dialect. 'Though there are none, or few, who pass.'

'Just as well to be far from the evil stinking cities,' Fafhrd interjected heartily. 'Do you know the mountain ahead, Father? Is there an easy way past it that leads north?'

At the word 'mountain' the aged man cringed. He did not answer.

'Is there something wrong about the path we are taking?' the Mouser asked quickly. 'Or something evil about that misty mountain?'

The aged man started to shrug his shoulders, held them contracted, looked again at the travelers. Friendliness seemed to fight with fear in his face, and to win, for he leaned forward and said hurriedly, 'I warn you, sons, not to venture farther. What is the steel of your swords, the speed of your steeds, against – but remember' – he raised his voice – 'I accuse no one.' He looked quickly from side to side. 'I have nothing at all to complain of.

To me the mountain is a great benefit. My fathers returned here because the land is shunned by thief and honest men alike. There are no taxes on this land – no money taxes. I question nothing.'

'Oh, well, Father, I don't think we'll go farther,' sighed the Mouser wilily. 'We're but idle fellows who follow our noses across the world. And sometimes we smell a strange tale. And that reminds me of a matter in which you may be able to give us generous lads some help.' He chinked the coins in his pouch. 'We have heard a tale of a demon that inhabits here – a young demon dressed in black and silver, pale, with a black beard.'

As the Mouser was saying these things the aged man was edging backward and at the finish he dodged inside and slammed the door, though not before they saw someone pluck at his sleeve. Instantly there came muffled angry expostulation in a girl's voice.

The door burst open. They heard the aged man say ' . . . bring it down upon us all.' Then a girl of about fifteen came running toward them. Her face was flushed, her eyes anxious and scared.

'You must turn back!' she called to them as she ran. 'None but wicked things go to the mountain – or the doomed. And the mist hides a great horrible castle. And powerful, lonely demons live there. And one of them—'

She clutched at Fafhrd's stirrup. But just as her fingers were about to close on it, she looked beyond him straight at Ahura. An expression of abysmal terror came into her face. She screamed, 'He! The black beard!' and crumpled to the ground.

The door slammed and they heard a bar drop into place.

They dismounted. Ahura quickly knelt by the girl, signed to them after a moment that she had only fainted. Fafhrd approached the barred door, but it would not open to any knocking, pleas, or threats. He finally solved the riddle by kicking it down. Inside he saw: the aged man cowering in a dark corner; a woman attempting to conceal a young child in a pile of straw; a very old woman sitting on a stool, obviously blind, but frightenedly peering about just the same; and a young man holding an ax in trembling hands. The family resemblance was very marked.

Fafhrd stepped out of the way of the young man's feeble ax-blow and gently took the weapon from him.

The Mouser and Ahura brought the girl inside. At sight of Ahura there were further horrified shrinkings.

They laid the girl on the straw, and Ahura fetched water and began to bathe her head.

Meanwhile, the Mouser, by playing on her family's terror and practically identifying himself as a mountain demon, got them to answer his questions. First he asked about the stone city. It was a place of ancient devil-worship, they said, a place to be shunned. Yes, they had seen the black monolith of Ahriman, but only from a distance. No, they did not worship Ahriman – see the fire-shrine they kept for his adversary Ormadz? But they dreaded Ahriman, and the stones of the devil-city had a life of their own.

Then he asked about the misty mountain, and found it harder to get satisfactory answers. The cloud always shrouded its peak, they insisted. Though once toward sunset, the young man admitted, he thought he had glimpsed crazily leaning green towers and twisted minarets. But there was danger up there, horrible danger. What danger? He could not say.

The Mouser turned to the aged man. 'You told me,' he said harshly, 'that my brother demons exact no money tax from you for this land. What kind of tax, then, do they exact?'

'Lives,' whispered the aged man, his eyes showing more white.

'Lives eh? How many? And when do they come for them?'

'They never come. We go. Maybe every ten years, maybe every five, there comes a yellow-green light on the mountain-top at night, and a powerful calling in the air. Sometimes after such a night one of us is gone – who was too far from the house when the green light came. To be in the house with others helps resist the calling. I never saw the light except from our door, with a fire burning bright at my back and someone holding me. My brother went when I was a boy. Then for many years afterwards the light never came, so that even I began to wonder whether it was not a boyhood legend or illusion.

'But seven years ago,' he continued quaveringly, staring at the

540

Mouser, 'there came riding late one afternoon, on two gaunt and death-wearied horses, a young man and an old – or rather the semblances of a young man and an old, for I knew without being told, knew as I crouched trembling inside the door, peering through the crack, that the masters were returning to the Castle Called Mist. The old man was bald as a vulture and had no beard. The young man had the beginnings of a silky black one. He was dressed in black and silver, and his face was very pale. His features were like—' Here his gaze flickered fearfully toward Ahura. 'He rode stiffly, his lanky body rocking from side to side. He looked as if he were dead.

'They rode on toward the mountain without a sideward glance. But ever since that time the greenish-yellow light has glowed almost nightly from the mountaintop, and many of our animals have answered the call – and the wild ones too, to judge from their diminishing numbers. We have been careful, always staying near the house. It was not until three years ago that my eldest son went. He strayed too far in hunting and let darkness overtake him.

'And we have seen the black-bearded young man many times, usually at a distance, treading along the skyline or standing with head bowed upon some crag. Though once when my daughter was washing at the stream she looked up from her clothes-pounding and saw his dead eyes peering through the reeds. And once my eldest son, chasing a wounded snow-leopard into a thicket, found him talking with the beast. And once, rising early on a harvest morning, I saw him sitting by the well, staring at our doorway, although he did not seem to see me emerge. The old man we have seen too, though not so often. And for the last two years we have seen little or nothing of either, until—' And once again his gaze flickered helplessly toward Ahura.

Meanwhile the girl had come to her senses. This time her terror of Ahura was not so extreme. She could add nothing to the aged man's tale.

They prepared to depart. The Mouser noted a certain veiled vindictiveness toward the girl, especially in the eyes of the woman with the child, for having tried to warn them. So turning in the doorway he said, 'If you harm one hair of the girl's head, we will return, and the black-bearded one with us, and the green light to guide us by and wreak terrible vengeance.'

He tossed a few gold coins on the floor and departed.

(And so, although, or rather because her family looked upon her as an ally of demons, the girl from then on led a pampered life, and came to consider her blood as superior to theirs, and played shamelessly on their fear of the Mouser and Fafhrd and Black-beard, and finally made them give her all the golden coins, and with them purchased seductive garments after fortunate passage to a faraway city, where by clever stratagem she became the wife of a satrap and lived sumptuously ever afterwards – something that is often the fate of romantic people, if only they are romantic enough.)

Emerging from the house, the Mouser found Fafhrd making a brave attempt to recapture his former berserk mood. 'Hurry up, you little apprentice-demon!' he welcomed. 'We've a tryst with the good land of snow and cannot lag on the way!'

As they rode off, the Mouser rejoined good-naturedly, 'But what about the camel, Fafhrd? You can't very well take it to the ice country. It'll die of the phlegm.'

'There's no reason why snow shouldn't be as good for camels as it is for men,' Fafhrd retorted. Then, rising in his saddle and turning back, he waved toward the house and shouted, 'Lad! You that held the ax! When in years to come your bones feel a strange yearning, turn your face to the north. There you will find a land where you can become a man indeed.'

But in their hearts both knew that this talk was a pretense, that other planets now loomed in their horoscopes – in particular one that shone with a greenish-yellow light. As they pressed on up the valley, its silence and the absence of animal and insect life now made sinister, they felt mysteries hovering all around. Some, they knew, were locked in Ahura, but both refrained from questioning her, moved by vague apprehensions of terrifying upheavals her mind had undergone.

Finally the Mouser voiced what was in the thoughts of both of them. 'Yes, I am much afraid that Anra Devadoris, who sought to make us his apprentices, was only an apprentice himself and apt, apprentice-wise, to take credit for his master's work. Black-beard is gone, but the beardless one remains. What was it Ningauble said? . . . no simple creature, but a mystery? . . . no single identity, but a mirage?'

'Well, by all the fleas that bite the Great Antiochus, and all the lice that tickle his wife!' remarked a shrill, insolent voice behind them. 'You doomed gentlemen already know what's in this letter I have for you.'

They whirled around. Standing beside the camel – he might conceivably have been hidden, it is true, behind a nearby boulder – was a pertly grinning brown urchin, so typically Alexandrian that he might have stepped this minute out of Rakotis with a skinny mongrel sniffing at his heels. (The Mouser half expected such a dog to appear at the next moment.)

'Who sent you, boy?' Fafhrd demanded. 'How did you get here?'

'Now who and how would you expect?' replied the urchin. 'Catch.' He tossed the Mouser a wax tablet. 'Say, you two, take my advice and get out while the getting's good. I think so far as your expedition's concerned, Ningauble's pulling up his tent pegs and scuttling home. Always a friend in need, my dear employer.'

The Mouser ripped the cords, unfolded the tablet, and read:

'Greetings, my brave adventurers. You have done well, but the best remains to be done. Hark to the calling. Follow the green light. But be very cautious afterwards. I wish I could be of more assistance. Send the shroud, the cup, and the chest back with the boy as first payment.'

'Loki-brat! Regin-spawn!' burst out Fafhrd. The Mouser looked up to see the urchin lurching and bobbing back toward the Lost City on the back of the eagerly fugitive camel. His impudent laughter returned shrill and faint.

'There,' said the Mouser, 'rides off the generosity of poor, penurious Ningauble. Now we know what to do with the camel.'

'Zutt!' said Fafhrd. 'Let him have the brute and the toys. Good riddance to his gossiping!'

'Not a very high mountain,' said the Mouser an hour later, 'but high enough. I wonder who carved this neat little path and who keeps it clear?'

As he spoke, he was winding loosely over his shoulder a long thin rope of the sort used by mountain climbers, ending in a hook.

It was sunset, with twilight creeping at their heels. The little path, which had grown out of nothing, only gradually revealing itself, now led them sinuously around great boulders and along the crests of ever steeper rock-strewn slopes. Conversation, which was only a film on wariness, had played with the methods of Ningauble and his agents – whether they communicated with one another directly, from mind to mind, or by tiny whistles that emitted a note too high for human ears to hear, but capable of producing a tremor in any brother whistle or in the ear of the bat.

It was a moment when the whole universe seemed to pause. A spectral greenish light gleamed from the cloudy top ahead – but that was surely only the sun's sky-reflected afterglow. There was a hint of all-pervading sound in the air, a mighty susurrus just below the threshold of hearing, as if an army of unseen insects were tuning up their instruments. These sensations were as intangible as the force that drew them onward, a force so feeble that they knew they could break it like a single spider-strand, yet did not choose to try.

As if in response to some unspoken word, both Fafhrd and the Mouser turned toward Ahura. Under their gaze she seemed to be changing momently, opening like a night flower, becoming ever more childlike, as if some master hypnotist were stripping away the outer, later petals of her mind, leaving only a small limpid pool, from whose unknown depths, however, dark bubbles were dimly rising.

They felt their infatuation pulse anew, but with a shy restraint on it. And their hearts fell silent as the hooded heights above, as she said, 'Anra Devadoris was my twin brother.'

7. *Ahura Devadoris*

'I never knew my father. He died before we were born. In one of her rare fits of communicativeness my mother told me, "Your father was a Greek, Ahura. A very kind and learned man. He laughed a great deal." I remember how stern she looked as she said that, rather than how beautiful, the sunlight glinting from her ringleted, black-dyed hair.

'But it seemed to me that she had slightly emphasized the word "Your". You see, even then I wondered about Anra. So I asked Old Berenice the housekeeper about it. She told me she had seen Mother bear us, both on the same night.

'Old Berenice went on to tell me how my father had died. Almost nine months before we were born, he was found one morning beaten to death in the street just outside the door. A gang of Egyptian longshoremen who were raping and robbing by night were supposed to have done it, although they were never brought to justice – that was back when the Ptolemies had Tyre. It was a horrible death. He was almost pashed to a pulp against the cobbles.

'At another time Old Berenice told me something about my mother, after making me swear by Athena and by Set and by Moloch, who would eat me if I did, never to tell. She said that Mother came from a Persian family whose five daughters in the old times were all priestesses, dedicated from birth to be the wives of an evil Persian god, forbidden the embraces of mortals, doomed to spend their nights alone with the stone image of the god in a lonely temple "halfway across the world", she said. Mother was away that day and Old Berenice dragged me down into a little basement under Mother's bedroom and pointed out three ragged gray stones set among the bricks and told me they came from the temple. Old Berenice liked to frighten me, although she was deathly afraid of Mother.

'Of course I instantly went and told Anra, as I always did.'

The little path was leading sharply upward now, along the spine of a crest. Their horses went at a walk, first Fafhrd's, then Ahura's, last the Mouser's. The lines were smoothed in Fafhrd's face, although he was still very watchful, and the Mouser looked almost like a quaint child.

Ahura continued, 'It is hard to make you understand my relationship with Anra, because it was so close that even the word "relationship" spoils it. There was a game we would play in the garden. He would close his eyes and guess what I was looking at. In other games we would change sides, but never in this one.

'He invented all sorts of versions of the game and didn't want to play any others. Sometimes I would climb up by the olive tree onto the tiled roof – Anra couldn't make it – and watch for an hour. Then I'd come down and tell him what I'd seen – some dyers spreading out wet green cloth for the sun to turn it purple, a procession of priests around the Temple of Melkarth, a galley from Pergamum setting sail, a Greek official impatiently explaining something to his Egyptian scribe, two henna-handed ladies giggling at some kilted sailors, a mysterious and lonely Jew – and he would tell me what kind of people they were and what they had been thinking and what they were planning to do. It was a very special kind of imagination, for afterwards when I began to go outside I found out that he was usually right. At the time I remember thinking that it was as if he were looking at the pictures in my mind and seeing more than I could. I liked it. It was such a gentle feeling.

'Of course our closeness was partly because Mother, especially after she changed her way of life, wouldn't let us go out at all or mix with other children. There was more reason for that than just her strictness. Anra was very delicate. He once broke his wrist and it was a long time healing. Mother had a slave come in who was skilled in such things, and he told Mother he was afraid that Anra's bones were becoming too brittle. He told about children whose muscles and sinews gradually turned to stone, so that they became living statues. Mother struck him in the face and drove him from the house – an action that cost her a dear friend, because he was an important slave.

'And even if Anra had been allowed to go out, he couldn't have. Once after I had begun to go outside I persuaded him to come with me. He didn't want to, but I laughed at him, and he could never stand laughter. As soon as we climbed over the garden wall he fell down in a faint and I couldn't rouse him from it, though I tried and tried. Finally I climbed back so I could open the door and drag him in, and Old Berenice spotted me and I had to tell her what had happened. She helped me carry him in, but afterwards she whipped me because she knew I'd never dare tell Mother I'd taken him outside. Anra came to his senses while she was whipping me, but was sick for a week afterwards. I don't think I ever laughed at him after that, until today.

'Cooped up in the house, Anra spent most of his time studying. While I watched from the roof or wheedled stories from Old Berenice and the other slaves, or later on went out to gather information for him, he would stay in Father's library, reading, or learning some new language from Father's grammars and translations. Mother taught both of us to read Greek, and I picked up speaking knowledge of Aramaic and scraps of other tongues from the slaves and passed them on to him. But Anra was far cleverer than I at reading. He loved letters as passionately as I did the outside. For him, they were alive. I remember him showing me some Egyptian hieroglyphs and telling me that they were all animals and insects. And then he showed me some Egyptian hieratics and demotics and told me those were the same animals in disguise. But Hebrew, he said, was best of all, for each letter was a magic charm. That was before he learned Old Persian. Sometimes it was years before we found out how to pronounce the languages he learned. That was one of my most important jobs when I started to go outside for him.

'Father's library had been kept just as it was when he died. Neatly stacked in canisters were all the renowned philosophers, historians, poets, rhetoricians, and grammarians. But tossed in a corner along with potsherds and papyrus scraps like so much trash, were rolls of a very different sort. Across the back of one of them my father had scribbled, derisively I'm sure, in his big impulsive hand, "Secret Wisdom!" It was those that from the first captured Anra's curiosity. He would read the respectable books in the canisters, but chiefly so he could go back and take a brittle roll from the corner, blow off the dust, and puzzle out a little more.

'They were very strange books that frightened and disgusted me and made me want to giggle all at once. Many of them were written in a cheap and ignorant style. Some of them told what

547

dreams meant and gave directions for working magic – all sorts of nasty things to be cooked together. Others – Jewish rolls in Aramaic – were about the end of the world and wild adventures of evil spirits and mixed-up, messy monsters – things with ten heads and jeweled cartwheels for feet, things like that. Then there were Chaldean star-books that told how all the lights in the sky were alive and their names and what they did to you. And one jerky, half illiterate roll in Greek told about something horrible, which for a long while I couldn't understand, connected with an ear of corn and six pomegranate seeds. It was in another of those sensational Greek rolls that Anra first found out about Ahriman and his eternal empire of evil, and after that he couldn't wait until he'd mastered Old Persian. But none of the few Old Persian rolls in Father's library were about Ahriman, so he had to wait until I could steal such things for him outside.

'My going outside was after Mother changed her way of life. That happened when I was seven. She was always a very moody and frightening woman, though sometimes she'd be very affectionate toward me for a little while, and she always spoiled and pampered Anra, though from a distance, through the slaves, almost as if she were afraid of him.

'Now her moods became blacker and blacker. Sometimes I'd surprise her looking in horror at nothing, or beating her forehead while her eyes were closed and her beautiful face was all taut, as if she were going mad. I had the feeling she'd been backed up to the end of some underground tunnel and must find a door leading out, or lose her mind.

'Then one afternoon I peeked into her bedroom and saw her looking into her silver mirror. For a long, long while she studied her face in it and I watched her without making a sound. I knew that something important was happening. Finally she seemed to make some sort of difficult inward effort and the lines of anxiety and sternness and fear disappeared from her face, leaving it smooth and beautiful as a mask. Then she unlocked a drawer I'd never seen into before and took out all sorts of little pots and vials and brushes. With these she colored and whitened her face and carefully smeared a dark, shining powder around her eyes and painted her lips reddish-orange. All this time my heart was pounding and my throat was choking up, I didn't know why. Then she laid down her brushes and dropped her chiton and felt of her throat and breasts in a thoughtful way and took up the mirror and looked at herself with a cold satisfaction. She was very beautiful, but it was a beauty that terrified me. Until now I'd always thought of her as hard and stern outside, but soft and loving within, if only you could manage to creep into that core. But now she was all turned inside out. Strangling my sobs, I ran to tell Anra and find out what it meant. But this time his cleverness failed him. He was as puzzled and disturbed as I.

'It was right afterwards that she became even stricter with me, and although she continued to spoil Anra from a distance, kept us shut up from the world more than ever. I wasn't even allowed to speak to the new slave she'd bought, an ugly, smirking, skinny-legged girl named Phryne who used to massage her and sometimes play the flute. There were all sorts of visitors coming to the house now at night, but Anra and I were always locked in our little bedroom high up by the garden. We'd hear them yelling through the wall and sometimes screaming and bumping around the inner court to the sound of Phryne's flute. Sometimes I'd lie staring at the darkness in an inexplicable sick terror all night long. I tried every way to get Old Berenice to tell me what was happening, but for once her fear of Mother's anger was too great. She'd only leer at me.

'Finally Anra worked out a plan for finding out. When he first told me about it, I refused. It terrified me. That was when I discovered the power he had over me. Up until that time the things I had done for him had been part of a game I enjoyed as much as he. I had never thought of myself as a slave obeying commands. But now when I rebelled, I found out not only that my twin had an obscure power over my limbs, so that I could hardly move them at all, or imagined I couldn't, if he were unwilling, but also that I couldn't bear the thought of him being unhappy or frustrated.

'I realize now that he had reached the first of those crises in his life when his way was blocked and he pitilessly sacrificed his dearest helper to the urgings of his insatiable curiosity.

'Night came. As soon as we were locked in I let a knotted cord out the little high window and wriggled out and climbed down. Then I climbed the olive tree to the roof. I crept over the tiles down to the square skylight of the inner court and managed to squirm over the edge – I almost fell – into a narrow, cobwebby space between the ceiling and the tiles. There was a faint murmur of talk from the dining room, but the court was empty. I lay still as a mouse and waited.'

Fafhrd uttered a smothered exclamation and stopped his horse. The others did likewise. A pebble rattled down the slope, but they hardly heard it. Seeming to come from the heights above them and yet to fill the whole darkening sky was something that was not entirely a sound, something that tugged at them like the Sirens' voices at fettered Odysseus. For a while they listened incredulously, then Fafhrd shrugged and started forward again, the others following.

Ahura continued, 'For a long time nothing happened, except occasionally slaves hurried in and out with full and empty dishes, and there was some laughter, and I heard Phryne's flute. Then suddenly the laughter grew louder and changed to singing, and there was the sound of couches pushed back and the patter of footsteps, and there swept into the court a Dionysiac rout.

'Phryne, naked, piped the way. My mother followed, laughing, her arms linked with those of two dancing young men, but clutching to her bosom a large silver wine-bowl. The wine sloshed over and stained purple her white silk chiton around her breasts, but she only laughed and reeled more wildly. After those came many others, men and women, young and old, all singing and dancing. One limber young man skipped high, clapping his heels, and one fat old grinning fellow panted and had to be pulled by girls, but they kept it up three times around the court before they threw themselves down on the couches and cushions. Then while they chattered and laughed and kissed and embraced and played pranks and watched a naked girl prettier than Phryne dance, my mother offered the bowl around for them to dip their wine cups.

'I was astounded – and entranced. I had been almost dead with fear, expecting I don't know what cruelties and horrors.

Instead, what I saw was wholly lovely and natural. The revelation burst on me, "So this is the wonderful and important thing that people do." My mother no longer frightened me. Though she still wore her new face, there was no longer any hardness about her, inside or out, only joy and beauty. The young men were so witty and gay I had to put my fist in my mouth to keep from screaming with laughter. Even Phryne, squatting on her heels like a skinny boy as she piped, seemed for once unmalicious and likeable. I couldn't wait to tell Anra.

'There was only one disturbing note, and that was so slight I hardly noticed it. Two of the men who took the lead in the joking, a young red-haired fellow and an older chap with a face like a lean satyr, seemed to have something up their sleeves. I saw them whisper to some of the others. And once the younger grinned at Mother and shouted, "I know something about you from way back!" And once the older called at her mockingly, "I know something about your great-grandmother, you old Persian you!" Each time Mother laughed and waved her hand derisively, but I could see that she was bothered underneath. And each time some of the others paused momentarily, as if they had an inkling of something, but didn't want to let on. Eventually the two men drifted out, and from then on there was nothing to mar the fun.

'The dancing became wilder and staggering, the laughter louder, more wine was spilled than drunk. Then Phryne threw away her flute and ran and landed in the fat man's lap with a jounce that almost knocked the wind out of him. Four or five of the others tumbled down.

'Just at that moment there came a crashing and a loud rending of wood, as if a door were being broken in. Instantly everyone was as still as death. Someone jerked around and a lamp snuffed out, throwing half the court into shadow.

'Then loud, shaking footsteps, like two paving blocks walking, sounded through the house, coming nearer and nearer.

'Everyone was frozen, staring at the doorway. Phryne still had her arm around the fat man's neck. But it was in Mother's face that the truly unbearable terror showed. She had retreated to the remaining lamp and dropped to her knees there. The whites showed around her eyes. She began to utter short, rapid screams, like a trapped dog.

'Then through the doorway clomped a great ragged-edged, square-limbed, naked stone man fully seven feet high. His face was just expressionless black gashes in a flat surface, and before him was thrust a mortary stone member. I couldn't bear to look at him, but I had to. He tramped echoingly across the room to Mother, jerked her up, still screaming, by the hair, and with the other hand ripped down her wine-stained chiton. I fainted.

'But it must have ended about there, for when I came to, sick with terror, it was to hear everyone laughing uproariously. Several of them were bending over Mother, at once reassuring and mocking her, the two men who had gone out among them, and to one side was a jumbled heap of cloth and thin boards, both crusted with mortar. From what they said I understood that the red-haired one had worn the horrible disguise, while satyr-face had made the footsteps by rhythmically clomping on the floor with a brick, and had simulated the breaking door by jumping on a propped-up board.

'"Now tell us your great-grandmother wasn't married to a stupid old stone demon back in Persia!" he jeered pleasantly, wagging his finger.

'Then came something that tortured me like a rusty dagger and terrified me, in a very quiet way, as much as the image. Although she was white as milk and barely able to totter, Mother did her best to pretend that the loathsome trick they'd played on her was just a clever joke. I knew why. She was horribly afraid of losing their friendship and would have done anything rather than be left alone.

'Her pretense worked. Although some of them left, the rest yielded to her laughing entreaties. They drank until they sprawled out snoring. I waited until almost dawn, then summoned all my courage, made my stiff muscles pull me onto the tiles, cold and slippery with dew, and with what seemed the last of my strength, dragged myself back to our room.

'But not to sleep. Anra was awake and avid to hear what had happened. I begged him not to make me, but he insisted. I had to tell him everything. The pictures of what I'd seen kept bobbing up in my wretchedly tired mind so vividly that it seemed to be happening all over again. He asked all sorts of questions, wouldn't let me miss a single detail. I had to relive that first thrilling revelation of joy, tainted now by the knowledge that the people were mostly sly and cruel.

'When I got to the part about the stone image, Anra became terribly excited. But when I told him about it all being a nasty joke, he seemed disappointed. He became angry, as if he suspected me of lying.

'Finally he let me sleep.

'The next night I went back to my cubbyhole under the tiles.'

Again Fafhrd stopped his horse. The mist masking the mountaintop had suddenly begun to glow, as if a green moon were rising, or as if it were a volcano spouting green flames. The hue tinged their upturned faces. It lured like some vast cloudy jewel. Fafhrd and the Mouser exchanged a glance of fatalistic wonder. Then all three proceeded up the narrowing ridge.

Ahura continued, 'I'd sworn by all the gods I'd never do it. I'd told myself I'd rather die. But . . . Anra made me.

'Daytimes I wandered around like a stupefied little ghost-slave. Old Berenice was puzzled and suspicious and once or twice I thought Phryne grimaced knowingly. Finally even Mother noticed and questioned me and had a physician in.

'I think I would have gotten really sick and died, or gone mad, except that then, in desperation at first, I started to go outside, and a whole new world opened to me.'

As she spoke on, her voice rising in hushed excitement at the memory of it, there was painted in the minds of Fafhrd and the Mouser a picture of the magic city that Tyre must have seemed to the child – the waterfront, the riches, the bustle of trade, the hum of gossip and laughter, the ships and strangers from foreign lands.

'Those people I had watched from the roof – I could touch almost anywhere. Every person I met seemed a wonderful mystery, something to be smiled and chattered at. I dressed as a slave-child, and all sorts of folk got to know me and expect my coming – other slaves, tavern wenches and sellers of sweetmeats, street merchants and scribes, errand boys and boatmen, seamstresses and cooks. I made myself useful, ran errands myself, listened delightedly to their endless talk, passed on gossip I'd heard, gave away bits of food I'd stolen at home, became a favorite. It seemed to me I could never get enough of Tyre. I scampered from morning to night. It was generally twilight before I climbed back over the garden wall.

'I couldn't fool Old Berenice, but after a while I found a way to escape her whippings. I threatened to tell Mother it was she who had told red-hair and satyr-face about the stone image. I don't know if I guessed right or not, but the threat worked. After that, she would only mumble venomously whenever I sneaked in after sunset. As for Mother, she was getting farther away from us all the time, alive only by night, lost by day in frightened brooding.

'Then, each evening, came another delight. I would tell Anra everything I had heard and seen, each new adventure, each little triumph. Like a magpie I repeated for him all the bright colors, sounds, and odors. Like a magpie I repeated for him the babble of strange languages I'd heard, the scraps of learned talk I'd caught from priests and scholars. I forgot what he'd done to me. We were playing the game again, the most wonderful version of all. Often he helped me, suggesting new places to go, new things to watch for, and once he even saved me from being kidnaped by a couple of ingratiating Alexandrian slave-dealers whom anyone but I would have suspected.

'It was odd how that happened. The two had made much of me, were promising me sweetmeats if I would go somewhere nearby with them, when I thought I heard Anra's voice whisper "Don't." I became cold with terror and darted down an alley.

'It seemed as though Anra were now able sometimes to see the pictures in my mind even when I was away from him. I felt ever so close to him.

'I was wild for him to come out with me, but I've told you what happened the one time he tried. And as the years passed, he seemed to become tied even tighter to the house. Once when Mother vaguely talked of moving to Antioch, he fell ill and and did not recover until she had promised we would never, never go.

'Meanwhile he was growing up into a slim and darkly handsome youth. Phryne began to make eyes at him and sought excuses to go to his room. But he was frightened and rebuffed her. However, he coaxed me to make friends with her, to be near her, even share her bed those nights when Mother did not want her. He seemed to like that.

'You know the restlessness that comes to a maturing child, when he seeks love, or adventure, or the gods, or all three. That restlessness had come to Anra, but his only gods were in those dusty, dubious rolls my father had labeled "Secret Wisdom!" I hardly knew what he did by day any more except that there were odd ceremonies and experiments mixed with his studies. Some of them he conducted in the little basement where the three gray stones were. At such times he had me keep watch. He no longer told me what he was reading or thinking, and I was so busy in my new world that I hardly noticed the difference.

'And yet I could see the restlessness growing. He sent me on longer and more difficult missions, had me inquire after books the scribes had never heard of, seek out all manner of astrologers and wise-women, required me to steal or buy stranger and stranger ingredients from the herb doctors. And when I did win such treasures for him, he would only snatch them from me unjoyfully and be twice as gloomy the evening after. Gone were such days of rejoicing as when I had brought him the first Persian rolls about Ahriman, the first lodestone, or repeated every syllable I had overheard of the words of a famous philosopher from Athens. He was beyond all that now. He sometimes hardly listened to my detailed reports, as if he had already glanced through them and knew they contained nothing to interest him.

'He grew haggard and sick. His restlessness took the form of a frantic pacing. I was reminded of my mother trapped in that blocked-off, underground corridor. It made my heart hurt to watch him. I longed to help him, to share with him my new exciting life, to give him the thing he so desperately wanted.

'But it was not my help he needed. He had embarked on a dark, mysterious quest I did not understand, and he had reached a bitter, corroding impasse where of his own experience he could go no farther.

'He needed a teacher.'

8. *The Old Man Without a Beard*

'I was fifteen when I met the Old Man Without a Beard. I called him that and I still call him that, for there is no other distinguishing characteristic my mind can seize and hold. Whenever I think of him, even whenever I look at him, his face melts into the mob. It is as if a master actor, after portraying every sort of character in the world, should have hit on the simplest and most perfect of disguises.

'As to what lies behind that too-ordinary face – the something you can sometimes sense but hardly grasp – all I can say is a satiety and an emptiness that are not of this world.'

Fafhrd caught his breath. They had reached the end of the ridge. The leftward slope had suddenly tilted upward, become the core of the mountain. While the rightward slope had swung downward and out of sight, leaving an unfathomable black abyss. Between, the path continued upward, a stony strip only few feet wide. The Mouser touched reassuringly the coil of rope over his shoulder. For a moment their horses hung back. Then, as if the faint green glow and the ceaseless murmuring that bathed them were an intangible net, they were drawn on.

'I was in a wine shop. I had just carried a message to one of the men-friends of the Greek girl Chloe, hardly older than myself, when I noticed him sitting in a corner. I asked Chloe about him. She said he was a Greek chorister and commercial poet down on his luck, or no, that he was an Egyptian fortuneteller, changed her mind again, tried to remember what a Samian pander had told her about him, gave him a quick puzzled look, decided that she didn't really know him at all and that it didn't matter.

'But his very emptiness intrigued me. Here was a new kind of mystery. After I had been watching him for some time, he turned around and looked at me. I had the impression that he had been aware of my inquiring gaze from the beginning, but had ignored it as a sleepy man a buzzing fly.

'After that one glance he slumped back into his former position, but when I left the shop he walked at my side.

'"You're not the only one who looks through your eyes, are you?" he said quietly.

'I was so startled by his question that I didn't know how to reply, but he didn't require me to. His face brightened without becoming any more individualized and he immediately began to talk to me in the most charming and humorous way, though his words gave no clue as to who he was or what he did.

'However, I gathered from hints he let fall that he possessed some knowledge of those odd sorts of things that always interested Anra and so I followed him willingly, my hand in his.

'But not for long. Our way led up a narrow twisting alley, and I saw a sideways glint in his eye, and felt his hand tighten on mine in a way I did not like. I became somewhat frightened and expected at any minute the danger warning from Anra.

'We passed a lowering tenement and stopped at a rickety three-story shack leaning against it. He said his dwelling was at the top. He was drawing me toward the ladder that served for stairs, and still the danger warning did not come.

'Then his hand crept toward my wrist and I did not wait any longer, but jerked away and ran, my fear growing greater with every step.

'When I reached home, Anra was pacing like a leopard. I was eager to tell him all about my narrow escape, but he kept interrupting me to demand details of the Old Man and angrily flirting his head because I could tell him so little. Then, when I came to the part about my running away, an astounding look of tortured betrayal contorted his features, he raised his hands as if to strike me, then threw himself down on the couch, sobbing.

'But as I leaned over him anxiously, his sobs stopped. He looked around at me, over his shoulder, his face white but composed, and said, "Ahura, I must know everything about him."

'In that one moment I realized all that I had overlooked for years – that my delightful airy freedom was a sham – that it was not Anra, but I, that was tethered – that the game was not a game, but a bondage – that while I had gone about so open and eager, intent only on sound and color, form and movement, he had been developing the side I had no time for, the intellect, the purpose, the will – that I was only a tool to him, a slave to be sent on errands, an unfeeling extension of his own body, a tentacle he could lose and grow again, like an octopus – that even my misery at his frantic disappointment, my willingness to do anything to please him, was only another lever to be coldly used against me – that our very closeness, so that we were only two halves of one mind, was to him only another tactical advantage.

'He had reached the second great crisis of his life, and again he unhesitatingly sacrificed his nearest.

'There was something uglier to it even than that, as I could see in his eyes as soon as he was sure he had me. We were like brother and sister kings in Alexandria or Antioch, playmates from infancy, destined for each other, but unknowingly, and the boy crippled and impotent – and now, too soon and horridly had come the bridal night.

'The end was that I went back to the narrow alley, the lowering tenement, the rickety shack, the ladder, the third story, and the Old Man Without a Beard.

'I didn't give in without a struggle. Once I was out of the house I fought every inch of the way. Up until now, even in the cubbyhole under the tiles, I had only to spy and observe for Anra. I had not to do things.

'But in the end it was the same. I dragged myself up the last rung and knocked on the warped door. It swung open at my touch. Inside, across a fumy room, behind a large empty table, by the light of a single ill-burning lamp, his eyes as unwinking as a fish's, and upon me, sat the Old Man Without a Beard.'

Ahura paused, and Fafhrd and the Mouser felt a clamminess descend upon their skins. Looking up, they saw uncoiling downward from dizzy heights, like the ghosts of constrictive snakes or jungle vines, thin tendrils of green mist.

'Yes,' said Ahura, 'there is always mist or smokiness of some sort where he is.

'Three days later I returned to Anra and told him everything – a corpse giving testimony as to its murderer. But in this instance the judge relished the testimony, and when I told him of a certain plan the Old Man had in mind, an unearthly joy shimmered on his face.

'The Old Man was to be hired as a tutor and physician for Anra. This was easily arranged, as Mother always acceded to Anra's wishes and perhaps still had some hope of seeing him stirred from his seclusion. Moreover, the Old Man had a mixture of unobtrusiveness and power that I am sure would have won him entry everywhere. Within a matter of weeks he had quietly established a mastery over everyone in the house – some, like Mother, merely to be ignored; others, like Phryne, ultimately to be used.

'I will always remember Anra on the day the Old Man came. This was to be his first contact with the reality beyond the garden wall, and I could see that he was terribly frightened. As the hours of waiting passed, he retreated to his room, and I think it was mainly pride that kept him from calling the whole thing off. We did not hear the Old Man coming – only Old Berenice, who was counting the silver outside, stopped her muttering. Anra threw himself back on the couch in the farthest corner of the room, his hands gripping its edge, his eyes fixed on the doorway. A shadow lurched into sight there, grew darker and more definite. Then the Old Man put down on the threshold the two bags he was carrying and looked beyond me at Anra. A moment later my twin's painful gasps died in a faint hiss of expired breath. He had fainted.

'That evening his new education began. Everything that had happened was, as it were, repeated on a deeper, stranger level. There were languages to be learned, but not any languages to be found in human books; rituals to be intoned, but not to any gods that ordinary men have worshiped; magic to be brewed, but not with herbs that I could buy or steal. Daily Anra was instructed in the ways of inner darkness, the sicknesses and unknown powers of the mind, the eon-buried emotions that must be due to insidious impurities the gods overlooked in the earth from which they made man. By silent stages our home became a temple of the abominable, a monastery of the unclean.

'Yet there was nothing of tainted orgy, of vicious excess about their actions. Whatever they did, was done with strict self-discipline and mystic concentration. There was no looseness anywhere about them. They aimed at a knowledge and a power, born of darkness, true, but one which they were willing to make any self-sacrifice to obtain. They were religious, with this difference: their ritual was degradation, their aim a world chaos played upon like a broken lyre by their master minds, their god the quintessence of evil, Ahriman, the ultimate pit.

'As if performed by sleepwalkers, the ordinary routine of our home went on. Indeed, I sometimes felt that we were all of us, except Anra, merely dreams behind the Old Man's empty eyes – actors in a deliberate nightmare where men portrayed beasts; beasts, worms; worms, slime.

'Each morning I went out and made my customary way through Tyre, chattering and laughing as before, but emptily, knowing that I was no more free than if visible chains leashed me to the house, a puppet dangled over the garden wall. Only at the periphery of my masters' intentions did I dare oppose them even passively – once I smuggled the girl Chloe a protective amulet because I fancied they were considering her as a subject for such experiments as they had tried on Phryne. And daily the periphery of their intentions widened – indeed, they would long since have left the house themselves, except for Anra's bondage to it.

'It was to the problem of breaking that bondage that they now devoted themselves. I was not told how they hoped to manage it, but I soon realized that I was to play a part.

'They would shine glittering lights into my eyes and Anra would chant until I slept. Hours or even days later I would awake to find that I had gone unconsciously about my daily business, my body a slave to Anra's commands. At other times Anra would wear a thin leather mask which covered all his features, so that he could only see, if at all, through my eyes. My sense of oneness with my twin grew steadily with my fear of him.

'Then came a period in which I was kept closely pent up, as if in some savage prelude to maturity or death or birth, or all three. The Old Man said something about "not to see the sun or touch the earth". Again I crouched for hours in the cubbyhole under the tiles or on reed mats in the little basement. And now it was my eyes and ears that were covered rather than Anra's. For hours I, whom sights and sounds had nourished more than food, could see nothing but fragmentary memories of the child-Anra sick, or the Old Man across the fumy room, or Phryne writhing on her belly and hissing like a snake. But worst of all was my separation from Aura. For the first time since our birth I could not see his face, hear his voice, feel his mind. I withered like a tree from which the sap is withdrawn, an animal in which the nerves have been killed.

'Finally came a day or night, I know not which, when the Old Man loosened the mask from my face. There could hardly have been more than a glimmer of light, but my long-blindfolded eyes made out every detail of the little basement with a painful clarity. The three gray stones had been dug out of the pavement. Supine beside them lay Anra, emaciated, pale, hardly breathing, looking as though he were about to die.'

The three climbers stopped, confronted by a ghostly green wall. The narrow path had emerged onto what must be the mountain's tablelike top. Ahead stretched a level expanse of dark rock, mist-masked after the first few yards. Without a word they dismounted and led their trembling horses forward into a moist realm which, save that the water was weightless, most resembled a faintly phosphorescent sea bottom.

'My heart leaped out toward my twin in pity and horror. I realized that despite all tyranny and torment I still loved him more than anything in the world, loved him as a slave loves the weak, cruel master who depends for everything on that slave, loved him as the ill-used body loves the despot mind. And I felt more closely linked to him, our lives and deaths interdependent, than if we had been linked by bonds of flesh and blood, as some rare twins are.

'The Old Man told me I could save him from death if I chose. For the present I must merely talk to him in my usual fashion. This I did, with an eagerness born of days without him. Save for an occasional faint fluttering of his sallow eyelids, Anra did not move, yet I felt that never before had he listened as intently, never before had he understood me as well. It seemed to me that all my previous speech with him had been crude by contrast. Now I remembered and told him all sorts of things that had escaped my memory or seemed too subtle for language. I talked on and on, haphazardly, chaotically, ranging swiftly from local gossip to world history, delving into myriad experiences and feelings, not all of them my own.

'Hours, perhaps days passed – the Old Man may have put some spell of slumber or deafness on the other inmates of the house to guard against interruption. At times my throat grew dry and he gave me drink, but I hardly dared pause for that, since I was appalled at the slight but unremitting change for the worse that was taking place in my twin and I had become possessed with the idea that my talking was the cord between life and Anra, that it created a channel between our bodies, across which my strength could flow to revive him.

'My eyes swam and blurred, my body shook, my voice ran the gamut of hoarseness down to an almost inaudible whisper. Despite my resolve I would have fainted, save that the Old Man held to my face burning aromatic herbs which caused me to come shudderingly awake.

'Finally I could no longer speak, but that was no release, as I continued to twitch my cracked lips and think on and on in a rushing feverish stream. It was as if I jerked and flung from the depths of my mind scraps of ideas from which Anra sucked the tiny life that remained to him.

'There was one persistent image – of a dying Hermaphroditus approaching Salmacis' pool, in which he would become one with the nymph.

'Farther and farther I ventured out along the talk-created channel between us, nearer and nearer I came to Anra's pale, delicate, cadaverous face, until, as with a despairing burst of effort I hurled my last strength to him, it loomed large as a green-shadowed ivory cliff falling to engulf me—'

Ahura's words broke off in a gasp of horror. All three stood still and stared ahead. For rearing up before them in the thickening mist, so near that they felt they had been ambushed, was a great chaotic structure of whitish, faintly yellowed stone, through whose narrow windows and wide-open door streamed a baleful greenish light, source of the mist's phosphorescent glow. Fafhrd and the Mouser thought of Karnak and its obelisks, of the Pharos lighthouse, of the Acropolis, of the Ishtar Gate in Babylon, of the ruins of Khatti, of the Lost City of Ahriman, of those doomful mirage-towers that seamen see where are Scylla and Charybdis. Of a truth, the architecture of the strange structure varied so swiftly and to such unearthly extremes that it was lifted into an insane stylistic realm all of its own. Mist-magnified, its twisted ramps and pinnacles, like a fluid face in a nightmare, pushed upward toward where the stars should have been.

9. *The Castle Called Mist*

'What happened next was so strange that I felt sure I had plunged from feverish consciousness into the cool retreat of a fanciful dream,' Ahura continued as, having tethered their horses, they mounted a wide stairway toward that open door which mocked alike sudden rush and cautious reconnoitering. Her story went on with as calm and drugged a fatalism as their step-by-step advance. 'I was lying on my back beside the three stones and watching my body move around the little basement. I was terribly weak, I could not stir a muscle, and yet I felt delightfully refreshed – all the dry burning and aching in my throat was gone. Idly, as one will in a dream, I studied my face. It seemed to be smiling in triumph, very foolishly I thought. But as I continued to study it, fear began to intrude into my pleasant dream. The face was mine, but there were unfamiliar quirks of expression. Then, becoming aware of my gaze, it grimaced contemptuously and turned and said something to the Old Man, who nodded matter-of-factly. The intruding fear engulfed me. With a tremendous effort I managed to roll my eyes downward and look at my real body, the one lying on the floor.

'It was Anra's.'

They entered the doorway and found themselves in a huge, many-nooked and niched stone room – though seemingly no nearer the ultimate source of the green glow, except that here the misty air was bright with it. There were stone tables and benches and chairs scattered about, but the chief feature of the place was the mighty archway ahead, from which stone groin-ings curved upward in baffling profusion. Fafhrd's and the Mouser's eyes momentarily sought the keystone of the arch, both because of its great size and because there was an odd dark recess toward its top.

The silence was portentous, making them feel uneasily for their swords. It was not merely that the luring music had ceased – here in the Castle Called Mist there was literally no sound, save what rippled out futilely from their own beating hearts. There was instead a fog-bound concentration that froze into the senses, as though they were inside the mind of a titanic thinker, or as if the stones themselves were entranced.

Then, since it seemed as unthinkable to wait in that silence as for lost hunters to stand motionless in deep winter cold, they passed under the archway and took at random an upward-leading ramp.

Ahura continued, 'Helplessly I watched them make certain preparations. While Anra gathered some small bundles of manuscripts and clothing, the Old Man lashed together the three mortar-crusted stones.

'It may have been that in the moment of victory he relaxed habitual precautions. At all events, while he was still bending over the stones, my mother entered the room. Crying out, "What have you done to him?" she threw herself down beside me and felt at me anxiously. But that was not to the Old Man's liking. He grabbed her shoulders and roughly jerked her back. She lay huddled against the wall, her eyes wide, her teeth chattering – especially when she saw Anra, in my body, grotesquely lift the lashed stones. Meanwhile the Old Man hoisted me, in my new, wasted form, to his shoulder, picked up the bundles, and ascended the short stair.

'We walked through the inner court, rose-strewn and filled with Mother's perfumed, wine-splashed friends, who stared at us in befuddled astonishment, and so out of the house. It was night. Five slaves waited with a curtained litter in which the Old Man placed me. My last glimpse was of Mother's face, its paint tracked by tears, peering horrifiedly through the half open door.'

The ramp issued onto an upper level and they found themselves wandering aimlessly through a mazy series of rooms. Of little use to record here the things they thought they saw through shadowy doorways, or thought they heard through metal doors with massy complex bolts whose drawing they dared not fathom. There was a disordered, high-shelved library, certain of the rolls seeming to smoke and fume as though they held in their papyrus and ink the seeds of a holocaust; the corners were piled with sealed canisters of greenish stone and age-verdigrised brass tablets. There were instruments that Fafhrd did not even bother to warn the Mouser against touching. Another room exuded a fearful animal stench; upon its slippery floor they noted a sprinkling of short, incredibly thick black bristles. But the only living creature they saw at the time was a little hairless thing that looked as if it had once sought to become a bear cub; when Fafhrd stooped to pet it, it flopped away whimpering. There was a door that was thrice as broad as it was high, and its height hardly that of a man's knee. There was a window that let upon a blackness that was neither of mist nor of night, and yet seemed infinite; peering in, Fafhrd could faintly see rusted iron handholds leading upward. The Mouser uncoiled his climbing rope to its full length and swung it around inside the window, without the hook striking anything.

Yet the strangest impression this ominously empty stronghold begot in them was also the subtlest, and one which each new room or twisting corridor heightened – a feeling of architectural inadequacy. It seemed impossible that the supports were equal to the vast weights of the great stone floors and ceilings, so impossible that they almost became convinced that there were buttresses and retaining walls they could not see, either invisible or existing in some other world altogether, as if the Castle Called Mist had only partially emerged from some unthinkable outside. That certain bolted doors seemed to lead where no space could be, added to this hinting.

They wandered through passages so distorted that, though they retained a precise memory of landmarks, they lost all sense of direction.

Finally Fafhrd said, 'This gets us nowhere. Whatever we seek, whomever we wait for – Old Man or demon – it might as well be in that first room of the great archway.'

The Mouser nodded as they turned back, and Ahura said, 'At least we'll be at no greater disadvantage there. Ishtar, but the Old Man's rhyme is true! "Each chamber is a slavering maw, each arch a toothy jaw." I always greatly feared this place, but never thought to find a mazy den that sure as death has stony mind and stony claws.

'They never chose to bring me here, you see, and from the night I left our home in Anra's body, I was a living corpse, to be left or taken where they wished. They would have killed me, I think, at least there came a time when Anra would, except it was necessary that Anra's body have an occupant – or my rightful body when he was out of it, for Anra was able to re-enter his own body and walk about in it in this region of Ahriman. At such times I was kept drugged and helpless at the Lost City. I believe that something was done to his body at that time – the Old Man talked of making it invulnerable – for after I returned to it, I found it seeming both emptier and stonier than before.'

Starting back down the ramp, the Mouser thought he heard from somewhere ahead, against the terrible silence, the faintest of windy groans.

'I grew to know my twin's body very well, for I was in it most of seven years in the tomb. Somewhere during that black period all fear and horror vanished – I had become habituated to death. For the first time in my life my will, my cold intelligence, had time to grow. Physically fettered, existing almost without sensation, I gained inward power. I began to see what I could never see before – Anra's weaknesses.

'For he could never cut me wholly off from him. The chain he had forged between our minds was too strong for that. No matter how far away he went, no matter what screens he raised up, I could always see into some sector of his mind, dimly, like a scene at the end of a long, narrow, shadowy corridor.

'I saw his pride – a silver-armored wound. I watched his ambition stalk among the stars as if they were jewels set on black velvet in his treasure house to be. I felt, almost as if it were my own, his choking hatred of the bland, miserly gods – almighty fathers who lock up the secrets of the universe, smile at our pleas, frown, shake their heads, forbid, chastise; and his groaning rage at the bonds of space and time, as if each cubit he could not see and tread upon were a silver manacle on his wrist, as if each moment before or after his own life were a silver crucifying nail. I walked through the gale-blown halls of his loneliness and glimpsed the beauty that he cherished – shadowy, glittering forms that cut the soul like knives – and once I came upon the dungeon of his love, where no light came to show it was corpses that were fondled and bones kissed. I grew familiar with his desires, which demanded a universe of miracles peopled by unveiled gods. And his lust, which quivered at the world as at a woman, frantic to know each hidden part.

'Happily, for I was learning at long last to hate him, I noted how, though he possessed my body, he could not use it easily and bravely as I had. He could not laugh, or love, or dare. He must instead hang back, peer, purse his lips, withdraw.'

More than halfway down the ramp, it seemed to the Mouser that the groan was repeated, louder, more whistlingly.

'He and the Old Man started on a new cycle of study and experience that took them, I think, to all corners of the world and that they were confident, I'm sure, would open to them those black realms wherein their powers would become infinite. Anxiously from my cramped vantage-point I watched their quest ripen and then, to my delight, rot. Their outstretched fingers just missed the next handhold in the dark. There was something that both of them lacked. Anra became bitter, blamed the Old Man for their lack of success. They quarreled.

'When I saw Anra's failure become final, I mocked him with my laughter, not of lips but of mind. From here to the stars he could not have escaped it – it was then he would have killed me. But he dared not while I was in his own body, and I now had the power to bar him from that.

'Perhaps it was my faint thought-laughter that turned his desperate mind to you and to the secret of the laughter of the Elder Gods – that, and his need of magical aid in regaining his body. For a while then I almost feared he had found a new avenue of escape – or advance – until this morning before the tomb, with sheer cruel joy, I saw you spit on his offers, challenge, and, helped by my laughter, kill him. Now there is only the Old Man to fear.'

Passing again under the massive multiple archway with its oddly recessed keystone, they heard the whistling groan once more repeated, and this time there was no mistaking its reality, its nearness, its direction. Hastening to a shadowy and particularly misty corner of the chamber, they made out an inner window set level with the floor, and in that window they saw a face that seemed to float bodiless on the thick fog. Its features defied recognition – it might have been a distillation of all the ancient, disillusioned faces in the world. There was no beard below the sunken cheeks.

Coming close as they dared, they saw that it was perhaps not entirely bodiless or without support. There was the ghostly suggestion of tatters of clothing or flesh trailing off, a pulsating sack that might have been a lung, and silver chains with hooks or claws.

Then the one eye remaining to that shameful fragment opened and fixed upon Ahura, and the shrunken lips twisted themselves into the caricature of a smile.

'Like you, Ahura,' the fragment murmured in the highest of falsettos, 'he sent me on an errand I did not want to run.'

As one, moved by a fear they dared not formulate, Fafhrd and the Mouser and Ahura half turned round and peered over their shoulders at the mist-clogged doorway leading outside. For three, four heartbeats they peered. Then, faintly, they heard one of the horses whinny. Whereupon they turned fully round, but not before a dagger, sped by the yet unshaking hand of Fafhrd, had buried itself in the open eye of the tortured thing in the inner window.

Side by side they stood, Fafhrd wild-eyed, the Mouser taut, Ahura with the look of someone who, having successfully climbed a precipice, slips at the very summit.

A slim shadowy bulk mounted into the glow outside the doorway.

'Laugh!' Fafhrd hoarsely commanded Ahura. 'Laugh!' He shook her, repeating the command.

Her head flopped from side to side, the cords in her neck

jerked, her lips twitched, but from them came only a dry croaking. She grimaced despairingly.

'Yes,' remarked a voice they all recognized, 'there are times and places where laughter is an easily-blunted weapon – as harmless as the sword which this morning pierced me through.'

Death-pale as always, the tiny blood-clot over his heart, his forehead crumbled in, his black garb travel-dusted, Anra Devadoris faced them.

'And so we come back to the beginning,' he said slowly, 'but now a wider circle looms ahead.'

Fafhrd tried to speak, to laugh, but the words and laughter choked in his throat.

'Now you have learned something of my history and my power, as I intended you should,' the adept continued. 'You have had time to weigh and reconsider. I still await your answer.'

This time it was the Mouser who sought to speak or laugh and failed.

For a moment the adept continued to regard them, smiling confidently. Then his gaze wandered beyond them. He frowned suddenly and strode forward, pushed past them, knelt by the inner window.

As soon as his back was turned Ahura tugged at the Mouser's sleeve, tried to whisper something – with no more success than one deaf and dumb.

They heard the adept sob, 'He was my nicest.'

The Mouser drew a dagger, preparing to steal on him from behind, but Ahura dragged him back, pointing in a very different direction.

The adept whirled on them. 'Fools!' he cried. 'Have you no inner eye for the wonders of darkness, no sense of the grandeur of horror, no feeling for a quest beside which all other adventurings fade in nothingness, that you should destroy my greatest miracle – slay my dearest oracle? I let you come here to Mist, confident its mighty music and glorious vistas would win you to my view – and thus I am repaid. The jealous, ignorant powers ring me round – you are my great hope fallen. There were unfavorable portents as I walked from the Lost City. The white, idiot glow of Ormadz faintly dirtied the black sky. I heard in the wind the senile clucking of the Elder Gods. There was a fumbling abroad, as if even incompetent Ningauble, last and stupidest of the hunting pack, were catching up. I had a charm in reserve to thwart them, but it needed the Old Man to carry it. Now they close in for the kill. But there are still some moments of power left me and I am not wholly yet without allies. Though I am doomed, there are still those bound to me by such ties that they must answer me if I call upon them. You shall not see the end, if end there be.' With that he lifted his voice in a great eerie shout: 'Father! Father!'

The echoes had not died before Fafhrd rushed at him, his great sword swinging.

The Mouser would have followed suit except that, just as he shook Ahura off, he realized at what she was so insistently pointing.

The recess in the keystone above the mighty archway. Without hesitation he unslipped his climbing rope, and running lightly across the chamber, made a whistling cast.

The hook caught in the recess.

Hand over hand he climbed up.

Behind him he heard the desperate skirl of swords, heard also another sound, far more distant and profound.

His hand gripped the lip of the recess, he pulled himself up and thrust in head and shoulders, steadying himself on hip and elbow. After a moment, with his free hand, he whipped out his dagger.

Inside, the recess was hollowed like a bowl. It was filled with a foul greenish liquid and incrusted with glowing minerals. At the bottom, covered by the liquid, were several objects – three of them rectangular, the others irregularly round and rhythmically pulsating.

He raised his dagger, but for the moment did not, could not, strike. There was too crushing a weight of things to be realized and remembered – what Ahura had told about the ritual marriage in her mother's family – her suspicion that, although she and Anra were born together, they were not children of the same father – how her Greek father had died (and now the Mouser guessed at the hands of what) – the strange affinity for stone the slave-physician had noted in Anra's body – what she had said about an operation performed on him – why a heart-thrust had not killed him – why his skull had cracked so hollowly and egg-shell easy – he had never seemed to breathe – old legends of other sorcerers who had made themselves invulnerable by hiding their hearts – above all, the deep kinship all of them had sensed between Anra and this half-living castle – the black, man-shaped monolith in the Lost City—

He saw Anra Devadoris, spitted on Fafhrd's blade, hurling himself closer along it, and Fafhrd desperately warding off Needle with a dagger.

As if pinioned by a nightmare, he helplessly heard the clash of swords rise toward a climax, heard it blotted out by the other sound – a gargantuan stony clomping that seemed to be following their course up the mountain, like a pursuing earthquake—

The Castle Called Mist began to tremble, and still he could not strike—

Then, as if surging across infinity from that utmost rim beyond which the Elder Gods had retreated, relinquishing the world to younger deities, he heard a mighty, star-shaking laughter that laughed at all things, even at this; and there was power in the laughter, and he knew the power was his to use.

With a downward sweep of his arm he sent his dagger plunging into the green liquid and tearing through the stone-crusted heart and brain and lungs and guts of Anra Devadoris.

The liquid foamed and boiled, the castle rocked until he was almost shaken from the niche, the laughter and stony clomping rose to a pandemonium.

Then, in an instant it seemed, all sound and movement ceased. The Mouser's muscles went weak. He half fell, half slid, to the floor. Looking about dazedly, making no attempt to rise, he saw Fafhrd wrench his sword from the fallen adept and totter back until his groping hand found the support of a table-edge, saw Ahura, still gasping from the laughter that had possessed her, go up and kneel beside her brother and cradle his crushed head on her knees.

No word was spoken. Time passed. The green mist seemed to be slowly thinning.

Then a small black shape swooped into the room through a high window and the Mouser grinned.

'Hugin,' he called luringly.

The shape swooped obediently to his sleeve and clung there, head down. He detached from the bat's leg a tiny parchment.

'Fancy, Fafhrd, it's from the commander of our rear guard,' he announced gaily. 'Listen:

'"To my agents Fafhrd and the Gray Mouser, funeral greetings! I have regretfully given up all hope for you, and yet – token of my great affection – I risk my own dear Hugin in order to get this last message through. Incidentally, Hugin, if given opportunity, will return to me from Mist – something I am afraid you will not be able to do. So if, before you die, you see anything interesting – and I am sure you will – kindly scribble me a memorandum. Remember the proverb: Knowledge takes precedence over death. Farewell for two thousand years, dearest friends. Ningauble.'"

'That demands drink,' said Fafhrd, and walked out into the darkness. The Mouser yawned and stretched himself, Ahura stirred, printed a kiss on the waxen face of her brother, lifted the trifling weight of his head from her lap, and laid it gently on the stone floor. From somewhere in the upper reaches of the castle they heard a faint crackling.

Presently Fafhrd returned, striding more briskly, with two jars of wine under his arm.

'Friends,' he announced, 'the moon's come out, and by its light this castle begins to look remarkably small. I think the mist must have been dusted with some green drug that made us see sizes wrong. We must have been drugged, I'll swear, for we never saw something that's standing plain as day at the bottom of the stairs with its foot on the first step – a black statue that's twin brother to the one in the Lost City.'

The Mouser lifted his eyebrows. 'And if we went back to the Lost City . . . ?' he asked.

'Why,' said Fafhrd, 'we might find that those fool Persian farmers, who admitted hating the thing, had knocked down the statue there, and broken it up, and hidden the pieces.' He was silent for a moment. Then, 'Here's wine,' he rumbled, 'to sluice the green drug from our throats.'

The Mouser smiled. He knew that hereafter Fafhrd would refer to their present adventure as 'the time we were drugged on a mountaintop.'

They all three sat on a table-edge and passed the two jars endlessly round. The green mist faded to such a degree that Fafhrd, ignoring his claims about the drug, began to argue that even it was an illusion. The crackling from above increased in volume; the Mouser guessed that the impious rolls in the library, no longer shielded by the damp, were bursting into flame. Some proof of this was given when the abortive bear cub, which they had completely forgotten, came waddling frightenedly down the ramp. A trace of decorous down was already sprouting from its naked hide. Fafhrd dribbled some wine on its snout and held it up to the Mouser.

'It wants to be kissed,' he rumbled.

'Kiss it yourself, in memory of pig-trickery,' replied the Mouser.

This talk of kissing turned their thoughts to Ahura. Their rivalry forgotten, at least for the present, they persuaded her to help them determine whether her brother's spells were altogether broken. A moderate number of hugs demonstrated this clearly.

'Which reminds me,' said the Mouser brightly, 'now that our business here is over, isn't it time we started, Fafhrd, for your lusty Northland and all that bracing snow?'

Fafhrd drained one jar dry and picked up the other.

'The Northland?' he ruminated. 'What is it but a stamping ground of petty, frost-whiskered kinglets who know not the amenities of life. That's why I left the place. Go back? By Thor's smelly jerkin, not now!'

The Mouser smiled knowingly and sipped from the remaining jar. Then, noticing the bat still clinging to his sleeve, he took stylus, ink, and a scrap of parchment from his pouch, and, with Ahura giggling over his shoulder, wrote:

'To my aged brother in petty abominations, greetings! It is with the deepest regret that I must report the outrageously lucky and completely unforeseen escape of two rude and unsympathetic fellows from the Castle Called Mist. Before leaving, they expressed to me the intention of returning to some one called Ningauble – you are Ningauble, master, are you not? – and lopping off six of his seven eyes for souvenirs. So I think it only fair to warn you. Believe me, I am your friend. One of the fellows was very tall and at times his bellowings seemed to resemble speech. Do you know him? The other fancied a gray garb and was of extreme wit and personal beauty, given to . . .'

Had any of them been watching the corpse of Anra Devadoris at this moment, they would have seen a slight twitching of the lower jaw. At last the mouth came open, and out leaped a tiny black mouse. The cub-like creature, to whom Fafhrd's fondling and the wine had imparted the seeds of self-confidence, lurched drunkenly at it, and the mouse began a squeaking scurry toward the wall. A wine jar, hurled by Fafhrd, shattered on the crack into which it shot; Fafhrd had seen, or thought he had seen, the untoward place from which the mouse had come.

'Mice in his mouth,' he hiccuped. 'What dirty habits for a pleasant young man! A nasty, degrading business, this thinking oneself an adept.'

'I am reminded,' said the Mouser, 'of what a witch told me about adepts. She said that, if an adept chances to die, his soul is reincarnated in a mouse. If, as a mouse, he managed to kill a rat, his soul passes over into a rat. As a rat, he must kill a cat; as a cat, a wolf; as a wolf, a panther; and, as a panther, a man. Then he can recommence his adeptry. Of course, it seldom happens that anyone gets all the way through the sequence and in any case it takes a very long time. Trying to kill a rat is enough to satisfy a mouse with mousedom.'

Fafhrd solemnly denied the possibility of any such foolery, and Ahura cried until she decided that being a mouse would interest rather than dishearten her peculiar brother. More wine was drunk from the remaining jar. The crackling from the rooms above had become a roar, and a bright red glow consumed the dark shadows. The three adventurers prepared to leave the place.

Meantime the mouse, or another very much like it, thrust its head from the crack and began to lick the wine-damp shards, keeping a fearful eye upon those in the great room, but especially upon the strutting little would-be bear.

The Mouser said, 'Our quest's done. I'm for Tyre.'

Fafhrd said, 'I'm for Ning's Gate and Lankhmar. Or is that a dream?'

The Mouser shrugged, 'Mayhap Tyre's the dream. Lankhmar sounds as good.'

Ahura said, 'Could a girl go?'

A great blast of wind, cold and pure, blew away the last lingering of Mist. As they went through the doorway they saw, outspread above them, the self-consistent stars.

SWORDS AGAINST WIZARDRY

CONTENTS

This book is dedicated to
HARRY OTTO FISCHER,
who first explored Quarmall
and who wrote ten thousand of these words,
here unchanged,
about that subterranean kingdom.

Additionally, Part Two of this novel –
Stardock – is dedicated to
those two hardy cragsmen,
Poul Anderson and Paul Turner.

I
IN THE WITCH'S TENT

The hag bent over the brazier. Its upward-seeking gray fumes interwove with strands of her downward dangling, tangled black hair. Its glow showed her face to be as dark, jagged-featured, and dirty as the new-dug root-clump of a blackapple tree. A half century of brazier heat and smoke had cured it as black, crinkly, and hard as Mingol bacon.

Through her splayed nostrils and slack mouth, which showed a few brown teeth like old tree stumps irregularly fencing the gray field of her tongue, she garglingly inhaled and bubblingly expelled the fumes.

Such of them as escaped her greedy lungs tortuously found their way to the tent's saggy roof, resting on seven ribs down-curving from the central pole, and deposited on the ancient rawhide their tiny dole of resin and soot. It is said that such a tent, boiled out after decades or preferably centuries of use, yields a nauseous liquid which gives a man strange and danger-ous visions.

Outside the tent's drooping walls radiated the dark, twisty alleys of Illik-Ving, an overgrown and rudely boisterous town, which is the eighth and smallest metropolis of the Land of the Eight Cities.

While overhead there shivered in the chill wind the strange stars of the world of Nehwon, which is so like and unlike our own world.

Inside the tent, two barbarian-clad men watched the crouch-ing witch across the brazier. The big man, who had red-blond hair, stared somber-eyed and intently. The little man, who was dressed all in gray, dropped his eyelids, stifled a yawn, and wrinkled his nose.

'I don't know which stinks worse, she or the brazier,' he murmured. 'Or maybe it's the whole tent, or this alley muck we must sit in. Or perchance her familiar is a skunk. Look, Fafhrd, if we must consult a sorcerous personage, we should have sought out Sheelba or Ningauble before ever we sailed north from Lankhmar across the Inner Sea.'

'They weren't available,' the big man answered in a clipped whisper. 'Shh, Gray Mouser, I think she's gone into trance.'

'Asleep, you mean,' the little man retorted irreverently.

The hag's gargling breath began to sound more like a death rattle. Her eyelids fluttered, showing two white lines. Wind stirred the tent's dark walls – or it might be unseen presences fumbling and fingering.

The little man was unimpressed. He said, 'I don't see why we have to consult anyone. It isn't as if we were going outside Nehwon altogether, as we did in our last adventure. We've got the papers – the scrap of ramskin parchment, I mean – and we know where we're going. Or at least you say you do.'

'Shh!' the big man commanded, then added hoarsely, 'Before embarking on any great enterprise, it's customary to consult a warlock or witch.'

The little man, now whispering likewise, countered with, 'Then why couldn't we have consulted a civilized one? – any member in good standing of the Lankhmar Sorcerers Guild. He'd at least have had a comely naked girl or two around, to rest your eyes on when they began to water from scanning his crabbed hieroglyphs and horoscopes.'

'A good earthy witch is more honest than some city rogue tricked out in black cone-hat and robe of stars,' the big man argued. 'Besides, this one is nearer our icy goal and its influences. You and your townsman's lust for luxuries! You'd turn a wizard's workroom into a brothel.'

'Why not?' the little man wanted to know. 'Both species of glamor at once!' Then, jerking his thumb at the hag, 'Earthy, you said? Dungy describes her better.'

'Shh, Mouser, you'll break her trance.'

'Trance?' The little man reinspected the hag. Her mouth had shut and she was breathing wheezingly through her beaky nose alone, the fume-sooty tip of which sought to meet her jutting chin. There was a faint high wailing, as of distant wolves, or nearby ghosts, or perhaps just an odd overtone of the hag's wheezes.

The little man sneered his upper lip and shook his head. His hands shook a little too, but he hid that. 'No, she's only stoned out of her skull, I'd say,' he commented judiciously. 'You shouldn't have given her so much poppy gum.'

'But that's the entire intent of trance,' the big man protested. 'To lash, stone, and otherwise drive the spirit out of the skull and whip it up mystic mountains, so that from their peaks it can spy out the lands of past and future, and mayhaps other-world.'

'I wish the mountains ahead of *us* were merely mystic,' the little man muttered. 'Look, Fafhrd, I'm willing to squat here all night – or at any rate for fifty more stinking breaths or two hundred bored heartbeats – to pleasure your whim. But has it occurred to you that we're in danger in this tent? And I don't mean solely from spirits. There are other rogues than ourselves in Illik-Ving, some perhaps on the same quest as ours, who'd dearly love to scupper us. And here in this blind leather hut we're deer on a skyline – or sitting ducks.'

Just then the wind came back with its fumblings and fingerings, and in addition a scrabbling that might be that of wind-swayed branch tips or of dead men's long fingernails a-scratch. There were faint growlings and wailings too, and with them stealthy footfalls. Both men thought of the Mouser's last warning. Fafhrd and he looked toward the tent's night-slitted skin door and loosened their swords in their scabbards.

At that instant the hag's noisy breathing stopped and with it all other sound. Her eyes opened, showing only whites – milky ovals infinitely eerie in the dark root-tangle of her sharp features and stringy hair. The gray tip of her tongue traveled like a large maggot around her lips.

The Mouser made to comment, but the out-thrust palmside of Fafhrd's spread-fingered hand was more compelling than any *shh*.

In a voice low but remarkably clear, almost a girl's voice, the hag intoned:

> '*For reasons sorcerous and dim*
> *You travel toward the world's frost rim . . .*'

'*Dim*' *is the key word there*, the Mouser thought. *Typical witchy say-nothing. She clearly knows naught about us except that we're headed north, which she could get from any gossipy mouth.*

> '*You north, north, north, and north must go*
> *Through dagger-ice and powder-snow . . .*'

More of the same, was the Mouser's inward comment. *But must she rub it in, even the snow? Brr!*

> '*And many a rival, envy-eyed,*
> *Will dog your steps until you've died . . .*'

Aha, the inevitable right-thrust, without which no fortune-tale is complete!

> '*But after peril's cleansing fire*
> *You'll meet at last your heart's desire . . .*'

And now pat the happy ending! Gods, but the stupidest palm-reading prostitute of Ilthmar could—

> '*And then you'll find—*'

Something silvery gray flashed across the Mouser's eyes, so close its form was blurred. Without a thought he ducked back and drew Scalpel.

The razor-sharp spear-blade, driven through the tent's side as if it were paper, stopped inches from Fafhrd's head and was dragged back.

A javelin hurtled out of the hide wall. This the Mouser struck aside with his sword.

Now a storm of cries rose outside. The burden of some was, 'Death to the strangers!' Of others, 'Come out, dogs and be killed!'

The Mouser faced the skin door, his gaze darting.

Fafhrd, almost as quick to react as the Mouser, hit on a somewhat irregular solution to their knotty tactical problem: that of men besieged in a fortress whose walls neither protect them nor permit outward viewing. At first step, he leaped to the tent's central pole and with a great heave drew it from the earth.

The witch, likewise reacting with good solid sense, threw herself flat on the dirt.

'We decamp!' Fafhrd cried. 'Mouser, guard our front and guide me!'

And with that he charged toward the door, carrying the whole tent with him. There was a rapid series of little explosions as the somewhat brittle old thongs that tied its rawhide sides to its pegs snapped. The brazier tumbled over, scattering coals. The hag was overpassed. The Mouser, running ahead of Fafhrd, threw wide the door-slit. He had to use Scalpel at once, to parry a sword thrust out of the dark, but with his other hand he kept the door spread.

The opposing swordsman was bowled over, perhaps a bit startled at being attacked by the tent. The Mouser trod on him. He thought he heard ribs snap as Fafhrd did the same, which seemed a nice if brutal touch. Then he was crying out, 'Veer left now, Fafhrd! Now to the right a little! There's an alley coming up on our left. Be ready to turn sharp into it when I give the word. Now!' And grasping the door's hide edges, the Mouser helped swing the tent as Fafhrd pivoted.

From behind came cries of rage and wonder, also a screeching that sounded like the hag, enraged at the theft of her home.

The alley was so narrow that the tent's sides dragged against buildings and fences. At the first sign of a soft spot in the dirt underfoot, Fafhrd drove the tent-pole into it, and they both dashed out of the tent, leaving it blocking the alley.

The cries behind them grew suddenly louder as their pursuers turned into the alley, but Fafhrd and the Mouser did not run off over-swiftly. It seemed certain their attackers would spend considerable time scouting and assaulting the empty tent.

They loped together through the outskirts of the sleeping city toward their own well-hidden camp outside it. Their nostrils sucked in the chill, bracing air funneling down from the best pass through the Trollstep Mountains, a craggy chain which walled off the Land of Eight Cities from the vast plateau of the Cold Waste to the north.

Fafhrd remarked, 'It's unfortunate the old lady was interrupted just when she was about to tell us something important.'

The Mouser snorted. 'She'd already sung her song, the sum of which was zero.'

'I wonder who those rude fellows were and what were their motives?' Fafhrd asked. 'I thought I recognized the voice of that ale-swiller Gnarfi, who has an aversion to bear-meat.'

'Scoundrels behaving as stupidly as we were,' the Mouser answered. 'Motives? – as soon impute 'em to sheep! Ten dolts following an idiot leader.'

'Still, it appears that someone doesn't like us,' Fafhrd opined.

'Was that ever news?' the Gray Mouser retorted.

II
STARDOCK

Early one evening, weeks later, the sky's gray cloud-armor blew away south, smashed and dissolving as if by blows of an acid-dipped mace. The same mighty northeast wind contemptuously puffed down the hitherto impregnable cloud wall to the east, revealing a grimly majestic mountain range running north to south and springing abruptly from the plateau, two leagues high, of the Cold Waste – like a dragon fifty leagues long heaving up its spike-crested spine from icy entombment.

Fafhrd, no stranger to the Cold Waste, born at the foot of these same mountains and childhood climber of their lower slopes, named them off to the Gray Mouser as the two men stood together on the crunchy hoarfrosted eastern rim of the hollow that held their camp. The sun, set for the camp, still shone from behind their backs onto the western faces of the major peaks as he named them – but it shone not with any romanticizing rosy glow, but rather with a clear, cold, detail-pinning light fitting the peaks' dire aloofness.

'Travel your eye to the first great northerly upthrust,' he told the Mouser, 'that phalanx of heaven-menacing ice-spears shafted with dark rock and gleaming green – that's the Ripsaw. Then, dwarfing them, a single ivory-icy tooth, unscalable by any sane appraisal – the Tusk, he's called. Another unscalable then, still higher and with south wall a sheer precipice shooting up a league and curving outward toward the needletop: he is White Fang, where my father died – the canine of the Mountains of the Giants.

'Now begin again with the first snow dome at the south of the chain,' continued the tall fur-cloaked man, copper-bearded and copper-maned, his head otherwise bare to the frigid air, which was as quiet at ground level as sea-deep beneath storm. 'The

Hint, she's named, or the Come On. Little enough she looks, yet men have frozen nighting on her slopes and been whirled to death by her whimsical queenly avalanches. Then a far vaster snow dome, true queen to the Hint's princess, a hemisphere of purest white, grand enough to roof the council hall of all the gods that ever were or will be – she is Gran Hanack, whom my father was first of men to mount and master. Our town of tents was pitched *there* near her base. No mark of it now, I'll guess, not even a midden.

'After Gran Hanack and nearest to us of them all, a huge flat-topped pillar, a pedestal for the sky almost, looking to be of green-shot snow but in truth all snow-pale granite scoured by the storms: Obelisk Polaris.

'Lastly,' Fafhrd continued, sinking his voice and gripping his smaller comrade's shoulder, 'let your gaze travel up the snow-tressed, dark-rocked, snowcapped peak between the Obelisk and White Fang, her glittering skirt somewhat masked by the former, but taller than they as they are taller than the Waste. Even now she hides behind her the mounting moon. She is Stardock, our quest's goal.'

'A pretty enough, tall, slender wart on this frostbit patch of Nehwon's face,' the Gray Mouser conceded, writhing his shoulder from Fafhrd's grip. 'And now at last tell me, friend, why you never climbed this Stardock in your youth and seized the treasure there, but must wait until we get a clue to it in a dusty, hot, scorpion-patrolled desert tower a quarter world away – and waste half a year getting here.'

Fafhrd's voice grew a shade unsure as he answered, 'My father never climbed her; how should I? Also, there were no legends of a treasure on Stardock's top in my father's clan . . . though there was a storm of other legends about Stardock, each forbidding her ascent. They called my father the Legend Breaker and shrugged wisely when he died on White Fang . . . Truly, my memory's not so good for those days, Mouser – I got many a mind-shattering knock on my head before I learned to deal all knocks first . . . and then I was hardly a boy when the clan left the Cold Waste – though the rough hard walls of Obelisk Polaris had been my upended playground . . .'

The Mouser nodded doubtfully. In the stillness they heard their tethered ponies munching the ice-crisped grass of the hollow, then a faint unangry growl from Hrissa the ice-cat, curled between the tiny fire and the piled baggage – likely one of the ponies had come cropping too close. On the great icy plain around them, nothing moved – or almost nothing.

The Mouser dipped gray lambskin-gloved fingers into the bottom of his pouch and from the pocket there withdrew a tiny oblong of parchment and read from it, more by memory than sight:

> *'Who mounts white Stardock, the Moon Tree,*
> *Past worm and gnome and unseen bars,*
> *Will win the key to luxury:*
> *The Heart of Light, a pouch of stars.'*

Fafhrd said dreamily, 'They say the gods once dwelt and had their smithies on Stardock and from thence, amid jetting fire and showering sparks, launched all the stars; hence her name. They say diamonds, rubies, smaragds – all great gems – are the tiny pilot models the gods made of the stars . . . and then threw carelessly away across the world when their great work was done.'

'You never told me that before,' the Mouser said, looking at him sharply.

Fafhrd blinked his eyes and frowned puzzledly. 'I am beginning to remember childhood things.'

The Mouser smiled thinly before returning the parchment to its deep pocket. 'The guess that a pouch of stars might be a bag of gems,' he listed, 'the story that Nehwon's biggest diamond is called the Heart of Light, a few words on a ramskin scrap in the topmost room of a desert tower locked and sealed for centuries – small hints, those, to draw two men across this murdering, monotonous Cold Waste. Tell me, Old Horse, were you just homesick for the miserable white meadows of your birth to pretend to believe 'em?'

'Those small hints,' Fafhrd said, gazing now toward White Fang, 'drew other men north across Nehwon. There must have been other ramskin scraps, though why they should be dis-covered at the same time, I cannot guess.'

'We left all such fellows behind at Illik-Ving, or Lankhmar even, before we ever mounted the Trollsteps,' the Mouser asserted with complete confidence. 'Weak sisters, they were, smelling loot but quailing at hardship.'

Fafhrd gave a small headshake and pointed. Between them and White Fang rose the tiniest thread of black smoke.

'Did Gnarfi and Kranarch seem weak sisters? – to name but two of the other seekers,' he asked when the Mouser finally saw and nodded.

'It could be,' the Mouser agreed gloomily, 'Though aren't there any ordinary travelers of this Waste? Not that we've seen a man-shaped soul since the Mingol.'

Fafhrd said thoughtfully, 'It might be an encampment of the Icy Gnomes . . . though they seldom leave their caves except at High Summer, now a month gone . . .' He broke off, frowning puzzledly. 'Now how did I know that?'

'Another childhood memory bobbing to the top of the black pot?' the Mouser hazarded. Fafhrd shrugged doubtfully.

'So, for choice, Kranarch and Gnarfi,' the Mouser con-cluded. 'Two strong brothers, I'll concede. Perhaps we should have picked a fight with 'em at Illik-Ving,' he suggested. 'Or perhaps even now . . . a swift march by night . . . a sudden swoop—'

Fafhrd shook his head. 'Now we're climbers, not killers,' he said. 'A man must be all climber to dare Stardock.' He directed the Mouser's gaze back toward the tallest mountain. 'Let's rather study her west wall while the light holds.

'Begin first at her feet,' he said. 'That glimmering skirt falling from her snowy hips, which are almost as high as the Obelisk – that's the White Waterfall, where no man may live.

'Now to her head again. From her flat tilted snowcap hang two great swelling braids of snow, streaming almost perpetually with avalanches, as if she combed 'em day and night – the Tresses, those are called. Between them's a wide ladder of dark rock, marked at three points by ledges. The topmost of the three ledge-banks is the Face – d'you note the darker ledges

marking eyes and lips? The midmost of the three is called the
Roosts; the lowermost – level with Obelisk's wide summit – the
Lairs.'

What lairs and roosts there?' the Mouser wanted to know.

'None may say, for none have climbed the Ladder,' Fafhrd
replied. 'Now as to our route up her – it's most simple. We
scale Obelisk Polaris – a trustworthy mountain if there ever was
one – then cross by a dippling snow-saddle (there's the danger-
stretch of our ascent!) to Stardock and climb the Ladder to her
top.'

'How do we climb the Ladder in the long blank stretches
between the ledges?' the Mouser asked with childlike innocence,
almost. 'That is, if the Lairers and Roosters will honor our
passports and permit us to try.'

Fafhrd shrugged. 'There'll be a way, rock being rock.'

'Why's there no snow on the Ladder?'

'Too steep.'

'And supposing we climb it to the top,' the Mouser finally
asked, 'how do we lift our black-and-blue skeletonized bodies
over the brim of Stardock's snowy hat, which seems to outcurve
and downcurve most stylishly?'

'There's a triangular hole in it somewhere called the Needle's
Eye,' Fafhrd answered negligently. 'Or so I've heard. But never
you fret, Mouser, we'll find it.'

'Of course we will,' the Mouser agreed with an airy certainty
that almost sounded sincere, 'we who hop-skip across shaking
snow bridges and dance the fantastic up vertical walls without
ever touching hand to granite. Remind me to bring a longish
knife to carve our initials on the sky when we celebrate the end
of our little upward sortie.'

His gaze wandered slightly northward. In another voice he
continued, 'The dark north wall of Stardock now – that looks
steep enough, to be sure, but free of snow to the very top. Why
isn't that our route – rock, as you say with such unanswerable
profundity, being rock.'

Fafhrd laughed unmockingly. 'Mouser,' he said, 'do you mark
against the darkening sky that long white streamer waving south
from Stardock's top? Yes, and below it a lesser streamer – can

you distinguish that? That second one comes through the Needle's Eye! Well, those streamers from Stardock's hat are called the Grand and Petty Pennons. They're powdered snow blasted off Stardock by the northeast gale, which blows at least seven days out of eight, never predictably. That gale would pluck the stoutest climber off the north wall as easily as you or I might puff dandelion down from its darkening stem. Stardock's self shields the Ladder from the gale.'

'Does the gale never shift around to strike the Ladder?' the Mouser inquired lightly.

'Only occasionally,' Fafhrd reassured him.

'Oh, that's great,' the Mouser responded with quite over-powering sincerity and would have returned to the fire, except just then the darkness began swiftly to climb the Mountains of the Giants, as the sun took his final dive far to the west, and the gray-clad man stayed to watch the grand spectacle.

It was like a black blanket being pulled up. First the glittering skirt of the White Waterfall was hidden, then the Lairs on the Ladder and then the Roosts. Now all the other peaks were gone, even the Tusk's and White Fang's gleaming cruel tips, even the greenish-white roof of Obelisk Polaris. Now only Stardock's snow hat was left and below it the Face between the silvery Tresses. For a moment the ledges called the Eyes gleamed, or seemed to. Then all was night.

Yet there was a pale afterglow about. It was profoundly silent and the air utterly unmoving. Around them, the Cold Waste seemed to stretch north, west, and south to infinity.

And in that space of silence something went whisper-gliding through the still air, with the faint rushy sound of a great sail in a moderate breeze. Fafhrd and the Mouser both stared all around wildly. Nothing. Beyond the little fire, Hrissa the ice-cat sprang up hissing. Still nothing. Then the sound, whatever had made it, died away.

Very softly, Fafhrd began, 'There is a legend . . .' A long pause. Then with a sudden headshake, in a more natural voice: 'The memory slips away, Mouser. All my mind-fingers couldn't clutch it. Let's patrol once around the camp and so to bed.'

*

From first sleep the Mouser woke so softly that even Hrissa, back pressed against him from his knees to his chest on the side toward the fire, did not rouse.

Emerging from behind Stardock, her light glittering on the Southern Tress, hung the swelling moon, truly a proper fruit of the Moon Tree. Strange, the Mouser thought, how small the moon was and how big Stardock, silhouetted against the moon-pale sky.

Then, just below the flat top of Stardock's hat, he saw a bright, pale blue twinkling. He recalled that Ashsha, pale blue and brightest of Nehwon's stars, was near the moon tonight and he wondered if he were seeing her by rare chance through the Needle's Eye, proving the latter's existence. He wondered too what great sapphire or blue diamond – perhaps the Heart of Light? – had been the gods' pilot model for Ashsha, smiling drowsily the while at himself for entertaining such a silly, lovely myth. And then, embracing the myth entirely, he asked himself whether the gods had left any of their full-scale stars, un-launched, on Stardock. Then Ashsha, if it were she, winked out.

The Mouser felt cozy in his cloak lined with sheep's-wool and now thong-laced into a bag by the horn hooks around its hem. He stared long and dreamily at Stardock until the moon broke loose from her and a blue jewel twinkled on top of her hat and broke loose too – now Ashsha surely. He wondered unfearfully about the windy rushing he and Fafhrd had heard in the still air – perhaps only a long tongue of a storm licking down briefly. If the storm lasted, they would climb up into it.

Hrissa stretched in her sleep. Fafhrd grumbled low in a dream, wrapped in his own great thong-laced cloak stuffed with eiderdown.

The Mouser dropped his gaze to the ghostly flames of the dying fire, seeking sleep himself. The flames made girl-bodies, then girl-faces. Next a ghostly pale green girl-face – perhaps an after-image, he thought at first – appeared beyond the fire, staring at him through close-slitted eyes across the flame tops. It grew more distinct as he gazed at it, but there was no trace of hair or body about it – it hung against the dark like a mask.

Yet it was weirdly beautiful: narrow chin, high-arched cheeks, wine-dark short lips slightly pouted, straight nose that went up without a dip into the broad, somewhat low forehead – and then the mystery of those fully lidded eyes seeming to peer at him through wine-dark lashes. And all, save lashes and lips, of palest green, like jade.

The Mouser did not speak or stir a muscle, simply because the face was very beautiful to him – just as any man might hope for the moment never to end when his naked mistress unconsciously or by secret design assumes a particularly charming attitude.

Also, in the dismal Cold Waste, any man treasures illusions, though knowing them almost certainly to be such.

Suddenly the eyes parted wide, showing only the darkness behind, as if the face were a mask indeed. The Mouser did start then, but still not enough to wake Hrissa.

Then the eyes closed, the lips puckered with taunting invitation; then the face began swiftly to dissolve as if it were being literally wiped away. First the right side went, then the left, then the center, last of all the dark lips and the eyes. For a moment the Mouser fancied he caught a winy odor; then all was gone.

He contemplated waking Fafhrd and almost laughed at the thought of his comrade's surly reactions. He wondered if the face had been a sign from the gods, or a sending from some black magician castled on Stardock, or Stardock's very soul perhaps – though then where had she left her glittering tresses and hat and her Ashsha eye? – or only a random creation of his own most clever brain, stimulated by sexual privation and tonight by beauteous if devilishly dangerous mountains. Rather quickly he decided on the last explanation and he slumbered.

Two evenings later, at the same hour, Fafhrd and the Gray Mouser stood scarcely a knife cast from the west wall of Obelisk Polaris, building a cairn from pale greenish rock-shards fallen over the millennia. Among this scanty scree were some bones, many broken, of sheep or goats.

As before, the air was still though very cold, the Waste empty, the set sun bright on the mountain faces.

From this closest vantage point the Obelisk was foreshortened into a pyramid that seemed to taper up forever, vertically. Encouragingly, his rock felt diamond-hard while the lowest reaches of the wall at any rate were thick with bumpy handholds and footholds, like pebbled leather.

To the south, Gran Hanack and the Hint were hidden. To the north White Fang towered monstrously, yellowish white in the sunlight, as if ready to rip a hole in the graying sky. Bane of Fafhrd's father, the Mouser recalled.

Of Stardock, there could be seen the dark beginning of the wind-blasted north wall and the north end of the deadly White Waterfall. All else of Stardock the Obelisk hid.

Save for one touch: almost straight overhead, seeming now to come from Obelisk Polaris, the ghostly Grand Pennon streamed southwest.

From behind Fafhrd and the Mouser as they worked came the tantalizing odor of two snow hares roasting by the fire, while before it Hrissa tore flesh slowly and savoringly from the carcass of a third she'd coursed down. The ice-cat was about the size and shape of a cheetah, though with long tufty white hair. The Mouser had bought her from a far-ranging Mingol trapper just north of the Trollsteps.

Beyond the fire the ponies eagerly chomped the last of the grain, strengthening stuff they'd not tasted for a week.

Fafhrd wrapped his sheathed longsword Graywand in oiled silk and laid it in the cairn, then held out a big hand to the Mouser.

'Scalpel?'

'I'm taking my sword with me,' the Mouser stated, then added justifyingly, 'it's but a feather to yours.'

'Tomorrow you'll find what a feather weighs,' Fafhrd foretold. The big man shrugged and placed by Graywand his helmet, a bear's hide, a folded tent, shovel and pickax, gold bracelets from his wrists and arms, quills, ink papyrus, a large copper pot, and some books and scrolls. The Mouser added various empty and near-empty bags, two hunting spears, skis, an unstrung bow with a quiver of arrows, tiny jars of oily paint and squares of parchment, and all the harness of the ponies, many of the items wrapped against damp like Graywand.

Then, their appetites quickening from the roast-fumes, the two comrades swiftly built two top courses, roofing the cairn.

Just as they turned toward supper, facing the raggedly gilt-edged flat western horizon, they heard in the silence the rushy sail-like noise again, fainter this time but twice: once in the air to the north and, almost simultaneously, to the south.

Again they stared around swiftly but searchingly, yet there was nothing anywhere to be seen except – again Fafhrd saw it first – a thread of black smoke very near White Fang, rising from a point on the glacier between that mountain and Stardock.

'Gnarfi and Kranarch, if it be they, have chosen the rocky north wall for their ascent,' the Mouser observed.

'And it will be their bane,' Fafhrd predicted, up-jerking his thumb at the Pennon.

The Mouser nodded with less certainty, then demanded, 'Fafhrd, what *was* that sound? You've lived here.'

Fafhrd's brow crinkled and his eyes almost shut. 'Some legend of great birds . . .' he muttered questioningly, ' . . . or of great fish – no, that couldn't be right.'

'Memory pot still seething all black?' the Mouser asked. Fafhrd nodded.

Before he left the cairn, the Northerner laid beside it a slab of salt. 'That,' he said, 'along with the ice-filmed pool and herbage we just passed, should hold the ponies here for a week. If we don't return, well, at least we showed 'em the way between here and Illik-Ving.'

Hrissa smiled up from her bloody tidbit, as if to say, 'No need to worry about me or my rations.'

Again the Mouser woke as soon as sleep had gripped him tight, this time with a surge of pleasure, as one who remembers a rendezvous. And again, this time without any preliminary star-staring or flame-gazing, the living mask faced him across the sinking fire: every same expression-quirk and feature – short lips, nose and forehead one straight line – except that tonight it was ivory pale with greenish lips and lids and lashes.

The Mouser was considerably startled, for last night he had stayed awake, waiting for the phantom girl-face – and even trying to make it come again – until the swelling moon had risen three handbreadths above Stardock . . . without any success whatever. His mind had known that the face had been an hallucination on the first occasion, but his feelings had insisted otherwise – to his considerable disgust and the loss of a quarter night's sleep.

And by day he had secretly consulted the last of the four short stanzas on the parchment scrap in his pouch's deepest pocket:

Who scales the Snow King's citadel
Shall father his two daughters' sons;
Though he must face foes fierce and fell,
His seed shall live while time still runs.

Yesterday that had seemed rather promising – at least the fathering and daughters part – though today, after his lost sleep, the merest mockery.

But now the living mask was there again and going through all the same teasing antics, including the shuddersome yet somehow thrilling trick of opening wide its lids to show not eyes but a dark backing like the rest of the night. The Mouser was enchanted in a shivery way, but unlike the first night he was full-mindedly alert and he tested for illusions by blinking and squinting his own eyes and silently shifting his head about in his hood – with no effect whatever on the living mask. Then he quietly unlaced the thong from the top hooks of his cloak – Hrissa was sleeping against Fafhrd tonight – and slowly reached out his hand and picked up a pebble and flicked it across the pale flames at a point somewhere below the mask.

Although he knew there wasn't anything beyond the fire but scattered scree and ringingly hard earth, there wasn't the faintest sound of the pebble striking anywhere. He might have thrown it off Nehwon.

At almost the same instant, the mask smiled tauntingly.

The Mouser was very swiftly out of his cloak and on his feet.

But even more swiftly the mask dissolved away – this time in one swift stroke from forehead to chin.

He quickly stepped, almost lunged, around the fire to the spot where the mask had seemed to hang, and there he stared around searchingly. Nothing – except a fleeting breath of wine or spirits of wine. He stirred the fire and stared around again. Still nothing. Except that Hrissa woke beside Fafhrd and bristled her moustache and gazed solemnly, perhaps scornfully, at the Mouser, who was beginning to feel rather like a fool. He wondered if his mind and his desires were playing a silly game against each other.

Then he trod on something. His pebble, he thought, but when he picked it up, he saw it was a tiny jar. It could have been one of his own pigment jars, but it was too small, hardly bigger than a joint of his thumb, and made not of hollowed stone but some kind of ivory or other tooth.

He knelt by the fire and peered into it, then dipped in his little finger and gingerly rubbed the tip against the rather hard grease inside. It came out ivory-hued. The grease had an oily, not winy odor.

The Mouser pondered by the fire for some time. Then with a glance at Hrissa, who had closed her eyes and laid back her moustache again, and at Fafhrd, who was snoring softly, he returned to his cloak and to sleep.

He had not told Fafhrd a word about his earlier vision of the living mask. His surface reason was that Fafhrd would laugh at such calf-brained nonsense of smoke-faces; his deeper reason the one which keeps any man from mentioning a pretty new girl even to his dearest friend.

So perhaps it was the same reason which next morning kept Fafhrd from telling his dearest friend what happened to him late that same night. Fafhrd dreamed he was feeling out the exact shape of a girl's face in absolute darkness while her slender hands caressed his body. She had a rounded forehead, very long eye-lashed eyes, in-dipping nose bridge, apple cheeks, an impudent snub nose – it *felt* impudent! – and long lips whose grin his big gentle fingers could trace clearly.

He woke to the moon glaring down at him aslant from the south. It shivered the Obelisk's interminable wall, turning rock-knobs to black shadow bars. He also woke to acute disappointment that a dream had been only a dream. Then he would have sworn that he felt fingertips briefly brush his face and that he heard a faint silvery chuckle which receded swiftly. He sat up like a mummy in his laced cloak and stared around. The fire had sunk to a few red ember-eyes, but the moonlight was bright and by it he could see nothing at all.

Hrissa growled at him reproachfully for a silly sleep-breaker. He damned himself for mistaking the after-image of a dream for reality. He damned the whole girl-less, girl-vision-breeding Cold Waste. A bit of the night's growing chill spilled down his neck. He told himself he should be fast asleep like the wise Mouser over there, gathering strength for tomorrow's great effort. He lay back and after some time he slumbered.

Next morning the Mouser and Fafhrd woke at the first gray of dawn, the moon still bright as a snowball in the west, and quickly breakfasted and readied themselves and stood facing Obelisk Polaris in the stinging cold, all girls forgotten, their manhood directed solely at the mountain.

Fafhrd stood in high-laced boots with newly-sharpened thick hobnails. He wore a wolfskin tunic, fur turned in but open now from neck to belly. His lower arms and legs were bare. Short-wristed rawhide gloves covered his hands. A rather small pack, wrapped in his cloak, rode high on his back. Clipped to it was a large coil of black hempen rope. On his stout unstudded belt, his sheathed ax on his right side balanced on the other a knife, a small waterskin, and a bag of iron spikes headed by rings.

The Mouser wore his ramskin hood, pulled close around his face now by its drawstring, and on his body a tunic of gray silk, triple layered. His gloves were longer than Fafhrd's and fur-lined. So were his slender boots, which were footed with crinkly behemoth hide. On *his* belt, his dagger Cat's Claw and his waterskin balanced his sword Scalpel, its scabbard thonged loosely to his thigh. While to his cloak-wrapped pack was secured a curiously thick, short, black bamboo rod headed with a spike at one end and at the other a spike and large hook, somewhat like that of a shepherd's crook.

Both men were deeply tanned and leanly muscular, in best trim for climbing, hardened by the Trollsteps and the Cold

Waste, their chests a shade larger than ordinary from weeks of subsisting on the latter's thin air.

No need to search out the best-looking ascent – Fafhrd had done that yesterday as they'd approached the Obelisk.

The ponies were cropping again, and one had found the salt and was licking it with his thick tongue. The Mouser looked around for Hrissa to cuff her cheek in farewell, but the ice-cat was sniffling out a spoor beyond the campsite, her ears a-prick.

'She makes a cat-parting,' Fafhrd said. 'Good.'

A faint shade of rose touched the heavens and the glacier by White Fang. Scanning toward the latter, the Mouser drew in his breath and squinted hard, while Fafhrd gazed narrowly from under the roof of his palm.

'Brownish figures,' the Mouser said at last. 'Kranarch and Gnarfi always dressed in brown leather, I recall. But I make them more than two.'

'I make them four,' Fafhrd said. 'Two strangely shaggy – clad in brown fur suits, I guess. And all four mounting from the glacier up the rock wall.'

'Where the gale will—' the Mouser began, then looked up. So did Fafhrd.

The Grand Pennon was gone.

'You said that sometimes—' the Mouser started.

'Forget the gale and those two and their rough-edged reinforcements,' Fafhrd said curtly. He faced around again at Obelisk Polaris. So did the Mouser.

Squinting up the greenish-white slope, head bent sharply back, the Mouser said, 'This morning he seems somewhat steeper even than that north wall and rather extensive upward.'

'Pah!' Fafhrd retorted. 'As a child I would climb him before breakfast. Often.' He raised his clenched right rawhide glove as if it held a baton, and cried, 'We go!'

With that he strode forward and without a break began to walk up the knobbly face – or so it seemed, for although he used handholds he kept his body far out from the rock, as a good climber should.

The Mouser followed in Fafhrd's steps and holds, stretching his legs farther and keeping somewhat closer to the cliff.

Midmorning and they were still climbing without a break. The Mouser ached or stung in every part. His pack was like a fat man on his back, Scalpel a sizable boy clinging to his belt. And his ears had popped five times.

Just above, Fafhrd's boots clashed rock-knobs and into rock-holes with an unhesitating mechanistic rhythm the Mouser had begun to hate. Yet he kept his eyes resolutely fixed on them. Once he had looked down between his own legs and decided not to do that again.

It is not good to see the blue of distance, or even the gray-blue of middle distance, below one.

So he was taken by surprise when a small white bearded face, bloodily encumbered, came bobbing up alongside and past him.

Hrissa halted on a ledgelet by Fafhrd and took great whistling breaths, her tufted belly-skin pressing up against her spine with each exhalation. She breathed only through her pinkish nostrils because her jaws were full of two snow hares, packed side by side, with dead heads and hind-quarters a-dangle.

Fafhrd took them from her and dropped them in his pouch and laced it shut.

Then he said, just a shade grandiloquently, 'She has proved her endurance and skill, and she has paid her way. She is one of us.'

It had not occurred to the Mouser to doubt any of that. It seemed to him simply that there were three comrades now climbing Obelisk Polaris. Besides, he was most grateful to Hrissa for the halt she had brought. Partly to prolong it, he carefully pressed a handful of water from his bag and stretched it to her to lap. Then he and Fafhrd drank a little too.

All the long summer day they climbed the west wall of the cruel but reliable Obelisk. Fafhrd seemed tireless. The Mouser got his second wind, lost it, and never quite got his third. His whole body was one great leaden ache, beginning deep in his bones and filtering outward, like refined poison, through his flesh. His vision became a bobbing welter of real and remembered rock-knobs, while the necessity of never missing one single grip or foot-placement seemed the ruling of an insane schoolmaster god. He silently cursed the whole maniacal Stardock project, cackling in his brain at the idea that the luring stanzas on the parchment could be anything but pipe dreams. Yet he would not cry quits or seek again to prolong the brief breathers they took.

He marveled dully at Hrissa's leaping and hunching up beside them. But by midafternoon he noted she was limping and once he saw a light blood-print of two pads where she'd set a paw.

They made camp at last almost two hours before sunset, because they'd found a rather wide ledge – and because a very light snowfall had begun, the tiny flakes sifting silently down like meal.

They made a fire of resin-pellets in the tiny claw-footed brazier Fafhrd packed, and they heated over it water for herb tea in their single narrow high pot. The water was a long time getting even lukewarm. With Cat's Claw the Mouser stirred two dollops of honey into it.

The ledge was as long as three men stretched out and as deep as one. On the sheer face of Obelisk Polaris that much space seemed an acre, at least.

Hrissa stretched slackly behind the tiny fire. Fafhrd and the Mouser huddled to either side of it, their cloaks drawn around them, too tired to look around, talk, or even think.

The snowfall grew a little thicker, enough to hide the Cold Waste far below.

After his second swallow of sweetened tea, Fafhrd asserted they'd come at least two-thirds of the way up the Obelisk.

The Mouser couldn't understand how Fafhrd could pretend to know that, any more than a man could tell by looking at the shoreless waters of the Outer Sea how far he'd sailed across it. To the Mouser they were simply in the exact center of a dizzily tip-tilted plain of pale granite, green-tinged and now snow-sprinkled. He was still too weary to outline this concept to Fafhrd, but he managed to make himself say, 'As a child you would climb up and down the Obelisk before breakfast?'

'We had rather late breakfasts then,' Fafhrd explained gruffly.

'Doubtless on the afternoon of the fifth day,' the Mouser concluded.

After the tea was drunk, they heated more water and left the hacked and disjointed bits of one of the snow hares in the fluid until they turned gray, then slowly chewed them and drank the dull soup. At about the same time Hrissa became a little interested in the flayed carcass of the other hare set before her nose – by the brazier to keep it from freezing. Enough interested to begin to haggle it with her fangs and slowly chew and swallow.

The Mouser very gently examined the pads of the ice-cat's paws. They were worn silk-thin, there were two or three cuts in them, and the white fur between them was stained deep pink. Using a feather touch, the Mouser rubbed salve into them, shaking his head the while. Then he nodded once and took from his pouch a large needle, a spool of thin thong, and a small rolled hide of thin, tough leather. From the last he cut with Cat's Claw a shape rather like a very fat pear and stitched from it a boot for Hrissa.

When he tried it on the ice-cat's hind paw, she let it be for a little, then began to bite at it rather gently, looking up queerly at the Mouser. He thought, then very carefully bored holes in it for the ice-cat's non-retracting claws, then drew the boot up the leg snugly until the claws protruded fully and tied it there with the drawstring he'd run through slits at the top.

Hrissa no longer bothered the boot. The Mouser made others, and Fafhrd joined in and cut and stitched one too.

When Hrissa was fully shod in her four clawed paw-mittens, she smelled each, then stood up and paced back and forth the length of the ledge a few times, and finally settled herself by the still-warm brazier and the Mouser, chin on his ankle.

The tiny grains of snow were still falling ruler-straight, frosting the ledge and Fafhrd's coppery hair. He and the Mouser began to pull up their hoods and lace their cloaks about them for the night. The sun still shone through the snowfall, but its light was filtered white and brought not an atom of warmth.

Obelisk Polaris was not a noisy mountain, as many are – a-drip with glacial water, rattling with rock slides, and even with rock strata a-creak from uneven loss or gain of heat. The silence was profound.

The Mouser felt an impulse to tell Fafhrd about the living

girl-mask or illusion he'd seen by night, while simultaneously Fafhrd considered recounting to the Mouser his own erotic dream.

At that moment there came again, without prelude, the rushing in the silent air and they saw, clearly outlined by the falling snow, a great flat undulating shape.

It came swooping past them, rather slowly, about two spear-lengths out from the ledge.

There was nothing at all to be seen except the flat, flakeless space the thing made in the airborne snow and the eddies it raised; it in no way obscured the snow beyond. Yet they felt the gust of its passage.

The shape of this invisible thing was most like that of a giant skate or stingray four yards long and three wide; there was even the suggestion of a vertical fin and a long, lashing tail.

'Great invisible fish!' the Mouser hissed, thrusting his hand down in his half-laced cloak and managing to draw Scalpel in a single sweep. 'Your mind was most right, Fafhrd, when you thought it wrong!'

As the snow-sketched apparition glided out of sight around the buttress ending the ledge to the south, there came from it a mocking rippling laughter in two voices, one alto, one soprano.

'A sightless fish that laughs like girls – most monstrous!' Fafhrd commented shakenly, hefting his ax, which he'd got out swiftly too, though it was still attached to his belt by a long thong.

They crouched there then for a while, scrambled out of their cloaks, and with weapons ready, awaited the invisible monster's return, Hrissa standing between them with fur bristling. But after a while they began to shake from the cold and so they perforce got back into their cloaks and laced them, though still gripping their weapons and prepared to throw off the upper lacings in a flash. Then they briefly discussed the weirdness just witnessed, insofar as they could, each now confessing his earlier visions or dreams of girls.

Finally the Mouser said, 'The girls might have been riding the invisible thing, lying along its back – and invisible too! Yet, what *was* the thing?'

This touched a small spot in Fafhrd's memory. Rather

unwillingly he said, 'I remember waking once as a child in the night and hearing my father say to my mother, " . . . like great thick quivering sails, but the ones you can't see are the worst." They stopped speaking then, I think because they heard me stir.'

The Mouser asked, 'Did your father ever speak of seeing girls in the high mountains – flesh, apparition, or witch, which is a mixture of the two; visible or invisible?'

'He wouldn't have mentioned 'em if he had,' Fafhrd replied. 'My mother was a very jealous woman and a devil with a chopper.'

The whiteness they'd been scanning turned swiftly to darkest gray. The sun had set. They could no longer see the falling snow. They pulled up their hoods and laced their cloaks tight and huddled together at the back of the ledge with Hrissa close between them.

Trouble came early the next day. They roused with first light, feeling battered and nightmare-ridden, and uncramped themselves with difficulty while the morning ration of strong herb tea and powdered meat and snow were stewed in the same pot to a barely uncold aromatic gruel. Hrissa gnawed her rewarmed hare's bones and accepted a little bear's fat and water from the Mouser.

The snow had stopped during the night, but the Obelisk was powdered with it on every step and hold, while under the snow was ice – the first-fallen snow melted by yesterday afternoon's meager warmth on the rock and quickly refrozen.

So Fafhrd and the Mouser roped together, and the Mouser swiftly fashioned a harness for Hrissa by cutting two holes in the long side of an oblong of leather. Hrissa protested somewhat when her forelegs were thrust through the holes and the ends of the oblong double-stitched together snugly over her shoulders. But when an end of Fafhrd's black hempen rope was tied around her harness where the stitching was, she simply lay down flat on the ledge, on the warm spot where the brazier had stood, as if to say, 'This debasing tether I will not accept, though humans may.'

But when Fafhrd slowly started up the wall and the Mouser

followed and the rope tightened on Hrissa, and when she had looked up and seen them still roped like herself, she followed sulkily after. A little later she slipped off a bulge – her boots, snug as they were, must have been clumsy to her after naked pads – and swung scrabbling back and forth several long moments before she was supporting her own weight again. Fortunately the Mouser had a firm stance at the time.

After that, Hrissa came on more cheerily, sometimes even climbing to the side ahead of the Mouser and smiling back at him – rather sardonically, the Mouser fancied.

The climbing was a shade steeper than yesterday with an even greater insistence that each hand- and foothold be perfect. Gloved fingers must grip stone, not ice; spikes must clash through the brittle stuff to rock. Fafhrd roped his ax to his right wrist and used its hammer to tap away treacherous thin platelets and curves of the glassy frozen water.

And the climbing was more wearing because it was harder to avoid tenseness. Even looking sideways at the steepness of the wall tightened the Mouser's groin with fear. He wondered *what if the wind should blow?* – and fought the impulse to cling flat to the cliff. Yet at the same time sweat began to trickle down his face and chest, so that he had to throw back his hood and loosen his tunic to his belly to keep his clothes from sogging.

But there was worse to come. It had looked as though the slope above were gentling, but now, drawing nearer, they perceived a bulge jutting out a full two yards some seven yards above them. The under-slope was pocked here and there – fine handholds, except that they opened down. The bulge extended as far as they could see to either side, at most points looking worse.

They found themselves the best and highest holds they could, close together, and stared up at their problem. Even Hrissa, a-cling by the Mouser, seemed subdued.

Fafhrd said softly, 'I mind me now they used to say there was an out-jutting around the Obelisk's top. His crown, I think my father called it. I wonder . . .'

'Don't you know?' the Mouser demanded, a shade harshly. Standing rigid on his holds, his arms and legs were aching worse than ever.

'O Mouser,' Fafhrd confessed, 'in my youth I never climbed Obelisk Polaris farther than halfway to last night's camp. I only boasted to raise our spirits.'

There being nothing to say to that, the Mouser shut his lips, though somewhat thinly. Fafhrd began to whistle a tuneless tune and carefully fished a small grapnel with five dagger sharp flukes from his pouch and tied it securely to the long end of their black rope still coiled on his back. Then stretching his right arm as far out as he might from the cliff, he whirled the grapnel in a smallish circle, faster and faster, and finally hurled it upward. They heard it clash against rock somewhere above the bulge, but it did not catch on any crack or hump and instantly came sliding and then dropping down, missing the Mouser by hardly a handbreadth, it seemed to him.

Fafhrd drew up the grapnel – with some delays, since it tended to catch on every crack or hump below them – and whirled and hurled it again. And again and again and again, each time without success. Once it stayed up, but Fafhrd's first careful tug on the rope brought it down.

Fafhrd's sixth cast was his first really bad one. The grapnel never went out of sight at all. As it reached the top of the throw, it glinted for an instant.

'Sunlight!' Fafhrd hissed happily. 'We're almost to the summit!'

'That "almost" is a whopper, though,' the Mouser commented, but even he couldn't keep a cheerful note out of his voice.

By the time Fafhrd had failed on seven more casts, all cheerfulness was gone from the Mouser again. His aches were horrible, his hands and feet were numbing in the cold, and his brain was numbing too, so that the next time Fafhrd cast and missed, he was so unwise as to follow the grapnel with his gaze as it fell.

For the first time today he really looked out and down. The Cold Waste was a pale blue expanse almost like the sky – and seeming even more distant – all its copses and mounds and tiny tarns having long since become pinpoints and vanished. Many leagues to the west, almost at the horizon, a jagged pale gold band showed where the shadows of the mountains ended.

Midway in the band was a blue gap – Stardock's shadow continuing over the edge of the world.

Giddily the Mouser snatched his gaze back to Obelisk Polaris . . . and although he could still see the granite, it didn't seem to count any more – only four insecure holds on a kind of pale green nothingness, with Fafhrd and Hrissa somehow suspended beside him. His mind could no longer accept the Obelisk's steepness.

As the urge to hurl himself down swelled in him, he somehow transformed it into a sardonic snort, and he heard himself say with daggerish contempt, 'Leave off your foolish fishing, Fafhrd! I'll show you now how Lankhmarian mountain science deals with a trifling problem such as this which has baffled all your barbarian whirling and casting!'

And with that he unclipped from his pack with reckless speed the thick black bamboo pike or crook and began cursingly with numb fingers to draw out and let snap into place its telescoping sections until it was four times its original length.

This tool of technical climbing, which indeed the Mouser had brought all the way from Lankhmar, had been a matter of dispute between them the whole trip, Fafhrd asserting it was a tricksy toy not worth the packing.

Now, however, Fafhrd made no comment, but merely coiled up his grapnel and thrust his hands into his wolf-skin jerkin against his sides to warm them and, mild-eyed, watched the Mouser's furious activity. Hrissa shifted to a perch closer to Fafhrd and crouched stoically.

But when the Mouser shakily thrust the narrower end of his black tool toward the bulge above, Fafhrd reached out a hand to help him steady it, yet could not refrain from saying, 'If you think to get a good enough hold with the crook on the rim to shinny up that stick—'

'Quiet, you loutish kibitzer!' the Mouser snarled and with Fafhrd's help thrust pike-end into a pock in the rock hardly a finger's length from the rim. Then he seated the spiked foot of the pole in a small, deep hollow just above his head. Next he snapped out two short recessed lever-arms from the base of the pole and began to rotate them. It soon became clear that they controlled a great screw hidden in the pole, for the latter lengthened until it stood firmly between the two pocks in the rock, while the stiff black shaft itself bent a little.

At that instant a sliver of rock, being pressed by the pole, broke off from the rim. The pole thrummed as it straightened and the Mouser, screaming a curse, slipped off his holds and fell.

It was good then that the rope between the two comrades was short and that the spikes of Fafhrd's boots were seated firmly, like so many demon-forged dagger-points, in the rock of his footholds – for as the strain came suddenly on Fafhrd's belt and on his rope-gripping left hand, he took it without plummeting after the Mouser, only bending his knees a little and grunting softly, while his right hand snatched hold of the vibrating pole and saved it.

The Mouser had not even fallen far enough to drag Hrissa from her perch, though the rope almost straightened between them. The ice-cat, her tufted neck bent sharply between foreleg and chest, peered down with great curiosity at the dangling man.

His face was ashen. Fafhrd made no mark of that, but simply handed him the black pole, saying, 'It's a good tool. I've screwed it back short. Seat it in another pock and try again.'

Soon the pole stood firm between the hollow by the Mouser's head and a pock a hand's width from the rim. The bow-like bend in the pole faced downward. Then they put the Mouser first on the rope, and he went climbing up and out along the pole, hanging from it back downward, his boot-edges finding tiny holds on the pole's section-shoulders – out into and over the vast, pale blue-gray space which had so lately dizzied him.

The pole began to bend a little more with the Mouser's weight, the pike end slipping a finger's span in the upper pock with a horrible tiny grating sound, but Fafhrd gave the screw another turn and the pole held firm.

Fafhrd and Hrissa watched the Mouser reach its end, where he paused briefly. Then they saw him reach up his left arm until it was out of sight to the elbow above the rim, meanwhile gripping with his right hand the crook and twining his legs around the shaft. He appeared to feel about with his left hand and find something. Then he moved out and up still further and very slowly his head and after it, in a sudden swift sweep, his right arm went out of sight above the rim.

For several long moments they saw only the bottom half of the bent Mouser, his dark crinkly-soled boots twined securely to the end of the pole. Then, rather slowly, like a gray snail, and with a final push of one boot against the top of the crook, he went entirely out of sight.

Fafhrd slowly paid out rope after him.

After some time the Mouser's voice, quite ghostly yet clear, came down to them: 'Hola! I've got the rope anchored around a boss big as a tree stump. Send up Hrissa.'

So Fafhrd put Hrissa on the rope ahead of him, knotting it to her harness with a sheepshank.

Hrissa fought desperately for a moment against being swung into space, but as soon as it was done hung deathly still. Then as she was drawn slowly up, Fafhrd's knot began to slip. The ice-cat swiftly snatched at the rope with her teeth and gripped it far back between her jaws. The moment she came near the rim, her clawed mittens were ready and she scrabbled and was dragged out of sight.

Soon word came down from the Mouser that Hrissa was safe and Fafhrd might follow. He frowningly tightened the screw another half turn, though the pole creaked ominously, and then very gently climbed out along it. The Mouser now kept the rope taut from above, but for the first stretch it could hardly take more than a few pounds of Fafhrd's weight off the pole.

The upper spike once again grated horribly a bit in its pock, but it still held firm. Helped more by the rope now, Fafhrd got his hands and head over the rim.

What he saw was a smooth, gentle rock slope, which could be climbed by friction, and at the top of it the Mouser and Hrissa standing backgrounded by blue sky and gilded by sunlight.

Soon he stood beside them.

The Mouser said, 'Fafhrd, when we get back to Lankhmar remind me to give Glinthi the Artificer thirteen diamonds from the pouch of them we'll find on Stardock's hat: one for each section and joint of my climbing pole, one each for the spikes at the ends and two for each screw.'

'Are there two screws?' Fafhrd asked respectfully.

'Yes, one at each end,' the Mouser told him and then made Fafhrd brace the rope for him so that he could climb down the slope and, bending all his upper body down over the rim, shorten the pole by rotating its upper screw until he was able to drag it triumphantly back over the top with him.

As the Mouser telescoped its sections together again, Fafhrd said to him seriously, 'You must thong it to your belt as I do my ax. We must not chance losing Glinthi's help on the rest of this journey.'

Throwing back their hoods and opening their tunics wide to the hot sun, Fafhrd and the Mouser looked around, while Hrissa luxuriously stretched and worked her slim limbs and neck and body, the white fur of which hid her bruises.

Both men were somewhat exalted by the thin air and filled brain-high with the ease of mind and spirit that comes with a great danger skilfully conquered.

Rather to their amazement, the southward swinging sun had climbed barely halfway to noon. Perils which had seemed demihours long had lasted minutes only.

The summit of Obelisk Polaris was a great rolling field of pale rock too big to measure by Lankhmar acres. They had arrived near the southwest corner, and the gray-tinted stone meadow seemed to stretch east and north almost indefinitely. Here and there were hummocks and hollows, but they swelled and dipped most gently. There were a few scattered large boulders, not many, while off to the east were darker indistinct shapes which might be bushes and small trees footed in cracks filled with blown dirt.

'What lies east of the mountain chain?' the Mouser asked. 'More Cold Waste?'

'Our clan never journeyed there,' Fafhrd answered. He frowned. 'Some taboo on the whole area, I think. Mist always masked the east on my father's great climbs – or so he told us.'

'We could have a look now,' the Mouser suggested.

Fafhrd shook his head. 'Our course lies there,' he said, pointing northeast, where Stardock rose like a giantess standing tall but asleep, or feigning sleep, looking seven times as big and high at least as she had before the Obelisk hid her top two days ago.

The Mouser said, a shade dolefully, 'All our brave work scaling the Obelisk has only made Stardock higher. Are you sure there's not another peak, perhaps invisible, on top of her?'

Fafhrd nodded without taking his eyes off her, who was empress without consort of the Mountains of the Giants. Her Tresses had grown to great swelling rivers of snow and now the two adventurers could see faint stirrings in them – avalanches slipping and tumbling.

The Southern Tress came down in a great dipping double curve toward the northwest corner of the mighty rock summit on which they stood.

At the top, Stardock's corniced snow hat, its upper rim glittering with sunlight as if it were edged around with diamonds, seemed to nod toward them a trifle more than it ever had before, and the demurely-eyed Face with it, like a great lady hinting at possible favors.

But the gauzy, long pale veils of the Grand and Petty Pennons no longer streamed from her Hat. The air atop Stardock must be as still at the moment as it was where they stood upon the Obelisk.

'What devil's luck that Kranarch and Gnarfi should tackle the north wall the one day in eight the gale fails!' Fafhrd cursed. 'But 'twill be their destruction yet – yes, and of their two shaggy-clad henchmen too. This calm can't hold.'

'I recall now,' the Mouser remarked, 'that when we caroused with 'em in Illik-Ving, Gnarfi drunken-claimed he could whistle up winds – had learned the trick from his grandmother – and could whistle 'em down too, which is more to the point.'

'The more reason for us to hasten!' Fafhrd cried, upping his pack and slipping his big arms through the wide shoulder straps. 'On, Mouser! Up, Hrissa! We'll have a bite and sup before the snow ridge.'

'You mean we must tackle that freezing, treacherous problem today?' demurred the Mouser, who would dearly have loved to strip and bake in the sun.

'Before noon!' Fafhrd decreed. And with that he set them a stiff walking pace straight north, keeping close to the summit's west edge, as if to countermand from the start any curiosity the Mouser might have about a peek to the east. The latter followed with only minor further protests; Hrissa came on limpingly, lagging at first far behind, but catching up as her limp went and her cat-zest for newness grew.

And so they marched across the great, strange rolling granite plain of Obelisk's top, patched here and there with limestone stretches white as marble. Its sun-drenched silence and uniformity became eerie after a bit. The shallowness of its hollows was deceptive: Fafhrd noted several in which battalions of armed men might have hidden a-crouch, unseen until one came within a spear's cast.

The longer they strode along, the more closely Fafhrd studied the rock his hobnails clashed. Finally he paused to point out a strangely rippled stretch.

'I'd swear that once was seabottom,' he said softly.

The Mouser's eyes narrowed. Thinking of the great invisible fishlike flier they had seen last evening, its raylike form undulating through the snowfall, he felt gooseflesh crawling on him.

Hrissa slunk past them, head a-weave.

Soon they passed the last boulder, a huge one, and saw, scarcely a bowshot ahead, the glitter of snow.

The Mouser said, 'The worst thing about mountain climbing is that the easy parts go so quickly.'

'Hist!' warned Fafhrd, sprawling down suddenly like a great four-legged water beetle and putting his cheek to the rock. 'Do you hear it, Mouser!'

Hrissa snarled, staring about, and her white fur bristled.

The Mouser started to stoop, but realized he wouldn't have to, so fast the sound was coming on: a general high-pitched drumming, as of five hundred fiends rippling their giant thick fingernails on a great stone drumhead.

Then, without pause, there came surging straight toward them over the nearest rock swelling to the southeast, a great wide-fronted stampede of goats, so packed together and their

613

fur so glossy white that they seemed for a flash like an onrushing of living snow. Even the great curving horns of their leaders were ivory-hued. The Mouser noted that a stretch of the sunny air just above their center shimmered and wavered as it will above a fire. Then he and Fafhrd were racing back toward the last boulder with Hrissa bounding ahead.

Behind them the devil's tattoo of the stampede grew louder and louder.

They reached the boulder and vaulted atop it, where Hrissa already crouched, hardly a pounding heartbeat before the white horde. And well it was that Fafhrd had his ax out the instant they won there, for the midmost of the great billies sprang high, forelegs tucked up and head bowed to present his creamy horns – so close Fafhrd could see their splintered tips. But in that same instant Fafhrd got him in his snowy shoulder with a great swashing deep-cleaving blow so heavy that the beast was carried past them to the side and crashed on the short slope leading down to the rim of the west wall.

Then the white stampede was splitting around the great boulder, the animals so near and packed that there was no longer room for leaping, and the din of their hooves and the gasping and now the frightened bleating was horrendous, and the caprid stench was stifling, while the boulder rocked with their passage.

In the worst of the bruit there was a momentary down-rushing of air, briefly dispelling the stench, as something passed close above their heads, rippling the sky like a long flapping blanket of fluid glass, while through the clangor could he heard for a moment a harsh, hateful laughter.

The lesser tongue of the stampede passed between the boulder and the rim, and of these goats many went tumbling over the edge with bleats like screams of the damned, carrying with them the body of the great billy Fafhrd had maimed.

Then as sudden in its departure as a snow squall that dismasts a ship in the Frozen Sea, the stampede was past them and pounding south, swinging east somewhat from the deadly rim, with the last few of the goats, chiefly nannies and kids, bounding madly after.

Pointing his arm toward the sun as if for a sword-thrust, the Mouser cried furiously, 'See there, where the beams twist all askew above the herd! It's the same flier as just now overpassed us and last night we saw in the snowfall – the flier who raised the stampede and whose riders guided it against us! Oh, damn the two deceitful ghostly bitches, luring us on to a goaty destruction stinking worse than a temple orgy in the City of Ghouls!'

'I thought this laughter was far deeper,' Fafhrd objected. 'It was not the girls.'

'So they have a deep-throated pimp – does that improve them in your eyes? Or your great flapping love-struck ears?' the Mouser demanded angrily.

The drumming of the stampede had died away even swifter than it had come and in the new-fallen silence they heard now a happy half-obstructed growling. Hrissa, springing off the boulder at stampede-end, had struck down a fat kid and was tearing at its bloodied white neck.

'Ah, I can smell it broiling now!' the Mouser cried with a great smile, his preoccupations altering in less than an instant. 'Good Hrissa! Fafhrd, if those be treelets and bushes and grass to the east – and they must be that, for what else feeds these goats? – there's sure to be dead wood – why, there may even be mint! – and we can . . .'

'You'll eat the flesh raw for lunch or not at all!' Fafhrd decreed fiercely. 'Are we to risk the stampede again? Or give the sniggering flier a chance to marshal against us some snow lions? – which are sure to be here too, to prey on the goats. And are we to present Kranarch and Gnarfi the summit of Stardock on a diamond-studded silver platter? – if this devil's lull holds tomorrow too and they be industrious strong climbers, not nice-bellied sluggards like one I could name!'

So, with only a gripe or two more from the Mouser, the kid was swiftly bled, gutted and skinned, and some of its spine-meat and haunches wrapped and packed for supper. Hrissa drank some more blood and ate half the liver and then followed the Mouser and Fafhrd as they set off north toward the snow ridge. The two men were chewing thin-sliced peppered collops of raw kid, but striding swiftly and keeping a wary eye behind for another stampede.

The Mouser expected now at last to get a view of the eastern depths, by peering east along the north wall of Obelisk Polaris, but here again he was foiled by the first great swell of the snow-saddle.

However, the northern view was fearsomely majestic. A full half league below them now and seen almost vertically on, the White Waterfall went showering down mysteriously, twinkling even in the shadow.

The ridge by which they must travel first curved up a score of yards, then dipped smoothly down to a long snow-saddle another score of yards below them, then slowly curved up into the South Tress, down which they could now plainly see avalanches trickling and tumbling.

It was easy to see how the northeast gale, blowing almost continually but missing the Ladder, would greatly pile up snow between the taller mountain and the Obelisk – but whether the rocky connection between the two mountains underlay the snow by only a few yards or by as much as a quarter league was impossible to know.

'We must rope again,' Fafhrd decreed. 'I'll go first and cut steps for us across the west slope.'

'What need we steps in this calm?' the Mouser demanded. 'Or to go by the west slope? You just don't want me to see the east, do you? The top of the ridge is broad enough to drive two carts across abreast.'

'The ridge-top in the wind's path almost certainly overhangs emptiness to the east and would break away,' Fafhrd explained. 'Look you, Mouser; do I know more about snow and ice or do you?'

'I once crossed the Bones of the Old Ones with you,' the Mouser retorted, shrugging. 'There was snow there, I recall.'

'Pooh, the mere spillings of a lady's powderbox compared to this. No, Mouser, on this stretch my word is law.'

'Very well,' the Mouser agreed.

So they roped up rather close – in order, Fafhrd, Mouser, and Hrissa – and without more ado Fafhrd donned his gloves and thonged his ax to his wrist and began cutting steps for them around the shoulders of the snow swell.

It was rather slow work, for under a dusting of powder snow the stuff was hard and for each step Fafhrd must make at least two cuts – first an in-chopping back hand one to make the step, then a down-chop to clear it. And as the slope grew steeper, he must make the steps somewhat closer together. The steps he made were rather small, at least for his great boots, but they were sure.

Soon the ridge and the Obelisk cut off the sun. It grew very chill. The Mouser closed his tunic and drew his hood around his face, while Hrissa, between her short leaps from step to step, performed a kind of tiny cat-jig on them, to keep her gloved paws from freezing. The Mouser reminded himself to stuff them a bit with lamb's wool when he renewed the salve. He had his pike out now, telescoped short and thonged to his wrist.

They passed the shoulder of the swell and came opposite the beginning of the snow-saddle, but Fafhrd did not cut steps up toward it. Rather, the steps he now was cutting descended at a sharper angle than the saddle dipped, though the slope they were crossing was becoming quite steep.

'Fafhrd,' the Mouser protested quietly, 'we're heading for Stardock's top, not the White Waterfall.'

'You said, "Very well,"' Fafhrd retorted between chops. 'Besides, who does the work?' His ax rang as it bit into ice.

'Look, Fafhrd,' the Mouser said, 'there are two goats crossing to Stardock along the saddletop. No, three.'

'We should trust goats? Ask yourself why they've been sent.' Again Fafhrd's ax rang.

The sun swung into view as it coursed southward, sending their three shadows ranging far ahead of them. The pale gray of the snow turned glittery white. The Mouser unhooded to the yellow rays. For a while the enjoyment of their warmth on the back of his head helped him keep his mouth shut, but then the slope grew steeper yet, as Fafhrd continued remorselessly to cut steps downward.

'I seem to recall that our purpose was to *climb* Stardock, but my memory must be disordered,' the Mouser observed. 'Fafhrd,

I'll take your word we must keep away from the top of the ridge, but do we have to keep away so *far*? And the three goats have all skipped across.'

Still, '"Very well," you said,' was all Fafhrd would answer, and this time there was a snarl in his voice.

The Mouser shrugged. Now he was bracing himself with his pike continuously, while Hrissa would pause studyingly before each leap.

Their shadows went less than a spear's cast ahead of them now, while the hot sun had begun to melt the surface snow, sending down trickles of ice water to wet their gloves and make their footing unsure.

Yet still Fafhrd kept cutting steps downward. And now of a sudden he began to cut them downward more steeply still, adding with taps of his ax a tiny handhold above each step – and these handholds were needed!

'Fafhrd,' the Mouser said dreamily, 'perhaps an ice-sprite has whispered to you the secret of levitation, so that from this fine takeoff you can dive, level out, and then go spiring to Stardock's top. In that case I wish you'd teach myself and Hrissa how to grow wings in an instant.'

'Hist!' Fafhrd spoke softly yet sharply at that instant. 'I have a feeling. Something comes. Brace yourself and watch behind us.'

The Mouser drove his pike in deep and rotated his head. As he did, Hrissa leaped from the last step behind to the one on which the Mouser stood, landing half on his boot and clinging to his knee – yet this done so dexterously the Mouser was not dislodged.

'I see nothing,' the Mouser reported, staring almost sunward. Then, words suddenly clipped: 'Again the beams twist like a spinning lantern! The glints on the icy ripple and wave. 'Tis the flier come again! Cling!'

There came the rushing sound, louder than ever before and swiftly mounting, then a great sea-wave of air, as of a great body passing swiftly only spans away; it whipped their clothes and Hrissa's fur and forced them to cling fiercely to their holds, though Fafhrd made a full-armed swipe with his ax. Hrissa snarled. Fafhrd almost louted forward off his holds with the momentum of his blow.

'I'll swear I scored on him, Mouser,' he snarled, recovering. 'My ax touched something besides air.'

'You harebrained fool!' the Mouser cried. 'Your scratches will anger him and bring him back.' He let go of the chopped ice-hold with his hand and, steadying himself by his pike, he searched the sun-bright air ahead and around for ripples.

'More like I've scared him off,' Fafhrd asserted, doing the same. The rushy sound faded and did not return; the air became quiet, and the steep slope grew very still; even the water-drip faded.

Turning back to the wall with a grunt of relief, the Mouser touched emptiness. He grew still as death himself. Turning his eyes only he saw that upward from a point level with his knees the whole snow ridge had vanished – the whole saddle and a section of the swell to either side of it – as if some great god had reached down while the Mouser's back was turned and removed that block of reality.

Giddily he clung to his pike. He was standing atop a newly created snow-saddle now. Beyond and below its raw, fresh-fractured white eastern slope, the silently departed great snow-cornice was falling faster and faster, still in one hill-size chunk.

Behind them the steps Fafhrd had cut mounted to the new snow rim, then vanished.

'See, I chopped us down far enough only in the nick,' Fafhrd grumbled. 'My judgment was faulty.'

The falling cornice was snatched downward out of sight, so that the Mouser and Fafhrd at last could see what lay east of the Mountains of the Giants: a rolling expanse of dark green that might be treetops except that from here even giant trees would be tinier than glass blades – an expanse even farther below them than the Cold Waste at their backs. Beyond the green-carpeted depression, another mountain range loomed like the ghost of one.

'I have heard legends of the Great Rift Valley,' Fafhrd murmured. 'A mountainsided cup for sunlight, its warm floor a league below the Waste.'

Their eyes searched.

'Look,' the Mouser said, 'how trees climb the eastern face of Obelisk almost to his top. Now the goats don't seem so strange.'

They could see nothing, however, of the east face of Stardock.

'Come on!' Fafhrd commanded. 'If we linger, the invisible growl-laughter flier may gather courage to return despite my ax-nick.'

And without further word he began resolutely to cut steps onward . . . and still a little down.

Hrissa continued to peer over the rim, her bearded chin almost resting on it, her nostrils a-twitch as if she faintly scented gossamer threads of meat-odor mounting from the leagues' distant dark green, but when the rope tightened on her harness, she followed.

Perils came thick now. They reached the dark rock of the Ladder only by chopping their way along a nearly vertical ice wall in the twinkly gloom under a close-arching waterfall of snow that shot out from an icy boss above them – perhaps a miniature version of the White Waterfall that was Stardock's skirt.

When they stepped at last, numb with cold and hardly daring to believe they'd made it, onto a wide dark ledge, they saw a jumble of bloody goat tracks in the snow around.

Without more warning than that, a long snowbank between that step and the next above reared up its nearest white end a dozen feet and hissed fearsomely, showing it to be a huge serpent with head as big as an elk's, all covered with shaggy snow-white fur. Its great violet eyes glared like those of a mad horse and its jaws gaped to show slashing-teeth like a shark's and two great fangs jutting a mist of pale ichor.

The furred serpent hesitated for two sways between the nearer, taller man with flashing ax and the farther, smaller one with thick black stick. In that pause Hrissa, with snarling hisses of her own, sprang forward past the Mouser on the downslope side and the furred serpent struck at this newest and most active foe.

Fafhrd got a blast of its hot acrid breath, and the vapor trail from its nearer fang bathed his left elbow.

The Mouser's attention was fixed on a fur-wisped violet eye as big as a girl's fist.

Hrissa looked down the monster's gaping dark red gullet

620

rimmed by slaver-swimming ivory knives and the two ichor-jetting fangs.

Then the jaws clashed shut, but in the intervening instant Hrissa had leaped back more swiftly even than she'd advanced.

The Mouser plunged the pike-end of his climbing pole into the glaring violet eye.

Swinging his ax two-handed, Fafhrd slashed at the furry neck just back of the horse-like skull, and there gushed out red blood which steamed as it struck the snow.

Then the three climbers were scrambling upward, while the monster writhed in convulsions which shook the rock and spattered with red alike the snow and its snow-white fur.

At what they hoped was a safe distance above it, the climbers watched it dying, though not without frequent glances about for creatures like it or other perilous beasts.

Fafhrd said, 'A hot-blooded serpent, a snake with fur – it goes against experience. My father never spoke of such; I doubt he ever met 'em.'

The Mouser answered, 'I'll wager they find their prey on the east slope of Stardock and come here only to lair or breed. Perhaps the invisible flier drove the three goats over the snow-saddle to lure this one.' His voice grew dreamy. 'Or perhaps there's a secret world inside Stardock.'

Fafhrd shook his head, as if to clear it of such imagination-snaring visions. 'Our way lies upward,' he said. 'We'd best be well above the Lairs before nightfall. Give me a dollop of honey when I drink,' he added, loosening his water bag as he turned and scanned up the Ladder.

From its base the Ladder was a dark narrow triangle climbing to the blue sky between the snowy, ever-tumbling Tresses. First there were the ledges on which they stood, easy at first, but swiftly growing steeper and narrower. Next an almost blank stretch, etched here and there with shadows and ripplings hinting at part-way climbing routes, but none of them connected. Then another band of ledges, the Roosts. Then a stretch still blanker than the first. Finally another ledge-band, narrower and shorter – the Face – and atop all what seemed a tiny pen-stroke of white ink: the brim of Stardock's pennonless snowy hat.

All the Mouser's aches and weariness came back as he squinted up the Ladder while feeling in his pouch for the honey jar. Never, he was sure, had he seen so much distance compressed into so little space by vertical foreshortening. It was as if the gods had built a ladder to reach the sky, and after using it had kicked most of the steps away. But he clenched his teeth and prepared to follow Fafhrd.

All their previous climbing began to seem book-simple compared to what they now struggled through, step by straining step, all the long summer afternoon. Where Obelisk Polaris had been a stern schoolmaster, Stardock was a mad queen, tireless in preparing her shocks and surprises, unpredictable in her wild caprices.

The ledges of the Lairs were built of rock that sometimes broke away at a touch, and they were piled with loose gravel. Also, the climbers made acquaintance with Stardock's rocky avalanches, which brought stones whizzing and spattering down around them without warning, so that they had to press close to the walls and Fafhrd regretted leaving his helmet in the cairn. Hrissa first snarled at each pelting pebble which hit near her, but when at last struck in the side by a small one, showed fear and slunk close to the Mouser, trying until rebuked to push between the wall and his legs.

And once they saw a cousin of the white worm they had slain rear up man-high and glare at them from a distant ledge, but it did not attack.

They had to work their way to the northernmost point of the topmost ledge before they found, at the very edge of the Northern Tress, almost underlying its streaming snow, a screechoked gulley which narrowed upward to a wide vertical groove – or chimney, as Fafhrd called it.

And when the treacherous scree was at last surmounted, the Mouser discovered that the next stretch of the ascent was indeed very like climbing up the inside of a rectangular chimney of varying width and with one of the four walls missing – that facing outward to the air. Its rock was sounder than that of the Lairs, but that was all that could be said for it.

Here all tricks of climbing were required and the utmost of main strength into the bargain. Sometimes they hoisted themselves by cracks wide enough for finger- and toeholds; if a crack they needed was too narrow, Fafhrd would tap into it one of his spikes to make a hold, and this spike must, if possible, be unwedged after use and recovered. Sometimes the chimney narrowed so that they could walk up it laboriously with shoulders to one wall and boot soles to the other. Twice it widened and became so smooth-walled that the Mouser's extensible climbing-pike had to be braced between wall and wall to give them a necessary step.

And five times the chimney was blocked by a huge rock or chockstone which in falling had wedged itself fast, and these fearsome obstructions had to be climbed around on the outside, generally with the aid of one of more of Fafhrd's spikes driven between chockstone and wall, or his grapnel tossed over it.

'Stardock has wept millstones in her day,' the Mouser said of these gigantic barriers, jerking his body aside from a whizzing rock for a period to his sentence.

This climbing was generally beyond Hrissa and she often had to be carried on the Mouser's back, or left on a chockstone or one of the rare paw-wide ledges and hoisted up when opportunity offered. They were strongly tempted, especially after they grew death-weary, to abandon her, but could not forget how her brave feint had saved them from the white worm's first stroke.

All this, particularly the passing of the chockstones, must be done under the pelting of Stardock's rocky avalanches – so that each new chockstone above them was welcomed as a roof, until it had to be surmounted. Also, snow sometimes gushed into the chimney, overspilling from one of the snowy avalanches forever whispering down the North Tress – one more danger to guard against. Ice water runneled too from time to time down the chimney, drenching boots and gloves and making all holds unsure.

In addition, there was less nourishment in the air, so that they had more often to halt and gasp deeply until their lungs were satisfied. And Fafhrd's left arm began to swell where the venomous mist from the worm's fang had blown around it, until he could hardly bend its swollen fingers to grip crack or rope. Besides, it itched and stung. He plunged it again and again into snow to no avail.

Their only allies on this most punishing ascent were the hot sun, heartening them by its glow and offsetting the growing frigidity of the thin still air, and the very difficulty and variety of the climb itself, which at least kept their minds off the emptiness around and beneath them – the latter a farther drop than they'd ever stood over on the Obelisk. The Cold Waste seemed like another world, poised separate from Stardock in space.

Once they forced themselves to eat a bite and several times sipped water. And once the Mouser was seized with mountain sickness, ending only when he had retched himself weary.

The only incident of the climb unrelated to Stardock's mad self occurred when they were climbing out around the fifth chockstone, slowly, like two large slugs, the Mouser first this time and bearing Hrissa, with Fafhrd close behind. At this point the North Tress narrowed so that a hump of the North Wall was visible across the snow stream.

There was a whirring unlike that of any rock. Another whirring then, closer and ending in a *thunk*. When Fafhrd scrambled atop the chockstone and into the shelter of the walls, he had a cruelly barbed arrow through his pack.

At cost of a third arrow whirring close by his head, the Mouser peeped out north with Fafhrd clinging to his heels and swiftly dragging him back.

''Twas Kranarch all right; I saw him twang his bow,' the Mouser reported. 'No sight of Gnarfi, but one of their new comrades clad in brown fur crouched behind Kranarch, braced on the same boss. I couldn't see his face, but 'tis a most burly fellow, short of leg.'

'They keep apace of us,' Fafhrd grunted.

'Also, they scruple not to mix climbing with killing,' the Mouser observed as he broke off the tail of the arrow piercing Fafhrd's pack and yanked out the shaft. 'Oh, comrade, I fear your sleeping cloak is sixteen times holed. And that little bladder of pine liniment – it got holed too. Ah, what fragrance!'

'I'm beginning to think those two men of Illik-Ving aren't sportsmen,' Fafhrd asserted. 'So . . . up and on!'

624

They were all dog-weary, even cat-Hrissa, and the sun was barely ten fingerbreadths (at the end of an outstretched arm) above the flat horizon of the Waste; and something in the air had turned Sol white as silver – he no longer sent warmth to combat the cold. But the ledges of the Roosts were close above now, and it was possible to hope they would offer a better camp site than the chimney.

So although every man and cat muscle protested against it, they obeyed Fafhrd's command.

Halfway to the Roosts it began to snow, powdery grains falling arrow-straight like last night, but thicker.

This silent snowfall gave a sense of serenity and security which was most false, since it masked the rockfalls which still came firing down the chimney like the artillery of the God of Chance.

Five yards from the top a fist-size chunk struck Fafhrd glancingly on the right shoulder, so that his good arm went numb and hung useless, but the little climbing that remained was so easy he could make it with boots and puffed-up, barely-usable left hand.

He peeped cautiously out of the chimney's top, but the Tress here had thickened up again, so that there was no sight of the North Wall. Also the first ledge was blessedly wide and so overhung with rock that not even snow had fallen on its inner half, let alone stones. He scrambled up eagerly, followed by the Mouser and Hrissa.

But even as they cast themselves down to rest at the back of the ledge, the Mouser wriggling out of his heavy pack and unthonging his climbing-pike from his wrist – for even *that* had become a torturesome burden – they heard a now-familiar rushing in the air and there came a great flat shape swooping slowly through the sun-silvered snow which outlined it. Straight at the ledge it came and this time it did not go past, but halted and hung there, like a giant devil fish nuzzling the sea's rim, while ten narrow marks, each of suckers in line, appeared in the snow on the ledge's edge, as of ten short tentacles gripping there.

From the center of this monstrous invisibility rose a smaller snow-outlined invisibility of the height and thickness of a man.

Midway up this shape was one visible thing: a slim sword of dark gray blade and silvery hilt pointed straight at the Mouser's breast.

Suddenly the sword shot forward, almost as fast as if hurled, but not quite, and after it, as swiftly, the man-size pillar, which now laughed harshly from its top.

The Mouser snatched up one-handed his unthonged climbing pike and thrust at the snow-sketched figure behind the sword.

The gray sword snaked around the pike and with a sudden sharp twist swept it from the Mouser's fatigue-slack fingers.

The black tool, on which Glinthi the Artificer had expended all the evenings of the Month of the Weasel three years past, vanished into the silvery snowfall and space.

Hrissa backed against the wall frothing and snarling, atremble in every limb.

Fafhrd fumbled frantically for his ax, but his swollen fingers could not even unsnap the sheath binding its head to his belt.

The Mouser, enraged at the loss of his precious pike to the point where he cared not a whit whether his foe was invisible or not, drew Scalpel from its sheath and fiercely parried the gray sword as it came streaking in again.

A dozen parries he had to make and was pinked twice in the arm and pressed back against the wall almost like Hrissa, before he could take the measure of his foe, now out of the snowfall and wholly invisible, and go himself on the attack.

Then, glaring at a point a foot above the gray sword – a point where he judged his foe's eyes to be (if his foe carried his eyes in his head) – he went stamping forward, beating at the gray blade, slipping Scalpel around it with the tiniest disengages, seeking to bind it with his own sword, and ever thrusting impetuously at invisible arm and trunk.

Three times he felt his blade strike flesh and once it bent briefly against invisible bone.

His foe leaped back onto the invisible flier, making narrow footprints in the slush gathered there. The flier rocked.

In his fighting rage the Mouser almost followed his foe onto that invisible, living, pulsating platform, yet prudently stopped at the brink.

And well it was he did so, for the flier dropped away like a skate in flight from a shark, shaking its slush into the snowfall. There came a last burst of laughter more like a wail, fading off and down in the silvery murk.

The Mouser began to laugh himself, a shade hysterically, and retreated to the wall. There he wiped off his blade and felt the stickiness of invisible blood, and laughed a wild high laugh again.

Hrissa's fur was still on end – and was a long time flattening.

Fafhrd quit trying to fumble out his ax and said seriously, 'The girls couldn't have been with him – we'd have seen their forms or footprints on the slush-backed flier. I think he's jealous of us and works against 'em.'

The Mouser laughed – only foolishly now – for a third time.

The murk turned dark gray. They set about firing the brazier and making ready for night. Despite their hurts and supreme weariness, the shock and fright of the last encounter had excited new energy from them and raised their spirits and given them appetites. They feasted well on thin collops of kid frizzled in the resin-flames or cooked pale gray in water that, strangely, could be sipped without hurt almost while it boiled.

'Must be nearing the realm of the Gods,' Fafhrd muttered. 'It's said they joyously drink boiling wine – and walk hurtlessly through flames.'

'Fire is just as hot here, though,' the Mouser said dully. 'Yet the air seems to have less nourishment. On what do you suppose the Gods subsist?'

'They are ethereal and require neither air nor food,' Fafhrd suggested after a long frown of thinking.

'Yet you just now said they drink wine.'

'Everybody drinks wine,' Fafhrd asserted with a yawn, killing the discussion and also the Mouser's dim, unspoken speculation as to whether the feebler air, pressing less strongly on heating liquid, let its bubbles escape more easily.

Power of movement began to return to Fafhrd's right arm and his left was swelling no more. The Mouser salved and bandaged his own small wounds, then remembered to salve Hrissa's pads and tuck into her boots a little pine-scented eider-down tweaked from the arrow-holes in Fafhrd's cloak.

When they were half laced up in their cloaks, Hrissa snuggled between them – and a few more precious resin pellets dropped in the brazier as a bedtime luxury – Fafhrd got out a tiny jar of strong wine of Ilthmar, and they each took a sup of it, imagining those sunny vineyards and that hot, rich soil so far south.

A momentary flare from the brazier showed them the snow falling yet. A few rocks crashed nearby and a snowy avalanche hissed, then Stardock grew still in the frigid grip of night. The climbers' eyrie seemed most strange to them, set above every other peak in the Mountains of the Giants – and likely all Nehwon – yet walled with darkness like a tiny room.

The Mouser said softly, 'Now we know what roosts in the Roosts. Do you suppose there are dozens of those invisible mantas carpeting around us on ledges like this, or a-hung from them? Why don't they freeze? Or does someone stable them? And the invisible folk, what of them? No more can you call 'em mirage – you saw the sword, and I fought the man-thing at the other end of it. Yet invisible! How's that possible?'

Fafhrd shrugged and then winced because it hurt both shoulders cruelly. 'Made of some stuff like water or glass,' he hazarded. 'Yet pliant and twisting the light less – and with no surface shimmer. You've seen sand and ashes made transparent by firing. Perhaps there's some heatless way of firing monsters and men until they are invisible.'

'But how light enough to fly?' the Mouser asked.

'Thin beasts to match thin air,' Fafhrd guessed sleepily.

The Mouser said, 'And then those deadly worms – and the Fiend knows what perils above.' He paused. 'And yet we must still climb Stardock to the top, mustn't we? Why?'

Fafhrd nodded. 'To beat out Kranarch and Gnarfi . . .' he muttered. 'To beat out my father . . . the mystery of it . . . the girls . . . O Mouser, could you stop here any more than you could stop after touching half of a woman?'

'You don't mention diamonds any more,' the Mouser noted. 'Don't you think we'll find them?'

Fafhrd started another shrug and mumbled a curse that turned into a yawn.

The Mouser dug in his pouch to the bottom pocket and brought out the parchment and blowing on the brazier read it all by the resin's last flaming:

Who mounts white Stardock, the Moon Tree,
    Past worm and gnome and unseen bars,
Will win the key to luxury:
    The Heart of Light, a pouch of stars.
The gods who once ruled all the world
    Have made that peak their citadel,
From whence the stars were one time hurled
    And paths lead on to Heav'n and Hell.
Comes, heroes, past the Trollstep rocks.
    Come, best of men, across the Waste.
For you, glory each door unlocks.
    Delay not, up, and come in haste.
Who scales the Snow King's citadel
    Shall father his two daughters' sons;
Though he must face foes fierce and fell,
    His seed shall live while time still runs.

The resin burnt out. The Mouser said, 'Well, we've met a worm and one unseen fellow who sought to bar our way – and two sightless witches who might be Snow King's daughters for all I know. Gnomes now – they would be a change, wouldn't they? You said something about Ice Gnomes, Fafhrd. What was it?'

He waited with an unnatural anxiety for Fafhrd's answer. After a bit he began to hear it: soft regular snores.

The Mouser snarled soundlessly, his demon of restlessness now became a fury despite all his aches. He shouldn't have thought of girls – or rather of one girl who was nothing but a taunting mask with pouting lips and eyes of black mystery seen across a fire.

Suddenly he felt stifled. He quickly unhooked his cloak and despite Hrissa's questioning mew felt his way south along the ledge. Soon snow, sifting like ice needles on his flushed face, told him he was beyond the overhang. Then the snow stopped. Another overhang, he thought – but he had not moved. He strained his eyes upward, and there was the black expanse of Stardock's topmost quarter silhouetted against a band of sky pale with the hidden moon and specked by a few faint stars. Behind him to the west, the snowstorm still obscured the sky.

He blinked his eyes and then he swore softly, for now the black cliff they must climb tomorrow was a-glow with soft scattered lights of violet and rose and palest green and amber. The nearest, which were still far above, looked tinily rectangular, like gleam-spilling windows seen from below.

It was as if Stardock were a great hostelry.

Then freezing flakes pinked his face again, and the band of sky narrowed to nothing. The snowfall had moved back against Stardock once more, hiding all stars and other lights.

The Mouser's fury drained from him. Suddenly he felt very small and foolhardy and very, very cold. The mysterious vision of the lights remained in his mind, but muted, as if part of a dream. Most cautiously he crept back the way he had come, feeling the radiant warmth of Fafhrd and Hrissa and the burnt-out brazier just before he touched his cloak. He laced it around him and lay for a long time doubled up like a baby, his mind empty of everything except frigid blackness. At last he slumbered.

Next day started gloomy. The two men chafed and wrestled each other as they lay, to get the stiffness a little out of them and enough warmth in them to rise. Hrissa withdrew from between them limping and sullen.

At any rate, Fafhrd's arms were recovered from their swelling and numbing, while the Mouser was hardly aware of his own arm's little wounds.

They breakfasted on herb tea and honey and began climbing the Roosts in a light snowfall. This last pest stayed with them all morning except when gusty breezes blew it back from Stardock. On these occasions they could see the great smooth cliff separating the Roosts from the ultimate ledges of the Face. By the glimpses they got, the cliff looked to be without any climbing routes whatever, or any marks at all – so that Fafhrd laughed at the Mouser for a dreamer with his tale of windows spilling colored light – but finally as they neared the cliff's base they began to distinguish what seemed to be a narrow crack – a hairline to vision – mounting its center.

They met none of the invisible flat fliers, either a-wing or a-perch, though whenever gusts blew strange gaps into the snowfall, the two adventurers would firm themselves on their perches and grip for their weapons, and Hrissa would snarl.

The wind slowed them little though chilling them much, for the rock of the Roosts was true.

And they still had to watch out for stony peltings, though these were fewer than yesterday, perhaps because so much of Stardock now lay below them.

They reached the base of the great cliff at the point where the crack began, which was a good thing, since the snowfall had grown so heavy that a hunt for it would have been difficult.

To their joy, the crack proved to be another chimney, scarcely a yard across and not much more deep, and as knobbly inside with footholds as the cliff outside was smooth. Unlike yesterday's chimney, it appeared to extend upward indefinitely without change of width and as far as they could see there were no chockstones. In many ways it was like a rock ladder half sheltered from the snow. Even Hrissa could climb here, as on Obelisk Polaris.

They lunched on food warmed against their skins. They were afire with eagerness, yet forced themselves to take time to chew and sip. As they entered the chimney, Fafhrd going first, there came three faint growling booms – thunder perhaps and certainly ominous, yet the Mouser laughed.

With never-failing footholds and opposite wall for back-brace, the climbing was easy, except for the drain on main strength, which required rather frequent halts to gulp down fresh stores of the thin air. Only twice did the chimney narrow so that Fafhrd had to climb for a short stretch with his body outside it; the Mouser, slighter framed, could stay inside.

It was an intoxicating experience, almost. Even as the day

grew darker from the thickening snowfall and as the crackling booms returned sharper and stronger – thunder now for sure, since they were heralded by brief palings up and down the chimney – snow-muted lightning flashes – the Mouser and Fafhrd felt as merry as children mounting a mysterious twisty stairway in a haunted castle. They even wasted a little breath in joking calls which went echoing faintly up and down the rugged shaft as it paled and gloomed with the lightning.

But then the shaft grew by degrees almost as smooth as the outer cliff and at the same time it began gradually to widen, first a handbreadth, then another, then a finger more, so that they had to mount more perilously, bracing shoulders against one wall and boots against the other and so 'walking' up with pushes and heaves. The Mouser drew up Hrissa and the ice-cat crouched on his pitching, rocking chest – no inconsiderable burden. Yet both men still felt quite jolly – so that the Mouser began to wonder if there might not be some actual intoxicant in air near Heaven.

Being a head or two taller than the Mouser, Fafhrd was better equipped for this sort of climbing and was still able to go on at that moment when the Mouser realized that his body was stretched almost straight between shoulders and boot soles – with Hrissa a-crouch on him like a traveler on a little bridge. He could mount no farther – and was hazy about how he had managed to come this far.

Fafhrd came down like a great spider at the Mouser's call and seemed not much impressed by the latter's plight – in fact, a lightning flash showed his great bearded face all a-grin.

'Abide you here a bit,' he said. ''Tis not so far to the top. I think I glimpsed it the last flash but one. I'll mount and draw you up, putting all the rope between you and me. There's a crack by your head – I'll knock in a spike for safety's sake. Meanwhile, rest.'

Whereupon Fafhrd did all of these things so swiftly and was on his upward way again so soon that the Mouser forebore to utter any of the sardonic remarks churning inside his rigid belly.

Successive lightning flashes showed the Northerner's long-limbed form growing smaller at a gratifyingly rapid rate until he looked hardly bigger than a trap spider at the end of his tube. Another flash and he was gone, but whether because he had reached the top or passed a bend in the chimney the Mouser couldn't be sure.

The rope kept paying upward, however, until there was only a small loop below the Mouser. He was aching abominably now and was also very cold, but gritted his teeth against the pain. Hrissa chose this moment to prowl up and down her small human bridge, restlessly. There was a blinding lightning flash and a crash of thunder that shook Stardock. Hrissa cringed.

The rope grew taut, tugging at the belt of the Mouser, who started to put his weight on it, holding Hrissa to his chest, but then decided to wait for Fafhrd's call. This was a good decision on his part, for just then the rope went slack and began to fall on the Mouser's belly like a stream of black water. Hrissa crouched away from it on his face. It came pelting endlessly, but finally its upper end hit the Mouser under the breastbone with a snap. The only good thing was that Fafhrd didn't come hurtling down with it. Another blinding mountain-shaking crash showed the upper chimney utterly empty.

'Fafhrd!' the Mouser called. '*Fafhrd!*' There came back only the echo.

The Mouser thought for a bit, then reached up and felt by his ear for the spike Fafhrd had struck in with a single offhand slap of his ax-hammer. Whatever had happened to Fafhrd, nothing seemed to remain to do but tie rope to spike and descend by it to where the chimney was easier.

The spike came out at the first touch and went clattering shrilly down the chimney until a new thunderblast drowned the small sound.

The Mouser decided to 'walk' down the chimney. After all, he'd come up that way the last few score of yards.

The first attempt to move a leg told him his muscles were knotted by cramp. He'd never be able to bend his leg and straighten it again without losing his purchase and falling.

The Mouser thought of Glinthi's pike, lost in white space, and he slew that thought.

Hrissa crouched on his chest and gazed down into his face

with an expression the next levin-glare showed to be sad yet critical, as if to ask, 'Where is this vaunted human ingenuity?'

Fafhrd had barely eased himself out of the chimney onto the wide, deep rock-roofed ledge at its top, when a door two yards high, a yard wide, and two spans thick had silently opened in the rock at the back of the ledge.

The contrast was most remarkable between the roughness of that rock and the ruler-flat smoothness of the dark stone forming the thick sides of the door and the lintel, jambs, and threshold of the doorway.

Soft pink light spilled out and with it a perfume whose heavy fumes were cargoed with dreams of pleasure barges afloat in a rippling sunset sea.

Those musky narcotic fumes, along with the alcoholic headiness of the thin air, almost made Fafhrd forget his purpose, but touching the black rope was like touching Hrissa and the Mouser at its other end. He unknotted it from his belt and prepared to secure it around a stout rock pillar beside the open door. To get enough rope to make a good knot he had to draw it up quite tight.

But the dream-freighted fumes grew thicker, and he no longer felt the Mouser and Hrissa in the rope. Indeed, he began to forget his two comrades altogether.

And then a silvery voice – a voice he knew well from having heard it laugh once and once chuckle – called, 'Come in, barbarian. Come in to me.'

The end of the black rope slipped from his fingers unnoticed and hissed softly across the rock and down the chimney.

Stooping a little, he went through the doorway which silently closed behind him just in time to shut out the Mouser's desperate call.

He was in a room lit by pink globes hanging at the level of his head. Their soft warm radiance colored the hangings and rugs of the room, but especially the pale spread of the great bed that was its only furniture.

Beside the bed stood a slim woman whose black silk robe concealed all of her except her face, yet did not disguise her body's sleek curves. A black lace mask hid the rest of her.

634

She looked at Fafhrd for seven thudding heartbeats, then sat down on the bed. A slender arm and hand clothed all in black lace came from under her robe and patted the spread beside her and rested there. Her mask never wavered from Fafhrd's face.

He shouldered out of his pack and unbuckled his ax belt.

The Mouser finished pounding all the thin blade of his dagger into the crack by his ear, using the firestone from his pouch for hammer, so that sparks showered from every cramped stroke of stone against pommel – small lightning flashes to match the greater flares still chasing up and down the chimney, while their thunder crashed an obbligato to the Mouser's taps. Hrissa crouched on his ankles, and from time to time the Mouser glared at her, as if to say, 'Well, cat?'

A gust of snow-freighted wind roaring up the chimney momentarily lifted the lean shaggy beast a span above him and almost blew the Mouser loose, but he tightened his pushing muscles still more and the bridge, arching upward a trifle, held firm.

He had just finished knotting an end of the black rope around the dagger's crossguard and grip – and his fingers and forearms were almost useless with fatigue – when a window two feet high and five wide silently opened in the back of the chimney, its thick rock shutter sliding aside, not a span away from the Mouser's inward shoulder.

A red glow sprang from the window and somewhat illumined four faces with piggy black eyes and with low hairless domes above.

The Mouser considered them. They were all four of extreme ugliness, he decided dispassionately. Only their wide white teeth, showing between their grinning lips which almost joined ear to swinish ear, had any claim to beauty.

Hrissa sprang at once through the red window and dis-appeared. The two faces between which she jumped did not flicker a black button-eye.

Then eight short brawny arms came out and easily pried the Mouser out and lifted him inside. He screamed faintly from a sudden increase in the agony of his cramps. He was aware of thick dwarfish bodies clad in hairy black jerkins and breeks – and one in a black hairy skirt – but all with thick-nailed splay-feet bare. Then he fainted.

When he came to, it was because he was being punishingly massaged on a hard table, his body naked and slick with warm oil. He was in a low, ill-lit chamber and still closely surrounded by the four dwarves, as he could tell from the eight horny hands squeezing and thumping his muscles before he ever opened his eyes.

The dwarf kneading his right shoulder and banging the top of his spine crinkled his warty eyelids and bared his beautiful white teeth bigger than a giant's in what might be intended for a friendly grin. Then he said in an atrocious Mingol patois, 'I am Bonecracker. This is my wife Gibberfat. Cosseting your body on the larboard side are my brothers Legcruncher and Breakskull. Now drink this wine and follow me.'

The wine stung, yet dispelled the Mouser's dizziness, and it was certainly a blessing to be free of the murderous massage – and also apparently of the cramp-lumps in his muscles.

Bonecracker and Gibberfat helped him off the slab while Legcruncher and Breakskull rubbed him quickly down with rough towels. The warm low-ceiling room rocked dizzily for a moment; then he felt wondrous fine.

Bonecracker waddled off into the dimness beyond the smoky torches. With never a question the Mouser followed the dwarf. Or were these Fafhrd's Ice Gnomes? he wondered.

Bonecracker pulled aside heavy drapes in the dark. Amber light fanned out. The Mouser stepped from rock-roughness onto down-softness. The drapes swished to behind him.

He was alone in a chamber mellowly lit by hanging globes like great topazes – yet he guessed they would bounce aside like puffballs if touched. There was a large wide couch and beyond it a low table against the arras-hung wall with an ivory stool set before it. Above the table was a great silver mirror, while on it were fantastic small bottles and many tiny ivory jars.

No, the room was not altogether empty. Hrissa, sleekly groomed, lay curled in a far corner. She was not watching the Mouser, however, but a point above the stool.

The Mouser felt a shiver creeping on him, yet not altogether one of fear.

A dab of palest green leaped from one of the jars to the point Hrissa was watching and vanished there. But then he saw a streak of reflected green appear in the mirror. The riddlesome maneuver was repeated, and soon in the mirror's silver there hung a green mask, somewhat clouded by the silver's dullness.

Then the mask vanished from the mirror and simultaneously reappeared unblurred hanging in the air above the ivory stool. It was the mask the mouser knew achingly well – narrow chin, high-arched cheeks, straight nose and forehead.

The pouty wine-dark lips opened a little and a soft throaty voice asked, 'Does my visage displease you, man of Lankhmar?'

'You jest cruelly, O Princess,' the Mouser replied, drawing on all his aplomb and sketching a courtier's bow, 'for you are Beauty's self.'

Slim fingers, half outlined now in pale green, dipped into the unguent jar and took up a more generous dab.

The soft throaty voice that so well matched half the laughter he had once heard in a snowfall, now said, 'You shall judge all of me.'

Fafhrd woke in the dark and touched the girl beside him. As soon as he knew she was awake too, he grasped her by the hips. When he felt her body stiffen, he lifted her into the air and held her above him as he lay flat on his back.

She was wondrous light, as if made of pastry or eiderdown, yet when he laid her beside him again, her flesh felt as firm as any, though smoother than most.

'Let us have a light, Hirriwi, I beg you,' he said.

'That were unwise, Faffy,' she answered in a voice like a curtain of tiny silver bells lightly brushed. 'Have you forgotten that now I am wholly invisible? – which might tickle some men, yet you, I think . . .'

'You're right, you're right, I like you real,' he answered, gripping her fiercely by the shoulders to emphasize his feelings, then guiltily jerking away his hands as he thought of how delicate she must be.

The silver bells clashed in full laughter, as if the curtain of them had been struck a great swipe. 'Have no fears,' she told him. 'My airy bones are grown of matter stronger than steel. It is a riddle beyond your philosophers and relates to the invisibility of my race and of the animals from which it sprang. Think how strong tempered glass can be, yet light goes through it. My cursed brother Faroomfar has the strength of a bear for all his slimness while my father Oomforafor is a very lion despite his centuries. Your friend's encounter with Faroomfar was no final test – but oh how it made him howl – Father raged at him – and then there are the cousins. Soon as this night be ended – which is not soon, my dear; the moon still climbs – you must return down Stardock. Promise me that. My heart grows cold at the thought of the dangers you've already faced – and was like ice I know not how many times this last three-day.'

'Yet you never warned us,' he mused. 'You lured me on.'

'Can you doubt why?' she asked. He was feeling her snub nose then and her apple cheeks, and so he felt her smile too. 'Or perhaps you resent it that I let you risk your life a little to win here to this bed?'

He implanted a fervent kiss on her wide lips to show her how little true that was, but she thrust him back after a moment.

'Wait, Faffy dear,' she said. 'No, wait, I say! I know you're greedy and impetuous, but you can at least wait while the moon creeps the width of a star. I asked you to promise me you would descend Stardock at dawn.'

There was a rather long silence in the dark.

'Well?' she prompted. 'What shuts your mouth?' she queried impatiently. 'You've shown no such indecision in certain other matters. Time wastes, the moon sails.'

'Hirriwi,' Fafhrd said softly, 'I must climb Stardock.'

'Why?' she demanded ringingly. 'The poem has been fulfilled. You have your reward. Go on, and only frigid fruitless perils await you. Return, and I'll guard you from the air – yes, and your companion too – to the very Waste.' Her sweet voice faltered a little. 'O Faffy, am I not enough to make you forego the conquest of a cruel mountain? In addition to all else, I love you – if I understand rightly how mortals use that word.'

'No,' he answered her solemnly in the dark. 'You are

wondrous, more wondrous than any wench I've known – and I love you, which is not a word I bandy – yet you only make me hotter to conquer Stardock. Can you understand that?'

Now there was silence for a while in the other direction.

'Well,' she said at length, 'you are masterful and will do what you will do. And I have warned you. I could tell you more, show you reasons counter, argue further, but in the end I know I would not break your stubbornness – and time gallops. We must mount our own steeds and catch up with the moon. Kiss me again. Slowly. So.'

The Mouser lay across the foot of the bed under the amber globes and contemplated Keyaira, who lay lengthwise with her slender apple green shoulders and tranquil sleeping face propped by many pillows.

He took up the corner of a sheet and moistened it with wine from a cup set against his knee and with it rubbed Keyaira's slim right ankle – so gently that there was no change in her narrow bosom's slow-paced rise and fall. Presently he had cleared away all the greenish unguent from a patch as big as half his palm. He peered down at his handwork. This time he expected surely to see flesh, or at least the green cosmetic on the underside of her ankle, but no, he saw through the irregular little rectangle he'd wiped only the bed's tufted coverlet reflecting the amber light from above. It was a most fascinating and somewhat unnerving mystery.

He glanced questioningly over at Hrissa, who lay on an end of the low table, the thin-glassed, fantastic perfume bottles standing around her, while she contemplated the occupants of the bed, her white tufted chin set on her folded paws. It seemed to the Mouser that she was looking at him with disapproval, so he hastily smoothed back unguent from other parts of Keyaira's leg until the peephole was once more greenly covered.

There was a low laugh. Keyaira propped on her elbows now, was gazing at him through slitted heavy-lashed eyelids.

'We invisibles,' she said in a humorous voice truly or feignedly heavy with sleep, 'show only the outward side of any cosmetic or raiment on us. It is a mystery beyond our seers.'

'You are Mystery's queenly self a-walk through the stars,' the Mouser pronounced, lightly caressing her green toes. 'And I the most fortunate of men. I fear it's a dream and I'll wake on Stardock's frigid ledges. How is it I am here?'

'Our race is dying out,' she said. 'Our men have become sterile. Hirriwi and I are the only princesses left. Our brother Faroomfar hotly wished to be our consort – he still boasts his virility – 'twas he you dueled with – but our father Oomforafor said, "It must be new blood – the blood of heroes." So the cousins and Faroomfar, he much against his will, must fly hither and yon and leave those little rhymed lures written on ramskin in perilous, lonely spots apt to tempt heroes.'

'But how can visibles and invisibles mate?' he asked.

She laughed with delight. 'Is your memory *that* short, Mouse?'

'I mean, have progeny,' he corrected himself, a little irked, but not much, that she had hit on his boyhood nickname. 'Besides, wouldn't such offspring be cloudy, a mix of seen and unseen?'

Keyaira's green mask swung a little from side to side.

'My father thinks such mating will be fertile and that the children will breed true to invisibility – that being dominant over visibility – yet profit greatly in other ways from the admixture of hot, heroic blood.'

'Then your father commanded you to mate with me?' the Mouser asked, a little disappointed.

'By no means, Mouse,' she assured him. 'He would be furious if he dreamt you were here, and Faroomfar would go mad. No, I took a fancy to you, as Hirriwi did to your comrade, when first I spied on you on the Waste – very fortunate that was for you, since my father would have got your seed, if you had won to Stardock's top, in quite a different fashion. Which reminds me, Mouse, you must promise me to descend Stardock at dawn.'

'That is not so easy a promise to give,' the Mouser said. 'Fafhrd will be stubborn, I know. And then there's that other matter of a bag of diamonds, if that's what a pouch of stars means – oh, it's but a trifle, I know, compared to the embraces of a glorious girl . . . still . . .'

'But if I say I love you? – which is only truth . . .'

'Oh, Princess,' the Mouser sighed, gliding his hand to her knee. 'How can I leave you at dawn? Only one night . . .'

'Why, Mouse,' Keyaira broke in, smiling roguishly and twisting her green form a little, 'do you not know that every night is an eternity? Has not any girl taught you that yet, Mouse? I am astonished. Think, we have half an eternity left us yet – which is also an eternity, as your geometer, whether white-bearded or dainty-breasted, should have taught you.'

'But if I am to sire many children—' the Mouser began.

'Hirriwi and I are somewhat like queen bees,' Keyaira explained, 'but think not of that. We have eternity tonight, 'tis true, but only if we make it so. Come closer.'

A little later, plagiarizing himself somewhat, the Mouser said softly, 'The sole fault of mountain climbing is that the best parts go so swiftly.'

'They can last an eternity,' Keyaira breathed in his ear. 'Make them last, Mouse.'

Fafhrd woke shaking with cold. The pink globes were gray and tossing in icy gusts from the open door. Snow had blown in on his clothes and gear scattered across the floor and was piled inches deep on the threshold, across which came also the only illumination – leaden daylight.

A great joy in him fought all these grim gray sights and conquered them.

Nevertheless he was naked and shivering. He sprang up and beat his clothes against the bed and thrust his limbs into their icy stiffness.

As he was buckling his ax belt, he remembered the Mouser down in the chimney, helpless. Somehow all night, even when he'd spoken to Hirriwi of the Mouser, he'd never thought of that.

He snatched up his pack and sprang out on the ledge. From the corner of his eye he caught something moving behind him. It was the massive door closing.

A titan gust of snow-fisted wind struck him. He grabbed the rough rock pillar to which he'd last night planned to tie the rope and hugged it tight. The gods help the Mouser below! Someone came sliding and blowing along the ledge in the wind and snow and hugged the pillar lower down.

The gust passed. Fafhrd looked for the door. There was no sign of it. All the piled snow was redrifted. Keeping close hold of pillar and pack with one hand, he felt over the rough wall with the other. Fingernails no more than eyes could discover the slightest crack.

'So you got tossed out too?' a familiar voice said gayly. '*I* was tossed out by Ice Gnomes, I'll have you know.'

'Mouser!' Fafhrd cried. 'Then you weren't—? I thought—'

'You never thought of me once all night, if I know you,' the Mouser said. 'Keyaira assured me you were safe and somewhat more than that. Hirriwi would have told you the same of me if you'd asked her. But of course you didn't.'

'Then you too—?' Fafhrd demanded, grinning with delight.

'Yes, Prince Brother-in-Law,' the Mouser answered him, grinning back.

They pommeled each other around the pillar a bit – to battle chill, but in sheer high spirits too.

'Hrissa?' Fafhrd asked.

'Warm inside, the wise one. They don't put out the cat here, only the man. I wonder, though . . . Do you suppose Hrissa was Keyaira's to begin with and that she foresaw and planned . . .' His voice trailed off.

No more gusts had come. The snowfall was so light they could see almost a league – up to the Hat above the snow-streaked ledges of the Face and down to where the Ladder faded out.

Once again their minds were filled, almost overpowered by the vastness of Stardock and by their own predicament: two half-frozen mites precariously poised on a frozen vertical world only distantly linked with Nehwon.

To the south there was a pale silver disk in the sky – the sun. They'd been abed till noon.

'Easier to fashion an eternity out of an eighteen-hour night,' the Mouser observed.

'We galloped the moon deep under the sea,' Fafhrd mused.

'Your girl promise to make you go down?' the Mouser asked suddenly.

Fafhrd nodded his head. 'She tried.'

'Mine too. And not a bad idea. The summit smells, by her account. But the chimney looks stuffed with snow. Hold my ankles while I peer over. Yes, packed solid all the way down. So—'

'Mouser,' Fafhrd said, almost gloomily, 'whether there's a way down or no, I must climb Stardock.'

'You know,' the Mouser answered, 'I am beginning to find something in that madness myself. Besides, the east wall of Stardock may hold an easy route to that lush-looking Rift Valley. So let's do what we can with the bare seven hours of light left us. Daytime's no stuff to fashion eternities.'

Mounting the ledges of the Face was both the easiest and hardest climbing they'd had yet to do. The ledges were wide, but some of them sloped outward and were footed with rotten shale that went skidding away into space at a touch, and now and again there were brief traverses which had to be done by narrow cracks and main strength, sometimes swinging by their hands alone.

And weariness and chill and even dizzying faintness came far quicker at this height. They had to halt often to drink air and chafe themselves. While in the back of one deep ledge – Stardock's right eye, they judged – they were forced to spend time firing the brazier with all the remaining resin-pellets, partly to warm food and drink, but chiefly to warm themselves.

Last night's exertions had weakened them too, they sometimes thought, but then the memories of those exertions would return to strengthen them.

And then there were the sudden treacherous wind gusts and the constant yet variable snowfall, which sometimes hid the summit and sometimes let them see it clear against the silvery sky, with great white out-curving brim of the Hat now poised threateningly above them – a cornice like that of the snow-saddle, only now they were on the wrong side.

The illusion grew stronger that Stardock was a separate world from Nehwon in snow-filled space.

Finally the sky turned blue and they felt the sun on their backs

– they had climbed above the snowfall at last – and Fafhrd pointed at a tiny nick of blue deep in the brim of the Hat – a nick just visible above the next snow-streaked rock bulge – and he cried, 'The apex of the Needle's Eye!'

At that, something dropped into a snowbank beside them, and there was a muffled clash of metal on rock, while from snow a notched and feathered arrow-end stuck straight up.

They dodged under the protective roof of a bigger bulge as a second arrow and a third clashed against the naked rock on which they'd stood.

'Gnarfi and Kranarch have beaten us, curse 'em,' Fafhrd hissed, 'and set an ambush for us at the Eye, the obvious spot. We must go roundabout and get above 'em.'

'Won't they expect that?'

'They were fools to spring their ambush too soon. Besides, we have no other tactic.'

So they began to climb south, though still upward, always keeping rock or snow between them and where they judged the Needle's Eye to be. At last, when the sun was dropping swiftly toward the western horizon, they came swinging back north again and still upward, stamping out steps now in the steepening bank of snow that reversed its curve above them to make the brim of the Hat that now roofed them ominously, covering two-thirds of the sky. They sweated and shook by turns and fought off almost continuous bouts of giddy faintness, yet still strove to move as silently and warily as they might.

At last they rounded one more snow bulge and found themselves looking down a slope at the great bare stretch of rock normally swept by the gale that came through the Needle's Eye to make the Petty Pennon.

On the outward lip of the exposed rock were two men, both clad in suits of brown leather, much scuffed and here and there ripped, showing the inward-turned fur. Lank, black-bearded, elk-faced Kranarch stood whipping his arms against his chest for warmth. Beside him lay his strung bow and some arrows. Stocky boar-faced Gnarfi knelt peeping over the rim. Fafhrd wondered where their two brown-clad bulky servitors were.

The Mouser dug into his pouch. At the same moment

644

Kranarch saw them and snatched up his weapon though rather more slowly than he would have in thicker air. With a similar slowness the Mouser drew out the fist-size rock he had picked up several ledges below for just such a moment as this.

Kranarch's arrow whistled between his and Fafhrd's heads. A moment later the Mouser's rock struck Kranarch full on his bow-shoulder. The weapon fell from his hand and that arm dangled. Then Fafhrd and the Mouser charged recklessly down the snow slope, the former brandishing his unthonged ax, the latter drawing Scalpel.

Kranarch and Gnarfi received them with their own swords, and Gnarfi with a dagger in his left hand as well. The battle that followed had the same dreamlike slowness as the exchange of missiles. First Fafhrd's and the Mouser's rush gave them the advantage. Then Kranarch's and Gnarfi's great strength – or restedness, rather – told, and they almost drove their enemy off the rim. Fafhrd took a slash in the ribs which bit through his tough wolfskin tunic, slicing flesh and jarring bone.

But then skill told, as it generally will, and the two brown-clad men received wounds and suddenly turned and ran through the great white pointy-topped triangular archway of the Needle's Eye. As he ran Gnarfi screeched, 'Graah! Kruk!'

'Doubtless calling for their shaggy-clad servants or bearers,' the Mouser gasped in surmise, resting sword arm on knee, almost spent. 'Farmerish fat country fellows those looked, hardly trained to weapons. We need not fear 'em greatly, I think, even if they come to Gnarfi's call.' Fafhrd nodded, gasping himself. 'Yet they climbed Stardock,' he added dubiously.

Just then there came galloping through the snowy archway on their hind legs with their nails clashing the windswept rock and their fang-edged slavering red mouths open wide and their great-clawed arms widespread – two huge brown bears.

With a speed which their human opponents had been unable to sting from them, the Mouser snatched up Kranarch's bow and sent two arrows speeding, while Fafhrd swung his ax in a gleaming circle and cast it. Then the two comrades sprang swiftly to either side, the Mouser wielding Scalpel and Fafhrd drawing his knife.

But there was no need for further fighting. The Mouser's first arrow took the leading bear in the neck, his second straight in its red mouth-roof and brain, while Fafhrd's ax sank to its helve between two ribs on the trailing bear's left side. The great animals pitched forward in their blood and death throes and rolled twice over and went tumbling ponderously off the rim.

'Doubtless both shes,' the Mouser remarked as he watched them fall. 'O those bestial men of Illik-Ving! Still, to charm or train such beasts to carry packs and climb and even give up their poor lives . . .'

'Kranarch and Gnarfi are no sportsmen, that's for certain now,' Fafhrd pronounced. 'Don't praise their tricks.' As he stuffed a rag into his tunic over his wound, he grimaced and swore so angrily that the Mouser didn't speak his quip: *Well, bears are only shortened bearers. I'm always right.*

Then the two comrades trudged slowly under the high tent-like arch of snow to survey the domain, highest on all Nehwon, of which they had made themselves masters – refusing from light-headed weariness to think, in that moment of triumph, of the invisible beings who were Stardock's lords. They went warily, yet not too much so, because Gnarfi and Kranarch had run scared and were wounded not trivially – and the latter had lost his bow.

Stardock's top behind the great toppling snow wave of the Hat was almost as extensive north to south as that of Obelisk Polaris, yet the east rim looked little more than a long bowshot away. Snow with a thick crust beneath a softer layer covered it all except for the north end and stretches of the east rim, where bare dark rock showed.

The surface, both snow and rock, was flatter even than that of the Obelisk and sloped somewhat from north to south. There were no structures or beings visible, nor signs of hollows where either might hide. Truth to tell, neither the Mouser nor Fafhrd could recall ever having seen a lonelier or barer place.

The only oddity they noticed at first were three holes in the snow a little to the south, each about as big as a hogshead but having the form of an equilateral triangle and apparently going down through the snow to the rock. The three triangular holes were the three corners of a larger equilateral triangle.

The Mouser squinted around closely, then shrugged. 'But a pouch of stars could be a rather small thing, I suppose,' he said. 'While a heart of light – no guessing its size.'

The whole summit was in bluish shadow except for the northernmost end and for a great pathway of golden light from the setting sun leading from the Needle's Eye all the way across the wind-leveled snow to the east rim.

Down the center of this sunroad went Kranarch's and Gnarfi's running footsteps, the snow flecked here and there with blood. Otherwise the snow ahead was printless. Fafhrd and the Mouser followed those tracks, walking east up their long shadows.

'No sign of 'em ahead,' the Mouser said. 'Looks like there *is* some route down the east wall, and they've taken it – at least far enough to set another ambush.'

As they neared the east rim, Fafhrd said, 'I see other prints making north – a spear's cast that way. Perhaps they turned.'

'But where to?' the Mouser asked.

A few steps more and the mystery was solved horribly. They reached the end of the snow and there on the dark bloodied rock, hidden until now by the wind-piled margin of the snow, sprawled the carcasses of Gnarfi and Kranarch, their middle clothes ripped away, their bodies obscenely mutilated.

Even as the Mouser's gorge rose, he remembered Keyaira's lightly-spoken words: 'If you had won to Stardock's top, my father would have got your seed in quite a different fashion.'

Shaking his head and glaring fiercely, Fafhrd walked around the bodies to the east rim and peered down.

He recoiled a step, then knelt and once more peered.

The Mouser's hopeful theory was prodigiously disproved. Never in his life had Fafhrd looked straight down half such a distance.

A few yards below, the east wall vanished inward. No telling how far the east rim jutted out from Stardock's heartrock.

From this point the fall was straight to the greenish gloom of the Great Rift Valley – five Lankhmar leagues, at least. Perhaps more.

He heard the Mouser say over his shoulder, 'A path for birds or suicides. Naught else.'

Suddenly the green below grew bright, though without showing the slightest feature except for a silvery hair, which might be a great river, running down its center. Looking up again, they saw that the sky had gone all golden with a mighty afterglow. They faced around and gasped in wonder.

The last sunrays coming through the Needle's Eye, swinging southward and a little up, glancingly illuminated a transparent, solid symmetric shape big as the biggest oak tree and resting exactly over the three triangular holes in the snow. It might only be described as a sharp-edged solid star of about eighteen points, resting by three of those on Stardock and built of purest diamond or some like substance.

Both had the same thoughts: that this must be a star the gods had failed to launch. The sunlight had touched the fire in its heart and made it shine, but for a moment only and feebly, not incandescently and forever, as it would have in the sky.

A piercingly shrill, silvery trumpet call broke the silence of the summit.

They swung their gaze north. Outlined by the same deep golden sunlight, ghostlier than the star, yet still clearly to be seen in some of its parts against the yellow sky, a tall slender castle lifted transparent walls and towers from the stony end of the summit. Its topmost spires seemed to go out of sight upward rather than end.

Another sound then – a wailing snarl. A pale animal bounded toward them across the snow from the northwest. Leaping aside with another snarl from the sprawled bodies, Hrissa rushed past them south with a third snarl tossed at them.

Almost too late they saw the peril against which she had tried to warn them.

Advancing toward them from west and north across the unmarked snow were a score of sets of footprints. There were no feet in those prints, nor bodies above them, yet they came on – right print, left print, appearing in succession – and ever more rapidly. And now they saw what they had missed at first because viewed end-on: above each paired set of prints a narrow-shafted, narrow-bladed spear, pointed straight toward them, coming on as swiftly as the prints.

They ran south with Hrissa, Fafhrd in the lead. After a half dozen sprinting steps the Northerner heard a cry behind him. He stopped and then swiftly spun around.

The Mouser had slipped in the blood of their late foes and fallen. When he got to his feet, the gray spear points were around him on all sides save the rim. He made two wild defensive slashes with Scalpel, but the gray spear points came in relentlessly. Now they were in a close semi-circle around him and hardly a span apart, and he was standing on the rim. They advanced another thrust and the Mouser perforce sprang back from them – and down he fell.

There was a rushing sound and chill air sluiced Fafhrd from behind and something sleekly hairy brushed his calves. As he braced himself to rush forward with his knife and slay an invisible or two for his friend, slender unseen arms clasped him from behind and he heard Hirriwi's silvery voice say in his ear, 'Trust us,' and a coppery-golden sister voice say, 'We'll after him,' and then he found himself pulled down onto a great invisible pulsing shaggy bed three spans above the snow, and they told him 'Cling!' and he clung to the long thick unseen hair, and then suddenly the living bed shot forward across the snow and off the rim and there tilted vertically so his feet pointed at the sky and his face at the Great Rift Valley – and then the bed plunged straight down.

The thin air roared past and his beard and mane were whipped back by the speed of that plunge, but he tightened his grip on the handfuls of invisible hair and a slender arm pressed him down from either side, so that he felt through the fur the throbbing heartbeat of the great invisible carpetlike creature they rode. And he became aware that somehow Hrissa had got under his arm, for there was the small feline face beside his, with slitted eyes and with beard-tuft and ears blown back. And he felt the two invisible girls' bodies alongside his.

He realized that mortal eyes, could such have watched, would have seen only a large man clasping a large white cat and falling headfirst through empty space – but he would be falling much faster than any man should fall, even from such a vast height.

Beside him Hirriwi laughed, as if she had caught his thought, but then the laughter broke off suddenly and the roaring of the wind died almost to utter silence. He guessed it was because the swiftly thickening air had deafened him.

The great dark cliffs flashing upward a dozen yards away were a blur. Yet below him the Great Rift Valley was still featurless green – no, the larger details were beginning to show now: forests and glades and curling hair-thin streams and little lakes like dewdrops.

Between him and the green below he saw a dark speck. It grew in size. It was the Mouser! – rather characteristically falling headfirst, straight as an arrow, with hands locked ahead of him and legs pressed together behind, probably in the faint hope that he might hit deep water.

The creature they rode matched the Mouser's speed and then gradually swung its plunge toward him, flattening out more and more from the vertical, so that the Mouser was pressed against them. Arms visible and invisible clasped him then, pulling him closer, so that all five of the plungers were crowded together on that one great sentient bed.

The creature's dive flattened still more then, halting its fall – there was a long moment while they were all pressed stomach-surgingly tight against the hairy back, while the trees still rushed up at them – and then they were coasting above those same treetops and spiraling down into a large glade.

What happened next to Fafhrd and the Mouser went all in a great tumbling rush, much too swiftly: the feel of springy turf under their feet and balmy air sluicing their bodies, quick kisses exchanged, laughing, shouted congratulations that still sounded all muffled like ghost voices, something hard and irregular yet soft-covered pressed into the Mouser's hands, a last kiss – and then Hirriwi and Keyaira had broken away and a great burst of air flattened the grass and the great invisible flier was gone and the girls with it.

They could watch its upward spiraling flight for a little, however, because Hrissa had gone away on it too. The ice-cat seemed to be peering down at them in farewell. Then she too vanished as the golden afterglow swiftly died in the darkening sky overhead.

They stood leaning together for support in the twilight. Then they straightened themselves, yawning prodigiously, and their hearing came back. They heard the gurgling of a brook and the twittering of birds and a small, faint rustle of dry leaves going away from them and the tiny buzz of a spiraling gnat.

The Mouser opened the invisible pouch in his hands.

'The gems seem to be invisible too,' he said, 'though I can feel 'em well enough. We'll have a hard time selling them – unless we can find a blind jeweler.'

The darkness deepened. Tiny cold fires began to glow in his palms: ruby, emerald, sapphire, amethyst, and pure white.

'No, by Issek!' the Gray Mouser said. 'We'll only need to sell them by night – which is unquestionably the best time for trade in gems.'

The new-risen moon, herself invisible beyond the lesser mountains walling the Rift Valley to the east, painted palely now the upper half of the great slender column of Stardock's east wall.

Gazing up at that queenly sight, Fafhrd said, 'Gallant ladies, all four.'

III
THE TWO BEST THIEVES
IN LANKHMAR

Through the mazy avenues and alleys of the great city of Lankhmar, Night was a-slink, though not yet grown tall enough to whirl her black star-studded cloak across the sky, which still showed pale, towering wraiths of sunset.

The hawkers of drugs and strong drinks forbidden by day had not yet taken up their bell-tinklings and thin, enticing cries. The pleasure girls had not lit their red lanterns and sauntered insolently forth. Bravos, desperados, procurers, spies, pimps, conmen, and other malfeasors yawned and rubbed drowsy sleep from eyes yet thick-lidded. In fact, most of the Night People were still at breakfast, while most of the Day People were at supper. Which made for an emptiness and hush in the streets, suitable to Night's slippered tread. And which created a large bare stretch of dark, thick, unpierced wall at the intersection of Silver Street with the Street of the Gods, a crossing-point where there habitually foregathered the junior executives and star operatives of the Thieves Guild; also meeting there were the few freelance thieves bold and resourceful enough to defy the Guild and the few thieves of aristocratic birth, sometimes most brilliant amateurs, whom the Guild tolerated and even toadied to, on account of their noble ancestry, which dignified a very old but most disreputable profession.

Midway along the bare stretch of wall, where none might conceivably overhear, a very tall and a somewhat short thief drifted together. After a while they began to converse in prison-yard whispers.

A distance had grown between Fafhrd and the Gray Mouser during their long and uneventful trek south from the Great Rift Valley. It was due simply to too much of each other and to an ever more bickering disagreement as to how the invisible jewels, gift of Hirriwi and Keyaira, might most advantageously be disposed of – a dispute which had finally grown so acrimonious that they had divided the jewels, each carrying his share. When they finally reached Lankhmar, they had lodged apart and each made his own contact with jeweler, fence or private buyer. This separation had made their relationship quite scratchy, but in no way diminished their absolute trust in each other.

'Greetings, Little Man,' Fafhrd prison-growled. 'So you've come to sell your share to Ogo the Blind, or at least give him a viewing? – if such expression may be used of a sightless man.'

'How did you know that?' the Mouser whispered sharply.

'It was the obvious thing to do,' Fafhrd answered somewhat condescendingly. 'Sell the jewels to a dealer who could note neither their night-glow nor daytime invisibility. A dealer who must judge them by weight, feel, and what they can scratch or be scratched by. Besides, we stand just across from the door to Ogo's den. It's very well guarded, by the by – at fewest, ten Mingol swordsmen.'

'At least give me credit for such trifles of common knowledge,' the Mouser answered sardonically. 'Well, you guessed right; it appears that by long association with me you've gained some knowledge of how my wit works, though I doubt that it's sharpened your own a whit. Yes, I've already had one conference with Ogo, and tonight we conclude the deal.'

Fafhrd asked equably, 'Is it true that Ogo conducts all his interviews in pitchy dark?'

'Ho! So there are some few things you admit not knowing! Yes, it's quite true, which makes any interview with Ogo risky work. By insisting on absolute darkness, Ogo the Blind cancels at a stroke the interviewer's advantage – indeed, the advantage passes to Ogo, since he is used by a lifetime of it to utter darkness – a long lifetime, since he's an ancient one, to judge by his speech. Nay, Ogo knows not what darkness is, since it's all he's ever known. However, I've a device to trick him there if need be. In my thick, tightly drawstringed pouch I carry fragments of brightest glow-wood, and can spill them out in a trice.'

Fafhrd nodded admiringly and then asked, 'And what's in that flat case you carry so tightly under your elbow? An elaborate false history of each of the jewels embossed in ancient parchment for Ogo's fingers to read?'

'There your guess fails! No, it's the jewels themselves, guarded in clever wise so that they cannot be filched. Here, take a peek.' And after glancing quickly to either side and overhead, the Mouser opened the case a handbreadth on its hinges.

Fafhrd saw the rainbow-twinkling jewels firmly affixed in artistic pattern to a bed of black velvet, but all closely covered by an inner top consisting of a mesh of stout iron wire.

The Mouser clapped the case shut. 'On our first meeting, I took two of the smallest of the jewels from their spots in the box and let Ogo feel and otherwise test them. He may dream of filching them all, but my box and the mesh thwart that.'

'Unless he steals from you the box itself,' Fafhrd agreed. 'As for myself, I keep my share of the jewels chained to me.' And after such precautionary glances as the Mouser had made, he thrust back his loose sleeve, showing a stout browned-iron bracelet snapped around his wrist. From the bracelet hung a short chain which both supported and kept tightly shut a small, bulging pouch. The leather of the pouch was everywhere sewed across with fine brown wire. He unclicked the bracelet, which opened on a hinge, then clicked it fast again.

'The browned-iron wire's to foil any cutpurse,' Fafhrd explained offhandedly, pulling down his sleeve.

The Mouser's eyebrows rose. Then his gaze followed them as it went from Fafhrd's wrist to his face, while the small man's expression changed from mild approval to bland inquiry. He asked, 'And you trust such devices to guard your half of the gems from Nemia of the Dusk?'

'How did you know my dealings were with Nemia?' Fafhrd asked in tones just the slightest surprised.

'Because she's Lankhmar's only woman fence, of course. All know you favor women when possible, in business as well as erotic matters. Which is one of your greatest failings, if I may say so. Also, Nemia's door lies next to Ogo's, though that's a trivial clue. You know, I presume, that seven Kleshite stranglers protect her somewhat overripe person? Well, at least then you know the sort of trap you're rushing into. Deal with a woman! – surest route to disaster. By the by, you mentioned "dealings". Does that plural mean this is not your first interview with her?'

Fafhrd nodded. 'As you with Ogo . . . Incidentally, am I to understand that you trust men simply because they're men? That were a greater failing than the one you impute to me. Anyhow, as you with Ogo, I go to Nemia of the Dusk a second time, to complete our deal. The first time I showed her the gems in a twilit chamber, where they appeared to greatest advantage, twinkling just enough to seem utterly real. Did you know, in passing, that she always works in twilight or soft gloom? – which accounts for the second half of her name. At all events, as soon as she glimpsed them, Nemia greatly desired the gems – her breath actually caught in her throat – and she agreed at once to my price, which is not low, as basis for further bargaining. However, it happens that she invariably follows the rule – which I myself consider a sound one – of never completing a transaction of any sort with a member of the opposite sex without first testing them in amorous commerce. Hence this second meeting. If the member be old or otherwise ugly, Nemia deputes the task to one of her maids, but in my case, of course . . .' Fafhrd coughed modestly. 'One more point I'd like to make: "overripe" is the wrong expression: "Full-bloomed" or "the acme of maturity" is what you're looking for.'

'Believe me, I'm sure Nemia is the fullest bloom – a late August flower. Such women always prefer twilight for the display of their "perfectly matured" charms,' the Mouser answered somewhat stifledly. He had for some time been hard put to restrain laughter, and now it appeared in quiet little bursts as he said, 'Oh, you great fool! And you've actually agreed to go to bed with her? And expect not to be parted from your jewels (including family jewels?), let alone not strangled, while at that disadvantage? Oh, this is worse than I thought.'

'I'm not always at such a disadvantage in bed as some people may think,' Fafhrd answered with quiet modesty. 'With me, amorous play sharpens instead of dulls the senses. I trust you have as much luck with a man in ebon darkness as I with a woman in soft gloom. Incidentally, why must you have two conferences with Ogo? Not Nemia's reason, surely?'

The Mouser's grin faded and he lightly bit his lip. With elaborate casualness he said, 'Oh, the jewels must be inspected by the Eyes of Ogo – *his* invariable rule. But whatever test is tried, I'm prepared to out-trick it.'

Fafhrd pondered, then asked, 'And what, or who are, or is, the Eyes of Ogo? Does he keep a pair of them in his pouch?'

'Is,' the Mouser said. Then with even more elaborate casualness, 'Oh, some chit of a girl, I believe. Supposed to have an intuitive faculty where gems are concerned. Interesting, isn't it, that a man as clever as Ogo should believe such superstitious nonsense? Or depend on the soft sex in any fashion. Truly, a mere formality.'

'"Chit of a girl",' Fafhrd mused, nodding his head again and yet again and yet again. 'That describes to a red dot on each of her immature nipples the sort of female you've come to favor in recent years. But of course the amorous is not at all involved in this deal of yours, I'm sure,' he added, rather too solemnly.

'In no way whatever,' the Mouser replied, rather too sharply. Looking around, he remarked, 'We're getting a bit of company, despite the early hour. There's Dickon of the Thieves Guild, that old pen-pusher and drawer of the floor plans of houses to be robbed – I don't believe he's actually worked on a job since the Year of the Snake. And there's fat Grom, their subtreasurer, another armchair thief. Who comes so dramatically a-slither? – by the Black Bones, it's Snarve, our overlord Glipkerio's nephew! Who's that he speaks to? – oh, only Tork the Cutpurse.'

'And there now appears,' Fafhrd took up, 'Vlek, said to be the Guild's star operative these days. Note his smirk and hear how his shoes creak faintly. And there's that gray-eyed, black-haired amateur, Alyx the Picklock – well, at least her boots don't squeak and I rather admire her courage in adventuring here, where the Guild's animosity toward freelance females is as ill a byword as that of the Pimps Guild. And, just now turning from the Street of the Gods, who have we but Countess Kronia of the Seventy-seven Secret Pockets, who steals by madness, not method.

There's one bone-bag I'd never trust, despite her emaciated charms and the weakness you lay to me.'

Nodding, the Mouser pronounced, 'And such as these are called the aristocracy of thiefdom! In all honesty I must say that notwithstanding your weaknesses – which I'm glad you admit – one of the two best thieves in Lankhmar now stands beside me. While the other, needless to say, occupies my ratskin boots.'

Fafhrd nodded back, though carefully crossing two fingers.

Stifling a yawn, the Mouser said, 'By the by, have you yet any thought about what you'll be doing after those gems are stolen from your wrist, or – though unlikely – sold and paid for? I've been approached about – or at any rate been considering a wander toward – in the general direction of the Eastern Lands.'

'Where it's hotter even than in this sultry Lankhmar? Such a stroll hardly appeals to me,' Fafhrd replied, then casually added, 'In any case, I've been thinking of taking ship – er – northward.'

'Toward that abominable Cold Waste once more? No, thank you!' the Mouser answered. Then, glancing south along Silver Street, where a pale star shone close to the horizon, he went on still more briskly, 'Well, it's time for my interview with Ogo – and his silly girl Eyes. Take your sword to bed with you, I advise, and look to it that neither Graywand nor your more vital blade are filched from you in Nemia's dusk.'

'Oh, so first twinkle of the Whale Star is the time set for your appointment too?' Fafhrd remarked, himself stirring from the wall. 'Tell me, is the true appearance of Ogo known to anyone? Somehow the name makes me think of a fat, old, and overlarge spider.'

'Curb your imagination, if you please,' the Mouser answered sharply. 'Or keep it for your own business, where I'll remind you that the only dangerous spider is the female. No, Ogo's true appearance is unknown. But perhaps tonight I'll discover it!'

'I'd like you to ponder that your besetting fault is over-curiosity,' said Fafhrd, 'and that you can't trust even the stupidest girl to be always silly.'

The Mouser turned impulsively and said, 'However tonight's interviews fall out, let's rendezvous after. The Silver Eel?'

Fafhrd nodded and they gripped hands together. Then each rogue sauntered toward his fateful door.

The Mouser crouched a little, every sense a-quiver, in space utterly dark. On a surface before him – a table, he had felt it out to be – lay his jewel box, closed. His left hand touched the box. His right gripped Cat's Claw and with that weapon nervously threatened the inky darkness all around.

A voice which was at once dry and thick croaked from behind him, 'Open the box!'

The Mouser's skin crawled at the horror of that voice. Nevertheless, he complied with the direction. The rainbow light of the meshed jewels spilled upward, dimly showing the room to be low-ceilinged and rather large. It appeared to be empty except for the table and, indistinct in the far left corner behind him, a dark low shape which the Mouser did not like. It might be a hassock or a fat, round, black pillow. Or it might be . . . The Mouser wished Fafhrd hadn't made his last suggestion.

From ahead of him a rippling, silvery voice quite unlike the first called, 'Your jewels, like no others I have ever seen, gleam in the absence of all light.'

Scanning piercingly across the table and box, the Mouser could see no sign of the second caller. Evening out his own voice, so it was not breathy with apprehension, but bland with confidence, he said, to the emptiness, 'My gems are like no others in the world. In fact, they come not from the world, being of the same substance as the stars. Yet you know by your test that one of them is harder than diamond.'

'They are truly unearthly and most beautiful jewels,' the sourceless silvery voice answered. 'My mind pierces them through and through, and they are what you say they are. I shall advise Ogo to pay your asking price.'

At that instant the Mouser heard behind him a little cough and a dry, rapid scuttling. He whirled around, dirk poised to strike. There was nothing to be seen or sensed, except for the hassock or whatever, which had not moved. The scuttling was no longer to be heard.

He swiftly turned back, and there across the table from him, her front illumined by the twinkling jewels, stood a slim naked girl with pale straight hair, somewhat darker skin, and over-large eyes staring entrancedly from a child's tiny-chinned, pouty-lipped face.

Satisfying himself by a rapid glance that the jewels were in their proper pattern under their mesh and none missing, he swiftly advanced Cat's Claw so that its needle point touched the taut skin between the small yet jutting breasts.

'Do not seek to startle me so again!' he hissed. 'Men – aye, and girls – have died for less.'

The girl did not stir by so much as the breadth of a fine hair; neither did her expression nor her dreamy yet concentrated gaze change, except that her short lips smiled, then parted to say honey-voiced, 'So you are the Gray Mouser. I had expected a crouchy, sear-faced rogue, and I find . . . a prince.' The very jewels seemed to twinkle more wildly because of her sweet voice and sweeter presence, striking opalescent glimmers from her pale irises.

'Neither seek to flatter me!' the Mouser commanded, catching up his box and holding it open against his side. 'I am inured, I'll have you know, to the ensorcelments of all the world's minxes and nymphs.'

'I speak truth only, as I did of your jewels,' she answered guilelessly. Her lips had stayed parted a little and she spoke without moving them.

'Are you the Eyes of Ogo?' the Mouser demanded harshly, yet drawing Cat's Claw back from her bosom. It bothered him a little, yet only a little, that the tiniest stream of blood, like a black thread, led down for a few inches from the prick his dirk had made.

Utterly unmindful of the tiny wound, the girl nodded. 'And I can see through you, as through your jewels, and I discover naught in you but what is noble and fine, save for certain small subtle impulses of violence and cruelty, which a girl like myself might find delightful.'

'There your all-piercing eyes err wholly, for I am a great villain,' the Mouser answered scornfully, though he felt a pulse of fond satisfaction within him.

The girl's eyes widened as she looked over his shoulder somewhat apprehensively, and from behind the Mouser the dry and thick voice croaked once more, 'Keep to business! Yes, I will pay you in gold your offering price, a sum it will take me some hours to assemble. Return at the same time tomorrow night and we'll close the deal. Now shut the box.'

The Mouser had turned around, still clutching his box, when Ogo began to speak. Again he could not distinguish the source of the voice, though he scanned minutely. It seemed to come from the whole wall.

Now he turned back. Somewhat to his disappointment, the naked girl had vanished. He peered under the table, but there was nothing there. Doubtless some trapdoor or hypnotic device . . .

Still suspicious as a snake, he returned the way he had come. On close approach, the black hassock appeared to be only that. Then as the door to the outside slid open noiselessly, he swiftly obeyed Ogo's last injunction, snapping shut the box, and departed.

Fafhrd gazed tenderly at Nemia lying beside him in perfumed twilight, while keeping the edge of his vision on his brawny wrist and the pouch pendant from it, both of which his companion was now idly fondling.

To do Nemia justice, even at the risk of imputing a certain cattiness to the Mouser, her charms were neither overblown, nor even ample, but only . . . sufficient.

From just behind Fafhrd's shoulder came a spitting hiss. He quickly turned his head and found himself looking into the crossed blue eyes of a white cat standing on the small bedside table beside a bowl of bronze chrysanthemums.

'Ixy!' Nemia called remonstratingly yet languorously.

Despite her voice, Fafhrd heard behind him, in rapid succession, the click of a bracelet opening and the slightly louder click of one closing.

He turned back instantly, to discover only that Nemia had meanwhile clasped on his wrist, beside the browned-iron bracelet, a golden one around which sapphires and rubies marched alternately in single file.

Gazing at him from betwixt the strands of her long dark hair, she said huskily, 'It is only a small token which I give to those who please me . . . greatly.'

Fafhrd drew his wrist closer to his eyes to admire his prize, but mostly to palpate his pouch with the fingers of his other hand, to assure himself that it bulged as tightly as ever.

It did, and in a burst of generous feeling he said, 'Let me give you one of my gems in precisely the same spirit,' and made to undo his pouch.

Nemia's long-fingered hand glided out to prevent. 'No,' she breathed. 'Let never the gems of business be mixed with the jewels of pleasure. Now if you should choose to bring me some small gift tomorrow night, when at the same hour we exchange your jewels for my gold and my letters of credit on Glipkerio, underwritten by Hisvin the Grain Merchant . . .'

'Right,' Fafhrd said briefly, concealing the relief he felt. He'd been an idiot to think of giving Nemia one of the gems – and with it a day's opportunity to discover its abnormalities.

'Until tomorrow,' Nemia said, opening her arms to him.

'Until tomorrow, then,' Fafhrd agreed, embracing her fervently, yet keeping his pouch clutched in the hand to which it was chained – and already eager to be gone.

The Silver Eel was far less than half filled, its candles few, its cupbearers torpid, as Fafhrd and the Gray Mouser entered simultaneously by different doors and made for one of the many empty booths.

The only eye to watch them at all closely was a gray one above a narrow section of pale cheek bordered by dark hair, peering past the curtain of the backmost booth.

When their thick table-candles had been lit and cups set before them and a jug of fortified wine, and fresh charcoal tumbled into the red-seeded brazier at table's end, the Mouser placed his flat box on the table and, grinning, said, 'All's set. The jewels passed the test of the Eyes – a toothsome wenchlet; more of her later. I get the cash tomorrow night – all my offering price! But you, friend, I hardly thought to see you back alive. Drink we up! I take it you escaped from Nemia's divan whole and sound in organs and limbs – as far as you yet know. But the jewels?'

'They came through too,' Fafhrd answered, swinging the pouch lightly out of his sleeve and then back in again. 'And I get my money tomorrow night . . . the full amount of my asking price, just like you.'

As he named those coincidences, his eyes went thoughtful.

They stayed that way while he took two large swallows of wine. The Mouser watched him curiously.

'At one point,' Fafhrd finally mused, 'I thought she was trying the old trick of substituting for mine an identical but worthlessly filled pouch. Since she'd seen the pouch at our first meeting, she could have had a similar one made up, complete with chain and bracelet.'

'But was she—?' the Mouser asked.

'Oh no, it turned out to be something entirely different,' Fafhrd said lightly, though some thought kept two slight vertical furrows in his forehead.

'That's odd,' the Mouser remarked. 'At one point – just one, mind you – the Eyes of Ogo, if she'd been extremely swift, deft, and silent, might have been able to switch boxes on me.'

Fafhrd lifted his eyebrows.

The Mouser went on rapidly, 'That is, if my box had been closed. But it was open, in darkness, and there'd have been no way to reproduce the varicolored twinkling of the gems. Phosphorus or glow-wood? Too dim. Hot coals? No, I'd have felt the heat. Besides, how get that way a diamond's pure white glow? Quite impossible.'

Fafhrd nodded agreement, but continued to gaze over the Mouser's shoulder.

The Mouser started to reach toward his box, but instead with a small self-contemptuous chuckle picked up the jug and began to pour himself another drink in a careful small stream.

Fafhrd shrugged at last, used the back of his forefingers to push over his own pewter cup for a refill, and yawned mightily, leaning back a little and at the same time pushing his spread-fingered hands to either side across the table, as if pushing away from him all small doubts and wonderings.

The fingers of his left hand touched the Mouser's box.

His face went blank. He looked down his arm at the box.

Then to the great puzzlement of the Mouser, who had just begun to fill Fafhrd's cup, the Northerner leaned forward and placed his head ear-down on the box.

'Mouser,' he said in a small voice, 'your box is buzzing.'

Fafhrd's cup was full, but the Mouser kept on pouring. Heavily fragrant wine puddled and began to run toward the glowing brazier.

'When I touched the box, I felt vibration,' Fafhrd went on bemusedly. 'It's buzzing. It's still buzzing.'

With a low snarl, the Mouser slammed down the jug and snatched the box from under Fafhrd's ear. The wine reached the brazier's hot bottom and hissed.

He tore the box open, opened also its mesh top, and he and Fafhrd peered in.

The candlelight dimmed, but by no means extinguished the yellow, violet, reddish, and white twinkling glows rising from various points on the black velvet bottom.

But the candlelight was quite bright enough also to show, at each such point, matching the colors listed, a firebeetle, glowwasp, nightbee, or diamondfly, each insect alive but delicately affixed to the floor of the box with silver wire. From time to time the wings or wingcases of some buzzed.

Without hesitation, Fafhrd unclasped the brown-iron bracelet from his wrist, unchained the pouch, and dumped it on the table.

Jewels of various sizes, all beautifully cut, made a fair heap.

But they were all dead black.

Fafhrd picked up a big one, tried it with his fingernail, then whipped out his hunting knife and with its edge easily scored the gem.

He carefully dropped it in the brazier's glowing center. After a bit it flamed up yellow and blue.

'Coal,' Fafhrd said.

The Mouser clawed his hands over his faintly twinkling box, as if about to pick it up and hurl it through the wall and across the Inner Sea.

Instead he unclawed his hands and hung them decorously at his sides.

'I am going away,' he announced quietly, but very clearly, and did so.

Fafhrd did not look up. He was dropping a second black gem in the brazier.

He did take off the bracelet Nemia had given him; he brought it close to his eyes, said, 'Brass . . . glass,' and spread his fingers to let it drop in the spilled wine. After the Mouser was gone, Fafhrd drained his brimming cup, drained the Mouser's and filled it again, then went on supping from it as he continued to drop the black jewels one by one in the brazier.

Nemia and the Eyes of Ogo sat cozily side by side on a luxurious divan. They had put on negligees. A few candles made a yellowish dusk.

On a low, gleaming table were set delicate flagons of wines and liqueurs, slim-stemmed crystal goblets, golden plates of sweetmeats and savories, and in the center two equal heaps of rainbow-glowing gems.

'What a quaint bore barbarians are,' Nemia remarked, delicately stifling a yawn, 'though good for one's sensuous self, once in a great while. This one had a little more brains than most. I think he might have caught on, except that I made the two clicks come so exactly together when I snapped back on his wrist the bracelet with the false pouch and at the same time my brass keepsake. It's amazing how barbarians are hypnotized by brass along with any odd bits of glass colored like rubies and sapphires – I think the three primary colors paralyze their primitive brains.'

'Clever, *clever* Nemia,' the Eyes of Ogo cooed with a tender caress. 'My little fellow almost caught on too when I made the switch, but he got interested in threatening me with his knife. Actually jabbed me between the breasts. I think he has a dirty mind.'

'Let me kiss the blood away, darling Eyes,' Nemia suggested. 'Oh, dreadful . . . dreadful.'

While shivering under her treatment – Nemia had a slightly

bristly tongue – Eyes said, 'For some reason he was quite nervous about Ogo.' She made her face blank, her pouty mouth hanging slightly open.

The richly draped wall opposite her made a scuttling sound and then croaked in a dry, thick voice, 'Open your box, Gray Mouser. Now close it. Girls, girls! Cease your lascivious play!'

Nemia and Eyes clung to each other laughing. Eyes said in her natural voice, if she had one, 'And he went away still thinking there was a real Ogo. I'm quite certain of that. My, they both must be in a froth by now.'

Sitting back, Nemia said, 'I suppose we'll have to take some special precautions against their raiding us to get their jewels back.'

Eyes shrugged, 'I have my five Mingol swordsmen.'

Nemia said. 'And I have my three and a half Kleshite stranglers.'

'Half?' Eyes asked.

'I was counting Ixy. No, but seriously.'

Eyes frowned for half a heartbeat, then shook her head decisively. 'I don't think we need worry about Fafhrd and the Gray Mouser raiding us back. Because we're girls, their pride will be hurt, and they'll sulk a while and then run away to the ends of the earth on one of those adventures of theirs.'

'Adventures!' said Nemia, as one who says, 'Cesspool and privies!'

'You see, they're really weaklings,' Eyes went on, warming to her topic. 'They have no drive whatever, no ambition, no true passion for money. For instance, if they did – and if they didn't spend so much time in dismal spots away from Lankhmar – they'd have known that the King of Ilthmar has developed a mania for gems that are invisible by day, but glow by night, and has offered half his kingdom for a sack of star-jewels. And then they'd never have had even to consider such an idiotic thing as coming to us.'

'What do you suppose he'll do with them? The King, I mean.'

Eyes shrugged. 'I don't know. Build a planetarium. Or eat them.' She thought a moment. 'All things considered, it might be as well if we got away from here for a few weeks. We deserve a vacation.'

Nemia nodded, closing her eyes. 'It should be absolutely the opposite sort of place to the one in which the Mouser and Fafhrd will have their next – ugh! – adventure.'

Eyes nodded too and said dreamily, 'Blue skies and rippling water, spotless beach, a tepid wind, flowers and slim slavegirls everywhere . . .'

Nemia said, 'I've always wished for a place that has no weather, only perfection. Do you know which half of Ilthmar's kingdom has the least weather?'

'Precious Nemia,' Eyes murmured, 'you're so civilized. And so very, very clever. Next to one other, you're certainly the best thief in Lankhmar.'

'Who's the other?' Nemia was eager to know.

'Myself, of course,' Eyes answered modestly.

Nemia reached up and tweaked her companion's ear – not too painfully, but enough.

'If there were the least money depending on that,' she said quietly but firmly, 'I'd teach you differently. But since it's only conversation . . .'

'Dearest Nemia.'

'Sweetest Eyes.'

The two girls gently embraced and kissed each other fondly.

The Mouser glared thin-lipped across a table in a curtained booth in the Golden Lamprey, a tavern not unlike the Silver Eel.

He rapped the teak before him with his fingertip, and the perfumed stale air with his voice, saying, 'Double those twenty gold pieces and I'll make the trip and hear Prince Gwaay's proposal.'

The very pale man opposite him, who squinted as if even the candlelight were a glare, answered softly, 'Twenty-five – and you serve him for one day after arrival.'

'What sort of ass do you take me for?' the Mouser demanded dangerously. 'I might be able to settle all his troubles in one day – I usually can – and what then? No, no preagreed service; I hear his proposal only. And . . . thirty-five gold pieces in advance.'

'Very well, thirty gold pieces – twenty to be refunded if you refuse to serve my master, which would be a risky step, I warn you.'

'Risk is my bed-mate,' the Mouser snapped. 'Ten only to be refunded.'

The other nodded and began slowly to count rilks onto the teak. 'Ten *now*,' he said. 'Ten when you join our caravan tomorrow morning at the Grain Gate. And ten when we reach Quarmall.'

'When we first glimpse the spires of Quarmall,' the Mouser insisted.

The other nodded.

The Mouser moodily snatched the golden coins and stood up. They felt very few in his fist. For a moment he thought of returning to Fafhrd and with him devising plans against Ogo and Nemia.

No, never! He realized he couldn't in his misery and self-rage bear the thought of even looking at Fafhrd.

Besides, the Northerner would certainly be drunk.

And two, or at most three, rilks would buy him certain tolerable and even interesting pleasures to fill the hours before dawn brought him release from this hateful city.

Fafhrd was indeed drunk, being on this third jug. He had burnt up all the black jewels and was now with the greatest delicacy and most careful use of the needle point of his knife, releasing unharmed each of the silver-wired firebeetles, glow-wasps, nightbees, and diamondflies. They buzzed about erratically.

Two cupbearers and the chucker-out had come to protest and now Slevyas himself joined them, rubbing the back of his thick neck. He had been stung and a customer too. Fafhrd had himself been stung twice, but hadn't seemed to notice. Nor did he now pay the slightest attention to the four haranguing him.

The last nightbee was released. It careened off noisily past Slevyas' neck, who dodged his head with a curse. Fafhrd sat back, suddenly looking very wretched. With varying shrugs the master of the Silver Eel and his three servitors made off, one cupbearer making swipes at the air.

Fafhrd tossed up his knife. It came down almost point first, but didn't quite stick in the teak. He laboriously scabbarded it, then forced himself to take a small sip of wine.

As if someone were about to emerge from the backmost booth, there was a stirring of its heavy curtains, which like all the others had stitched to them heavy chain and squares of metal, so that one guest couldn't stab another through them, except with luck and the slimmest stilettos.

But at that moment a very pale man, who held up his cloak to shield his eyes from the candlelight, entered by the side door and made to Fafhrd's table.

'I've come for my answer, Northerner,' he said in a voice soft yet sinister. He glanced at the toppled jugs and spilled wine. 'That is, if you remember my proposition.'

'Sit down,' Fafhrd said. 'Have a drink. Watch out for the glowwasps – they're vicious.' Then, scornfully, 'Remember! Prince Hasjarl of Marquall – Quarmall. Passage by ship. A mountain of gold rilks. Remember!'

Keeping on his feet, the other amended, 'Twenty-five rilks. Provided you take ship with me at once and promise to render a day's service to my prince. Thereafter by what further agreement you and he arrive at.'

He placed on the table a small golden tower of precounted coins.

'Munificent!' Fafhrd said, grabbing it up and reeling to his feet. He placed five of the coins on the table and shoved the rest in his pouch, except for three more, which scattered dulcetly across the floor. He corked and pouched the third wine jug. Coming out from behind the table, he said, 'Lead the way, comrade,' gave the squinty-eyed man a mighty shove toward the side door, and went weaving after him.

In the backmost booth, Alyx the Picklock pursed her lips and shook her head disapprovingly.

IV
THE LORDS OF QUARMALL

The room was dim, almost maddeningly dim to one who loved sharp detail and the burning sun. The few wall-set torches that provided the sole illumination flamed palely and thinly, more like will-o'-the-wisps than true fire, although they released a pleasant incense. One got the feeling that the dwellers of this region resented light and only tolerated a thin mist of it for the benefit of strangers.

Despite its vast size, the room was carved all in somber solid rock – smooth floor, polished curving walls, and domed ceiling – either a natural cave finished by man or else chipped out and burnished entirely by human effort, although the thought of that latter amount of work was nearly intolerable. From numerous deep niches between the torches, metal statuettes and masks and jeweled objects gleamed darkly.

Through the room, bending the feeble bluish flames, came a perpetual cool draft bringing acid odors of damp ground and moist rock which the sweet spicy scent of the torches never quite masked.

The only sounds were the occasional rutch of rock on wood from the other end of the long table, where a game was being played with black and white stone counters – that and, from beyond the room, the ponderous sighing of the great fans that sucked down the fresh air on its last stage of passage from the distant world above and drove it through this region . . . and the perpetual soft thudding of the naked feet of the slaves on the heavy leather tread-belts that drove those great wooden fans . . . and the very faint mechanic gasping of those slaves.

After one had been in this region for a few days, or only a few hours, the sighing of the fans and the soft thudding of the feet and the faint gaspings of the tortured lungs seemed to drone out only the name of this region, over and over.

'Quarmall . . .' they seemed to chant. 'Quarmall . . . Quarmall is all . . .'

The Gray Mouser, upon whose senses and through whose mind these sensations and fancies had been flooding and flitting, was a small man strongly muscled. Clad in gray silks irregularly woven, with tiny thread-tufts here and there, he looked restless as a lynx and as dangerous.

From a great tray of strangely hued and shaped mushrooms set before him like sweetmeats, the Mouser disdainfully selected and nibbled cautiously at the most normal looking, a gray one. Its perfumy savor masking bitterness offended him and he spat it surreptitiously into his palm and dropped that hand under the table and flicked the wet chewed fragments to the floor. Then, while he sucked his cheeks sourly, the fingers of both his hands began to play as slowly and nervously with the hilts of his sword Scalpel and his dagger Cat's Claw as his mind played with his boredoms and murky wonderings.

Along each side of the long narrow table, in great highbacked chairs widely spaced, sat twelve scrawny old men, bald or shaven of dome and chin, and chicken fluted of jowl, and each clad only in a neat white loincloth. Eleven of these stared intently at nothing and perpetually tensed their meager muscles until even their ears seemed to stiffen, as though concentrating mightily on realms unseen. The twelfth had his chair half turned and was playing across a far corner of the table the board-game that made the occasional tiny rutching noises. He was playing it with the Mouser's employer Gwaay, ruler of the Lower Levels of Quarmall and younger son to Quarmal, Lord of Quarmall.

Although the Mouser had been three days in Quarmall's depths he had come no closer to Gwaay than he was now, so that he knew him only as a pallid, handsome, soft-spoken youth, no realer to the Mouser, because of the eternal dimness and the invariable distance between them, than a ghost.

The game was one the Mouser had never seen before and quite tricky in several respects.

The board looked green, though it was impossible to be

certain of colors in the unending twilight of the torches, and it had no perceptible squares or tracks on it, except for a phosphorescent line midway between the opponents, dividing the board into two equal fields.

Each contestant started the game with twelve flat circular counters set along his edge of the board. Gwaay's counters were obsidian-black, his ancient opponent's marble-white, so the Mouser was able to distinguish them despite the dimness.

The object of the game seemed to be to move the pieces randomly forward over uneven distances and get at least seven of them into your opponent's field first.

Here the trickiness was that one moved the pieces not with the fingers but only by looking at them intently. Apparently, if one gazed only at a single piece, one could move it quite swiftly. If one gazed at several, one could move them all together in a line or cluster, but more sluggishly.

The Mouser was not yet wholly convinced that he was witnessing a display of thought-power. He still suspected threads, soundless air-puffings, surreptitious joggings of the board from below, powerful beetles under the counters, and hidden magnets! – for Gwaay's pieces at least could by their color be some sort of loadstone.

At the present moment Gwaay's black counters and the ancient's white ones were massed at the central line, shifting only a little now and then as the push-of-war went first a nail's breadth one way, then the other. Suddenly Gwaay's rearmost counter circled swiftly back and darted toward an open space at the board's edge. Two of the ancient's counters moved to block it. Six of Gwaay's other counters formed a wedge and thrust across the midline through the weak point thus created. As the ancient's two detached counters returned to oppose them, Gwaay's end-running counter sped across. The game was over – Gwaay gave no sign of this, but the ancient began fumblingly to return the pieces to their starting positions with his fingers.

'Ho, Gwaay, that was easily won!' the Mouser called out cockily. 'Why not take on two of them together? The oldster must be a sorcerer of the Second Rank to play so weakly – or even a doddering apprentice of the Third.'

The ancient shot the Mouser a venomous gaze. 'We are, all twelve of us, sorcerers of the First Rank and have been from our youth,' he proclaimed portentously. 'As you should swiftly learn were one of us to point but a little finger against you.'

'You have heard what he says,' Gwaay called softly to the Mouser without looking at him.

The Mouser, daunted no whit, at least outwardly, called back, 'I still think you could beat two of them together, or seven – or the whole decrepit dozen! If they are of First Rank, you must be of Zero or Negative Magnitude.'

The ancient's lips worked speechlessly and bubbled with froth at the affront, but Gwaay only called pleasantly. 'Were but three of my faithful magi to cease their sorcerous concentrations, my brother Hasjarl's sendings would burst through from the Upper Levels and I would be stricken with all the diseases in the evil compendium, and a few others that exist in Hasjarl's putrescent imagination alone – or perchance I should be erased entirely from this life.'

'If nine out of twelve must be forever a-guarding you, they can't get much sleep,' the Mouser observed, calling back.

'Times are not always so troublous,' Gwaay replied tranquilly. 'Sometimes custom or my father enjoins a truce. Sometimes the dark inward sea quiets. But today I know by certain signs that a major assault is being made on the liver and lights and blood and bones and rest of me. Dear Hasjarl has a double coven of sorcerers hardly inferior to my own – Second Rank, but High Second – and he whips them on. And I am as distasteful to Hasjarl, oh Gray Mouser, as the simple fruits of our manure beds are to your lips. Tonight, furthermore, my father Quarmal casts his horoscope in the tower of the Keep, high above Hasjarl's Upper Levels, so it befits I keep all rat-holes closely watched.'

'If it's magical helpings you lack,' the Mouser retorted boldly, 'I have a spell or two that would frizzle your elder brother's witches and warlocks!' And truth to tell the Mouser had parchment-crackling in his pouch one spell – though one spell only – which he dearly wanted to test. It had been given him by his own wizardly mentor and master Sheelba of the Eyeless Face.

Gwaay replied, more softly than ever, so that the Mouser felt that if there had been a yard more between them he would not have heard, 'It is your work to ward from my physical body Hasjarl's sword-sendings, in particular those of this great champion he is reputed to have hired. My sorcerers of the First Rank will shield off Hasjarl's sorcerous *billets-doux*. Each to his proper occupation.' He lightly clapped his hands together. A slim slavegirl appeared noiselessly in the dark archway beyond him. Without looking once at her, Gwaay softly commanded, 'Strong wine for our warrior.' She vanished.

The ancient had at last laboriously shuffled the black and white counters into their starting positions and Gwaay regarded his thoughtfully. But before making a move, he called to the Mouser, 'If time still hangs heavy on your hands, devote some of it to selecting the reward you will take when your work is done. And in your search overlook not the maiden who brings you the wine. Her name is Ivivis.'

At that the Mouser shut up. He had already chosen more than a dozen expensive be-charming objects from Gwaay's drawers and niches and locked them in a disused closet he had discovered two levels down. If this should be discovered, he would explain that he was merely making an innocent preselection pending final choice, but Gwaay might not view it that way and Gwaay was sharp, judging from the way he'd noted the rejected mushroom and other things.

It had not occurred to the Mouser to preempt a girl or two by locking her in the closet also, though it was admittedly an attractive idea.

The ancient cleared his throat and said chucklingly across the board, 'Lord Gwaay, let this ambitious sworder try his sorcerous tricks. Let him try them on me!'

The Mouser's spirits rose, but Gwaay only raised palm and shook his head slightly and pointed a finger at the board; the ancient began obediently to think a piece forward.

The Mouser's spirits fell. He was beginning to feel very much alone in this dim underworld where all spoke and moved in whispers. True, when Gwaay's emissary had approached him in Lankhmar, the Mouser had been happy to take on this solo job.

It would teach his loud-voiced sword-mate Fafhrd a lesson if his small gray comrade (and brain!) should disappear one night without a word . . . and then return perchance a year later with a brimful treasure chest and a mocking smile.

The Mouser had even been happy all the long caravan trip from Lankhmar south to Quarmall, along the Hlal River and past the Lakes of Pleea and through the Mountains of Hunger. It had been a positive pleasure to loll on a swaying camel beyond reach of Fafhrd's hugeness and disputatious talk and boisterous ways, while the nights grew ever bluer and warmer and strange jewel-fiery stars came peering over the southern horizon.

But now he had been three nights in Quarmall since his secret coming to the Lower Levels – three nights and days, or rather one hundred and forty-four interminable demi-hours of buried twilight – and he was already beginning in his secretest mind to wish that Fafhrd were here, instead of half a continent away in Lankhmar – or even farther than that if he'd carried out his misty plans to revisit his northern homeland. Someone to drink with, at any rate – and even a roaring quarrel would be positively refreshing after seventy-two hours of nothing but silent servitors, tranced sorcerers, stewed mushrooms, and Gwaay's unbreakable soft-tongued equanimity.

Besides, it appeared that all Gwaay wanted was a mighty sworder to nullify the threat of this champion Hasjarl was supposed to have hired as secretly as Gwaay had smuggled in the Mouser. If Fafhrd were here, he could be Gwaay's sworder, while Mouser would have better opportunity to peddle Gwaay his magical talents. The one spell he had in his pouch – he had got it from Sheelba in return for the tale of the Perversions of Clutho – would forever establish his reputation as an archimage of deadly might, he was sure.

The Mouser came out of his musings to realize that the slavegirl Ivivis was kneeling before him – for how long she had been there he could not say – and proffering an ebony tray on which stood a squat stone jug and a copper cup.

She knelt with one leg doubled, the other thrust behind her as in a fencing lunge, stretching the short skirt of her green tunic, while her arms reached the tray forward.

Her slim body was most supple – she held the difficult pose effortlessly. Her fine straight hair was pale as her skin – both a sort of ghost color. It occurred to the Mouser that she would look very well in his closet, perhaps cherishing against her bosom the necklace of large black pearls he had discovered piled behind a pewter statuette in one of Gwaay's niches.

However, she was kneeling as far away from him as she could and still stretch him the tray, and her eyes were most modestly downcast, nor would she even flicker up their lids to his gracious murmurings – which were all the approach he thought suitable at this moment.

He seized the jug and cup. Ivivis drooped her head still lower in acknowledgment, then flitted silently away.

The Mouser poured a finger of blood-red, blood-thick wine and sipped. Its flavor was darkly sweet, but with a bitter undertaste. He wondered if it were fermented from scarlet toadstools.

The black and white counters skittered rutchingly in obedience to Gwaay's and the ancient's peerings. The pale torch flames bent to the unceasing cool breeze, while the fanslaves and their splayed bare feet on the leather belts and the great unseen fans themselves on their ponderous axles muttered unendingly, 'Quarmall . . . Quarmall is downward tall . . . Quarmall . . . Quarmall is all . . .'

In an equally vast room many levels higher yet still underground – a windowless room where torches flared redder and brighter, but their brightness nullified by an acrid haze of incense smoke, so that here too the final effect was exasperating dimness – Fafhrd sat at the table's foot.

Fafhrd was ordinarily a monstrously calm man, but now he was restlessly drumming fist on thumb-root, on the verge of admitting to himself that he wished the Gray Mouser were here, instead of back in Lankhmar or perchance off on some ramble in the desert-patched Eastern Lands.

The Mouser, Fafhrd thought, might have more patience to unriddle the mystification and crooked behavior-ways of these burrowing Quarmallians. The Mouser might find it easier to endure Hasjarl's loathsome taste for torture, and at least the little gray fool would be someone human to drink with!

Fafhrd had been very glad to be parted from the Mouser and from his vanities and tricksiness and chatter when Hasjarl's agent had contacted him in Lankhmar, promising large pay in return for Fafhrd's instant, secret, and solitary coming. Fafhrd had even dropped a hint to the small fellow that he might take ship with some of his Northerner countrymen who had sailed down across the Inner Sea.

What he had not explained to the Mouser was that, as soon as Fafhrd was aboard her, the longship had sailed not north but south, coasting through the vast Outer Sea along Lankhmar's western seaboard.

It had been an idyllic journey, that – pirating a little now and then, despite the sour objections of Hasjarl's agent, battling great storms and also the giant cuttlefish, rays, and serpents which swarmed ever thicker in the Outer Sea as one sailed south. At the recollection Fafhrd's fist slowed its drumming and his lips almost formed a long smile.

But now this Quarmall! This endless stinking sorcery! This torture-besotted Hasjarl! Fafhrd's fist drummed fiercely again.

Rules! – he mustn't explore downward, for that led to the Lower Levels and the enemy. Nor must he explore upward – that way was to Father Quarmal's apartments, sacrosanct. None must know of Fafhrd's presence. He must satisfy himself with such drink and inferior wenches as were available in Hasjarl's limited Upper Levels. (They called these dim labyrinths and crypts *upper!*)

Delays! – they mustn't muster their forces and march down and smash brother-enemy Gwaay; that was unthinkable rashness. They mustn't even shut off the huge treadmill-driven fans whose perpetual creaking troubled Fafhrd's ears and which sent the life-giving air on the first stages of its journey to Gwaay's underworld, and through other rock-driven wells sucked out the stale – no, those fans must never be stopped, for Father Quarmal would frown on any battle-tactic which suffocated valuable slaves; and from anything Father Quarmal frowned on, his sons shrank shuddering.

Instead, Hasjarl's war-council must plot years-long campaigns weaponed chiefly with sorcery and envisioning the conquest of Gwaay's Lower Levels a quarter tunnel – or a quarter mushroom field – at a time.

Mystifications! – mushrooms must be served at all meals but never eaten or so much as tasted. Roast rat, on the other hand, was a delicacy to be crowed over. Tonight Father Quarmal would cast his own horoscope and for some reason that superstitious starsighting and scribbling would be of incalculable cryptic consequence. All maids must scream loudly twice when familiarities were suggested to them, no matter what their subsequent behavior. Fafhrd must never get closer to Hasjarl than a long dagger's cast – a rule which gave Fafhrd no chance to discover how Hasjarl managed never to miss a detail of what went on around him while keeping his eyes fully closed almost all the time.

Perhaps Hasjarl had a sort of short-range second sight, or perhaps the slave nearest him ceaselessly whispered an account of all that transpired, or perhaps – well, Fafhrd had no way of knowing.

But somehow Hasjarl could see things with his eyes shut.

This paltry trick of Hasjarl's evidently saved his eyes from the irritation of the incense smoke, which kept those of Hasjarl's sorcerers and of Fafhrd himself red and watering. However, since Hasjarl was otherwise a most energetic and restless prince – his bandy-legged misshapen body and mismated arms forever a-twitch, his ugly face always grimacing – the detail of eyes tranquilly shut was peculiarly jarring and shiversome.

All in all, Fafhrd was heartily sick of the Upper Levels of Quarmall though scarcely a week in them. He had even toyed with the notion of double-crossing Hasjarl and hiring out to his brother or turning informer for his father – although they might, as employers, be no improvement whatever.

But mostly he simply wanted to meet in combat this champion of Gwaay's he kept hearing so much of – meet him and slay him and then shoulder his reward (preferably a shapely maiden with a bag of gold in her either hand) and turn his back forever on the accursed dim-tunneled whisper-haunted hill of Quarmall!

In an excess of exasperation he clapped his hand to the hilt of his longsword Graywand.

Hasjarl saw that, although Hasjarl's eyes were closed, for he quickly pointed his gnarly face down the long table at Fafhrd, between the ranks of the twenty-four heavily robed, thickly bearded sorcerers crowded shoulder to shoulder. Then, his eyelids still shut, Hasjarl commenced to twitch his mouth as a preamble to speech and with a twitter-tremble as overture called, 'Ha, hot for battle, eh, Fafhrd boy? Keep him in the sheath! Yet tell me, what manner of man do you think this warrior – the one you protect me against – Gwaay's grim manslayer? He is said to be mightier than an elephant in strength, and more guileful than the very Zobolds.' With a final spasm Hasjarl managed, still without opening his eyes, to look expectantly at Fafhrd.

Fafhrd had heard all this sort of worrying time and time again during the past week, so he merely answered with a snort:

'Zutt! They all say that about anybody. I know. But unless you get me some action and keep these old flea-bitten beards out of my sight—'

Catching himself up short, Fafhrd tossed off his wine and beat with his pewter mug on the table for more. For although Hasjarl might have the demeanor of an idiot and the disposition of a ocelot, he served excellent ferment of grape ripened on the hot brown southern slopes of Quarmall hill . . . and there was no profit in goading him.

Nor did Hasjarl appear to take offense – or if he did, he took it out on his bearded sorcerers, for he instantly began to instruct one to enunciate his runes more clearly, questioned another as to whether his herbs were sufficiently pounded, reminded a third that it was time to tinkle a certain silver bell thrice, and in general treated the whole two dozen as if they were a roomful of schoolboys and he their eagle-eyed pedagogue – though Fafhrd had been given to understand that they were all magi of the First Rank.

The double coven of sorcerers in turn began to bustle more

nervously, each with his particular spell – touching off more stinks, jiggling black drops out of more dirty vials, waving more wands, pin-stabbing more figurines, finger-tracing eldritch symbols more swiftly in the air, mounding up each in front of him from his bag more noisome fetishes, and so on.

From his hours of sitting at the foot of the table, Fafhrd had learned that most of the spells were designed to inflict a noisome disease upon Gwaay; the Black Plague, the Red Plague, the Boneless Death, the Hairless Decline, the Slow Rot, the Fast Rot, the Green Rot, the Bloody Cough, the Belly Melts, the Ague, the Runs, and even the footling Nose Drip. Gwaay's own sorcerers, he gathered, kept warding off these malefic spells with counter-charms, but the idea was to keep on sending them in hopes that the opposition would some day drop their guard, if only for a few moments.

Fafhrd rather wished Gwaay's gang were able to reflect back the disease-spells on their dark-robed senders. He had become weary even of the abstruse astrologic signs stitched in gold and silver on those robes, and of the ribbons and precious wires knotted cabalistically in their heavy beards.

Hasjarl, his magicians disciplined into a state of furious busyness, opened wide his eyes for a change and with only a preliminary lip-writhe called to Fafhrd, 'So you want action, eh, Fafhrd boy?'

Fafhrd, mightily irked at the last epithet, planted an elbow on the table and wagged that hand at Hasjarl and called back, 'I do. My muscles cry to bulge. You've strong-looking arms, Lord Hasjarl. What say you we play the wrist game?'

Hasjarl tittered evilly and cried, 'I go but now to play another sort of wrist game with a maid suspected of commerce with one of Gwaay's pages. She never screamed even once . . . then. Wouldst accompany me and watch the action, Fafhrd?' And he suddenly shut his eyes again with the effect of putting on two tiny masks of skin – yet shut them so firmly there could be no question of his peering through the lashes.

Fafhrd shrank back in his chair, flushing a little. Hasjarl had divined Fafhrd's distaste for torture on the Northerner's first night in Quarmall's Upper Levels and since then had never missed an opportunity to play on what Hasjarl must view as Fafhrd's weakness.

To cover his embarrassment, Fafhrd drew from under his tunic a tiny book of stitched parchment pages. The Northerner would have sworn that Hasjarl's eyelids had not flickered once since closing, yet now the villain cried, 'The sigil on the cover of that packet tells me it is something of Ningauble of the Seven Eyes. What is it, Fafhrd?'

'Private matters,' the latter retorted firmly. Truth to tell, he was somewhat alarmed. The contents of the packet were such as he dared not permit Hasjarl see. And just as the villain somehow knew, there was indeed on the top parchment the bold black figure of a seven-fingered hand, each finger bearing an eye for a nail – one of the many signs of Fafhrd's wizardly patron.

Hasjarl coughed hackingly. 'No servant of Hasjarl has private matters,' he pronounced. 'However, we will speak of that at another time. Duty calls me.' He bounded up from his chair and fiercely eyeing his sorcerers cried at them barkingly, 'If I find one of you dozing over his spells when I return, it were better for him – aye, and for his mother too – had he been born with slave's chains on his ankles!'

He paused, turning to go, and pointing his face at Fafhrd again, called rapidly yet cajolingly, 'The girl is named Friska. She's but seventeen. I doubt not she will play the wrist game most adroitly and with many a charming exclamation. I will converse with her, at length. I will question her, as I twist the crank, very slowly. And she will answer, she will comment, she will describe her feelings, in sounds if not in words. Sure you won't come?' And trailing an evil titter behind him, Hasjarl strode rapidly from the room, red torches in the archway outlining his monstrous bandy-legged form in blood.

Fafhrd ground his teeth. There was nothing he could do at the moment. Hasjarl's torture chamber was also his guard barrack. Yet the Northerner chalked up in his mind an intention, or perhaps an obligation.

To keep his mind from nasty unmanning imaginings, he began carefully to reread the tiny parchment book which

Ningauble had given him as a sort of reward for past services, or an assurance for future ones, on the night of the Northerner's departure from Lankhmar.

Fafhrd did not worry about Hasjarl's sorcerers overlooking what he read. After their master's last threat they were all as furiously and elbow-jostlingly busy with their spells as so many bearded black ants.

Quarmall was first brought to my attention (*Fafhrd read in Ningauble's little handwritten, or tentacle-writ book*) by the report that certain passageways beneath it ran deep under the Sea and extended to certain caverns wherein might dwell some remnant of the Elder Ones. Naturally I dispatched agents to probe the truth of the report: two well-trained and valuable spies were sent (also two others to watch them) to find the facts and accumulate gossip. Neither pair returned nor did they send messages or tokens in explanation, or indeed word of any sort. I was interested; but being unable at that time, to spare valuable material on so uncertain and dangerous a quest, I bided my time until information should be placed at my disposal (as it usually is).

After twenty years my discretion was rewarded. (*So went the crabbed script as Fafhrd continued to read.*) An old man, horribly scarred and peculiarly pallid, was fetched to me. His name was Tamorg, and his tale interesting in spite of the teller's incoherence. He claimed to have been captured from a passing caravan when yet a small lad and carried into captivity within Quarmall. There he served as a slave on the Lower Levels, far below the ground. Here there was no natural light, and the only air was sucked down into the mazy caverns by means of large fans, treadmill-driven; hence his pallor and otherwise unusual appearance.

Tamorg was quite bitter about these fans, for he had been chained at one of those endless belts for a longer time than he cared to think about. (He really did not know exactly how long, since there was, by his own statement, no measure of time in the Lower Levels.) Finally he was released from his onerous walking, as nearly as I could glean from his garbled tale, by the invention or breeding of a specialized type of slave who better served the purpose.

From this I postulate that the Masters of Quarmall are sufficiently interested in the economics of their holdings to improve them: a rarity among overlords. Moreover, if these specialized slaves were bred, the life-span of these overlords must perforce be longer than ordinary; or else the cooperation between father and son is more perfect than any filial relationship I have yet noted.

Tamorg further related that he was put to more work digging, along with eight other slaves likewise taken from the treadmills. They were forced to enlarge and extend certain passages and chambers; so for another space of time he mined and buttressed. This time must have been long, for by close cross-questioning I found that Tamorg digged and walled, single-handed, a passage a thousand and twenty paces long. These slaves were not chained, unless maniacal, nor was it necessary to bind them so; for these Lower Levels seem to be a maze within a maze, and an unlucky slave once strayed from familiar paths stood small chance of retracing his steps. However, rumor has it, Tamorg said, that the Lords of Quarmall keep certain slaves who have memorized each a portion of the ever-extending labyrinth. By this means they are able to traverse with safety and communicate one level to the other.

Tamorg finally escaped by the simple expedient of accidentally breaking through the wall whereat he dug. He enlarged the opening with his mattock and stooped to peer. At that moment a fellow workman pushed against him and Tamorg was thrust head-foremost into the opening he had made. Fortunately it led into a chasm at the bottom of which ran a swift but deep underground stream, into which Tamorg fell. As swimming is an art not easily forgotten, he managed to keep afloat until he reached the outer world. For several days he was blinded by the sun's rays and felt comfortable only by dim torchlight.

I questioned him in detail about the many interesting phenomena which must have been before him constantly but he was very unsatisfactory, being ignorant of all observational methods. However I placed him as gatekeeper in the palace of D – whose coming and going I desired to check upon. So much for that source of information.

My interest in Quarmall was aroused (*Ningauble's book went on*) and my appetite whetted by this scanty meal of facts, so I applied myself toward getting more information. Through my connection with Sheelba I made contact with Eeack, the Overlord of Rats; by holding out the lure of secret passages to the granaries of Lankhmar, he was persuaded to visit me. His visit proved both barren and embarrassing. Barren because it turned out that rats are eaten as a delicacy in Quarmall and hunted for culinary purposes by well-trained weasels. Naturally, under such circumstances, any rat within the walls of Quarmall stood little chance of doing liaison work except from the uncertain vantage of a pot. Eeack's personal cohort of countless rats, evil-smelling and famished, consumed all edibles within reach of their sharp teeth; and out of pity for the plight in which I was left Eeack favored me by cajoling Scraa to wake and speak with me.

Scraa (*Ningauble's notes continued*) is one of those eon-old roaches who existed contemporaneously with those monstrous reptiles which once ruled the world, and whose racial memories go back into the mistiness of time before the Elder Ones retreated from the surface. Scraa presented me the following short history of Quarmall neatly inscribed on a peculiar parchment composed of cleverly welded wingcases flattened and smoothed most subtly. I append his document and apologize for his somewhat dry and prosy style.

'The city-state of Quarmall houses a civilization almost unheard of in the sphere of anthropoid organization. Perhaps the closest analogy which might be made is to that of the slave-making ants. The domain of Quarmall is at the present day limited to the small mountain, or large hill, on which it stands; but like a radish the main portion of it lies buried beneath the surface. This was not always so.

'Once the Lords of Quarmall ruled over broad meadows and vast seas; their ships swam between all known ports and their caravans marched the routes from sea to sea. Slowly from the fertile valleys and barren cliffs, from the desert spots and the open sea the grip of Quarmall loosened; not willingly but ever forced did the Lords of Quarmall retreat. Inexorably they were driven, year by year, generation by generation, from all their possessions and rights; until finally they were confined to that last and staunchest stronghold, the impregnable castle of Quarmall. The cause of this driving is lost in the dimness of fable; but it was probably due to those most gruesome practices which even to this day persuade the surrounding countryside that Quarmall is unclean and cursed.

'As the Lords of Quarmall were pushed back, driven in spite of their sorceries and valor, they burrowed under that last, vast stronghold ever deeper and ever broader. Each succeeding Lord dug more deeply into the bowels of the small mount on which sat the Keep of Quarmall. Eventually the memory of past glories faded and was forgotten and the Lords of Quarmall concentrated on their mazy tunneling to the exclusion of the outer world. They would have forgotten the outer world entirely but for their constant and ever increasing need of slaves and of sustenance for those slaves.

'The Lords of Quarmall are magicians of great repute and adepts in the practice of the Art. It is said that by their skill they can charm men into bondage both of body and of soul.'

So much did Scraa write. All in all it is a very unsatisfactory bit of gossip: hardly a word about those intriguing passageways which first aroused my interest; nothing about the conformation of the Land or its inhabitants; not even a map! But then poor ancient Scraa lives almost entirely in the past – the present will not become important to him for another eon or so.

However I believe I know two fellows who might be persuaded to undertake a mission there . . . (*Here Ningauble's notes ended, much to Fafhrd's irritation and suspicious puzzlement – and carking shamed discomfort too, for now he must think again of the unknown girl Hasjarl was torturing.*)

Outside the mount of Quarmall the sun was past meridian and shadows had begun to grow. The great white oxen threw their weight against the yoke. It was not the first time nor would it be the last, they knew. Each month as they approached this mucky stretch of road the master whipped and slashed them frantically, attempting to goad them into a speed which they, by nature, were unable to attain. Straining until the harness creaked, they obliged as best they could: for they knew that when this spot was passed the master would reward them with a bit of salt, a rough caress, and a brief respite from work. It was unfortunate that this particular piece of road stayed mucky long after the rains had ceased; almost from one season to the next. Unfortunate that it took a longer time to pass.

Their master had reason to lash them so. This spot was accounted accursed among his people. From this curved eminence the towers of Quarmall could be spied on; and more important these towers looked down upon the road, even as one looking up could see them. It was not healthy to look on the towers of Quarmall, or to be looked upon by them. There was sufficient reason for this feeling. The master of the oxen spat surreptitiously, made an obvious gesture with his fingers, and glanced fearfully over his shoulder at the sky-thrusting lacy-topped towers as the last mudhole was traversed. Even in this fleeting glance he caught the glimpse of a flash, a brilliant scintillation, from the tallest keep. Shuddering, he leaped into the welcome covert of the trees and thanked the gods he worshiped for his escape.

Tonight he would have much to speak of in the tavern. Men would buy him bowls of wine to swill, and bitter beer of herbs. He could lord it for an evening. Ah! but for his quickness he might even now be plodding soulless to the mighty gates of Quarmall; there to serve until his body was no more and even after. For tales were told of such charmings, and of other things, among the elders of the village: tales that bore no moral but which all men did heed. Was it not only last Serpent Eve that young Twelm went from the ken of men? Had he not jeered at these very tales and, drunken, braved the terraces of Quarmall? Sure, and this was so! And it was also true that his less brave companion had seen him swagger with bravado to the last, the highest terrace, almost to the most; then when Twelm, alarmed at some unknown cause, turned to run, his twisted-arched body was pulled willy-nilly back into the darkness. Not even a scream was heard to mark the passing of Twelm from this earth and the ken of his fellowmen. Juln, that less brave or less foolhardy companion of Twelm, had spent his time thenceforth in a continual drunken stupor. Nor would he stir from under roofs at night.

All the way to the village the master of the oxen pondered. He tried to formulate in his dim peasant intellect a method by which he might present himself as a hero. But even as he painfully constructed a simple, self-aggrandizing tale, he bethought himself of the fate of that one who had dared to brag of robbing Quarmall's vineyards; the one whose name was spoken only in a hushed whisper, secretly. So the driver decided to confine himself to facts, simple as they were, and trust to the atmosphere of horror that he knew any manifestation of activity in Quarmall would arouse.

While the driver was still whipping his oxen, and the Mouser watching two shadow-men play a thought-game, and Fafhrd swilling wine to drown the thought of an unknown girl in pain – at the same time Quarmal, Lord of Quarmall, was casting his own horoscope for the coming year. In the highest tower of the Keep he labored, putting in order the huge astrolabe and the other massive instruments necessary for his accurate observations.

Through curtains of broidery the afternoon sun beat hotly into the small chamber; beams glanced from the polished surfaces and scintillated into rainbow hues as they reflected askew. It was warm, even for an old man lightly gowned, and Quarmal stepped to the windows opposite the sun and drew the broidery aside, letting the cool moor-breeze blow through his observatory.

He glanced idly out the deep-cut embrasures. In the distance down past the terraced slopes he could see the little, curved brown thread of road which led eventually to the village.

Like ants the small figures on it appeared: ants struggling through some sticky trap; and like ants, even as Quarmal watched, they persisted and finally disappeared. Quarmal sighed as he turned away from the windows. Sighed in a slight disappointment because he regretted not having looked a moment sooner. Slaves were always needed. Besides, it would have been an opportunity for trying out a recently invented instrument or two.

Yet it was never Quarmal's way to regret the past, so with a shrug he turned away.

For an old man Quarmal was not particularly hideous until his eyes were noticed. They were peculiar in their shape and the ball was rich ruby-red. The dead-white iris had that nauseous sheen of pearly iridescence found only in the sea dwellers among living creatures; this character he inherited from his mother, a mer-woman. The pupils, like specks of black crystal, sparkled with incredible malevolent intelligence. His baldness was accentuated by the long tufts of coarse black hair which grew symmetrically over each ear. Pale, pitted skin hung loosely on his jowls, but was tightly drawn over the high cheekbones. Thin as a sharpened blade, his long jutting nose gave him the appearance of an old hawk or kestrel.

If Quarmal's eyes were the most arresting feature in his countenance, his mouth was the most beautiful. The lips were full and ruddy, remarkable in so aged a man, and they had that peculiar mobility found in some elocutionists and orators and actors. Had it been possible for Quarmal to have known vanity, he might have been vain about the beauty of his mouth; as it was this perfectly molded mouth served only to accentuate the horror of his eyes.

He looked up veiledly now through the iron rondures of the astrolobe at the twin of his own face pushing forth from a windowless square of the opposite wall: it was his own waxen life-mask, taken within the year and most realistically tinted and blackly hair-tufted by his finest artist, save that the white-irised eyes were of necessity closed – though the mask still gave a feeling of peering. The mask was the last in several rows of such, each a little more age-darkened than the succeeding one. Though some were ugly and many were elderly-handsome, there was a strong family resemblance between the shut-eyed faces, for there had been few if any intrusions into the male lineage of Quarmall.

There were perhaps fewer masks than might have been expected, for most Lords of Quarmall lived very long and had sons late. Yet there were also a considerable many, since Quarmall was such an ancient rulership. The oldest masks were of a brown almost black and not wax at all but the cured and mummified face skins of those primeval autocrats. The arts of flaying and tanning had early been brought to an exquisite degree of perfection in Quarmall and were still practiced with jealously prideful skill.

Quarmal dropped his gaze from the mask to his lightly-robed body. He was a lean man, and his hips and shoulders still gave evidence that once he had hawked, hunted, and fenced with the best. His feet were high-arched and his step was still light. Long and spatulate were his knob-knuckled fingers, while fleshy muscular palms gave witness to their dexterity and nimbleness, a necessary advantage to one of his calling. For Quarmal was a sorcerer, as were all the Lords of Quarmall from the eon-mighty past. From childhood up through manhood each male was trained into his calling, like some vines are coaxed to twist and thread a difficult terrace.

As Quarmal returned from the window to attend his duties he pondered on his training. It was unfortunate for the House of Quarmall that he possessed two instead of the usual single heir. Each of his sons was a creditable necromancer and well skilled in other sciences pertaining to the Art; both were exceedingly ambitious and filled with hatred. Hatred not only for one another but for Quarmal their father.

Quarmal pictured in his mind Hasjarl in his Upper Levels below the Keep and Gwaay below Hasjarl in his Lower Levels . . . Hasjarl cultivating his passions as if in some fiery circle of Hell, making energy and movement and logic carried to the ultimate the greatest goods, constantly threatening with whips and tortures and carrying through those threats, and now hiring a great brawling beast of a man to be his sworder . . . Gwaay nourishing restraint as if in Hell's frigidest circle, trying to reduce all life to art and intuitive thought, seeking by meditation to compel lifeless rock to do his bidding and constrain Death by the power of his will, and now hiring a small gray man like Death's younger brother to be his knifer . . . Quarmal thought of Hasjarl and Gwaay and for a moment a strange smile of fatherly pride bent his lips and then he shook his head and his smile became stranger still and he shuddered very faintly.

It was well, thought Quarmal, that he was an old man, far past his prime, even as magicians counted years, for it would be unpleasant to cease living in the prime of life, or even in the twilight of life's day. And he knew that sooner or later, in spite of all protecting charms and precautions, Death would creep silently on him or spring suddenly from some unguarded moment. This very night his horoscope might signal Death's instant escapeless approach; and though men lived by lies, treating truth's very self as lie to be exploited, the stars remained the stars.

Each day Quarmal's sons, he knew, grew more clever and more subtle in their usage of the Art which he had taught them. Nor could Quarmal protect himself by slaying them. Brother might murder brother, or the son his sire, but it was forbidden from ancient times for the father to slay his son. There were no very good reasons for this custom, nor were any needed. Custom in the House of Quarmall stood unchallenged, and it was not lightly defied.

Quarmal bethought him of the babe sprouting in the womb of Kewissa, the childlike favorite concubine of his age. So far as his precautions and watchfulness might have enforced that babe was surely his own – and Quarmal was the most watchful and cynically realistic of men. If that babe lived and proved a boy – as omens foretold it would be – and if Quarmal were given but twelve more years to train him, and if Hasjarl and Gwaay should be taken by the fates or each other . . .

Quarmal clipped off in his mind this line of speculation. To expect to live a dozen more years with Hasjarl and Gwaay growing daily more clever-subtle in their sorceries – or to hope for the dual extinguishment of two such cautious sprigs of his own flesh – were vanity and irrealism indeed!

He looked around him. The preliminaries for the casting were completed, the instruments prepared and aligned; now only the final observations and their interpretation were required. Lifting a small leaden hammer Quarmal lightly struck a brazen gong. Hardly had the resonance faded when the tall, richly appareled figure of a man appeared in the arched doorway.

Flindach was Master of the Magicians. His duties were many but not easily apparent. His power carefully concealed was second only to that of Quarmal. A wearied cruelty sat upon his dark visage, giving him an air of boredom which ill matched the consuming interest he took in the affairs of others. Flindach was not a comely man: a purple wine mark covered his left cheek, three large warts made an isosceles triangle on his right, while his nose and chin jutted like those of an old witch. Startlingly, with an effect of mocking irreverence, his eyes were ruby-whited and pearly-irised like those of his lord; he was a younger offspring of the same mer-woman who had birthed Quarmal – after Quarmal's father had done with her and following one of Quarmal's bizzare customs, he had given her to *his* Master of Magicians.

Now those eyes of Flindach, large and hypnotically staring, shifted uneasily as Quarmal spoke: 'Gwaay and Hasjarl, my sons, work today on their respective Levels. It would be well if they were called into the council room this night. For it is the night on which my doom is to be foretold. And I sense premonitorily that this casting will bear no good. Bid them dine together and permit them to amuse one another by plotting at my death – or by attempting each other's.'

He shut his lips precisely as he finished, and looked more evil than a man expecting Death should look. Flindach, used to terrors in the line of business, could scarcely repress a shudder at the glance bestowed on him; but remembering his position he made the sign of obeisance, and without a word or backward look departed.

The Gray Mouser did not once remove his gaze from Flindach as the latter strode across the domed dim sorcery chamber of the Lower Level until he reached Gwaay's side. The Mouser was mightily intrigued by the warts and wine mark on the cheeks of the richly-robed witch-faced man, and by his eerie red-whited eyes, and he instantly gave this charming visage a place of honor in the large catalog of freak-faces he stored in his memory vaults.

Although he strained his ears, he could not hear what Flindach said to Gwaay or what Gwaay answered.

Gwaay finished the telekinetic game he was playing by sending all his black counters across the midline in a great rutching surge that knocked half his opponent's white counters tumbling into his loinclothed lap. Then he rose smoothly from his stool.

'I sup tonight with my beloved brother in my all-revered father's apartments,' he pronounced mellowly to all. 'While I am there and in the escort of great Flindach here, no sorcerous spells may harm me. So you may rest for a space from your protective concentrations, oh my gracious magi of the First Rank.' He turned to go.

The Mouser, inwardly leaping at the chance to glimpse the sky again, if only by chilly night, rose springily too from his chair and called out, 'Ho, Prince Gwaay! Though safe from spells, will you not want the warding of my blades at this dinner party? There's many a great prince never made king 'cause he was served cold iron 'twixt the ribs between the soup and the fish. I also juggle most prettily and do conjuring tricks.'

Gwaay half turned back. 'Nor may steel harm me while my sire's hand is stretched above,' he called so softly that the Mouser felt the words were being lobbed like feather balls barely as far as his ear. 'Stay here, Gray Mouser.'

His tone was unmistakably rebuffing, nevertheless the Mouser, dreading a dull evening, persisted, 'There is also the matter of that serious spell of mine of which I told you, Prince – a spell most effective against magi of the *Second* Rank and lower, such as a certain noxious brother employs. Now were a good time—'

'Let there be no sorcery tonight!' Gwaay cut him off sternly, though speaking hardly louder than before. ''Twere an insult to my sire and to his great servant Flindach here, a Master of Magicians, even to think of such! Bide quietly, swordsman, keep peace, and speak no more.' His voice took on a pious note. 'There will be time enough for sorcery and swords, if slaying there must be.'

Flindach nodded solemnly at that and they silently departed. The Mouser sat down. Rather to his surprise, he noted that the twelve aged sorcerers were already curled up like pillbugs on their sides on their great chairs and snoring away. He could not even while away time by challenging one of them to the thought-game, hoping to learn by playing, or to a bout at conventional chess. This promised to be a most glum evening indeed.

Then a thought brightened the Mouser's swarthy visage. He lifted his hands, cupping the palms, and clapped them lightly together as he had seen Gwaay do.

The slim slavegirl Ivivis instantly appeared in the far archway. When she saw that Gwaay was gone and his sorcerers slumbering, her eyes became bright as a kitten's. She scampered to the Mouser, her slender legs flashing, seated herself with a last bound on his lap, and clapped her lissome arms around him.

Fafhrd silently faded back into a dark side passage as Hasjarl came hurrying along the torchlit corridor beside a richly robed official with hideously warted and mottled face and red eyeballs, on whose other side strode a pallid comely youth with strangely ancient eyes. Fafhrd had never before met Flindach or, of course, Gwaay.

Hasjarl was clearly in a pet, for he was grimacing insanely and twisting his hands together furiously as though pitting one in murderous battle against the other. His eyes, however, were tightly shut. As he stamped swiftly past, Fafhrd thought he glimpsed a bit of tattooing on the nearest upper eyelid.

Fafhrd heard the red-eyeballed one say, 'No need to run to your sire's banquet-board, Lord Hasjarl. We're in good time.' Hasjarl answered only a snarl, but the pale youth said sweetly, 'My brother is ever a baroque pearl of dutifulness.'

Fafhrd moved forward, watched the three out of sight, then turned the other way and followed the scent of hot iron straight to Hasjarl's torture chamber.

It was a wide, low-vaulted room and the brightest Fafhrd had yet encountered in these murky, misnamed Upper Levels.

To the right was a low table around which crouched five squat brawny men more bandy-legged than Hasjarl and masked each to the upper lip. They were noisily gnawing bones snatched from a huge platter of them, and swilling ale from leather jacks. Four of the masks were black, one red.

Beyond them was a fire of coals in a circular brick tower half as high as a man. The iron grill above it glowed redly. The coals brightened almost to white, then grew more deeply red again, as a twisted half-bald hag in tatters slowly worked a bellows.

Along the walls to either side, there thickly stood or hung various metal and leather instruments which showed their foul purpose by their ghostly hand-and-glove resemblance to various outer surfaces and inward orifices of the human body: boots, collars, masks, iron maidens, funnels, and the like.

To the left a fair-haired pleasingly plump girl in white under tunic lay bound to a rack. Her right hand in an iron half-glove stretched out tautly toward a machine with a crank. Although her face was tear-streaked, she did not seem to be in present pain.

Fafhrd strode toward her, hurriedly slipping out of his pouch and onto the middle finger of his right hand the massy ring Hasjarl's emissary had given him in Lankhmar as token from his master. It was of silver, holding a large black seal on which was Hasjarl's sign: a clenched fist.

The girl's eyes widened with new fears as she saw Fafhrd coming.

Hardly looking at her as he paused by the rack, Fafhrd turned toward the table of masked messy feasters, who were staring at him gape-mouthed by now. Stretching out toward them the back of his right hand, he called harshly yet carelessly, 'By authority of this sigil, release to me the girl Friska!' From mouth-corner he muttered to the girl, 'Courage!'

The black-masked creature who came hurrying toward him like a terrier appeared either not to recognize at once Hasjarl's sign or else not to reason out its import, for he said only, wagging a greasy finger, 'Begone, barbarian. This dainty morsel

693

is not for you. Think not to quench your rough lusts here. Our Master—'

Fafhrd cried out, 'If you will not accept the authority of the Clenched Fist one way, then you must take it the other.' Doubling up the hand with the ring on it, he smashed it against the torturer's suet-shining jaw so that he stretched himself out on the dark flags, skidded a foot, and lay quietly.

Fafhrd turned at once toward the half-risen feasters and slapping Graywand's hilt but not drawing it, he planted his knuckles on his hips and, addressing himself to the red mask, he barked out rather like Hasjarl, 'Our Master of the Fist had an afterthought and ordered me to fetch the girl Friska so that he might continue her entertainment at dinner for the amusement of those he goes to dine with. Would you have a new servant like myself report to Hasjarl your derelictions and delays? Loose her quickly and I'll say nothing.' He stabbed a finger at the hag by the bellows, 'You! – fetch her outer dress.'

The masked ones sprang to obey quickly enough at that, their tucked-up masks falling over their mouths and chins. There were mumblings of apology, which he ignored. Even the one he had slugged got groggily to his feet and tried to help.

The girl had been released from her wrist-twisting device, Fafhrd supervising, and she was sitting up on the side of the rack when the hag came with a dress and two slippers, the toe of one stuffed with oddments of ornament and such. The girl reached for them, but Fafhrd grabbed them instead and, seizing her by the left arm, dragged her roughly to her feet.

'No time for that now,' he commanded. 'We will let Hasjarl decide how he wants you trigged out for the sport,' and without more ado he strode from the torture chamber, dragging her beside him, though again muttering from mouth-side, 'Courage.'

When they were around the first bend in the corridor and had reached a dark branching, he stopped and looked at her frowningly. Her eyes grew wide with fright; she shrank from him, but then firming her features she said fearful-boldly, 'If you rape me by the way, I'll tell Hasjarl.'

'I don't mean to rape but rescue you, Friska,' Fafhrd assured her rapidly. 'That talk of Hasjarl sending to fetch you was but my trick. Where's a secret place I can hide you for a few days? – until we flee these musty crypts forever! I'll bring you food and drink.'

At that Friska looked far more frightened. 'You mean Hasjarl didn't order this? And that you dream of escaping from Quarmall? Oh, stranger, Hasjarl would only have twisted my wrist a little longer, perhaps not maimed me much, only heaped a few more indignities, certainly spared my life. But if he so much as suspected that I had sought to escape from Quarmall . . . Take me back to the torture chamber!'

'That I will not,' Fafhrd said irkedly, his gaze darting up and down the empty corridor. 'Take heart, girl. Quarmall's not the wide world. Quarmall's not the stars and the sea. Where's a secret room?'

'Oh, it's hopeless,' she faltered. 'We could never escape. The stars are a myth. Take me back.'

'And make myself out a fool? No,' Fafhrd retorted harshly. 'We're rescuing you from Hasjarl and from Quarmall too. Make up your mind to it, Friska, for I won't be budged. If you try to scream I'll stop your mouth. *Where's a secret room?*' In his exasperation he almost twisted her wrist, but remembered in time and only brought his face close to hers and rasped, '*Think!*' She had a scent like heather underlying the odor of sweat and tears.

Her eyes went distant then and she said in a small voice, almost dreamlike, 'Between the Upper and the Lower Levels there is a great hall with many small rooms adjoining. Once it was a busy and teeming part of Quarmall, they say, but now debated ground between Hasjarl and Gwaay. Both claim it, neither will maintain it, not even sweep its dust. It is called the Ghost Hall.' Her voice went smaller still. 'Gwaay's page once begged me meet him a little this side of there, but I did not dare.'

'Ha, that's the very place,' Fafhrd said with a grin. 'Lead us to it.'

'But I don't remember the way,' Friska protested. 'Gwaay's page told me, but I tried to forget . . .'

Fafhrd had spotted a spiral stair in the dark branchway. Now he strode instantly toward it, drawing Friska along beside him.

'We know we have to start by going down,' he said with rough cheer. 'Your memory will improve with motion, Friska.'

The Gray Mouser and Ivivis had solaced themselves with such kisses and caresses as seemed prudent in Gwaay's Hall of Sorcery, or rather now of Sleeping Sorcerers. Then, at first coaxed chiefly by Ivivis, it is true, they had visited a nearby kitchen, where the Mouser had readily wheedled from the lumpish cook three large thin slices of medium-rare unmistakable rib-beef, which he had devoured with great satisfaction.

At least one of his appetites mollified, the Mouser had consented that they continue their little ramble and even pause to view a mushroom field. Most strange it had been to see, betwixt the rough-finished pillars of rock, the rows of white button-fungi grow dim, narrow, and converge toward infinity in the ammonia-scented darkness.

At this point they had become teasing in the talks, he taxing Ivivis with having many lovers drawn by her pert beauty, she stoutly denying it, but finally admitting that there was a certain Klevis, page to Gwaay, for whom her heart had once or twice beat faster.

'And best, Gray Guest, you keep an eye open for him,' she had warned, wagging a slim finger, 'for certain he is the fiercest and most skillful of Gwaay's swordsmen.'

Then to change this topic and to reward the Mouser for his patience in viewing the mushroom field, she had drawn him, they going hand in hand now, to a wine cellar. There she had prettily begged the aged and cranky butler for a great tankard of amber fluid for her companion. It had proved to the Mouser's delight to be purest and most potent essence of grape with no bitter admixture whatever.

Two of his appetites now satisfied, the third returned to the Mouser more hotly. Hand-holding became suddenly merely tantalizing and Ivivis' pale green tunic no more an object for admiration and for compliments to her, but only a barrier to be got rid of as swiftly as possible and with the smallest necessary modicum of decorousness.

Himself taking the lead, he drew her as directly as he could recall the route, and with little speech, toward the closet he had preemptied for his loot, two levels below Gwaay's Hall of Sorcery. At last he found the corridor he sought, one hung to either side with thick purple arras and lit by infrequent copper chandeliers which hung each from the rock ceiling on three copper chains and held three thick black candles.

This far Ivivis followed him with only the fewest flirtatious balkings and a minimum of wondering, innocent-eyed questions as to what he intended and why such haste was needful. But now her hesitations became convincing, her eyes began to show a genuine uneasiness, or even fearfulness, and when he stopped by the arras-slit before the door to his closet and with the courtliest of lecherous smirks he could manage indicated to her that they had reached their destination, she drew sharply back, stifling an exclamation with the flat of her hand.

'Gray Mouser,' she whispered rapidly, her eyes at once frightened and beseeching, 'there is a confession I should have made earlier and now must make at once. By one of those malign and mocking coincidences which haunt all Quarmall, you have chosen for your hidey-hole the very chamber where—'

Well it was for the Gray Mouser then that he took seriously Ivivis' look and tone, that he was by nature sense-aware and distrustful, and in particular that his ankles now took note of a slight yet unaccustomed draft from under the arras. For without other warning a fist pointed with a dark dagger punched through the arras-slit at his throat.

With the edge of his left hand, which had been raised to indicate to Ivivis their bedding-place, the Mouser struck aside the black-sleeved arm.

The girl exclaimed, not loudly, 'Klevis!'

With his right hand the Mouser caught hold of the wrist going by him and twisted it. With his spread left hand he simultaneously rammed his attacker in the armpit.

But the Mouser's grip, made by hurried snatch, was imperfect. Moreover, Klevis was not minded to resist and have his arm dislocated or broken in that fashion. Spinning with the Mouser's twist, he also went into a deliberate forward somersault.

The net result was that Klevis lost his cross-gripped dagger, which clattered dully on the thick-carpeted floor, but tore loose unhurt from the Mouser and after two more somersaults came lightly to his feet, at once turning and drawing rapier.

By then the Mouser had drawn Scalpel and his dirk Cat's Claw too, but held the latter behind him. He attacked cautiously, with probing feints. When Klevis counterattacked strongly, he retreated, parrying each fierce thrust at the last moment, so that again and again the enemy blade went whickering close by him.

Klevis lunged with especial fierceness. The Mouser parried, high this time and not retreating. In an instant they were pressed body to body, their rapiers strongly engaged near their hilts and above their heads.

By turning a little, the Mouser blocked Klevis' knee driven at his groin. While with the dirk Klevis had overlooked, he stabbed the other from below, Cat's Claw entering just under Klevis' breastbone to pierce his liver, gizzard, and heart.

Letting go his dirk, the Mouser nudged the body away from him and turned.

Ivivis was facing them, with Klevis' punching-dagger gripped ready for a thrust.

The body thudded to the floor.

'Which of us did you propose to skewer?' the Mouser asked.

'I don't know,' the girl answered in a flat voice. 'You, I suppose.'

The Mouser nodded. 'Just before this interruption, you were saying, "The very chamber where—" What?'

'—where I often met Klevis, to be with him,' she replied.

Again the Mouser nodded. 'So you loved him and—'

'Shut up, you fool!' she interrupted. '*Is he dead?*' There were both deep concern and exasperation in her voice.

The Mouser backed along the body until he stood at the head of it. Looking down, he said, 'As mutton. He was a handsome youth.'

For a long moment they eyed each other like leopards across the corpse. Then, averting her face a little, Ivivis said, 'Hide the body, you imbecile. It tears my heartstrings to see it.'

Nodding, the Mouser stooped and rolled the corpse under the arras opposite the closet door. He tucked in Klevis' rapier beside him. Then he withdrew Cat's Claw from the body. Only a little dark blood followed. He cleaned his dirk on the arras, then let the hanging drop.

Standing up, he snatched the punching-dagger from the brooding girl and flipped it so that it too vanished under the arras.

With one hand he spread wide the slit in the arras. With the other he took hold of Ivivis' shoulder and pressed her toward the doorway which Klevis had left open to his undoing.

She instantly shook loose from his grip, but walked through the doorway. The Mouser followed. The leopard look was still in both their eyes.

A single torch lit the closet. The Mouser shut the door and barred it.

Ivivis snarled at him, summing it up: 'You owe me much, Gray Stranger.'

The Mouser showed his teeth in an unhumorous grin. He did not stop to see whether his stolen trinkets had been disturbed. It did not even occur to him, then, to do so.

Fafhrd felt relief when Friska told him that the darker slit at the very end of the dark, long, straight corridor they'd just entered was the door to the Ghost Hall. It had been a hurrying, nervous trip, with many peerings around corners and dartings back into dark alcoves while someone passed, and a longer trip vertically downward than Fafhrd had anticipated. If they had now only reached the top of the Lower Levels, this Quarmall must be bottomless! Yet Friska's spirits had improved considerably. Now at times she almost skipped along in her white chemise cut low behind. Fafhrd strode purposefully, her dress and slippers in his left hand, his ax in his right.

The Northerner's relief in no wise diminished his wariness, so that when someone rushed from an inky tunnel-mouth they were passing, he stroked out almost negligently and he felt and heard his ax crunch halfway through a head.

He saw a comely blond youth, now most sadly dead and his comeliness rather spoiled by Fafhrd's ax, which still stood in the great wound it had made. A fair hand opened and the sword it had held fell from it.

'Hovis!' he heard Friska cry; 'O gods! O gods that are not here. Hovis!'

Lifting a booted foot, Fafhrd stamped it sideways at the youth's chest, at once freeing his ax and sending the corpse back into the tunneled dark from which the live man had so rashly hurtled.

After a swift look and listen all about, he turned toward Friska where she stood white-faced and staring.

'Who's this Hovis?' he demanded, shaking her lightly by the shoulder when she did not reply.

Twice her mouth opened and shut again, while her face remained as expressionless as that of a silly fish. Then with a little gasp she said, 'I lied to you, barbarian. I have met Gwaay's page Hovis here. More than once.'

'Then why didn't you warn me, wench?' Fafhrd demanded. 'Did you think I would scold you for your morals, like some city graybeard? Or have you no regard at all for your men, Friska?'

'Oh, do not chide me,' Friska begged miserably. 'Please do not chide me.'

Fafhrd patted her shoulder. 'There, there,' he said. 'I forget you were shortly tortured and hardly of a mind to remember everything. Come on.'

They had taken a dozen steps when Friska began to shudder and sob together in a swiftly mounting crescendo. She turned and ran back, crying, 'Hovis! Hovis, forgive me!'

Fafhrd caught her before three steps. He shook her again and when that did not stop her sobbing, he used his other hand to slap her twice, rocking her head a little.

She stared at him dumbly.

He said not fiercely but somberly, 'Friska, I must tell you that Hovis is where your words and tears can never again reach him. He's dead. Beyond recall. Also, I killed him. That's beyond recall too. But you are still alive. You can hide from Hasjarl. Ultimately, whether you believe it or not, you can escape with me from Quarmall. Now come on with me, and no looking back.'

She blindly obeyed, with only the faintest of moanings.

*

The Gray Mouser stretched luxuriously on the silver-tipped bearskin he'd thrown on the floor of his closet. Then he lifted on an elbow and, finding the black pearls he'd pilfered, tried them against Ivivis' bosom in the pale cool light of the single torch above. Just as he'd imagined, the pearls looked very well there. He started to fasten them around her neck.

'No, Mouser,' she objected lazily. 'It awakens an unpleasant memory.'

He did not persist, but lying back again, said unguardedly, 'Ah, but I'm a lucky man, Ivivis. I have you and I have an employer who, though somewhat boresome with his sorceries and his endless mild speaking, seems a harmless enough chap and certainly more endurable than his brother Hasjarl, if but half of what I hear of that one is true.'

The voice of Ivivis briskened. 'You think Gwaay harmless? – and kinder than Hasjarl? La, that's a quaint conceit. Why, but a week ago he summoned my late dearest friend, Divis, then his favorite concubine, and telling her it was a necklace of the same stones, hung around her neck an emerald adder, the sting of which is infallibly deadly.'

The Mouser turned his head and stared at Ivivis. 'Why did Gwaay do that?' he asked.

She stared back at him blankly. 'Why, for nothing at all, to be sure,' she said wonderingly. 'As everyone knows, that is Gwaay's way.'

The Mouser said, 'You mean that, rather than say, "I am wearied of you," he killed her?'

Ivivis nodded. 'I believe Gwaay can no more bear to hurt people's feelings by rejecting them than he can bear to shout.'

'It is better to be slain than rejected?' the Mouser questioned ingenuously.

'No, but for Gwaay it is easier on his feelings to slay than to reject. Death is everywhere here in Quarmall.'

The Mouser had a fleeting vision of Klevis' corpse stiffening behind the arras.

Ivivis continued, 'Here in the Lower Levels we are buried

before we are born. We live, love, and die buried. Even when we strip, we yet wear a garment of invisible mold.'

The Mouser said, 'I begin to understand why it is necessary to cultivate a certain callousness in Quarmall, to be able to enjoy at all any moments of pleasure snatched from life, or perhaps I mean from death.'

'That is most true, Gray Mouser,' Ivivis said very soberly, pressing herself against him.

Fafhrd started to brush aside the cobwebs joining the two dust-filmed sides of the half open, high, nail-studded door, then checked himself and bending very low ducked under them.

'Do you stoop too,' he told Friska. 'It were best we leave no signs of our entry. Later I'll attend to our footprints in the dust, if that be needful.'

They advanced a few paces, then stood hand in hand, waiting for their eyes to grow accustomed to the darkness. Fafhrd still clutched in his other hand Friska's dress and slippers.

'This is the Ghost Hall?' Fafhrd asked.

'Aye,' Friska whispered close to his ear, sounding fearful. 'Some say that Gwaay and Hasjarl send their dead to battle here. Some say that demons owing allegiance to neither—'

'No more of that, girl,' Fafhrd ordered gruffly. 'If I must battle devils or liches, leave me my hearing and my courage.'

They were silent a space then while the flame of the last torch twenty paces beyond the half shut door slowly revealed to them a vast chamber low-domed with huge, rough black blocks pale-mortared for a ceiling. It was set out with a few tatter-shrouded furnishings and showed many small closed doorways. To either side were wide rostra set a few feet above floor level, and toward the center there was, surprisingly, what looked like a dried-up fountain pool.

Friska whispered, 'Some say the Ghost Hall was once the harem of the father lords of Quarmall during some centuries when they dwelt underground between Levels, ere this Quarmal's father coaxed by his sea-wife returned to the Keep. See, they left so suddenly that the new ceiling was neither finish-polished, nor final cemented, nor embellished with drawings, if such were purposed.'

Fafhrd nodded. He distrusted that unpillared ceiling and thought the whole place looked rather more primitive than Hasjarl's polished and leather-hung chambers. That gave him a thought.

'Tell me, Friska,' he said. 'How is it that Hasjarl can see with his eyes closed? Is it that—'

'Why, do you not know that?' she interrupted in surprise. 'Do you not know even the secret of his horrible peeping? He simply—'

A dim velvet shape that chittered almost inaudibly shrill swooped past their faces and with a little shriek Friska hid her face in Fafhrd's chest and clung to him tightly.

In combing his fingers through her heather-scented hair to show her no flying mouse had found lodgment there and in smoothing his palms over her bare shoulders and back to demonstrate that no bat had landed there either, Fafhrd began to forget all about Hasjarl and the puzzle of his second sight – and his worries about the ceiling falling in on them too.

Following custom, Friska shrieked twice, very softly.

Gwaay languidly clapped his white, perfectly groomed hands and with a slight nod motioned for the waiting slaves to remove the platters from the low table. He leaned lazily into the deep-cushioned chair and through half-closed lids looked momentarily at his companion before he spoke. His brother across the table was not in a good humor. But then it was rare for Hasjarl to be other than in a pet, a temper, or more often merely sullen and vicious. This may have been due to the fact that Hasjarl was a very ugly man, and his nature had grown to confirm to his body; or perhaps it was the other way around. Gwaay was indifferent to both theories; he merely knew that in one glance all his memory had told him of Hasjarl was verified; and he again realized the bitter magnitude of his hatred for his brother. However, Gwaay spoke gently in a low, pleasant voice:

'Well, how now, Brother, shall we play at chess, that demon

game they say exists in every world? 'Twill give you a chance to lord it over me again. You always win at chess, you know, except when you resign. Shall I have the board set before us?' and then cajolingly, 'I'll give you a pawn!' and he raised one hand slightly as if to clap again in order that his suggestion might be carried out.

With the lash he carried slung to his wrist Hasjarl slashed the face of the slave nearest him, and silently pointed at the massive and ornate chessboard across the room. This was quite characteristic of Hasjarl. He was a man of action and given to few words, at least away from his home territory.

Besides, Hasjarl was in a nasty humor. Flindach had torn him from his most interesting and exciting amusement: torture! And for what? thought Hasjarl: to play at chess with his priggish brother; to sit and look at his pretty brother's face; to eat food that would surely disagree with him; to wait the answer to the casting, which he already knew – had known for years; and finally to be forced to smile into the horrible blood-whited eyes of his father, unique in Quarmall save for those of Flindach, and toast the House of Quarmall for the ensuing year. All this was most distasteful to Hasjarl and he showed it plainly.

The slave, a bloody welt swift-swelling across his face, carefully slid the chessboard between the two. Gwaay smiled as another slave arranged the chessmen precisely on their squares; he had thought of a scheme to annoy his brother. He had chosen the black as usual and he planned a gambit which he knew his avaricious opponent couldn't refuse; one Hasjarl would accept to his own undoing.

Hasjarl sat grimly back in his chair, arms folded. 'I should have made you take white,' he complained. 'I know the paltry tricks you can do with black pebbles – I've seen you as a girl-pale child darting them through the air to startle the slaves' brats. How am I to know you will not cheat by fingerless shifting your pieces while I deep ponder?'

Gwaay answered gently, 'My paltry powers, as you most justly appraise them, Brother, extend only to bits of basalt, trifles of obsidian and other volcanic rocks conformable to my nether level. While these chess pieces are jet, Brother, which in your great scholarship you surely know is only a kind of coal, vegetable stuff pressed black, not even in the same realm as the very few materials subject to my small magickings. Moreover, for you to miss the slightest trick with those quaint slave-surgeried eyes of yours, Brother, were matter for mighty wonder.'

Hasjarl growled. Not until all was ready did he stir; then, like an adder's strike, he plucked a black rook's pawn from the board and with a sputtering giggle, snarled: 'Remember, Brother? It was a pawn you promised! Move!'

Gwaay motioned the waiting slave to advance his king's pawn. In like manner Hasjarl replied. A moment's pause and Gwaay offered his gambit: pawn to king-bishop's fourth! Eagerly Hasjarl snatched the apparent advantage and the game began in earnest. Gwaay, his face easy-smiling in repose, seeming to be less interested in the game than in the shadow play of the flickering lamps on the figured leather upholsterings of calfskin, lambskin, snakeskin, and even slaveskin and nobler human hide; seeming to move offhand, without plan, yet confidently. Hasjarl, his lips compressed in concentration, was intent on the board, each move a planned action both mental and physical. His concentration made him for the moment oblivious of his brother, oblivious of all but the problem before him; for Hasjarl loved to win beyond all computation.

It had always been this way; even as children the contrast was apparent. Hasjarl was the elder; older by only a few months which his appearance and demeanor lengthened to years. His long, misshapen torso was ill-borne on short bandy legs. His left arm was perceptibly longer than the right; and his fingers, peculiarly webbed to the first knuckle, were gnarled and stubby with brittle striated nails. It was as if Hasjarl were a poorly reconstructed puzzle put together in such fashion that all the pieces were mismated and awry.

This was particularly true of his features. He possessed his sire's nose, though thickened and coarse-pored; but this was contradicted by the thin-lipped, tightly compressed mouth continually pursed until it had assumed a perpetual sphincter-like appearance. Hair, lank and lusterless, grew low on his forehead; and low, flattened cheekbones added yet another contradiction.

As a lad, led by some perverse whim, Hasjarl had bribed, coaxed, or more probably browbeaten one of the slaves versed in surgery to perform a slight operation on his upper eyelids. It was a small enough thing in itself, yet its implications and results had affected the lives of many men unpleasantly, and never ceased to delight Hasjarl.

That merely the piercing of two small holes, centered over the pupil when the eyes were closed, could produce such qualms in other people was incredible; but it was so. Feather-weight grommets of sleekest gold, jade or – as now – ivory – kept the holes from growing shut.

When Hasjarl peered through these tiny apertures it gave the effect of an ambush and made the object of his gaze feel spied upon; but this was the least annoying of his many irritating habits.

Hasjarl did nothing easily but he did all things well. Even in swordplay his constant practice and overly long left arm made him the equal of the athletic Gwaay. His administration of the Upper Levels over which he ruled was above all things economical and smooth; for woe betide the slave who failed in the slightest detail of his duties. Hasjarl saw and punished.

Hasjarl was well nigh the equal of his teacher in the practice of the Art; and he had gathered about him a band of magicians almost the caliber of Flindach himself. But he was not happy in his prowess so hardly won, for between the absolute power which he desired and the realization of that desire stood two obstacles: the Lord of Quarmall whom he feared above all things; and his brother Gwaay whom he hated with a hatred nourished on envy and fed by his own thwarted desires.

Gwaay, antithetically, was supple of limb, well-formed and good to look upon. His eyes, wide-set and pale, were deceptively gentle and kindly; for they masked a will as strong and capable of action as coiled spring-steel. His continual residence in the Lower Levels over which he ruled gave to his pallid smooth skin a peculiar waxy luster.

Gwaay possessed that enviable ability to do all things well, with little exertion and less practice. In a way he was much worse than his brother: for while Hasjarl slew with tortures and slow pain and an obvious personal satisfaction, he at least attached some importance to life because he was so meticulous in its taking; whereas Gwaay smiling gently would slay, without reason, as if jesting. Even the group of sorcerers which he had gathered about him for protection and amusement was not safe from his fatal and swift humors.

Some thought that Gwaay was a stranger to fear, but this was not so. He feared the Lord of Quarmall and he feared his brother; or rather he feared that he would be slain by his brother before he could slay him. Yet so well were his fear and hatred concealed that he could sit relaxed, not two yards from Hasjarl, and smile amusedly, enjoying every moment of the evening. Gwaay flattered himself on his perfect control over all emotion.

The chess game had developed beyond the opening stage, the moves coming slower, and now Hasjarl rapped down a rook on the seventh rank.

Gwaay observed gently, 'Your turreted warrior rushes deep into my territory, Brother. Rumor has it you've hired a brawny champion out of the north. With what purpose, I wonder, in our peace-wrapped cavern world? Could he be a sort of living rook?' He poised, hand unmoving over one of his knights.

Hasjarl giggled. 'And if his purpose is to slash pretty throats, what's that to you? I know naught of this rook-warrior, but 'tis said – slaves' chat, no doubt – that you yourself have had fetched a skilled sworder from Lankhmar. Should I call him a knight?'

'Aye, two can play at a game,' Gwaay remarked with prosy philosophy and lifting his knight, softly but firmly planted it at his king's sixth.

'I'll not be drawn,' Hasjarl snarled. 'You shall not win by making my mind wander.' And arching his head over the board, he cloaked himself again with his all-consuming calculations.

In the background slaves moved silently, tending the lamps and replenishing the founts with oil. Many lamps were needed to light the council room, for it was low-ceiled and massively beamed, and the arras-hung walls reflected little of the yellow rays and the mosaic floor was worn to a dull richness by countless footsteps in the past. From the living rock this room had been carved; long forgotten hands had set the huge cypress beams and inlaid the floor so cunningly. Those gay, time-faded tapestries had been hung by the slaves of some ancient Lord of Quarmall, who had pilfered them from a passing caravan, and so with all the rich adornments. The chessmen and the chairs, the chased lamp sconces and the oil which fed the wicks, and the slaves which tended them: all was loot. Loot from generations back when the Lords of Quarmall plundered far and wide and took their toll from every passing caravan.

High above that warm, luxuriously furnished chamber where Gwaay and Hasjarl played at chess, the Lord of Quarmall finished the final calculations which would complete his horoscope. Heavy leather hangings shut out the stars that had but now twinkled down their benisons and dooms. The only light in that instrument-filled room was the tiny flare of a single taper. By such scant illumination did custom bid the final casting be read, and Quarmal strained even his keen vision to see the Signs and Houses rightly.

As he rechecked the final results his supple lips writhed in a sneer, a grimace of displeasure. *Tonight or tomorrow*, he thought with an inward chill. *At most, late on the morrow*. Truly, he had little time.

Then, as if pleased by some subtle jest, he smiled and nodded, making his skinny shadow perform monstrous gyrations on the curtains and brasured wall.

Finally Quarmal laid aside his crayon, and taking the single candle lighted by its flame seven larger tapers. With the aid of this better light he read once more the horoscope. This time he made no sign of pleasure or any other emotion. Slowly he rolled the intricate diagramed and inscribed parchment into a slender tube, which he thrust in his belt; then rubbing together his lean hands he smiled again. At a nearby table were the ingredients which he needed for his scheme's success: powders, oils, tiny knives, and other materials and instruments.

The time was short. Swiftly he worked, his spatulate fingers performing miracles of dexterity. Once he went on an errand to the wall. The Lord of Quarmall made no mistakes, nor could he afford them.

It was not long before the task was completed to his satisfaction. After extinguishing the last lit candles, Quarmal, Lord of Quarmall, relaxed into his chair and by the dim light of a single taper summoned Flindach, in order that his horoscope might be announced to those below.

As was his wont, Flindach appeared almost at once. He presented himself confronting his master with arms folded across his chest, and head bowed submissively. Flindach never presumed. His figure was illuminated only to the waist, above that shadow concealed whatever expression of interest or boredom his warted and wine-marked face might show. In like manner the pitted yet sleeker countenance of Quarmal was obscured, only his pale irises gleamed phosphorescent from the shadows like two minute moons in a dark bloody sky.

As if he were measuring Flindach, or as if he saw him for the first time, Quarmal slowly raised his glance from foot to forehead of the figure before him, and looking direct into the shaded eyes of Flindach so like his own, he spoke. 'O Master of Magicians, it is within your power to grant me a boon this night.'

He raised a hand as Flindach would have spoken and swiftly continued: 'I have watched you grow from boy to youth and from youth to man; I have nurtured your knowledge of the Art until it is only second to my own. The same mother carried us, though I her firstborn and you the child of her last fertile year – that kinship helped. Your influence within Quarmall is almost equal to mine. So I feel that some reward is due your diligence and faithfulness.'

Again Flindach would have spoken, but was dissuaded by a gesture. Quarmal spoke more slowly now, and accompanied his words with staccato taps on the parchment roll. 'We both well know, from hearsay and direct knowledge, that my sons plot my death. And it is also true that in some manner they must be thwarted, for neither of the twain is fit to become the Lord of Quarmall; nor does it seem probable that either will ever reach such wisdom. Under their warring, Quarmall would die of inanition and neglect, as has died the Ghost Hall. Furthermore, each of them, to buttress his sorceries, has secretly hired a sworded champion from afar – you've seen Gwaay's – and this is the beginning of the bringing of free mercenaries into Quarmall and the sure doom of our power.' He stretched a hand toward the dark close-crowded rows of mummied and waxen masks and he asked rhetorically, 'Did the Lords of Quarmall guard and preserve our hidden realm that its councils might be entered, crowded, and at last be captured by foreign captains?

Now a far more secret matter,' he continued, his voice sinking. 'The concubine Kewissa carries my seed: male-growing, by all omens and oracles – though this is known only to Kewissa and myself, and now to you, Flindach. Should this unborn sprout reach but boyhood brotherless, I might die content, leaving to you his tutelage in all confidence and trust.'

Quarmal paused and sat impassive as an effigy. 'Yet to forestall Hasjarl and Gwaay becomes more difficult each day, for they increase in power and in scope. Their own innate wickedness gives them access to regions and demons heretofore but imagined by their predecessors. Even I, well versed in necromancy, am often appalled.' He paused and quizzically looked at Flindach.

For the first time since he had entered Flindach spoke. His voice was that of one trained in the recitation of incantations, deep and resonant. 'Master, what you speak is true. Yet how will you encompass their plots? You know, as well as I, the custom that forbids what is perhaps the only means of thwarting them.'

Flindach paused as if he would say more, but Quarmal quickly intervened. 'I have concocted a scheme, which may or may not succeed. The success of it depends almost entirely upon your cooperation.' He lowered his voice almost to a whisper, beckoning for Flindach to step closer. 'The very stones may carry tales, O Flindach, and I would that this plan were kept entirely secret.' Quarmal beckoned again, and Flindach stepped still nearer until he was within arm's reach of his master. Half stooping, he placed himself in such a position that his ear was close to Quarmal's mouth. This was closer than ever he remembered approaching Quarmal, and strange qualms filled his mind, recrudescences of childish old wives' tales. This ancient ageless man with eyes pearl-irised as his own seemed to Flindach not like half brother at all, but like some strange, merciless half father. His burgeoning terror was intensified when he felt the sinewy fingers of Quarmal close on his wrist and gently urge him closer, almost to his knees, beside the chair.

Quarmal's lips moved swiftly, and Flindach controlled his urge to rise and flee as the plan was unfolded to him. With a sibilant phrase, the final phrase, Quarmal finished and Flindach realized the full enormity of that plan. Even as he comprehended it, the single taper guttered and was extinguished. There was darkness absolute.

The chess game progressed swiftly; the only sounds, except the ceaseless shuffle of naked feet and the hiss of lamp wicks, were the dull click of the chessmen and the staccato cough of Hasjarl. The low table off which the twain had eaten was placed opposite the broad arched door which was the only apparent entrance to the council chamber.

There was another entrance. It led to the Keep of Quarmall; and it was toward this arras-concealed door that Gwaay glanced most often. He was positive that the news of the casting would be as usual, but a certain curiosity whelmed him this evening; he felt a faint foreshadowing of some untoward event, even as wind blows gusty before a storm.

An omen had been vouchsafed Gwaay by the gods today; an omen that neither his necromancers nor his own skill could interpret to his complete satisfaction. So he felt that it would be wise to await the development of events prepared and expectant.

Even as he watched the tapestry behind which he knew was the door whence would step Flindach to announce the consequences of the casting, that hanging bellied and trembled as if some breeze blew on it, or some hand pushed against it lightly.

Hasjarl abruptly threw himself back in his chair and cried in his high-pitched voice, 'Check with my rook to your king, and mate in three!' He dropped one eyelid evilly and peered triumphantly at Gwaay.

Gwaay, without removing his eyes from the still swaying

tapestry, said in precise, mellow words. 'The knight interposes, Brother, discovering check. I mate in two. You are wrong again, my comrade.'

But even as Hasjarl swept the men with a crash to the floor, the arras was more violently disturbed. It was parted by two slaves and the harsh gong-note, announcing the entrance of some high official, sounded.

Silently from betwixt the hanging stepped the tall lean form of Flindach. His shadowed face, despite the disfiguring wine mark and the treble mole, had a great and solemn dignity. And in its somber expressionlessness – an expressionlessness curiously mocked by a knowing glitter deep in the black pupils of the pearl-irised crimson-balled eyes – it seemed to forebode some evil tiding.

All motion ceased in that long low hall as Flindach, standing in the archway framed in rich tapestries, raised one arm in a gesticulation demanding silence. The attendant well-trained slaves stood at their posts, heads bowed submissively; Gwaay remained as he was, looking directly at Flindach; and Hasjarl, who had half-turned at the gong note, likewise awaited the announcement. In a moment, they knew, Quarmal their father would step from behind Flindach and smiling evilly would announce his horoscope. Always this had been the procedure; and always, since each could remember, Gwaay and Hasjarl had at this moment wished for Quarmal's death.

Flindach, arm lifted in dramatic gesture, began to speak.

'The casting of the horoscope has been completed and the finding has been made. Even as the Heavens foretell is the fate of man fulfilled. I bring this news to Hasjarl and Gwaay, the sons of Quarmal.'

With a swift motion Flindach plucked a slender parchment tube from his belt and, breaking it with his hands, dropped it crumpled at his feet. In almost the same gesture he reached behind his left shoulder and stepping from the shadow of the arch drew a peaked cowl over his head.

Throwing wide both arms, Flindach spoke, his voice seeming to come from afar:

'Quarmal, Lord of Quarmall, rules no more. The casting is

fulfilled. Let all within the walls of Quarmall mourn. For three days the place of the Lord of Quarmall will be vacant. So custom demands and so shall it be. On the morrow, when the sun enters his courtyard, that which remains of what was once a great and puissant lord will be given to the flames. Now I go to mourn my master and oversee the obsequies and prepare myself with fasting and with prayer for his passing. Do you likewise.'

Flindach slowly turned and disappeared into the darkness from which he had come.

For the space of ten full heartbeats Gwaay and Hasjarl sat motionless. The announcement came as a thunderclap to both. Gwaay for a second felt an impulse to giggle and smirk like a child who has unexpectedly escaped punishment and is instead rewarded; but in the back of his mind he was half-convinced that he had known all along the outcome of the casting. However, he controlled his childish glee and sat silent, staring.

On the other hand Hasjarl reacted as might be expected of him. He went through a series of outlandish grimaces and ended with an obscene half smothered titter. Then he frowned, and turning said to Gwaay, 'Heard you not what said Flindach? I must go and prepare myself!' and he lurched to his feet and paced silently across the room, out the broad-arched door.

Gwaay remained sitting for another few moments, frowning eyes narrowed in concentration, as if he were puzzling over some abtruse problem which required all his powers to solve. Suddenly he snapped his fingers and, motioning for his slaves to precede him, made ready for his return to the Lower Levels, whence he had come.

Fafhrd had barely left the Ghost Hall when he heard the faint rattle and clink of armed men moving cautiously. His bemusement with Friska's charms vanished as if he had been soused with ice water. He shrank into the deeper darkness and eavesdropped long enough to learn that these were pickets of Hasjarl, guarding against an invasion from Gwaay's Lower Levels – and not tracking down Friska and himself as he'd first feared. Then he made off swiftly for Hasjarl's Hall of Sorcery, grimly pleased that his memory for landmarks and turnings seemed to work as well for mazy tunnels as for forest trails and steep zigzag mountain escalades.

The bizarre sight that greeted him when he reached his goal stopped him on the stony threshold. Standing shin-deep and stark naked in a steaming marble tub shaped like a ridgy seashell, Hasjarl was berating and haranguing the great roomful around him. And every man jack of them – sorcerers, officers, overseers, pages bearing great fringy towels and dark red robes and other apparel – was standing quakingly still with cringing eyes, except for the three slaves soaping and laving their Lord with tremulous dexterity.

Fafhrd had to admit that Hasjarl naked was somehow more consistent – ugly everywhere – a kobold birthed from a hot-spring. And although his grotesque child-pink torso and mismated arms were a-writhe and a-twitch in a frenzy of apprehension, he had dignity of a sort.

He was snarling, 'Speak, all of you, is there a precaution I have forgotten, a rite omitted, a rat-hole overlooked that Gwaay might creep through? Oh, that on this night when demons lurk and I must mind a thousand things and dress me for my father's obsequies, I should be served by wittols! Are you all deaf and dumb? Where's my great champion, who should ward me now? Where are my scarlet grommets? Less soap there, you – take that! You, Essem, are we guarded well above? – I don't trust Flindach. And, Yissim, have we guards enough below? – Gwaay is a snake who'll strike through any gap. Dark Gods, defend me! Go to the barracks, Yissim, get more men, and reinforce our downward guards – and while you're there, I mind me now, bid them continue Friska's torture. Wring the truth from her! She's in Gwaay's plots – this night has made me certain. Gwaay knew my father's death was imminent and laid invasion plans long weeks agone. Any of you may be his purchased spies! Oh, where's my champion? *Where are my scarlet grommets?*'

Fafhrd, who'd been striding forward, quickened his pace at mention of Friska. A simple inquiry at the torture chamber would reveal her escape and his part in it. He must create diversions. So he halted close in front of pink wet steaming Hasjarl and said boldly, 'Here is your champion, Lord. And he counsels not sluggy defense, but some swift stroke at Gwaay! Surely your mighty mind has fashioned many a shrewd attacking stratagem. Launch you a thunderbolt!'

It was all Fafhrd could do to keep speaking forcefully to the end and not let his voice trail off as his attention became engrossed in the strange operation now going on. While Hasjarl crouched stock-still with head a-twist, an ashen-faced bath-slave had drawn out Hasjarl's left upper eyelid by its lashes and was inserting into the hole in it a tiny flanged scarlet ring or grommet no bigger than a lentil. The grommet was carried on the tip of an ivory wand as thin as a straw and the whole deed was being done by the slave with the anxiety of a man refilling the poison pouches of an untethered rattlesnake – if such an action might be imagined for purposes of comparison.

However, the operation was quickly completed, and then on the right eye too – and evidently with perfect satisfaction, since Hasjarl did not slash the slave with the soapy wet lash still dangling from his wrist – and when Hasjarl straightened up he was grinning broadly at Fafhrd.

'You counsel me well, champion,' he cried. 'These other fools could do nothing but shake. There *is* a stroke long-planned that I'll try now, one that won't violate the obsequies. Essem, take slaves and fetch the dust – you know the stuff I mean – and meet me at the vents! Girls, sluice these suds off with tepid water. Boy, give me my slippers and my toweling robe! – those other clothes can wait. Follow me, Fafhrd!'

But just then his red-grommeted gaze lit on his four-and-twenty bearded and hooded sorcerers standing apprehensive by their chairs.

'Back to your charms at once, you ignoramuses!' he roared at them. 'I did not tell you to stop because I bathed! Back to your charms and send your plagues at Gwaay – red, black and green, nose drip and bloody rot – or I will burn your beards off to the eyelashes as prelude to more dire torturings! Haste, Essem! Come, Fafhrd!'

*

The Gray Mouser at that same moment was returning from his closet with Ivivis when Gwaay, velvet-shod and followed by barefoot slaves, came around a turn in the dim corridor so swiftly there was no evading him.

The young Lord of the Lower Levels seemed preternaturally calm and controlled, yet with the impression that under the calm was naught but quivering excitement and darting thought – so much so that it would hardly have surprised the Mouser if there had shone forth from Gwaay an aura of Blue Essence of Thunderbolt. Indeed, the Mouser felt his skin begin to prickle and sting as if just such an influence were invisibly streaming from his employer.

Gwaay scanned the Mouser and the pretty slavegirl in a flicker and spoke, his voice dancing rapid and gaysome.

'Well, Mouser, I can see you've sampled your reward ahead of time. Ah, youth and dim retreats and pillowed dreams and amorous hostessings – what else gilds life or makes it worth the guttering sooty candle? Was the girl skillful? Good! Ivivis, dear, I must reward your zeal. I gave Divis a necklace – would you one? Or I've a brooch shaped like a scorpion, ruby-eyed—'

The Mouser felt the girl's hand quiver and chill in his and he cut in quickly with, 'My demon speaks to me, Lord Gwaay, and tells me it's a night when the Fates walk.'

Gwaay laughed. 'Your demon has been listening behind the arras. He's heard tales of my father's swift departure.' As he spoke a drop formed at the end of his nose, between his nostrils. Fascinated, the Mouser watched it grow. Gwaay started to lift the back of his hand to it, then shook it off instead. For an instant he frowned, then laughed again.

'Aye, the Fates trod on Quarmall Keep tonight,' Gwaay said, only now his gay rapid voice was a shade hoarse.

'My demon whispers me further that there are dangerous powers abroad this night,' the Mouser continued.

'Aye, brother love and such,' Gwaay quipped in reply, but now his voice was a croak. A look of great startlement widened his eyes. He shivered as with a chill and drops pattered from his nose. Three hairs came loose from his scalp and fell across his eyes. His slaves shrank back from him.

716

'My demon warns me we'd best use my Great Spell quickly against those powers,' the Mouser went on, his mind returning as always to Sheelba's untested rune. 'It destroys only sorcerers of the Second Rank and lower. Yours, being of the First Rank, will be untouched. But Hasjarl's will perish.'

Gwaay opened his mouth to reply, but no words came forth, only a moaning nightmarish groan like that of a mute. Hectic spots shone forth high on his cheeks, and now it seemed to the Mouser that a reddish blotch was crawling up the right side of his chin, while on the left black spots were forming. A hideous stench became apparent. Gwaay staggered and his eyes brimmed with a greenish ichor. He lifted his hand to them and its back was yellowish crusted and red-cracked. His slaves ran.

'Hasjarl's sendings!' the Mouser hissed. 'Gwaay's sorcerers still sleep! I'll rouse 'em! Support him, Ivivis!' And turning he sped like the wind down corridor and up ramp until he reached Gwaay's Hall of Sorcery. He entered it, clapping and whistling harshly between his teeth, for true enough the twelve scrawny loinclothed magi were still curled snoring on their wide high-backed chairs. The Mouser darted to each in turn, righting and shaking him with no gentle hands and shouting in his ear, 'To your work! Anti-venom! Guard Gwaay!'

Eleven of the sorcerers roused quickly enough and were soon staring wide-eyed at nothingness, though with their bodies rocking and their heads bobbing for a while from the Mouser's shaking – like eleven small ships just overpassed by a squall.

He was having a little more trouble with the twelfth, though this one was coming awake, soon would be doing his share, when Gwaay appeared of a sudden in the archway with Ivivis at his side, though not supporting him. The young Lord's face gleamed as silvery clear in the dimness as the massy silver mask of him that hung in the niche above the arch.

'Stand aside, Gray Mouser, I'll jog the sluggard,' he cried in a rippingly bright voice and snatching up a small obsidian jar tossed it toward the drowsy sorcerer.

It should have fallen no more than halfway between them. Did he mean to wake the ancient by its shattering? the Mouser wondered. But then Gwaay stared at it in the air and it quickened its speed fearfully. It was as if he had tossed up a ball, then batted it. Shooting forward like a bolt fired point-blank from a sinewy catapult it shattered the ancient's skull and spattered the chair and the Mouser with his brains.

Gwaay laughed, a shade high-pitched, and cried lightly, 'I must curb my excitement! I must! I must! Sudden recovery from two dozen deaths – or twenty-three and the Nose Drip – is no reason for a philosopher to lose control. Oh, I'm a giddy fellow!'

Ivivis cried suddenly, 'The room swims! I see silver fish!'

The Mouser felt dizzy himself then and saw a phosphorescent green hand reach through the archway toward Gwaay – reach out on a thin arm that lengthened to yards. He blinked hard and the hand was gone – but now there were swimmings of purple vapor.

He looked at Gwaay and that one, frowny-eyed now, was sniffling hard then sniffling again, though no new drop could be seen to have formed on his nose-end.

Fafhrd stood three paces behind Hasjarl, who looked in his bunched and high-collared robe of earth-brown toweling rather like an ape.

Beyond Hasjarl on the right there trotted on a thick wide roller-riding leather belt three slaves of monstrous aspect: great splayed feet, legs like an elephant's, huge furnace-bellows chests, dwarfy arms, pinheads with wide toothy mouths and with nostrils bigger than their eyes or ears – creatures bred to run ponderously and nothing else. The moving belt disappeared with a half twist into a vertical cylinder of masonry five yards across and reemerged just below itself, but moving in the opposite direction, to pass under the rollers and complete its loop. From within the cylinder came the groaning of the great wooden fan which the belt whirled and which drove life-sustaining air downward to the Lower Levels.

Beyond Hasjarl on the left was a small door as high as Fafhrd's head in the cylinder. To it there mounted one by one, up four narrow masonry steps, a line of dusky, great-headed dwarves. Each bore on his shoulder a dark bag which when he reached the window he untied and emptied into the clamorous shaft, shaking it out most thoroughly while he held it inside, then folding it and leaping down to give place to the next bag-bearer.

Hasjarl leered over his shoulder at Fafhrd. 'A nosegay for Gwaay!' he cried. ''Tis a king's ransom I strew on the downward gale: powder of poppy, dust of lotus and mandragora, crumble of hemp. A million lewdly pleasant dreams, and all for Gwaay! Three ways this conquers him: he'll sleep a day and miss my father's funeral, then Quarmall's mine by right of sole appearance yet with no bloodshed, which would mar the rites; his sorcerers will sleep and my infectious spells burst through and strike him down in stinking jellied death; his realm will sleep, each slave and cursed page, so we'll conquer all merely by marching down after the business of the funeral. Ho, swifter there!' And seizing a long whip from an overseer, he began to crack it over the squat cones of the tread-slaves' heads and sting their broad backs with it. Their trot changed to a ponderous gallop, the moan of the fan rose in pitch, and Fafhrd waited to hear it shatter crackingly, or see the belt snap, or the rollers break on their axles.

The dwarf at the shaft-window took advantage of Hasjarl's attention being elsewhere to snatch a pinch of powder from his bag and bring it to his nostrils and sniff it down, leering ecstatically. But Hasjarl saw and whipped him about the legs most cruelly. The dwarf dutifully emptied his bag and shook it out while making little hops of agony. However he did not seem much chastened or troubled by his whipping, for as he left the chamber Fafhrd saw him pull his empty bag over his head and waddle off breathing deeply through it.

Hasjarl went on whip-cracking and calling, 'Swifter, I say! For Gwaay a drugged hurricane!'

The officer Yissim raced into the room and darted to his master.

'The girl Friska's escaped!' he cried. 'Your torturers say your champion came with your seal, telling them you had ordered her release – and snatched her off! All this occurred a quarter day ago.'

'Guards!' Hasjarl squealed. 'Seize the Northerner! Disarm and blind the traitor!'

But Fafhrd was gone.

The Mouser, in company with Ivivis, Gwaay and a colorful rabble of drug-induced hallucinations, reeled into a chamber similar to the one from which Fafhrd had just disappeared. Here the great cylindrical shaft ended in a half turn. The fan that sucked down the air and blew it out to refresh the Lower Levels was set vertically in the mouth of the shaft and was visible as it whirled.

By the shaft-mouth hung a large cage of white birds, all lying on its floor with their feet in the air. Besides these telltales, there was stretched on the floor of the chamber its overseer, also overcome by the drugs whirlwinding from Hasjarl.

By contrast, the three pillar-legged slaves ponderously trotting their belt seemed not affected at all. Presumably their tiny brains and monstrous bodies were beyond the reach of any drug, short of its lethal dose.

Gwaay staggered up to them, slapped each in turn, and commanded, 'Stop!' Then he himself dropped to the floor.

The groaning of the fan died away, its seven wooden vanes became clearly visible as it stopped (though for the Mouser they were interwoven with scaly hallucinations), and the only real sound was the slow gasping of the tread-slaves.

Gwaay smiled weirdly at them from where he sprawled and he raised an arm drunkenly and cried, 'Reverse! About face!' Slowly the tread-slaves turned, taking a dozen tiny steps to do it, until they all three faced the opposite direction on the belt.

'Trot!' Gwaay commanded them quickly. Slowly they obeyed and slowly the fan took up again its groaning, but now it was blowing air up the shaft against Hasjarl's downward fanning.

Gwaay and Ivivis rested on the floor for a space, until their brains began to clear and the last hallucinations were chased from view. To the Mouser they seemed to be sucked up the shaft through the fan blades: a filmy horde of blue and purple wraiths armed with transparent saw-toothed spears and cutlasses.

Then Gwaay, smiling in highest excitement with his eyes, said softly and still a bit breathlessly, 'My sorcerers . . . were not overcome . . . I think. Else I'd be dying . . . Hasjarl's two dozen deaths. Another moment . . . and I'll send across the level . . . to reverse the exhaust fan. We'll get fresh air through it. And put more slaves on this belt here – perchance I'll blow my brother's nightmares back to him. Then lave and robe me for my father's fiery funeral and mount to give Hasjarl a nasty shock. Ivivis, as soon as you can walk, rouse my bath girls. Bid them make all ready.'

He reached across the floor and grasped the Mouser strongly at the elbow. 'You, Gray One,' he whispered, 'prepare to work this mighty rune of yours which will smite down Hasjarl's warlocks. Gather your simples, pray your demonic prayers – consulting first with my twelve arch-magi . . . if you can rouse the twelfth from his dark hell. As soon as Quarmal's lich is in the flames, I'll send you word to speak your deadly spell.' He paused and his eyes gleamed with a witchy glare in the dimness. 'The time has come for sorcery and swords!'

There was a tiny scrabbling as one of the white birds staggered to its feet on the cage-bottom. It gave a chirrup that was rather like a hiccup, yet still had a note of challenge in it.

All that night through, all Quarmall was awake. Into the Ordering Room of the Keep, a magician came crying, 'Lord Flindach! The mind-casters have incontrovertible advertisements that the two brothers war against each other. Hasjarl sends sleepy resins down the shafts, while Gwaay blows them back.'

The warty and purple-blotched face of the Master of Magicians looked up from where he sat busy at a table surrounded by a small host awaiting orders.

'Have they shed blood?' he asked.

'Not yet.'

'It is well. Keep enchanted eyes on them.'

Then, gazing sternly in turn from under his hood at those whom he addressed, the Master of Magicians gave his other orders:

To two magicians robed as his deputies: 'Go on the instant to

Hasjarl and Gwaay. Remind them of the obsequies and stay with them until they and their companies reach the funeral court-yard.'

To a eunuch: 'Hasten to your master Brilla. Learn if he requires further materials or assistance building the funeral pyre. Help will be furnished him at once and without stint.'

To a captain of slingers: 'Double the guard on the walls. Yourself make the rounds. Quarmall must be entirely secure from outward assaults and escapes from within on this coming morn.'

To a richly-clad woman of middle years: 'To Quarmal's harem. See that his concubines are perfectly groomed and clad, as if their Lord himself meant to visit them at dawn. Quiet their apprehensions. Send to me the Ilthmarix Kewissa.'

In Hasjarl's Hall of Sorcery, that Lord let his slaves robe him for the obsequies, while not neglecting to direct the search for his traitorous champion Fafhrd, to instruct the shaftwatchers in the precautions they must take against Gwaay's attempts to return the poppy dust, perchance with interest, and to tutor his sorcerers in the exact spells they must use against Gwaay once Quarmal's body was devoured by the flames.

In the Ghost Hall, Fafhrd munched and drank with Friska a small feast he'd brought. He told her how he'd fallen into disfavor with Hasjarl and he mulled plans for his escape with her from the realm of Quarmall.

In Gwaay's Hall of Sorcery, the Gray Mouser conferred in turn with the eleven skinny wizards in their white loin-cloths, telling them nothing of Sheelba's spell, but securing from each the firm assurance that he was a magus of the First Rank.

In the steam room of Gwaay's bath, that Lord recuperated his flesh and faculties shaken by disease spells and drugs. His girls, supervised by Ivivis, brought him fragrant oils and elixirs, and scrubbed and laved him as he directed languidly yet precisely. The slender forms, blurred and silvered by the clouds of steam, moved and posed as in a languorous ballet.

*

The huge pyre was finally completed, and Brilla heaved a sigh of relief and contentment with the knowledge of work well done. He relaxed his fat, massive frame onto a bench against the wall and spoke to one of his companions in a high-pitched feminine voice:

'Such short notice, and at such a time, but the gods are not to be denied and no man can cheat his stars. It is shameful, though, to think that Quarmal will go so poorly attended: only a half dozen Lankhmarts, an Ilthmarix, and three Mingols – and one of those blemished. I always told him he should keep a better harem. However the male slaves are in fine fettle and will perhaps make up for the rest. Ah! but it's a fine flame the Lord will have to light his way!' Brilla wagged his hand dolefully and, snuffling, blinked a tear from his piggy eye; he was one of the few who really regretted the passing of Quarmal.

As High Eunuch to the Lord, Brilla's position was a sinecure and, besides, he had always been fond of Quarmal since he could remember. Once when a small chubby boy Brilla had been rescued from the torments of a group of larger, more virile slaves who had freed him at the mere passing-by of Quarmal. It was this small incident, unwotted or long forgotten by Quarmal, which had provoked a life-long devotion in Brilla.

Now only the gods knew what the future held. Today the body of Quarmal would be burned and what would happen after that was better left unpondered, even in the innermost thoughts of a man. Brilla looked once more at his handiwork, the funeral pyre. Achieving it in six short hours, even with hosts of slaves at his command, had taxed his powers. It towered in the center of the courtyard, even higher than the arch of the great gate thrice the stature of a tall man. It was built in the form of a square pyramid, truncated midway; and the inflammable woods that composed it were completely hidden by somber-hued drapes.

A runway was built from the ground across the vast courtyard to the topmost tier on each of the four sides; and at the top was a sizable square platform. It was here that the litter containing the body of Quarmal would be placed, and here the sacrificial victims be immolated. Only those slaves of proper age and talents were permitted to accompany their Lord on his long journey beyond the stars.

Brilla approved of what he saw and, rubbing his hands, looked about curiously. It was only on such occasions as this that one realized the immensity of Quarmall, and these occasions were rare; perhaps once in his life a man would see such an event. As far as Brilla could see small bands of slaves were lined, rank on rank, against the walls of the courtyard, even as was his own band of eunuchs and carpenters. There were the craftsmen from the Upper Levels, skilled workmen all in metal and in wood; there were the workers from the fields and vineyards all brown and gnarled from their labors; there were the slaves from the Lower Levels, blinking in the unaccustomed daylight, pallid and curiously deformed; and all the rest who served in the bowels of Quarmall, a representative group from each level.

The size of the turnout seemed to contradict the dawn's frightening rumors of secret war last night between the Levels, and Brilla felt reassured.

Most important and best placed were the two bands of henchmen of Hasjarl and Gwaay, one group on each side of the pyre. Only the sorcerers of the twain were absent, Brilla noted with a pang of unease, though refusing to speculate why.

High above all this mass of mixed humanity, atop the towering walls, were the ever silent, ever alert guards; standing quietly at their posts, slings dangling ready to hand. Never yet had the walls of Quarmall been stormed and never had a slave once within those close-watched walls passed into the outer world alive.

Brilla was admirably placed to observe all that occurred. To his right, projecting from the wall of the courtyard, was the balcony from which Hasjarl and Gwaay would watch the consuming of their father's body; to his left, likewise projecting, was the platform from which Flindach would direct the rituals. Brilla sat almost next to the door whence the prepared and purified body of Quarmal would be borne for its final fiery cleansing. He wiped the sweat fom his flabby jowls with the hem of his under tunic and wondered how much longer it would be before things started. The sun could not be far from the top of the wall now, and with its first beams the rites began.

Even as he wondered there came the tremendous, muffled vibration of the huge gong. There was a craning of necks and a rustling as many bodies shifted; then silence. On the left balcony the figure of Flindach appeared.

Flindach was cowled with the Cowl of Death and his garments were of heavy woven brocades, somber and dull. At his waist glittered the circular fan-bladed Golden Symbol of Power, which while the Chair of Quarmall was vacant, Flindach as High Steward must keep inviolate.

He lifted his arms toward the place where the sun would in a moment appear and intoned the Hymn of Greeting; even as he chanted, the first tawny rays struck into the eyes of those across the courtyard. Again that muffled vibration, which shook the very bones of those closest it, and opposite Flindach, on the other balcony, appeared Gwaay and Hasjarl. Both were garbed alike but for their diadems and scepters. Hasjarl wore a sapphire-jeweled silver band on his forehead and in his hand was the scepter of the Upper Levels, crested with a clenched fist; Gwaay wore a diadem inlaid with rubies and in his hand was his scepter surmounted by a worm, dagger-transfixed. Otherwise the twain were dressed identically in ceremonial robes of darkest red, belted with broad leather girdles of black; they wore no weapons nor were any other ornaments permissible.

As they seated themselves upon the high stools provided, Flindach turned toward the gate nearest Brilla and began to chant. His sonorous voice was answered by a hidden chorus and reechoed by certain of the bands in the courtyard. For the third time the monstrous gong was sounded and as the last echoes faded the body of Quarmal, litter-borne, appeared. It was carried by the six Lankhmar slavegirls and followed by the Mingols; this small band was all that remained of the many who had slept in the bed of Quarmal.

But where, Brilla asked himself with a heart-bounding start, was Kewissa the Ilthmarix, the old Lord's favorite? Brilla had ordered the marshaling of the girls himself. She could not—

Slowly through a lane of prostrate bodies the litter progressed toward the pyre. The carcass of Quarmal was propped in a sitting posture, and it swayed in a manner horribly suggestive of life as the slavewomen staggered under their unaccustomed load. He was garbed in robes of purple silk and his brow bore the golden bands of Quarmall's Lord. Those lean hands, once so active in the practice of necromancy and incantations, were folded stiffly over the Grammarie which had been his bible during life. On his wrist, hooded and chained, was a great gyrfalcon, and at the feet of its dead master lay his favorite coursing leopard, quiet in the quietness of death. Even as was the falcon hooded, so with wax-like lids were the once awesome eyes of Quarmal covered; those eyes which had seen so much of death were now forever dead.

Although Brilla's mind was still agitated about Kewissa, he spoke a word of encouragement to the other girls as they passed, and one of them flung him a wistful smile; they all knew it was an honor to accompany their master into the future, but none of them desired it particularly; however there was little they could do about it except follow directions. Brilla felt sorry for them all; they were so young, had such luscious bodies and were capable of giving so much pleasure to a man, for he had trained them well. But custom must be fulfilled. Yet how then had Kewissa—? Brilla shut off that speculation.

The litter moved on up the ramp. The chanting grew in volume and tempo as the top of the pyre was reached, and the rays of the sun, now shining full onto the dead countenance of Quarmal, as the litter turned toward it, reflected from the bright hair and white skin of the Lankhmar slavegirls, who had with their companions thrown themselves at the feet of Quarmal.

Suddenly Flindach dropped his arms and there was silence, a complete and total silence startling in its contrast to the measured chant and clashing gongs.

Gwaay and Hasjarl sat motionless, staring intently at the figure that had once been the Lord of Quarmall.

Flindach again raised his arms and from the gate opposite to that from whence had come the body of Quarmal, there leaped eight men. Each bore a flambeau and was naked but for a purple cowl which obscured his face. To the accompaniment of harsh gong notes they ran swiftly to the pyre, two on each side and, thrusting their torches into the prepared wood, cast themselves over the flames they created and clambering up the pyramid embraced the slavegirls wantonly.

Almost at once the flames ate into the resinous and oil-impregnated wood. For a moment through the thick smoke the interlocking writhing forms of the slaves could be perceived, and the lean figure of dead Quarmal staring through closed lids directly into the face of the sun. Then, incensed by the heat and acrid fumes, the great falcon screamed in vicious anger and wing-flapping rose from the wrist of its master. The chains held fast; but all could see the arm of Quarmal lifted high in a gesture of sublime dismissal before the smoke obscured. The chanting reached crescendo and abruptly ended as Flindach gave the sign that the rites were finished.

As the eager flames swiftly consumed the pyre and the burden it bore, Hasjarl broke the silence which custom had enjoined. He turned toward Gwaay, fingering the knuckly knob of his scepter and with an evil grin he spoke.

'Ha! Gwaay, it would have been a merry thing to have seen you leching in the flames. Almost as merry as to see our sire gesticulating after death. Go quickly, Brother! There's yet a chance to immolate yourself and so win fame and immortality.' And he giggled, slobbering.

Gwaay had just made an unapparent sign to a page nearby and the lad was hurrying away. The young Lord of the Lower Levels was in no manner amused by his brother's ill-timed jesting, but with a smile and shrug he replied sarcastically, 'I choose to seek death in less painful paths. Yet the idea is a good one; I'll treasure it.' Then suddenly in a deeper voice: 'It had been better that we were both stillborn than to fritter our lives away in futile hatreds. I'll overlook your dream-dust and your poppy hurricanes, and e'en your noisome sorceries, and make a pact with you, O Hasjarl! By the somber gods who rule under Quarmall's Hill and by the Worm which is my sign I swear that from my hand your life is sacrosanct; with neither spells nor steel nor venoms will I slay thee!' Gwaay rose to his feet as he finished and looked directly at Hasjarl.

Taken unaware, Hasjarl for a second sat in silence; a puzzled expression crossed his face; then a sneer distorted his thin lips and he spat at Gwaay:

'So! You fear me more even than I thought. Aye! And rightly so! Yet the blood of yon old cinder runs in both our bodies, and there is a tender spot within me for my brother. Yes, I'll pact with thee, Gwaay! By the Elder Ones who swim in lightless deeps and by the Fist that is my token, I'll swear your life is sacrosanct – until I crush it out!' And with a final evil titter Hasjarl, like a malformed stoat, slid from stool and out of sight.

Gwaay stood quietly listening, gazing at the space where Hasjarl had sat; then, sure his brother was well gone, he slapped his thighs mightily and, convulsed with silent laughter, gasped to no one in particular, 'Even the wiliest hares are caught in simple snares,' and still smiling he turned to watch the dancing flames.

Slowly the variegated groups were herded into the passageways whence they had come and the courtyard was cleared once again, except for those slaves and priests whose duties kept them there.

Gwaay remained watching for a time, then he too slipped off the balcony into the inner rooms. And a faint smile yet clung to his mouth corners as if some jest were lingering in his mind pleasantly.

' . . . And by the blood of that one whom it is death to look upon . . .'

So sonorously invoked the Mouser, as with eyes closed and arms outstretched he cast the rune given him by Sheelba of the Eyeless Face which would destroy all sorcerers of less than First Rank of an undetermined distance around the casting point – surely for a few miles, one might hope, so smiting Hasjarl's warlocks to dust.

Whether his Great Spell worked or not – and in his inmost heart he strongly mistrusted that it would – the Mouser was very pleased with the performance he was giving. He doubted Sheelba himself could have done better. What magnificent deep chest tones! – even Fafhrd had never heard him declaim so.

He wished he could open his eyes for just a moment to note

the effect his performance was having on Gwaay's magicians – they'd be staring open-mouthed for all their supercilious boasting, he was sure – but on this point Sheelba's instructions had been adamant: eyes tightly shut while the last sentences of the rune were being recited and the great forbidden words spoken; even the tiniest blink would nullify the Great Spell. Evidently magicians were supposed to be without vanity or curiosity – what a bore!

Of a sudden in the dark of his head, he felt contact with another and a larger darkness, a malefic and puissant darkness, of which light itself is only the absence. He shivered. His hair stirred. Cold sweat prickled his face. He almost stuttered midway through the word 'slewerisophnak'. But concentrating his will, he finished without flaw.

When the last echoing notes of his voice had ceased to rebound between the domed ceiling and floor, the Mouser slit open one eye and glanced surreptitiously around him.

One glance and the other eye flew open to fullness. He was too surprised to speak.

And whom he would have spoken to, had he not been too surprised, was also a question.

The long table at the foot of which he stood was empty of occupants. Where but moments before had sat eleven of the very greatest magicians of Quarmall – sorcerers of the First Rank, each had sworn on his black Grammarie – was only space.

The Mouser called softly. It was possible that these provincial fellows had been frightened at the majesty of his dark Lankh-marian delivery and had crawled under the table. But there was no answer.

He spoke louder. Only the ceaseless groan of the fans could be sensed, though hardly more noticeable after four days hearing them than the coursing of his blood. With a shrug the Mouser relaxed into his chair. He murmured to himself, 'If those slick-faced old fools run off, what next? Suppose all Gwaay's henchmen flee?'

As he began to plan out in his mind what strategy of airy nothing to adopt if that should come to pass, he glanced somberly at the wide high-backed chair nearest his place, where had sat the boldest-seeming of Gwaay's arch-magi. There was only a loosely crumpled white loincloth – but in it was what gave the Mouser pause. A small pile of flocculent gray dust was all.

The Mouser whistled softly between his teeth and raised himself the better to see the rest of the seats. On each of them was the same: a clean loincloth, somewhat crumpled as if it had been worn for a little while, and within the cloth that small heap of grayish powder.

At the other end of the long table, one of the black counters, which had been standing on its edge, slowly rolled off the board of the thought-game and struck the floor with a tiny *tick*. It sounded to the Mouser rather like the last noise in the world.

Very quietly he stood up and silently walked in his ratskin moccasins to the nearest archway, across which he had drawn thick curtains for the Great Spell. He was wondering just what the range of the spell had been, *where* it had stopped, if it had stopped at all. Suppose, for instance, that Sheelba had underestimated its power and it disintegrated not only sorcerers, but . . .

He paused in front of the curtains and gave one last over-the-shoulder glance. Then he shrugged, adjusted his sword-belt, and, grinning far more bravely than he felt, said to no one in particular, 'But they assured me that they were the *very* greatest sorcerers.'

As he reached toward the curtain, heavy with embroidery, it wavered and shook. He froze, his heart leaping wildly. Then the curtains parted a little and there was thrust in the saucy face of Ivivis, wide-eyed with excited curiosity.

'Did your Great Spell work, Mouser?' she asked him breathlessly.

He let out his own breath in a sigh of relief. 'You survived it, at all events,' he said and reaching out pulled her against him. Her slim body pressing his felt very good. True, the presence of almost any living being would have been welcome to the Mouser at this moment, but that it should be Ivivis was a bonus he could not help but appreciate.

'Dearest,' he said sincerely, 'I was feeling that I was perchance the last man on Earth. But now—'

'And acting as if I were the last girl, lost a year,' she retorted tartly. 'This is neither the place nor the time for amorous consolations and intimate pleasantries,' she continued, half mistaking his motives and pushing back from him.

'Did you slay Hasjarl's wizards?' she demanded, gazing up with some awe into his eyes.

'I slew *some* sorcerers,' the Mouser admitted judiciously. 'Just how many is a moot question.'

'Where are Gwaay's?' she asked, looking past the Mouser at the empty chairs. 'Did he take them all with him?'

'Isn't Gwaay back from his father's funeral yet?' the Mouser countered, evading her question, but as she continued to look into his eyes, he added lightly, 'His sorcerers are in some congenial spot – I hope.'

Ivivis looked at him queerly, pushed past, hurried to the long table, and gazed up and down the chair seats.

'Oh, *Mouser!*' she said reprovingly, but there was real awe in the gaze she shot him.

He shrugged. 'They swore to me they were of First Rank,' he defended himself.

'Not even a fingerbone or skullshard left,' Ivivis said solemnly, peering closely at the nearest tiny gray dust pile and shaking her head.

'Not even a gallstone,' the Mouser echoed harshly. 'My rune was dire.'

'Not even a tooth,' Ivivis re-echoed, rubbing curiously if somewhat callously through the pile. 'Nothing to send their mothers.'

'Their mothers can have their diapers to fold away with their baby ones,' the Mouser said irascibly though somewhat uncomfortably. 'Oh, Ivivis, sorcerers don't have mothers!'

'But what happens to our Lord Gwaay now his protectors are gone?' Ivivis demanded more practically. 'You saw how Hasjarl's sendings struck him last night when they but dozed. And if anything happens to Gwaay, then what happens to us?'

Again the Mouser shrugged. 'If my rune reached Hasjarl's

twenty-four wizards and blasted them too, then no harm's been done – except to sorcerers, and they all take their chances, sign their death warrants when they speak their first spells – 'tis a dangerous trade.

'In fact,' he went on with argumentative enthusiasm, 'we've gained. Twenty-four enemies slain at cost of but a dozen – no, eleven total casualties on our side – why, that's a bargain any warlord would jump at! Then with the sorcerers all out of the way – except for the Brothers themselves, and Flindach – that warty blotchy one is someone to be reckoned with! – I'll meet and slay this champion of Hasjarl's and we'll carry all before us. And if . . .'

His voice trailed off. It had occurred to him to wonder why he himself hadn't been blasted by his own spell. He had never suspected, until now, that he might be a sorcerer of the First Rank – having despite a youthful training in country-sorceries only dabbled in magic since. Perhaps some metaphysical trick or logical fallacy was involved . . . If a sorcerer casts a rune that midway of the casting blasts *all* sorcerers, *provided the casting be finished*, then does he blast himself, or . . . ? Or perhaps indeed, the Mouser began to think boastfully, he was unknown to himself a magus of the First Rank, or even higher, or—

In the silence of his thinking, he and Ivivis became aware of approaching footsteps, first a multitudinous patter but swiftly a tumult. The gray-clad man and the slavegirl had hardly time to exchange a questioning apprehensive look when there burst through the draperies, tearing them down, eight or nine of Gwaay's chiefest henchmen, their faces deathpale, their eyes staring like madmen's. They raced across the chamber and out the opposite archway almost before the Mouser could recover from where he'd dodged out of their way.

But that was not the end of the footsteps. There was a last pair coming down the black corridor and at a strange unequal gallop, like a cripple sprinting, and with a squushy slap at each tread. The Mouser crossed quickly to Ivivis and put an arm around her. He did not want to be standing alone at this moment, either.

Ivivis said, 'If your Great Spell missed Hasjarl's sorcerers, and

their disease-spells struck through to Gwaay, now unde-
fended . . .'

Her whisper trailed off fearfully as a monstrous figure clad in
dark scarlet robes lurched by swift convulsive stages into view.
At first the Mouser thought it must be Hasjarl of the Mismated
Arms, from what he'd heard of that one. Then he saw that its
neck was collared by gray fungus, its right check crimson, its left
black, its eyes dripping green ichor and its nose spattering clear
drops. As the loathy creature took a last great stride into the
chamber, its left leg went boneless like a pillar of jelly and its
right leg, striking down stiffly though with a heel splash, broke
in midshin and the jagged bones thrust through the flesh. Its
yellow-crusted, red-cracked scurfy hands snatched futilely at the
air for support and its right arm brushing its head carried away
half the hair on that side.

Ivivis began to mewl and yelp faintly with horror and she
clung to the Mouser, who himself felt as if a nightmare were
lifting its hooves to trample him.

In such manner did Prince Gwaay, Lord of the Lower Levels
of Quarmall, come home from his father's funeral, falling
in a stenchful, scabrous, ichorous heap upon the torn-down
richly embroidered curtains immediately beneath the pristine-
handsome silver bust of himself in the niche above the arch.

The funeral pyre smoldered for a long time, but of all the
inhabitants in that huge and ramified castle-kingdom Brilla the
High Eunuch was the only one who watched it out. Then he
collected a few representative pinches of ashes to preserve; he
kept them with some dim idea that they might perhaps act as
some protection, now that the living protector was forever gone.

Yet the fluffy-gritty gray tokens did not much cheer Brilla as
he wandered desolately into the inner rooms. He was troubled
and eunuch-like be-twittered by thoughts of the war between
brothers that must now ensue before Quarmall had again a
single master. Oh, what a tragedy that Lord Quarmal should
have been snatched so suddenly by the Fates with no chance to
make arrangement for the succession! – though what that
arrangement might have been, considering custom's strictures

in Quarmall, Brilla could not say. Still, Quarmal had always seemed able to achieve the impossible.

Brilla was troubled too, and rather more acutely, by his guilty knowledge that Quarmal's concubine Kewissa had evaded the flames. He might be blamed for that, though he could not see where he had omitted any customary precaution. And burning would have been small pain indeed to what the poor girl must suffer now for her transgression. He rather hoped she had slain herself by knife or poison, though that would doom her spirit to eternal wandering in the winds between the stars that make them twinkle.

Brilla realized his steps were taking him to the harem and he halted a-quake. He might well find Kewissa there and he did not want to be the one to turn her in.

Yet if he stayed in this central section of the Keep, he would momentarily run into Flindach and he knew he would hold back nothing when gimleted by that arch-sorcerer's stern witchy gaze. He would have to remind him of Kewissa's defection.

So Brilla bethought him of an errand that would take him to the nethermost sections of the Keep, just above Hasjarl's realm. There was a storeroom there, his responsibility, which he had not inventoried for a month. Brilla did not like the Dark Levels of Quarmall – it was his pride that he was one of the elite who worked in or at least near sunlight – but now, by reason of his anxieties, the Dark Levels began to seem attractive.

This decision made, Brilla felt slightly cheered. He set off at once, moving quite swiftly, with a eunuch's peculiar energy, despite his elephantine bulk.

He reached the storeroom without incident. When he had kindled a torch there, the first thing he saw was a small girl-like woman cowering among the bales of drapery. She wore a lustrous loose yellow robe and had the winsome triangular face, moss-green hair, and bright blue eyes of an Ilthmarix.

'Kewissa,' he whispered shudderingly yet with motherly warmth. 'Sweet chick . . .'

She ran to him. 'Oh, Brilla, I'm so frightened,' she cried softly as she pressed against his paunch and hid herself in his great-sleeved arms.

'I know, I know,' he murmured, making little clucking noises as he smoothed her hair and petted her. 'You were always frightened of flames, I remember now. Never mind, Quarmal will forgive when you meet beyond the stars. Look you, little duck, it's a great risk I run, but because you were the old Lord's favorite I cherish you dearly. I carry a painless poison . . . only a few drops on the tongue, then darkness and the windy gulfs . . . A long leap, true, but better far than what Flindach must order when he discovers—'

She pushed back from him. 'It was Flindach who commanded me not to follow My Lord to his last hearth!' she revealed wide-eyed and reproachful. 'He told me the stars directed otherwise and also that this was Quarmal's dying wish. I doubted and feared Flindach – he with face so hideous and eyes so horridly like My Dear Lord's – yet could not but obey . . . with some small thankfulness, I must confess, dear Brilla.'

'But what reason earthly or unearthly . . . ?' Brilla stammered, his mind a-whirl.

Kewissa looked to either side. Then, 'I bear Quarmal's quickening seed,' she whispered.

For a bit this only increased Brilla's confusion. How could Quarmal have hoped to get a concubine's child accepted as Lord of All when there were two grown legitimate heirs? Or cared so little for the land's security as to leave alive even an unborn bastard? Then it occurred to him – and his heart shook at the thought – that Flindach might be seeking to seize supreme power, using Kewissa's babe and an invented death wish of Quarmal as his pretext along with those Quarmal-eyes of his. Palace revolutions were not entirely unknown in Quarmall. Indeed, there was a legend that the present line had generations ago clambered dagger-fisted to power by that route, though it was death to repeat the legend.

Kewissa continued, 'I stayed hidden in the harem. Flindach said I'd be safe. But then Hasjarl's henchmen came searching in Flindach's absence and in defiance of all customs and decencies. I fled here.'

This continued to make a dreadful sort of sense, Brilla thought. If Hasjarl suspected Flindach's impious snatch at power, he would instinctively strike at him, turning the fraternal strife into a three-sided one involving even – woe of woes! – the sunlit apex of Quarmall, which until this moment had seemed so safe from war's alarums . . .

At that very instant, as if Brilla's fears had conjured up their fruition, the door of the storeroom opened wide and there loomed in it an uncouth man who seemed the very embodiment of battle's barbarous horrors. He was so tall his head brushed the lintel; his face was handsome yet stern and searching-eyed; his red-gold hair hung tangledly to his shoulders; his garment was a bronze-studded wolfskin tunic; longsword and massy short-handled ax swung from his belt, and on the longest finger of his right hand Brilla's gaze – trained to miss no detail of decor and now fear-sharpened – noted a ring with Hasjarl's clenched-fist sigil.

The eunuch and the girl huddled against each other, quivering.

Having assured himself that these two were all he faced, the newcomer's countenance broke into a smile that might have been reassuring on a smaller man or one less fiercely accoutered. Then Fafhrd said, 'Greetings, Grandfather. I require only that you and your chick help me find the sunlight and the stables of this benighted realm. Come, we'll plot it out so you may satisfy me with least danger to yourselves.' And he swiftly stepped toward them, silently for all his size, his gaze returning with interest to Kewissa as he noted she was not child but woman.

Kewissa felt that and although her heart was a-flutter, piped up bravely, 'You dare not rape me! I'm with child by a dead man!'

Fafhrd's smile soured somewhat. Perhaps, he told himself, he should feel complimented that girls started thinking about rape the instant they saw him, still he was a little irked. Did they deem him incapable of civilized seduction because he wore furs and was no dwarf? Oh well, they quickly learned. But what a horrid way to try to daunt him!

Meanwhile tubby-fat Grandfather, who Fafhrd now realized was hardly equipped to be that or father either, said fearful-mincing, 'She speaks only the truth, oh Captain. But I will be o'erjoyed to aid you in any—'

736

There were rapid steps in the passage and the harsh slither of steel against stone. Fafhrd turned like a tiger. Two guards in the dark-linked hauberks of Hasjarl's guards were pressing into the room. The fresh-drawn sword of one had scraped the door-side, while a third behind them cried sharply now. 'Take the Northern turncoat! Slay him if he shows fight. I'll secure old Quarmal's concubine.'

The two guards started to run at Fafhrd, but he, counterfeiting even more the tiger, sprang at them twice as suddenly. Graywand coming out of his scabbard swept sideways up, fending off the sword of the foremost even as Fafhrd's foot came crushing down on that one's instep. Then Graywand's hilt crashed backhand into his jaw, so that he lurched against his fellow. Meanwhile Fafhrd's ax had come into his left hand and at close quarters he stroked it into their brains, then shouldering them off as they fell, he drew back the ax and cast it at the third, so that it lodged in his forehead between the eyes as he turned to see what was amiss, and he dropped down dead.

But the footsteps of a fourth and perhaps a fifth could be heard racing away. Fafhrd sprang toward the door with a growl, stopped with a foot-stamp and returned as swiftly, stabbing a bloody finger at Kewissa cowering into the great bulk of blanching Brilla.

'Old Quarmal's girl? With child by him?' he rapped out and when she nodded rapidly, swallowing hard, he continued, 'Then you come with me. Now! The castrado too.'

He sheathed Graywand, wrenched his ax from the sergeant's skull, grabbed Kewissa by the upper arm and strode toward the door with a devilish snarling head-wave to Brilla to follow.

Kewissa cried, 'Oh mercy, sir! You'll make me lose the child.'

Brilla obeyed, yet twittered as he did, 'Kind Captain, we'll be no use to you, only encumber you in your—'

Fafhrd, turning suddenly again, spared him one rapid speech, shaking the bloody ax for emphasis: 'If you think I don't understand the bargaining value or hostage-worth of even an unborn claimant to a throne, then your skull is as empty of brains as your loins are of seed – and I doubt that's the case. As for you, girl,' he added harshly to Kewissa, 'if there's anything but bleat under your green ringlets, you know you're safer with a stranger than with Hasjarl's hellions and that better your child miscarry than fall into their hands. Come, I'll carry you.' He swept her up. 'Follow, eunuch; work those great thighs of yours if you love living.'

And he made off down the corridor, Brilla trotting ponderously after and wisely taking great gasping breaths in anticipation of exertions to come. Kewissa laid her arms around Fafhrd's neck and glanced up at him with qualified admiration. He himself now gave vent to two remarks which he'd evidently been saving for an unoccupied moment.

The first, bitterly sarcastic: ' . . . if he shows fight!'

The second, self-angry: 'Those cursed fans must be deafening me, that I didn't hear 'em coming!'

Forty loping paces down the corridor he passed a ramp leading upward and turned toward a narrower darker corridor.

From just behind, Brilla called softly yet rapidly, penurious of breath. 'That ramp led to the stables. Where are you taking us, My Captain?'

'Down!' Fafhrd retorted without pausing in his lope. 'Don't panic, I've a hidey-hole for the two of you – and even a girl-mate for little Prince-mother Greenilocks here.' Then to Kewissa, gruffly, 'You're not the only girl in Quarmall who wants rescuing, nor yet the dearest.'

The Mouser, steeling himself for it, knelt and surveyed the noisome heap that was Prince Gwaay. The stench was abominably strong despite the perfumes the Mouser had sprinkled and the incense he had burned but an hour ago. The Mouser had covered with silken sheets and fur robes all the loathsomeness of Gwaay except for his plagues-stricken pillowed-up face. The sole feature of his face that had escaped obvious extreme contagion was the narrow handsome nose, from the end of which there dripped clear fluid, drop by slow drop, like the ticking of a water clock, while from below the nose proceeded a continual small nasty retching which was the only reasonably sure sign that Gwaay was not wholly moribund. For a while

Gwaay had made faint straining moanings like the whispers of a mute, but now even those had ceased.

The Mouser reflected that it was very difficult indeed to serve a master who could neither speak, write, nor gesticulate – particularly when fighting enemies who now began to seem neither dull nor contemptible. By all counts Gwaay should have died hours since. Presumably only his steely sorcerous will and consuming hatred of Hasjarl kept his spirit from fleeing the horrid torment that housed it.

The Mouser rose and turned with a questioning shrug toward Ivivis, who sat now at the long table hemming up two hooded black voluminous sorcerer's robes, which she had cut down at the Mouser's direction to fit him and herself. The Mouser had thought that since he now seemed to be Gwaay's sole remaining sorcerer as well as champion, he should be prepared to appear dressed as the former and to boast at least one acolyte.

In answer to the shrug, Ivivis merely wrinkled her nostrils, pinched them with two dainty fingertips, and shrugged back. True, the Mouser thought, the stench was growing stronger despite all his attempts to mask it. He stepped to the table and poured himself a half cup of the thick blood-red wine, which he'd begun unwillingly to relish a little, although he'd learned it was indeed fermented from scarlet toadstools. He took a small swallow and summed up:

'Here's a pretty witch's kettle of problems. Gwaay's sorcerers blasted – all right, yes, by me, I admit it. His henchmen and soldiers fled – to the lowest loathy dank dim tunnels, I think, or else gone over to Hasjarl. His girls vanished save for you. Even his doctors fearful to come nigh him – the one I dragged here fainting dead away. His slaves useless with dread – only the tread-beasts at the fans keep their heads, and they because they haven't any! No answer to our message to Flindach suggesting that we league against Hasjarl. No page to send another message by – and not even a single picket to warn us if Hasjarl assaults.'

'You could go over to Hasjarl yourself,' Ivivis pointed out.

The Mouser considered that. 'No,' he decided, 'there's something too fascinating about a forlorn hope like this. I've always wanted to command one. And it's only fun to betray the wealthy and victorious. Yet what strategy can I employ without even a skeleton army?'

Ivivis frowned. 'Gwaay used to say that just as sword-war is but another means of carrying out diplomacy, so sorcery is but another means of carrying out sword-war. Spell-war. So you could try your Great Spell again,' she concluded without vast conviction.

'Not I!' the Mouser repudiated. 'It never touched Hasjarl's twenty-four or it would have stopped their disease-spells against Gwaay. Either they are of First Rank or else I'm doing the spell backwards – in which case the tunnels would probably collapse on me if I tried it again.'

'Then use a different spell,' Ivivis suggested brightly. 'Raise an army of veritable skeletons. Drive Hasjarl mad, or put a hex on him so he stubs his toe at every step. Or turn his soldiers' swords to cheese. Or vanish their bones. Or transmew all his maids to cats and set their tails afire. Or—'

'I'm sorry, Ivivis,' the Mouser interposed hurriedly to her mounting enthusiasm. 'I would not confess this to another, but . . . that was my only spell. We must depend on wit and weapons alone. Again I ask you, Ivivis, what strategy does a general employ when his left is o'erwhelmed, his right takes flight, and his center is ten times decimated?'

A slight sweet sound like a silver bell chinked once, or a silver string plucked high in the harp, interrupted him. Although so faint, it seemed for a moment to fill the chamber with auditory light. The Mouser and Ivivis gazed around wonderingly and then at the same moment looked up at the silver mask of Gwaay in the niche above the arch before which Gwaay's mortal remains festered silken-wrapped.

The shimmering metal lips of the statua smiled and parted – so far as one might tell in the gloom – and faintly there came Gwaay's brightest voice, saying: 'Your answer: he attacks!'

The Mouser blinked. Ivivis dropped her needle. The statua continued, its eyes seeming to twinkle, 'Greetings, hostless captain mine! Greetings, dear girl. I'm sorry my stink offends you – yes, yes, Ivivis, I've observed you pinching your nose at my poor carcass this last hour through – but then the world teems with loathiness. Is that not a black death-adder gliding now through the black robe you stitch?'

With a gasp of horror Ivivis sprang cat-swift up and aside from the material and brushed frantically at her legs. The statua gave a naturally silver laugh, then quickly said, 'Your pardon, gentle girl, I did but jest. My spirits are too high, too high – perchance because my body is so low. Plotting will curb my feyness. Hist now, hist!'

In Hasjarl's Hall of Sorcery his four-and-twenty wizards stared desperately at a huge magic screen set up parallel to their long table, trying with all their might to make the picture on it come clear. Hasjarl himself, dire in his dark red funeral robes, gazing alternately with open eyes and through the grommeted holes in his upper lids, as if that perchance might make the picture sharper, stutteringly berated them for their clumsiness and at intervals conferred staccato with his military.

The screen was dark gray, the picture appearing on it in pale green witch-light. It stood twelve feet high and eighteen feet long. Each wizard was responsible for a particular square yard of it, projecting on it his share of the clairvoyant picture.

This picture was of Gwaay's Hall of Sorcery, but the best effect achieved so far was a generally blurred image showing the table, the empty chairs, a low mound on the floor, a high point of silver light, and two figures moving about – these last mere salamander-like blobs with arms and legs attached, so that not even the sex could be determined, if indeed they were human at all or even male or female.

Sometimes a yard of the picture would come clear as a flower-bed on a bright day, but it would always be a yard with neither of the figures in it or anything of more interest than an empty chair. Then Hasjarl would bark sudden for the other wizards to do likewise, or for the successful wizard to trade squares with someone whose square had a figure in it, and the picture would invariably get worse and Hasjarl would screech and spray spittle, and then the picture would go completely bad, swimming everywhere or with squares all jumbled and overlapping like an unsolved puzzle, and the twenty-four sorcerers would have to count off squares and start over again while Hasjarl disciplined them with fearful threats.

Interpretations of the picture by Hasjarl and his aides differed considerably. The absence of Gwaay's sorcerers seemed to be a good thing, until someone suggested they might have been sent to infiltrate Hasjarl's Upper Levels for a close-range thaumaturgic attack. One lieutenant got fearfully tongue-lashed for suggesting the two blob-figures might be demons seen unblurred in their true guise – though even after Hasjarl had discharged his anger, he seemed a little frightened by the idea. The hopeful notion that all Gwaay's sorcerers had been wiped out was rejected when it was ascertained that no sorcerous spells had been directed at them recently by Hasjarl or any of his wizards.

One of the blob-figures now left the picture entirely and the point of silvery light faded. This touched off further speculation, which was interrupted by the entry of several of Hasjarl's torturers looking rather battered and a dozen of his guards. The guards were surrounding – with naked swords aimed at his chest and back – the figure of an unarmed man in a wolfskin tunic with arms bound tight behind him. He was masked with a red silk eye-holed sack pulled down over his head and hair, and a black robe trailed behind him.

'We've taken the Northerner, Lord Hasjarl!' the leader of the dozen guards reported joyously. 'We cornered him in your torture room. He disguised himself as one of those and tried to lie his way through our lines, humped and going on his knees, but his height still betrayed him.'

'Good, Yissim – I'll reward you,' Hasjarl approved. 'But what of my father's treacherous concubine and the great castrado who were with him when he slew three of your fellows?'

'They were still with him when we glimpsed him near Gwaay's realm and gave chase. We lost 'em when he doubled back to the torture room, but the hunt goes on.'

'Find 'em, you were best,' Hasjarl ordered grimly, 'or the sweets of my reward will be soured entire by the pains of my displeasure.' Then to Fafhrd, 'So, traitor! Now I will play with you the wrist game – aye, and a hundred others too, until you are wearied of sport.'

Fafhrd answered loudly and clearly through his red mask, 'I'm no traitor, Hasjarl. I was only tired of your twitching and of your torturing of girls.'

There came a sibilant cry from the sorcerers. Turning, Hasjarl saw that one of them had made the low mound on the floor come clear, so that it was clearly seen as a stricken man covered to his pillowed head.

'Closer!' Hasjarl cried – all eagerness, no threat – and perhaps because they were neither startled nor threatened, each wizard did his work perfectly, so that there came greenpale onto the screen Gwaay's face, wide as an oxcart and team, the plagues visible by the huge pustules and crustings and fungoid growths if not by their colors, the eyes like great vats stewing with ichor, the mouth a quaking boghole, while each drop that fell from the nose-tip looked a gallon.

Hasjarl cried thickly, like a man choking with strong drink, 'Joy, oh joy! My heart will break!'

The screen went black, the room dead silent, and into it from the further archway there came gliding noiselessly through the air a tiny bone-gray shape. It soared on unflapping wings like a hawk searching its prey, high above the swords that struck at it. Then turning in a smooth silent curve, it swooped straight at Hasjarl and, evading his hands that snatched at it too late, tapped him on the breast and fell to the floor at his feet.

It was a dart folded from parchment on which lines of characters showed at angles. Nothing more deadly than that.

Hasjarl snatched it up, pulled it crackingly open, and read aloud:

'Dear Brother. Let us meet on the instant in the Ghost Hall to settle the succession. Bring your four-and-twenty sorcerers. I'll bring one. Bring your champion. I'll bring mine. Bring your henchmen and guards. Bring yourself. I'll be brought. Or perhaps you'd prefer to spend the evening torturing girls. Signed (by direction) Gwaay.'

Hasjarl crumpled the parchment in his fist and peering over it thoughtful-evil, rapped out staccato: 'We'll go! He means to play on my brotherly pity – that would be sweet. Or else to trap us, but I'll out-trick him!'

Fafhrd called boldly, 'You may be able to best your death-rotten brother, oh Hasjarl, but what of his champion? – cunninger than Zobold, more battle-fierce than a rogue elephant! Such a one one can cut through your cheesy guards as easy as I bested 'em one-to-five in the Keep, and be at your noisy throat! You'll need me!'

Hasjarl thought for a heartbeat, then turning toward Fafhrd said, 'I'm not mind-proud. I'll take advice from a dead dog. Bring him with us. Keep him bound, but bring his weapons.'

Along a wide low tunnel that trended slowly upward and was lit by wall-set torches flaming no bluer-brighter than marsh gas and as distant-seeming each from the next as coastal beacons, the Mouser striding swiftly yet most warily led a strange short cortege.

He wore a black robe with peaked black hood that thrown forward would hide his face entirely. Under it he carried at his belt his sword and dagger and also a skin of the blood-red toadstool wine, but in his fingers he bore a thin black wand tipped with a silver star, to remind him that his primary current role was Sorcerer Extraordinary to Gwaay.

Behind him trotted two-abreast four of the great-legged tiny-headed tread-slaves, looking almost like dark walking cones, especially when silhouetted by a torch just passed. They bore between them, each clutching a pole-end in both dwarfish hands, a litter of bloodwood and ebony ornately carved, whereon rested mattressed and covered by furs and silks and richly embriodered fabrics the stenchful, helpless flesh and dauntless spirit of the young Lord of the Lower Levels.

Close behind Gwaay's litter followed what seemed a slightly smaller version of the Mouser. It was Ivivis, masquerading as his acolyte. She held a fold of her hood as a sort of windbreak in front of her mouth and nose, and frequently she sniffed a handkerchief steeped in spirits of camphor and ammonia. Under her arm she carried a silver gong in a woolen sack and a strange thin wooden mask in another.

The splayed calloused feet of the tread-slaves struck the stony floor with a faint *hrush*, over which came at long regular intervals Gwaay's gargly retching. Other sound there was none.

The walls and low ceiling teemed with pictures, mostly in yellow ocher, of demons, strange beasts, bat-winged girls, and other infernal beauties. Their slow looming and fading was nightmarish, yet gently so. All in all, it was one of the pleasantest journeys the Mouser could recall, equal of a trip he had once made by moonlight across the roofs of Lankhmar to hang a wilting wreath on a forgotten tower-top statue of the God of Thieves, and light a small blue fire of brandy to him.

'Attack!' he murmured humorously and wholly to himself. 'Forward, my big-foot phalanx! Forward, my terror-striking war-cat! Forward, my dainty rearguard! Forward, my host!'

Brilla and Kewissa and Friska sat quiet as mice in the Ghost Hall beside the dried-up fountain pool yet near the open door of the chamber that was their appointed hiding place. The girls were whispering together, head leaned to head, yet that was no noisier than the squeaking of mice, nor was the occasional high sigh Brilla let slip.

Beyond the fountain was the great half open door through which the sole faint light came questing and through which Fafhrd had brought them before doubling back to draw off the pursuit. Some of the cobwebs stretching across it had been torn away by Brilla's ponderous passage.

Taking that door and the one to their hiding place as two opposite corners of the room, the two remaining opposite corners were occupied by a wide black archway and a narrow one, each opening on a large section of stony floor raised three steps above the still larger floor section around the dried-up pool. Elsewhere in the wall were many small doors, all shut, doubtless leading to onetime bed chambers. Over all hung the pale mortared great black slabs of the shallowly domed ceiling. So much their eyes, long accustomed to the darkness, could readily distinguish.

Brilla, who recognized that this place had once housed a harem, was musing melancholically that now it had become a kind of tiniest harem again, with eunuch – himself – and pregnant girl – Kewissa – gossiping with restless high-spirited girl – Friska – who was fretting for the safety of her tall barbarian lover. Old times! He wanted to sweep up a bit and find some draperies, even if rotten ones, to hang and spread, but Friska had pointed out that they mustn't leave clues to their presence.

There came a faint sound through the great door. The girls quit their whispering and Brilla his sighs and musings, and they listened with all their beings. Then more noises came – footsteps and the knock of a sheathed sword against the wall of a tunnel – and they sprang silently up and scurried back into their hiding chamber and silently shut the door behind them, and the Ghost Hall was briefly alone with its ghosts once more.

A helmeted guard in the hauberk of Hasjarl's guards appeared in the great door and stood peering about with arrow nocked to the taut string of a short bow he held crosswise. Then he motioned with his shoulder and came sneaking in followed by three of his fellows and by four slaves holding aloft yellowly flaming torches, which cast the monstrous shadows of the guardsmen across the dusty floor and the shadows of their heads against the curving far wall, as they spied about for signs of trap or ambush.

Some bats swooped about and fled the torchlight through the archways.

The first guardsman whistled then down the corridor behind him and waved an arm and there came two parties of slaves, who applied themselves each to a side of the great door, so that it groaned and creaked loudly at its hinges, and they pushed it open wide, though one of them leaped convulsively as a spider fell on him from the disturbed cobwebs, or he thought it did.

Then more guards came, each with a torch-slave, and moved about calling softly back and forth, and tried all the shut doors and peered long and suspiciously into the black spaces beyond the narrow archway and the wide one, but all returned quite swiftly to form a protective semicircle around the great door and enclosing most of the floor space of the central section of the Ghost Hall.

Then into that shielded space Hasjarl came striding, surrounded by his henchmen and followed at heel by his two dozen
sorcerers closely ranked. With Hasjarl too came Fafhrd, still
arm-bound and wearing his red bag-mask and menaced by the
drawn swords of his guards. More torchslaves came too, so that
the Ghost Hall was flaringly lit around the great door, though
elsewhere a mixture of glare and black shadow.

Since Hasjarl wasn't speaking, no one else was. Not that the
Lord of the Upper Levels was altogether silent – he was
coughing constantly, a hacking bark, and spitting gobbets of
phlegm into a fiery embroidered kerchief. After each small
convulsion he would glare suspiciously around him, drooping
evilly one pierced eyelid to emphasize his wariness.

Then there was a tiny scurrying and one called, 'A rat!'
Another loosed an arrow into the shadows around the pool
where it rasped stone, and Hasjarl demanded loudly why his
ferrets had been forgotten – and his great hounds too, for that
matter, and his owls to protect him against poison-toothed bats
Gwaay might launch at him – and swore to flay the right hands
of the neglectful ones.

It came again, that swift-traveling rattle of tiny claws on
smooth stone, and more arrows were loosed futilely to skitter
across the floor, and guards shifted position nervously, and in
the midst of all that Fafhrd cried, 'Up shields, some of you, and
make walls to either side of Hasjarl! Have you not thought that a
dart, and not a paper one this time, might silently wing from
either archway and drive through your dear Lord's throat and
stop his precious coughing forever?'

Several leaped guiltily to obey that order and Hasjarl did not
wave them away and Fafhrd laughed and remarked, 'Masking a
champion makes him more dreadsome, oh Hasjarl, but tying his
hands behind him is not so apt to impress the enemy – and has
other drawbacks. If there should now come suddenly a-rush that
one wilier than Zobold, weightier than a mad elephant to
tumble and hurl aside your panicky guards—'

'Cut his bonds!' Hasjarl barked and someone began to saw
with a dagger behind Fafhrd's back. 'But don't give him his
sword or ax! Yet hold them ready for him!'

Fafhrd writhed his shoulders and flexed his great forearms and began to massage them and laughed again through his mask.

Hasjarl fumed and then ordered all the shut doors tried once more. Fafhrd readied himself for action as they came to the one behind which Friska and the two other were hidden, for he knew it had no bolt or bar. But it held firm against all shoving. Fafhrd could imagine Brilla's great back braced against it, with the girls perhaps pushing at his stomach, and he smiled under the red silk.

Hasjarl fumed a while longer and cursed his brother for his delay and swore he had intended mercy to his brother's minions and girls, but now no longer. Then one of Hasjarl's henchmen suggested Gwaay's dart-message might have been a ruse to get them out of the way while an attack was launched from below through other tunnels or even by way of the air-shafts, and Hasjarl seized that henchman by the throat and shook him and demanded why, if he had suspected that, he hadn't spoken earlier.

At that moment a gong sounded, high and silver-sweet, and Hasjarl loosed his henchman and looked around wonderingly. Again the silvery gong-note, then through the wider black archway there slowly stepped two monstrous figures each bearing a forward pole of an ornately carved black and red litter.

All of those in the Ghost Hall were familiar with the tread-slaves, but to see them anywhere except on their belts was almost as great and grotesque a wonder as to see them for the first time. It seemed to portend unsettlements of custom and dire upheavals, and so there was much murmuring and some shrinking.

The tread-slaves continued to step ponderously forward and their mates came into view behind them. The four advanced almost to the edge of the raised section of floor and set the litter down and folded their dwarfed arms as well as they could, hooking fingers to fingers across their gigantic chests, and stood motionless.

Then through the same archway there swiftly paced the figure of a rather small sorcerer in black robe and hood that hid his features, and close behind him like his shadow a slightly smaller figure identically clad.

The Black Sorcerer took his stand to one side of the litter and a little ahead of it, his acolyte behind him to his right, and he lifted alongside his cowl a wand tipped with glittering silver and said loudly and impressively, 'I speak for Gwaay, Master of Demons and Lord of All Quarmall! – as we will prove!'

The Mouser was using his deepest thaumaturgic voice, which none but himself had ever heard, except for the occasion on which he had blasted Gwaay's sorcerers – and come to think of it, that had ended with no one else having heard either. He was enjoying himself hugely, marveling greatly at his own audacity.

He paused just long enough, then slowly pointed his wand at the low mound on the litter, threw up his other arm in an imperious gesture, palm forward, and commanded, 'On your knees, vermin, all of you, and do obeisance to your sole rightful ruler, Lord Gwaay, at whose name demons blench!'

A few of the foremost fools actually obeyed him – evidently Hasjarl had cowed them all too well – while most of the others in the front rank goggled apprehensively at the muffled figure in the litter – truly, it was an advantage having Gwaay motionless and supine, looking like Death's horridest self: it made him a more mysterious threat.

Searching over their heads from the cavern of his cowl, the Mouser spotted one he guessed to be Hasjarl's champion – gods, he was a whopper, big as Fafhrd! – and knowledgeable in psychology if that red silk bag-mask were his own idea. The Mouser didn't relish the idea of battling such a one, but with luck it wouldn't come to that.

Then there burst through the ranks of the awed guards, whipping them aside with a short lash, a hunch-shouldered figure in dark scarlet robes – Hasjarl at last! and coming to the fore just as the plot demanded.

Hasjarl's ugliness and frenzy surpassed the Mouser's expectations. The Lord of the Upper Levels drew himself up facing the litter and for a suspenseful moment did naught but twitch, stutter, and spray spittle like the veriest idiot. Then suddenly he got his voice and barked most impressively and surely louder than any of his great hounds:

'By right of death – suffered lately or soon – lately by my father, star-smitten and burned to ash – soon by my impious brother, stricken by my sorceries – and who dare not speak for himself, but must fee charlatans – I, Hasjarl, do proclaim myself sole Lord of Quarmall – and of all within it – demon or man!'

Then Hasjarl started to turn, most likely to order forward some of his guards to seize Gwaay's party, or perhaps to wave an order to his sorcerers to strike them down magically, but in that instant the Mouser clapped his hands together loudly. At that signal, Ivivis, who'd stepped between him and the litter, threw back her cowl and opened her robe and let them fall behind her almost in one continuous gesture – and the sight revealed held everyone spell-bound, even Hasjarl, as the Mouser had known it would.

Ivivis was dressed in a transparent black silk tunic – the merest blackly opal gleaming over her pale flesh and slimly youthful figure – but on her face she wore the white mask of a hag, female yet with mouth a-grin showing fangs and with fiercely staring eyes red-balled and white-irised, as the Mouser had swiftly repainted them at the direction of Gwaay, speaking from his silver statua. Long green hair mixed with white fell from the mask behind Ivivis and some thin strands of it before her shoulders. Upright before her in her right hand she held ritualistically a large pruning knife.

The Mouser pointed straight at Hasjarl, on whom the eyes of the mask were already fixed, and he commanded in his deepest voice, 'Bring that one here to me, oh Witch-Mother!' and Ivivis stepped swiftly forward.

Hasjarl took a backward step and stared horror-enchanted at his approaching nemesis, all motherly-cannibalistic above, all elfin-maidenly below, with his father's eyes to daunt him and with the cruel knife to suggest judgment upon himself for the girls he had lustily done to death or lifelong crippledness.

The Mouser knew he had success within his grasp and there remained only the closing of the fingers.

At that instant there sounded from the other end of the chamber a great muffled gong-note deep as Gwaay's had been silvery-high, shuddering the bones by its vibrancy. Then from either side of the narrow black archway at the opposite end of the hall from Gwaay's litter there rose to the ceiling with a hollow roar twin pillars of white fire, commanding all eyes and shattering the Mouser's spell.

The Mouser's most instant reaction was inwardly to curse such superior stage-management.

Smoke billowed out against the great black squares of the ceiling, the pillars sank to white jets, man-high, and there strode forward between them the figure of Flindach in his heavily embroidered robes and with the Golden Symbol of Power at his waist, but with the Cowl of Death thrown back to show his blotched warty face and his eyes like those of Ivivis' mask. The High Steward threw wide his arms in a proud imploring gesture and in his deep and resonant voice that filled the Ghost Hall recited thus:

'Oh Gwaay! Oh Hasjarl! In the name of your father burned and beyond the stars, and in the name of your grandmother whose eyes I too bear, think of Quarmall! Think of the security of this your kingdom and of how your wars ravage her. Forego your enmities, abjure your brotherly hates, and cast your lots now to settle the succession – the winner to be Lord Paramount here, the loser instantly to depart with great escort and coffers of treasure, and journey across the Mountains of Hunger and the desert and the Sea of the East and live out his life in the Eastern Lands in all comfort and high dignity. Or if not by customary lot, then let your champions battle to the death to decide it – all else to follow the same. Oh Hasjarl, oh Gwaay, I have spoken.' And he folded his arms and stood there between the two pale flame pillars still burning high as he.

Fafhrd had taken advantage of the shocks to seize his sword and ax from the ones holding them nervelessly, and to push forward by Hasjarl as if properly to ward him standing alone and unshielded in front of his men. Now Fafhrd lightly nudged Hasjarl and whispered through his bag-mask, 'Take him up on it, you were best. I'll win your stuffy loathy catacomb kingdom for you – aye, and once rewarded depart from it swifter ever than Gwaay!'

Hasjarl grimaced angrily at him and turning toward Flindach shouted, '*I* am Lord Paramount here, and no need of lots to determine it! Yes, and I have my arch-magi to strike down any who sorcerously challenge me! – and my great champion to smite to mincemeat any who challenge me with swords!'

Fafhrd threw out his chest and glared about through red-ringed eyeholes to back him up.

The silence that followed Hasjarl's boast was cut as if by keenest knife when a voice came piercingly dulcet from the unstirring low mound on the litter, cornered by its four impassive tread-slaves, or from a point just above it.

'I, Gwaay of the Lower Levels, am Lord Paramount of Quarmall, and not my poor brother there, for whose damned soul I grieve. And I have sorceries which have saved my life from the evilest of his sorceries and I have a champion who will smite his champion to chaff!'

All were somewhat daunted at that seemingly magical speaking except Hasjarl, who giggled sputteringly, twitching a-main, and then as if he and his brother were children alone in a playroom, cried out, 'Liar and squeaker of lies! Effeminate boaster! Puny charlatan! *Where* is this great champion of yours? Call him forth! Bid him appear! Oh, confess it now, he's but a figment of your dying thoughts! Oh, ho, ho, ho!'

All began to look around wonderingly at that, some thoughtful, some apprehensive. But as no figure appeared, certainly not a warlike one, some of Hasjarl's men began to snigger with him. Others of them took it up.

The Gray Mouser had no wish to risk his skin – not with Hasjarl's champion looking a meaner foe every moment, side-armed with ax like Fafhrd and now apparently even acting as counselor to his lord – perhaps a sort of captain-general behind the curtain, as he was behind Gwaay's – yet the Mouser was almost irresistibly tempted by this opportunity to cap all surprises with a master surprise.

And in that instant there sounded forth again Gwaay's eerie bell-voice, coming not from his vocal cords, for they were rotted away, but created by the force of his deathless will marshaling the unseen atomies of the air:

'From the blackest depths, unseen by all, in very center of the Hall – Appear, my champion!'

That was too much for the Mouser. Ivivis had reassumed her hooded black robe while Flindach had been speaking, knowing that the terror of her hag-mask and maiden-form was a fleeting thing, and she again stood beside the Mouser as his acolyte. He handed her his wand in one stiff gesture, not looking at her, and lifting his hands to the throat of his robe, he threw it and his hood back and dropped them behind him, and drawing Scalpel whistling from her sheath leaped forward with a heelstamp to the top of the three steps and crouched glaring with sword raised above head, looking in his gray silks and silver a figure of menace, albeit a rather small one and carrying at his belt a wineskin as well as a dagger.

Meanwhile Fafhrd, who had been facing Hasjarl to have a last word with him, now ripped off his red bag-mask, whipped Graywand screaming from his sheath, and leaped forward likewise with an intimidating stamp.

Then they saw and recognized each other.

The pause that ensued was to the spectators more testimony to the fearsomeness of each – the one so dreadful-tall, the other metamorphosed from sorcerer. Evidently they daunted each other greatly.

Fafhrd was the first to react, perhaps because there had been something hauntingly familiar to him all along about the manner and speech of the Black Sorcerer. He started a gargantuan laugh and managed to change it in the nick into a screaming snarl of, 'Trickster! Chatterer! Player at magic! Sniffer after spells. Wart! *Little Toad!*'

The Mouser, mayhap the more amazed because he had noted and discounted the resemblance of the masked champion to Fafhrd, now took his comrade's cue – and just in time, for he was about to laugh too – and boomed back, 'Boaster! Bumptious brawler! Bumbling fumbler after girls! Oaf! Lout! *Big Feet!*'

The taut spectators thought these taunts a shade mild, but the spiritedness of their delivery more than made up for that.

Fafhrd advanced another stamp, crying, 'Oh, I have dreamed

of this moment. I will mince you from your thickening toenails to your cheesy brain!'

The Mouser bounced for his stamp, so as not to lose height going down the steps, and skirled out the while, 'All my rages find happy vent. I will gut you of each lie, especially those about your northern travels!'

Then Fafhrd cried, 'Remember Ool Hrusp!' and the Mouser responded. 'Remember Lithquil!' and they were at it.

Now for all most of the Quarmallians knew, Lithquil and Ool Hrusp might be and doubtless were places where the two heroes had earlier met in fight, or battlefields where they had warred on opposing sides, or even girls they had fought over. But in actuality Lithquil was the Mad Duke of the city of Ool Hrusp, to humor whom Fafhrd and the Mouser had once staged a most realistic and carefully rehearsed duel lasting a full half hour. So those Quarmallians who anticipated a long and spectacular battle were in no wise disappointed.

First Fafhrd aimed three mighty slashing blows, any one enough to cleave the Mouser in twain, but the Mouser deflected each at the last moment strongly and cunningly with Scalpel, so that they whished an inch above his head, singing the harsh chromatic song of steel on steel.

Next the Mouser thrust thrice at Fafhrd, leaping skimmingly like a flying fish and disengaging his sword each time from Graywand's parry. But Fafhrd always managed to slip his body aside, with nearly incredible swiftness for one so big, and the thin blade would go hurtlessly by him.

This interchange of slash and thrust was but the merest prologue to the duel, which now carried into the area of the dried-up fountain pool and became very wild-seeming indeed, forcing the spectators back more than once, while the Mouser improvised by gushing out some of his thick blood-red toadstool wine when they were momentarily pressed body-to-body in a fierce exchange, so that they both appeared sorely wounded.

There were three in the Ghost Hall who took no interest in this seeming masterpiece of duels and hardly watched it. Ivivis was not one of them – she soon threw back her hood, tore off her hag-mask, and came following the fight close, cheering on the

Mouser. Nor were they Brilla, Kewissa and Friska – for at the sound of swords the two girls had insisted on opening their door a crack despite the eunuch's solicitous apprehensions and now they were all peering through, head above head, Friska in the midst agonizing at Fafhrd's perils.

Gwaay's eyes were clotted and the lids glued with ichor, and the tendons were dissolved whereby he might have lifted his head. Nor did he seek to explore with his sorcerous senses in the direction of the fight. He clung to existence solely by the thread of his great hatred for his brother, all else of life was to him less than a shadow-show; yet his hate held for him all of life's wonder and sweetness and high excitement – it was enough.

The mirror image of that hate in Hasjarl was at this moment strong enough too to dominate wholly his healthy body's instincts and hungers and all the plots and images in his crackling thoughts. He saw the first stroke of the fight, he saw Gwaay's litter unguarded, and then as if he had seen entire a winning combination of chess and been hypnotized by it, he made his move without another cogitation.

Widely circling the fight and moving swiftly in the shadows like a weasel he mounted the three steps by the wall and headed straight for the litter.

There were no ideas in his mind at all, but there were some shadowy images distortedly seen as from a great distance – one of himself as a tiny child toddling by night along a wall to Gwaay's crib, to scratch him with a pin.

He did not spare a glance for the tread-slaves and it is doubtful if they even saw, or at least took note of him, so rudimentary were their minds.

He leaned eagerly between two of them and curiously surveyed his brother. His nostrils drew in at the stench and his mouth contracted to its tightest sphincter yet still smiled.

He plucked a wide dagger of blued steel from a sheath at his belt and poised it above his brother's face, which by its plagues was almost unrecognizable as such. The honed edges of the dagger were tiny hooks directed back from the point.

The sword-clashing below reached one of its climaxes, but Hasjarl did not mark it.

He said softly, 'Open your eyes, Brother. I want you to speak once before I slay you.'

There was no reply from Gwaay – not a motion, not a whisper, not a bubble of retching.

'Very well,' Hasjarl said harshly, 'then die a prim shut-mouth,' and he drove down the dagger.

It stopped violently a hairbreadth above Gwaay's upper cheek and the muscles of Hasjarl's arm driving it were stabbingly numbed by the jolt they got.

Gwaay did open his eyes then, which was not very pleasant to behold since there was nothing in them but green ichor.

Hasjarl instantly closed his own eyes, but continued to peer down through the holes in his upper lids.

Then he heard Gwaay's voice like a silver mosquito by his ear saying, 'You have made a slight oversight, dear brother. You have chosen the wrong weapon. After our father's burning you swore to me my life was sacrosanct – until you killed me by crushing. "Until I crush it out," you said. The gods hear only our words, Brother, not our intentions. Had you come lugging a boulder, like the curious gnome you are, you might have accomplished your aim.'

'Then I'll have you crushed!' Hasjarl retorted angrily, leaning his face closer and almost shouting. 'Aye, and I'll sit by and listen to your bones crunch – what bones you have left! You're as great a fool as I, Gwaay, for you too after our father's funeral promised not to slay me. Aye, and you're a greater fool, for now you've spilled to me your little secret of how you may be slain.'

'I swore not to slay you with spells or steel or venom or with my hand,' the bright insect voice of Gwaay replied. 'Unlike you, I said nothing at all of crushing.'

Hasjarl felt a strange tingling in his flesh while in his nostrils there was an acrid odor like that of lightning mingling with the stink of corruption.

Suddenly Gwaay's hands thrust up to the palms out of his overly rich bedclothes. The flesh was shredding from the finger bones which pointed straight up, invokingly.

Hasjarl almost started back, but caught himself. He'd die, he told himself, before he'd cringe from his brother. He was aware of strong forces all about him.

There was a muffled grating noise and then an odd faintly pattering snowfall on the coverlet and on Hasjarl's neck . . . a thin snowfall of pale gritty stuff . . . grains of mortar . . .

'Yes, you will crush me, dear brother,' Gwaay admitted tranquilly. 'But if you would know *how* you will crush me, recall my small special powers . . . or else *look up!*'

Hasjarl turned his head, and there was the great black basalt slab big as the litter rushing down, and the one moment of life left Hasjarl was consumed in hearing Gwaay say, 'You are wrong, again, my comrade.'

Fafhrd stopped a sword-slash in midcourse when he heard the crash and the Mouser almost nicked him with his rehearsed parry. They lowered their blades and looked, as did all others in the central section of the Ghost Hall.

Where the litter had been was now only the thick basalt slab mortar-streaked with the litter-poles sticking out from under, and above in the ceiling the rectangular white hole whence the slab had been dislodged. The Mouser thought, *That's a larger thing to move by thinking than a checker or jar, yet the same black substance.*

Fafhrd thought, *Why didn't the whole roof fall? – there's the strangeness.*

Perhaps the greatest wonder of the moment was the four tread-slaves still standing at the four corners, eyes forward, fingers locked across their chests, although the slab had missed them only by inches in its falling.

Then some of Hasjarl's henchmen and sorcerers who had seen their Lord sneak to the litter now hurried up to it, but fell back when they beheld how closely the slab approached the floor and marked the tiny rivulet of blood that ran from under it. Their minds quailed at the thought of those brothers who had hated each other so dearly, and now their bodies locked in an obscene interpenetrating and commingling embrace.

Meanwhile Ivivis came running to the Mouser and Friska to Fafhrd to bind up their wounds, and were astonished and mayhap a shade irked to be told there were none. Kewissa and Brilla came too and Fafhrd with one arm around Friska reached out the wine-bloody hand of the other and softly closed it around Kewissa's wrist, smiling at her friendlily.

Then the great muffled gong-note sounded again and the twin pillars of white flame briefly roared to the ceiling to either side of Flindach. They showed by their glare that many men had entered by the narrow archway behind Flindach and now stood around him: stout guardsmen from the companies of the Keep with weapons at the ready, and several of his own sorcerers.

As the flame-pillars swiftly shrank, Flindach imperiously raised hand and resonantly spoke:

'The stars which may not be cheated foretold the doom of the Lord of Quarmall. All of you heard those two' – he pointed toward the shattered litter – 'proclaim themselves Lord of Quarmall. So the stars are twice satisfied. And the gods, who hear our words to each tiniest whisper, and order our fates by them, are content. It remains that I reveal to you the next Lord of Quarmall.'

He pointed at Kewissa and intoned, '*The next Lord of Quarmall but one* sleeps and waxes in the womb of her, wife of the Quarmal so lately honored with burnings and immolations and ceremonious rites.'

Kewissa shrank and her blue eyes went wide. Then she began to beam.

Flindach continued, 'It still remains that I reveal to you *the next Lord of Quarmall*, who shall tutor Queen Kewissa's babe until he arrives at manhood a perfect king and all-wise sorcerer, under whom our buried realm will enjoy perpetual inward peace and outward-raiding prosperity.'

Then Flindach reached behind his left shoulder. All thought he purposed to draw forward the Cowl of Death over his head and brows and hideous warty winy cheeks for some still more solemn speaking. But instead he grasped his neck by the short hairs of the nape and drew it upward and forward and his scalp and all his hair with it, and then the skin of his face came off with his scalp as he drew his hand down and to the side, and there was revealed, sweat-gleaming a little, the unblemished face and jutting nose and full mobile smiling lips of Quarmal, while his terrible blood-red white-irised eyes gazed at them all mildly.

'I was forced to visit Limbo for a space,' he explained with a solemn yet genial fatherly familiarity, 'while others were Lords of Quarmall in my stead and the stars sent down their spears. It was best so, though I lost two sons by it. Only so might our land be saved from ravenous self-war.'

He held up for all to see the limp mask with empty lash-fringed eyeholes and purple-blotched left cheek and wart-triangled right. He said, 'And now I bid you all honor great and puissant Flindach, the loyalest Master of Magicians a king ever had, who lent me his face for a necessary deception and his body to be burned for mine with waxen mask of mine to cover his poor head-front, which had sacrificed all. In solemnly supervising my own high flaming obsequies, I honored only Flindach. For him my women burned. This his face, well preserved by my own skills as flayer and swift tanner, will hang forever in place of honor in our halls, while the spirit of Flindach holds my chair for me in the Dark World beyond the stars, a Lord Paramount there until I come, and eternally a Hero of Quarmall.'

Before any cheering or hailing could be started – which would have taken a little while, since all were much bemused – Fafhrd cried out, 'Oh cunningest king, I honor you and your babe so highly and the Queen who carries him in her womb that I will guard her moment by moment, not moving a pace from her, until I and my small comrade here are well outside Quarmall – say a mile – together with horses for our conveyance and with the treasures promised us by those two late kings.' And he gestured as Quarmal had toward the crushed litter.

The Mouser had been about to launch at Quarmal some subtly intimidating remarks about his own skills as a sorcerer in blasting Gwaay's eleven. But now he decided that Fafhrd's words were sufficient and well-spoken, save for the slighting reference to himself, and he held his peace.

Kewissa started to withdraw her hand from Fafhrd's, but he tightened his grip just a little and she looked at him with understanding. In fact, she called brightly to Quarmal, 'Oh Lord Husband, this man saved my life and your son's from

759

Hasjarl's fiends in a storeroom of the Keep. I trust him,' while Brilla, dabbing tears of joy from his eyes with his undersleeve, seconded her with, 'My very dear Lord, she speaks only nakedest truth, bare as a newborn babe or new-wed wife.'

Quarmal raised his hand a little, reprovingly, as if such speaking were unnecessary and somewhat out of place, and smiling thinly at Fafhrd and the Mouser said, 'It shall be as you have spoken. I am neither ungenerous nor unperceptive. Know that it was not altogether by chance that my late sons unbeknown to each other hired you two friends – also mutually unknowing – to be their champions. Furthermore know that I am not altogether unaware of the curiosities of Ningauble of the Seven Eyes or of the spells of Sheelba of the Eyeless Face. We grandmaster sorcerers have a— But to speak more were only to kindle the curiosity of the gods and alert the trolls and attract the attention of the restless hungry Fates. Enough is enough.'

Looking at Quarmal's slitted eyes, the Mouser was glad he had not boasted and even Fafhrd shivered a little.

Fafhrd cracked whip above the four-horse team to set them pulling the high-piled wagon more briskly through this black sticky stretch of road deeply marked with cart tracks and the hoofprints of oxen, a mile from Quarmall. Friska and Ivivis were turned around on the seat beside him to wave as long a farewell as they might to Kewissa and the eunuch Brilla, standing at the roadside with four impassive guardsmen of Quarmall, to whom they had but now been released.

The Gray Mouser, sprawled on his stomach atop the load, waved too, but only with his left hand – in his right he held a cocked crossbow while his eyes searched the trees about for sign of ambush.

Yet the Mouser was not truly apprehensive. He thought that Quarmal would hardly be apt to try any tricks against such a proven warrior and sorcerer as himself – or Fafhrd too, of course. The old Lord had shown himself a most gracious host during the last few hours, plying them with rare wines and loading them with rich gifts beyond what they'd asked or what the Mouser had purloined in advance, and even offering them other girls in addition to Ivivis and Friska – benison which they'd rejected, with some inward regrets, after noting the glares in the eyes of those two. Twice or thrice Quarmal had smiled in too tiger-friendly a fashion, but at such times Fafhrd had stood a little closer to Kewissa and emphasized his light but inflexible grip on her, to remind the old Lord that she and the prince she carried were hostages for his and the Mouser's safety.

As the mucky road curved up a little, the towers of Quarmall came into view above the treetops. The Mouser's gaze drifted to them and he studied the lacy pinnacles thoughtfully, wondering whether he'd ever see them again. Suddenly the whim seized him to return to Quarmall straightway – yes, to slip off the back of the load and run there. What did the outer world hold half so fine as the wonders of that subterranean kingdom? – its mazy mural-pictured tunnelings a man might spend his life tracing . . . its buried delights . . . even its evils beautiful . . . its delicious infinitely varied blacks . . . its hidden fan-driven air . . . Yes, suppose he dropped down soundlessly this very moment . . .

There was a flash, a brilliant scintillation from the tallest keep. It pricked the Mouser like a goad and he loosed his hold and let himself slide backward off the load. But just at that instant the road turned and grew firm and the trees moved higher, masking the towers, and the Mouser came to himself and grabbed hold again before his feet touched the road and he hung there while the wheels creaked merrily and cold sweat drenched him.

Then the wagon stopped and the Mouser dropped down and took three deep breaths and then hastened forward to where Fafhrd had descended too and was busy with the harness of the horses and their traces.

'Up again, Fafhrd, and whip up!' he cried. 'This Quarmal is a cunninger witch than I guessed. If we waste time by the way, I fear for our freedom and our souls!'

'You're telling me?' Fafhrd retorted. 'This road winds and there'll be more sticky stretches. Trust a wagon's speed? – pah! We'll uncouple the four horses and taking only simplest victuals and the smallest and most precious of the treasure, gallop across the moor away from Quarmall straight as the crow flies. That way we *should* dodge ambush and outrun ranging pursuit. Friska, Ivivis! Spring to it, all!'